10 PLATOON
–
BLITZKRIEG

By

Evan S James

Grosvenor House
Publishing Limited

This book is published by
Grosvenor House Publishing Ltd
Link House
140 The Broadway, Tolworth, Surrey, KT6 7HT.
www.grosvenorhousepublishing.co.uk

This book reflects the recorded actions of historical figures
at specific times and places as part of the story.
The characters and actions of 10 Platoon and
the West Staffordshire Regiment are completely fictitious,
and any resemblance to people or events,
past or present, is purely coincidental.

A CIP record for this book
is available from the British Library

Paperback ISBN 978-1-83615-160-9
Hardback ISBN 978-1-83615-161-6
eBook ISBN 978-1-83615-162-3

PROLOGUE

This book is based on actual historical events and characters. The words spoken, and actions taken by these characters are able to be reproduced because they were either captured at the time, or subsequently recorded after the events to which they refer. Where records of conversations do not exist, their words have been "assumed" from the outcome of the events, or subsequent actions taken. The post event accounts of these characters, where they exist, can be followed in the Epilogue at the end of the book.

The West Staffordshire Regiment is fictitious; which by extrapolation means that the individual members, and the actions of 10 Platoon, are also fictitious.

This book reflects the social standards, language and attitudes of the time; in an almost exclusively male military service environment, under the conditions created by a continent at war.

PART 1
PRELUDE TO WAR

Wednesday 23 August 1939 –
Khodynka Airfield, Moscow, Russia.

The propellors on the Focke-Wulf Condor had shuddered to a halt only seconds before the door in the fuselage was opened and metal steps were clipped into place. The smell of aviation fuel from the warm engines hung heavily in the air as Hitler's Foreign Minister, Joachim von Ribbentrop, gingerly descended the rungs of the flimsy metal ladder, aware that everyone present was watching, and that a stumble at this point would destroy the persona he had worked so hard to create. As he stepped onto the airstrip followed by the members of the German delegation, a Soviet military band struck up *Deutschlandlied*. Swastika banners displayed by the honour guard flapped in the breeze; having been hurriedly sourced from a Soviet film studio where they had been used in the production of an anti-Nazi propaganda movie a short time before. Now repurposed to herald a change of political intent, they greeted the German Foreign Minister to Moscow.

Ribbentrop stepped into the waiting black limousine, followed by his delegation; the door held open by a Russian soldier standing rigidly to attention. With hardly a sound from the engine, the vehicle moved off on the short drive to Red Square. The Germans were ushered into the luxuriously decorated room in the Kremlin where their Russian counterparts were waiting. The walls were wood panelled to shoulder height, their dark polished surface glowing in the light from wall and table lamps. From above a crackling log fire, a huge painting of Lenin overlooked the proceedings. The Russian Foreign Minister, Vyacheslav Molotov greeted von Ribbentrop with a handshake; closely followed by the Russian Premier, Joseph Stalin. The presence of the Premier took von Ribbentrop a little by surprise, but his attendance reinforced the importance and symbolism of the meeting.

Molotov directed von Ribbentrop to the single seat at the long desk upon which the non-aggression pact rested. It was a simple one-page document, decorated by both swastika and hammer and sickle emblems, with a short passage of less than three hundred words in the appropriate national language under the corresponding emblem. The pact would run for ten years, stressing the strengthening of the cause of peace between Germany and Russia, both parties desisting from any acts of violence, aggression or attacks on each other. Von Ribbentrop was handed a pen, slowly and

1

deliberately signing in the appropriate place under the German language text. As von Ribbentrop stood up, Molotov took the vacated seat, signing under the Russian text. Flashbulbs popped as von Ribbentrop and Molotov posed with a handshake under the picture of Lenin. Stalin then took his turn for a photograph in the same pose with von Ribbentrop. The signatories celebrated at a reception with caviar, vodka and champagne.

The celebrations were mirrored in Berlin, as Hitler now felt confident that his planned actions in Poland would be free from any Russian interference on his eastern flank. In consideration of previous appeasement gestures from the Western Powers, von Ribbentrop had assured Hitler that Britain and France would not have the political resolve to do anything meaningful on his western flank. All the pieces of the jigsaw were now in place.

Thursday 31 August 1939 – Gleiwitz Radio Station, Eastern Germany.

Alfred Helmut Naujocks pulled the left sleeve of his scruffy jacket back from his wrist to check the time on his watch. The watch was German Army issue; the jacket had originally been meant for wear by someone with slightly longer arms than his. It was a few minutes before 8 p.m. as two cars approached the Gleiwitz Radio Station, four miles from the Polish border inside Germany. The car tyres crunched gently on the loose gravel as they wound their way through the tree lined approach road, the wooden gates of the transmission station lying open in front of them. Above the surrounding pine trees, the transmitter mast could be clearly seen, the setting sun flicking between the wooden struts as the cars approached the three-storey building. From a white painted flagpole in the centre of the courtyard, a swastika flag hung limply in the warm late summer air.

The time had been carefully chosen when most people would be at home, thus increasing the size of any potential listening audience, and would also facilitate their escape in the gathering darkness. Naujocks leaned forward and pulled down the sun visor on his side of the car as the angle of the setting sun reached just the right height to dazzle him. The driver did the same almost simultaneously.

The Head of the Gestapo, Reinhard Heydrich himself, had telephoned Naujocks at 4 p.m. that afternoon, giving the codeword "*Grossmutter gestorben*" (Grandmother has died), triggering the operation. This was it, he thought to himself, as he closed his eyes and shook his head slightly to restore his vision from the glare of the sun. The chance to do his master's personal bidding and earn respect and advancement. The SS seemed to work that way, but such clandestine operations also caused distrust and personal loathing between its members. In his mind, Naujocks pictured himself reporting to Heydrich on a mission completed successfully, receiving the praise of his superiors and the envy of his subordinates. He was jerked back from his fantasy as the cars stopped abruptly in a swirl of dust on the paved surface outside the building. They came to rest one behind the other, opposite the closed wooden door of the station.

Naujocks stepped from the front passenger seat closely followed by the driver and two rear seat passengers, all four dressed in rough clothes specifically sourced for the occasion to create the impression of anti-German agitators or Polish insurgents. From the second car, having stopped a few yards behind, three men got out, again all similarly dressed. As Naujocks and his team bounded up the steps to the building, the crew of the second car struggled to remove a limp body from the boot of their vehicle. Franciszek Honiok was a 43-year-old unmarried Catholic farmer and German Silesian, well known to the authorities for sympathizing with the Poles. He had been arrested the previous day by the Gestapo, and anaesthetised only a few hours prior. He was alive but completely unresponsive, making him awkward to lift. His would-be comrades cursed and strained as they pulled Honiok's ample farmer's frame from the confines of the vehicle boot, unconcerned as his head and body thumped sickeningly off the lip of the boot frame and lock.

Naujocks and his three accomplices burst through the door and into the broadcast studio. The station manager rose to his feet in shock, subsequently being manhandled into the basement along with his operating staff. Threatening the operators with pistols but not uttering a word, two of the intruders pushed the operators' faces against the wall and held them there as their hands were tied behind their backs. The slightest movement from the prisoners was met with forearms pushed into the back of their necks, and pistols pointed into their faces. Naujocks remained in the broadcast studio with the group's Polish speaker, Karl Hornack. Hornack leaned down so his mouth was close to the wire mesh of the station's microphone and nodded at Naujocks who fired his pistol into the ceiling before Hornack spoke in Polish.

"Attention! This is Gliwice. The broadcasting station is in Polish hands."

The sound of the gunshot told the hostage takers in the basement it was time to leave. They released their grip on the operators, pushing them away roughly before turning and running back up the stairs to the broadcast studio. Naujocks waited in the doorway with pistol in hand, gesturing his accomplices outside and pulling the door closed behind him once they had passed. Lying on the station steps was the limp body of Honiok, carefully positioned by the occupants of the second car. Naujocks paused over the unconscious man before raising his pistol and firing three rounds into the unconscious Honiok's chest. Blood splattered onto the victim's face as the bullets tore into his heart and lungs. Naujocks calmly returned the pistol to his holster as he walked the few yards to the car, the door lying open and the engine already running. It moved off with a swirl of dust before he had time to close the door.

Shortly after 8 p.m. the German News Agency reported an attack on Gleiwitz radio broadcasting station by Polish partisans, who had forced their way into the studio and broadcast a statement in Polish. The report stated that several such incidents had taken place along the border with Poland, some involving Polish soldiers alongside the partisans. In all cases, the Poles had been overpowered by German police who opened fire on them, killing several.

Using these seemingly unprovoked attacks against German facilities, with the bodies of dead Polish soldiers and partizans as evidence, Hitler would subsequently justify the invasion of Poland. The dead bodies were those of concentration camp inmates, or undesirables such as Honiok, carefully dressed to resemble Polish soldiers or partisans, before being transported to the scene and shot. As the newspapers were printing their front pages describing the attacks, nearly one and a half million German troops stood ready to cross the Polish border at 4.45 a.m. on Friday 1 September.

Friday 1 September 1939 –
Free City of Danzig, Baltic Coast, Northern Germany.

The Polish Post Office in Danzig had opened in 1920 under the terms of the Versailles Treaty which ended the Great War, and its buildings were considered Polish property. The ornate brick and stained-glass entrance was surmounted with the Polish national eagle, and a large sign declaring the building's function. As tensions between Poland and Germany grew throughout August, a Polish combat engineer, Lieutenant Konrad Guderski, had reinforced the building in preparation for possible hostilities, and trained the staff in defensive duties. The Post Office staff had been supplemented by ten Reservist non-commissioned officers in mid-August, bringing the number of employees on the morning of 1 September to fifty-six. This included the building caretaker and his 10-year-old daughter Erwina who lived in the complex. A cache of weapons had been smuggled in and secretly stored inside, consisting of three machine guns, forty other firearms and three chests of hand grenades.

At 4 a.m. the telephone and electricity lines to the building were suddenly cut from outside, and at 4:43 a.m. the German Battleship Schleswig-Holstein slipped her moorings in the port of Danzig, moving a short distance to lie opposite the Polish military depot on the Westerplatte peninsula. As a training ship for German Naval Cadets, the arrival and continued presence of the vessel in Danzig since 25 August had drawn no suspicion. Being launched in

1906 she was a naval relic, obsolete even before the Great War had begun. The high-profile arrival, with flags flying and cadets carefully arranged on the deck disguised both her intent, and the presence of two hundred and twenty-five Marines hidden below decks. The Westerplatte depot served as an unloading area for Polish military hardware and ammunition; outwardly unimpressive, consisting of a barracks, mess and warehouses, protected by a ring of blockhouses and barbed wire. Despite being limited by treaty to a garrison of eighty-eight, the growing tensions meant the Polish garrison had secretly been increased to two hundred and ten, supported by an armoury of machine guns, mortars and anti-tank weapons.

To coincide precisely with the time that German troops were crossing the Polish border, Captain Gustav Kleikamp ordered all guns on the Schleswig-Holstein to open fire on the depot. Within seven minutes, five tons of explosive fell on Westerplatte, smashing trees, blowing craters in the earth and damaging the buildings and blockhouses. When the ship's guns fell silent, and the dust from the explosions still hung in the air, the ground assault began. As the German Marines moved along the peninsula, following their out-of-date maps, they came under fire from all sides when attempting to scale the perimeter wall of the depot. Machine gun fire from unseen positions tore through their ranks at a range of forty yards. The Marines fought for an hour to gain a foothold in the depot, but were forced to withdraw when casualties became too great. Watching from the Schleswig-Holstein, Captain Kleikamp ordered another bombardment as the Marines broke clear, landing a further forty-six tons of explosive on the depot. The second assault began shortly before 9 a.m. initially meeting with greater success, before this too was forced to withdraw after the mortal wounding of the Commanding Officer, Leutnant Henningsen.

A simultaneous morning attack plan was initiated against the Post Office by the Danzig Police in armoured cars, supported by local German Stormtrooper and SS volunteers. Having been notified in advance, journalists from local newspapers and the state radio station arrived to cover the event. The first attack was repelled, although some Germans managed to temporarily enter the building through the front entrance. A second attack through a hole blasted in the wall of an adjacent building was also unsuccessful, although Lieutenant Guderski was killed in the fighting.

At 11 a.m. reinforcements were requested from the German units fighting at the Westerplatte. A mortar team arrived and fire was directed onto the building, but was too inaccurate to influence the situation. The Germans declared a two-hour ceasefire at 3 p.m. during which they offered surrender terms to the Poles in the Post Office, whilst simultaneously digging under the walls of the building and loading 1,200 lbs of explosive in the void. When the ceasefire period elapsed at 5 p.m. without a Polish surrender, the Germans detonated the mine, collapsing the wall, and occupying the building on the subsequent assault.

The Polish defenders who survived the explosion were forced into the cellar from where they continued their resistance; until the Germans pumped petrol into the cellar and set it alight with a hand grenade. The first to emerge from the building was the Post Office Director, waving a white towel. He was met with a volley of shots, killing him instantly. The next out was a Polish Army Reserve Officer who was set alight with a flame thrower, dying in agony as he rolled on the ground trying to extinguish the flames. The screams of a child were heard as the caretaker brought out Erwina whose clothes were on fire. The caretaker, Erwina and those that filed out behind were taken prisoner.

Friday 1 September 1939 –
Whittington Barracks, Staffordshire, England.

It was fifteen minutes before 11 a.m. The officer and non-commissioned officer instructors in the company office were becoming uneasy as they nervously looked at their watches; wary of the approaching parade start time of 11 o'clock and quietly reminding the Company Second in Command that they needed to leave very soon. As was the custom before every recruit passing out parade, the instructors had gathered together to mark the end of the three-month training course by drinking a toast to the newly trained soldiers, prior to them leaving the Depot and joining their battalions.

The chatter of the families assembled in the stands outside was clearly audible through the partially opened windows as they excitedly waited to see their sons, on what was for many the most important event in their young lives to date. Exactly at the arranged time, the Regimental Band began playing to entertain the waiting families, starting the formal events for the parade sequence, and triggering those present in the office to look at their watches again. Just prior to everyone gathering, the Company Clerk had been neatly arranging two bottles of port and glasses ready for the toast, when the Company Commander received a telephone call and hurried from the office. The poured port now sat untouched awaiting his return.

"We'll give the Company Commander two more minutes and then you have to go." said the Second in Command attempting to settle the growing unease, cognisant of the requirement for those in attendance to be somewhere else. Just as he finished speaking, the office door opened and Major Harvey stepped through, looking pale and flustered. The waiting gathering sprang to attention as he entered the office. He took off his cap and laid it on the clerk's desk along with his swagger stick.

"Gentlemen, my apologies for keeping you waiting." began Harvey in a calming voice that belied his appearance, before taking a deep breath and continuing. "But I have just been informed that Germany invaded Poland at dawn this morning." After a few seconds of stunned silence, he continued.

"I am expecting all leave to be cancelled, and I know some of you have made plans for time with your families; but those plans are likely to change." He waited a few more seconds for the information to sink in before continuing. "Don't tell the soldiers just yet. Let them enjoy lunch with their families and the Commanding Officer will address them later when more information may be available." He moved slowly to the table where the port was waiting and lifted a glass; each of those present following his lead. When everyone had a drink in hand, he raised his glass in the usual tribute. "To the next generation."

The repeated tribute from those in the room was half hearted. The instructors set down their empty glasses and hurriedly left to join their soldiers formed up outside, waiting excitedly to begin their parade. Harvey set down his empty glass and lifted another full one, immediately downing that as well.

"Oh Christ, not again." he murmured to a now empty room. He lifted his hat and stick from the clerk's desk and closed the door of the office as he left.

* * *

As he stood on parade, Private Martin Kyle had searched along the rows of faces in the stands for his mother, until he spotted the flowery dress that she wore to every special occasion. Just as he identified her, she waved, as if sensing that he had seen her. He marked the spot in his head, now knowing where to find her after the parade.

It had been practiced so many times that his participation in the event seemed to be removed from reality. Determined not to make a mistake, his concentration was so intense that he didn't have the presence of mind to appreciate what was happening or enjoy the occasion marking the culmination of three months' work. His fully conscious mind only returned when the backslapping and handshakes began as nervous energy overflowed from the recruits when the parade was dismissed by the Adjutant. Pushing his way through his celebrating colleagues, Kyle hurried back towards the stands to find his mother. He recognised her dress in the area of the stands he remembered and broke into a run, as fast as his studded boots would allow on the parade ground surface. She was standing with her back to him, talking with a man in uniform when she heard his call. Turning her head at the sound of Martin's voice, she gently touched the uniformed sleeve of the man beside her as if to excuse her departure, and ran to meet him. She flung her arms around him as they met, then still holding his shoulders, pushed him to arm's length.

"Let me have a look at you." She paused as she looked him up and down. "So smart and so handsome." she said proudly. The uniformed man had approached at a slower pace, and sensing his proximity, she turned, touched him again on the arm and introduced him to her son. "Martin, this is Seamus McCann. He has been a family friend for years." Martin immediately noticed the crown insignia on his lower sleeve, denoting a Warrant Officer Class 2. Not appreciating the niceties of military rank, she was somewhat surprised when Martin sprang to attention as appropriate when about to be addressed by a Warrant Officer.

"Very pleased to meet you again, son." McCann spoke in a broad Southern Irish accent and held out his hand. Martin relaxed and shook McCann's offered hand replying, "Sir." His hand was dwarfed by that of McCann's, his firm grip reflecting a muscular frame with broad shoulders. His complexion indicated a combination of outdoor life and a fondness for alcohol, which had reddened his cheeks and nose.

"Don't worry about the Sir, Martin." joked McCann with a huge grin. "Today, I'm just Seamus. I'll be Sir next time, once you've joined the battalion proper, after your leave." McCann put his arm around Kyle's shoulder, gently guiding him in the direction of the dining hall. "Now, let's get your mother some lunch, and something to drink for you and me." continued McCann with a beaming smile. As Kyle moved in the direction of the cookhouse, McCann gently slapped him on the back as he passed. "Lead the way, son." he said.

There was a short queue at the door of the dining hall which moved quickly as the newly trained soldiers and their families made their way inside. The dining hall had been smartened up from what Kyle had come to expect from the previous three months. Tablecloths had been placed on the tables with small bunches of flowers in vases placed in the centre of each. Cutlery and seating had been arranged to provide six settings at each table. Only the unmistakeable smell of mass-produced Army food remained the same.

As they passed through the door, McCann and Kyle removed their headdress, hanging them on the rows of hooks on the wall for that purpose. Now uncovered, Martin noticed a scar running from behind McCann's left ear to the crown of his head. He had a full head of hair but the mark was clearly visible despite this. The excited chatter of the gathering families was building up as they sorted out their groups and took their seats. McCann selected a free table and strode towards it. He pulled out a chair and gestured to Kyle's mother.

"There you are, Elizabeth." he said as she sat down, and then pushed her chair in towards the table. Kyle sat on his mother's left and McCann sat on her right. Kyle felt a hand on his shoulder and looked round to see his friend Private Kenneth Watts. They had been allocated adjoining beds in the barrack room on the day of their arrival and had formed a solid friendship as they trained together.

"Mind if we sit here, mate?" asked Watts, gesturing at the unoccupied seats opposite with a nod of his head.

"Fire away Ken, mate." replied Kyle. Watts hurriedly sat down beside his friend, swiftly followed by a heavily set woman who made a sigh of relief as she slumped into the next available seat. Kyle glanced across and smiled. She was a woman who made an instant impression; in that she wore her make-up a little too thick and her clothes a little too tight.

"Martin, this is my mum." said Watts, gesturing to the woman who had just sat down. Kyle half rose from his seat as a courtesy as he spoke.

"Pleased to meet you Mrs Watts, I'm Martin Kyle." and touching his mother on the upper arm to get her attention continued, "This is my mum and Mr McCann." She had been talking quietly to McCann and turned at her son's touch to respond to the introduction.

"Hello, I'm Elizabeth Kyle." As she spoke, McCann stood up, nodding his head forward in a respectful gesture before he spoke.

"Seamus McCann. I'm glad you could make it today. The boys did very well. Very smart."

"Oh yes. I thought they were wonderful." gushed Mrs Watts. As she spoke, she reached across and rubbed her son's face, pulling his head towards her to try and kiss him. He resisted, visibly embarrassed by his mother's actions in front of his friend. "Were you part of the parade, Mr McCann?" she asked.

"Not today, Mrs Watts." he replied. "I'm here to represent D Company, and meet the new soldiers who will be joining us after their leave." Growing impatient with the small talk, he remembered his priority and changed the subject. "Now, what can I get everyone to drink?" With everyone having given their orders, Kyle stood up to help. "Sit yourself down, son." said McCann. "This is your day, so just relax and enjoy it."

As Kyle sat back down, McCann made his way to a makeshift bar that had been set up in the corner of the dining hall. As McCann stood in the queue, Kyle saw Major Harvey approach him, followed by a distinctly warm greeting. Being obvious acquaintances, the two men chatted boisterously, interspersed with raucous laughter as they waited to be served by the barman. The two ladies at the table were talking loudly across the two friends, now feeling trapped between them.

"He has put on so much weight, I hardly recognised him." exaggerated Mrs Watts, throwing her head back with an annoying, shrill laugh. This time she did succeed in landing a kiss on her son as she swung forward again in the chair. She licked the tips of the fingers on her left hand and pushed an unruly tuft of hair back from his face without realising she had done it; an action obviously completed so many times it had ceased to register with her anymore. Kyle saw McCann gesturing at him from the bar, and jumped at the opportunity to leave the table.

"Give us a hand with these glasses, son." gestured McCann as Kyle approached. He had three glasses clamped in a triangle with his huge hands. Kyle lifted the remaining two and followed after him back towards the table.

"The last time I saw you was after....you barely came up to my waist." The obvious break in McCann's sentence gave away his change of mind in what he was about to say. He tried to recover the situation. "Now the boy has become a man, and we're having a drink together."

They had just sat down when the Depot instructors arrived at the table to serve food; the tradition being that the instructors served the newly trained soldiers their lunch after the passing out parade. Corporal Hutchinson, a Section Commander who Kyle had grown to respect greatly because of his patience and dedication, whispered in his ear as he set down his food.

"What the hell are you doing sitting with Genghis?" Kyle looked up at him, the confused expression on his face prompting further explanation from Hutchinson. "Sergeant Major McCann. Genghis McCann. He's a madman."

"He's a family friend. Seems really nice actually." whispered Kyle in response.

"He's a bloody maniac." said Hutchinson in an exasperated tone; his volume rising above a whisper. "Why do you think we call him Genghis?"

"Everything alright, Corporal?" said McCann, having picked up on his nickname being uttered.

"Yes, Sir. Just congratulating Private Kyle on passing out, Sir." lied Hutchinson quickly and confidently, before hurriedly moving away to continue his serving duties.

The table settled into silence as they ate their food. Kyle watched McCann, now intrigued after the comments from Corporal Hutchinson. He ate slowly and deliberately, taking great care to prepare every forkful of food before gently putting it in his mouth. On his left, both members of the Watts household were attacking their food as if in a race. Kyle had noticed many times the speed at which his friend ate during training, nothing unusual with young men experiencing hard physical work, but now saw it was a family trait.

With the meal finished and the tables cleared by the instructors, McCann offered another round of drinks and got up to make his way to the bar. Without waiting to be asked this time, Kyle followed. Sensing that his presence at the parade and obvious closeness to Kyle's mother may need some clarity, McCann used the time waiting in the bar queue to fill in some gaps.

"I served with your father in the Great War." he began. "I was a newly enlisted Private soldier in 1917, and he was the Lance Corporal in my section." He paused and smiled to himself as the memories returned, subconsciously raising his hand to run his finger along the scar on his head. "We got promoted together; him to Corporal and me to Lance Corporal. We believed we had the best section in the whole Army." He paused slightly as if choosing how much of the story he would reveal. "We were inseparable, and I was Best Man at your parents' wedding when we got some leave in the summer of 1918."

Kyle felt there was more to come, but the story was curtailed by their arrival at the front of the queue where McCann ordered a repeat round for the table. Kyle picked up the first drinks served and made his way back to the table, where his mother and Mrs Watts were still engaged in lively chatter. McCann arrived a few moments later and as he sat down, a loud, gruff voice echoed through the dining hall.

"Ladies and Gentlemen, can I have your attention please?" It was the Depot Regimental Sergeant Major. The chatter in the room decreased, but without achieving the perfect silence he had expected, the Regimental Sergeant Major repeated the request, this time with a greater emphasis on the "Please". There was a scraping of chair legs on the floor as the guests orientated themselves to look towards the origin of the intrusion, and the room fell silent. Bemused glances were exchanged as the Depot Commanding Officer strode in, positioning himself right in the centre of the hall. The Regimental Sergeant Major saluting smartly as he passed.

"Relax everyone please." requested the Commanding Officer in a nasally monotone voice. He paused momentarily, then visibly gathered himself before speaking again. "I have an announcement to make that will affect us all." He paused again, as if not wanting to disclose what he had to say. Then he quietly cleared his throat. "This morning at dawn, German soldiers crossed the border with Poland in what seems to be a deliberate and full-scale invasion of that country." There was an audible gasp from those seated and a short burst of murmured conversation. The Commanding Officer held his hands up and gestured for the room to be quiet before continuing. "Details are limited at this time, but I have no doubt you will get more from the newspapers and radio in due course." In order to exploit the silence just created, he continued immediately. "I'm afraid to say that all military leave has been cancelled, and those newly trained soldiers who were expecting to go on a period of leave today before joining their battalions, will unfortunately not be doing so." A louder murmur broke out that the raised hands of the Commanding Officer this time failed to quell.

"Pay attention everyone." intervened the Regimental Sergeant Major loudly, immediately bringing the hall to silence again.

"All those soldiers who passed out today will be moving to join their battalions on Sunday morning." the Commanding Officer continued. "The preparations must begin immediately, and all guests are kindly requested to depart."

Kyle's mother gripped his hand tightly under the table. He looked round at her, but she had her eyes closed and her head bowed. The dining hall suddenly erupted into a clamour of voices and movement. McCann got up, and placing his hands on Mrs Kyle's upper arms gently helped her to her feet.

"Come on, Elizabeth. Let's get you out of here." he said quietly. "The boys will have some preparation to do." She rose to her feet as if in a trance, before suddenly snapping back to her senses and placing her hands on each side of her son's face.

"Telephone and tell me what's happening." she ordered, as she looked directly into his eyes.

"Yes, Mum. As soon as I know anything." Kyle stuttered in reply.

"Come on, Elizabeth. Let's get you home." spoke McCann soothingly. He looked at Kyle with pursed lips and nodded gently as he turned his mother away and led her towards the door. The families were being ushered out by the instructors, their tables and chairs left in disarray; their drinks unfinished. Watching their families leave, the newly trained soldiers gathered in the middle of the hall, deflated, and uncertain what to do next. The Regimental Sergeant Major brought order to the situation.

"Right, you lot. Get yourselves back to your platoon blocks, quick as you can."

Sunday 3 September 1939 –
Lichfield Train Station, Staffordshire, England.

The tailgates of the Bedford transport vehicles swung open with a metallic clunk as each one came to a stop in a single line behind the others. Voices of non-commissioned officers yelled for the occupants to get out. The two soldiers nearest the back jumped down, kit bags and equipment being passed the length of the vehicle and out the back to those waiting. The rest of the occupants jumped down in turn, searching to find their labelled bags and put on their packs and webbing equipment. Once they had sorted themselves out, they were ushered into the station and formed up on the platform. Outside the newspaper kiosk, an advertising poster displayed the headline *"Hitler Invades Poland"* in large black letters.

Two Military Policemen who had been standing outside the entrance, followed the soldiers into the station and took up positions at the exits to deter or prevent any potential deserters; their red topped caps in stark contrast to the khaki of everyone else. A train stood ready, passenger carriages filling almost the complete length of the platform, its engine hissing steam as if impatient to depart. Sergeant Major McCann paced slowly up and down in front of the ranks of waiting soldiers. He looked at the young, pale faces of the men; mostly the newly trained recruits that had passed out only forty-eight hours before. Included also were some of the instructors returning to their battalions after finishing their Depot postings, and here and there, some soldiers from other Regiments and Corps who had been recalled from leave in the area. McCann knew exactly how they were feeling, having himself stood nervously on a railway platform as a newly trained soldier, bound for France twenty-two years previously.

As Captain Roberts approached, McCann brought the parade to attention. He saluted smartly and announced the parade present. Roberts, who himself had been on leave, knew McCann well. Both served together in D Company; Roberts as Second in Command and McCann as Company Sergeant Major. Captain Roberts returned the salute then looked at his watch.

12

"Fall the men out, Sergeant Major." Roberts ordered. "Give them five minutes with their families, then get them on the train."

On command, the parade dismissed, some soldiers heading straight to the newspaper stand to buy the paper and cigarettes. Some of the families who lived close by had come to see their loved ones depart. As the parade fell out, Watts' mother rushed to embrace her son. She took quick but short steps, her pace constricted by a pencil skirt. She pulled his face towards hers as he tried to resist, a failed kiss smearing her lipstick across his cheek. She tried to rub it off, but unsure of how much remained, he rubbed the area himself inspecting his fingers to measure his degree of success. His sudden movement in avoiding the kiss caused his cap to slide from his head and land on the platform. His mother picked it up and placed it back on his head, pushing it down hard as if to ensure it would stay in place. The pressing action squeezed his unruly hair tuft from under the cap, leaving it protruding across his forehead.

"That hair of yours. Always that bit at the front." she tutted, licking her fingers and pushing it back underneath the cap.

A whistle sounded, easing Watts' immediate discomfort as his mother jumped at the sound and released her grip on him. Shouts from non-commissioned officers to board the train were greeted by whimpers of distress from mothers, wives and children as they realised their time together was at an end. Kyle had told his mother the time and place of his departure as she had requested, but she was nowhere to be seen. He looked around nervously for her, the whistle blast heightening his sense of unease at her absence. Corporal Hutchinson moved among the families on the platform gently separating the final embraces and ushering the soldiers onto the train. McCann and Roberts stood together on the quickly emptying platform as the soldiers boarded the train.

"Don't worry, Mrs Watts. I'll look after him." Hutchinson reassured her as he guided her son towards the open doors of the waiting carriages. Kyle saw his friend climb in and reluctantly followed him on board, pulling the door shut behind him, then turning and sliding the window down. Using the extra height of the carriage, Kyle leaned out, scanning the remaining crowd for a sight of his mother. He then heard her voice shouting out McCann's name as she ran onto the platform.

"Where is he, Seamus?" she pleaded as she approached McCann, grasping his sleeve. McCann turned and shouted as loud as he could.

"Private Kyle. Make yourself known." Kyle leaned further out the open window waving frantically.

"Mum, over here!" he yelled above the noise.

McCann grabbed her hand and pushing through the families gathered on the platform edge, led her to where her son was leaning through the window. She threw her arms around his neck, her weight unbalancing him, almost pulling him from the train.

13

"I thought I had missed you." she sobbed, as much in relief at finding him as in sadness at his departure.

"Don't worry, Mum. I'll be alright." Kyle responded reassuringly.

"I've had him sent to D Company where I can keep an eye on him." McCann assured her. "He'll be alright, just as he says."

She held both her son's hands, saying nothing. Words seemed pointless now. She just wanted to hold him for as long as she could. McCann and Roberts were the last to board as the guard waved a green flag and the train slowly moved off. The remaining families on the platform broke into a cheer as the carriages started to move. Those on board waved their caps from open windows in response. Kyle's mother continued to hold his hands as the train moved, walking faster as it gathered speed. When she could no longer keep up, their hands slipped apart. Kyle looked back to see her waving before the steam and smoke from the engine blurred the scene.

The guard watched until the train cleared the station and returned to his office, leaving the forlorn relatives still standing on the platform. He crossed the threadbare carpet to the stove and filled the teapot from the kettle that was always kept boiling on top. He slumped down in his battered brown leather chair, checking his pocket watch against the clock on the wall. It was 11:15 a.m. Leaning over to the sideboard, he switched on the wireless before settling back into his chair. The unmistakable voice of the Prime Minister crackled from the speaker.

"I am speaking to you from the cabinet room at 10 Downing Street. This morning, the British Ambassador in Berlin handed the German Government a final note stating that unless we heard from them by 11 o'clock that they were prepared at once to withdraw their troops from Poland, a state of war would exist between us. I have to tell you now that no such undertaking has been received, and that consequently, this country is at war with Germany."

Sunday 3 September 1939 –
Aldershot, Southern England.

With his cap placed between his head and the window as a makeshift pillow, Martin Kyle had been able to sleep for most of the journey. It had been a frantic few days, and he was using the enforced break to catch up; wakening intermittently when the train stopped to see the station names on the journey south. As the brakes screeched again, he opened his eyes just enough to see the sign indicating Aldershot. Watts was lying across two seats opposite, and as far as Kyle could establish had slept the whole journey. He heard voices approaching from adjacent carriages calling for all West Staffords to get off the train.

"This is us, mate." he said wearily as he shook Watts awake. Corporal Hutchinson appeared through the carriage door, walking between the seats and shaking awake anyone he found still asleep. Seeing Kyle and Watts awake but inactive he hurried them along.

"Right, boys. Get your stuff and get yourselves outside. Make sure you don't leave anything behind." His voice continued down the carriage repeating his call for all West Staffords to get off, before fading as he moved into the next carriage. As Kyle and Watts stepped down from the train, they could see other soldiers already forming into ranks in the middle of the platform.

"Hurry up and fall in." Sergeant Major McCann's voice was unmistakable even with all the noise of a busy railway platform. It had the desired effect, as Kyle and Watts scurried to join the gathering group. Non-commissioned officers pointed at individuals as they counted the formed ranks, then counted again; and once content that everyone who should be there was on parade, the group was marched off the platform and out of the station to a line of waiting trucks. It was the usual melee as kit and equipment was loaded, and the soldiers climbed up to take their seats in the back of the Bedford trucks. The tailgate was raised and locked, and a thump of a hand on the vehicle side panel indicated to the driver that loading was complete and he could move off.

Having slept well on the train, Kyle was refreshed enough to take in the surroundings through the open canvas flap in the gathering gloom of early evening. Some young children waved as the convoy passed. Kyle found it amusing and waved back, much to the excitement of the children who had managed to elicit a response. After a fifteen-minute journey, the vehicles entered Aldershot Garrison, a red and white barrier being raised to let them pass. When through the barrier, the vehicles stopped and orders to dismount were shouted.

Watts and Kyle found themselves feeling lost, standing idly with the other newly trained soldiers, as those who were familiar with Aldershot collected their baggage and equipment and moved off to their accommodation. Corporal Hutchinson produced a list of names, calling out those at the top of the alphabet first, giving them a platoon number and the name of their Sergeant. He then directed them towards three Sergeants who were standing chatting outside the guardroom. Half a dozen names had been called before it was Kyle's turn.

"Kyle, 10 Platoon, Sergeant Preston." shouted Hutchinson.

Kyle acknowledged the instruction, lifted his equipment and began walking towards the group of Sergeants, who had started to form lines of the new soldiers allocated to them. His slow pace invited encouragement from one of the Sergeants.

"Don't bloody walk. Run." demanded an unknown voice. Kyle broke into a run heading directly towards the gruff Scotsman who had just berated him, coming to a halt a foot away.

"Are you Tenpiltoon?" inquired Sergeant Preston, running the words together in his broad Scottish accent.

"Yes, Sergeant. Private Kyle." he replied.

"Stand there and don't talk." said Preston, as they were joined by another soldier that Kyle recognised from Depot training as Private McEnearney. McEnearney grimaced at Kyle as he passed, as if to silently question what they had done wrong to get such gruff treatment. Sergeant Preston accepted a cigarette from one of the other Sergeants that were collecting their new arrivals. All three huddled together to light their cigarettes from the same match. Kyle could see Watts was the last new arrival awaiting designation, and heard him being assigned to 10 Platoon by Corporal Hutchinson. Kyle gestured for him to hurry over, and he joined the line behind McEnearney and Kyle before Sergeant Preston had returned to his position. When Preston turned back, he saw three soldiers where there had previously been two.

"Are you Tenpiltoon?" Preston asked, addressing Watts.

"No, Sergeant. Private Watts." he answered with a wavering voice.

There was a few seconds' pause as Preston's neck seemed to swell and overflow his tunic collar. Barely controlling his obvious rage, Preston grabbed Watts by the front of his tunic pulling him up on to his toes, a not unimpressive feat considering that Watts was dressed in marching order and still holding his kit bag. Watts felt the heat of Preston's breath on his face with a whiff of cigarette smoke and alcohol as Preston's mouth came within inches of his nose.

"You cheeky little bastard." Preston hissed slowly through gritted teeth before regaining control of his temper and demonstrably releasing his grip, letting Watts drop back down onto his feet. Gathering himself further, he stared hard at Watts for several seconds.

"Corporal McIlwaine." Preston yelled without breaking his eye contact with Watts, before turning and clearing the three steps into the Guardroom in a single bound. Raised voices could be heard from inside.

"What did you say that for?" Kyle whispered accusingly at Watts as they found themselves alone.

"He asked me if my name was Templeton." replied Watts, incredulous that his apparently only correct answer had seemingly caused some yet to be experienced unpleasant event.

"He asked if you were 10 Platoon, you bloody fool. He's Scottish." replied Kyle, sensing that any impending punishment was about to be shared equally by association, despite himself and McEnearney having no part in the exchange that had just taken place.

"We're for it now." added McEnearney, with a note of impending doom in his voice. A Corporal emerged from the Guardroom hurriedly fixing his belt and headdress as if he had been stung by a bee.

"Which one of you is Watts?" he asked.

"That's me, Corporal." replied Watts sheepishly, turning his head towards the rapidly advancing non-commissioned officer. McIlwaine stopped in front of him. He was a diminutive individual with a pocked face from teenage acne and eyebrows that joined in the middle.

"Get yourself into the Guardroom now." yelled Corporal McIlwaine, his upper body leaning forward with the effort and saliva spraying from his lips as he shouted the command. Watts moved faster than either of his colleagues had seen him move before. As Watts and Corporal McIlwaine disappeared up the steps and into the Guardroom, Sergeant Preston re-emerged, pulling another soldier by the arm.

"Take these two to 1 Section block and get them settled in." he directed, roughly pushing the newcomer towards the waiting Kyle and McEnearney. "Watts will be along later." he growled, turning back towards the Guardroom steps.

"Welcome to 10 Platoon." said the newcomer through a beaming smile, straightening his headdress and a thick lensed pair of wire rimmed glasses that had shifted when his body jerked forward from the push by Sergeant Preston. "I'm Smith, but everyone calls me Smudger. I see you've already met Sergeant Preston." he remarked, nodding his head in the direction of the departing Sergeant.

"Is he always like this?" Kyle questioned, hoping for a reply in the negative.

"Not all the time." replied Smith. "He's never completely calm, but is always worse if he's had a drink. Best just to stay out of his way if you know or think he has been on it." Kyle and McEnearney looked at each other, both silently asking the other what they had gotten themselves into.

"Now, who is who?" asked Smith.

"I'm Martin Kyle, and this is Tom McEnearney." replied Kyle with a nod of his head towards his comrade.

"Grab your kit and follow me." Smith cheerfully quipped as he moved off. Kyle and McEnearney hastily lifted their kit bags and hurried after Smith who was already moving at a fast walk down the gently sloping road towards the centre of the camp. They passed single storey wooden huts on each side of the road as they struggled to keep pace with Smith under the burden of their equipment and kit bags. Dim lights shone through the curtained windows of the huts, with the occasional sound of men talking and laughing. Smith suddenly turned right, pushing open the door to one of the huts.

Kyle and McEnearney followed him in to a small hall with three doors; two directly facing and one on the right-hand side. Entering the door on the right they were immediately struck by the smell of floor polish carried on hot air. The hut had ten metal framed beds, five down each side, with a wardrobe sized wooden locker to the right side of each bed. In the middle of the room were two tables with some wooden chairs arranged around them, a table on either side of a black stove in which logs were burning. There were single windows behind each bed with a larger double window in the middle of the gable wall at the far end. Two soldiers sat at one of the tables, smoking and playing cards; another lying fully clothed on his bed, feet crossed with his hands behind his head. None paid any attention as the new arrivals walked in.

Smith walked to the furthest end of the room and pointed at two unmade beds, one on each side of the hut. The sheets and blankets were neatly folded in blocks at the end of the mattress furthest from the wall. A yellow stained pillow lay at the head of each bed.

"Take your pick. They're both free." he said, pointing at the two unmade beds. Both of the new arrivals threw their kit bag onto their chosen bed and unbuckled their equipment, dropping it to the floor. Smith ran through the ground rules.

"There is a kit layout pinned inside the locker door. That's the way your uniform and equipment must be laid out for inspection. Your bed must be made up the same as everyone else, and each person is responsible for keeping the area around his own bedspace clean."

Kyle opened his locker door to see a printed page attached to the inside with two drawing pins at the top and bottom, the corners of the paper beginning to curl inwards with age. It was a diagram of where each piece of clothing and equipment was to be stored or hung up inside the locker.

"The non-commissioned officers stay in the rooms you passed on the way in, and the next hut down is the ablutions." continued Smith. Gesturing for them to follow, he moved back towards the middle of the room, stopping at the soldier who was lying on his bed; a muscular and somewhat dishevelled looking individual. "This is Private Bell, known to everyone as Dinger." said Smith. Bell opened his eyes and raised his head to look at the new arrivals, grunting his acknowledgement. "Martin Kyle and Tom McEnearney. Just arrived from Depot." offered Smith as a way of introduction.

"Welcome to 1 Section." muttered Bell as he closed his eyes and lay back down again, in an apparent state of exhaustion.

"Always tired and always hungry is our Dinger." explained Smith, leaning over and patting him on the lower leg. "No matter how much sleep he gets, or how much he eats." Bell raised his hands in the air, as if surrendering in grudging acceptance of Smith's personal assessment as the trio moved off. As Bell's hands were exposed, Kyle noticed they were huge, and his knuckles were covered in callouses and warts. "These two gentlemen are Privates McCafferty and Orpin." continued Smith as he introduced the two card players, indicating with his hand which was which. McCafferty offered a wide grin, exposing a set of badly discoloured teeth for a man only just in his twenties. He had obviously not used a toothbrush for a considerable time. He had particularly bright ginger hair, made starker by an unhealthy looking white skin tone.

"D...do any of you p...play cards?" he asked in a stuttering broad Liverpool accent, tapping the deck on the table to straighten it before beginning to shuffle. "Y...You're more than welcome to j...join in."

"Leave the boys alone, La La; at least wait until they get paid to make it worth your while." giggled Orpin in a droning nasal voice, very obviously from the English Midlands. "You don't want to be playing with him lads, unless you know how to spot a cheat." Both players looked at each other and laughed at the barbed accusation.

"The non-commissioned officers live in here." gestured Smith towards the two separate doors as he continued the block tour back the way they had entered. "Lance Corporal Tetlow stays in here. He's the Section Second in Command." said Smith, tapping the door with the toe of his boot, "And we are getting a new Section Commander on return from a Depot posting. A Corporal Hutchinson." Tapping the other door, Smith pursed his lips and shrugged his shoulders to display the name meant nothing to him.

"We know Corporal Hutchinson from Depot." chirped Kyle, speaking for both himself and Private McEnearney, somewhat relieved that at least he had a familiar face to associate with his new surroundings. "He was on the train with us from Lichfield."

"Well, I hope he knows his stuff, because Tetlow is a useless bloody nightmare." explained Smith. "He's on platoon guard duty tonight with a lot of the other lads, but you'll meet him tomorrow. Been in the Army for twelve years and reached the dizzy heights of Lance Corporal. Say no more! He's a creature, but you'll find that out for yourselves quickly enough." He ran through the names of the other Sergeants in the company; Sergeant Toner in 11 Platoon and Sergeant Allen in 12 Platoon. Then the Corporals in 10 Platoon; McIlwaine and Hill in 2 Section and Thomas and White in 3 Section.

Moving back outside, he immediately turned right into the next hut in the row. A sign on the door read *10 Platoon Ablutions* written in chalk on a black painted board. Smith pushed open the door which led into a small porch. On the wall inside the porch was a noticeboard with some documents pinned to it.

"This is the block jobs list." he said. "It shows who is responsible for cleaning the showers, toilets and accommodation blocks and emptying the bins on what day. The cleaning materials are in the store just there." he continued, pointing to a narrow wooden locker, hidden when the main door was opened. "Sergeant Preston produces the roster, and if you get on the wrong side of him, you'll get extra block jobs in return. Your names are not on the cleaning roster yet," continued Smith, running his finger down the list of names, "but I suggest you get familiar with the routine and see how it's done for when it's your turn."

Stepping through the second door into the ablutions, there was a central island of white ceramic washbasins, five in a row and back-to-back, separated by a line of cracked and discoloured mirrors, one over each sink. A line of six urinals ran along the wall on the left, with a universal cistern on the wall above from which the sound of trickling water was continuous. A line of saloon doored toilet cubicles was on the right. Kyle was struck by a smell of stale urine, and noticing his reaction to the smell, Smith reassured him.

"It always gets a bit ripe later in the day, but it smells fresh enough after cleaning in the morning." Following Smith around the washbasins they passed through another door at the opposite end of the room. "On the left is the showers and a bath, and on the right is the laundry and drying room." A wave of heat came from the drying room as Smith pushed open the door, carrying with it the smell of wet woollen clothes.

"This ablution block is for the whole platoon. You're just lucky that your barrack room is next door. The other two sections have to come across the road from the barrack rooms opposite; rain, hail or shine!" He turned and made his way back towards the barrack room they had just left, followed by Kyle and McEnearney, stopping outside the door without entering.

"Get yourselves unpacked and settled in. I'll collect you when I come off guard tomorrow morning at half seven and take you to the cookhouse for breakfast. Be washed and shaved and dressed as you are now. The Commanding Officer wants to speak to the whole battalion in the cinema at 9 o'clock, so something big must be happening."

Kyle and McEnearney watched for a few seconds as Smith hurried up the slope towards the guardroom, then went back inside the barrack room. Bell was still lying on his bed, cutting slices from an apple with a penknife, and the card game continued uninterrupted. Kyle unclipped the fastener on the top of his kit bag and began to pull the contents out onto the bed. Referring to the locker plan, he began to arrange his clothing and equipment in accordance with the diagram. He felt empty inside, just as he did when he started training at the Depot, but told himself this would pass in a few days like before, once he knew his way around and settled into a routine.

Monday 4 September 1939 –
Aldershot Garrison, Southern England.

The cinema was a wooden structure with a line of small windows running the length of each side just below the level of the panelled ceiling. Blackout curtains used during film screenings had been pulled aside to let in the light, and their drawstrings tied around cleats at shoulder height on the wall. There was a stage at one end running the full width of the building, and with a similar black curtain covering the complete wall. Six wooden steps on either side allowed access up to the stage floor level, where four chairs now sat in the middle of the stage. The Battalion Officers occupied armchairs in the first row of seats, the rows behind being folded out wooden slatted chairs arranged facing towards the stage, with a ten feet wide space left empty down the middle for access. The room buzzed with the sound of voices, undoubtedly discussing their thoughts on the impending announcement.

Kyle and McEnearney had been collected by Smith and taken to the cookhouse that morning as arranged, and although the food was not as good as they were served at Depot, and eating time was restricted due to the numbers trying to get fed, they had eaten heartily on porridge, bacon and bread. The section was now seated together in the cinema in the same row; the musty smell of damp and cigarette smoke from impregnated uniforms pervading the space. This was the first time the new arrivals had got to see their section colleagues. Corporal Hutchinson sat in the seat closest to the central gap, and as Kyle leaned forward to look along the ranks, Hutchinson caught his eye, smiled and winked. An unknown Lance Corporal sat next to Hutchinson that Kyle assumed must be Tetlow. He looked older than others of a similar rank, as Smith had alluded to, but there was something about his bearing that made him seem detached and disinterested. He slouched in his seat with his legs stretched out in front and was probing inside his nose with his index finger, which he then examined carefully before wiping it on the backrest of the seat in front of him. Sensing someone was looking at him, Tetlow quickly turned his head and stared straight at Kyle who had been mesmerised by his actions. Kyle instantly averted his gaze and then slowly turned his head away in an attempt to disguise that he had been watching. Feeling very self-conscious that Tetlow was still staring at him, he startled when he felt a tap on his shoulder, turning abruptly round in his chair to see Watts grinning at him from the row behind.

"How are you settling in?" Watts enquired.

"Bit early to say for sure, but so far so good. I'm in 1 Section. The others seem nice enough." he replied. "How about you?"

"I'm in 2 Section. They all seem friendly."

"What happened to you last night when they took you to the guardroom?" asked Kyle. Watts half smiled and shrugged his shoulders.

"Got accused of being insubordinate to Sergeant Preston. After a bit of yelling and shouting, they made me take my boots off and put on a pair with double soles that were much too large. Weighed a bloody ton they did! Then the Corporal held a stick out level in front of me at waist height, and I had to mark time making sure I touched the stick with my thighs each time."

McEnearney, who was sitting on Kyle's left had turned to listen to the story and both he and Kyle began to laugh as they pictured Watts being punished.

"It might be funny to you now, but it wasn't at the time." Watts continued. The sweat was running down my back and between the cheeks of my ass." This made Kyle and McEnearney laugh even more. "Every time I didn't touch the stick with my leg, Corporal McIlwaine made me go faster. He only stopped when I fell in a heap on the floor and couldn't do any more." Their attention was drawn to the front of the stage from where a voice boomed around the cinema.

"Company Sergeant Majors, report to me!" It was the Regimental Sergeant Major, the sound of whom made everyone in the cinema stop talking. Four Warrant Officers hurriedly approached, each springing to attention in turn as they stopped in front of the Regimental Sergeant Major. He scribbled some notes in a grubby notebook as each of the Warrant Officers reported, then dismissed them before climbing the steps up onto the stage. Quiet chatting began again, eliciting an order for silence from the Regimental Sergeant Major. He stared around the room, as if daring anyone else to talk, before stamping his feet nosily on the wooden stage and springing to attention.

"Sit Up." he snapped loudly.

Chairs screeched as everyone in the cinema adjusted their seated posture to sit bolt upright with their arms straight and clenched fists resting on their knees. Then there was complete silence. Three officers walked down the central aisle between the rows of chairs, the Commanding Officer leading, followed by the Battalion Second in Command and the Adjutant, the second two officers carrying a large board with an easel. They climbed the steps on the left side up onto the stage. The Regimental Sergeant Major took a single pace forward with his left foot as they approached, then stamped his right foot in line to come to the position of attention again. He saluted, which was returned by the Commanding Officer.

"Sir, apart from those on essential duties or bedded down in the Medical Centre, the battalion is present, Sir." he declared in a voice loud enough to be heard by all present.

"Thank you, RSM. Please have the men sit easy." replied the Commanding Officer. With another drill movement, the Regimental Sergeant Major turned forty-five degrees to his right before announcing "Sit Easy." At this command everyone in the cinema relaxed their posture and assumed a more comfortable position in their chairs. The two accompanying officers set up the easel and the board at the back of the stage, then along with the Regimental Sergeant Major occupied the pre-positioned armchairs. The Commanding Officer moved to the front of the stage and walked slowly back and forth with his hands behind his back, looking around the cinema, but at no one in particular, before he spoke.

"You will probably already know that Hitler's forces invaded Poland on Friday morning, and that at eleven fifteen yesterday morning the Prime Minister declared that Britain was once again at war with Germany. I have subsequently received notice that the battalion will be moving overseas in the near future, to somewhere in France, and my guess is this will happen within the next few weeks." A low murmur broke out around the cinema, quickly dying as the Commanding Officer continued.

"In preparation, we will be entering a period of intensive training that the Battalion Second in Command has designed, and he will brief you all on that later this morning. Needless to say, it will involve range work, tactical exercises, patrolling and route marching to prepare us for whatever tasks lie ahead." He paused for a few seconds before continuing. "An advance party will depart later this week to prepare the way and get everything arranged for our arrival. A contingent from the Quartermaster's Department and a Corporal from each platoon will travel ahead to sort out the new barracks, get to know the area, and then be responsible for bringing everyone else up to speed when we eventually get there." Another murmur washed across the audience.

"I urge you to make the most of the next few weeks." he continued. "To some, it will just be revision of long held skills, but to others, and especially any recent arrivals, this may well be the first time you have taken part in training of this complexity and intensity. Learn it well." He paused again. "That is all that I can tell you now; but rest assured that as soon as any more information becomes available, I will pass it on." He turned to look at the Regimental Sergeant Major who was rising from his seat at the unspoken signal.

"Sit Up." barked the RSM as soon as he was standing, the audience once again assuming the seated position of attention. The Commanding Officer returned the Regimental Sergeant Major's salute before he descended the steps at the side of the stage and walked down the aisle through the still braced soldiers. The Regimental Sergeant Major watched until the Commanding Officer had left the building before allowing the men to sit easy. In the time it took for the Commanding Officer to leave, the Second in Command had set up the board at the front of the stage. He pulled back a cloth cover so the audience could see the carefully ruled table inscribed on the board. The officers on the front row took out their notebooks and began to copy down the information.

"Right, this is how the programme will work." the Second in Command began his brief, his voice displaying the confidence of an officer who knew his business.

* * *

Kyle, Watts and McEnearney were stood at ease in the corridor outside the Company Commander's Office. Sergeant Preston had told them to report to the Company Sergeant Major immediately after lunch for their new arrivals' interview with Major Crawley. Three Corporals were already waiting in the corridor ahead of them when they arrived. Company Sergeant Major McCann appeared from inside the Company Commander's Office and closed the door behind him.

"Right, you three. Stand at attention and turn to the right." he growled at the Corporals; his Irish accent accentuated by his obvious bad mood. "March to the time I call out. Go straight in, then left wheel in front of the OC's desk." He opened the office door, holding it wide with his left hand.

"Quick March. Left, right, left, right, left, right, left." The three Corporals filed in past him; he followed them in, still calling out the time, and closed the door behind them.

The three Privates remained awkwardly silent in the corridor, muffled voices coming from inside the Company Commander's office. Kyle leaned forward and strained his ears trying to make out what was being said, but to no avail. They startled as the door suddenly opened, almost feeling guilty they had been caught out trying to listen in. The Company Sergeant Major's voice preceded the three Corporals back out through the door. "Left, right, left, right, halt." The three Corporals stood perfectly still as McCann closed the office door behind them.

"Look at me." McCann said in a calmer voice, the Corporals turning their heads to comply. "Don't get big-headed with all that shite about being the best Corporals we have in the company, and being representatives of the regiment with the French." He moved closer to them, staring at the individuals in turn as he spoke. The calmer demeanour disappeared again, his voice rising to the pre-interview level as he stared directly into their eyes one after the other. "I know what you're like." continued McCann addressing all three, before singling out one with a snap of his head bringing his face within inches of the individual. "Especially you, Corporal Thomas!" He moved his head away and paused for effect. "Don't fuck this up. Any reports of bad behaviour, drunkenness, theft or raping nuns and I'll pull your bloody arms and legs out! Understood?"

"Yes, Sir." the three Corporals answered back in unison. Stepping back, having made his point perfectly clear, McCann paused for a few seconds. "Now disappear and get your kit packed. Move!" As the three Corporals scurried away, McCann glared at the three waiting Privates when he passed, before knocking on the Company Commander's door and going back into the office.

"Bloody Hell." whispered McEnearney as the door closed. "He seems a level headed and understanding bloke." Kyle was about to interject with his personal, but as yet limited, exposure to McCann, when the door opened sharply. McCann pulled Watts forward and moved him from the left to the centre of the group to match an order that had obviously just been agreed with the waiting Company Commander.

"Stand at attention and turn to the right." McCann ordered. The three soldiers complied. "March to the time I call out." He repeated the same instructions as he had given the Corporals. "Go straight in, then left wheel in front of the OC's desk." He opened the office door, holding it wide with his left hand as he yelled, "Quick March. Left, right, left, right, left, right, left." The three soldiers entered the office, wheeled left and marked time as instructed by McCann, before halting and turning right to face the Company Commander's desk.

"Salute." yelled McCann. The soldiers saluted and returned to the position of attention as they had done countless times at the Training Depot. When McCann stood them at ease, Kyle glanced around him without moving his head. The Officer Commanding sat behind a green leather surfaced wooden desk. On it rested a silver photo frame, inkwell and telephone, and three wooden document trays labelled "In", "Pending", and "Out." His peaked cap and swagger stick sat off to one side. Various framed posed photographs of groups of seated officers decorated the walls behind him. A trench coat hung on a wooden coat stand in the corner of the office. McCann took up a position to the right of the desk where he could see both the Officer Commanding and the soldiers.

Major Crawley was a narrow-shouldered individual, almost painfully thin. His hair was receding, particularly visible to those standing while he was seated. As the soldiers saluted, he looked up with a wide toothy smile. One of his top incisors was slightly twisted and had discoloured to a coffee-colour. The corresponding incisor in the lower jaw was set back from the others, again discoloured. Before he spoke, he let out a deep nasally sniff, as if something was lodged in his sinus and he was trying to dislodge it.

"Watts, Kyle, McEnearney." he said confidently but with the hint of a lisp, pointing at each from left to right as he said the name. McCann stepped forward and adjusted the order of the three files on the officer's desk to match the order in which the soldiers stood.

"That's it now, Sir. Kyle, Watts and McEnearney." The look on McCann's face was a mix of frustration and resignation as he stepped back to the side of the desk again, shaking his head almost imperceptibly at how something agreed barely sixty seconds earlier had still gone array. Major Crawley leafed through the corresponding file before questioning each soldier in turn, whether they had been a volunteer or conscripted, if they had any family connections to the regiment, how they found the experience at Depot, if they took part in sport or had any other skills that could be useful in Army life. Kyle declared his father's service with the Regiment in the Great War, but found Major Crawley somewhat dismissive of the fact. As he spoke, Kyle felt his eyes drawn to the twisted discoloured teeth, which added to the slightly scatter-brained impression that Crawley exuded. Every so often during the conversation he would let out another deep nasal sniff.

McEnearney had been in a different platoon than Kyle and Watts during training, so it came as a bit of a surprise to them when he declared he spoke French. Major Crawley couldn't disguise his delight at the revelation, seeing all kinds of opportunities unfolding when the battalion eventually got to France.

"I think Private McEnearney will be extremely useful. Don't you agree, Sergeant Major?" It was meant as a statement rather than a question, but McCann felt a compulsion to answer.

"He'll be bloody marvellous, Sir." came the response as McCann hid the sarcasm in his voice but not in his face, scowling directly at McEnearney. With the interview finished, and the three soldiers lined up back in the corridor outside the Company Commander's Office, Sergeant Major McCann took the opportunity to set some ground rules for the newest members of D Company.

"I've never heard so much shite talked in all my life!" McCann exploded at McEnearney. "French? Where did you learn to speak bloody French?"

"My mother is French, Sir." McEnearney stammered in his defence. "My father was originally from Ireland and they met when he served in France during the Great War. He didn't want to return home due to the Civil War, so they lived in Jersey. I was born and raised there."

"I don't see much Irish in you. Are you sure you weren't adopted?" McCann quizzed sarcastically. Receiving no reaction from McEnearney, he persisted in his original line of questioning. "And your mother taught you to speak French?"

"Fluent French, Sir, yes." replied McEnearney confidently.

"You'd better not be telling me bloody lies!" snapped McCann as he raised his pace stick and held it just under McEnearney's nose. "The truth will become all too obvious very soon. As the Company Commander said, he has big plans for you. If you don't speak French, you better bloody well learn, and fast." McCann stepped back from McEnearney and addressed all three soldiers as he walked up and down in front of them, his stick under his left arm and his right arm behind his back.

"Listen to me, Gentlemen, and listen well." He paused for effect, calmly addressing the wall above their heads as opposed to the soldiers themselves in a well-rehearsed speech that all new arrivals had received since McCann assumed his post. "I have eyes and ears everywhere. Everything you do wrong will find its way back to me, so, I suggest you discipline yourselves or I will discipline you." His air of calmness abruptly disappeared. "And I'll give you one guess which will be more unpleasant." he yelled. "Now get back to your duties! Move." Without waiting for further instruction, the three soldiers ran down the corridor and out of the building.

* * *

The rest of the section was in the barrack room collecting their webbing equipment when Kyle and McEnearney came in.

"How did it go with Creepy?" Orpin asked inquisitively as he fastened his equipment. Both Kyle and McEnearney stared at him blankly and then at each other, hoping the other would understand the question and give an answer. "Creepy Crawley, the Company Commander." repeated Orpin somewhat exasperated at seeing their confusion.

"Oh, he was fine." replied Kyle. "Seems a bit easily confused though."

"I would agree," replied Orpin, "But he's also easily pleased, which makes things better for us." he continued. "Although, he can't cope with pressure very well. Falls apart when given responsibility."

"He was delighted when I said I could speak French." McEnearney beamed.

"You don't want to advertise that too widely." advised Orpin. "You'll be bloody tortured by the rest of the boys wanting stuff when we get to France. Anyway, get your webbing equipment on. We're expected at the armoury to collect weapons for handling and safety tests this afternoon as we're on the range tomorrow."

Tuesday 5 September 1939 –
Aldershot Firing Range, Southern England.

Sergeant Preston had split the platoon into its three sections, with one operating the target frames in the butts, one on the firing point and the other in the troop shelter waiting their turn to shoot. Preston was a man of limited mental agility and was happiest when simple routines were in place. He hated the complexity that officers invariably added to any situation and had subsequently developed a dislike for all commissioned ranks. The fact that a steady drizzle was falling made him even happier as the shooting detail lay on the wet grass while he kept dry under his rain cape. He saw this as a way of toughening up the men, made better in that he suffered minimal discomfort himself whilst doing so. As his platoon pet, Sergeant Preston had assigned Corporal McIlwaine to manage the butt party, where some degree of protection from the elements was afforded under the cover of the raised sand backstop. McIlwaine had subsequently selected his close friend Lance Corporal Tetlow to assist, knowing they could stay dry all day, not have to fire their weapons, and thus not have to clean them at the end of the training.

Private Cockcroft sat behind the firing line where a field telephone connected him to the butt party. His job was to trigger the raising and lowering of the targets upon command of Sergeant Preston. As a gesture to the longevity of his task, Sergeant Preston had allowed him to put on his rain cape. Cockcroft was a five-year veteran and skilled in the art of avoiding arduous duties. He had been involved in a range accident some years before when he had broken his jaw and lost most of his front teeth. This had left him difficult to understand when talking generally, but more specifically, when using communication devices or when he got excited or agitated. His affliction earned him the platoon nickname of "Wobbly Gob", and in a running 10 Platoon joke at Cockcroft's expense, he was always assigned jobs that required some form of verbal communication. As Sergeant Preston ordered targets up and down for the firers to engage, Cockcroft called the corresponding phone in the butts to initiate the required action. It had been working well all morning with the targets appearing and disappearing on request.

Sergeant Preston had just ordered a change of magazine for the firers and signalled Cockcroft with a movement of his hand that he wanted the targets up. Cockcroft dutifully signalled the butts, but received no answer to his ring. He became aware of Sergeant Preston getting more animated, vigorously repeating the signal for targets up, while giving Cockcroft dagger looks. Cockcroft immediately repeated the call, becoming increasingly frantic in his efforts as he saw Sergeant Preston purposefully striding towards him. Expecting a physical rebuke, he got to his feet and dropped the telephone handset as Preston approached. Preston pushed him away from the telephone, kneeled down beside the instrument and dialled the butts himself, obviously fully apportioning the blame for the failure on Cockcroft; but as before, there was no response. With a yell of frustration, Preston threw the handset to the ground and stomped back towards the soldiers waiting to fire, ordering them to unload their weapons. He then returned to Cockcroft and grabbing him by his upper arm pushed him in the direction of the butts.

"Go and find out what that idiot McIlwaine has done to the telephone, and get it fixed." he hissed at Cockcroft, who took off at a half run towards the butts. In the firing detail, Private Smith took the opportunity to rest his rifle on the ground and took out a handkerchief to wipe the rain off his glasses.

"They probably don't understand what Wobbly Gob is saying on the telephone." he said to no one in particular. A murmur of agreement spread among the resting group as they welcomed the unexpected break from firing. Seeing Cockcroft moving at somewhat less than running speed, Sergeant Preston yelled at him to hurry up. Cockcroft made a token gesture to display extra effort by moving his legs faster but taking shorter steps and not actually increasing his speed. As he approached the butts, he heard the sound of raucous laughter; and coming to a stop on the mantle, he looked down into the target operating area. The butt party were scattered around the area in seated or lying positions convulsed in laughter. Cockcroft's garbled request for an explanation fell on deaf ears, subsequent louder requests becoming more garbled as his frustration increased on receiving no response. He turned in the direction of Sergeant Preston and raised his outstretched arms to signal his inability to resolve the problem. Preston set out at a run towards the butts.

"What's the bloody problem?" yelled Preston as he arrived beside Cockcroft on the mantle. Cockcroft didn't answer, simply pointing down into the butts at the soldiers who were still helpless with laughter. Sergeant Preston strode along the mantle to the edge, and took the steps down into the butts two at a time. Corporal McIlwaine was seated beside the field telephone clutching his abdomen, barely able to breathe with laughter. He could only utter the occasional word between outbursts as he tried to respond to the

Sergeant's questions. Preston fought back the desire to laugh himself as his anger subsided, and although he could make little sense of what was being said he heard enough to understand the word "Penny." Penny was the nickname for Private Farthing, so called after the vintage bicycle, and Preston looked around for him. Farthing was sitting at the far end of the butts and the only one not laughing. He had been one of the first conscripts when the mechanism had been reintroduced in March 1939, and was clearly not cut out for life in the Army. His naive, gentle nature and slightness of build made him a target for anyone who wished to take advantage of him. Lance Corporal Tetlow, being such an individual, continually singled him out and made his life a misery. Any of his peers who tried to stand up for him received the same treatment from Tetlow, and they had since given up trying. Preston, sensing that Farthing had been the subject of some unfortunate event, adopted an approachable posture, sitting down beside him.

"What happened here, Farthing?" he asked in a conciliatory tone.

Farthing paused for a few seconds to gather his thoughts before replying. He explained that he needed to urinate but that Corporal McIlwaine would not allow him to leave the area of the butts while firing was taking place. As he declared he could not hold on until the end of the section practice, McIlwaine had directed him to relieve himself against the brick wall of the target shed.

"I couldn't hold on any longer, Sergeant, so I went against the wall." He paused again as the subsequent events returned to his mind. "My piss ran down the slope to where the section had stacked their webbing and soaked into Lance Corporal Tetlow's kit." Preston let out a snigger at the thought, and then controlled himself in consideration of Farthing's feelings.

"And he didn't take that very well?" surmised Preston with a hint of joviality in his voice.

"No, Sergeant. He told me to give him my rifle. Then he dropped his trousers, held it between his legs and shit into the breech." Preston snorted with laughter, unable to contain himself any longer, and then quickly suppressed it in an unusual display of empathy. "He then pushed the bolt forward ramming the shit up the barrel." continued Farthing. Preston's self-control broke and he descended into uncontrolled laughter, putting his hand on Farthing's shoulder in a display of apology at finding humour in his unfortunate circumstances. As he started to regain control, the bemused look on Farthing's face started him off again, this time only louder and harder as he completely abandoned any semblance of impartiality. "But how am I going to get my rifle cleaned, Sergeant?" queried Farthing while Preston was still in the throes of laughter. Preston did not attempt to answer until he was sure that he had composed himself again. Taking a deep breath and a cough to clear his throat, he yelled for Corporal McIlwaine who quickly appeared at his side. Lifting Farthing's dirty rifle and moving beyond the soldier's hearing, Preston hissed in McIlwaine's ear.

"That clown Tetlow doesn't know where to draw the line." He threw the rife at McIlwaine, who caught it awkwardly, trying to keep it as far away from his body as he could. "This happened under your supervision, so you and Tetlow can clean his shit out of this rifle. I suggest you get some boiling water when the NAAFI van arrives and pour it down the barrel." Preston stormed off towards the steps at the side of the range, before stopping and turning his head back towards Corporal McIlwaine and pointing at Lance Corporal Tetlow. "One day he is going to go too far and someone will get hurt. Now get these bloody targets ready for the next practice." he added, remembering the purpose of his personal intervention.

Wednesday 6 September 1939 –
Aldershot Firing Range, Southern England.

The two Bedford lorries carrying 10 Platoon stopped in a cloud of dust and exhaust fumes. The gaggle of voices and laughter from inside was interrupted as harsh voices yelled for the men to dismount. The canvas flaps were cast aside and the soldiers jumped to the ground, where they were ushered into their respective sections by the Corporals. Sergeant Preston brought them to attention then paced up and down in front of them as he addressed the platoon.

"Keep quiet and pay attention." he began. "This is the grenade range, where those of you who have never used it before, or have not used it for a while, will be able to familiarise yourselves before we progress on to live fire platoon attack training." He paused and stood still to emphasise the next statement. "Grenades are highly dangerous. There is no room for joking or messing about. Do exactly what you are told, when you are told, or I will come down on you like a ton of shite." He waited for any sarcastic comment as an opportunity to reinforce his threat, but to his mild disappointment, no one responded. "I want you through in sections, beginning with 1 Section, then 2, then 3. The recent arrivals and those unfamiliar with this weapon are to go through first. Helmets and empty webbing only to be worn. Leave your weapons and other equipment in the troop shelter with the waiting sections." He gave the order to fall out and the platoon moved to the troop shelter to prepare their equipment. Preston walked in the opposite direction towards the range to get ready for the first practice.

* * *

Outside the troop shelter, Corporal Hutchinson lined up the section and checked each man's webbing in turn to ensure their ammunition pouches were empty. He heard Sergeant Preston shouting at him from the range to get a move on.

"You'll be put into pairs at the range, Dinger." he whispered into Bell's ear as he checked his pouches. "Pair off with Farthing and keep him away from Tetlow. This is not the place for anything to go wrong."

"I've got him, Corporal." replied Bell. As the section approached the range, Sergeant Preston told them to get into pairs as Hutchinson had predicted, Bell gently grabbing Farthing by the elbow. "You pair up with me, Penny." he said grinning at Farthing. Sergeant Preston checked their ammunition pouches were empty before handing each man a grenade from a metal box.

"Put this in your left ammunition pouch and don't touch it until I call you forward." he ordered. Once the section had all been given a grenade, Preston closed and sealed the box with the two spring levers on the front. "Right, first two forward. Follow me." he said. As new arrivals, Kyle and McEnearney were at the front as instructed, and moved on to the range behind Sergeant Preston.

The area was made up of three separate levels. The middle level had two small trenches with a raised front wall constructed of railway sleepers. The lower level in front of the trenches was an open area of raked sand some twenty yards square, with a wooden target representing an enemy soldier hammered into the ground in the middle. A watchtower was set further back on the third level, with open ladders to an observation platform, which was also constructed of railway sleepers. A Conducting Officer with the rank of Captain was positioned on the platform to control the operation of the range.

Sergeant Preston jumped into the furthest trench followed by Kyle. McEnearney jumped into the nearest trench where Lance Corporal Tetlow was waiting.

"Do exactly as I tell you, when I tell you." Tetlow hissed at McEnearney. "Understand, lad?"

"Yes, Corporal." replied McEnearney, nodding his head. The Conducting Officer in the tower then spoke through a loudhailer.

"Trench number one, stand by. Trench number two, take cover." Tetlow roughly pulled McEnearney below the parapet of the trench, the pair hunkering down in the confines of the hole. Tetlow gestured for McEnearney to put his fingers in his ears. He dutifully obliged. Sergeant Preston remained standing with Kyle in trench number one.

"Take the grenade out of your pouch and hold it in your right hand." Preston slowly and calmly instructed. Kyle did so, and got to handle the grenade properly for the first time. The green metal shell was divided into cubes about half an inch square, with a silver-coloured metal lever running down one side. A metal split pin held the lever in place, with an inch diameter wire ring on the end. "Position the lever in the web of your right hand and wrap your fingers around the grenade." Preston continued. Kyle twisted the grenade until the lever was positioned as ordered. Preston raised his arm in the air to signal the watchtower he was ready.

"Trench number one, throw." was the response from the tower to Preston's signal. Sergeant Preston calmly and slowly continued.

"When I say so, I want you to pull out the pin with your left hand by putting your finger through the ring and pulling hard. As long as you keep the strike lever in place by holding tight with your right hand, the grenade will not go off." Kyle nodded, feeling too nervous to answer verbally. "I want you to throw the grenade like you would throw a stone, aiming to land it at the bottom of the target in front." Kyle nodded again. "When you throw, the strike lever will fly off, igniting the fuse which lasts for four seconds." continued Preston. "Shout grenade as you throw, watch where the grenade lands and then duck down into the trench." Kyle nodded a bit faster as his nervousness and excitement mixed together.

After what seemed an age, Sergeant Preston continued. "Pull the pin." Kyle pulled, but the pin wouldn't come loose. Preston reached out and straightened the split in the retaining pin to make it easier to pull. "Pull the pin." he repeated calmly. There was a click as the pin came free. "Now look at the target, and throw the grenade just like you would throw a stone." Kyle heard a metallic ping as the grenade left his hand and the strike lever disconnected from the grenade body. He immediately ducked down into the trench. He heard Preston shout "Grenade" and looking up he saw the Sergeant still standing and looking towards the target before dropping down beside him in the trench. Preston signalled for him to put his fingers in his ears.

Kyle felt assaulted by the explosion; which although expected, was much louder than he was prepared for. The ground seemed to conduct the shock through his body a split second before the noise reached his ears, and he felt himself flinch in fright. Small stones landed around them in the trench, striking his helmet as if to prove its worth. Sergeant Preston helped him to his feet and they surveyed the scene. A dark grey smoke cloud was dispersing in the light breeze. The explosion had created a blackened hole a foot wide in the sand about six feet from the target, which on initial impression seemed unaffected.

"Did I hit it, Sergeant?" asked Kyle quizzingly, almost upset the target remained standing.

"You certainly did. Look closely." replied Preston. Kyle squinted in the sunlight and was able to see tiny beams of light through perforations in the target. "You ruined his day!" said Preston, giving him a friendly shove.

"Trench number two, stand by. Trench number one, take cover." came from the tower. Preston sat down in the trench and Kyle slumped down beside him.

"Remember to shout "Grenade" next time, and watch where the grenade lands before taking cover." Preston calmly reminded him as they sat squashed together.

"Sorry, Sergeant." replied Kyle, in a somewhat deflated tone.

"Don't worry yourself, son. I forgot as well on my first time." replied Preston with a broad smile.

"Trench number two, throw." came from the tower again. Kyle heard Lance Corporal Tetlow going through the instructions with McEnearney the way Sergeant Preston had done with him. When Tetlow shouted "Grenade", Preston gestured for Kyle to put his fingers in his ears. Although still surprised by the violence of the explosion, Kyle was more prepared for the effects second time around. At the sound of the explosion, Preston lifted a handful of loose stones and gravel from the bottom of the trench and threw it into the air in the direction of the other trench. An exclamation of "Bloody Hell" in Tetlow's voice came from the other trench as the stones fell around the occupants. Preston and Kyle giggled quietly to themselves at the success of the prank. Sergeant Preston got Kyle and McEnearney out of the trenches and led them off the range towards the waiting detail. The two young soldiers grinned at each other, elated by the combination of excitement and danger they had both just experienced.

"Right, next two." requested Sergeant Preston; Privates Bell and Farthing dutifully stepping forward, before being led away towards the range. Bell saw Lance Corporal Tetlow waiting beside his trench and quickly moved in his direction, forcing Farthing to go with Sergeant Preston; happy that he had complied with Corporal Hutchinson's instructions. Kyle and McEnearney stood among the other section members waiting their turn.

"How did it go, boys?" asked Orpin on seeing their beaming smiles.

"Fun but frightening at the same time." replied Kyle.

"It was great." added McEnearney. "I want another go."

"Just wait until we do the live firing platoon attacks. You'll get all the chances you want to throw grenades." continued Orpin.

"Y...You sure w...will." added McCafferty, who despite orders to the contrary had removed the grenade from his pouch and was straightening the split pin on the ring pull.

"You don't want to be doing that, La La!" chastised Orpin. "Wait until you are in the trench in case the bloody thing comes loose." The sound of exploding grenades could be heard from the range as the second detail were put through their rotation. Sergeant Preston reappeared with Bell and Farthing, both soldiers grinning from ear to ear. McCafferty quickly returned the grenade to his pouch on seeing Preston approach.

"Orpin and McCafferty, you're next." ordered Preston, gesticulating with a flick of his head for them to follow him. "Those who have been through can go back to the troop shelter and send 2 Section down next." As Orpin and McCafferty made off towards the range, those who had been through already, trudged back up the range road to the troop shelter.

The shelter was a single storey brick building with a flat, poured concrete roof. The facia of the bricks had started to sheer off with age and weathering, and gathered in small mounds around the base of the structure. The wooden door was so old and rotten that it didn't close properly, scraping on the floor and sticking when either nearly fully open or nearly fully closed.

The inside was painted white, which had flaked and bubbled due to damp coming through the bricks. Slatted bench seating was present around all four walls. A disused pot-bellied stove remained inactive in the middle of the room, rust stained lines on the flue showing where water had been leaking through the roof and running down in rivulets. The only light came through two filthy windows in the same wall as the door. As the soldiers entered, the smell of damp and cigarette smoke was overpowering. Private Bell relayed the message from Sergeant Preston to Corporal McIlwaine, triggering grudging compliance from 2 Section as cigarettes were put out and equipment was put on. Kyle took the chance to speak to Watts as he was putting on his equipment.

"How's it going, mate?" he asked.

"All good mate, thanks." Watts replied in his irrepressible good humour. "How are things for you?"

"Like starting Depot all over again. Just taking the time to find where I fit in. Who to trust, and who to avoid. You'll enjoy the grenade range mind. Good fun." replied Kyle.

"Looking forward to it." enthused Watts as he swung his equipment over his shoulders and fastened the buckle. "See you at lunch."

Those that had returned from the range took the places on the benches of those departing. They could hear Corporal McIlwaine forming his section up outside the shelter and marching them off to the range. The shelter door opened as Corporal Hutchinson, Orpin, McCafferty and Smith came in, having hurried back from the range, the section reunited again after their training. Private Bell recovered his small pack that had been left in the shelter while he was away. He reached into his trouser pocket and took out a penknife, then sitting down beside Kyle, placed the small pack on his lap. Opening the knife, he placed his left hand on the pack and much to Kyle's mixture of curiosity and revulsion, began to trim the surface of his warts.

"You don't want to be doing that, mate. You'll just make them worse." Orpin chirped as he undid his buckle and took off his webbing equipment. Without a verbal reaction, Bell closed the knife and replaced it in his pocket. He reached into his small pack through the side without opening the straps and pulled out a red apple. He polished it vigorously on his trousers until it shone, and took a noisy bite.

"You're keen on your fruit, Dinger." remarked Kyle.

"I was born and raised on a farm." replied Bell between mouthfuls. "Got a liking for it since childhood."

"Why are you in the Army then?" queried Kyle. "You weren't conscripted, were you?"

"Too much like hard work on the farm." replied Bell. "All I did was work and sleep."

"And the Army is easier?" queried Kyle again.

"Much easier." Bell paused. "I get more time to relax, but I've started to turn soft since I joined up. I used to be much stronger and fitter than I am now."

"We were both conscripted on the last call up." said Kyle gesturing towards McEnearney. "Although my dad served in the West Staffords during the Great War."

"That's how you know the Company Sergeant Major then." blurted Corporal Hutchinson more in statement than in question as the story fell into place for him.

"My dad and him were mates, Corporal. He was Best Man when my folks got married." answered Kyle.

"Bloody Hell!" exclaimed Bell as bits of chewed apple flew out of his mouth. "You're friends with Genghis?"

"Not exactly friends. More like a family acquaintance. And why does everybody call him Genghis anyway?" queried Kyle with a hint of frustration in his voice.

"Don't worry. You'll see soon enough." offered Bell in a cheeky reply as the rest of the gathering giggled.

"I think Sergeant Preston is after his title." Orpin continued.

"Be fair now, he hasn't been too bad recently!" replied Bell in his defence.

"H...he's just not c...consistent." joined in McCafferty. "I...I wo... would be happier if he just behaved the same each t...time."

"Exactly right, La La." agreed Bell. "You never know what Sergeant Preston you are going to meet from one minute to the next."

"Well, he...he's in a good m...mood today, and l...long may it continue." replied McCafferty.

Bell reached into his pocket and took out his knife again. He opened the blade, wiped it on his trousers and started to cut off the remaining flesh from around the core of his apple, holding the cut fruit between the blade and his thumb as he put it in his mouth.

"Has no one else noticed this?" Kyle thought to himself. He glanced across at Corporal Hutchinson who was gently shaking his head in disbelief at Bell's disregard for basic hygiene.

"Now look at Tetlow for example." began Bell again as he continued to shave the remaining flesh from his apple. "Apart from being an arse like Sergeant Preston, at least he's a consistent arse. No good and bad days with him, just bad." Everyone nodded in agreement. "I heard he shit in your rifle yesterday, Penny." continued Bell, looking for confirmation.

"That's right." replied Farthing. "And he wasn't too pleased when Sergeant Preston made him clean it.

"H...he won't be h...happy that he got in trouble with Sergeant Preston." McCafferty interjected.

"Right again, La La." said Bell encouragingly, pointing his penknife at him in reinforcement. He then turned his penknife pointer towards Farthing.

"You had better watch yourself around him, Penny. Stay out of his way as far as possible." continued Bell, disguising the fact that Corporal Hutchinson had already taken steps to keep them apart.

"That man has the most disgusting habits." added Farthing; much to the surprise of everyone in the shelter that he had voiced an opinion on anything. "Have you noticed that he's always scratching his arse then smelling his fingers?" The whole shelter descended into helpless laughter at the statement.

"Dear God, Penny." stated Bell above the laughing. "Can't say I've ever noticed."

"You just watch him, Dinger. He does it when he thinks no one is looking." replied Farthing.

"I'll pay special attention when he comes back for lunch." Bell replied enthusiastically. Kyle leaned over and whispered in Bell's ear.

"I get the Dinger Bell and Penny Farthing names, but why do you call McCafferty La La?" Bell didn't reply directly, but shouted across the shelter to where McCafferty was sitting.

"McCafferty, tell Kyle here what your first name is."

"La...La...Lawrence." came the unquestioning answer.

"All clear now?" asked Bell.

"Perfectly clear." said Kyle in reply, a smile breaking across his face. The noise of a vehicle approaching distracted the section from their conversation.

"Sounds like lunch is here, boys!" exclaimed Bell, rising to his feet.

"Just stay where you are." Corporal Hutchinson raised his hand and his voice to prevent an exodus from the shelter; then opened the door and stepped outside. Bell slumped back down on the bench, chastised and deflated. Vehicle doors were heard opening and closing and Corporal Hutchinson engaged someone in conversation. The sound of metal sliding on metal was followed by the sound of the doors closing again and the vehicle departing. Corporal Hutchinson shouted for two men to come outside, and McCafferty and Orpin, who were closest, dutifully obliged. A few seconds later they reappeared carrying a green painted metal box, which they placed in the corner of the shelter on Corporal Hutchinson's direction.

The remainder of the platoon filtered into the shelter as they finished their range rotation. Sergeant Preston was the last to appear and after having checked the contents of the metal haybox, allowed Lance Corporal Tetlow to distribute the food. Tetlow was left standing alone beside the haybox having ladled out the stew. As the men sat on the benches and ate from their mess tins balanced on their knees, they glanced at each other expectantly, while keeping Tetlow in their peripheral vision. He was particularly active, openly scratching around his groin, but with no indication that he would go any further.

"He's not going to do it, Penny." Bell whispered to Farthing.

"Just wait. He'll do it when he thinks no one is watching." Farthing whispered back. "Don't stare at him. He'll sense that we're watching."

After a particularly vigorous scratch, Tetlow raised his hand towards his face. Farthing tapped Bell's foot with his own to attract his attention. There was a palpable sigh of disappointment when he only tucked his fingers into his tunic and pulled it away from his neck; for him to then gently rub his fingers on his nostrils. The section let out a snorting sound in unison, created by suppressed laughter and disgust combined. Tetlow looked round accusingly at the sudden sound, but only saw the men with their heads down over their mess tins, now in silence. It didn't register with him that no one was speaking as they tried to muffle the sound of their laughter by not breathing.

"Told you." uttered Farthing, the seemingly innocuous words setting them all off laughing again just as they were getting themselves under control. Tetlow sensed something was going on. He took a loaf of bread from the haybox and approached the seated section.

"Anyone for bread?" he asked, breaking off a lump with his scratching hand and offering it to those seated in turn. The soldiers just murmured their negative reply without even raising their heads to look at him lest they would descend into laughter again. Tetlow then singled out Bell, who he knew to be perpetually hungry. "Bread, Dinger?" he offered, holding out a lump of bread with his offending hand.

"No thanks, Corporal. I'm stuffed!" quickly retorted Bell while patting his stomach, causing more suppressed laughter from the section. In the absence of any takers, Tetlow pushed the bread into his own mouth and licked his fingers, as if to demonstrate what everyone else was missing out on. Kyle felt he was going to burst as he tried to suppress his laughter, being almost jealous of Bell who seemed to be able to keep his emotions under complete control while at the same time as goading Lance Corporal Tetlow. Even though only a few days had passed, Kyle was beginning to enjoy the company of his new comrades, and feel settled.

* * *

"Right, get your equipment on and everyone line up outside." Sergeant Preston left to a murmur of discontent as the platoon begrudgingly put on their equipment and helmets, lifted their rifles and made their way out of the shelter as ordered. Preston had opened the grenade box and was standing with two un-primed grenades, one in each hand. He repeatedly tossed the grenade in his right hand about a foot into the air and caught it again while he waited for everyone to gather around him.

"To prove I am the best soldier in 10 Platoon, I can throw a grenade further than any of you." he announced boastfully. He waited for a reaction from the gathered platoon but got only silence. However, not to be denied the opportunity to prove his worth, he pressed on with his planned demonstration.

37

"40 Watts. Get yourself down the range road until I say stop." he demanded. Watts took off at a jog and had gone about forty yards when Preston shouted on him to stop and turn around. Then after scratching a line in the dust on the road with his boot, he took a short run up and launched the grenade down the road with a grunt of effort. The grenade tumbled through the air watched by the platoon, landing a few feet short of where Watts was standing.

"Stand exactly where the grenade landed, Watts." Preston shouted to the young soldier. Watts moved forward and stood on the spot as directed.

"Which one of you girls is going to take me on?" challenged Preston smugly, confident that his throw could not be beaten. He stood grinning arrogantly as a murmur broke out among the ranks of the platoon questioning which one of them would have the best chance of beating the Platoon Sergeant. Corporal Hutchinson quietly spoke to Bell.

"You're a strong bugger, Dinger. Have a go!" A chorus of "Go on Dinger." and "You can take him." gathered momentum from the platoon; erupting into a cheer as Bell handed his rifle to the soldier beside him and stepped forward to formally accept the challenge as the platoon representative. Preston tossed him the second grenade as he approached, which he caught neatly. He threw it up in the air and caught it again to mimic Sergeant Preston, much to the delight of his watching colleagues who clapped and cheered.

"Take as much run up as you need, but throw before the line." Preston reminded him. The cheers of encouragement got louder as Bell walked backwards from the line to give himself five yards of a run up, growing into a crescendo as he took a few steps forward and released the grenade with a grunt. The observers fell silent for a few seconds as the grenade arced into the air, with the noise building again as they gauged the flight and knew it would be a close call. Whistles and whoops of delight sounded as the grenade flew over Watts' head, landing three yards behind him. Bell stood facing the celebrating soldiers and took a bow, basking in his victory.

"Does that mean you're not the best soldier in 10 Platoon then, Sergeant?" Bell asked with feigned innocence, exacerbated by renewed cheering from the watching soldiers. Preston's face went purple with anger, a sign the experienced soldiers knew only too well meant he would not take his defeat with good grace. A hush descended as they awaited the inevitable retribution for his humiliation.

"Due to Private Bell being a smart arse," began Preston, "the last section down to the grenade range and back to here will be on guard duty next week." He stood expectantly with his hands on his hips waiting for the response. As the penny dropped, the non-commissioned officers began yelling for their men to move, eventually the whole platoon ending up running towards the range to shouts of encouragement from their Corporals running among them. As the first soldiers reached the trenches and tried to turn round, a scrum developed as those arriving just behind them tried to hold them back so they could catch up. Some good-natured wrestling began accompanied by raucous laughter, until they separated again and ran back up the hill towards Sergeant Preston. The platoon reformed in their sections in front of the Sergeant, the men leaning on their rifles, red faced and out of breath, but still in good humour.

"I can't decide who came last, so let's go again." said Preston smugly, gesturing towards the grenade range with both hands as if to shoo them away. "Move yourselves!" he yelled. The platoon set off down towards the range again, with a lot less bravado this time; forming up afterwards in a considerably worse state than after the first run. "Now we're getting somewhere, but I still can't decide." Preston enthused as he rubbed his hands together and surveyed the degradation in morale he had caused. "1 Section step forward." he continued. The line of soldiers in 1 Section took a pace forward. "You see that tree fifty yards away?" he pointed to a lone tree standing in rough ground at the side of the range road. "Leopard crawl out, touch it and then run back." The section moved to the side of the road and lay down on the grass facing the direction of the target tree, their rifles held out in front across their forearms.

"Go." shouted Preston, and they began to crawl. After a few yards, expletives rose from the crawling soldiers as thistles and brambles entwined in the long grass began to pull at their uniforms and sting their hands and faces. "Keep going." ordered Preston from his position on the road as he saw and heard their anguish.

"Quick as you can, lads." encouraged Corporal Hutchinson as he crawled faster, some choosing to follow the path of flattened foliage he was making through the undergrowth. "The sooner we get there, the sooner this stops!" When he reached the tree, he stood up and encouraged his section again. "On me, let's go back together." He was quickly joined by the others and they sprinted back the way they had come, arriving back as a complete section. No sooner had they made it to the road when Sergeant Preston called forward 2 Section and they began their ordeal.

Corporal Hutchinson gathered his section at the troop shelter.

"Help each other." he instructed, as the soldiers paired off and began to remove the brambles and thistles from their uniforms and equipment.

"Christ, I'm in agony." groaned Lance Corporal Tetlow, as he pulled the trapped brambles from Private Bell's battledress, sucking air through his teeth as the thorns jagged his hands.

"I thought the Sergeant was your mate, Corporal!" teased Bell as he returned the favour on Tetlow's uniform. His comment was met with a grunt of derision from Tetlow.

"You don't want to be doing that again, La La." Orpin stated the obvious as McCafferty and him paired off to remove the unwanted greenery.

"N...Not bloody likely!" replied McCafferty.

Having sorted themselves out as best they could, Corporal Hutchinson took his section back to the road where 3 Section had just finished their run and had joined 2 Section in trying to tidy themselves up. Vehicle engines announced the arrival of two Bedford trucks, which the platoon quickly began to board, handing their rifles to those who had climbed in first before hauling themselves up. As there were not enough seats for everyone, some stood, holding on to the roof supports to steady themselves as the vehicles rode the bumps in the range road on the way back to camp. There was none of the usual banter, almost complete silence, apart from the striking of matches to light cigarettes that were passed around.

* * *

McCafferty sat on the end of his bed. He had stripped down to his underwear, dropping his battledress in a pile on the floor. He was inspecting his bare arms and legs, pulling out thorns with his thumb and forefinger as he discovered them still imbedded in his skin from that afternoon's activity with the brambles.

"Are you coming to the NAAFI tonight, La La?" asked Orpin.

"M...might g...go to the cinema instead." came the response. "O...only a p...penny to get in."

"But you've seen that film already." said Orpin, exasperated. "You'd be better going to the cinema in town in that case. More modern films, and women!"

"B...but it's m...more expensive to get in." replied McCafferty.

"Suit yourself, La La." said Orpin, giving up. "What about the NAAFI tonight, boys?" he continued, turning his attention to Kyle and McEnearney.

"We're up for that." replied McEnearney cheerfully, glancing at Kyle who was nodding his approval.

* * *

Orpin waved as Kyle and McEnearney entered the NAAFI, indicating for them to join his group. Farthing and Smith were at the table already.

"Grab a seat, boys." said Orpin sliding along the slatted bench to make room for the new arrivals. Kyle and McEnearney sat down. The NAAFI was a brick-built structure, the inside having been painted white. There was no ceiling, visible wooden beams holding up the corrugated metal roof. There were trestle tables down each side at right angles to the wall, with wooden slatted benches on each side of the tables. A wood panelled bar was in the corner, behind which a barman was pulling pints from a hand pull. A queue had already formed.

Seeing that Orpin, Smith and Farthing had drinks already, Kyle offered McEnearney a beer and went to the bar.

"Nice place." said McEnearney in a tone that was unclear whether he was being sarcastic or not.

"It's cheap and cheerful." added Orpin. "But it can get a bit loud later and at that stage you're better going down town."

Kyle returned and set a drink down in front of McEnearney when he felt a hand on his shoulder. Turning round he saw Watts and Corporal Hutchinson standing behind him.

"Look who I found outside. Mind if we join you?" asked Hutchinson, being conscious that Watts was 2 Section and not wanting to intrude. No one in particular answered, but the shuffling along to make room on the benches portrayed a unanimous reply. Watts quickly sat down beside Kyle, beaming his usual smile.

"What can I get you, 40?" asked Hutchinson.

"Just a mug of tea for me please, Corporal. I don't drink alcohol." came the reply. Kyle knew this from Depot training, but it was obviously news to the others around the table. "My mum didn't approve of alcohol." Watts quickly added seeing the quizzical looks of the others.

"Tea it is, 40." confirmed Hutchinson. "Everyone else good for drinks?" he added, looking around the table. Everyone else confirmed they were currently happy.

"Did he just call you 40?" Kyle asked Watts.

"Yes. It seems that I have a platoon nickname already." confirmed Watts proudly. "Sergeant Preston started using it after the range today. 40 Watts he called me. He said it's because I'm like a 40-Watt bulb; not very bright." All those around the table burst into laughter, except Watts who just looked confused. Through the laughter, Kyle asked him what had happened on the range to generate such a derogatory nickname.

"Well, I was with Sergeant Preston in the trench. He told me to hold the grenade in my right hand, which I did, and pull the pin with my left hand." The table fell silent, hanging on Watts' every word. "He then said to throw it like I would throw a stone." continued Watts. "I'm left-handed so I threw the pin, which was in my left hand." The table erupted in laughter again.

"Shit the bed, Ken, what happened next?" enquired Kyle through convulsions of laughter.

"Sergeant Preston grabbed my right hand and squeezed my fingers tight around the grenade. He then told me to throw the grenade with my right hand when he said throw again."

"I hope you remembered to shout grenade." added Farthing, enjoying that someone else was the centre of attention rather than him.

"That's the thing. I did remember." added Watts, somewhat surprised at his presence of mind in light of the situation.

"You didn't shout pin when you threw the pin then?" questioned Smith, which started the laughter again. Hutchinson returned from the bar as the laughter was subsiding.

"I take it from the laughter that 40 has told you the story?" Hutchinson enquired. They all nodded, still smiling at Watts' predicament. "That's how Wobbly Gob got injured; on a grenade range."

"What happened to him, Corporal? Did he throw the pin as well?" asked Kyle, elbowing Watts to keep the embarrassment going.

"Much worse than that." continued Hutchinson. "He pulled the pin but wasn't holding the strike lever in. It flew off and hit him in the face, making him drop the grenade into the trench." There was a collective gasp from those around the table as they imagined themselves in such a situation. "Sergeant Preston was the instructor at the time, and a Corporal then. He pushed Cockcroft out of the way, lifted the live grenade and threw it out of the trench." Total silence gripped the table as they waited for the rest of the story. "The grenade exploded in the air and Cockcroft took a bit of shrapnel in the face."

"Bloody Hell. No wonder Sergeant Preston was so strict on the range this morning." added Kyle. "Maybe that's why he's such a bugger all the time."

"He is the way he is because he's trying to prepare you for combat." answered Hutchinson. "He wants you to become a team, to all think the same way, to look after each other and be able to rely on each other to do the right thing at the right time." Again, there was silence, waiting for Hutchinson to go on. "He's making you do things that you might have to do when fighting, so that you know you can do them if you have to."

"I never looked at it that way before." said Orpin, who had been in 10 Platoon the longest, and subject to Preston's methods for longer than the others. "It makes sense now."

"Especially as we're off to France soon and don't know what we'll face there." added Hutchinson. All those round the table were suddenly pensive and thoughtful, before Corporal Hutchinson lightened the mood. "Right, drinks are on me. What does everyone want?"

Having taken the order, Hutchinson took Watts to the bar with him to help carry the drinks.

"I'll be looking at Sergeant Preston a different way from now on." said Smith.

"Me too." added Farthing. "I just thought he was being a bastard for the sake of it." The others nodded their agreement.

Watts appeared carrying a tray of beer glasses and passed them out to those who had ordered. As Farthing lifted his glass to his lips, he saw Lance Corporal Tetlow and Corporal McIlwaine standing in the corner of the room looking directly at him. Tetlow's face was contorted, his lips pressed tightly together and his eyes narrowed. Farthing looked away, but sensed Tetlow was still staring at him, periodically glancing back to see the same expression on his face.

With almost two pints consumed, Farthing excused himself from the table and went to the toilet block, adjoining the NAAFI. The door was wedged open on the tiled floor, allowing in some fresh air to dilute the smell of stale urine. Large individual ceramic urinals hung in a row along the wall. As Farthing relieved himself and was fixing his clothing, he heard the door scrape over the tiles and slam shut. He felt an arm across his face as he was pulled back and his head pressed against someone's chest. He tried to pull the arm away but he was clasped too tightly.

"I hear you've been talking about me, boy." Tetlow's unmistakable voice whispered in his ear. Fear gripped Farthing's whole body and he froze. "It's time you grew up a bit, and I've got something here in my battledress for you." hissed Tetlow. Pushing his hand down the back of his own trousers, Tetlow then rubbed his middle finger along Farthing's upper lip, leaving a brown greasy streak. "There, now you're a big boy and you've grown a moustache." he uttered as he released his grip and pushed Farthing to the floor, leaving him sprawling on the tiles.

Corporal Hutchinson saw Tetlow returning to the NAAFI. He suddenly had a bad feeling and hurried to the toilet block. Farthing was leaning over a wash basin splashing water on his face, the basin full of vomit.

"Everything alright, Penny?" Hutchinson asked.

"Yes, Corporal." Farthing mumbled back. "Don't think that beer has agreed with me, that's all."

"Get yourself sorted out. I'll get one of the lads to go back to the accommodation block with you." Hutchinson returned to the NAAFI and took Orpin aside. "Penny's in the toilets being sick. Take him back to the block and get him into bed."

"No problem, Corporal." replied Orpin as he turned to leave. "I'll make sure he's alright."

Thursday 7 September 1939 – Aldershot Garrison, Southern England.

"Sit Up." The Regimental Sergeant Major's voice echoed around the cinema and the room fell silent. The Commanding Officer strode down the centre aisle and up the steps at the side on to the stage. He returned the Regimental Sergeant Major's salute and asked him to sit the men at ease. The battalion had been assembled immediately after breakfast and it was clear that a significant development was about to be disclosed. The Commanding Officer looked around the audience before he began to speak, as if trying to capture something in his memory that was about to be lost to him.

"Gentlemen, I have received notification of the date that the battalion will be moving to France." There was no sound from the assembly as they all waited to hear the date. "I can't tell you when or from where we will depart for security reasons, but I will say that it can be measured in days rather than weeks." A murmur swept around the cinema. "With this date now set, we will be stepping up the training programme to include live firing platoon and company attacks, building on the low-level training that you have been conducting recently." He paused before continuing.

"There is no suitable training area in the vicinity, so we will be moving to Salisbury Plain this coming weekend, and a movement instruction will be distributed to the companies later today." Another murmur went round the audience. "You already know that an Advance Party left for France yesterday to prepare the way for us, and when there, we will receive significant reinforcement from training depots across the country, who are currently busy with the latest mobilisation intakes. This reinforcement in officers and soldiers will bring us up to full fighting strength, for whatever tasks lie ahead." He then took the opportunity to give his personal thoughts on the state of the conflict.

"In relation to the conduct of the war, our Polish allies continue to fight courageously against the Germans in the east, while our French allies are preparing to give Hitler a bloody nose in the west."

Thursday 7 September 1939 –
Free City of Danzig, Baltic Coast,
Northern Germany.

Every day since the initial attack, Polish radio proudly announced *"Westerplatte broni sie nadal!"* (Westerplatte still fights on). The garrison had endured the sporadic shelling from Schleswig-Holstein, German infantry assaults, and dive bombing by Stukas. The previous day, a railway tanker wagon filled with fuel had been pushed close to the perimeter defences and detonated to try and dislodge the Poles. Smoke hung continuously in the air above the depot as the remaining fuel burned off and the wrecked facilities smouldered; yet the defenders still held out.

Another bombardment from Schleswig-Holstein began before dawn on 7 September, and signalled a renewed infantry assault. Pushing further into the complex than before, the Germans left another tanker wagon which they detonated as they withdrew, destroying the remaining perimeter defences. There was nothing now left to prevent the next assault entering the main complex; when defeat would be inevitable.

In consideration of these circumstances, the decision was made to surrender, and at 09.30 a.m. a white flag was displayed from the first floor of the shattered barrack block. Major Henryk Sucharski, the Depot Commander, gathered what remained of his men together, thanked them for their fortitude and offered a prayer to their fallen comrades. He began to sing the traditional hymn for military funerals *"Spij, kolego"* (Sleep, my friend), his men joining in with their final act of reverence and defiance. The sound of the singing could be heard by the Germans as they entered the Depot to take the surrender.

Thursday 7 September 1939 –
Rhine Valley, Western Germany.

In France, which like Britain, had declared war against Germany on 3 September, the declaration was a largely symbolic act. France was too far from Poland to offer physical aid in driving back the invaders, but one possibility offered itself; an invasion of Western Germany by French troops. As direct action in Poland was not possible geographically, it was hoped this advance would force the Germans to withdraw military assets from Poland to counter the threat in the west. Failing that, it would at least give France a foothold in enemy territory in the war that must inevitably come her way. The French did not want to violate the neutrality of Belgium by taking armed forces across its territory, and as a result, could only attack Germany along their mutual border; a limited front.

Consequently, in compliance with the Allied promise to assist Poland if invaded, eleven French divisions advanced along a twenty-mile-wide front near Saarbrücken, and facing almost no resistance, captured around twenty German villages. The villages had been evacuated by the German Army before the French arrived, but they left behind minefields and booby-trapped houses to inflict casualties and slow down the invading French. Having advanced to a depth of five miles, the French halted short of the carefully prepared German defences of the Seigfried Line. They felt that any further advance would mean abandoning their own very expensive fixed defences of the Maginot Line, from which France had a long-held strategy to fight a defensive war. Subsequently, the French divisions were ordered to withdraw back to their barracks along the Maginot Line, leaving only a small holding force in the captured territory.

The attack initially caused some consternation in the German High Command, but Hitler had been convinced by von Ribbentrop that the Allies would do nothing meaningful, and was proven to be correct. Contrary to the hopes of the French and British, the attack did not result in the diversion of any German troops from Poland. Only when Poland was defeated were German troops sent back west, and on 16 October they launched a counter-offensive in Saarland. The tiny French holding force withdrew, leaving the Germans to reoccupy the captured territory.

Friday 8 September 1939 –
Bydgoszcz, Northern Poland.

As the German Army occupied more of rural Poland on their advance towards Warsaw, sporadic armed resistance by Polish militia provoked disproportionate measures against the civilian population. On 7 September, military and police units in the town of Bydgoszcz took civilian hostages with the threat of public execution in retaliation against further such resistance. Unaware of the significance of their detention, a group of hostage Boy Scouts aged twelve to sixteen, laughed and played games together. When, on Friday 8 September, a German soldier was wounded in a sniper attack, forty hostages were taken to the market square in Bydgoszcz. The Boy Scouts remained blissfully unaware of their fate, continuing to joke and play until they were lined up against a wall and machine guns were set up. Suddenly realising their fate, the younger boys began to cry. Physically supported by the older Scouts, who began to sing the Polish National Anthem, the children were cut down in a hail of bullets. Witnessing the atrocity, a local priest who ran to administer the last rites to the dying children was shot dead in the attempt.

Monday 11 September 1939 – Salisbury Plain, Southern England.

A life size recreation of a German trench system had been constructed on the extensive firing ranges on Salisbury Plain to allow exercising units to practice their tactics in an environment as close as possible to what they might expect in France; with barbed wire entanglements protecting trenches and dugouts, manned by straw filled dummies to represent the enemy defenders. Lines of white tape marked safe passages through the wire obstacles, and deep dugouts were also marked off with tape, indicating where grenades could be dropped inside. To ensure control and safety, a permanently established training team conducted the exercises, thus allowing Section and Platoon Commanders to be exercised and tested alongside their soldiers.

The companies had been briefed on the mechanism of platoon and company attacks, and walked through the training area by the training team the previous day. They were now expected to exercise with live ammunition. With A, B and C Companies having been put through the exercise earlier that day, 10, 11 and 12 Platoons of D Company were now waiting their turn; bayonets fixed, live rounds in their magazines and live grenades distributed. 10 Platoon was called forward first, 1 and 2 Sections to lead side by side, with 3 Section behind. An infantry Captain instructor from the training team gave the final briefing before the exercise began.

"Forward sections make ready." At his command, 1 and 2 Sections cocked their weapons, putting a round into the chamber of their rifles. "Rear section, do not make ready until you have passed through the forward sections." he emphasised. On a whistle blast the forward sections moved off at a brisk walk. Kyle looked down the line as they set off, the bayonets glinting in the sun as the men moved forward. Corporal Hutchinson kept the section line straight, slowing down those moving forward too quickly, while Sergeant Preston followed just behind, keeping the two sections in line with each other. 3 Section followed, thirty yards behind Sergeant Preston.

Kyle saw the stuffed heads of the German dummies begin to appear in the trenches as they got closer, when there was a sudden shout from the instructor to take cover. The men dashed forward a few yards and dived to the ground as they had practised the previous day. "Open fire." was the next command; safety catches being flicked off and the targets engaged. Kyle felt his ears start to whistle with the sound of the discharging rounds, soil being kicked up from the edge of the enemy trench as the bullets struck home. He was firing as fast as he could re-cock his rifle, until he pulled the trigger and nothing happened. He realised then that he had emptied the magazine very quickly and rolled onto his side to get access to his pouches to reload.

"Cease Fire." was the next command heard, then "Sections forward." At this, both sections jumped to their feet and ran forward to the edge of the barbed wire entanglement before diving to the ground again. "Grenadiers forward." came the next command from the instructor. Orpin and Bell had been issued with the grenades in 1 Section, and crawled through the gaps in the wire towards the trenches, where white tape squares marked the points they were to attack. Both dropped their grenades into the marked pits, then squirmed back before lying flat on the ground. The explosions went off almost simultaneously, followed shortly by the grenades posted by 2 Section, debris shooting harmlessly into the air from the deep pits.

"Sections forward." was heard again, and scrambling to their feet the advancing sections weaved through the wire and jumped into the enemy trenches. As they landed inside, they began to bayonet the straw filled dummies that represented the enemy, screaming aggressively as they had been taught the previous day. Kyle noticed Lance Corporal Tetlow knock a dummy off its frame with the power of his bayonet strike, then stamp on its head when it hit the ground. Looking up, Kyle saw the members of 3 Section jump over their heads, having been ordered forward; followed by the sound of their own assault on the enemy in the second line of trenches."

With a feeling of elation driven by adrenaline, the platoon was directed back to the start line when the attack was complete. Sweating and out of breath, they formed in a semicircle around the instructor for his assessment on their efforts. He congratulated them on their enthusiasm and aggression, but pointing out, similar to those who had exercised previously, their expenditure of ammunition was too great, and should the enemy counterattack, then they would have only their bayonets with which to fight back.

The instructor then gave the watching D Company hierarchy the chance to add their comments. Company Sergeant Major McCann reiterated the comment on the rate of fire observation, then reminded each soldier to count his rounds and replace his magazine when the tenth bullet was still in the rifle breech, so as not to be caught with an empty rifle during a magazine change. Kyle thought this was directed at him personally, having been seen trying to fire an empty weapon, but noticed others nod their agreement and felt he was not alone in making such an error. As the platoon left the range, Major Crawley turned to McCann.

"I thought that went really well, Sergeant Major, don't you think?" he asked.

"There's just one problem, Sir." replied McCann. "The straw dummies weren't firing back."

The platoons and companies continually practised attacks on the trenches over the next two days, their confidence and aggression growing each time. The West Staffords left Salisbury Plain on Wednesday evening, to allow the next battalion on the training roster to use the ranges.

Friday 15 September 1939 –
Aldershot Garrison, Southern England.

Most of the battalion had already received overseas inoculations as they were due to replace their sister battalion, the North Staffords, in India, before being diverted to France after the declaration of war with Germany. Any new recruits, or those that had been on attached duties elsewhere, had now been called forward to receive their injections. The rest of the company was preparing for a forced march in Field Service Marching Order, and Kyle and McEnearney were lying on their beds watching the rest of the section preparing their equipment.

"I hate needles," said McEnearney to no one in particular, "but at least we'll miss the forced march."

"Give me the forced march any day." Orpin replied. "It will all be over in two hours, while you guys will suffer all weekend." McEnearney looked at Orpin quizzingly, encouraging an explanation. "That's why they give you the injections on a Friday, because you suffer all weekend but are well enough to start work by Monday."

"Is it that bad?" asked McEnearney.

"I h...had the shits for t...two d...days, and my arm was s...sore for a month." added McCafferty.

"So sore he couldn't lift it. I had to help him get dressed for a couple of days. Correct, La La?" quizzed Orpin, discretely winking at McCafferty.

"C...correct." confirmed McCafferty, playing along with the story. "C...couldn't t...tie my b...boots or w...wipe my arse."

"Bloody Hell, is it really that bad?" said Kyle, sitting up and taking notice as the conversation progressed.

"At least you'll get to meet Butterface, and that will make it all worthwhile." added Orpin, grinning at McCafferty.

"Who's Butterface?" enquired McEnearney, intrigued.

"Captain Knox, the Nursing Officer in the Medical Centre. You'll know her when you see her." continued Orpin, looking at McCafferty again and still grinning. "You better go, boys. Don't want to be late and get on the wrong side of Butterface."

* * *

The smell of disinfectant caught their nostrils immediately Kyle and McEnearney entered the Medical Centre. There was a short, tiled corridor leading to a waist high reception desk at the far end, with an arched entrance to a waiting room on the right. They looked in as they passed and saw Private Watts and Corporal Hutchinson sitting on wooden chairs arranged around the perimeter of the room. The walls behind the reception desk were shelved and held green coloured files, separated by alphabet dividers.

As they approached the desk, they saw a female in uniform reaching up to retrieve a file from the top shelf. McEnearney leaned over the desk to get a better look. She was standing on tip toes and her heels had come out of her court shoes. His gaze moved up her legs, noticing very defined calf muscles with a stocking line up the back. Her thighs and hips were outlined by a figure-hugging khaki skirt; with a beige shirt showing a narrow waist and shoulders. Her blonde hair was gathered in a bun. Hearing the duo approach, she turned round, displaying an ample chest.

"Can I help you?" she asked. The request broke McEnearney's trance and he looked up from her chest to her face. She was wearing thick glasses that made her eyes seem very small, and her bottom teeth were visible, indicating an underbite on her lower jaw. Wrinkles around her lips and eyes indicated an age more advanced than her body had suggested. Receiving no reply from the two soldiers, she pushed her glasses up higher on her nose with the back of her left wrist and repeated the question. Somewhat taken aback that her face did not match his expectations from her body, McEnearney blurted out that they were reporting for inoculations. "I'm not a mind reader, so give me your name and service number." she replied sourly.

"2466877 Private McEnearney." came the standard reply. Looking McEnearney directly in the eyes, she tapped the officer insignia on her shoulder with a pencil she had lifted from the desk. "Sorry, Ma'am." McEnearney added quickly.

"2465122 Private Kyle Ma'am." said Kyle immediately. "Recently arrived from Depot." he continued, as an attempted excuse to explain their unfamiliarity with the Nursing Officer's rank.

Captain Knox noted their details and directed them both to the waiting room, where they took a seat next to Watts and Corporal Hutchinson. The room had slatted wooden chairs on three sides, the fourth wall having two doors with wooden slides at head height showing "engaged" and "vacant" notifications, depending on where the slide was. Watts was his normal cheerful self, welcoming his friends with a broad smile. No sooner had they sat down, than Captain Knox came through the arch from reception carrying a bundle of green files. She called out Corporal Hutchinson's name, and he rose and followed her through one of the doors. Sensing those remaining in the waiting room were staring at her, Knox deliberately stared back as she moved the door sign to "engaged" and closed it behind her.

McEnearney fiddled with his cap nervously, prompting a question from Watts.

"Everything alright, mate?" he quizzed.

"Just a bit nervous." replied McEnearney. "I hate needles, and the older lads in the section said these injections can be really bad."

"How bad?" asked Watts, suddenly concerned.

"One of them couldn't move his arm for days, and said it was sore for a month." added McEnearney. "He had to be helped getting dressed it was that bad."

"You're left-handed aren't you, Ken?" Kyle joined in. "So maybe you should get the injection in your right arm." he added.

"Good idea. Thanks, mate." Watts replied enthusiastically, seeing the logic in protecting the subsequent mobility of his preferred arm.

A few minutes later, the door to the consultation room opened and Corporal Hutchinson came out, fastening the buckle on his battledress blouse. He nodded and smiled to the waiting trio as he left the waiting room. Captain Knox called Watts' name from the consultation room, and jumping to his feet, he hurried inside. Those waiting outside heard her tell Watts to take a seat before the door closed behind him.

With Watts gone, McEnearney felt free to talk openly. "My God, she's some specimen." he blurted out quietly, still looking at the door as if waiting for her to reappear.

"What are you on about?" quizzed Kyle.

"That nurse." continued McEnearney. "There's just something about her."

"She's old enough to be your mother." Kyle protested, screwing his face up at the realisation of his friend's attraction for a substantially older woman.

"If she was my mother, I'd let her bath me every night." whispered McEnearney, both of them bursting out laughing at the thought. They were still giggling when the door opened again and Watts appeared. Watts pointed at his right shoulder and gave a thumbs up as he passed.

"Private McEnearney." summoned the voice from the consultation room.

"Wish me luck." whispered McEnearney with a smile and a wink as he got to his feet and went inside.

"Close the door, Private," ordered Captain Knox as he entered. "and have a seat." Without looking up, she pointed to a seat on the opposite side to the desk she was sitting at. Neither said anything for a few moments as she leafed through an open file on the desk in front of her.

"Take off your battledress blouse and roll up your left sleeve." she eventually said, looking up. As he complied, Captain Knox got up and went to a basin on the wall behind her desk. McEnearney smelt carbolic soap as the nurse washed her hands, drying them on a small towel which hung on a metal frame below the sink. She then walked across the room to a small metal table. He watched mesmerised as she moved, staring at her legs as she prepared his inoculation on the table. She returned to the desk and set down a silver kidney dish containing a sheathed needle and syringe.

McEnearney stared at the top of her head as she pushed his shirt sleeve up and cleaned his arm with cotton wool and alcohol. He leaned towards her slightly and breathed deeply, enjoying the waft of perfume mixed with the smell of the alcohol. With her left hand keeping his shirt pushed up, she reached back for the syringe, popped off the sheath and stuck the needle into his arm. He wanted to flinch at the sudden sharp pain but was determined not to show any reaction. She set the syringe back in the dish and used the cotton wool to press on the injection site, holding his arm in her hand and pressing with her thumb. He felt her cold hand on his skin, determined to enjoy every second of physical contact.

"All done." she said. "It may be a bit sore around the site for a few days, and you may get a temperature, like having the flu." She released the pressure on the cotton wool, and satisfied that any bleeding had stopped, dropped it into the kidney dish with the empty syringe. "Any symptoms lasting more than a few days, then come back."

"It won't be sore for a month then?" McEnearney asked.

"I would suggest not." Captain Knox replied in a dismissive tone. "Give me your paybook and put your tunic back on." He reached into the top pocket of his battledress blouse and handed over his paybook, rolling his sleeve back down as she flicked to the appropriate page. He watched her filling in the inoculation record in his book as he buttoned his blouse, replacing it in his pocket when she handed it back.

"Send in Private..." there was a slight pause as she checked the name on the front of the remaining file, before completing her sentence, "Kyle."

"I'll wait for you here." McEnearney whispered to Kyle as he left the consulting room, and ushered him in.

* * *

Kyle and McEnearney were lying on their beds when the rest of the section returned from the forced march. Orpin and McCafferty appeared as if they had been out for a morning walk. Farthing was in a poor physical state, breathing heavily and sweating profusely. He collapsed onto his bed, obviously exhausted.

"Well boys, did you meet Butterface?" asked Orpin before he had even unbuckled his equipment. "Get you going, did she?"

51

"She was professional, albeit a bit spikey at times." replied Kyle.

"Nothing special." added McEnearney.

"Don't talk bollocks. She had you going, didn't she?" continued Orpin cheerfully.

"Alright, she was lovely, except..." began McEnearney.

"Except what?" goaded Orpin.

"Her face and body don't match." added McEnearney.

"Exactly." exulted Orpin, delighted that his questioning had revealed the expected answer. "That's where she gets her name from. Everything about her is beautiful.... but her face." He paused for a reaction to his play on words joke but none came, so he tried a different angle. "My mate who is a Corporal in A Company said his Platoon Commander has been there. Said she was insatiable, and he was lucky to escape in one piece."

McEnearney visibly perked up at the thought, his reaction spotted by Orpin. "Don't get any ideas in that direction young man. She's reserved for officers."

"Why do officers seem to have all the fun?" asked McEnearney with distinct disappointment in his voice.

"Because they're officers, and rank has its privilege." replied Orpin. "She likes young officers; gets them drunk at Regimental Dinners and has her way with them I was told."

"W...we better w...warn the new Platoon Commander w...when he arrives then." McCafferty joined in, both him and Orpin laughing at the thought.

Saturday 16 September 1939 –
Aldershot Garrison, Southern England.

Kyle and McEnearney were a bit off colour at breakfast, and now fully appreciated the logic behind inoculations being given on a Friday.

"I heard you moaning a bit during the night." McEnearney remarked to Kyle.

"My bloody arm was agony and I woke up every time I rolled on it." replied Kyle, rubbing it gently. "I think I'll go back to bed after breakfast and try to get some more sleep."

"Mine's not too bad, just a bit tender to touch." responded McEnearney. "I think the nurse liked me and was especially gentle." Kyle just shook his head gently in disbelief. "Look what the cat dragged in." continued McEnearney as Watts slumped down beside them, looking absolutely miserable.

"God, please kill me now!" he muttered as his colleagues giggled at his obvious discomfort. "I can't move my right arm at all and I've sweated buckets all night. Haven't slept a wink."

"Sit tight." replied Kyle. "I'll get you some breakfast." He got up and went back to the serving hatch to get Watts some food, returning with bacon, bread and jam, and a mug of tea. "Get some of that in you and you'll feel better." he told Watts encouragingly. Watts ate and drank using only his left arm, moving his mouth towards the food rather than the food towards his mouth. His right arm hung loose by his side.

Orpin and McCafferty appeared, having finished their block jobs, and now ready for their breakfast. "How are we all feeling today, boys?" chirped Orpin gleefully as he set his food down, already knowing the answer from the demeanour around the table, and not expecting a reply.

"I t...told you s...so." added McCafferty. "S...she's a b...butcher that nurse."

"Just think. You'll have to wipe your arse with a numb arm when the diarrhoea starts." added Orpin enthusiastically, at which both him and McCafferty elbowed each other and laughed.

"Right. We're off." said McEnearney, gesturing for Watts and Kyle to get up. "I'm going to the NAAFI to get a newspaper. Anyone coming?"

"I'll come with you, mate." said Watts.

"Not me. I'm off for a lie down." replied Kyle.

McEnearney helped the struggling Watts with his headdress on the cookhouse steps, and they set off at a very slow pace towards the NAAFI. Kyle went in the opposite direction back towards the barrack room.

"I'm starting to feel a bit better with the food and fresh air." Watts said as he breathed heavily in and out. A gentle rain was starting to fall and Watts turned his face upwards, enjoying the cooling effect on his skin.

"We can get another mug of tea in the NAAFI and you'll be your normal self again." encouraged McEnearney as Watts brightened up a bit, and they began to walk faster as the rain got heavier. As they rounded the corner of the cookhouse, Major Crawley and Sergeant Major McCann suddenly appeared in front of them. Both sprang to attention, McEnearney saluting, and Watts trying to, but unable to move his right arm.

"Don't you learn to salute officers at Depot any more, Watts?" yelled McCann; enraged at the apparent lack of respect towards Major Crawley. "Salute the Company Commander!" he demanded.

"I can't, Sir. My arm is sore after an injection yesterday." stuttered Watts in his defence.

"My arm is sore, Sir." repeated McCann, mocking Watts in a put-on childish voice. "I hope the Germans will understand and go easy on you." he added. "Well, I can fix that with a bit of manual labour to loosen you up." continued McCann, reverting to his harsh Irish accent. "Get your arse over to the Warrant Officers' Mess and report to the Mess Sergeant. Tell him I sent you for some manual labour. You can water the garden."

"But, Sir, it's raining." answered Watts, as he tried to point out the futility of the suggested punishment.

"Well put your rain cape on then!" responded McCann, either missing or choosing to ignore the point Watts was making. McEnearney grinned at the stupidity of the situation, his expression quickly noticed by McCann.

"And you can help him, Frenchie!" said McCann as he moved off with Major Crawley.

Sunday 17 September 1939 –
Western Approaches, Atlantic Ocean.

After some German U-Boat successes against British shipping in the Western Approaches, the Admiralty deployed the aging aircraft carrier HMS Courageous with a destroyer escort screen to conduct anti-submarine patrols in the area and offer some protection to merchant vessels. HMS Courageous was originally a Battle Cruiser, before being converted into an aircraft carrier in May 1928. A hangar and flight deck had been installed by removing the original 15-inch guns, meaning that she had to rely on her screening escorts for protection against surface ships.

The head of the German U-Boat fleet, Admiral Donitz, had ordered all his boats to converge in the Western Approaches to attack the convoys, which included Otto Schuhart in U-29 and Ernst-Gunther Heinicke in U-53. On 17 September, Heinicke attacked and sank the Kafristan, a 5,000-ton British freighter, with a combination of gunfire and torpedoes; triggering the dispatch of Swordfish biplanes from Courageous, and two of her destroyer escorts to the area of the sinking.

Meanwhile, further east, Schuhart in U-29 was still searching for the convoys. While running submerged, he spotted one of the Swordfish biplanes through the ship's periscope; which being three hundred miles out in the open sea, could only mean that an aircraft carrier had to be close by. When a smoke plume was spotted on the horizon, Schuhart ordered his crew to battle stations and adjusted his course for an interception. Remaining submerged because of the circling aircraft and accompanying destroyer screen, Schuhart tracked the aircraft carrier from afar for another ninety minutes, gradually falling further away however, due to his slower submerged speed. On the verge of losing contact, HMS Courageous suddenly stopped and turned into the wind to launch its aircraft, presenting U-29 with a perfect side on target. Ten minutes later Schuhart attacked, launching three torpedoes from a distance of 3,000 yards.

Watching through the periscope as the torpedoes made their run, Schuhart was startled when a destroyer came into view just five hundred yards away. He immediately ordered a dive to one hundred and eighty-feet expecting attack, but the destroyer sailed by, unaware of the submarine's presence. Now under silent running routine and diving to a depth never before attempted, the creaking of the protesting hull was suddenly interrupted by two huge explosions as the torpedoes struck home. The U-29 crew could not contain their elation and began cheering, despite knowing that an attack by the destroyer escorts was surely only minutes away. Both destroyer escorts attacked relentlessly until their depth charges were exhausted, the ordeal lasting four hours before U-29 could make good her escape.

Eyewitness accounts from the Dutch passenger liner Veendam that was passing nearby, described a huge white cloud engulfing the Courageous, followed by two explosions shooting pieces of steel into the sky. The Courageous, which sank in less than fifteen minutes, was the first British warship to be lost to enemy action in the war, with the loss of 519 lives from her crew of 1,260 officers and ratings. Such heavy losses were attributed to the speed at which Courageous sank, trapping the men between the decks. The Veendam and British freighter Collingsworth mounted a rescue, pulling survivors from the oily waters.

Wednesday 20 September 1939 – Grodno, Eastern Poland.

On Sunday 17 September, with the prior knowledge and agreement of the Germans, Russian forces crossed the border into eastern Poland. The invading soldiers and both the Polish Army and civilian population they encountered were all equally confused as to the intentions of the Russian Army. A Russian propaganda effort implied the reason for intervention to be a protective measure for the Polish people who had been left without a Government by the German invasion. By implication, rumours rapidly spread that they were coming to fight against the Germans, yet despite stories of maltreatment of civilians and executions of captured Polish officers in particular, the human need for hope often outweighed the truth.

With perhaps a better understanding of the situation than lesser politicised citizens, local Communist groups in the city of Grodno staged an uprising, encouraged by a Russian Airforce leaflet drop. Subsequently disavowed of their naivety, local Police, Scouts, Firemen and civilian volunteers assisted Polish military units in putting down the uprising, subsequently bolstering the number of defenders and assisting in building barricades with paving stones lifted from the streets.

The first Russian forces arrived in the city on the morning of 20 September, when a dozen tanks, unaccompanied by infantry, rumbled into the city square. Small arms fire rained down upon them from the surrounding buildings, but deflected harmlessly off the vehicles' armour. The tanks moved slowly through the narrow streets, shooting high explosive shells into the buildings where resistance was identified; but once isolated, and without the close protection of infantry, many were disabled in grenade attacks against the weak points on their tracks by courageous Poles who crawled within grenade throwing range. Stranded crews attempted to fight off further attacks from under the protection of their armour using the onboard machine guns; but the Scouts made use of their diminutive frames to duck and move below the level of the tank hull guns, setting the crippled machines alight by smashing petrol bombs into their engine compartments. As the flames took hold, the tank crews tried to escape through the top hatches, only to be shot down by the defenders in the buildings overlooking them as they emerged. Black, oily smoke columns rose into the sky from the burning machines; stored ammunition exploding harmlessly with muffled bangs inside the crew compartments as the flames ignited the propellant in the shells.

Schoolchildren and students resupplied the defenders on the front lines and strongpoints with ammunition from the armoury in the army barracks by running shuttles behind the cover of the barricades. Women brought food and drink to the fighters and evacuated the wounded to care for them in their own homes. Thirteen-year-old Tadeusz Jasiński was one of the Scouts stalking the tanks in the confines of the city streets. Dodging the Russian bullets, he had crawled forward with a petrol bomb until close enough to attack a vehicle, before throwing the bomb and diving to the ground for cover from the expected explosion. In the excitement of the moment, he had forgotten to light the rag in the neck of the bottle, the glass smashing harmlessly against the steel of the enemy tank. He was pulled to his feet by a Russian soldier who had witnessed the attempted attack, and tied to the front of the tank as a human shield.

When the tank was later destroyed, his smashed body was cut loose and taken home to his mother, where she held him tightly, supporting his head, and rocking him like a baby to ease his suffering. She whispered to him, telling him to rejoice that the Polish Army was coming to their rescue with banners flying, singing as they marched. He died in her arms.

The Russians renewed their attack later in the day, aiming to capture the bridges over the river Niemen. The defenders allowed the tanks access to the bridges before attacking the front vehicle with anti-tank weapons, blocking the road and then picking off the vehicles trapped in the column behind. That night, the order was given to evacuate the city under cover of darkness and move north to Lithuania; those who remained behind, either through choice or necessity, falling under Russian occupation. Soviet records state that six hundred Poles were killed in the fighting for Grodno, which did not include the students, Scouts and prisoners of war who died in mass executions after the surrender of the city. Twenty-nine Polish officers were summarily executed along with the Commander of the Grodno Garrison, Brigadier General Olszyna-Wilczynski, who was dragged from his staff car and shot at the side of the road.

Friday 22 September 1939 –
Brest-Litowsk, Eastern Poland.

As neither of the advancing German or Russian armies had been told of the Molotov-Ribbentrop Pact, some clashes had taken place between German and Soviet troops, each mistaking the other for Poles. By the evening of 14 September, the Germans had fought their way to the gates of Brest-Litowsk on the river Bug. When infantry attacks over the next few days failed to take the city due to supply shortages and bad weather hampering critical Luftwaffe support, the Germans began to invest the city. This was the trigger for the Poles to withdraw, and they escaped under cover of darkness during the night of 16 / 17 September, leaving only their wounded behind. The Germans marched in unopposed at 8 a.m. on 17 September.

On 20 September, a Soviet armoured car approached a German roadblock in the north of the city at Turna. The incumbent Russian officer was escorted directly to the Corps Headquarters, where he was welcomed personally by German General Heinz Guderian. This meeting resulted in agreement around a subsequent demarcation line and a timetable for German withdrawal back across the river Bug. Extending the discussions to cover a lunch together, the two officers parted with a formally agreed handover date of 22 September having been set.

At 4 p.m. on the agreed date, German General Guderian and Soviet Brigadier General Krivoshein stood side by side on a hastily constructed wooden platform outside the German Corps Headquarters on Union of Lublin Street; a German Battle Flag fluttering in the breeze. Guderian looked resplendent in his tailor-made field grey greatcoat with the red lapel facings of a German General Officer. Krivoshein wore a simple belted leather trench coat to keep out the chill of the autumn afternoon. They conversed in French, neither being proficient in the national language of the other.

A substantial civilian crowd had gathered, lining the street opposite the building, clapping and cheering as firstly German infantry units marched past, goose-stepping proudly and arrogantly before the watching Generals. Then came a motorised unit towing artillery pieces followed by tanks; their tracks clattering loudly on the cobbled street. The procession was then repeated in the same order by the Russians, each unit that passed drawing smart salutes from both Generals. German and Russian soldiers mixed awkwardly for the newsreel cameras, swapping cigarettes and sweets in the universal language of soldiers everywhere. When the parade had passed, Guderian and Krivoshein turned to face the flagpole behind and saluted as the German Battle Flag was lowered to the sound of the German National Anthem, being replaced by the Hammer and Sickle to the sound of The Internationale. The officers shook hands and departed, Guderian joining his men as they crossed back west over the river Bug.

PART 2

THE PHONEY WAR

**Saturday 23 September 1939 –
Cherbourg Harbour, Channel Coast, France.**

The sea seemed to boil around the keel and turned brown with silt as the ferry manoeuvred against the dock in Cherbourg. The West Staffords had been transported from Southampton by a civilian vessel, taken out of trade for the role of moving the British Expeditionary Force to France. They had departed Aldershot during the night, with almost no notice, as a security measure against German spies who were, according to the newspapers, hiding behind every hedge in southern England. It was just getting light when a Tanoy announcement instructed all passengers to assemble on the deck. As they gathered, it was a first glimpse of France for many, and an unwelcome return for those that had fought there only twenty-one years previously. The two Royal Navy destroyers that had escorted them against the U-Boat threat, sounded their klaxons in a farewell gesture on successful completion of their task, and turned away back towards England.

Most men had slept where they could find space on the deck to lie down, partly in fear of a U-Boat attack, and partly because the interior of the ship smelt of warm oil and stale food. McCafferty never left the handrail, vomiting for the complete duration of the crossing.

"Nearly there now, La La." Orpin reassured him as he prized him off the handrail and helped him towards the area on the deck where the platoon was forming up prior to disembarking.

"Christ, you look awful." said Bell as McCafferty joined the gathering platoon. He just nodded in acknowledgement, unable to answer, his head buried in his lifejacket and breathing heavily through clenched teeth. "Bet you got sick on the Birkenhead ferry going on your holidays." continued Bell, trying to lighten the situation. He got no response.

With the platoon assembled, they were marched down a steep gangplank onto the dock. There were wooden slats across the gangplank to give grip, but not being designed for studded Army boots, many soldiers held the rope rails for support as they descended. Only the sound of squawking seagulls welcomed them as they dropped their lifejackets in a pile at the bottom of the gangplank and stepped onto French soil. Having been under strict orders to wear it at all times, Kyle was glad to be rid of his lifejacket, as it both felt and smelt damp; leaving a lingering odour on his battledress for many hours after its removal. A field kitchen had been set up on the docks. Tins of meat and vegetables had been emptied out into a boiler and heated, the chefs ladling it into the mess tins of those who wanted it.

With the now expected shouting from the non-commissioned officers, the battalion was put into companies before being marched away from the docks. Some French dockers paused their work to watch with a morbid interest, joined by a scattering of early rising civilians as the battalion marched out of the dock gates and through the town to the railway station. Boots echoed on the almost empty streets; lights going on in house windows as the occupants were woken up by the noise. The station was similar to the railway stations in England, except the signs were in French. As they boarded the train, corned beef sandwiches wrapped in greaseproof paper were handed out for the journey. Then the chaos began, as soldiers pushed their way into carriages designed for six, with seats being reserved for fictitious friends in the hope of ending up with more space.

Orpin found an empty carriage and ushered McCafferty in. He lay down and curled up across two seats with his eyes closed; Kyle, Bell and McEnearney filling the vacant spaces. Kyle sat by the window as the train moved away, fascinated at his first sight of a foreign country. He saw the cranes of the port in the distance silhouetted against the brightening sky, and the terraced houses of the port workers that reminded him of the workers' houses around the potteries in Stafford. French soldiers crammed the platforms of the stations leading away from Cherbourg as they waited on their own troop trains. Looking around the carriage, everyone else had fallen asleep almost instantly. McCafferty seemed comfortable at last, lying across two seats, but Kyle thought he looked even more pale than usual, if that was possible. As the train moved into the countryside, he rested his head against the window and closed his eyes.

* * *

Kyle woke with a start at the sound of the carriage door opening. Bell saw that he had disturbed him and felt obliged to indicate that he was going to look for the toilet by mouthing the words so as not to waken the others. Kyle nodded his understanding, and then feeling the urge himself got up and followed, gently closing the carriage door behind him. They moved down the corridor as the train swayed from side to side, pushing past groups of soldiers talking and smoking.

Surprisingly, there was no queue outside the toilet at the end of the carriage, Bell entering and sliding across the catch inside the door. Kyle looked out through the window of the carriage door as he waited. They were now well away from Cherbourg and travelling through what seemed to be endless fields of gently swaying grain. Farmers were harvesting on horse drawn machinery, while manual labourers were loading the cut produce onto carts with long pitchforks. Bell emerged from the toilet eating the sandwiches he had been given at Cherbourg station.

"There's no paper in there, mate. I've just wiped my arse with the greaseproof paper off my sandwiches." he said between mouthfuls. "Didn't really wipe it; just spread it evenly everywhere." he giggled.

Kyle closed the door and locked it. He lifted the wooden toilet lid to reveal a heavily soiled porcelain bowl with no seat, and the sleepers of the rail track rushing past below. "No requirement to flush then." he thought to himself, relieved he only needed to urinate. Now uneasy about touching anything, he registered there was no mechanism to flush anyway, and no facility for hand washing.

***

After just short of six hours travelling, the view from the carriage window had become heavily industrialised. Factory chimneys belched smoke into an already overcast early afternoon sky. The screeching brakes and station signs indicated they were at their destination of Lille; and soon, shouts to get off could be heard the length of the train. Lille station was much busier than Cherbourg. Unfamiliar smells and accents mixed with the universal sound of shunting trains and escaping steam. Little attention was paid to the British soldiers lined up on the platform, by either the scurrying civilians or the French soldiers who seemed to be everywhere. Only the occasional child twisted their head to stare, soon pulled away by their parents or elder siblings.

A selection of military trucks and very obviously hastily green painted civilian commercial lorries were lined up outside the station for the final leg of the journey to their new home; a French Army barracks, unused since the German occupation of Lille finished at the end of the Great War. The canvas flaps of the trucks were secured closed for the journey to the barracks, but once inside, as the men climbed down from the vehicles, they got the impression of a Victorian jail rather than an Army barracks. Dark three-story stone buildings surrounded a large square, the barracks protected by a high stone perimeter wall. The battalion representatives that had been sent ahead stood waiting, and on rejoining their platoons, quickly led the men into their allocated accommodation. Cream painted corridors with paved floors ran the full length of all storeys in each building, joined by staircases at each end. Rifle racks were built into the fabric of the stone walls in the corridors outside the rooms, each furnished with five sets of metal framed bunk beds. Their boots echoed off the stone floors and walls as the platoons were led to their designated areas, then divided into their sections, one section per room.

As they took off their equipment and grabbed the bunk of their choice, Kyle's impression was of a cold, soulless place, feeling and smelling damp. Notice was shouted that food was being served in the cookhouse and the men quickly unpacked their mess tins and cutlery. Once outside, they were directed towards the open end of the large square into a high-ceilinged wooden structure, laid out inside with rows of trestle tables. Chefs stood behind the serving bay with huge pots of steaming stew and trays of French crusty loaves, cut into six-inch lengths. 1 Section managed to get a table together, hungrily dipping their bread into the stew.

"The chefs are French Army." McEnearney said. "I heard them talking and asked what was going on. They are here along with medics and mechanics to provide our support until our own people can be brought across."

"Maybe we'll get some decent food in that case." Bell chipped in.

"I don't think so." added Farthing, obviously disappointed at the meal. "This is just Maconochie's Meat and Vegetables, British Army rations heated up by a Frenchman."

"Well, maybe they'll heat it up differently, in a French sort of way." added Orpin, which elicited a giggle round the table.

"I'm not sure I like this place." Farthing continued. "Have you seen the toilets?" he asked no one in particular. No one else had visited the toilets in the rush to get into the rooms and then down for dinner. "Take a look in on your way back." he added depressingly.

* * *

As Farthing had suggested, a section visit to the toilets took place on the return from dinner. The urinals were a continuous porcelain structure about three yards long, but in place of the expected cubicles there were just porcelain trays with a hole in the base and two raised steps. There were dividing walls between the trays but no doors for any privacy.

"How the hell do those work?" Bell asked.

"I've seen these before when in France with my mother." McEnearney explained. "You stand with your feet on the raised steps and squat over the hole. When you flush, the water runs around the tray and your feet stay dry on the steps."

"Bloody Hell." said Bell in response to the explanation. "Welcome to France."

Sunday 24 September 1939 – Lille, Northern France.

With no cinema or suitable large building in the barracks, the Commanding Officer spoke to the battalion in the cookhouse immediately after breakfast. There was a constant background noise from the chefs who continued to work in the kitchens, clearing up after breakfast and preparing for the next meal. The Commanding Officer was visibly irritated with the distraction, but continued as best he could.

"Now that we are physically here supporting our allies, the battalion will be assuming responsibility for a section of the defensive line close to the Belgian border, currently occupied by the French." Apart from the noise from the kitchen, there was silence as the gathering waited to hear the specific details. "Our first job will be to improve the defensive positions, making them as strong as possible to hold any German attack, and as comfortable as possible in case we have to spend an extended period of time there."

"Sounds like a re-run of the last war." Orpin whispered to those around the table; attracting dagger looks from the Company Sergeant Major who was nearby and overheard. The Commanding Officer continued.

"During this immediate period, we will be supported by French logistic units including chefs, medical personnel and vehicle mechanics, until we are brought up to full strength and our own support units arrive." There was a feint murmur around the room.

"Just like the cooks said last night." whispered McEnearney. The Commanding Officer continued with his briefing.

"If we find ourselves here for some time, then a programme of home and local leave will be initiated, and I will encourage friendly competition with intercompany sports events. In the meantime, get settled in and have some rest today. Work begins tomorrow."

Monday 25 September 1939 – France / Belgium Border.

A mixture of military and civilian vehicles had brought the battalion to the site of the proposed fixed defences on the Belgian border. Royal Engineer Officers were briefing the Company Commanders on the defensive plan for the area while the soldiers waited in the vehicles. Although the weather was mild, a steady rain was falling which made the prospect of digging trenches all the more daunting. Morale within 10 Platoon was not good as they listened to the rain beating on the canvas cover of their transport, knowing that soon they would be working outside. All too quickly, the order came to get out of the vehicles; cigarettes being quickly extinguished and rain capes put on. The area was arable land and sheep moved back and forth as they grazed, sometimes being inquisitive and venturing close to the working soldiers; only to be spooked and running off at a sudden noise or movement. Defence stores of sandbags, steel pickets, barbed wire and metal meshing had been pre-dumped for the construction efforts.

French soldiers had been in the location previously, but only for a very short time. A start had been made to the proposed trench system, but little attention paid to the latrines which were already overflowing, leaving human waste lying on the surface of the ground. The pressing task was to divert a nearby fast-flowing stream into the area where the latrines would be sited, creating a water filled pit with a continuous flow through; and then screen off the area with canvas sheeting. 10 Platoon were assigned this task and Sergeant Preston split the sections down to conduct the separate requirements. 1 and 2 Sections together dug the pit that was to become the latrine. 3 Section dug the new inflow water course from the latrine pit towards the river, and the outflow from the latrine pit back into the river further downstream. Once the latrine pit was deep enough, the water courses were connected and the platoon stood and watched as the latrine slowly filled up. A fallen tree from a nearby wood was stripped of bark and branches and fixed across the full length of the pit as a seat.

Once the latrines were complete, 10 Platoon joined the rest of the company digging the main trench system and filling sandbags. Long metal pickets were driven into the earth just inside the dug trenches and metal meshing was slid into the gap to prevent the walls from crumbling inwards. The sandbags were then built up to form machine gun bays and firing steps inside the trench. Until communication trenches and underground sleeping bays could be created, those working on the position would be required to sleep in the holes they had dug. The priority was to create a defensible line, and the niceties of comfort would not be considered before the completion of a position that could be effectively fought from. The company had been briefed they would work for two days before being relieved by another work party, and this would mean two nights sleeping in the open until they were able to return to barracks.

* * *

It had rained all day without a break and the wind was getting stronger, so when a very welcome hot meal was delivered just as it was getting dark, the men slumped exhausted into the half-finished trenches to get some degree of protection from the weather. Sergeant Preston had gathered the platoon and they sat together as they ate, their utensils scraping noisily off their mess tins as they devoured the hot food. It was only when they had stopped working that the wet and cold took hold of their bodies.

"I'm so tired I feel sick." complained Orpin, stretching his arms above his head to relieve the tension in his back.

"I can't feel my hands." added Farthing, making fists then straightening his hands to try and restore his circulation.

"It's holding those bloody pickets as they are hammered in." Bell explained. "The vibration makes your hands go numb."

Company Sergeant Major McCann was checking on all the platoons and arrived in 10 Platoon's area. He squeezed in between the men who were sitting on the sandbag firing step.

"What's happening?" he quizzed to no one in particular, trying to offer a mechanism to start a conversation.

"Just not used to hard labour, Sir." replied Sergeant Preston. "Sore backs and hands everywhere."

"I bloody hated digging trenches." added McCann. "Tried every trick in the book to avoid it."

"What tricks were those, Sir?" asked Bell in anticipation, hoping to get a tip on how to avoid work from a veteran soldier.

"I'm sure you could probably tell me!" McCann replied with a grin. Bell feigned disappointment. "Just work smarter, not harder." McCann continued. "My hands used to hurt like hell after holding pickets, but if you get an empty sandbag looped around it, and two men pulling in opposite directions, the picket is held steady and the vibration doesn't go through your hands when it's hammered in."

"Clever!" replied Bell. "We'll try that tomorrow."

McCann stood up and took Sergeant Preston out of earshot. "I need two men from the platoon on sentry duty tonight, Jock. I suggest four hours per section from now until dawn."

"Aye, Sir. No problem." answered Preston. "Leave it with me." As McCann moved off, Preston called the Section Commanders together to work out the roster.

Tuesday 26 September 1939 – France / Belgium Border.

Although the rain had stopped during the night, the trenches had already begun to fill with water; a steady wind making it feel colder than it was in reality. The men had slept seated on the firing step, huddled together to keep upright and for warmth. Their uniforms were still wet from the rain the previous day, their webbing equipment shrinking and stiffening due to the moisture and making it difficult to access the contents.

The men were unusually happy to be put back to work, as the physical activity warmed them up and began to dry their uniforms. The platoon was assigned wiring duties; creating barbed wire obstacles in front of the trenches to slow down or trap any attacking force. Using Company Sergeant Major McCann's advice for holding pickets, these were hammered about one foot into the ground, and then coils of barbed wire strung between them to create the obstacles. McEnearney and Farthing were holding the pickets as Bell hammered them in, and being on the surface of the ground as opposed to digging trenches, were able to observe the landscape rather than the mud walls of a trench. Corned beef sandwiches and hot tea was delivered for lunch, and the wiring teams sat together as they ate.

"You were a farmer, Dinger." began McEnearney. "What are those stone wall circles in the field behind?"

"Those are sheep pens, Tom mate." replied Bell. "The sheep go into them at night or during bad weather to keep warm and dry. They look like continuous circles from here, but there will be an opening on the far side for the animals to enter and leave." The conversation was interrupted by shouts to get back to work and the teams returned to their wiring duties. Not long after they restarted work, the rain began again, soaking the wiring teams exposed on the open ground.

* * *

After another miserable dinner of barely warm stew in the flooded trenches, Farthing and McEnearney were assigned to sentry duty. They stood in the rain and the dark for an hour before their relief appeared.

"I'm soaked and cold." complained Farthing. "Why don't we check out those sheep pens rather than sit in a flooded trench for the rest of the night?"

"Let's have a look." replied McEnearney. "If it's shit, then we can just go back to the trench. Nothing ventured, nothing gained." When relieved on sentry duty, they quietly sneaked away from the trenches towards the nearest pen. The stone walls were about three feet high, and had a small opening just as Bell had said. As they ventured inside, three startled sheep bolted out past them and disappeared into the darkness, making them jump in fright. The farmer had placed some straw in the pen and the two men gathered it up into a makeshift mattress, lying tightly against the stone wall for protection from the wind and rain.

"This is better." said McEnearney cheerfully. "Let's get our head down here, and as long as we report back to the platoon before dawn, no one will be any the wiser." They tightened their rain capes around their necks, pulled their legs up underneath, and were soon asleep.

Wednesday 27 September 1939 –
Lille, Northern France.

The sound of sheep in the pen woke the two soldiers before dawn. As they stirred and stretched, the sheep that had ventured back during the night took fright again and ran from the structure. The soldiers gathered their senses and checked they had left nothing behind before leaving the pen, quietly making their way back towards the platoon trenches. The rain had stopped during the night and the wind had dropped. The sound of bird calls from the nearby wood signalled the approaching dawn. As they neared the area of the trench, the sound of someone snoring guided them in.

"I bet that's Dinger snoring." whispered Farthing.

"Better than having a compass to find your way back." replied McEnearney. They sat down on the lip of the trench rather than climb down inside, knowing that everyone would be awake soon. The sentries returned as the sun came up, closely followed by Sergeant Preston who formally roused the still sleeping men.

"Good news, boys." began Preston. "We're getting relieved early, which means breakfast in barracks." Being stiff, wet and cold, a half-hearted cheer of relief rather than celebration was all the platoon could muster in response to the welcome development.

* * *

The vehicles stopped in the square outside the barrack block and the men ran inside to drop their equipment before going for breakfast. The cookhouse buzzed with excited chatter, and morale increased immeasurably as they sat down to bacon, bread, jam and warm tea. The routine of equipment cleaning awaited, before taking a shower, with the prospect of a few hours in a clean bed and the rest of the day off.

Men huddled around ceramic sinks in the laundry room, scrubbing their webbing equipment with bristle brushes to get the dirt out, before hanging it up in the drying room. Some left their dirty uniforms on the floor beside their beds to clean later, while some decided that they would wash their clothes in the shower alongside themselves. McEnearney and Farthing stripped in their rooms, and wrapping a towel around themselves went to the showers. The shower block was tiled on all surfaces except the ceiling, which held pipework in the shape of a large square. From this pipework, three showerheads hung down each leg of the square, allowing up to twelve people to use the facility at once.

They hung their towels on the hooks outside the shower and entered the steam filled room. They grinned at each other as the warm water ran over them, lathering up soap to scrub themselves, when Farthing suddenly stopped and pointed at McEnearney's chest. A black lump the size of a fingernail was imbedded in his skin. McEnearney gripped it to pull it out, causing it to wiggle and embed itself further in his flesh. Both men yelled at the shock of the moving creature, which drew the attention of everyone else in the shower. Having worked on a farm, Bell immediately identified the creature as a sheep tick.

"Don't try to pull it out, Tom mate." he told McEnearney quickly, who was pulling at the creature burrowing into him. "The head will break off and cause an infection." Farthing let out another yell as he found a similar creature on himself; Bell giving the same advice to him. "You need to go to the Medical Centre and have them removed with tweezers so the head comes out as well." he advised. The two friends ran to their room and put their PT vests and shorts on over their wet bodies, then hurried to the Medical Centre. There was a very overweight Medical Corps Sergeant at the reception desk who confirmed Bell's identification of the creatures, poking the ticks with a pencil and causing them to burrow in further; much to the distress of Farthing and McEnearney. He recorded the soldiers' service numbers and names.

"Been away from home too long and getting friendly with sheep then?" he asked sarcastically as he retrieved their files. The pair didn't answer. "The British medics are not here yet, but the French medics will sort you out." he added. "Wait in there," he said, pointing to a seated area, "but don't sit down or touch anything."

"Bloody sheep ticks!" whispered McEnearney to Farthing as they stood in the middle of the waiting room. "We must have got them by sleeping in the pen."

"Oh God, just get these things out of me." added Farthing, his voice reflecting his revulsion at the situation. A French medic appeared out of one of the consulting rooms and went to the reception desk. He stared at the two friends standing in the middle of the room, looking them up and down as he passed.

"He seems a bit weird." remarked Farthing.

"Distinctly effeminate." answered McEnearney. "I hope he picks you and not me." His attempt at humour fell flat. The medic came back with two files, and in broken English asked Farthing to identify his. Farthing pointed to the file bearing his name. The medic went to the other consulting room and entered without knocking; emerging seconds later and gesturing for Farthing to follow him into his own room. McEnearney was left alone for only a minute before the other consulting room door opened and he was waved inside by a different French medic. In broken English, he was told to remain standing and undress, at which point McEnearney declared that he understood the language.

The demeanour of the medic changed instantly. He explained that McEnearney's clothes needed to be checked first, and any ticks removed. McEnearney undressed, and between them they checked his clothing, finding nothing. The medic explained that sheep ticks were very common in mild, wet weather and that they needed to be removed properly and not just pulled out; just as Private Bell had said. He showed McEnearney the special tweezers and how they worked, and within seconds the tick on his chest had been removed. The medic inspected his body from the top down getting him to raise his arms and finding another tick in his armpit. He pulled his buttocks apart and inspected around his groin before working down his legs, finding another tick on the back of his knee.

McEnearney was told to get dressed again and advised to check for ticks in the uniform he had worn in the field; making sure to wash it thoroughly. He thanked the medic and they both left the consulting room at precisely the same time as Farthing emerged from his examination, followed by the other medic. Farthing appeared to be in some distress; he was visibly pale and had a far away, vacant look on his face, as if his mind was somewhere else.

Unaware that McEnearney understood the language, Farthing's medic smugly and loudly spoke to his colleague.

"Cul comme un garçon chinois de quatorze ans." At the same time making a sidewards movement with his hand, the middle finger extended. The other medic shook his head quickly, and gestured with his hands for his colleague to stop talking. McEnearney looked accusingly at the vocal medic before leading Farthing out of the waiting room, stopping when outside and asking him what had happened.

"He got me to strip naked and stand in the middle of the room." Farthing began. "After he had inspected my clothes, he took out the tick with tweezers and then checked the rest of me. He got me to bend over and spent a lot of time checking around my arse and groin." He stopped talking for a short period as if unwilling to relate the story. "Then he put something inside me and pulled it out again, like a finger or a thumb."

"Bloody Hell, mate." said McEnearney. "Trust you to get the pervert medic." he continued. "You did make a big impression though, as he told his mate that you had an arse like a fourteen-year-old Chinese boy." At this point McEnearney could control himself no longer, and burst out laughing.

Wednesday 27 September 1939 – Warsaw, Poland.

Having been under siege and bombed almost continuously for fourteen days, at 2 p.m. the sky cleared of enemy planes and the streets of Warsaw fell silent. A ceasefire had been declared in order to allow negotiations around terms for a surrender of the capital. Polish General Tadeusz Kutrzeba had travelled by car through the shattered streets to Sulejwek, a small town nine miles east of Warsaw, to the local Primary School; now the headquarters of the German 1st Corps. Already struggling to cope with the enormity of the decision that lay ahead of him, Kutrzeba's situation seemed even more surreal as he made his way down the corridors of the building, passing low fixed coat hooks on the walls and child size chairs and desks.

He was led to an office occupied by German Lieutenant General Walter Petzel, who got to his feet as Kutrzeba entered. Without ceremony, Petzel began reading the terms he had drawn up, and despite containing the phrase "unconditional capitulation", Kutrzeba nodded his agreement in the lack of any viable alternative. Petzel offered his hand, which, still in a state of shock, Kutrzeba accepted, before saluting and departing.

On driving back to his headquarters through Warsaw's remaining defensive positions, Kutrzeba surveyed the city. Churches, museums and art galleries, once the pride of Warsaw, lay in ruins. Statues of Poland's leaders and scholars were decapitated or lay completely smashed at the base of their plinths. Rows of disturbed earth from hasty burials covered the parks where children once played and friends met to talk and walk their dogs. With the lull in the fighting, a pale and dust covered civilian population had emerged from their cellars, and now wandered aimlessly through their destroyed properties. Some stood below broken pipes to catch the trickling water in pots, while others hacked flesh from bloated dead horses lying in the street to feed their families. When his vehicle stopped, the smell of putrefaction and smoke hit his nostrils as he opened the car door.

Thursday 28 September 1939 –
Warsaw, Poland.

The next morning, Kutrzeba travelled to the suburb of Rakowiec, on the south-western edge of the city, to the Headquarters of the German 8th Army. The command post was in the ruins of the Skoda factory, where German General Johannes Blaskowitz had assembled his staff inside an Opel Blitz bus. The relative comfort of the vehicle contrasted sharply to the twisted metal girders and smashed brickwork of the factory in which it stood. As Kutrzeba climbed the three steps into the bus, Blaskowitz and his waiting staff officers stood up as one. On the table awaiting his signature was the surrender document, detailing the terms agreed the previous afternoon. With this simple act, the fighting in Warsaw would come to an end. Over the next hours, the orders to facilitate the surrender were sent around the city; and 140,000 Polish soldiers passed into captivity.

Friday 29 September 1939 –
Lille, Northern France.

The whole battalion had been told to wait behind in the cookhouse after dinner for a presentation by the Medical Officer, Captain Walker. There was loud chatter as the men waited for the event to begin; mostly around what the subject of the presentation would be. The chairs had all been turned to face the same direction, so some soldiers sat with their backs to the dining tables. The Regimental Sergeant Major called for order as the Medical Officer prepared to speak. He was a very young Captain, obviously not long qualified, who found himself swept up in the conscription process, and made responsible for the provision of medical services to a battalion of infantry soldiers. The fat Medical Sergeant was also in attendance. His name was Parker, which naturally attracted the nickname of "Nosey".

Captain Walker began to speak quietly, as he was used to in a medical setting, only to be immediately interrupted by shouts from the back of the room that he could not be heard. He cleared his throat and began again, his voice obviously straining with the required volume. As he spoke, the room became transfixed. The subject was sexually transmitted diseases, how they could be caught and what symptoms to watch for. Cognisant of the problems that had been created during the last war with soldiers catching sexual diseases from the local brothels, the presentation had been requested by the Commanding Officer before he would allow the men any leave.

With the audience in a stunned silence after the Medical Officer's delivery, the Medical Sergeant took over; contraception being the subject of his presentation. Whistles and laughter erupted from the assembly as he talked about contraceptive techniques and how to use condoms; but despite the distractions he continued, and as an able speaker, received a round of applause from the audience when he had finished.

Farthing looked down the line of seated soldiers and saw Lance Corporal Tetlow laughing and slapping his thigh in merriment at the content and style of the Medical Sergeant's presentation. Farthing tapped McEnearney on the shoulder and pointed at Tetlow.

"He doesn't need this lecture." he whispered. "His personality is the best contraceptive ever!"

Tuesday 3 October 1939 –
Naval Headquarters, Berlin, Germany.

Kapitanleutnant Gunter Prien sat in a dark green leather chair, undecided if he was uncomfortable due to the chair or the nervous excitement of his circumstances. He uncrossed his legs and crossed them the opposite way to see if that would help. The highly polished marble floored corridor was completely empty, except for chairs like the one he was currently sitting on, positioned at intervals down the corridor outside office doors like the one he was sitting outside. A large painting of Hitler seemed to stare at him from the facing wall. On the coffee table beside him, he had placed his black Naval cap and a file marked "Geheim". Secret Operation Order *North Sea Number 16* had been given to him exactly forty-eight hours earlier by Admiral Donitz, head of the German Navy's U-Boat Arm, in the office he again now waited outside.

He had been ordered to consider it carefully and return today to give his answer. The contents described Donitz' strategic aim to weaken the British blockade over the North Sea, making it less hazardous for German surface raiders. The operation order laid out details of an attack on the Royal Navy inside the defences of Scapa Flow, a natural harbour in the Orkney Islands. It proposed a two-pronged assault, starting with an attack inside the harbour, forcing the British Home Fleet to disperse around alternative ports in the vicinity until Scapa Flow could be made safe again. Secondly, mines would be placed in likely relocation ports at Loch Ewe, the Firth of Forth and the Firth of Clyde to potentially inflict further damage on the fleet as it dispersed.

Naval Intelligence Services had gathered as much information as possible on Scapa Flow. Aerial photographs of the defences had been ordered from the Luftwaffe, showing in detail the blockships and steel netting across the seven entrances to the harbour. The photographs also showed the entire British Home Fleet at anchor. For sixteen days, U-14 had scouted the perimeter defences around the Orkneys and measured tidal conditions, all adding to the information that Donitz had used to formulate the details of his plan. He had concluded that any penetration attempt would have to be conducted on the surface, therefore on a moonless night, and at high tide when the currents were weakest. These required conditions thus dictated the date of the attack; the night of 13 / 14 October.

The plan was so detailed that even the path to be taken by the attacking U-Boat was described; through Holm Sound at the eastern end, and then Kirk Sound, navigating between the sunken blockships and through into Scapa Flow. Kirk Sound was only five hundred yards wide and forty-five feet deep at its deepest; this deep path through the channel restricted by three sunken blockships, while a fourth lay on its side further obstructing any passage attempts. The attacking Captain would have to steer his vessel right next to the blockship where any error or drift in the current would either result in a collision with the blockship or the U-Boat being grounded on the shore.

Prien knew the details intimately, having thought of little else for the previous forty-eight hours. He had made up his mind to accept the mission after his first read through the file. Subsequent study had not changed his opinion that it was probably a suicide mission, but he was captured by the thought of the file's concluding paragraph guaranteeing the *"Acclaim of the Fuhrer and the German Nation"* if he managed to pull it off. Admiral Donitz had personally selected Prien for this mission; as it was his brainchild and he felt he was entitled to choose its commander. He had met Prien on a few occasions, being struck by his incisive intelligence and instinctive thrust – like a hunter who outwits his prey and strikes just at the right moment. He was also clean cut, cocky, and a fanatical Nazi; the perfect attributes required to create a National Socialist naval hero.

Donitz finished signing the documents his Adjutant had presented to him and pushed them back across his desk.

"Kapitanleutnant Prien is waiting, Herr Admiral. Shall I show him in?" the Adjutant asked. Donitz nodded his approval, placed the cap back on his pen and tidied his desk in preparation to receive the young officer. The Adjutant opened the office door and announced Prien by his rank and surname. Prien approached Donitz's desk, stopped three feet short and gave a straight arm salute as he clicked his heels together. He stared straight ahead, not looking at the Admiral.

"Yes, or no?" asked Donitz without any pleasantries.

"Yes, Herr Admiral." came the immediate reply from Prien. The mood of both men changed instantly. Donitz thumped the desk with the palm of his hand and stood up. Prien removed his hat and tucked it under his left arm, a wide smile beaming across his face. Donitz moved round to the front of his desk and shook Prien's hand warmly.

"Very well." he said in a voice hushed by relief as he nodded his approval. "Get your boat ready."

Sunday 8 October 1939 –
Kiel Naval Dockyards, Northern Germany.

It was a beautiful clear morning. At a few minutes to 10 o'clock, Prien stood on the pier with U-Boat Command Staff Officer Kapitan von Friedeburg, looking at U-47 with its crew lined on the deck. Neither had spoken much, the mutual understanding of the mission and the risks it entailed requiring no words. Prien looked at his watch and confirmed it was time to go. Kapitan von Friedeburg wished him luck; the officers saluted each other and Prien walked across the gangway to his boat. The diesel engines roared into life and U-47 slipped out of Kiel docks without fanfare or ceremony. Over the previous five days, all sensitive equipment, secret papers and code books, including the Enigma cypher machine, had been removed from the vessel. None of this would be required as the submarine would be on radio silence for the duration of the mission. U-47 was to use a new secret weapon for the first time on operations, the currently used steam powered torpedoes being replaced by the newly developed, wakeless G7e electrically powered torpedoes. These weapons had been developed under total secrecy and the German Navy wanted to keep them secret, hence explosives had been rigged to scuttle the vessel at a moment's notice should there be the slightest danger of capture.

All German surface vessels and U-boats operating around the Orkney islands had been withdrawn to maintain the clandestine nature of the mission. If it all went wrong, no one was to know of the attempt; and Prien had not briefed the crew where they were going to maintain security. Donitz had updated the Naval Supreme Commander, Grand Admiral Raeder, verbally to prevent information leaks. Travelling on the surface by night and remaining submerged during the day, it would take four days for U-47 to reach Scapa Flow.

Tuesday 10 October 1939 –
Lille, Northern France.

Just after midday, a reinforcement of trained soldiers arrived, three of the group being posted to 10 Platoon. It was decided to keep them together as far as possible to assist in the settling in process, and all three were assigned to

1 Section. Corporal Hutchinson stood beside Sergeant Preston as the new soldiers dismounted the vehicles; a late lunch had been arranged and Corporal Hutchinson took them to the cookhouse. The new soldiers introduced themselves as Hamill, Millar and Moore, and a welcome interview with the Company Commander was arranged for the next morning. Hamill had been recalled to service, having previously been a Regular soldier for eight years; not being required to attend a training Depot and being posted directly to the battalion. Millar and Moore had been conscripted from civilian life; were fresh from Depot training, and incredibly naive about life, let alone Army life. Hamill was required to undergo a medical examination so that his records could be brought up to date, and an appointment had been made for his review that afternoon.

After they had eaten, Corporal Hutchinson took all three soldiers on a tour of the barracks, dropping Hamill off at the Medical Centre before taking the others back to the platoon accommodation. Hamill had been issued with his previous records which he handed to the Medical Sergeant at reception. He was asked to wait in the seated area. After a few minutes, Sergeant Parker invited him to a consulting room.

"I see you have previous service." he began.

"Eight years, mostly in India." Hamill replied.

"And you have been recalled to service from civilian employment?" Parker continued.

"I worked in a furniture warehouse for a year before recall." Hamill elaborated.

"I was Territorial Army myself and got mobilised." added Parker, his tone displaying his annoyance at his circumstances. "Married with no dependent children." he read out loud from Hamill's file.

"That's correct." Hamill confirmed.

"Jump on the scales and we'll make a start." ordered Parker.

***

Along with questions on his general health, the examination covered height, weight, blood pressure and heart rate measurements, along with an eyesight test. On completion, Hamill was invited to take a seat opposite the desk.

"You're two stone overweight." said Parker, pointing at Hamill's stomach, "But that will come off over the next few months with normal military life." Being told he was overweight, especially by a nearly obese Medical Sergeant did not sit well with Hamill.

"I'll be a stone lighter by this time tomorrow." he replied curtly. Sergeant Parker lifted his eyes from the file, staring at Hamill through his eyebrows, a look of distain on his face.

"Are you going to cut your head off?" he asked sarcastically.

"I'll bet you ten bob, if you wish." challenged Hamill.

"Ten bob you'll be a stone lighter by tomorrow afternoon?" quizzed Parker, checking he had understood the offer correctly.

"By this time tomorrow." confirmed Hamill confidently.

"You're on there, mate." replied the Medical Sergeant, knowing of no method of losing a stone in twenty-four hours.

"I'll see you tomorrow then, Sergeant." confirmed Hamill.

"Bring your money." replied Parker.

Wednesday 11 October 1939 – Lille, Northern France.

It was morning NAAFI break and both Hamill and Orpin had called into the ablutions on their way back. Orpin was using the urinal, Hamill was using a tray. Orpin let his mind wander as he relieved himself, imagining he was anywhere else but in Lille. The sound of a grunt followed by a gasp of relief came from the area of the trays, and a smell that could be described as that of a decomposing body hit Orpin's nostrils and then the back of his throat. He gagged and his face screwed up.

"Jesus Christ mate, what the..." He didn't get to finish his sentence as he closed his mouth in an involuntary reaction against the choking odour. Looking into the open cubicle, he saw Hamill squatting over the hole in the tray, an enormous pile of excrement around his feet, and getting bigger as diarrhoea followed the solids. On the verge of retching, Orpin ran towards the door and put his head outside to breathe. "You need to see the Medical Officer, mate." he shouted back from outside, as much in disgust as concern for his colleague.

"Don't worry." replied Hamill. "I'm going there right now."

* * *

The Medical Sergeant looked up from the reception desk as Hamill went in.

"I'm here to get weighed." demanded Hamill.

"Are you sure?" questioned Sergeant Parker. "You don't look any thinner."

"Just weigh me please." repeated Hamill impatiently. Parker recovered his file, and indicating for Hamill to follow him, they went into a consulting room.

"Be my guest." said Sergeant Parker, indicating for Hamill to get on the scales as he checked the file for his recorded weight from the previous day. Leaning over to take the new reading, he asked Hamill to get off and on again. He then balanced the scales again.

"These aren't the scales we used yesterday." said Parker, obviously unnerved by the new reading. "We were in the other room."

"Let's go there then." replied Hamill merrily. They crossed the waiting area and entered the same consulting room they had occupied the previous day.

"Try now." said Parker, confident that the same scales would give a different reading. Hamill stepped on again, and Parker took the reading.

"You're over a stone lighter!" said the exasperated medic. "How the hell did you do it?"

"Never you mind how I did it. Where's my money?" asked Hamill, holding out his hand. Sergeant Parker took out his wallet and removed a ten shilling note, reluctantly handing it to Hamill.

"Thanks for your time and the use of your facilities." Hamill quipped as he put the money in his pocket.

* * *

The members of 1 Section were mostly lying on their beds after dinner. Hamill came in whistling and sat down on the end of his bed.

"Who's for a drink?" he questioned. "I'm buying." The room suddenly came to life, everyone getting to their feet at the offer of free drink. The whole section left the room in high spirits, full of excited chatter as they made their way to the NAAFI.

Being a hastily converted bedroom in one of the blocks, the NAAFI was not particularly welcoming, with stone walls and very little natural light. A trestle table had been set up in the corner to represent a bar, with an Army blanket spread over the top. No draught beer was on offer, only locally brewed bottled beer. The section took up a full table with a few seats being moved from adjacent tables so they could all sit together. Hamill arrived with a tray full of bottles.

"What's the occasion?" asked Orpin, the others hanging on his words for the reply.

"I won a bet with the Medical Sergeant." answered Hamill truthfully. "I bet him ten bob that I could lose a stone in weight within twenty-four hours."

"Ten bob?" exclaimed Farthing. "That's a week's pay!"

"Never mind that." interrupted Smith. "How did you lose a stone in weight?"

"You see, I've always had this problem." began Hamill. "I only shit once every eight days. Always have. Like clockwork." The table fell completely silent, wondering what was coming next in the story. "I thought this was normal until I got married. I only realised I was different when the wife shit nearly every day. I thought there was something wrong with her." The table descended into howls of laughter. "I knew I would have to go sometime today," he continued, "so when I was called fat by the medic, I thought, I'll teach you, you cheeky fat bastard."

"And you made the bet knowing you would shit out the extra stone." Orpin finished the story for him, having witnessed the event that morning in the ablutions.

"Correct." confirmed Hamill with a broad smile. The table was in uproar, attracting inquisitive looks from others present in the NAAFI.

"That's unbelievable." chipped in McEnearney when he could control his laughter.

"Regular as clockwork, every seven days." repeated Hamill. "It would be better if it was every eight days, then it would be the same day each week and easier to remember." The table fell about laughing again.

"Well, here's to your infrequent but regular bowels." said Orpin, holding up his bottle in a toast.

"To your infrequent but regular bowels." repeated everyone present, returning the toast and clinking their bottles together at arm's length in the middle of the table.

Thursday 12 October 1939 –
Orkney Islands, North Sea.

By the evening of 12 October, U-47 was 1.8 nautical miles from the Orkneys, when Prien ordered the boat to the relative safety of the ocean floor. Lying static at a depth of three hundred feet, Prien gathered every member of his forty-man crew for briefing. The air was humid and stale from the submerged journey that day, and the submariners were now into their fourth day without washing, which added a certain sharpness to each inhalation of breath. There was an uncomfortable silence as the crew waited expectantly for Prien to speak. The only sound was the dripping of condensation onto the metal floor and the creaking of the structural ribs under the pressure of the water pressing on the hull, pushing the boat into the sediment on the seabed. Without any introduction or narrative, Prien simply made his announcement.

"Tomorrow, we shall enter Scapa Flow. No one knows of our mission and if the boat is lost, no one will know of our fate. We have the chance to avenge the humiliation of 1919, and I am confident we shall succeed." The message was met with absolute silence by the crew. Every German sailor knew of the scuttling of the Imperial Fleet in Scapa Flow in June 1919, shortly after the end of the Great War, and although all hands were elated at the chance to purge the shame, the inherent danger of the mission did not escape them.

Friday 13 October 1939 –
Royal Military College Sandhurst, Surrey, England.

It had been eighteen months since Student Officer William Dudley Chadwick walked through the gates of Royal Military College Sandhurst, past the square, squat solid stone guardhouse where his course joining documentation was checked, then directed up the long road towards Old College building. He vividly remembered the birds singing in the trees beside the lake that stretched below the road on his left. It was April 1938 and he was doing what was expected of him, to become an officer in the Army and serve his country. Now his final day had come. The lessons on fieldcraft and leadership and the forced marches across Salisbury Plain loaded down with equipment. All were finished. The endless firing ranges and weapon cleaning. The platoon attacks against a compliant enemy who died when they were told. The cleaning of bedrooms, pressing of uniforms and polishing of equipment. All finished. Sometimes it felt he had only been there weeks, and other times it felt as if he had been there for years.

In his mind he had questioned his career choice; something that had been slowly eating at his consciousness for many months. He had fought to overcome his reticence, convincing himself that everyone must feel like this sometime, and to give life in the Army a chance to settle. But his feelings grew stronger rather than weaker, and he had become convinced that the Army was not for him; or he was not for the Army. He had not been able to decide which, and it didn't matter now anyhow, as his options had been overtaken by events. Britain had been at war with Germany for over a month and no one was going to listen to his career choice doubts now. Here he was on the drill square outside Old College on his Commissioning Parade, about to become an officer in the West Staffordshire Regiment, whether he wanted to or not.

A shiny black staff car pulled gently to a halt and an orderly stepped forward to open the door. As the Inspecting General stepped from the vehicle, he was met by the College Commander, exchanging salutes and a few short words before making their way up the King's Walk to the inspection dais. As the Inspecting General's foot hit the first step of the dais, the command was given to present arms and Student Officer Chadwick was jolted back to reality. As the Inspecting General looked out over the parade, the weapons and uniforms had changed since he himself stood where the Student Officers now stood, but little else had. The towering pillars guarding the entrance to Old College, the array of cannon captured from Napoleon at Waterloo lining the edges of the parade square, the excited chatter of the families proudly watching their sons being commissioned, he remembered it all very well.

The Adjutant approached on his white horse and requested "Permission for Sandhurst to March Past." The Inspecting General gave his permission and the Adjutant expertly turned his horse around to face the waiting Student Officers. "Sandhurst will March Past in Quick Time." he barked. The band struck up and the parade stepped off, wheeling first to the right and then to the left as they positioned themselves to march the full length of the square, giving an "Eyes Right" as they passed the Inspecting General. They returned to their original position on the parade, being dressed off by the Company Sergeant Major to straighten the ranks for the General's Inspection. The General dismounted the dais and approached the lines of waiting Student Officers under the guise of inspection, but in reality to allow him to speak directly to some of the officers about to commission. The band played appropriate non-martial music to entertain the spectators while the Inspecting General moved among the ranks on parade.

"What Regiment are you joining?" The General had stopped in front of Chadwick and was addressing him directly.

"The West Staffordshire Regiment, Sir." answered Chadwick, looking above the General's head and not at him, as protocol directed.

"Ah, a fine Regiment. I'm sure you will do very well there." came the reply; in a tone that struck Chadwick as impersonal and without feeling or meaning. The General moved off down the line chatting to some officers on the way and came back up the second rank. Stopping directly behind Chadwick, he spoke to a Student Officer in the next rank.

"What Regiment are you joining?"

"The Royal Sussex Regiment, Sir." came the reply.

"Ah, a fine Regiment. I'm sure you will do very well there." repeated the General in the same unfeeling tone. Chadwick pursed his lips to suppress a grin and then held his breath as he tried to stifle a laugh of derision. Something had to give, and a snort came down his nose. A face appeared from behind over his left shoulder, and a mouth pressed close to his ear. The metal tip of a pace stick, used to measure the length of a drill step, was stuck into his lower back.

"What the fuck do you think you are doing, Mister fucking Chadwick, Sir?" hissed the unmistakeable voice of the College Sergeant Major. "Don't fucking dare speak." The College Sergeant Major had been following behind the General and the College Commander on their inspection. It was a surprise to Chadwick to hear him whisper, yet this whisper still portrayed all the venom that the Student Officers had become accustomed to receiving for the last eighteen months when he had yelled in their faces, their noses almost touching, at the slightest misdemeanour on the drill square. His routine and frequent use of swearwords added colour and feeling to the simplest situation. "If the General wants to be a fucking clown, then he can be a fucking clown. He's a fucking General, and it's not for you to fucking comment one way or the other, Sir." Chadwick stood suitably chastised and embarrassed, only daring to breathe again when he was sure the College Sergeant Major had moved on. The General finished his inspection and returned to the dais.

"Sandhurst will march past in slow time." yelled the Adjutant albeit indistinctly as he fought to keep his horse facing the right way; although through continuous rehearsal, everyone knew what drill movement was coming next and the specific words of the command did not actually matter. The band struck up again and the parade moved off in slow time. The same orders were given as before and the same manoeuvres brought the half company before the Inspecting Officer on the dais. The command for eyes right was given again and the heads of the student officers snapped to the right as they passed the General. Just before the command was given for eyes front, Chadwick saw the College Sergeant Major standing at the side of the dais pointing his pace stick directly at him. As their eyes met, the College Sergeant Major mouthed the word "Fucker" at him. Chadwick was relieved when the eyes front command was given and he could break eye contact. On returning to the starting position the formation was again dressed off by the Company Sergeant Major.

A microphone on a stand was placed in front of the dais and the General rose to address the parade. There was a clearly audible murmur from the watching families as the Inspecting Officer approached the microphone, which quickly settled to complete silence as he prepared to speak. He waited for a few seconds as if for dramatic effect.

"We are once again at war with Germany," he began, "and those of you who are commissioning into your regiments today, will almost certainly be leading your men against the enemy on the field of battle in the near future." Chadwick felt sick. "Leading your men…" the General had said, and this is what Chadwick felt most uneasy about. He questioned his suitability to lead men when he doubted his own motives. He had convinced himself that he could do the few years that were expected of him, appeasing his father who had held a commission in the West Staffordshire Regiment, and served with distinction in the Great War.

His father had then served in Ireland, only to be shot in the back in an ambush by the Irish Republican Army during the War of Irish Independence, and confined to a wheelchair by his injuries. As he grew more bitter and frustrated at his confinement, he began to live his life through his son, constant pressure being applied to have the full military career that he had been denied. And so, it had ended up here. About to become an officer in his father's former regiment, with no want or desire for the role or the responsibility, and without the courage to tell his father of his feelings. The General had stopped speaking and polite applause rippled through the watching parents and dignitaries. "Stand by." was whispered down the ranks as a trigger to concentrate again in anticipation of the coming commands.

"Sandhurst will Advance in Review Order. By the centre, Quick March." yelled the Adjutant, his horse dancing again at the shock of the abrupt noise. The band struck up the British Grenadiers March, and the whole of the Senior Division moved forward as a single body for fourteen paces, snapping to a halt in unison in front of the dais. The Adjutant gently spurred his horse, bringing it between the front rank of the Senior Division and the dais. Saluting by raising his sword vertically in front of his face with his hand almost touching his chin, then dropping it to his waist, the Adjutant asked the Inspecting Officer for permission to march off. The General nodded his approval and the Adjutant repeated the salute with his sword. Gently tweaking the reigns with his left hand, his horse did a neat about turn to face the line of Student Officers.

"Sandhurst will March Off in Slow Time. Inwards Turn." At the Adjutant's command, half the Senior Division turned left, the other half turning right, to face each other in the middle. Being one of the smallest on the parade, Chadwick was directly in the centre of the Division as it turned inwards, now standing face to face with three of his course colleagues who had turned in the opposite direction. They grinned at each other in relief that they were seconds away from completing the course. As the Adjutant ordered "Slow March", the two opposite facing columns wheeled left and right respectively, ending up six abreast facing the entrance to Old College. Each step took them closer to the huge doors, which were swung open from the inside as the column approached. Up the steps they went, between the columns and through the doors into the entrance hall behind. Chadwick felt the excitement of those around him as the Student Officers passed through the doors and were symbolically commissioned as officers in the British Army. He felt no such excitement himself, but a sense of dread at what lay ahead.

"Keep moving and keep quiet." whispered the Sergeant inside the entrance as the new officers passed through the door. They broke formation and spread out to make room as more officers came up the steps and into the hall behind them. As the last of the Senior Division passed through the doors, the Adjutant followed them up the steps on his horse, the sound of the metal shod hooves on the marble floor echoing around the stone walls. The Sergeant signalled to his orderlies to close the doors and held the horse's bridle as the Adjutant dismounted.

"Congratulations, Gentlemen." the Adjutant said, sounding distinctly relieved the ceremony was over. "That went very well. Now get out the back door, collect your guests and make your way to lunch."

* * *

William could feel a distinct tension in the air as he sat with his parents in the main dining hall in Old College. Their silence was in stark contrast to the lively chatter that filled the room as the other newly commissioned officers excitedly related their experience of officer training to their parents and guests. His father broke the silence but didn't look at his son as he spoke, continuing to concentrate on his plate as he ate his meal.

"I was good friends with your Company Commander, Major Morrisey. We served together in France and Ireland as junior officers you know."

"Yes, Father, I know." William replied. He had been told this a dozen times before and suspected the conversation trigger was just the beginning of something more than small talk. Major Morrisey had himself spoken of their acquaintance during scheduled progress interviews that William had attended during his training, and had asked as to his father's wellbeing.

"He wrote to me to say how you were getting along." his father continued. William sensed his mother's posture change and knew she was becoming uncomfortable.

"James, I don't think this is the right time." she said as firmly as she dared, to a man she was evidently walking on eggshells with all the time.

"This is absolutely the right time!" he blurted out as his fist thumped the table, making the cutlery and glasses jump. The dining room fell silent as everyone looked round at the source of the outburst, but returned to their own conversations after a few seconds when the potential for further entertainment did not develop. "This is absolutely the right time." his father repeated much more slowly and calmly, taking his wife's hand and squeezing it gently as a sign of apology. He now looked William straight in the eye. "I find it difficult to accept that your personal feelings around military service have to come to my attention in a letter from your Company Commander rather than from your own admission." He raised his hand to stifle a reply as he saw William about to speak. "For God's sake why did you not speak to me about this before, and I could have straightened you out?" The intensity of his voice increased as anger began to grow in him again, once more raising his hand to prevent an answer to his question.

But William had no intention of interrupting him. He knew from the earliest days of his childhood that words had no impact on his father when he was in this frame of mind; when his frustration at losing his career and his physical independence overrode his ability to see things from others' point of view. He wondered how his mother had managed to put up with it for so long.

"Do you have any idea how much you have embarrassed me?" hissed his father from between clenched teeth. William lifted his napkin from his lap, gently wiped his lips, then folded it and placed it on the table. He stood up, the chair legs giving a protesting scrape on the tiled floor as it was pushed back. He placed his hand on his mother's shoulder and kissed her cheek.

"I'll write when I get settled." he whispered to her, before walking away without any acknowledgement to his father. The noise of chattering families abruptly disappeared as the dining room door swung closed behind him. He didn't remember the start of the walk back to his room, the jumbled buzzing of emotions in his head driving all other thoughts aside. As he climbed the stairs and turned into the long corridor of classrooms that led to the Student Officers' bedrooms, the echo of his nailed boots on the stone floor resounded in the silent, empty space. Without thinking he collected his mail from his pigeon hole at the entrance to his platoon accommodation as he had done countless times before, pushed open his unlocked door and very deliberately flung himself onto his bed. He lay looking at the ceiling of the room, familiar with every crack and blemish in the plaster, a view he had studied for more hours than he could imagine as he had lain awake wrestling with his thoughts for the past eighteen months. Turning to the side he reached out and picked up the two items of mail he had placed on his bedside table as he came in. The first was a final mess bill, including the cost of the lunch he had just endured with his parents. He let it drop to the floor. The second was an official looking letter addressed to Second Lieutenant William Chadwick, The West Staffordshire Regiment. He swung his feet off the bed and sat up, sliding his finger under the flap of the letter to open it.

It was from a Captain Greer, his Adjutant to be, welcoming him into his new regiment. After two weeks leave, he was to report for duty at the Regimental Headquarters in Whittington Barracks, Staffordshire, to assume the appointment of Platoon Commander of 10 Platoon, D Company, 1st Battalion, The West Staffordshire Regiment. From there, arrangements would be made for his onward movement to his battalion. He knew the battalion had been preparing to go to India, but had recently been sent to France after the declaration of war, and that his remaining time in England would be short.

Friday 13 October 1939 –
Orkney Islands, North Sea.

Aboard U-47, the rest of the day passed very slowly waiting on the seabed. With the lights extinguished, those not on duty were sent to their bunks as they waited for nightfall; but few could sleep. The crew on watch who remained awake, wrapped their boots in cloth to minimise noise as they moved around the boat, in the hope of allowing those off duty to rest. At 4 p.m. everyone was woken up and a lavish dinner of veal cutlets and green cabbage was served, the men eating as much as they could, as only cold food and chocolate would be available from then on until the mission was completed. At 5 p.m. the tables, crockery and cutlery were cleared away, torpedoes were checked and the scuttling charges primed in case of impending capture.

Smoking and unnecessary talking were now prohibited, as at 7 p.m. Prien gave the order to surface. The vessel groaned and shuddered as it begrudgingly left the grip of the North Sea mud, as if somehow it knew what danger lay ahead and wanted to stay safely enveloped in its comfortable bed. Operating under red light to protect their night vision, the crew kept the boat level as the Engineer called out the ever-decreasing depth from the gauge; until at 7:15, after a periscope check of the area, U-47 broke the surface. There was a rush of cold, fresh air and sea water as the hatch was opened and Prien, now clad in cumbersome oilskins, climbed the ladder onto the conning tower. His initial reaction was that of disbelief. He had expected the safety of darkness but found the sky was ablaze with the shimmering glow of the Northern Lights, the wet hull of the boat glistening in the display. He almost ordered an immediate retreat to safety beneath the surface, but steadied his nerve on reflection that any enemy vessel would be much more obvious than his submarine with its low profile. He whispered back through the hatch for the lookouts to quickly take post, and then for the ballast tanks to be partially flooded to lower the boat's profile even further. The boat remained motionless and silent until Prien was content that they had not been detected, then ordered it slowly forward in the direction of Scapa Flow.

Almost four hours later, the boat was approaching Holm Sound. Prien was still deeply concerned about the light levels and had been contemplating conducting the attack submerged in order to avoid detection. He was unexpectedly given the chance to test his idea when a merchant ship was spotted by the bridge watch and Prien ordered the boat to dive. At periscope depth he aligned the merchant vessel in the crosshairs as it passed him and immediately lost all depth perception against the glittering horizon. He knew at that point a submerged attack was not feasible in the prevailing light conditions, and his attack would have to be made from the surface despite the increased likelihood of detection.

Once he was sure the merchant vessel was gone, Prien surfaced again at 11:31 p.m. He took a few moments to fix his position and proceeded towards Kirk Sound, switching from the diesel engines to the quieter electric motors. He whispered steering adjustments as the boat approached the gap between the Thames and Soriano blockships, when the vessel was suddenly gripped by the tide as it flowed through the space between the ships and into Scapa Flow. The U-Boat lurched to the side as if pulled by a giant magnet, heading uncontrollably towards the huge metal mooring cables that held the blockship hulks together. Shouting for full power from the engines to counteract the current, Prien attempted to steer the boat directly at the mid-point between the ships where he hoped the sag in the cables would give him the depth of water needed to pass. The sound of metal scraping on metal reverberated throughout the vessel as the keel of the boat rubbed on the mooring cable, rising slightly in the water before dipping back down to starboard as the engines pushed the hull up, over and clear of the obstruction. The noise stopped, but the momentum needed to clear the cable now pushed the boat onto the raised channel bed behind the blockship, and U-47 ran aground. Prien quickly called for the engines to stop as the boat was driven further into the raised bed by the frantically turning propellers.

The crew now performed a standard procedure of trying to rock the boat free using forward and backward thrust against opposite rudder angles, but to no avail. If they could not work themselves free before dawn, the boat would have to be destroyed and the crew would become prisoners of war. As a feeling of helplessness began to spread among the crew, the Engineer recalled partially flooding the ballast tanks to lower the boat's silhouette prior to the approach. Prien reacted instantly to the reminder and ordered the ballast tanks blown out. The boat gently lifted free of the sand and Prien steered hard to port, bringing the vessel back into the current that had caused the problem in the first place; now using the power of the tide to take him away from the obstacles. He fought to steady the boat in the rushing current until the channel widened and the power of the tide dispersed, allowing U-47 to sail serenely into St Mary's Bay, the dark, eerie openness of Scapa Flow lying before it.

The bridge watch could clearly see the shoreline about thirty yards away, identifying parked trucks with sentries guarding them, illuminated by the Northern Lights. The sentries were certainly not expecting any attempt to enter the mooring, and boredom had dulled their attention to such a level that U-47 remained unnoticed. Aware of how sound travelled over water and the proximity of the enemy, those on bridge watch were almost frightened to breathe. They could clearly hear the murmur of the guards talking amongst themselves and knew any sound from them would be similarly audible. They became mesmerised by the tension of the situation when their trance was suddenly shattered as a beam of light swept the conning tower from front to back. Assuming a searchlight had found them, the sailors instinctively dropped below the lip of the tower, expecting a hail of bullets to rake the boat. The light disappeared as abruptly as it had appeared and gingerly raising their heads, the watch saw the distinctive light pattern of a vehicle as it moved through the dips and turns of the coast road, its engine noise fading and rising as it entered into and re-emerged from dead ground. Prien instructed that a note be made in the log. It read "14 October, 00.27. Entered Scapa Flow."

Saturday 14 October 1939 –
Scapa Flow, Orkney Islands, North Sea.

With the Northern Lights still dancing in the sky, visibility was extremely good. Prien, his Watch Officer, Oberleutnant Engelbert Endrass, and the lookouts all scoured the horizon, each one wanting to be the first to locate the British Home Fleet at anchor. The boat continued westwards for fifteen minutes, covering a distance of over three miles, and the feelings of both those on the conning tower and those waiting expectantly in the body of the boat became uneasy. Prien, believing the lookouts had simply missed the British ships due to the lighting conditions, ordered the boat around and headed back east. Another fifteen minutes of fruitless search almost returned them to Kirk Sound. Still nothing was seen, and the euphoria felt at gaining entry to the anchorage was turning to bitter disappointment.

Prien was almost in a state of desperation. The intelligence reports clearly stated Scapa Flow was full of battleships and the aerial photographs had confirmed this. He pictured the photographs in his mind and as a last resort he decided to search the as yet unobserved northeast corner of the anchorage. He gave the new bearing and lifted his binoculars to his eyes again. As the boat moved north, the dark silhouette of a large ship contrasted against the gentle glow of the calm water. Having studied the silhouettes of all the ships believed to be at anchor in Scapa Flow, Prien quickly identified the Royal Oak. About one thousand yards behind the Royal Oak was another vessel with only a bow outline showing. Prien convinced himself, more out of hope than visible evidence, this second vessel was HMS Repulse. It was in reality HMS Pegasus, an antiquated sea plane carrier, its normally distinct outline obscured behind the massive structure of Royal Oak.

A buzz ran through the crew as they prepared themselves for action, each man at his battle station, calm but hyper-alert, all their nerves gone. The only sound audible again was the condensation dripping onto the steel floor, as each man strained his senses waiting for orders. U-47 closed to 3,500 yards when the order was received to make the four bow tubes ready while Endrass did the calculations for the surface targeting. A ship the size of Royal Oak stationary at 3,500 yards was a certain kill with two torpedoes. The second two, Endrass targeted at what he thought was Repulse. The order to open tube doors was enacted and the water flooded in, although it seemed an eternity before Endrass gave the order to launch torpedoes. The clear notification of "Number one away." then "Number two away." was heard all through the boat. Prien glanced at his watch. It was 00:55 a.m. The call of "Number three away." should have been followed by confirmation that number four was also away, but the notification never came. Number four had misfired and was still in the tube; but the other three torpedoes were running.

Nearly all the 1,219 crew onboard Royal Oak were asleep. Arthur Smith, a seventeen years old Boy Sailor, was on aircraft lookout above the four-inch gun deck. The sky was cloudless and the stars were clearly visible. He watched as streaks of greenish yellow light shot across the northern horizon, as if the Northern Lights were putting on a show just for him. He had just buried his chin deeper into his duffle coat to keep out the chill when a loud explosion came from the starboard bow and the ship leapt up from the water. As he regained his balance, Smith looked round to see a column of water rising into the air and washing over the deck. The port anchor released; its chain running unchecked across the fo'csle deck and making a tremendous noise as the links were pulled through the hawsepipe. Voices all over the ship shouted for "Action Stations" as the klaxon alarm wailed. The Officer of the Watch and some other crewmen were running frantically across the deck trying to find out what had happened. Smith climbed down from the lookout onto the deck to join his gun crew in his designated action station.

As an eyewitness, he tried to make it known that the waterspout would suggest an explosion outside the ship, and thought it might have been a torpedo. The captain of the gun crew slapped him across the ear and corrected his assumption.

"How could it have been a torpedo?" he questioned. "We're in Scapa Flow." When a further fifteen minutes had elapsed with no damage reported and no further explosions, "Fall Out" was sounded and Smith returned to his lookout position, while the remainder of the crew returned to their hammocks.

Alf Fordham, a musician in the Royal Marines, jumped from his bunk as the muffled explosion and sudden movement of the ship woke him up. An announcement came over the ship's Tannoy to "Take magazine temperatures" and Fordham noticed a worried Gunnery Officer hurrying past. Half-truths and supposition spread rapidly that the noise could have been a slippage of the anchor chains or an exploding tin of paint. Others said they heard it was a bomb dropped from a high-flying German plane that had narrowly missed, and showered the deck with water. Whatever the cause, no special precautions were deemed necessary and none were ordered; the men returning to their beds.

Prien had been staring at his watch, counting down the seconds inside his head. The time for the first torpedo strike had passed and nothing had been heard. Exactly as Endrass had briefed him for the stated time of the second strike, an explosion occurred. The crew performed silent celebrations at the sound of the explosion and prepared for the next strike; but nothing came. Prien raised his binoculars and examined the Royal Oak. There appeared to be no damage and no frantic activity on deck. He concluded that both the torpedoes aimed at Royal Oak had suffered technical issues, as Endrass could not have miscalculated so much as to miss such a large static target at this range; and that the explosion heard had been a strike on Repulse. Expecting a surface ship reaction from the British, Prien ordered the reloading of tubes one to three for a potential fighting withdrawal to Kirk Sound and attempted escape. As the boat moved into its turn, he thought there was nothing to lose and possibly everything to be gained from another attack. The stern tube was loaded, and as U-47 turned its back on the Royal Oak another torpedo was released as the boat headed for escape. Now watching from the rear of the conning tower, both Prien and Endrass stared at each other in disbelief as the calculated strike time passed and no explosion was heard. Prien thumped his gloved hand on the lip of the conning tower four times in sheer frustration, then stood motionless. Endrass had seen this reaction in his captain before and knew that Prien's mind was working at tremendous speed, calculating options, risks and possible results.

"What's the torpedo state?" Prien called down inside to the Engineer. The reply came back that tubes one and two were nearly ready and that tube four had been repaired. "Turn the boat around and report when tubes ready." he snapped sharply. With a smirk on his face, he looked at Endrass almost accusingly. "I will take you closer. The situation has not changed."

He then leaned against the handrail to steady himself, the boat heaving as it turned sharply back again. With torpedo tubes one, two and four reported ready, Prien took the boat to within 3,000 yards of the Royal Oak. Endrass checked his calculations again, finding them correct and gave Prien a confirmatory nod. Endrass gave the order to fire. From below, he heard the Engineer reporting "Number one away." "Number two away." "Number four away." Prien looked at his watch. It was 1:13 a.m.

All three torpedoes struck within a space of ten seconds, ripping enormous holes in the starboard side of the Royal Oak. The cordite magazines ignited instantly sending orange flames flashing through the confined passageways of the ship. The first torpedo hit amidships, below the Boys' Mess Deck, killing and maiming many of the young sailors in their hammocks. The second torpedo hit further aft, tearing a hole in the armoured deck, killing many men in the Stokers' Mess Deck. The remainder of the crew tumbled from their bunks and hammocks with the heaving of the vessel. Royal Oak began to list almost instantly, allowing thick fuel oil from the ruptured tanks to spill into the sea.

Arthur Smith was back at his aircraft lookout position when the three explosions rocked the ship. As the vessel began to list, he watched as chaos unfolded around him, and seeing men jumping into the water, he realised that would be his only route of escape. He made his way down to the deck and had the presence of mind to take off his duffle coat as he knew the weight would drag him under. With cold and shaking hands he struggled with the toggles, only shedding the garment as the water reached his feet. With no time to remove his trousers and boots, he dived in and began to swim away from the stricken ship.

Alf Fordham jumped from his bunk again, and began to get dressed just as a tongue of orange flame came through the passageway door, into the space he had been sleeping only seconds before. He ran in the opposite direction past the Officers' Quarters and found a ladder he knew would take him to the quarter deck. His haste to escape made him miss the rungs as his hands and feet lost their coordination; banging his knees and shins as he strived to recover his balance. He saw stars as he looked up, and a few seconds later tumbled out onto the deck.

Nineteen years old Ken Conway was pushed from his hammock and told to get out. He made his way down a smoke-filled gangway becoming disorientated as the ship listed and his vision became increasingly obscured by the smoke. A torch beam flicked from side to side in front of him and he made his way towards it. A Petty Officer was standing at the foot of ladders to the deck and was pushing sailors up the steps to escape. He was yelling for men to make their way towards his torch and remained at his post to show the way out for as many men as he could. As Conway reached the ladder the Petty Officer told him to make his way aft to the Daisy by walking down the ship's side. The Daisy was a tender that had been moored alongside Royal

Oak, and as Conway reached the deck, he could see a stream of men moving like monkeys on all fours down the steeply angled side of the ship towards the tender. Before he got close enough to board, Daisy separated from the crippled Royal Oak; Johnnie Duthie, a crewman on the Daisy, saving the tender by cutting the rope holding her to the stricken battleship. On seeing this, the more experienced men pushed the younger sailors over the side into the water and shouted at them to swim towards the Daisy.

At nineteen years old, Norman Thackery was old enough to drink, and had been ashore that night. The alcohol had aided a very restful sleep from which he was only woken by the second attack. His bunk was on the port side of the ship and the area did not suffer initial damage from the torpedo strikes on the starboard side. The men in that area waited for orders, but none came. It was only when the listing of the ship became very noticeable and the shouts of the crew became louder that they decided to take their own action. Terribly burnt men began to appear amongst them, being helped away from the site of the attack by less wounded shipmates and medical personnel. Thackery was dumbstruck as a sailor wearing just a vest was helped past him. His hair was completely gone and the skin on his face, neck and arms looked like melted wax.

"Don't look at him, son." whispered the medic who was helping him along. Thackery turned his head away and closed his eyes, but could not unsee the horror he had witnessed. The electricity generators were swamped by the rising water, failed, and the lights went out. A discernible increase in panicked screams could be heard from the men trapped inside as the ship was plunged into darkness. It was only when the electric failed that Thackery became aware of light from a porthole above him. He pushed it open and climbed through, now standing on the once vertical side of the ship. He walked away from the direction of roll and felt barnacles on his bare feet, as the usually submerged keel became exposed when the ship began to capsize. Now running, he leapt into the water.

Corporal (Royal Marines) Henry Daniel Jordan was holding open a red-hot hatch cover above his head, releasing the men trapped behind it. Unable to hold the hatch any longer with burnt hands, the cover eventually fell, decapitating him.

As the ship listed further to starboard, the 15-inch shells weighing half a ton each came off their racks, landing on the steel floors with almighty bangs and rolling to rest against the nearest upright surface. As the ship rolled the gun barrels swivelled in the same direction, adding momentum to the listing of the vessel. Open hatches now slid below the waterline, further increasing the rate of roll as the water flooded in. Royal Oak capsized thirteen minutes after the torpedoes had struck, sealing the fate of those who had not yet made it to the decks.

Hundreds of men were in the freezing water, fighting for their lives. Poor swimmers and injured men grasped at anything or anyone around them in panic, often pulling other sailors to their death along with them as they sank. As Royal Oak capsized, the wave it created lifted Arthur Smith and somersaulted him through the water. He kicked desperately hoping to find the surface and popped up again covered in oil and coughing to clear his lungs. As the water cleared from his ears, he became aware the screaming and yelling of men in the last moments of their lives had ceased, and a deathly silence had descended. He struck out in the direction he believed would take him to the shore, feeling himself kicking faster and faster but slowly sinking as cold and exhaustion began to take their toll. Grasping in desperation at some debris that was floating alongside he found another sailor clinging motionless to the wood, his energy spent.

Smith tried to encourage him as they swam for a while towards the land, but when he closed his eyes to ease the irritation from the oil, found himself alone when he reopened them. His unknown associate had slipped silently beneath the surface, as the effects of cold and exhaustion overcame him. Smith became aware of the weight of his boots but although he was able to reach the laces, was unable to untie them due to the slimy coating of oil. He thought of his father who had taught him to swim at age five by throwing him into the deep end of their local pool. He thought of his mother and how she would react to the news of his death. Just as he was about to succumb to the cold and exhaustion, he heard a voice call out "Here's another one" as he was grabbed by the shoulders and hauled unceremoniously into a boat manned, to his surprise, by four RAF Airmen. They were stationed aboard the Pegasus and had launched a boat to search for survivors when the Royal Oak sank.

Norman Thackery was treading water. Starting to tire, he reached out for a floating wooden spar to support himself, only to have his hands pushed away by a sailor who had already claimed it as his own and was in no mind to share. Thackery fought to stay afloat, pushing his head back as far as possible to keep his nose and mouth above the surface. The noises of distressed men around him came and went as the waves lapped over his ears, intermittently silencing their cries for help. The sailor on the spar loosened his grip, weakened by either cold or wounds, and slipped silently to his death in the dark water. Thackery didn't hesitate to take his place on the floating debris.

The faces of the conning tower watch on U-47 were illuminated by the flashes of light from the continuing explosions, the sounds of which only arrived several seconds later. Even if they wanted to, they were mesmerised and could not look away. Prien studied the scene through his binoculars. He could see men running across the decks of the doomed ship and jumping over the rails. The unmistakable cries from hundreds of men in distress reached them across the surface of the water and they continued to watch in silence as frantic rescue efforts began. Hand held lamps from crews of small boats flicked across the surface searching for survivors, while huge searchlight beams probed the sky for the enemy aircraft thought to be responsible for the bombing of Royal Oak. The British were not even contemplating the possibility of a torpedo attack from inside Scapa Flow. The sound of Prien's voice broke the trance.

"He's finished. It's time to leave." As he gave the order to turn the boat around, he glanced at his watch and noted the time at 1:28 a.m. Heading at top speed towards the exit at Kirk Sound, the crew frantically worked to reload the remaining torpedoes in the event of a surface fleet reaction by the British. The tide was ebbing fast when U-47 reached Kirk Sound, the currents now running at a speed of ten knots, and Prien knew he had broken off the attack just in time. Reducing the boat's speed enough to allow a reaction to steering commands, Prien took the southern channel between blockship Minich and the shore of Lamb Holm, as recommended by Donitz' intelligence report. The boat passed within touching distance of the blockship, and once clear resumed top speed towards Holm Sound and the open sea. At 2:15 a.m. Prien's log entry read "We are once more outside." He ordered the boat to submerge and gathered the crew for briefing, telling them what they had achieved, and that he had never doubted the success of their mission. He saluted their bravery and allowed them to cheer. When the cheering stopped, through a broad grin he announced, "We are going home."

Monday 16 October 1940 –
Lille, Northern France.

To supplement the fixed defensive position being created on the France / Belgium border, patrols were conducted in front of the trenches to familiarise the defenders with the ground over which the enemy would most likely advance. These patrols were tasked with the identification of likely approaches for armoured vehicles, including natural obstacles and choke points for potential artillery targeting. Corporal Thomas from 3 Section, who had been sent to France early with the reconnaissance team, was responsible for conducting these patrols for 10 Platoon. Ten soldiers, including all the new arrivals, had been gathered in a small classroom for a briefing by Corporal Thomas before the patrol. The new arrivals included Hamill, Moore, Kyle, McEnearney, Millar and some others from 2 Section, one of which was Watts. Using an aerial photograph pinned to a board, Thomas showed the route they would be patrolling; paying special attention to the proximity of the enemy, the possibility of meeting enemy patrols and the dangers of booby traps and trip wires. He briefed those present to leave all personal possessions behind in case they were captured by the Germans and unwittingly gave away important information. As the briefing finished and the soldiers made their way to the waiting transport, Orpin approached Corporal Thomas on his own.

"Are we not miles from the enemy, Corporal? We're on the border with Belgium, not Germany." he whispered so that no one else would hear.

"I'm just going to have some fun with the new arrivals." Thomas replied. "Do what I do and play along." A huge grin came over Orpin's face as he realised what Thomas was up to. He had always been one for practical jokes and pushing the limits of discipline. Tonight's patrol was to be no exception.

* * *

An hour later, the lorry carrying the patrol stopped and switched off its lights. Thomas got out from the cab and made his way to the back of the vehicle.

"No lights, no smoking and no talking." he whispered as he silently let down the tailgate for the men to dismount. He steadied each one as they jumped down, pointing towards a hedge line beside the road for them to take cover. When the last man was out, and the lorry had left, Thomas joined them in the hedge and gave a final briefing.

"Intelligence reports tell us that the Germans have set up trip wires attached to grenades on the lanes and hedge gaps in this area. If you see me or the person in front stepping over, then do exactly the same." They all nodded nervously; concerned faces looking at each other for reassurance. "I will lead off with Private Orpin second. The rest of you follow along in a line." he whispered. "Stay within view of the person in front. If you get separated, just stay where you are and we'll come back for you."

Thomas moved off deliberately slowly to give the impression of an imminent threat of detection by the enemy. The night sky was clear and moonlight made for good visibility, allowing the group to see clearly what the patrol commander was doing. Every so often he would signal for everyone to lie down as if they were hiding from an enemy patrol. Orpin could hardly contain his amusement at the Corporal's behaviour, but played along with the performance, his repetition of Thomas's actions being transferred down the line of the following, and increasingly nervous, soldiers.

Suddenly, Thomas held his hand up for the patrol to stop. He looked round at those following and pointed at the ground, drawing an imaginary line with the closed fingers of his left hand to indicate the presence of a trip wire. He carefully and deliberately stepped up and over the imaginary obstacle, closely followed by Orpin who made the same exaggerated gesture. The two men moved forward about ten yards and giggled quietly together as they watched the rest of the patrol step over the non-existent wire.

After an hour of patrol activity, Thomas stopped and crouched down. He pointed towards what once would have been a large manor house, but which had since fallen into dereliction. He signalled for the patrol to follow, and made his way towards the crumbling building. Stopping the patrol at the bottom of the steps up to what had once been the grand entrance, he disappeared into the house. A few minutes later he reappeared and with a wave of his arm, ushered the patrol to follow him inside. Once back inside the building again he switched on his torch. The glowing light revealed a sweeping staircase, the beam from the torch not strong enough to reach the top. He led the men past the staircase and into a large room with a huge fireplace in the middle of the wall. The windows on the opposite wall to the fireplace had been boarded up years before. Adjoining what had probably been the formal dining room was a smaller room at the far end past the fireplace. A now empty doorway separated the two rooms.

Thomas detailed Private Hamill to be a sentry on the grand entrance, and the others to get a small fire going in the fireplace. As Hamill took up his sentry post, he quietly asked a question as he passed Corporal Thomas.

"What's going on, Corporal? You've said the place is crawling with Germans yet we're still in France and are carrying empty rifles." Thomas noticed the medal ribbon on Hamill's battledress denoting active service in India, and knew he had been caught out by an experienced soldier.

"Just go along with the story for now." he whispered to Hamill. "I'll explain shortly." Without a word, Hamill stepped outside for his sentry duty and Thomas moved towards the now flickering fire. The patrol made makeshift seats with their equipment and sat in a semi-circle around the fireplace. No sooner had they settled down, lit cigarettes and began to warm up, when Moore stood up.

"Where can I have a piss, Corporal?" he asked meekly.

"Go out past the sentry and left along the front of the house." Thomas directed. "But stay close to the wall and be quiet. There could be a German patrol close by." Moore set off towards the sentry, and as soon as he was outside, Thomas signalled that everyone else was to remain where they were and stay quiet. He grabbed Orpin by the arm. "Come with me." he said, the two men silently following the unsuspecting Moore, who by this time had undone his braces and dropped his trousers to his knees. They could hear the stream of urine splashing against the wall of the house as they sneaked up behind him.

"Hände schnell hoch!" shouted Thomas in a guttural tone at the top of his voice, when two yards behind the unsuspecting Moore.

"English swine!" added Orpin in his best German accent.

Moore yelled in fright, yanking up his trousers while continuing to urinate, and running past his two tormentors, back into the house. As Thomas and Orpin stumbled into the dining room in convulsions of laughter, Moore stood alone, the rest of the group lying on the floor helpless, having heard the prank unfold through the boarded-up windows.

"You bunch of bastards." yelled Moore, as more calls of "Hande hoch, English swine." were repeated from the group, adding to the noise level of the laughter. It was minutes before Corporal Thomas had gathered himself enough to give a full explanation of the night's antics to the men, most of them feeling a bit stupid at stepping over imaginary trip wires. With that, the fire was stoked up and Moore was able to dry his urine-soaked trousers.

Tea was brewed and biscuits and chocolate that the men had carried were passed around as everyone relaxed.

"I was brought here by the French liaison officer while on the reconnaissance." explained Thomas as everyone sat together. "He tried a similar German patrol trick with French conscripts, and that's where I got the idea." He continued with a request. "Don't say anything when you get back, and I'll try it again when the next batch of new recruits arrive."

"Don't worry, Corporal." Moore added. "I won't be telling anyone I pissed my trousers in front of an imaginary German patrol." The comment started everyone laughing again.

"The guide also told me the story of this house," Thomas continued, "as he grew up in this area and remembered it from before the Great War." He went on to relate the story of how the Germans had used the house as a headquarters when they occupied the Lille area, destroying it just prior to their withdrawal. "Like kids everywhere, they believed the house was haunted." Thomas continued, then paused, waiting for a request to tell the rest of the story. He was very quickly encouraged.

"The poor stable hand was in love with the rich owner's daughter, but she spurned his attention." he began. "In his despair, he threw himself off the roof to end his life, but only broke his back and survived, being crippled from the waist down." The group sat in absolute silence, mesmerised by the story. The light from the fire lit up their faces as they listened intently, casting moving shadows on the wall behind as the flames flickered. "Afterwards, he could only get about by dragging himself around with his arms, and would attract people's attention by grabbing their lower leg. The local kids said his ghost haunted the house, his crippled body scraping over the ground as he pulled himself along, then grabbing their legs to get attention."

"You don't want to be in here alone in that case." added Orpin, still playing his role in the whole charade by building up the story.

"What a load of bollocks!" added Watts, being uncharacteristically opinionated; obviously unnerved by the story and wanting to show some bravado.

"Well, if you don't believe in ghosts, then you'll be quite safe." Thomas replied, making a mental note of Watts' strong dismissal of the story. "Two hours rest and then we are back doing what we came here to do." he ordered. "So, get your heads down and make the most of it."

"And no snoring, English swine!" added Orpin in his German accent to continue Moore's embarrassment.

⁎

A sentry roster had been produced by Corporal Thomas to cover the resting period, some of the group getting thirty minutes duty each. Watts was on duty just inside the main entrance at the bottom of the stairs when he heard a gentle scraping sound, then a pause and the scraping sound again. At first, he ignored it, believing it was overgrown shrubs rubbing against the boarded-up windows in the breeze. But then it became too regular. A scrape then a pause, then a scrape, then a pause.

He thought it was coming from the dining room where the patrol was asleep and quietly entered the area so as not to waken anyone. Then he heard the sound again; a scrape followed by a pause and then another scrape. There were sounds of men asleep, and some movement as they rolled over to find comfort on the hard floor, but nothing to match the rhythmic scraping. Then he heard it again, but louder. It seemed to be coming from the smaller room at the end of the dining room; a scrape followed by a pause, then another scrape. Some of the men were lying sleeping across the empty doorway and Watts gently stepped over them to get access to the room, when a hand grabbed his ankle. Watts screamed and tried to pull his leg away, looking down and seeing a ghostly luminous face staring back up at him.

"Mummy, mummy!" he yelled, stepping on the sleeping men as he yanked his leg free and stumbled backwards. Chaos ensued as the sleeping men were woken by Watts' shouts and being trampled on as he tried to get away. As Watts made good his escape, Corporal Thomas was in convulsions of laughter, the sleepers coming to their senses and seeing his face lit up with his torch. Orpin appeared from the attached room, also in convulsions of laughter, rubbing two loose floor tiles together to make a scraping noise.

Monday 6 November 1939 – Lille, Northern France.

Second Lieutenant Chadwick had arrived late on Sunday night. He had been met by the Duty Officer, a Lieutenant Coburn, who took him to his room, met him for breakfast next morning and escorted him to the Battalion Headquarters to see the Adjutant for his formal welcome interview. The Union Jack and the Regimental Flag hung limply on white flagpoles outside the Battalion Headquarters building, and a brass plaque with the words "1st Battalion, The West Staffordshire Regiment" had been attached to the wall. The Duty Officer saluted the Adjutant as he entered the office and presented his duty report for events and occurrences over the weekend. He then announced that Chadwick had arrived as expected and was waiting outside. Lieutenant Coburn gestured for Chadwick to go into the office as he left.

Chadwick marched in and halted in front of the Adjutant's desk, saluting smartly. The Adjutant acknowledged the compliment and gave permission for Chadwick to relax. He stood up, introduced himself as Captain Greer, shook Chadwick's hand and asked him to take a seat in one of the armchairs in the corner of the room. Greer closed a file that was sitting on his desk, which Chadwick noticed had his name on the front.

"You've had a bit of a journey to get here." Captain Greer began as he sat down beside Chadwick. "Sandhurst to Whittington and now Lille. Posted to us just at an awkward time unfortunately." he continued. "Well, you're here now and that's what matters." With the niceties over, Captain Greer began the formal routine for a new arrival, explaining officer duty rosters, behavioural expectations and regimental customs and traditions, where even minor infringements would lead to extra duties on the roster.

"We are a bit restricted in the Officers' Mess at present." Greer continued. "We have a small ante room along the corridor here, where we can get tea during the day and drinks in the evening, but we share the dining room with the non-commissioned officers and other ranks due to space limitations." Chadwick had been taken to a screened off section of the cookhouse that morning for breakfast, the rationale now clear. "Far from ideal," Captain Greer continued, "but better than nothing."

Chadwick got the impression the meeting was drawing to a conclusion.

"The Commanding Officer is not here at present, he's at a briefing at Brigade," Greer went on, "and I'll arrange your formal welcome interview with him over the next few days. But for now, Major Crawley will be expecting you and I'll let you get away to see him." Greer stood up signifying the end of the conversation, quickly followed by Chadwick, who saluted and requested permission to carry on. "Please do." Greer replied.

Thursday 9 November 1939 –
Lille, Northern France.

D Company had been gathered on the central parade square for a briefing by the Company Commander, with the three platoons forming three sides of a hollow square. Second Lieutenant Chadwick took his place as 10 Platoon Commander for the first time on a parade. As Major Crawley approached, the Second in Command, Captain Roberts, brought the company to attention and saluted smartly. Crawley asked him to stand the parade at ease, which he did, and the men relaxed. Moving to the centre of the open end of the hollow square, so that he could be seen and heard by all those on parade, Major Crawley made the announcement that the company had been gathered to hear.

"It is my pleasure to announce that D Company has been selected to represent the West Staffordshire Regiment at a Remembrance Day Parade in Lille this Saturday. To this end, we have been relieved from the defensive works routine to prepare." He paused and there was a feint murmur of relief at being excused the activity they all hated. Crawley continued. "To facilitate this, I will be going to see the Mayor of Lille today to make arrangements."

He paused again. "The company will spend today on uniform preparation under your non-commissioned officers, and we will hold a rehearsal tomorrow, once I agree the format of the parade with the mayor later."

"Oh great!" someone in 10 Platoon whispered, but loud enough for Sergeant Preston who was standing at the rear of the platoon to hear.

"Shut up, everywhere!" he whispered back; loud enough for the platoon to hear but not loud enough to disturb the Company Commander who continued with his briefing.

"The new Commanding Officer will attend the parade as Guest of Honour of the mayor, so it is vital that we put on a good show. I have asked him to grant an evening pass to Lille after the parade as a reward, and he has agreed." A spontaneous cheer went up from the assembled company.

***

Company Sergeant Major McCann had been told to bring Private McEnearney along to the meeting with the mayor as a translator. McCann, McEnearney and the Company Commander were in the car on the way to Lille, with McCann driving, Major Crawley map reading in the front passenger seat and McEnearney in the back. The sight of military staff cars was not unusual, normally carrying staff officers to and from briefings at the various headquarters that had sprung up all over Northern France. Military Police at road junctions or soldiers on foot in towns or cities generally saluted staff cars as they went past, as most would be transporting officers in the back seat. McEnearney was enjoying the experience of watching the city go by and seeing soldiers spring to attention and salute as the car passed, so much so that he began to salute back, pretending he was the staff officer being driven about.

He sensed McCann looking at him and caught the stare of the Sergeant Major in the mirror. As their eyes met, McCann could not disguise a smile as he shook his head at the antics of McEnearney in the back seat.

"This map is wrong!" exclaimed Major Crawley in frustration. "The Town Hall is obviously not marked in the right place."

"It's back there, Sir." said McEnearney to Major Crawley, pointing to the way they had come. "The building marked Hotel de Ville. We've passed it twice already." Major Crawley was furious at having been shown up. His face portrayed it, but he said nothing. McCann went round the block again and stopped the car in the middle of the square outside the building. The Town Hall was a grand structure, made of red brick and white stone with a huge belfry on the left corner. Major Crawley was out of the car first and rushed up the steps to the arched entrance, and a set of dark wood double doors. He pushed first and then pulled the door on the left, but it was locked. McCann and McEnearney followed him up, obeying a sign that said "Entrée" to go through the door on the right.

"Right, son. This is your moment of greatness." said McCann to McEnearney as they entered the building. Just inside was a middle-aged lady wearing a white blouse and black pencil skirt. Her greying hair was gathered in a bun at the back of her head.

"Major Crawley?" she asked the two soldiers in a delightfully precise French accent. Just as she spoke, Crawley came through the door and pushed past McEnearney who was attempting to identify his Company Commander to the host. She led the way down a high arched-ceilinged corridor, the sound of her dainty steps on the marble tiles quickly drowned out by three pairs of military boots; stopping at an unusually large solid wood door with shining brass handles. Knocking three times, and not waiting for a response, she pushed open the door and introduced the military guests, then took a seat at a conference table in the corner of the room.

The mayor was sitting behind a polished desk, and rose as the guests entered. He had straggly white hair resting on the collar of his black suit, which was shiny from wear and smelt strongly of moth balls. His white shirt was stained yellow where it met his neck and was an inch too small, the gap badly hidden by the knot in an equally stained and shiny black tie. He was badly shaved, with little tufts of hair on his lip below his nostrils and on his throat where either bad eyesight or an unsteady hand had missed them. His teeth were stained and with noticeable gaps between each. Some were partly gold. He had a huge beaming smile which accentuated his dental state. He gestured for the military party to sit at the conference table with his clerk, who set a page with agenda points in front of the mayor.

Before the meeting could begin, Major Crawley told McEnearney to make it clear that he had been made personally responsible by the Commanding Officer for the arrangements of the day. McEnearney translated the comments, then saw the mayor and clerk glance at each other in bemusement.

"Tell them they can now continue." he told McEnearney, who translated the instructions word for word. The mayor looked down at the table and pushed his long hair back with his hand before looking up again, his composure regained. Returning to the agenda, the route of the marching contingent was discussed. Sergeant Major McCann produced a city map with a proposed marching route marked, finishing at the main square outside the city hall. The mayor nodded his agreement as McCann traced the marked route with his finger. McCann offered the services of the Padre for a religious input, and the Battalion Bugler for the sounding of the Last Post, at which the mayor appeared delighted. The mayor confirmed that the local Police would control the traffic on the route and the Police band would play the National Anthems of both countries. He asked McCann if he could keep the marked map; McCann being more than happy to oblige. The mayor offered an official invitation to both the Commanding Officer and Major Crawley to attend lunch in the Town Hall after the ceremony, at which stage Major Crawley interrupted again, stating that the menu should have no fish or garlic, and gesturing that the clerk should make notes. McEnearney translated and the clerk wrote on her pad.

With the meeting concluding, the mayor took McEnearney by the arm and spoke to him privately. He snapped his fingers at the clerk for the use of her pad and McEnearney wrote on it, before going through the words he had written with the mayor, who nodded throughout the conversation. After bidding farewell, the party left the office. As the clerk led the way out, McCann let Major Crawley move slightly ahead, then asked McEnearney what his private conversation with the mayor had been about.

"The mayor wants to greet the Commanding Officer in English and with respect to Regimental tradition. He wanted me to write out the words so he could practice." he answered.

"That's fine." McCann replied, quite relieved. "I thought he was maybe complaining about the behaviour of the Company Commander."

"Never mentioned it." replied McEnearney quickly; perhaps too quickly.

Friday 10 November 1939 –
Lille, Northern France.

D Company had been squeezed into the remaining transport that was not being used to support the defensive works effort, and was being driven to the outskirts of Lille.

"How did the visit with Creepy and Genghis go yesterday?" Orpin asked McEnearney as they bounced around in the back of the truck.

"You were right about the Company Commander." McEnearney replied. "He falls apart when under pressure. Made a bit of a fool of himself yesterday."

"How do you mean?" enquired Orpin.

"Kept sticking his nose in where it wasn't welcome and making demands." answered McEnearney. "Annoyed the mayor a bit."

"How do you know that?" asked Orpin, now intrigued by the route the conversation was taking.

"Because he told me so when we spoke privately." whispered McEnearney so no one else would hear. "He said he had been a soldier in the Great War and met officers like that before; and knew exactly how to deal with them." Orpin got no further information as the truck came to an abrupt stop, jolting everyone inside.

The vehicles had stopped in a semi-rural location on the edge of the city and the company was dismounted, sized off and put into three ranks. The weather was bright, but with a November chill in the air as they stood in the road waiting for something to happen. Scattered farm buildings stood on the high ground on either side, with stoned lanes running to them from the road. Animals roamed in the fields between the road and the farm buildings. Sergeant Major McCann walked up and down the formation, moving soldiers between ranks to get the sizing absolutely correct. He stopped in front of Private Smith who was in the front rank.

"Do you need those glasses, Smith?" he queried.

"Yes, Sir." Smith replied. McCann grabbed him roughly by the shoulder, pushing him into the centre rank and pulling another soldier into his place in the front rank.

"That's better." he continued. "Can't have someone wearing glasses in the front rank." Finally happy with the make-up of the formation, he told them to remember where they were standing and who was on either side of them so they could form up the following day in the same order.

"Be quiet and listen in to the Company Commander." McCann shouted as Major Crawley stood up on the verge beside the road to brief the company on the arrangements for the parade. He began with an outline of the planned events, covering the parade route from where they currently were into the city centre, the format of the ceremony with the National Anthems and then the sounding of the Last Post by the Battalion Bugler. He reminded the company that the Commanding Officer was attending and had granted his request for an evening pass to Lille after the parade.

As he spoke, a horse that had been grazing in the field behind him moved closer, curious at the unusual gathering. As it stood watching over the wire fence around the field it began to urinate, its huge penis emerging and quivering in the cold air, steam rising from the hot urine. Completely unaware of the events unfolding behind him, Major Crawley continued to speak as giggles began to break out among the formation, shoulders rocking as the soldiers tried to stifle their desire to laugh out loud. Unable to hold themselves together, some soldiers began to snigger, the whole parade quickly descending into chaos.

McCann saw what was happening, and controlling his own desire to laugh, apologised to Major Crawley for interrupting his briefing, ordered the parade to about turn and face the opposite direction; then quietly explained the reason for his actions to the Company Commander. A visibly annoyed Crawley moved his position to the other side of the road, back in front of the assembly, and attempted to continue with his briefing. But the image of the horse was too difficult to suppress, and some giggles began to ripple through the ranks again as Crawley was talking. With his anger growing still further at what he felt was insubordination, Crawley's patience broke.

"If this behaviour continues, then your evening off will be in jeopardy!" he blurted.

"Must be another change of plan. I thought we were going to Lille." said an unidentified voice from the middle of the parade, triggering loud laughter to begin again.

"Right, that's enough!" McCann yelled, moving between the ranks pointing his pace stick into the faces of suspected individuals. There was not a sound from anyone. "Keep this up and I will make your life shite." McCann continued.

With order restored and Major Crawley's briefing concluded, the company were loaded back on the transport and driven the short distance into the city. McCann had recovered his poise by the time the vehicles stopped again and the men had dismounted. Using his pace stick, he pointed out the route the parade would take when entering the town square, the place they would halt in front of the Town Hall, and explained the format of the remainder of the ceremony.

* * *

Lance Corporal Tetlow deliberately sat beside Sergeant Preston on the transport back to camp.

"What's the plan for tomorrow night, Sergeant?" Tetlow whispered.

"I'm open to any suggestions." Preston replied, twisting his position on the vehicle bench to face Tetlow, and suspecting from the question there was already a plan in the making.

"My mate from A Company has given me directions to a local knocking shop." Tetlow stated, hoping to gauge Preston's reaction. With facial interest expressed by Preston raising his eyebrows, Tetlow continued with the suggestion. "Said it's off the popular soldier run, very discreet and a good selection of girls. Something to suit every taste, so to speak."

"Tomorrow night would be ideal." began Preston. "With the other companies on defensive works rotation, we will have the town to ourselves." Tetlow nodded his agreement. "Keep it to yourself and 1 Section for now." said Preston. "I'll lay on some transport."

Saturday 11 November 1939 –
Lille, Northern France.

Sergeant Preston was awake earlier than usual to get ready for what was to be a busy day, and was shaving in the ablution block when Corporal McIlwaine came to find him. McIlwaine was the Duty Non-Commissioned Officer and had come to report an issue in the cookhouse.

"What's the problem that you can't fix it yourself?" asked Preston in frustration.

"It's the French chef, Sergeant." related McIlwaine. "He hasn't started making breakfast yet, and he's just yelling at me in French and waving his arms about."

"Get McEnearney and meet me there in a few minutes." replied Preston, who hurriedly finished shaving and went to get into uniform.

The chef was repeating the yelling and arm waving performance to Sergeant Preston when McEnearney arrived looking somewhat dishevelled, as he had just been pulled from his bed by Corporal McIlwaine.

"Find out what the problem is, lad." Preston requested as McEnearney approached, the soldier quickly trying to speak with the excitable chef. McEnearney visibly had to calm the chef down with hand gestures before he could engage in any conversation. After a few moments, both men approached Preston, the chef now looking very sheepish after his outburst, twisting his chef's cap nervously in his hands.

"He has a personal issue and says he needs to go home, Sergeant." McEnearney related to Preston.

"I would suggest that we all want to go home." answered Preston sarcastically. "What's his problem?"

"Well, it's a bit embarrassing." McEnearney continued reluctantly. "He's at an age where he hasn't been able to please his wife for a while, if you know what I mean."

"No, I don't know what you mean!" replied Preston, now getting extremely impatient at the situation.

"He can't get it up, Sergeant." whispered McEnearney as if he didn't want the chef to hear. "Hasn't been able to for a year." he continued.

"And why is that suddenly a problem now?" questioned Preston, getting more frustrated by the second.

"Well, it's up now, and he says he needs to go home." related McEnearney bluntly. Preston burst out laughing at the absurdity of the situation, then recovered himself as he saw the embarrassed look on the chef's face on realising his personal problem was found to be amusing.

"Tell him I sympathise with his problem," added Preston, "but I need someone to cook breakfast for D Company this morning." McEnearney began to explain to the chef who was becoming emotional, covering his face with his crumpled cap.

"Lance Corporal Tetlow might be able to do it." interjected Corporal McIlwaine. "He worked in a hotel kitchen before he joined the Army."

"Go and get him right now." Preston ordered.

* * *

McIlwaine and Tetlow appeared a few minutes later, Tetlow unshaven and unwashed, his hair unruly.

"Did you work in a hotel kitchen before?" Preston asked.

"Yes, Sergeant." replied Tetlow, rather surprised at such a random question.

"Can you prepare one hundred breakfasts?" questioned Preston.

"Certainly can, Sergeant, if I can be excused the parade this morning." he replied, not missing the opportunity to do a trade-off.

"You're on. Get started then." said Preston before turning to McEnearney. "Tell the chef he can go home, but I want him back to prepare lunch for the company after the parade." McEnearney related the instruction and the chef embraced him, kissing him on both cheeks before he hurried away.

"He said he'll be back in a few hours." McEnearney confirmed.

"A few hours?" repeated Preston. "His wife's a lucky girl!" he added. Content that the problem was resolved, Preston rushed away to ensure everything was in place for the day ahead, his plans already delayed by the cookhouse interruption.

Once alone, Tetlow turned to McIlwaine. "I did work in a hotel kitchen, but I was the porter, not the chef." he added with a cheeky smile.

"Why did you say you could cook a hundred breakfasts then?" asked McIlwaine.

"I would have said anything to get off that parade." Tetlow replied. "Anyway, I've seen it done dozens of times." he continued. "How difficult can it be?"

* * *

With the rest of the battalion deployed to the defensive works, the only soldiers left in barracks were from D Company. They had started to queue for breakfast outside the cookhouse door, which was usually locked until the specified meal time; but that morning still remained locked ten minutes later. The new Commanding Officer, Lieutenant Colonel Chambers arrived accompanied by Major Crawley and Company Sergeant Major McCann. Seeing the queue, McCann went through the back door of the cookhouse to see what was causing the delay. To his surprise, Lance Corporal Tetlow was behind the service area, a cigarette hanging from his lower lip, stirring porridge in a large pot and scrambled egg in a shallow tray.

"What the hell are you doing in here, Corporal?" McCann asked.

"Replacement chef, Sir." Tetlow answered confidently, continuing to stir the food.

"Are you ready to serve yet?" quizzed McCann. "There's a queue outside."

"That's me ready to go now, Sir." confirmed Tetlow, wiping his hands down the chef's apron that he had found and put on. McCann went to the cookhouse door and slid back the bolt on the inside; the soldiers streaming in for their food.

Kyle was one of the first in the queue and selected both a plate and a bowl from the stack at the hatch with the intention of getting porridge along with eggs and bacon. As Kyle approached the porridge pot, ash from the cigarette Tetlow was smoking fell off into the pot. Without a second thought, Tetlow simply stirred the ash into the contents with the ladle he was using to serve. Changing his mind on the porridge, Kyle held out his plate for eggs and bacon instead.

"Scrambled eggs?" asked Tetlow, scooping up a helping from the tray with a large spoon.

"Yes please, Corporal." replied Kyle. Tetlow slapped a spoonful onto his plate.

"Bacon?" asked Tetlow.

"Yes please, Corporal." replied Kyle again. Holding the same spoon that he used for the eggs in his right hand, Tetlow reached behind with his left hand and scratched his arse, then used it to push slices of bacon onto the spoon.

"I've changed my mind, Corporal. I'm happy with just the eggs." Kyle quickly added before Tetlow could put the bacon on his plate. Not making the link between his actions and Kyle's choices, Tetlow dropped the bacon back into the tray and returned to the porridge pot to serve the next soldier in line.

McCann had rejoined the Commanding Officer and Company Commander in the food queue. Colonel Chambers selected porridge and eggs and sat in the screened off section of the cookhouse reserved for Officers and Sergeants. Crawley and McCann joined him after making their food selection. Colonel Chambers remarked to McCann that at least the weather was fair for the parade, and it was likely no one would get wet. They exchanged some recollections of parades they had experienced in appalling weather, and it transpired they had both participated together in one such occasion.

Colonel Chambers tasted his porridge, and his facial expression immediately portrayed his opinion. He began to gently stir the contents of his bowl, revealing dried lumps where the mixture had not been mixed properly in the preparation process. Pushing it aside, he lifted some scrambled eggs on his fork and put them in his mouth. He felt sharp edges, which he immediately identified as egg shells, discreetly picking them from his tongue and wiping them on the edge of his plate. On closer inspection of the remaining eggs on his plate, he saw shell fragments mixed right through the serving. He pushed that plate away also.

As a participant in the parade, the Padre had come for breakfast and joined the table. He had greasy black hair parted in the side, very prominent teeth, and glasses with thick lenses that made his eyes look enormous. His double chin was squeezed up by his shirt and tie, and wobbled every time he moved his head. A smell of stale sweat pervaded from him.

The Padre sat down beside Crawley, both of them facing Colonel Chambers across the table, and began to eat noisily. Chambers watched mesmerised as they devoured the badly prepared porridge, and quite happily picked shell pieces from their mouths as they crunched the scrambled eggs. Crawley occasionally let out one of his deep nasal sniffs, and the Padre spat saliva and pieces of food from his mouth as he insisted on speaking while eating; unable to close his lips properly due to his dental prominence. Colonel Chambers started to find himself subconsciously disliking both men.

"I say, Crawley, that's one of your men serving this morning is it not?" asked the Padre. Fat from the bacon ran down his chin as he spoke. McCann saw the confused look on his Company Commander's face and answered for him.

"That's right Padre, Sir. He's a last-minute replacement." McCann added quickly. Noticing that the Commanding Officer had hardly touched the food, McCann offered to get him some fruit, which Chambers quickly accepted. He left the table to find some.

"I hope the lunch today is better than the breakfast." Chambers remarked sourly. "I take it you have everything in hand, Crawley?"

Major Crawley let out another nasal sniff. "I took one of my soldiers along for the liaison visit on Thursday." he replied. "He's half French and can speak the language like a native." Crawley added.

"And you requested no fish or garlic for lunch today?" Chambers asked.

"I was very clear on that, Colonel." Crawley replied. McCann returned with two apples for the Commanding Officer.

"Sir, the Adjutant is outside with the staff car for yourself and the Padre." he reported.

"Right, Padre. Let's get moving." said Colonel Chambers, lifting his fruit from the table. As they left, Corporal McIlwaine, standing beside the service area in his role as Duty Non-Commissioned Officer, was being bombarded with complaints about the quality of the breakfast.

* * *

As D Company waited to get on the transport to be driven to the parade forming up point, Kyle noticed a differently dressed individual. He was wearing a dark blue uniform with a blue dress helmet, a large Regimental badge on the front, a spike on top and a silvered metal link chinstrap.

"Who's that?" Kyle asked Orpin, pointing at the soldier in the unusual uniform.

"That's Dink, the Battalion Bugler." replied Orpin. "He's here to play the Last Post at the Remembrance Service."

"Why is he called Dink?" Kyle asked, puzzled at the unusual nickname.

"He has buck teeth. When he lifts the bugle to his lips it hits his teeth first and makes a "dink" noise before any other sound comes out." explained Orpin with a smile. "You'll hear later. Happens every time."

"I'll listen out for that." Kyle added as both had a giggle at the prospect. Their joviality was interrupted by shouts to hurry up and get on the vehicles.

* * *

While D Company were moving towards the parade form up location, the Commanding Officer, Padre and Adjutant arrived at the Town Hall. They were met by an immaculately dressed, but painfully thin bespectacled clerk, and were taken to meet the mayor before the parade. As they entered the mayor's office, he stood up and came from behind his desk to greet them. Across his right shoulder and running to the waist on his left side was a French tricolour sash, its bright red, white and blue colours contrasting sharply with the same dark suit he had worn for the liaison meeting a few days before. Great War medals were displayed proudly on his left breast. He approached the Commanding Officer and embraced him, adding a kiss on both cheeks. The smell of his mothball suit combined with wine and garlic from the mayor's breath made Colonel Chambers almost gag, but he performed a cursory hug in reciprocation.

The mayor spoke in French as the embrace finished, and the clerk stepped forward, translating in perfect English. "The mayor welcomes the Commanding Officer of the West Staffordshire Regiment to our town on this historic date."

"Please tell him that we are delighted to be here and renew our alliance against a common enemy." Colonel Chambers replied, bowing his head slightly in appreciation at the mayor's comments. The clerk translated Chamber's response into French for the mayor who flashed his toothy grin and nodded gently the whole way through the translation. The mayor then whispered to the clerk, triggering a short but obviously strained conversation between the two officials. Visibly displaying with his body language that it was against his better judgement, the clerk complied with the mayor's wishes.

"The mayor would like to welcome you in your own language and Regimental tradition." relayed the clerk, gesturing to the mayor that he could now speak.

"God save the King," said the mayor in a heavy French accent, with an extended pause between "God" and "save", with "the" and "King" joined together as if a single word. He looked very pleased with himself that he had managed to get it right as Chambers smiled and nodded his approval. Then drawing himself up to full height he continued, "and fuck the Pope".

Colonel Chambers spluttered and stuttered before gathering himself and asking the clerk to thank the mayor for his warm welcome and considerate use of English. Turning to the Adjutant, Chambers hissed, "Find out where he got that from."

With the mayor still smiling at his mastery of English, the clerk suggested the party have a glass of wine before moving outside to take their place on the dais for the parade.

* * *

The parade entered the city along the route that had been agreed and rehearsed, Major Crawley at the head followed by Captain Roberts and the three platoons behind. Company Sergeant Major McCann brought up the rear. The rehearsed route required a right wheel as the parade entered the square in front of the Town Hall, then a left wheel to take them past the dais on which stood the mayor and the Commanding Officer. Many of the citizens of Lille had turned out to watch, lining the route and clapping loudly as the parade passed. When the parade reached the point for Major Crawley to give the command to right wheel and turn into the square, he continued to march straight ahead. Captain Roberts called out to him to give the command, but his voice was lost in the applause from the spectators. In compliance with the agreed route, Roberts gave the command himself and began the right wheel into the square. The parade followed, leaving Major Crawley marching on his own along the wrong route.

Following the planned left wheel to take the parade past the dais, Captain Roberts gave the command "Eyes Right" as the parade approached the mayor and the Commanding Officer. Roberts saluted smartly and those on parade jerked their heads to the right to acknowledge the dignitaries; Company Sergeant Major McCann giving "Eyes Front" as the last man passed the dais. Captain Roberts halted the parade and turned them to face the direction of the dais, moving to take up his command position in front of the three ranks. At this point, Major Crawley approached from the opposite direction, having marched the wrong way round the square on his own, coming to a halt in front of the company and saluting. The Commanding Officer put his left hand over his eyes in disbelief, but for most of those watching, the moment passed unnoticed as they were unaware of the parade format.

The Police band struck up "La Marseillaise", to which the townspeople sang heartily, followed by the National Anthem, after which the Commanding Officer invited the mayor to inspect the parade. They descended from the dais and the mayor walked quickly between the ranks, stopping only to exchange an understanding look with those who wore Great War ribbons on their uniform. The Padre then conducted a short religious service, followed by a similar oration in French from the local priest. Silence fell across the square as the time approached eleven o'clock, and the bell in the tower beside the Town Hall struck.

At this, the Regimental Bugler raised the instrument to his lips, and the expected "dink" sound immediately preceded the rendition of the Last Post.

"Told you so." whispered Orpin to Kyle who was standing beside him. Kyle suppressed a giggle.

* * *

As the dignitaries made their way into the Town Hall for lunch, the parading troops were driven back to barracks. The conversations in the back of the trucks were full of excitement at the prospect of a night out in Lille, and at the performance of the Company Commander.

"Did you see the state of Creepy on the parade?" asked Orpin to no one in particular.

"Bloody idiot." replied Hamill, being a veteran of many such events. "What the hell was he doing?"

"I'm sure the boss will give him what for later." chipped in Corporal Hutchinson. "He'll have bad breath burns on his face." Everyone in the back of the lorry agreed, and chuckled to themselves at the prospect.

"You've got to hand it to him mind." added Smith. "He knows how to make a first impression, does Creepy."

* * *

The dignitaries were seated on each side of a long thin polished wood table in the formal dining room inside the Town Hall. With high vaulted ceilings and tall stained-glass windows, the room was flooded with natural light in the bright autumn sunshine. With uniforms of Police and Fire Service mixing with the civilian members of the council, all the branches of the civic authorities were represented; the room buzzing with conversation. As special guests, the clerk sat between the mayor and Colonel Chambers in the centre of one side, with the Padre and Major Crawley opposite. White jacketed waiters entered carrying the plated lunch, setting the food down simultaneously in front of the mayor and his guests.

The smell of garlic immediately hit Colonel Chambers, and he looked down to see three small fish complete with heads and tails surrounded by some croquette potatoes and green beans.

The clerk looked at Major Crawley. "Fish in garlic as ordered." he said. The mayor nodded and smiled a knowing, toothy grin at Crawley across the table.

* * *

As the soldiers who had paraded that morning left the cookhouse, after what was an immaculate lunch prepared by a very grateful French chef, the Commanding Officer's staff car drew up outside the Battalion Headquarters building. The Commanding Officer let the car depart and from a distance the soldiers could see a very animated conversation between Colonel Chambers and Major Crawley. After a few minutes, Major Crawley saluted as the Commanding Officer broke off and entered the building. Crawley looked completely dejected as he stood alone for a few seconds before making his way towards the Officers' Mess Ante Room, in dire need of a drink.

* * *

Lance Corporal Tetlow had spread the word around 1 Section that a special event had been arranged in Lille that night, and the men had gathered in the NAAFI after dinner. Sergeant Preston arrived shortly after everyone else and having got himself a beer, joined the rest of the group.

"Where are we going, Sergeant?" asked Orpin, keen to know what the plan was.

"Don't worry, boys, I have arranged for us to visit a house of ill repute in town." whispered Preston so that no one outside the group would hear.

"You mean a brothel?" asked Orpin, slightly louder than he intended. Preston indicated for him to keep his voice down. "Have they all not been placed off limits due to the risk of sexual disease?" Orpin continued more quietly.

"That's only because the officers want to keep them for themselves." added Tetlow. "They don't want to have to share the ladies with the likes of us. And anyway, you can't catch VD if you drink plenty."

"That's good to know." added Orpin sarcastically. "Where did you come by that information?"

"The Medical Sergeant told me!" Tetlow snapped back. "He just doesn't want everyone to know, so kept it quiet at his lecture."

"I believe you." Bell joined in. "I'm definitely up for it."

"Look, anyone who wants to come is welcome." continued Preston getting frustrated. "Or you can stay here if you wish." Lance Corporal Murray, the Company Clerk came through the NAAFI door and gave Sergeant Preston a thumbs up signal. "Right, we're off. Drink up." said Preston emptying his bottle and setting it on the table. There was a flurry to finish their drinks and those who had decided to go rushed out the door. Watts had joined the group, and seeing him looking dejected that his pals from 1 Section had abandoned him, Sergeant Preston invited him along. "Come on, 40. We'll look after you." he said. Smiling, Watts followed Preston out the door to the waiting truck. Preston closed the tailgate and told those on board to be quiet going past the gate sentry. Someone kicked a wooden crate in the dark which made a clinking noise. "I left some beer in there. Don't open it until we're out the gate." Preston instructed. Corporal Tetlow and Sergeant Preston climbed into the cab beside Lance Corporal Murray and the vehicle moved off.

Once out the gate, those in the back of the vehicle opened the beer bottles by holding the cap against the side panels of the truck and hitting downwards with the flat of their hand. As Corporal Tetlow directed Corporal Murray with a hand drawn map, Sergeant Preston could hear the men in the back shouting and laughing as they enjoyed the free beer. He smiled to himself as he felt a team spirit was forming. The truck moved slowly through narrow streets, well off the beaten track; Tetlow squinting in the dark to see street names.

"Stop here and turn the lights off." he said abruptly to the driver. "This is the place, Sergeant." he confirmed to Preston, who jumped down from the cab and moved to the back of the vehicle. Telling those inside to keep the noise down, Preston gently released the tailgate latches, lowering it slowly rather than let it clunk open.

"Get out and keep quiet." he whispered as the men climbed down from the truck, when he heard the sound of an unseen rolling beer bottle from inside the vehicle. The noise stopped for a second as the bottle fell from the truck, before smashing on the cobbled street and triggering the local dogs to bark at the noise.

"So much for being discreet." Orpin remarked as he joined the group who had dismounted the vehicle already. Once everyone was out, the truck drove off and Tetlow led the way in single file down the street he had identified. There was no street lighting, only dim house lights that leaked through curtains, but enough to confirm they were going in the right direction. The sound of raised voices grabbed Tetlow's attention at the same time as he saw a red light in a street level window. The door to the house opened and the voices immediately got louder. A middle aged, heavily set woman dragged a dishevelled looking much smaller man out into the street, the man falling to the pavement under the force of the woman's ejection.

The soldiers picked up the elderly, unshaven man, to be immediately struck with the smell of stale urine and alcohol. The woman continued to berate him in French as the soldiers held him upright.

"This seems to be the place." Tetlow said gleefully. On seeing the soldiers, and realising they were potential clients, the woman's attitude completely changed.

"Come in, come in." she said in English with a heavy French accent, ushering the men inside to what was a dimly lit reception area, similar to that of a hotel; with a chest high desk, some seating around the walls and hooks for coats and hats. She made a final rude gesture to the man she had ejected and closed the door behind her.

"Welcome, Tommies." she said holding her arms wide as if in an offered embrace. "Your friends were here last week and had a very good time." Delighted that the host could speak English, Sergeant Preston asked about the old man that had just been thrown out. "He wants to enjoy the girls, but he has no money." she began. "If he has money, he can stay and enjoy the girls." She gestured towards a beaded curtain. "Go through, go through." she said, gently encouraging the group to move inside.

They emerged into a café scene with the walls covered in draped curtains. There was a bar in the corner and chairs arranged around circular tables; a strong smell of perfume and cigarette smoke hanging in the air. She encouraged them to take a seat and the men spread themselves around the tables. An elderly man came from behind the bar to arrange drinks. Once everyone had been served, the room suddenly filled with girls giggling and chatting amongst themselves; wearing nothing but G-Strings and feather boas to cover their breasts.

They immediately went to the tables and either sat beside the soldiers or in some cases sat on their knees, putting their arms around them or running their fingers through their hair. They flirted as best they could with limited language skills, McEnearney being continually pestered to translate. Individually the soldiers were enticed to the bar to buy their girl a drink, with champagne being invariably ordered for both. The host carefully watched who seemed to be getting along well, and moved the girls around if she felt there was no attraction forming. Lance Corporal Tetlow was enjoying himself immensely, with a young girl on each knee.

"Remember, lads," he said loudly, "make sure you drink plenty to protect yourself from any diseases." Encouraged by the girls, he stood up and took off his battledress blouse and shirt, exposing an unusually hairy back. The girls squealed in shock as much as delight as he lifted one under each arm to demonstrate his strength.

"Bloody Hell, he's like the gorilla at the zoo." Orpin exclaimed on seeing his hairy back and subsequent antics. The host reappeared and spoke into Tetlow's ear. He nodded and the girls stood up, the host leading them all towards the reception area. Tetlow slapped each one on the buttocks as they made their way out, causing them to flinch and laugh out loud.

"First one to break." said Hamill to Corporal Hutchinson.

"Like a biscuit dipped in tea." Hutchinson replied.

Without waiting to be encouraged by the host, Orpin quickly followed, as if he had been waiting to see how the system worked. As a non-drinker, Watts had been persuaded to try the champagne by a motherly type who had taken a shine to his boyish appearance. He declared that it tasted like lemonade, drinking heartily, and being unaccustomed to alcohol, he was now asleep in a chair. The motherly type that had been unwittingly responsible for his unconscious state, pushed his unruly hair away from his forehead and gently kissed him, before looking around the group for someone else. On seeing her actions, Corporal Hutchinson remembered Watts' mother doing the same with him at the railway station in Lichfield. The girl in question then attached herself to McEnearney, unknowingly fulfilling his penchant for older women.

Hutchinson and Hamill had agreed to remain sober and watch out for the others as the group got more drunk and rowdier by the minute, McEnearney taking on the role of matchmaker by translating ever more suggestive conversations between the men and the girls. Conscious of his stutter, McCafferty was delighted to find a girl that spoke no English whatsoever, and did not expect him to converse. Bell had selected a girl with rural looks, his taste in the opposite sex developed from when he worked on the farm. Farthing was too shy to be choosy, and had attracted a hugely overweight girl who continually pulled his face into her chest, much to his

111

embarrassment. Being the most senior, Sergeant Preston had selected the oldest of the girls. She wore heavy makeup with bright red lipstick and displayed a confidence and poise that suggested she had been in this profession for a considerable time. Preston introduced himself as Jock, and confirmed her name as Simone.

As each man reached the appropriate level of drunkenness, the host would approach and suggest they take their choice of girl upstairs. Hutchinson and Hamill were left alone to observe the host in action and take care of the sleeping Watts.

"She speaks good English." said Corporal Hutchinson to Hamill. "Must have done a roaring trade at the end of the last war."

"I would suggest she speaks good German as well." added Hamill. "Lille was occupied for years." The last to be approached by the host was Farthing, who was quickly pulled to his feet by his acquaintance and led to reception.

"She'll probably kill him and eat him." Hutchinson joked as he watched the diminutive Farthing being led away by the overweight girl.

"She'll leave some size of a shit behind." added Hamill. "And I would know."

The host took the appropriate payment at the reception desk before the girls were allowed upstairs, Farthing's girl pulling him impatiently by the hand as she climbed the stairs to her room. The room did not have a wooden door, just a heavy curtain that the girl pulled aside and then closed behind them as they entered. There was a heavy smell of stale perfume, a double bed against the far wall, an exposed clothes rail upon which a selection of dresses hung, and a toilet and washbasin in the corner, with a curtain on a rail for privacy. He took off his battledress blouse and hung it on a hook on the wall near the curtain door. His acquaintance sat on the bed and patted the mattress beside her, indicating for him to sit down. Nerves then got the better of him and he pointed at the toilet in a request to use the facility. She nodded and gestured her permission with a wave of her hand.

The white ceramic toilet bowl had a mosaic appearance through age cracking, with a wooden seat and a wall mounted cistern at head height, activated by a chain with a wooden handle on the end. He pulled the curtain closed behind him. Conscious of making a noise by urinating when standing, he decided to sit instead, releasing his braces and dropping his trousers. As he crouched down and leaned forward, the movement made him break wind. He automatically clenched his buttocks together and sat bolt upright to prevent further escape of gas, cursing himself in embarrassment, and hoping the noise had not travelled as far as the waiting girl on the bed. To prevent further noises, he reached around and held his buttocks apart to facilitate the silent escape of any remaining gas as he continued to urinate. Managing to finish without further mishap, he flushed the toilet and washed his hands in a similarly age cracked sink, drying them on a small hand towel hanging from the enamelled metal sink support. When he pulled the curtain back, the girl was already in bed. As he approached, she folded the covers down on the opposite side of the bed as an invitation to join her.

* * *

The men began to gather in the reception area where Hamill and Hutchinson were waiting. Watts had woken up by this stage and was experiencing his first hangover. They heard the truck return, and those already waiting moved outside to board the vehicle. Farthing appeared at the top of the stairs, his acquaintance clinging around his neck as if she did not want him to leave. They came down the stairs still entwined together, until about six steps from the bottom when their legs got tangled and they fell the rest of the way. Farthing landed first with the girl landing on top of him, and being considerably heavier, her weight completely knocked the wind out of him. He lay at the bottom of the stairs gasping for air, as the girl struggled to lift her ample frame off the squashed soldier. Both Hutchinson and Hamill were in convulsions of laughter while Farthing turned blue from lack of oxygen. Hamill helped the girl to her feet and Hutchinson lifted Farthing into an upright position.

"Up you get, Penny." he blurted out between howls of laughter. Farthing continued to gasp until he suddenly took a deep breath and his colour returned. The girl hugged and kissed him while he was still helpless before going back upstairs. When able to breathe normally, he was directed outside to the waiting transport.

Sergeant Preston was the last to appear, buttoning his battledress blouse as he descended the stairs. The last three left to join those waiting outside, passing the ejected vagrant they had encountered on the way in. He was urinating against the wall of the next house while drinking wine directly from a bottle. Preston suddenly stopped at the back of the vehicle, tapping the pockets of his battledress blouse.

"My wallet's gone." he said with an element of distress in his voice. "I had it when I paid before going upstairs, so it must be inside." He turned quickly and made his way back to the house. McEnearney quickly jumped down from the truck and followed him, in case any translation was required. By the time McEnearney re-entered the house, Preston and the host were having a heated exchange. He was accusing Simone of taking his wallet from his tunic when in her room. The host's understanding of English had suddenly disappeared, and McEnearney's attempt at translation was rebuffed by her waving arms. Preston lost his patience and began to climb the stairs, at which point the host's understanding of English returned.

"I know you are not allowed to be here." she shouted as she lifted the handset on the telephone sitting on the reception counter. "Leave or I will call the Police." Preston stopped and came back down the stairs. He knew that if the Police got involved, everyone who had been there that night would be disciplined for breaking out of bounds rules.

"Come on." he said to McEnearney as he left. As they stepped outside, Preston stopped and asked McEnearney how much money he had. McEnearney opened his wallet and Preston took out some money. "I'll give you this back tomorrow." he said. Grabbing hold of the vagrant, who was now sitting on the pavement, and with the previous conversation with the host about the vagrant in mind, he asked McEnearney to translate.

"Take this money and go inside." he began, with McEnearney translating as ordered. "You must ask for Simone, and only Simone." he continued; McEnearney again translating. The vagrant's face lit up and he mumbled something that even McEnearney did not understand. Helping him to his feet and pressing the money into his grubby hand, Preston ushered him towards the door. "Remember, only Simone." he reminded him. The vagrant smiled and nodded showing a set of rotten teeth, then grabbed Preston's hand, shaking it warmly before entering the house. "Let's see how clever Simone is when that dirty, filthy bastard is lying on top of her!" Preston told McEnearney, wiping the hand the vagrant had touched on his trousers. They waited for a few moments to ensure the vagrant was not ejected, and then happy that the plan had worked, laughed together as they went back to the vehicle.

* * *

On the journey back to camp, as the men recounted their sexual experiences to each other, McEnearney noticed how quiet Farthing was. Paying closer attention in the darkness, McEnearney saw he bore a similar expression from his experience with the French medic.

"Is everything alright, Penny?" he asked.

"I've just had another finger shoved up my arse." Farthing explained, to the accompaniment of uproar in the back of the truck.

"I hope you got the courtesy of a kiss this time at least." Bell added.

"What is it with these French?" Farthing asked in despair.

"What is it with your arse more like?" McEnearney replied. The uproar at Farthing's expense resumed, those seated beside him rubbing their hands roughly through his hair. Despite being the topic of their amusement, Farthing began to feel he was at last becoming part of the team.

Monday 13 November 1939 –
Lille, Northern France.

Lance Corporal Tetlow and Private McEnearney had been ordered to report to the Company Sergeant Major immediately after breakfast, having been identified as the two most prominent individuals involved in the disastrous visit by the Commanding Officer on 11 November. As they waited outside Sergeant Major McCann's office, they could hear the Company Commander's raised voice in the office next door. When it went quiet, McCann emerged and then entered his own office, staring at the two miscreants as he passed. He left the door open and sat behind his desk before calling them in. They marched in, coming to attention in front of McCann's desk. They looked straight ahead, but could feel his stare burning into them as he sat in silence.

"Gentlemen." he began calmly, "Let me start by saying that a number of things did not go according to plan on Saturday." He paused to let the fact sink in. "However, your individual actions contributed significantly to portraying D Company in the worst possible light to the new Commanding Officer." He paused again. "Thanks to you, the Commanding Officer will make our lives difficult for a while, but I will make your lives shite!" his voice rising as the sentence concluded.

"Lance Corporal Tetlow." he began. "You lied to the Platoon Sergeant, ruined the breakfast for everyone, including the Commanding Officer, and could have poisoned the entire company." McCann stood up, and leaning across the desk, moved his face as close as possible to Tetlow's. "If it was up to me, I'd have you busted and posted to the Shetland Islands as the fucking pissed mattress storeman!" he yelled.

McCann sat back down before addressing McEnearney. "And as for you, Frenchie, coming from a good Catholic like myself," he paused as he stared at McEnearney and slowly rose out of his seat again, "the Pope is not the only one fucked!" he yelled. Sitting down again, he composed himself before he continued. "Rest assured, that every shitty job that comes our way will have your names written all over it. Now get out of my sight!"

Wednesday 15 November 1939 – Lille, Northern France.

1 Section were lying on their beds after lunch. Wednesday afternoons were PT afternoons, and the men were taking the opportunity for a rest before getting changed into their PT kit. Bell came into the room in uniform, taking off his cap to reveal a completely bald head. It was a while before the laughing stopped and anyone could enquire as to his circumstances. He related how he had discovered tiny lice like creatures in his pubic hair that morning and had gone to the medical centre.

"The Medical Officer had a look through a magnifying glass and said I had pubic lice." Bell related. "He then started to question me about where I had been and if I had been sexually active."

"I bet you got them off that girl in Lille." Orpin quickly added. "What did you tell him?"

"Don't worry, I said nothing about Saturday night. I told him I started to feel itchy after guard duty and sleeping in the guardroom." Bell continued. "I was sent to the shower with soap and a razor and told to shave off my body hair, even my eyebrows."

"Oh yes. I didn't notice that." said Orpin, looking more closely.

"Apparently I didn't need to shave my head, but they didn't make that clear at the time." Bell rubbed the palm of his hand over his bald head to reinforce the point as laughter broke out again. The levity was interrupted by Corporal Hutchinson shouting in the corridor to get on parade outside for PT. This sparked a flurry of activity as the section hurriedly got changed into PT kit.

***

As the PT session came to an end, the instructor had the platoon run past the guardroom on their way back to the accommodation. A work party was busy removing all the bedding and mattresses from the guardroom and throwing them on a fire that had been lit behind the building. When the platoon halted outside the accommodation block, the Medical Sergeant was waiting with a cardboard box on the ground beside him.

"There has been an outbreak of lice in the barracks." he began. "Everyone must use this special shampoo for the next two weeks." he continued, holding up a bottle in his right hand. "As you come past me, lift a bottle from the box and use it every time you have a shower." The men filed past and took a bottle each before going inside the block. Kyle took off the lid and had a sniff.

"God, that's vile." he said, moving his head away sharply.

"Only one good thing will come from this." added Orpin as he sniffed the contents of his bottle and screwed up his face. "Lance Corporal Tetlow will smell nicer than normal."

Monday 27 November 1939 –
Lille, Northern France.

Sergeant Preston was having a cigarette with the Company Clerk at the door of the Platoon Headquarters building when he heard Lieutenant Chadwick calling for him from inside.

"What the hell does he want now?" Preston asked Lance Corporal Murray, not expecting an answer. He dropped his cigarette on the ground and rubbed his foot on it to extinguish the butt. Pulling his headdress from his belt where he had tucked it in, he placed it on his head as he made his way back into the building. Murray just shrugged his shoulders at the question and carried on smoking; glad he was not involved in any decision-making processes. He did what he was told, when he was told and was content with that.

Sergeant Preston came smartly to attention in front of Lieutenant Chadwick, wondering what job was coming his way next. He saluted and waited for the officer to speak.

"The Commanding Officer has decided to have an inter-company boxing competition on Christmas Eve." Lieutenant Chadwick began, without even looking up from the documents on his desk. He then raised his head to engage Preston. "Who is the best boxer in the Platoon?" A smile came over Preston's face as he recalled the last such competition.

"Easy, Sir. Private Smith by a mile, Sir."

"Smith with the glasses?" Chadwick enquired somewhat bemused. "But he can't see a thing without them. How can he box anybody?"

"Doesn't need to see who he is fighting, Sir. As long as there is a blurred figure in front of him, Smith will hit it until it falls over." Preston confirmed with a self-satisfied grin.

"Dear God!" Chadwick shook his head gently. "Get him off whatever he is doing. The Company Sergeant Major has organised some training for the company team over the next four weeks, starting tomorrow morning. Tell Smith to report to Company Headquarters after breakfast."

"I'll arrange that, Sir. Anything else?" asked Preston.

"No thank you, Sergeant. That's all for now." replied Chadwick. Preston saluted smartly and left the office, pleased with himself that he had got away with such an easy task; and had been offered an historically lucrative opportunity.

Tuesday 28 November 1939 –
Lille, Northern France.

The next morning, Private Smith and two other soldiers from 11 and 12 Platoons stood at ease outside Company Headquarters as ordered. The Company Physical Training Instructor, Corporal Wainwright, appeared from the side of the building, marching in an exaggerated fashion in an attempt to overstate his perceived self-importance. He came to a halt in front of the three soldiers and began to rant about how ugly and unfit they looked and how he would turn them into fighting machines over the next four weeks. Smith had already zoned out in his head but managed to keep a facial expression of being interested. He had heard the same drivel every time he had "volunteered" for the inter-company boxing competition, and had perfected his "interested" face as a result.

He had been a county boxing champion before joining the Army, the local fame of which had smoothed his enlistment, despite poor uncorrected vision that should have precluded him at an early stage in the selection process. His test had been fudged by a sympathetic Medical Sergeant to give him an acceptable level of eyesight for enlistment. Smith had somewhat lost his passion for boxing since joining the Army, but his reputation and previous performances in such competitions meant his automatic selection. Doing what he now disliked however, was infinitely easier than the trouble that would come his way from Sergeant Preston if he refused.

Corporal Wainwright paced up and down in front of the selected boxers explaining the programme to be conducted over the next four weeks, his chest pushed out and his stomach pulled in to emphasise his physique.

"Bloody Hell. He loves himself," whispered the soldier on Smith's left. "We're in the shit for the next month."

"Turn to your left. Double March." Corporal Wainwright bellowed; and the aspiring boxers began their training programme with a run.

Thursday 30 November 1939 –
Helsinki, Finland.

At 9:20 a.m. through the first rays of dawn, a lone Russian Tupolev SB-2 bomber appeared over Helsinki. As it circled the city, flying low enough to drop leaflets, the twin engines protested at the slow speed manoeuvre which made the inhabitants of Helsinki look upwards towards the noise; the red star markings on its wings and fuselage clearly visible. With the leaflet drop complete, the aircraft gained height and speed, turning away to drop five bombs on Malmi Airport before turning for home. Thousands of leaflets fluttered to the ground, urging the citizens of Helsinki to rise up and overthrow the "Oppressive Mannerheim led Government". The attack signalled the failure of months of discussion between the Finnish and Russian delegations, over the sovereignty of tiny islands in the Gulf of Finland; a dispute that had continued since Finland won its independence from Russia during the upheaval and subsequent civil war which followed the Russian Revolution in 1917.

As dawn gave way to full daylight, the morning was crisp and clear with an almost cloudless sky; apart from a cloudbank in the direction of Estonia to the south. At 10:30 a.m. reflected beams of light flashed from the glass domed noses of a further nine SB-2s as they descended from the cover of the clouds and levelled off in three rows of three aircraft, heading in the direction of Helsinki. The first row of aircraft released their bombs over the harbour, aiming at the crowded docks. The bombs detonated in a textbook pattern of straight lines, shooting columns of water into the air and creating large waves which bobbed the smaller boats in the harbour as they spread out from the points of impact. But despite no military interference from the Finns, and perfect weather conditions, not a single bomb struck the target shipping. The second row of aircraft banked away towards the heart of the city, heading for the railway station, releasing their bomb load as they flew over the facility. Again, not a single bomb landed on the station, but the public square in front of the building took most of the impacts, killing scores of civilians who were running for cover. The last three aircraft split away to attack the airport, where they set fire to a hangar and raked the facility with machine gun fire.

With almost all their heavy bombs gone, the formation split into small groups from which they terrorised the city at will, dropping a multitude of small incendiary devices which started fires over a wide area and stretched the city's fire fighting resources beyond their limit. As they departed, the aircraft gunners used the last of their ammunition to strafe a workers' housing development and released the last of their high explosive bombs; ironically damaging the Russian Legation building in the city centre. As the sound of the aircraft engines faded to the east, the eerie silence gave way to the moans of the wounded in the square in front of the station, and the high-pitched shrieks of terrified children. The bells of a stationary fire tender failed to clear a path through the chaos of the rubble strewn streets, but continued to sound anyway. Much too late, the wail of air raid sirens began, and some anti-aircraft shells exploded in a now empty sky.

With his ego soaring from capturing an area of eastern Poland of 100,000 square miles and thirteen million people, at a cost of less than 1,000 battle casualties; Stalin paid little attention to his Generals' suggested preparations for the Finnish Campaign. He felt that in terms of manpower and equipment he had all the elements necessary for his own version of the German Blitzkrieg. He envisaged his armoured columns slicing through the main lines of Finnish resistance, followed by massed infantry attacks to exploit the breakthrough; all covered by tactical air support and lavish supplies of artillery. Stalin's only declared concern was control of the forward units advancing too quickly and mistakenly blundering over the Finnish border into neutral Sweden. But the German doctrine they tried to imitate had been tailored to central European conditions, with open plains, good road networks and communication and supply centres close behind the front lines. In Finland, the topography could not have been worse for the use of such tactics.

The land they were invading was split by lakes, rivers and swamps, and almost entirely covered by forests, crisscrossed by minor tracks and with no natural shelter. Only the Karelian Isthmus in the south and the adjoining area around Lake Ladoga were suited to the manoeuvre warfare of a modern army. The Finns expected this was where the heaviest blow would fall and prepared accordingly, constructing an eighty-mile-long defensive network in three lines of mutually supporting bunkers, some made from reinforced concrete, others log roofed earthworks. Tank traps and choke points of mines and barbed wire created killing areas covered by artillery and machine gun fire. It soon became known as the Mannerheim Line, named after the Army Commander in Chief who the Russians felt had a disproportionate influence on Finnish Government decisions. The defensive posture included a scorched earth policy; burning any structure that could provide shelter for the enemy in the coming winter. All access to fresh water was denied by poisoning the wells with animal carcasses or horse manure. Some partially destroyed buildings were sewn with boobytraps under toilet seats and attached to kitchen utensils, to kill or maim Russian troops attracted by the prospect of cover from the elements.

In consideration of the climate, the date of late November had been deliberately selected by Stalin for the attack, the smaller bogs and lakes being frozen and therefore accessible for tanks; but before there was any significant snowfall to hinder the expected rapid advance. Russian ground forces struck before dawn at eight points along the full length of the Finnish border; with armoured columns in a massive ground assault, coupled with air raids to hamper communications and terrorise the civilian population. The attackers were encumbered with propaganda posters and brass bands, Stalin having been convinced by his political advisors that the Finnish population would greet them as liberators and not invaders. However, the Russians lacked the doctrinal drive that had been trained into German commanders; such initiative being curtailed by the political commissars who reviewed every command before releasing it to the combat formations. Lacking this freedom to exercise initiative, the Russian Generals would resort to the tactics of the Great War, relying on mass frontal attacks against the slightest sign of enemy resistance. Their vehicle columns towed hundreds of flat trajectory field guns, useless for anything other than very close-range engagements as they could not fire over the height of the trees; and modern anti-tank guns, even though the Finns had no armoured vehicles at this stage in the conflict. These weapons were subsequently captured intact and used against their former owners, to devastating effect. Russian infantry had no ski training, despite the snow being waist deep in most regions. In their packs they carried ski training manuals; being expected to learn on the job. The green painted tanks and brown uniformed soldiers were to make ideal targets against the snow-covered terrain.

The Finns knew they could not sustain a defence against the might of Russia for any conceivable length of time; their strategy being to hold out long enough for aid to arrive from the Western Allies. The concept was one of honourable annihilation, and was unfortunately wholly dependent on the political will of the already dithering French and British Governments. When the Russians struck simultaneously all along the length of the border, the Finns were taken by surprise and were forced to redeploy a third of their available force to meet the unexpected threat in the north, denuding the forces concentrated in the Isthmus to meet the predicted main Russian thrust. On the initial day of the invasion, landing parties captured the practically uninhibited islands in the Gulf of Finland that had been the original cause of the dispute.

From the moment Russian tanks crossed the border into Finland, the armoured and mechanised columns became jammed bumper to bumper. The buffer zone between the border and the Mannerheim Line was the site of continuous delaying actions by the Finns, with even the slightest engagement causing disproportionate delay and confusion among the Russian commanders, far beyond the size of the enemy force involved.

Sunday 3 December 1939 – South Atlantic Ocean.

The merchant ship SS Tairoa had left Durban on 27 November bound for England, carrying meat, cheese, and butter. Captain William Starr had put the ship's company on alert on 2 December, having picked up a distress message from another merchant vessel, the SS Doric Star, stating they were under attack and giving their position. That position was a mere one hundred and fifty miles north of his own ship, about half a day's run ahead on the same route. Starr knew, as did his crew, that a German surface raider had been stalking the South Atlantic, attacking merchant vessels. On picking up the message from Doric Star, he had decided to turn westwards hoping to put distance between his ship and the German raider. Starr was unaware however, that Captain Langsdorff on board the German Pocket Battleship, the Admiral Graff Spee, had already seen the smoke from Tairoa's coal fired boilers and was steaming directly towards his vessel. It was just past 4 p.m. when the lookout spotted the Graff Spee closing at tremendous speed. Starr immediately gave his radio operator, Fred Cummins, their exact position and the wording of the message to be sent, "Under attack by enemy vessel."

Cummins ran to his cabin and had just finished sending the message when he was almost blown out of his seat as a shell struck the Tairoa. It had entered a neighbouring cabin in which an officer was sleeping with his legs drawn up to his body, who would have lost his legs to the blast had he not been in this position. Cummins gathered himself and repeated the message as a second shell burst in the captain's empty cabin. As he repeated the message for a third time, the radio set exploded in a shower of sparks and smoke, throwing him across the room as much by shock as by the force of the blast. The third shell had impacted just outside the radio cabin, tearing through the wall and destroying the radio set. Dazed but unhurt, Cummins managed to crawl out onto the deck, where four seamen, hit by shell splinters, were screaming and writhing in their own blood. His mind told him to rush forward to help, but his legs felt paralysed, refusing to obey what his brain was telling them. By the time he regained control of his limbs, other crew members were tending the wounded.

Still standing upright and exposed on the open bridge, Captain Starr yelled to lower the lifeboats. The Graff Spee came close enough for Starr to identify a tattered Swastika standard, before she opened fire with three-inch pom-poms which tore pieces from the Tairoa's deck, sending splinters flying in all directions, and damaging all but two of the lifeboats. Starr had by now come down to the deck where he gave the order to abandon ship, before dashing to his cabin to gather the ship's confidential papers. As the two remaining lifeboats were being lowered, gunfire sporadically raked the vessel. Cowering men struggled on the shattered and debris strewn deck to carry the wounded to the lifeboats, some now bleeding profusely.

Under the covering fire, a two-boat boarding party from the Spee was already in the water and approaching the Tairoa from both forward and aft. Chief Steward Smith had followed Captain Starr down from the bridge and met him on the deck as he threw the confidential papers into the water; but they were too late for the lifeboats which were by this time well away from the ship. Smith was attending to a wounded seaman, a lad of seventeen whose hand had been shattered by a shell splinter, his two remaining fingers hanging by slivers of skin, when another shell hit the deck. The blast flung him into the deck rails, impacting against the metal bars on his right-hand side. His world suddenly went quiet. He could see the injured man he had been treating, lying prostrate on the deck, his mouth open in screams of agony, but he registered no sound other than a feint buzzing in his ears. He could see the pom-pom guns on the Spee were still firing, causing wood splinters to leap from the deck around him; but no sound accompanied their violent, deadly dance. Searing pain suddenly gripped his ears and he instinctively cupped his hands to cover them. Blood from his burst eardrums began to trickle down his wrists when he felt the muzzle of a pistol being shoved in his back. Turning around shocked and dazed, his face met that of a German officer from the boarding party.

One of the German launches had rapidly caught up with the lifeboats and escorted them back to the Tairoa. The escaping men were ushered back on board the crippled ship and lined up on the deck, the wounded being supported by their shipmates or laid on blankets if too badly injured to stand. Once assembled, the boarding party officer addressed Captain Starr, giving him ten minutes for his men to pack their personal belongings and be back on deck.

With an assortment of suitcases and kit bags, the men from the Tairoa were ferried to the Spee in the German launches, where they were again lined up on the deck before being led below. The dull thud of torpedoes being launched signalled to the captive crew that their ship was being finished off; before the engines of the Spee roared into life and the battleship sped away from the scene towards its supply ship Altmark, waiting for her mid-way between Africa and South America. At the planned rendezvous the prisoners would be transferred, where they would join many scores of captured merchantmen from other victims of the Spee, held captive below the decks of the Altmark.

Wednesday 6 December 1939 –
Karelian Isthmus, Southern Finland.

Due to the successful Finnish delaying tactics, it was not until 6 December that probing Russian reconnaissance reached the Mannerheim Line; the first artillery supported attacks being launched that night to test the defences. As the defensive positions held firm, increasing numbers of Russian tanks, infantry and artillery were thrown into the battle as they arrived, their attacks sweeping across the line looking for weak points they could exploit. Every Russian unit thrown against the line was badly mauled, three fifths of the tanks committed to the battle being destroyed. Witnessing the huge material advantage the Russians possessed, Mannerheim correctly predicted that the defences would undoubtedly be overcome, but only at the time when the Russians were prepared to accept the enormous casualties required to do so.

While choosing to fight a defensive battle in fixed positions across the southern Isthmus, Finnish doctrine for the defence of the forested and desolate area north of Lake Ladoga was dictated by terrain. The Finns were trained and equipped to fight in small groups, using their initiative and turning the constraints of the forest to their advantage. Hit and run ambushes by long range patrols, exceptional camouflage skills and physical conditioning against the harsh environment since childhood were the advantages the average Russian officer or soldier could never hope to match.

In a corridor fifty miles wide, north of Lake Ladoga, were two good roads that led from the Russian border to the Finnish interior, converging on the village of Tolvajärvi. The village was only a further day's march away from accessing the primary Finnish road and rail network running both north and south. In effect, the capture of Tolvajärvi constituted a back door to the Isthmus and the rear of the Mannerheim Line. With the main Russian armoured thrust held up by the defensive line in the Isthmus and casualties mounting, the Russians attempted to skirt round the fixed defences by exploiting this thinly defended area north of the lake.

A series of rapid outflanking manoeuvres by the attackers and equally rapid withdrawals by the defenders completely destabilised the front in this sector. The Finns were battered for nearly a week, being shelled continuously, and overrun by armour, against which, in this early stage in the war, they had no effective weapons. The weather conditions had been unkind, with less than expected snowfall to hamper Russian infantry manoeuvres and denying the Finns their ski mobility advantage. When not engaged in combat, they were retreating or digging new defensive positions that were almost immediately bypassed; from which exhaustion, cold and hunger took them to the point of being ineffective as a fighting force. Within this first week of the war, the Finns in this sector had retreated for forty miles under constant attack and the Russians were over halfway to accessing the transport links that would split the Finnish defences wide open.

General Mannerheim knew he had to act quickly and decisively to avoid disaster. He had concentrated his reserves behind the fixed defences on the Isthmus to repel any breakthrough in the area where he felt the war would be won or lost. He was now forced to packet them out to the flashpoints along the border north of Lake Ladoga, hoping local counterattacks could quickly stem the isolated incursions by the Russians before the developing situation got out of hand. Once the Russians had been stopped, the reserves would then be returned to their primary role behind the Mannerheim Line.

At 4 a.m. on 6 December, Colonel Paavo Talvela arrived at Mannerheim's Headquarters to be given command of "Group Talvela" with a mission to retake control of the roads in the Tolvajärvi area and halt the enemy drive west. When all his allocated forces had been concentrated, Talvela would still have less than half the manpower of his opponent, no armour, no air support bar sparse reconnaissance flights, and so few mortars and guns as to be almost negligible. However, Mannerheim had chosen his man wisely, and despite the obvious disparity in the combat strength of the opposing forces, Talvela was eager to give it a try.

He had received his military education in Germany during the Great War and returned to Finland during that country's civil war, where he commanded a battalion in the Ladoga – Karelia area, becoming intimately familiar with the geography. Talvela requested that a regiment of Jaegers be assigned to him, and picked JR16, commanded by his friend and veteran of civil war battles in the area, Colonel Aaro Pajari. When his request was granted, he immediately telephoned Pajari, ordering him to the front at Tolvajärvi to get a true assessment of the situation.

***

Lieutenant Colonel Pajari arrived at Tolvajärvi by car at 10 p.m. As he sat in the slow-moving vehicle, he watched through steamed up windows as hunched and dejected Finnish soldiers shuffled past in the opposite direction; an army on the verge of total collapse. Having been warned to expect Pajari, Lieutenant Colonel Räsänen, the sector commander, had assembled his staff officers to brief Pajari on the situation. After the briefing, Pajari left the headquarters, deliberately searching out and speaking to the local commanders and a handful of men, insisting that they speak freely so he could get a true picture of the situation. He studied the ground and read the latest intelligence reports on enemy strength and likely intentions. On the return journey he arranged his notes into a brief for Colonel Talvela, adding his personal assessment to the facts he had gathered. He closed his notebook, pulled the collar of his coat up around his neck and used the travel time to get some sleep, not knowing when he would next get the opportunity.

Thursday 7 December 1939 –
Tolvajärvi, Southern Finland.

By the time Pajari managed to report back to Talvela it was 3 a.m. His long friendship with Talvela enabled him to report the situation exactly as he saw it, without question or fear of rebuke. He related how, despite a reasonably upbeat brief by the staff officers, the defenders of Tolvajärvi were physically exhausted and discipline was hanging by a thread; fearing one more push by the Russians would break it. He assessed the enemy, the Russian 139th Division, to be well led and well trained by the way they executed successive flanking attacks, denying the Finns the time and space to stabilise and re-form. Pajari concluded that a near miracle would be needed to stem the Russian flow, regain the initiative and push them back. Talvela referred Pajari back to the map he had used in his briefing; stabbing his finger at the area on the western shore of Lake Tolvajärvi, he advised that this was the place to make a stand. Through his personal experience, Talvela knew this terrain was favourable for defence, and it was here the battle would either turn or be lost. He more asked than ordered Pajari to go back and take command, handing him a sealed letter for Lieutenant Colonel Räsänen. He also handed over a sheet of paper on which had been transcribed the units of artillery and infantry that had been detached from the strategic reserve in the isthmus, and their expected arrival times at Tolvajärvi. As Pajari scanned the information, he noticed his own unit, the 16th Jaegers was due to arrive later that day. Pajari gathered up his briefing materials, shook hands with Talvela, saluted smartly and left.

Feelings of both excitement and trepidation fought for control of his mind as he returned to his car for the drive back to Tolvajärvi. There was no sleep to be had on this journey. He nibbled on chocolate as he planned his defence of the sector, scribbling in his notebook as he positioned his forces in his head. It was late afternoon before he arrived back at Tolvajärvi, and the sun was already setting. Räsänen was waiting with his equipment and personal belongings packed, having expected to be relieved of command. Pajari handed him the letter from Talvela, and the two men parted without a word passing between them.

Pajari received a situational update from the Chief of Staff, which had deteriorated significantly since his visit the day before. The two men then set about positioning the reinforcing units that had already started to arrive. As the new arrivals began to dig in at their assigned positions, fleeing soldiers from the forward units appeared among them, threatening to infect them with their panic. As a commander, Pajari felt it necessary to do what commanders had done in this situation for hundreds of years. He left his headquarters, and by walking among his men looking relaxed and confident, he steadied their nerves. The panic ran its course, and those men who had fled returned to duty with their comrades, suitably ashamed of themselves.

Friday 8 December 1939 –
Tolvajärvi, Southern Finland.

Colonel Talvela had by now arrived at the front, and at the formal situational conference earlier that evening, both he and Pajari agreed that although the situation had stabilised, some form of offensive action was necessary to regain the initiative and prove that the Russians could be beaten. From intelligence updates, Talvela had identified an encamped enemy position strung out along a supply route a short distance behind the Russian front lines. He assessed they would feel safe, unseen behind the semi frozen Lake Tolvajärvi which separated them from the Finns, and might offer an easier target than the dug in Russian front line. Pajari led the fighting patrol himself, ambushing a force three times the size of his own and inflicting enormous casualties. The only Finnish casualty was himself, collapsing on the return journey and having to be carried back on an improvised stretcher. He had been suffering from a long-term heart condition that he had hidden from his superiors in case they took away his command. News of the successful ambush spread rapidly among the defenders all along the Tolvajärvi sector. The Russians, rocked by the attack, attempted no further significant offensive action for the next two days.

Sunday 10 December 1939 –
Tolvajärvi, Southern Finland.

Attempting a reconnaissance in force during the dark, a Russian infantry battalion had marched undetected through the tree choked wilderness on the Finns' left flank and fell upon Pajari's only supply line. At 11 p.m. on the night of 10 – 11 December, the Russians struck from the forest north of Lake Tolvajarvi, taking the Finns completely by surprise. There were no fixed defensive works and few combat troops; mostly cooks, storekeepers and medical personnel, centred on a headquarters bunker complex that was being used as a communication and supply hub. As the Russians streamed out of the forest, the first facility to be overrun was a field kitchen, where large vats of sausage soup were simmering. As the panic-stricken cooks scattered, the attackers paused at the smell of the food and began to eat, the initial momentum of the attack being lost and giving the Finns the vital time required to stabilise themselves and organise their resistance.

By pure chance, Colonel Pajari happened to be in the vicinity as his startled men sped past him. He physically grabbed men as they ran past, ordering them to stand fast. Inspired by his leadership and bravery, a makeshift force of about one hundred men was formed, made up from the fleeing cooks, supplemented with clerks, medics and storekeepers from the headquarters; and Pajari personally led them back the way they had come. With only his voice to control the action, he kept the men close together, stopping them at the edge of the clearing where the field kitchen was situated. Watching from the cover of the trees, he saw the Russians standing around the simmering pots, helping themselves to the soup. They had slung their weapons and retrieved their mess tins, which were now filled with hot food that was such a rarity among the Russian units. As they stood chatting and laughing amongst themselves in groups, they had not bothered to post sentries or begin to think how their breakthrough could be exploited.

Pajari silently spread his men out along the edge of the clearing in the cover of the tree line, and at his command, a volley of fire slammed into the eating Russians. Not wanting to become engaged in a tactical firefight, that as support troops they were not trained for, the Finns charged from the tree line into the confused Russians with fixed bayonets, using their aggression at close quarters to cancel out any tactical advantage the Russian combat troops would have. Those Russians that had filled their mess tins and moved away from the kitchen were overcome before they could reach their weapons. Those remaining closer to the kitchen had only time to unsling their weapons and fire sporadically before the Finnish wave crashed into them.

As if consumed by rage, the Finns slashed and stabbed at any part of a Russian that presented itself as a target, using the butts of their rifles to disable the enemy before driving their bayonets into their helpless bodies. Each time their blades struck home, they shouted "Hakkaa Päälle!" a war cry from the 17th Century, meaning "Cut them down" but translated and implemented by some as "No quarter". The clearing echoed with their cries, mixed with the screams of the wounded and dying, as if the surrounding trees and lying snow were trying to contain the sound of the evolving slaughter and hide it from the world. Two hastily summoned Finnish frontline companies arrived from the east, trapping the Russians in a furious melee. After two hours the fighting stopped. A handful of Russians had been taken prisoner, the remaining survivors scattering into the forest.

As Colonel Pajari organised the scene, he saw a terrified Russian being tormented by his Finnish captors. They circled around his cowering figure, kicking and threatening him with their knives. He was whimpering like an injured and confused animal on the edge of hysteria as he scurried on all fours away from one tormentor into the path of another, who repeated the treatment. Pajari instructed an officer to stop the torment and interrogate the prisoner, who was prodded at knifepoint into the command bunker of the complex. Keen to continue their entertainment, his tormentors followed him inside. They stooped to get through the door, entering the log roofed and moss floored bunker. Lanterns hung from the ceiling and a smokeless stove made the structure surprisingly warm and welcoming.

The prisoner was pushed onto a wooden chair in front of a trestle table, upon which maps and documents were arranged. The officer sat opposite him across the table, taking out a packet of cigarettes which he shook until a single cigarette presented itself from the open corner of the wrapping. He offered it to the prisoner who gingerly reached out a hand to take it. His demeanour changed as he inhaled the smoke, offering information about his unit strength and where in Finland they believed they were. He was wearing a padded uniform, now encrusted with dirt, thick felt boots and a thinner material felt cap. One of the Finnish soldiers who had followed him into the bunker crept up behind the prisoner and jerked off the felt cap he was wearing.

He yelped in fright at the sudden movement and jumped out of the seat, much to the amusement of the gathering. The officer barked some orders and the soldiers quietened down. With the removal of the cap, the lice infestation in the prisoner's hair became obvious, and the soldier who had snatched it from his head quickly threw it back onto the prisoner's lap. Sitting again and twisting his returned cap in anguish with both hands, he continued to complain about his shortage of food, his state of hygiene and how badly conscripts like himself were treated by their officers and non-commissioned officers. It was a tale that every captured Russian recited, and reinforced the success of the tactics that the Finns had employed.

He reached inside his filthy tunic, producing a tattered photograph of a woman and two small children, which he set on the table in front of the officer, flattening out the creases with his hands. As tears began to roll down his cheeks, he told how he was a conscripted farm labourer from near Leningrad, had not heard from his family since the campaign had begun, and feared he would never see them again. He wiped his face with the back of his hand, leaving clean streaks where his tears had washed away the dirt. The bunker fell into total silence. Their conscience pricked at how they had behaved, every one of the watching soldiers took out a cigarette and placed them in a small pile on the table in front of the prisoner. He got an encouraging slap on the back and turned his head to face his new friends, offering a wide smile of stained, broken or missing teeth.

Throughout the remainder of the night, Sergeant Miinalainen scoured the forest with a team of soldiers carrying powerful torches. When the presence of fleeing Russians was suspected, the lights were switched on, picking out the dark shapes against the snow. Sergeant Miinalainen concluded the previously unfinished work with his sub machine gun. By 4 a.m. the fighting had petered out almost completely, only the occasional rifle shot ringing out in the otherwise silent forest.

Dawn revealed nearly one hundred bodies around the kitchen; Finns and Russians mingled together in death throes among the bullet riddled cooking pots; those cut down in the first volley still with sausages between their frozen lips. From the Russian battalion of eight hundred men, only a few dozen made it back to their own lines. Finnish Propaganda had a field day, terming the engagement "The Sausage Wars".

Wednesday 13 December 1939 –
South Atlantic Ocean.

At 5:30 a.m. five short bursts on the alarm buzzers roused the twenty-seven remaining merchantmen prisoners on board the Graff Spee. There was a brief moment of silence before the clatter of boots running on the steel passageways and climbing or descending ladders to action stations obscured the crackling orders from the battleship's loudspeakers. The lookouts had identified three masted vessels on the horizon, about fifteen miles away, and early deliberations identified what was believed to be a heavy cruiser and two light cruisers. Through his glasses, Captain Hans Wilhelm Langsdorff saw the battle ensigns of three British ships and gave the order to open fire. The Spee shuddered as the first salvo of eleven-inch shells left the turrets, quickly followed by a second and a third. The third salvo had left the guns before the first shells landed in the sea around the heavy cruiser HMS Exeter, sending huge spouts of water into the air. Flashes of light announced the Exeter's reply and tense moments passed before her shells hit the water in front of the Spee; a second salvo landing closer as the gunners found their range. As Exeter and the Spee traded blows, the light cruisers HMS Ajax and Achilles, commanded by Commodore Henry Harwood, Commander in Chief, South America, rushed to close the distance to the Spee so their lighter guns could come within range. The heavy guns of both the Spee and Exeter found their mark at almost the same time; shells exploding on both ships. Direct hits on Exeter's bridge and gun turrets almost put the cruiser out of control, but she continued to fight, buying time for the smaller cruisers to close on their adversary. Spee's eleven-inch guns found their target again and again, hitting Exeter one hundred times; until listing and on fire she turned away towards the Falkland Islands.

While the Spee's big guns traded blows with Exeter, Langsdorff's gunners frantically engaged the rapidly closing Ajax and Achilles with their smaller armaments. The two light cruisers approached closer than the heavier guns on Spee could be depressed, the shells simply passing over them and exploding in the sea beyond. Achilles was by this point firing blindly, with her gun control mechanism having been put out of action, but shells from Ajax wrecked the Spee's control tower which housed the gun direction-finding instruments, killing many of the gunnery officers.

Collation of early damage reports confirmed to Langsdorff that the Exeter had badly damaged his ship before she retired, gaping holes now showing in the hull and many crew members dead. He called for smoke, anxious to break away from the two light cruisers and find a better tactical position from which to continue the fight. Thick black smoke now covered the battle scene, reducing visibility to zero in the pockets where it clung to the sea surface. As Ajax and Achilles continued their pursuit, they were engaged as they appeared between the pockets of smoke, two further hits on

Ajax silencing her guns completely. Now laying their own smoke, the light cruisers withdrew out of range, using torpedoes to harry the Spee from afar as they tracked her course westwards towards South America.

As the morning worn on, Langsdorff began to restore some order to his ship; sixty-one wounded sailors were treated, and thirty-six dead arranged on the deck. Subsequent reports revealed that damage to the guns could be repaired while still at sea, but low ammunition stocks would preclude another meaningful engagement. Most worrying however, was the hull damage that would endanger the ship in rough waters, and the required plating work could not be conducted at sea. His signallers were listening in on the frequency of the pursuing British cruisers who were sending frequent signals with the exact position and course of the Spee.

Langsdorff believed the messages were being sent to Royal Navy reinforcements who he envisaged were speeding to the scene from all over the South Atlantic. His mind was made up. He would head for shore to the safest option port – Montevideo, at the mouth of the River Plate in Uruguay. With no requirement to maintain radio silence now that the enemy knew exactly where he was, Langsdorff signalled German Naval High Command, detailing his situation, damage, and casualty figures. He neither expected nor received any orders by way of reply, German doctrine delegating combat decisions to the captain on the spot. The Spee dropped anchor in Montevideo harbour just before midnight.

Thursday 14 December 1939 – Montevideo Harbour, Uruguay.

Through the German Embassy, Langsdorff requested facilities for repairs and that the Uruguayan Government allow his ship to stay longer than the twenty-four hours that international law granted any combatant ship in a neutral harbour. The reply was not what he wanted to hear; that no repair facilities were available at present, but that an extension of stay could easily be arranged, with an offer of up to seventy-two hours should that be found necessary. He knew immediately that the Uruguayan stance favoured the British, each hour that passed bringing British reinforcements closer. At 4:30 p.m. the British merchantmen prisoners were assembled and told they could leave the ship, their initial exuberance dampened as they filed onto the deck past a perfectly arranged row of coffins draped in German battle flags; the human cost of the previous day's engagement. The British officers respectfully saluted as they passed. Their reverence continued as they stared in amazement at the damaged ship, now becoming fully aware how lucky they had been to avoid death or injury themselves in the violent engagement.

The whole of the port side was riddled with holes, the forward eleven-inch guns sagged in their turret mountings and the ship's spotter plane was reduced to a burned skeleton. The smell of cordite and burnt metal still carried on the wind. The German sailors who worked on the damaged deck did so in almost slow motion. They were drained both mentally and physically from the battle, and their subsequent efforts to repair the damage and keep the ship seaworthy. They looked accusingly at the British merchantmen from tired, sunken eyes, their pale faces reflecting their shock from seeing their colleagues terribly wounded or blown to pieces by high explosive shells. Despite the Spee and her crew being responsible for the sinking of their own ships, the British merchantmen felt a wave of sympathy and sorrow wash over them as they absorbed the scene of destruction. Sailors were sailors regardless of their country of origin or political belief, and an appreciation of their mutual privations bound them together across national boundaries. They followed their escort to a gangplank that had been secured between the ship and the quay, where the guard simply raised his hand to usher them off the vessel.

As they made their way down the gangplank a cheer rose from a crowd of Uruguayans that had gathered on the quayside. Members of the British Embassy staff were waiting to greet them, the Naval Attaché shaking hands with each man as they stepped ashore. Debriefing of the released prisoners quickly revealed the existence of the Altmark, with three hundred British prisoners on board. A detailed description of the ship was signalled to the Admiralty, from where Winston Churchill's personal command to find her and liberate the prisoners was flashed to all warships in the Western Approaches.

Friday 15 December 1939 – Montevideo, Uruguay.

As the sun rose on 15 December, neither Captain Langsdorff nor Commodore Harwood had slept. The accounts of the released prisoners combined with shore observation had confirmed the extent of the damage to the Spee. Although this information began to create a situational appreciation for Harwood, messages from the Admiralty had told the Commodore that only HMS Cumberland, a County Class heavy cruiser, would be available almost immediately to supplement his force, but that Spee equivalent sized vessels, Renown and Ark Royal, would not reach him for many days.

Attempting to influence Langsdorff's thought process, Harwood sent a message to the Civil Authorities in Montevideo requesting that they assure him of adequate security measures for the crews of Renown and Ark Royal who would be taking shore leave on the following day – Saturday 16 December. He knew this false information would leak out through the German intelligence services in the Uruguayan Government and subsequently be reported to Langsdorff. Harwood supplemented the false report deception by getting his ships, now reinforced with the arrival of HMS Cumberland, to deliberately perform overt manoeuvres that would give the appearance of a much larger force. These manoeuvres were indeed observed by the lookouts on Spee, and combined with the leaked security provision request, convinced Langsdorff that he was hemmed in by a much superior British force.

Harwood had also been in touch with the British Embassy requesting that pressure be applied to extend the grace period for Spee to remain in neutral Montevideo; an attempt to keep the Germans in port until his promised reinforcements arrived. Whether by accident or design, the British freighter Dunster Grange slowly and very visibly departed Montevideo harbour that evening, triggering the regulations of the Hague Convention that no warship of a combatant power was permitted to depart within twenty-four hours of an enemy state merchant ship. Designed to prevent hostile actions within territorial waters of neutral nations, this in effect trapped the Spee in harbour for another day.

Langsdorff dictated a dispatch to German Naval High Command, siting that despite the presence of British Naval vessels which would most likely preclude his escape, permission was requested for an attempted breakout in the direction of Buenos Aires and the much more pro-German Argentine administration. Clarification was also sought as to whether the ship should be scuttled or interned, should the prospect of damaging British naval assets through an engagement not be possible. A prompt reply laid out his options, granting him permission to attempt a breakout or to destroy his ship if meaningful combat with the British vessels could not be conducted. Internment was not to be considered. Throughout the day, the crew of the Spee had worked frantically to repair the damage to their ship and make her seaworthy, but as the sun fell that evening, the overwhelming feeling among the weary Germans who watched the last minutes of daylight running out, was that their own time was also running out.

Sunday 17 December 1939 –
Montevideo, Uruguay.

On 16 December, the delay on the Spee's enforced departure caused by the sailing of Dunster Grange had been used to bury the German dead. The freed British merchantmen attended the ceremony, laying wreaths on the graves of the enemy sailors. Captain Langsdorff stood pensive and white faced as he laid his men to rest.

Only minutes into the new day of Sunday, using what he regarded as the last safe opportunity to brief his officers, Langsdorff gathered them together and gave his orders. His plan was initiated almost immediately, the ships documents being burned, gun ranging apparatus and sighting equipment destroyed by beating with hammers and heavier mechanical equipment blown apart by grenades. The remaining unfired torpedoes were prepared for detonation in the engine room and munitions bunkers. As dawn broke, thousands of people crowded the quayside, knowing that the Spee had to depart that day, and expecting to see a showdown with the Royal Navy. Among the onlookers were British Naval and Diplomatic staff, scanning the Spee through powerful binoculars. Outwardly, all appeared quiet on board, belying the activity below decks. A German tanker, the Tacoma, had pulled alongside and the onlookers saw crates being ferried between the tanker and the battleship, giving the impression the Spee was being reprovisioned for a voyage. This process continued for twelve hours, and each time the boats unloaded their crates and returned to the Tacoma, they were full of sailors from the Spee, secreted on board out of sight of the onlookers. As the light started to fade, nearly one thousand sailors had been taken from the Spee to the safety of the Tacoma.

Without ceremony, the Spee slipped her moorings and began to move down river towards the open sea, the Tacoma in her wake. The scene was further graced by two German freighters that had steamed from Buenos Aires and lay alongside the Tacoma. Spee's engines stopped, and the vessel gently came to rest. The remaining crew were quickly ferried to the freighters, Captain Langsdorff being the last to leave his ship. He gently caressed Spee's hull as his farewell gesture before stepping into the launch to be taken away. It was 8:30 p.m.

No sooner had the launch moved off than a pillar of black smoke shot into the air, as if chased from the ship by the huge explosion which followed a split second behind. Smaller but no less violent explosions followed in close succession all along the length of the vessel. As Langsdorff stepped onto the deck of the Tacoma, the last charge exploded in the Spee's stern, sending the huge gun barrels tumbling through the air to splash into the sea near the ship's hull. Fires in the fuel tanks broke through the deck, and thick oily smoke billowed into the sky. As the fire took hold, an eerie glow silhouetted the superstructure of the ship against the night sky to the crowds still lining Montevideo quayside. A British aircraft circling the area reported to Commodore Harwood in HMS Ajax that the Spee had been destroyed.

Thursday 21 December 1939 –
Lille, Northern France.

"What are we going to do, Sergeant?" asked Lance Corporal Murray as he stood with the Platoon Sergeant in the Company Clerk's office. He had just been informed that the company boxers were ordered to report to the Medical Officer for a pre-boxing medical the next morning.

"How the hell did this happen?" enquired Sergeant Preston, not really expecting an answer. "The Medical Officer has never done pre-boxing medicals before." he added.

"It's that new PT Instructor, Corporal Wainwright." Murray replied. "He's far too bloody keen. They'll find out Smith can't see properly without his glasses and he'll be kicked off the team. The Company Sergeant Major will be furious, as Smith is a dead cert to win at his weight."

"He's a dead cert to win at any bloody weight." Sergeant Preston sighed. "I've a ton of money bet on him already. Nearly every soldier in the company has chipped in."

"What are we going to do, Sergeant?" asked Lance Corporal Murray again; not one for changing his approach to a problem.

"Right. I'll have a word with the Medical Sergeant. I know he likes to do dirty deals and I'm going to test his integrity." Sergeant Preston's eyes narrowed as the plan formed in his head. "Put the word out to the Section Commanders and get me someone else from the platoon as close to Smith's height and weight as possible. I'll send them for the examination tomorrow instead." He sat down as he worked out the finer details of the deception. "When you get the replacement, make sure he has Smith's number and date of birth learned off pat." he added. "And keep Smith in his barrack room out of sight until the examination is over." Preston got up and put on his headdress. "I'm off to the Medical Block." he said, as Lance Corporal Murray scurried out of the office after him to find the Section Commanders.

Friday 22 December 1939 –
Lille, Northern France.

"Name, Rank and Number?" asked the Medical Sergeant at the reception desk.

"Smith J, Private, 2301773, Sergeant." came the reply. Private Moore stood bolt upright at the Medical Sergeant's desk. He had worked on his uniform the previous evening while memorising Smith's details; determined not to provide any excuse for further inquisition due to a less than perfect appearance. He fixed his gaze straight ahead, determined to avoid eye contact with the Medical Sergeant.

"Take these documents and have a seat outside the Medical Officer's consulting room." said Sergeant Parker, handing over a light green-coloured file and gesturing in the direction of the waiting area. After Sergeant Preston's visit the day before, Parker knew the soldier in front of him was not Private Smith, but a favour owed was hard currency in the Sergeants' Mess, and he could always deny culpability if everything went sour. The second part of the favour would be slightly trickier to arrange however, and certainly carried a greater degree of direct association.

Moore took a seat as ordered. The black painted panel on the door had Captain Walker's name written in chalk. He glanced at the name on the file that the Medical Sergeant had given him. 2301773 Smith J Private. The rank was written in pencil for ease of adjustment should the file's owner ever be promoted. Moore had never liked doctors and was even more unhappy than usual given his present circumstances. It was the smell he thought. He was fine until he got the antiseptic smell. "Why do all doctors' surgeries always smell the same?" he asked himself out loud. He was about to have a look inside the file in case there was any information that would support the rouse, when the consulting room door opened and Moore sprang to his feet.

"Step inside, Private," asked the Medical Officer, "and take a seat." He took the file from Moore as he entered.

"What's your service number and date of birth?" asked Captain Walker without looking at Moore.

"2301773, 21 January 1919, Sir." replied Moore without hesitation; the Medical Officer checking the details against the file as he spoke to ensure he had the correct patient.

"Have you boxed before, Smith?" he asked, now engaging Moore with eye contact.

"Yes, Sir. Many times." bluffed Moore, steadily growing in confidence that all seemed to be going well.

"Stand behind the line on the floor and look at the chart on the wall opposite." ordered Walker. Moore did as requested. This was it; he thought. Get this done and get away as quickly as possible. "Place your left hand over your left eye and read the second line up from the bottom of the chart." Walker droned without any tone or emotion in his voice. Moore began quickly and then remembered that the real Private Smith would have some reduced vision recorded on his chart; deliberately slowing and stumbling over the last few letters. "Can you read anything from the bottom line?" asked Captain Walker, again in the same toneless, emotionless voice. Moore deliberately repeated the stumbling, hesitant performance; replacing "O" for "C" and "R" for "K" to enhance the ploy. The test was then repeated with his right eye covered by his right hand; with a similar stuttering performance from Moore.

"Remain standing and undo the buttons on your shirt." asked the Medical Officer. Moore undid his battledress blouse and hung it over the back of the chair, unhooked his braces from his shoulders and unbuttoned his shirt. Captain Walker put a stethoscope in his ears and set the microphone on Moore's chest. "Deep breaths in and out now until I say stop." Moore did as asked, and the doctor listened firstly to his heart and then pulled his shirt open by the collar to listen to his lungs from the back. "Right. Have a seat and breathe normally." he said as he returned to his desk.

"You're medically fit to fight on Sunday, Smith," said Walker as he scribbled some notes in the file. "What weight do you box at?" Moore felt his heart sink and a cold flush run through his body. He had no knowledge of boxing and felt he was on the verge of being caught out. In the absence of a reply the doctor looked up from his writing. "Well, what weight?" he repeated, his usual toneless voice now showing some impatience. Moore felt he would vomit right there and then.

"Same as last time, Sir." he blurted out, feeling instant relief at his ability to deflect the question. The Medical Officer opened the file again and leafed through the pages.

"Featherweight?" he queried.

"Yes, Sir. Featherweight." Moore reinforced quickly.

"Get stripped off and stand on the scales." Walker ordered, as he continued to make notes in the file. Moore was now in virgin territory. His mind was racing again, confidence gone. He had no idea what was about to happen and could not prepare for it in any way. He stepped on the scales in only his issue underwear and the doctor moved the bar and weights to reach a balance. "You're a couple of pounds over to fight at Featherweight, Smith," said the Medical Officer, "and you will have difficulty losing that before Sunday. But don't worry, I'll give you something to assist. Get dressed again."

Moore slowly got dressed as the doctor left the room, sitting back down again when fully clothed. He felt a flush of relief that he seemed to have pulled off the bluff but had a degree of trepidation at what may be coming next. The doctor came back and sat at his desk. He was stirring a glass that was half full of water with a salt sediment in the bottom. He continued to stir vigorously, occasionally holding the glass up to the light to observe the swirling contents. Once the water went clear he stood up and walked across the room towards the waiting soldier.

"Drink this in one go." he said as he handed the glass to Moore. Moore took the glass from the doctor with a grimace and swirled the contents himself. He could see a few crystals still in the bottom of the glass that were caught in a spiral of fluid as the swirling liquid created a whirlpool effect. As he raised the glass to his lips he got a distinctly salty waft from the liquid. Closing his eyes as he prepared himself for what he assumed would be a vile taste, he took hurried gulps from the glass and was almost finished when the extreme saltiness finally impacted and he began to gag. Captain Walker had been hovering in expectation of the reaction and steadied the glass at Moore's lips with his hand as the last dregs poured into his mouth.

"Wasn't too bad now, was it?" he asked.

"No, Sir. Delicious in fact." replied Moore, in an attempt at sarcasm, since the doctor knew it tasted terrible.

"I need you to drink a pint of water every hour for the next three hours." he said, in a tone that recognised Moore's sarcasm. "I suggest you don't stray too far from the barrack room either." He looked knowingly at Moore as he gestured him towards the door.

* * *

Moore was in a hurry to get his first drink, as the salty medicine had left a terrible taste in his mouth. He was quite pleased with himself when he arrived back in his barrack room to be met by both Smith and Sergeant Preston who had been waiting on him.

"All done and fit to fight." said Moore merrily to the reception party, before jumping onto his top bunk and taking his water bottle from his webbing equipment that was slung on the metal frame. Pulling out the cork, he took a long satisfying drink from the container, pleased to get the salty taste from his mouth. "No guard duty for a month as you promised, Sergeant." he said smugly, replacing the cork in his water bottle. He tapped the cork home with the palm of his hand and lay back on his bed, putting his hands behind his head on the pillow and crossing his feet.

"That was the deal, Moore, you cocky little bastard, and I'll stick to it." replied Sergeant Preston. He turned away and left the barrack room, satisfied that the first part of his plan had worked. Smith would be fighting on Sunday, and Preston knew his bet was safe. Smith sat down on his own bunk which directly faced Moore's.

"Thanks for doing that, mate." he blurted out meekly. Moore pushed his head back even further into his hands.

"No drama, Smudger." he replied. "Easy street for me for a whole month. Do me a favour mate and fill my canteen for me please. The doc said I had to drink lots of water for a few hours." Smith's bed gave a metallic squeak as he stood up and took Moore's water bottle from his outstretched hand. Moore was still smiling at the prospect of a guard free month when Smith returned and handed his canteen back.

"You going for dinner, mate?" asked Smith.

"Don't feel hungry, Smudger." Moore replied. "Must be that stuff the doc gave me is ruining my appetite. He said it would help me lose weight before the fight on Sunday. I'll go for a bit of a run or wander down the NAAFI later and see if that brings my appetite back."

"I'll bring you back an apple in case you get hungry." Smith said as he put on his headdress and left on his way to the cookhouse."

"Thanks, mate." replied Moore sleepily as he settled back to enjoy some peace and quiet before the rest of the section appeared after dinner. He took another long drink from his canteen and left it beside him on the bed as he closed his eyes.

* * *

Smith had discreetly placed an apple inside his battledress blouse, as taking food from the canteen was frowned upon. As he entered the block, most of the section had already returned and were noisily sorting out their equipment and uniforms for washing after a week of training. Moore's bed was empty, except for the canteen that was lying on the grey wool blanket.

"Anyone seen Moore?" he asked to no one in particular. A murmur of negative disinterest was his reply. He took out the apple from his blouse and placed it in his locker so no one could see, before lying down on his bed. Just as he lay back, Moore appeared beside him wearing his white PT vest and dark blue shorts.

"Alright Smudger, mate?" Moore enquired. "How was dinner? Still the usual slops?"

"Normal hard bread with a choice of smelly cheese or jam." replied Smith. "How are you feeling now?"

"Just had the most massive shit ever." said Moore. "Came on me all of a sudden during my run, had to put a bit of a sprint on and nearly didn't make it to the ablutions. It was so big the end was touching the tray and still attached to my arse at the same time."

"I don't need to know the gory details of what came out of your arse, mate." replied Smith sourly as he screwed up his face at the thought. "There's an apple in my locker for you if you want it." he whispered. "You better take it now as I'm on guard tonight and I'm not leaving it open with this lot about." He tilted his head to the left twice, gesturing towards the rest of the room occupants.

"I'll keep it for later thanks, Smudger. There's still some gurgling going on down below." said Moore as he took the fruit from Smith's locker, polishing it on the front of his vest, before returning to his bed. He assumed his favourite position of hands behind his head and feet crossed, the apple balanced on his chest.

Smith unhooked his webbing equipment from the bedframe and swung it across his shoulders so that his arms went between the support straps and the load fell nicely into place. He fastened the waistbelt buckle, tucked his headdress into his blouse and took his greatcoat from his locker before closing and locking it.

"That's me off on guard duty now, mate." he confirmed to Moore. "Don't forget to keep drinking like the doctor said." He walked the length of the barrack room and took his rifle from the rack in the wall. As he stepped out into the evening air, he could feel the chill of approaching winter. His breath condensed on his glasses and persisted for a few seconds before disappearing and restoring his full vision.

* * *

Corporal Thomas checked his watch against the clock on the wall of the guardroom.

"Right, Smudger. Security check now." he said as he made a note in the guardroom log against the appropriate time. Smith got to his feet from a wooden chair he had placed in front of the stove, unhooking his greatcoat from the wall peg and putting it on to keep in some of the heat from the burning logs. Lifting his rifle from the rack, he stepped out into the now distinctly frosty darkness. He breathed in deeply, glad at the freshness of the air contrasting to the stale, sweaty atmosphere of the guardroom. He always felt dirty when he was on guard duty, preferring to try and sleep in a chair rather than lie fully clothed on the stained mattresses with a dark grey woollen Army blanket draped over him. He knew his route off by heart as he went from building to building, checking the locked doors and looking through the windows for signs of fire or intruders. He set the edge of his hand against the glass then rested his forehead against it to cut out the glare from ambient lighting, enabling him to see any signs of movement or the glow of a possible fire inside the buildings.

He heard the sound of boots on the path running towards him before he saw who it was. It was Private Dusty Millar who had come across Smith by chance on his way to the guardroom.

"Come quick, Smudger. Moore is very sick." blurted Millar.

"Go and tell Corporal Thomas in the guardroom and then get the Duty Medic. I'll meet you back in the section room." replied Smith, pushing Millar in the direction of the guardroom. He came across Orpin and McCafferty in convulsions of laughter just outside the door to the barrack room.

"Don't go in there, Smudger." Orpin struggled to tell him, almost unable to speak he was laughing so hard. Despite the warning, the smell hit Smith the instant he entered the section room, and he covered his nose and mouth with his hand in a futile attempt to keep out the stench. Moore's bunk was splattered with diarrhoea and there was a trail of excrement up the middle of the room between the beds. Smith felt his stomach heave as the smell seemed to dissolve on his tongue and he began to taste it as well as smell it. He hurried outside where Orpin and McCafferty were still laughing.

"What the hell happened? Where's Moore?" he demanded.

"He's gone to the ablution block." blurted out Orpin. "I was lying on my bunk below him and he was lying on his own bed still in his PT kit. I heard him eating an apple, then he went quiet and I thought he was asleep." Orpin paused to gather himself. "The next thing I knew, he let out a yell and shit was flying everywhere, all over the bed and floor. He jumped out of bed still shitting, and I felt the heat from it as the stream of shit just missed my face. Moore slipped in the puddle on the floor, landing on his back, before running the length of the block, leaving a trail of shit after him."

"Has anyone been to check on him?" Smith asked. Orpin and McCafferty looked at each other and then at Smith like two scolded puppies. "Bloody good friends you are!" Smith continued angrily. Just as he was about to go to the ablutions himself to check on Moore, Corporal Thomas, Millar and the Duty Medic arrived.

"What the hell's happening here?" asked Corporal Thomas.

"Moore shit all over the place, Corporal." said Orpin. "He's in the ablutions now."

"Take the medic there with you now, Smith." Corporal Thomas ordered, before entering the barrack room to see for himself. As Orpin and McCafferty heard him gagging at the smell, they started to laugh again. Corporal Thomas emerged retching, to the obvious pleasure of Orpin who laughed even harder.

"I don't know what you're finding so funny, Orpin. Get a mop and bucket, get back in there and get it cleaned up." said Corporal Thomas. The grin was instantly wiped from Orpin's face, to the increased enjoyment of McCafferty who picked up the amusement where Orpin had left off. "And you're helping, La La, so get moving." added Thomas. Both men, now completely deflated, trudged away.

Smith and the medic had gone to the ablutions. The smell met them as they entered.

"Dear God!" said the medic, screwing up his face and recoiling at the odour.

"You in here, mate?" asked Smith as he looked into the cubicles in turn.

"In here, Smudger." came the weak reply. Smith followed the sound and gingerly looked in to see Moore crouched over the hole in the tray, pale as a ghost and shivering, his shorts round his ankles.

"What the hell happened?" asked Smith, noticing that Moore's lower legs, shorts and PT pumps were covered in diarrhoea.

"I felt a bit better and ate the apple you got me. Then I fell asleep just lying on the bed. I woke up as I started shitting myself, jumped out of bed and ran here. I just couldn't hold anything in."

"Don't worry yourself about it, mate." said the medic. "Have you stopped shitting now?"

"I think so, yeah." confirmed Moore.

"Get yourself in the shower, clothes and all, and I'll get you something clean to wear." suggested Smith. The medic helped Moore to his feet as Smith left to get Moore some clean clothes. He returned to the block to find Orpin and McCafferty trying to clean up the mess under the supervision of Corporal Thomas.

"Just use the shitty blankets to wipe the floor before you try to mop it." Thomas directed, with his hand over his mouth and nose. "Then throw the blankets outside." Orpin and McCafferty were visibly and audibly gagging as they tried to absorb the diarrhoea with the blankets. Carefully stepping around them, Smith lifted some clothes and a towel from Moore's locker before heading back to the ablutions. The medic had put Moore in the shower, where he stood, still shivering.

"He was saying the Medical Officer gave him something to drink for rapid weight loss." said the medic to Smith as he returned. "That's what's happened. It's been a bowel clearance solution. He should be alright by tomorrow morning, but make sure he drinks plenty." Smith helped Moore get dried and dressed.

"Let's get you back to bed." he said, supporting him with an arm around his chest. By the time they got back to the block, Orpin and McCafferty had cleared up the mess and were mopping the floor. All the windows had been opened to let in fresh air, a distinctly cold but welcome breeze disturbing the open curtains.

Saturday 23 December 1939 – Lille, Northern France.

"How are you feeling this morning?" asked Smith when he heard Moore was awake. "I heard you getting up a few times in the night."

"Just had a few dribbles, but at least I got a warning." replied Moore. "My ass is in tatters. It's too sore to wipe, so I just have to dab it instead." Now that the seriousness of the situation had passed, both men were able to giggle at Moore's circumstances as they got dressed for breakfast.

Moore realised he was ravenous when he entered the cookhouse and was met by the smell of bacon. Having only eaten an apple since lunchtime the day before, he gladly accepted everything on offer. Smith collected his breakfast and sat down to eat, but Moore remained standing.

"Not sitting down?" Smith asked.

"I'm still a bit tender, so I'll just stand up for now." Moore replied, and they both had another snigger at his predicament. They were joined by Lance Corporal Murray the Company Clerk, who had been privy to the deception from the start.

"All set for the big fight tomorrow, Smudger?" he asked.

"Ready as I'll ever be." Smith replied.

"The Clerk from A Company says they have a really good team." Murray added. "Sergeant Preston is a bit worried, as he has a small fortune resting on you."

"I've never lost an Army bout and I'm not going to start now." Smith added confidently. "Tell Sergeant Preston not to worry. His money is safe."

* * *

Both Sergeant Major McCann and Sergeant Preston were at the Medical Centre to witness the boxing team weigh in. Sergeant Major Patton from A Company was present to watch his own team. D Company boxers went first, and met their weight restrictions with no issues; Sergeant Parker who conducted the individual tests completely ignoring the fact that a different Private Smith was being weighed. Preston then stayed behind to witness the A Company weigh in, and ensure all was in order. The Medical Sergeant struck up a conversation with Sergeant Major Patton as they waited.

"I knew the trainer of the British Boxing Team at the 1936 Olympics in Berlin." he began. "Up to all sorts of tricks those Olympic teams." he said, shaking his head slowly in a display of apparent disbelief. Patton's ears pricked up at the prospect of gaining an advantage.

"What did they get up to then, Nosey?" he asked in a nonchalant way, as if he was only vaguely interested.

"Apparently the Germans made their boxers give blood on the morning of their fight." Parker replied; with an inclination of disbelief in his voice. "They said it made them move faster and breathe easier. Some theory about allowing faster circulation and a faster flow of oxygen to the muscles." he continued.

"Did it work then?" asked Patton, still trying to be nonchalant.

"Who can say for sure?" continued Parker. "But they won two golds, two silvers and a bronze, while the British won bugger all." Patton said nothing, his mind working overtime. A few minutes passed before Patton spoke again.

"Would you be able to do it for our boxers?" he asked quietly.

"What, you mean take blood?" quizzed Parker.

"Yip. Tomorrow morning before the competition." Patton confirmed. Parker said nothing for a few seconds then shook his head.

"No. The Medical Officer would never agree." he replied.

"I could have the team in here tomorrow morning early. No one will know, and I'll make it worth your while." suggested Patton. "Anything to beat those bastards from D Company."

"I could do it myself I suppose, and no one would be any the wiser." Parker said, as if thinking out loud, then changed his mind. "No. It's too risky. The Medical Officer would have my guts for garters if he found out." he concluded.

"Name your price, Nosey." Patton continued. "Anything you want." Parker remained quiet for a few seconds.

"Right. I'll do it. A tin of cigarettes for each man. Have the team here at 7 o'clock tomorrow morning." When Sergeant Major Patton went to brief his team, Parker nodded discreetly to Preston who was still watching from the Medical Centre doorway. Preston nodded back and left.

* * *

That afternoon, Sergeant Major McCann had gathered D Company on the parade square. He briefed them on the arrangements for the boxing match on Christmas Eve and the lunch on Christmas Day; when by tradition, the Regimental Officers served lunch to the non-commissioned ranks. Finally, he announced that the company was required to provide two volunteers for a sniper protection duty from 24 – 26 December on the Maginot Line.

"Lance Corporal Tetlow and Private McEnearney, take one step forward." he ordered. The two soldiers complied. "You have just volunteered." he continued, a beaming self-satisfied smile across his face.

Sunday 24 December 1939 –
Lille, Northern France.

Sergeant Preston diverted his route to breakfast via the Medical Centre. He saw the boxers from A Company being let in discreetly by Sergeant Parker and was very pleased with himself that the final part of his plan was in operation. Everything rested on the individual performance of the company boxers now, and there was nothing he could do about that.

Preston took a table after collecting his breakfast. He was quickly joined by Sergeants Toner and Allen, the other two Platoon Sergeants in D Company; and Sergeant Kane from 2 Platoon in A Company.

"Alright, lads?" Kane quizzed the other Sergeants. "Team all set for the contest tonight?" he asked cheerily to no one specifically; as if already confident in the outcome.

"I saw your boys at the Medical Centre this morning." Preston said to Kane, hoping to put him on the spot unexpectedly.

"Just some last-minute preparation." replied Kane, immediately going on the defensive.

"Just booking their beds on the ward for tonight after the fight then?" Sergeant Toner answered back quickly. The three Sergeants from D Company all began to laugh as Kane was visibly annoyed by the remark.

"Well, we'll see tonight, won't we?" replied Kane sharply, lifting his plate and moving to another table. The D Company Sergeants continued to laugh as they started to eat.

"What were A Company doing at the Medical Centre this morning, Jock?" Toner asked Preston between mouthfuls of food. "I got the impression you know and were just trying to make Kane uncomfortable."

"I know exactly what was happening." Preston dropped his voice to a whisper. "They were donating blood as they believe it will make them fight better tonight."

"And will it?" Toner asked, confused at the concept.

"Will it shite!" Preston replied. "Nosey Parker convinced them it was a tried and tested procedure, and they fell for it. They'll be weak as piss for about twenty-four hours." The three men laughed louder, and enjoyed their breakfast even more.

Sunday 24 December 1939 –
Maginot Line, France / Germany Border.

Lance Corporal Tetlow and Private McEnearney, along with those selected for the sniper protection duty from the other platoons across the battalion, were collected in a transport vehicle driven by soldiers from the Scottish infantry regiment that was being given some leave over Christmas. The journey began in the early afternoon, but was timed so the relief could be conducted in darkness to reduce the chance of being observed by the enemy. With the canvas cover secured closed, everyone inside became completely disorientated very quickly as to which way they were heading.

After a number of hours travel, the vehicle stopped, turning off its lights and engine. Two soldiers were then dispatched by a Scottish Corporal who had ridden in the cab, and told to walk to their relief positions. The vehicle journey continued until Tetlow's and McEnearney's turn came; and they climbed out of the vehicle to find themselves beside a sparse wood on a wide vehicle track. They were struck with the biting cold as soon as they dismounted. The Scottish Corporal explained where and how far they had to go, and set a bearing on Lance Corporal Tetlow's compass.

They moved into the wood and waited for a few minutes after the vehicle had moved off, listening for the sound of any other vehicle or patrols, and letting their eyes become accustomed to the dark. Lance Corporal Tetlow checked his compass and they set off. The night was clear and the destination, a cottage on a hill, was clearly visible in the moonlight, albeit still some distance away. As they approached, the cottage seemed deserted, but as they got close, a door opened and a dim light was visible inside. They entered, to be greeted by two Scottish soldiers, and a mug of hot tea thrust into their hand.

The soldiers they were relieving provided security protection for a French sniper team who operated from the upper floor of the cottage. The cottage had been fitted out to give the impression of a derelict building. The front windows which faced the border, were covered in hessian material with only tiny, almost invisible slits for observation. The windows at the rear were covered in heavy net curtains. There was a pot-bellied stove in the middle of the wall on the right side, a dining table, a double bed and a wooden staircase in the furthest corner, which led to the upper level of the cottage. The Scottish Corporal took Tetlow on a tour around the building to explain how the facility operated.

The French sniper team had been removed and a replacement team not yet provided; so, they began the tour upstairs. Three firing positions had been created for the snipers along the length of the building, shooting out through deliberately broken slates, disguised among the overall dilapidated state of the roof. They had a double bed and a small stove similar to the one downstairs. The Scottish Corporal explained that the stoves could only be lit at night using the provided charcoal, so what little smoke the charcoal produced could not be seen, and had to be extinguished before dawn. Movement inside the house during the day was to be kept to a minimum, and away from the windows to avoid casting a shadow on the hessian. The outside toilet was only to be used at night, any daytime excretions were to be collected in the chamber pot provided, which could be emptied when dark. They went outside to see the toilet, which was a small wooden shed with a plank suspended across a long drop pit. A rope with a knot in the end hung from the ceiling, to be held for extra stability if required while using the facility. It smelt terrible in the depths of winter, and Tetlow imagined it would be unbearable in the heat of the summer.

Once back inside, all four soldiers sat around the table. It was explained that the German border was less than a mile away and that both Allied and German patrols moved around the area; with aerial reconnaissance flights overhead frequently. The Maginot Line itself, was some miles further to the rear. The current incumbents reinforced that the security procedures just outlined must be rigidly adhered to, because if the cottage was identified as, or suspected of being, a sniper location, then it would be attacked or shelled by the Germans.

When there were no further questions, the Scottish Corporal confirmed on his map the position that Tetlow and McEnearney had been dropped off, as that was where they would be picked up when the vehicle returned later that night. They departed with a handshake, saying they would return in three days to take the cottage back. Lance Corporal Tetlow and Private McEnearney were left to their own devices. They looked at each other with a degree of unease and smiled nervously.

Sunday 24 December 1939 – Lille, Northern France.

A work party had built a makeshift boxing ring in the centre of the cookhouse as it was the only location large enough to hold the event. The dining tables and chairs had been rearranged around the ring to provide a view of the contest from all sides. A row of easy chairs was placed at the front for the officers. Most soldiers from the battalion had gathered to cheer on their own company boxers and the facility was packed. The Regimental Sergeant Major brought the room to attention as the Commanding Officer and the other Regimental Officers entered. The officers were wearing Mess Dress, their bright red jackets contrasting sharply with the khaki of the soldiers' battledress. The Battalion Second in Command took to the ring to welcome everyone and start the proceedings. As a former boxer himself, the Quartermaster was the referee for the evening, dressed in a white shirt and white trousers that looked distinctly tight; obviously procured when he was younger and leaner.

The soldiers from 10 Platoon had all arrived early, and secured themselves front row seats to watch Smith box. Soldiers from the other platoons clapped and cheered as their respective boxers made their way to the ring, led by their Company Physical Training Instructor. Those who were witnessing a boxing competition for the first time were surprised by the noise and bitter company rivalry that was on display from the audience.

The featherweight contest was announced, and Corporal Wainwright led Private Smith to the ring. The D Company soldiers clapped and shouted their encouragement as Smith walked past his colleagues and the seated officers. Still wearing his glasses, Smith winked knowingly at Private Moore as he walked by, acknowledging the distress endured by his comrade which had enabled him to fight. The Medical Officer was seated beside the Padre and looked puzzled as Smith went past, not remembering having conducted a fit to box medical examination on a soldier with glasses. He turned to the Padre as if he was about to raise his concerns, only to find the Padre fully entered into the spirit of the contest, shouting his encouragement to Smith.

His opponent was a fighter from A Company; and this was the bout on which a considerable amount of money had been bet. The A Company boxer was brimming with confidence, strutting around the ring, punching his gloves together and rallying support from his company colleagues. Smith stood quietly in his own corner with his head down. As the fighters were called together in the centre of the ring for the briefing by the referee, Corporal Wainright removed Smith's glasses, putting them into the pocket on his shirt for safekeeping. When the bell sounded and the boxers faced off, the Padre became vocal.

"Kill the bastard." he yelled, as Smith dispensed with any boxing style and simply pummelled his opponent with a flurry of punches.

"That's a bit unusual for a Padre!" whispered the Commanding Officer into the Padre's ear, taken aback by such an unexpected outburst of profanity.

"It's December 24th, Colonel." answered the Padre. "The good Lord allows me an annual quota of expletives which gets renewed on the first of January." The Commanding Officer began to laugh at the Padre's rationale. "I wouldn't want to waste any by not using them." he continued with a broad smile. "And besides, I have a bet placed on Smith to win." Colonel Chambers just shook his head gently.

As the bell went to end the first round, Smith returned to his corner and sat down on the hastily provided stool, sipping the water offered by Corporal Wainwright. In his opponent's corner things were not so calm, the boxer slumping into his seat as if exhausted. Sergeant Kane had left his place in the audience and was in heated discussion with his now puffy faced boxer, obviously concerned that the bout was not going his way. He was demonstrating hooks and uppercuts as he spoke, trying to show his boxer what was needed to turn the contest around.

The bell went to start the second round, and Smith was up and across the ring in a flash. Sensing his opponent was slow to come out of his corner and assume a guard, he launched another flurry of punches, landing on the other boxer's head and body. The noise level rose as Smith's relentless blows struck home, without reply from his opponent. Blood squirted from the A Company boxer's nose, which splashed over both boxers as Smith's punches continued unabated. The referee had seen enough, and stepped between the two fighters to end the contest. He took Smith by the wrist and raised his arm in the air to signify the winner. Those in attendance from D Company jumped to their feet to celebrate. Smith moved back to his corner where Corporal Wainwright returned his glasses. As the boxers left the ring, Smith raised his fist in acknowledgement of the support from his D Company colleagues. The Medical Officer stared hard at him as he passed, and was then summoned to examine his damaged opponent.

Monday 25 December 1939 – Lille, Northern France.

As the weather was cold but dry, the battalion was gathered on the parade square for the Christmas Day religious service. The officers and soldiers had been arranged to form three sides of a square, with a dais placed in the centre of the open end from which the Padre conducted the service. An Order of Service showing the format of the event and the words of the hymns had been printed and distributed, so the soldiers could follow the service and have no excuse not to sing the selected hymns. At the conclusion of the first hymn the Padre mildly berated the gathering for not singing loudly enough, requesting a better effort for the second hymn. As the second hymn began, loud tuneless singing could be heard from the front of the D Company contingent.

"What the hell is that noise?" whispered Bell to Farthing who stood beside him.

"I think it's Creepy." Farthing replied, as a ripple of laughter at Major Crawley's tuneless efforts began to sweep through the assembled company.

"Sounds like someone set fire to the milking parlour." replied Bell as he tried to suppress a giggle.

* * *

All non-commissioned ranks were seated in the cookhouse. The tables had been arranged in long lines for ease of service and bottles of beer placed beside each setting. The officers were gathered around the serving hatches to commence serving. As the starter was ready, every officer took a bowl of soup in each hand and served the seated soldiers, the serving sequence carefully controlled by the Quartermaster. 1 Section had arranged to sit together, splitting up so they faced each other across the table, drinking their beer as they eagerly awaited their lunch. A continuous stream of officers began to serve their table, both sides at once, each officer serving two soldiers at a time before going back to the hatch for the next collection. The Adjutant and Lieutenant Chadwick served Kyle,

McEnearney, Orpin and McCafferty on one side, slightly ahead of the other side, where Moore, Bell, Hamill and Farthing were still waiting. The Padre stepped between Moore and Bell, setting down a bowl of soup in front of each. As he served Moore, he tilted the bowl and the soup washed up over his thumb.

"Your thumb has gone in my soup, Padre." said Moore.

"Thank you, Private." replied the Padre, setting the bowl down in front of Moore and licking his thumb. As he leaned over Bell to serve his soup; the strong smell of body odour wafted in his face as the Padre's armpit came close.

"That smell caught the back of my throat when I breathed in there." said Bell with his face screwing up. "That would make a goat vomit." he added.

Moore left his soup untouched and watched in anticipation of a replacement starter as the Padre returned to the hatch; before lifting two more bowls and continuing to serve other soldiers. The look of disappointment on Moore's face attracted a comment by Orpin.

"You don't want to be eating that." he said. "His thumb could have been up his nose or scratched his bollocks or anything."

"Not after what your guts have been through the last few days." Bell chipped in with his own observation. Moore, pushed the bowl away, untouched.

"If you don't want that, then I'll have it." said Bell, reaching across the table and exchanging Moore's full bowl for his already empty one.

"How can you eat that knowing that the Padre's thumb has been in it?" Moore asked.

"You don't know where the chef's thumb has been, and I'm sure that was in it at some stage as well." replied Bell. "What you don't know doesn't hurt."

* * *

When dinner was over, the Padre stood up to talk.

"Wait 'till you hear this." Orpin said to those around him. "Same speech every year." He mimicked the Padre. "Cook's done a wonderful job." Those within earshot laughed as Orpin was able to copy the Padre's voice almost perfectly. The Padre rapped the table with a spoon to get everyone's attention, and the room fell silent.

"As we are able to eat and enjoy a drink together today, let us not forget the meaning of Christmas." he began in his unemotional drone. "We remember our loved ones at home, and pray that we will be returned to them soon." He then gave a ten-minute sermon to his captive audience before pausing to let the words sink in. "And finally, on behalf of you all, I would like to thank the cook, who has done a wonderful job." Orpin grinned and took a seated bow as his prediction was proven correct; those around him descending into convulsions of laughter, and attracting a stern look from the Padre.

As the soldiers enjoyed their lunch, Major Crawley and Company Sergeant Major McCann left the barracks in a staff car.

Monday 25 December 1939 –
Maginot Line, France / Germany Border.

Tetlow and McEnearney spent a quiet but uneasy first shift in their new surroundings, jumping at every sound that an old building makes as it cools down on a winter's night. With bully beef straight from the tin for breakfast and again for lunch, by mid-afternoon the two soldiers found themselves completely bored and discussing the Christmas lunch they had missed in barracks. The sound of distant aircraft engines brought them to the hessian covered windows, where kneeling down and squinting through the observation slits, they watched the forming vapour trails as opposing reconnaissance and accompanying fighter aircraft chased each other through the clear blue sky.

"Bloody RAF." said Tetlow sarcastically, as if he wished the pilots could hear. "Couldn't give the poor bloody Germans any peace, even on Christmas Day."

"Listen, I hear women's voices." said McEnearney almost in a whisper.

"Bollocks." replied Corporal Tetlow. "There are no women around here."

"No. Listen." repeated McEnearney, raising his finger to his mouth in a signal for Tetlow to stay quiet.

"Bloody hell, you're right." muttered Tetlow, jumping to his feet and rushing to the back window. He gently moved the net curtain to give him a clear view. "Shit, there are two women coming up the path." McEnearney pulled the curtain aside on the other window as if disbelieving Corporal Tetlow. The sound of their voices got louder as they approached.

"What the hell are we going to do, Corporal?" asked McEnearney. Tetlow just looked at him and shook his head. Both men moved away from the windows and stood motionless in the middle of the room. The door knocked and they looked at each other, almost not daring to breathe. McEnearney raised his hands in a gesture asking the Corporal for a decision when the door knocked again, but louder, with a female voice asking "Halo." in an expectant tone.

"You speak the lingo. See what they want." whispered Tetlow. McEnearney shook his head, declining the request; but Tetlow gestured with a nod of his head towards the door, reinforcing the order with a scowl.

"Qui est la?" McEnearney spoke through the door, asking who was there. A flurry of responses from two female voices came in reply. "They say they are cold and to let them in." McEnearney translated.

"Tell them we are English soldiers." ordered Tetlow.

"Nous sommes des soldats Anglais." responded McEnearney as instructed. Another flurry of responses was heard. "They think we are Scottish and want to come in." McEnearney translated again.

"Tell them we cannot let them in." replied Tetlow.

"Nous ne pouvons pas vous laisser entrer." explained McEnearney, almost apologetically. There was no response for a few seconds until a single female voice replied. McEnearney looked at Tetlow wide eyed, almost in shock as he translated.

"They say English soldiers are no fun, because Scottish soldiers know how to keep them warm!"

"Let them in." ordered Tetlow immediately, "Before they change their minds and go away." McEnearney slid open the door bolts and lifted the latch, opening the door just a fraction so he could look out. The door burst open, almost knocking him off his feet, as two teenage girls pushed their way inside, laughing and talking both at once. One carried a wicker basket with a cloth over the top which she set on the kitchen table, obviously familiar with the layout of the cottage, and turned to face the shocked soldiers. Delighted they had found someone who spoke their language, they bombarded McEnearney with questions which he could barely answer before the next question was asked. Tetlow just watched with his mouth open. They wore brightly coloured dresses, mostly hidden under farm labourers' jackets tied with twine, and military style leather ankle boots, which were obviously too big for them. Tetlow guessed they were sixteen or seventeen years old.

McEnearney gestured for them to sit down at the table as he tried to get a word in between their chatter; which they eventually did and quietened down as they sat. They had fresh youthful faces, red tinged with the cold. The cloth was removed from the basket, and the elder of the girls produced a bottle of wine, cheese and bread which she set on the table. Tetlow got some glasses that he had seen sitting on a sideboard and using the cloth from the basket, gave them a cursory wipe before pouring the wine. McEnearney was deep in conversation by this time, the girls giggling as they spoke.

"Ask them how the Scottish kept them warm." Tetlow encouraged McEnearney, who dismissed him with a raised hand as he continued his conversation. Realising he had to be patient, Tetlow gulped down some wine and topped up the glasses. After a few minutes, McEnearney broke off from his conversation with the girls to give Corporal Tetlow an update on how the situation was developing.

"They are farm workers on the land around here." explained McEnearney. "Both are city girls from Lille, sent to help the farmers when the male labourers were mobilised into the Army." He took a drink of wine before he continued. "They are Gabrielle and Celine." McEnearney continued; indicating which was which with his hand. Tetlow nodded to the girls and repeated their names. They giggled at his pronunciation. "They first met the Scots who were also helping on the farm, and are apparently regular visitors here!"

"I like Celine." said Tetlow, looking lustfully at her over the rim of his glass as he sipped his wine.

"That's good, because it would appear that she likes you too." continued McEnearney.

Celine broke off a piece of bread and handed it across the table to Tetlow. He reached to take it, but she didn't let it go; instead, standing up and moving towards the attic stairs, pulling Tetlow after her still clutching the bread. He just managed to lift his glass before he left the table. He gave a cheeky wink to McEnearney as he followed Celine up the stairs.

Now feeling slightly awkward at the developments, McEnearney raised his glass to Gabrielle. She responded, clinking the glasses together and took a sip of wine. McEnearney downed his wine in one go, stood up and moved behind her. He put his hands on her waist and pulled her to her feet, directing her towards the bed in the corner of the room. She giggled and sat down on the edge of the bed beside him, being careful not to spill her wine. He took the glass gently from her hand and set it down on the bedside table. She looked at him in fake surprise as he pulled her down beside him on the bed.

Seconds later, the noise of a car engine outside the cottage made McEnearney sit bolt upright. He jumped off the bed in blind panic and ran to the back window, carefully pulling the net curtains aside to look out. Major Crawley was stepping out of the passenger side of a staff car, with Company Sergeant Major McCann still sitting in the driver's seat.

"Get down here now, Corporal. Creepy's here!" yelled McEnearney as he pulled Gabrielle up from the bed and ushered her towards the attic stairs. He put the wine bottle and his empty glass in the wicker basket as he passed the table, pushing it into Gabrielle's arms as he forced her up the steps. She met Tetlow on his way down, buttoning his battledress, and they wrestled past each other on the narrow staircase. Both soldiers were dressed and waiting as Crawley and McCann came in the door, springing to attention and saluting.

"Merry Christmas. We weren't expecting to see you, Sirs." said Tetlow jovially, hoping his demeanour would hide the utter panic he felt inside.

"I bet you weren't." replied McCann dryly. "Show the Company Commander around and tell him what's going on." Lance Corporal Tetlow led Major Crawley on a tour of the cottage, explaining that the French sniper team who they were meant to be guarding had been called away. McCann made his way to where the soldiers had stored their equipment, lifting their rifles and checking them for cleanliness. He noticed the bread and cheese on the table, but saying nothing immediately he made his way to where McEnearney was still standing by the bed.

"Where did the fresh food come from, lad?" he asked quietly, but with a hint of menace.

"The Jocks left it behind, Sir." replied McEnearney quickly and confidently. "It was for the sniper, but he got called away and they said we could have it."

"And did the Jocks have lipstick on?" questioned McCann calmly and assuredly.

"Don't know what you mean, Sir!" blurted out McEnearney, feeling the nerves rise in his stomach.

"The glass of wine on the bedside table has lipstick marks on it." continued McCann in the same menacing tone. McEnearney was dumbstruck, struggling to think of an answer when Major Crawley returned with Lance Corporal Tetlow.

"Everything seems in order here, Sergeant Major." chirped Crawley, pleased at the brief from Corporal Tetlow and what he had seen. "Shall we go upstairs and see where the sniper operates from, Sergeant Major?" Crawley asked McCann. Tetlow and McEnearney glanced at each other, resigned to the fact the game was up if McCann agreed.

"I don't think so, Sir." replied McCann quickly. "The sniper wouldn't be too happy with us looking through his stuff when he's not here, if you see my point, Sir."

"Fully understand." came the curt reply from Crawley. "Anyway, we better get going before it gets too dark. Other teams to visit as well." He reached into his battledress blouse pocket and took out a bar of chocolate, placing it on the kitchen table. "I rescued that from the Christmas lunch." he added, before making his way towards the door. McCann followed without a word, and Tetlow and McEnearney slumped onto the dining chairs, placing their forearms on the table and resting their foreheads on them.

"Christ, that was close." sighed Tetlow without lifting his head, and they both began to snigger. Their relief was short lived as McCann reappeared through the door. Both soldiers sprang to attention as he approached. McCann slowly circled them without saying a word, placing his face inches from theirs in turn. Neither reacted, continuing to stare straight ahead.

"He might be fucking stupid." hissed McCann, gesturing with his thumb back out the door to where the Company Commander was sitting in the car. "But I'm not." He continued to circle the now perplexed soldiers. "I knew you two bastards had women in here the second I walked in. I could smell them!" He walked around the table again before continuing. "However, in your position, I would have done exactly the same." McCann paused to let the admission sink in. "So, have your fun, and then get them out." He was gone as quickly as he came in, slamming the door behind him. Tetlow and McEnearney sat down, stunned at what had just happened. Tetlow reacted first by rubbing his hands together with a huge smile on his face.

"Let the party continue." he said happily. They looked at each other and burst out laughing.

* * *

Gabrielle and Celine had waited until it was dark before leaving, so as not to be seen. Tetlow and McEnearney watched them slowly disappear into the distance, lit by light from a full moon. Having been a bright cloudless day, the temperature plummeted when it got dark and the pair lit the stove using the charcoal as instructed. The charcoal glowed, giving out heat with very little light. In the darkness, they pulled two dining chairs close to the stove to make the most of the meagre output, staring at the glowing embers as if mesmerised by the changing intensity and colours.

They began to talk about home and what their respective families would be doing on Christmas Day. It transpired that Tetlow had been the youngest in a family of seven siblings, and described a continuous battle for everything he got when growing up; from food to clothes. He declared that he never had new clothes until he joined the army. McEnearney was seeing Tetlow in a different light, far removed from the arrogant bully he had judged him to be. With no one to show off to, he was a friendly, affable character. McEnearney began to understand why he behaved as he did, treating others as he had been treated himself as a child. As an only child himself, McEnearney had no concept of sibling rivalry and appreciated for the first time how good his childhood had been. He began to recite tales of his youth in Jersey, when Tetlow suddenly put his finger to his lips to quieten him. Both sat in silence as McEnearney wondered what had happened.

Then he heard a feint rhythmic metallic clink, too regular to be naturally occurring. Tetlow had already moved to the door when they heard German voices, followed by the sound of nailed boots on the wooden veranda. A torch beam flicked across the window and into the room through the net curtains. Tetlow pressed his back against the door and McEnearney slid silently to the floor behind the table, keeping his eyes on Tetlow. Corporal Tetlow silently signalled him to get his rifle that he had left leaning against the kitchen table. Without making a sound, McEnearney grabbed his rifle and lay on the floor, pointing his weapon at the window. There was a clunk followed by what they assumed to be a profanity, as the rim of a helmet hit the glass, the German getting too close to the window as he tried to look in. A gloved hand then rubbed the glass, squeaking in the grime in a vain attempt to get a better view inside. The light from the torch flicked across a face, blurred features suddenly visible through the dirty glass and net curtains.

McEnearney thought he was going to be sick. His heart was pounding so fast he was convinced the Germans would hear it. The torch beam then searched around the room, flicking across the furniture. Tetlow noticed his helmet and gas mask bag sitting on the table. He began to signal to McEnearney to retrieve them, but realised any movement would give them away and changed his mind. The torch beam moved steadily along the line of the table, dancing over the helmet without stopping. The torch was switched off, followed by the sound of boots approaching the door.

Tetlow suddenly realised the bolts had not been engaged after the girls had left, quickly reaching down and then up to silently slide them into place. No sooner had the bolts been engaged than the door latch moved as a German tried to open it from the outside. Tetlow went cold as the latch was operated three or four times without success. McEnearney fought against a fear he had never experienced before, feeling almost paralysed, before gathering his senses, silently cocking his rifle and disengaging the safety catch with his thumb to prepare for action. Again, the latch moved, this time accompanied by a firm thump, as a shoulder was used to try and overcome the door's resistance. McEnearney put pressure on the trigger as he was certain he would have to fire. He felt tingles in his face and his breathing increased, gripping the rifle tighter as he prepared himself. The German voices then increased in number and volume, before getting quieter as they moved away.

Corporal Tetlow slid down the door and sat on the floor. McEnearney rested his forehead on the butt of his rifle. Neither spoke for what seemed like an age as their breathing rate returned to normal.

"I think we'll sleep one at a time tonight. Two hours about." said Tetlow.

Wednesday 10 January 1940 –
Munster, Northwest Germany.

Major Helmut Reinberger was regretting the amount of beer he had drunk the night before in the Officers' Mess at his base in Munster. He had enjoyed the company of an old friend, Major Erich Hoenmanns, an experienced Great War pilot and Commandant of the nearby Loddenheide Airfield. He had complained to Hoenmanns about the prospect of a long train journey to Cologne the next day for a staff conference; Hoenmanns immediately seizing upon the excuse to fly Reinberger to Cologne, and use the opportunity to visit his wife who lived in the city.

Reinberger shivered as he watched his friend do the pre-flight inspection on the waiting Me-108, and was having serious second thoughts. His breath condensed in the cold morning air and he closed his eyes to try and ease the pain in his head. He did not relish the experience of being tossed around in the small, single engine communications plane while still suffering the effects of last night's beer; but was also doubting his own wisdom in accepting his friend's offer in the first place. He clutched the yellow leather briefcase he was carrying a bit tighter, as if to protect the contents.

The conference he was due to attend had been arranged to clarify the Army's proposals for the relief of parachutists being dropped into Belgium at the beginning of the planned invasion of the west. The documents he carried gave dates, timings, troop strengths, deployment sequences and objectives. He knew that carrying secret documents by air without specific permission was forbidden, but at this late stage he could not make alternative arrangements. Neither could he disappoint his friend who, buoyed by the prospect of seeing his wife, was happily whistling a Luftwaffe marching song as he inspected the exterior fuselage of the plane before climbing into the cockpit.

When given the sign to alight, Reinberger set the briefcase on the back seat of the aircraft as he hauled himself in beside the pilot. As a trained parachutist, he was not unfamiliar with the metallic, oily smell of an aircraft interior, which seemed even more pronounced that morning in contrast to the fresh chill breeze he had experienced while waiting outside. He reluctantly strapped himself in, and undoubtedly would have felt worse had he known that Hoenmanns had flown this type of aircraft only once before. Hoenmanns pushed a folded map onto his passenger's lap as the single engine spluttered into life, revved up and then settled back to a steady, rhythmic drone. The pilot rotated the machine on the left wheel, turning into the prevailing wind to keep the engine cool as he completed his pre-flight checks on the control surfaces. His head moved from left to right to observe the ailerons, rudder and elevator as he pushed the stick side to side and front to back. As the aircraft turned, Reinberger became aware of the darkening skies in the distance, along the route the friends were to take.

The bumps of the grass runway seemed to transfer directly into Reinberger's throbbing head as the aircraft accelerated for take-off, and he felt distinct relief as the wheels left the ground and the vibration stopped. The aircraft quickly gained height before the pilot banked to set a course south west for Cologne, one hundred miles away, a journey which should take less than an hour. Unused to map reading in a moving aircraft, Reinberger felt even worse as he tried to relate ground features to the map through the gathering clouds.

He could sense Hoenmanns forcing the machine lower and lower as the clouds turned to a solid bank of freezing fog. Soon they were flying blind and trying to calculate their position by compass bearing and airspeed. At age fifty-two, and with thirty years' flying experience behind him, Hoenmanns turned west to locate the Rhine, and once orientated again, proposed to follow the river south towards Cologne. Reinberger agreed this was the best course of action and stared through the frosted windows hoping to see the river. He rested his forehead against the cold Perspex of the canopy and the nausea reduced. He closed his eyes momentarily as he knew that Hoenmanns couldn't see him, and felt better than he had all morning despite their predicament.

Forcing his eyes open again he saw the river; shining silver in the beams of sunlight that occasionally penetrated the fog. He tapped his friend on the shoulder and pointed to the river below. Hoenmanns smiled, nodded and banked the aircraft left to follow the river south. By his time and distance calculations, the buildings now fleetingly visible below were Cologne. As he circled to get a definite landmark fix, Hoenmanns tried to trim the aircraft controls to enable slow flight and prepare for landing, but being unfamiliar with the specifics of the aircraft interior, he mistakenly moved the lever cutting the fuel supply. The engine spluttered and stopped. His years of experience took over, and as the aircraft plummeted towards the ground with the extra weight of iced up wings, Hoenmanns instantly selected a possible emergency landing site and steered the stricken machine towards it as best he could.

Reinberger was at first unaware what was happening. It was the silence created by the stalling of the engine that alerted him to something being wrong. He turned to look at Hoenmanns who by then was already fighting with the controls to reduce the rate of descent of the aircraft. His mouth opened to ask a question, but no sound came out as he realised that he was about to experience a crash landing. Crossing his arms in front of his face he rested his head against the instrument panel and lifted his feet off the aircraft floor. He tried to follow his parachute training and fought against the natural reaction to stiffen his body for impact. When it came, he felt as if an enormous unseen force had tried to push him through the floor of the aircraft. As his body recoiled upwards after the impact, he was immediately flung forwards against the instrument panel as the aircraft stopped suddenly, his forearms absorbing the blow.

The noise of the impact had been tremendous, but now there was almost complete silence. Reinberger became aware of the feint whirring sound of the aircraft instruments powering down as the battery died. Almost scared to move, he slowly lifted his head and visually checked he was still in one piece. Hoenmanns had managed to land the aircraft on its wheels an instant before it struck trees, the impact of which had pulled both wings away from the fuselage. He was almost stung into action as his head cleared. He hammered with the flat palm of his hand on the cockpit canopy release and slid it back. He quickly released his harness, leaned to the side and swung his legs out of the cockpit. There was no wing as he expected to break his fall and he winded himself further by landing flat on his back on the grass. He heard a dull thump and a moan of pain as Hoenmanns also fell the full height of the airframe to the ground. The impact had completely detached the engine from the aircraft and both men met in the space where it once was. They embraced carefully and each assured the other he was uninjured. The plane had come down in farmland, and they noticed a building nearby across the open field in which Hoenmanns had tried to land. As they started to move towards it, a man came running across the field, dressed in the clothes expected of a farm labourer.

Engelbert Lambrichts had heard the aircraft circling as the pilot tried to orientate himself. The sound of aircraft was not unusual in this area, and he had paid little attention until the engine had suddenly cut out. He had then observed the machine attempt to land, and heard the crash as the trees stopped the forward momentum. As he approached the site of the crash, he noticed the two officers coming towards him and slowed his run to a walk. He also noticed the swastika painted on the tail of the smashed machine. As they met, Hoenmanns asked in German where they were. Lambrichts stamped his foot on the ground and replied they were in Belgium. He pointed to the south and said "Vucht". Hoenmanns was familiar with the border area and instantly knew what had happened. He had been following the line of the river Meuse, not the Rhine as he believed, and had crossed through Dutch airspace into Belgium. The buildings he had seen were in fact the town of Vucht, not Cologne. He turned to Reinberger, his face ashen, and told him they had landed in Belgium.

Reinberger felt he was about to feint. His mind would not function. He could not even reply. A sense of terror gripped his whole body. For what seemed an age, but in reality, was only seconds, he felt neutralised; unable to think or act. He grabbed Hoenmanns' arm and told him to go to the farmhouse with their new companion where he would catch him up; before turning and running back to the crashed aircraft. Hoenmanns did as he was asked and putting him arm across Lambrichts' shoulders, gently led him towards the farmhouse and away from the crash site.

Reinberger hauled himself back into the cockpit of the destroyed aircraft and kneeling on the front seat, looked on the back seat where he had left his briefcase. It was gone. He felt panic gripping him again, but caught sight of the yellow leather case underneath the seat he was kneeling on, having been tossed forward as the aircraft hit the trees. He reached down, grabbed it and released the catch on the flap. Pulling out the documents, he placed them on the pilot's seat and reached into his trouser pocket for his cigarette lighter. He didn't smoke himself but kept a lighter for utility purposes. He flicked open the lid and spun the wheel with him thumb. It sparked but did not light. He tried again. And again. Nothing. One more attempt failed before he threw it as far as he could across the field in sheer frustration.

Jumping to the ground, he raced after Hoenmanns shouting on him to stop. Also being a non-smoker, Hoenmanns had no cigarette lighter, and on making the sign of striking a match at Lambrichts, the farm hand understood the request and reached into his jacket pocket. He handed across a battered matchbox which Reinberger grabbed and sprinted back towards the aircraft, as Hoenmanns and Lambrichts continued towards the house.

The sound of tyres on the loose gravel of the farmhouse driveway alerted Hoenmanns to the arrival of two uniformed men on bicycles. Sergeant Frans Habets and Corporal Gerard Rubens from the Belgian Border Police had also witnessed the aircraft in distress, and noted the German identification markings as it glided to earth. Habets spoke to Lambrichts and then quickly directed Rubens towards the crash site, urging him to hasten with both his raised voice and arm gestures. Rubens set off at a jogging pace in the direction of the crashed aircraft. Habets took his pistol from the holster on his belt and by waving the weapon, indicated his wish that Hoenmanns should continue towards the house. He pushed him in the lower back as he passed to emphasise who was now in control of the situation.

Reinberger had heard the raised voice of Habets, and seeing the jogging shape of Rubens setting off in his direction, he grabbed the documents from the seat and jumped out of the aircraft again, careful to keep the fuselage of the machine between himself and the approaching border guard. Crouching as low as possible he ran down a hedge line taking him in the opposite direction to the approaching danger. He slid to a halt behind a thick section of the vegetation and backed himself into the foliage for cover. Fighting to control his gasping breaths, he slid open the matchbox he had received from Lambrichts to see only a single match inside. He cursed inwardly realising he had only one chance to destroy the documents. Shielding the box and the match from the wind with his body as best he could, he pulled the match head across the striking surface.

Rubens arrived at the crash site. He had drawn his pistol and held the weapon in front of him as he silently crept his way around the wreckage. His hand shook violently, and he subconsciously held his breath. He had fired his pistol when being trained on the weapon, but had never before drawn it in anger let alone fired it at another person. He called out gently as if expecting to receive a reply from the German who he knew was somewhere close. He suddenly thought his quarry might also be armed, and cursed himself for his stupidity in giving away his presence. Having completely circled the wreckage, he reached up with his left hand and grasped the canopy ledge. With the wing gone, his boots made a scraping noise as he tried to gain leverage on the fuselage to lift himself up, his pistol and head appearing simultaneously at the canopy opening as he heaved with his left arm. The cockpit was empty apart from the open yellow briefcase and the discarded map. He collected both and eased himself back to the ground.

The phosphorus ignited first time and Reinberger held the match at an angle to allow the flame to take hold. He lifted a single sheet from the document pile and presented the corner to the flame. As the paper darkened and then burned, he placed it on the ground and held more single sheets in each hand above the strengthening flame. One by one they were consumed.

His slowly building sense of relief was shattered as a boot slammed down into the burning papers. Rubens had seen a wisp of smoke coming from the hedge line and managed to approach unnoticed as Reinberger was engrossed in his task. Reinberger fell backwards in shock and scurried away on his hands and knees for a few seconds before rising to his feet and sprinting off. Rubens was taken unawares at the German's reaction, but as he regained his composure, he raised his pistol and took aim at the fleeing officer. Closing his eyes, he snatched rather than squeezed the trigger. He opened his eyes to see the German still running. Taking a deep breath, he tried to steady his shaking hands, but although he was able to keep his eyes open, he again snatched the trigger on his second shot. Reinberger stopped and Rubens thought he had hit him; but the German raised his hands above his head, turned around and slowly began to walk back towards the somewhat relieved guard. Rubens finished stamping out the still smouldering documents as Reinberger approached.

* * *

At the border guardhouse in Meclelen-aan-de-Maas, Captain Arthur Rodrique looked at the pile of singed and blackened documents sitting on his desk. He knew they must be important as the detained officers had attempted to destroy them; and he was now waiting for members of the Belgian Intelligence Service to collect both the documents and the detainees. A Belgian soldier with a rifle and fixed bayonet stood between the seated Germans across the room from Rodrique. He had tried to communicate in what little German he knew, but the officers had shunned all his attempts to gain any information. It was just a matter of waiting until he could be rid of them both, along with the documents. He stood up and crossed to a wood burning stove behind his desk. Using a metal poker, he lifted the lid and taking split logs from a stack beside the stove, pushed more wood inside. The slightly damp logs sparked and hissed as the flames took hold.

The uncomfortable silence that pervaded the room was broken as Hoenmanns indicated that he wanted to use the toilet. Rodrique opened the office door and shouted for his colleague who was manning the reception desk, but no one came. In frustration he asked the soldier to bring Hoenmanns and moved down the corridor to indicate the location of the toilet. As the three men were in the corridor, a scream of pain was heard from the office. Rodrique pushed past Hoenmanns, who deliberately tried to impede him, to find Reinberger standing beside the stove clutching his left hand. The stove lid was raised and flames leapt from the opening where Reinberger had stuffed the captured documents that Rodrique had left lying on his desk. Rodrique pushed him aside and plunged his hand into the flames, snatching the lit papers from the fire. With his bare hands, he patted out the flames from the burning documents on the surface of the desk.

Hoenmanns, the soldier and the reception guard were now all in the office on hearing the commotion. Reinberger was bent double clutching a very badly burned left hand from opening the hot stove lid. Rodrique was also injured after his retrieval of the documents from the flames. Rodrique yelled at the reception officer to take the documents to reception and lock them in his desk. He quickly gathered them and scurried away. Addressing the two Germans, Rodrique ordered them to sit back down, but as Reinberger passed him he felt pressure on his revolver holster as the German tried to undo the flap catch and snatch the weapon. In an automatic reaction, Rodrique struck back viciously with his right elbow which caught Reinberger directly in the face, sending him spinning to the ground. As the German raised his head from the tiled floor a Belgian bayonet appeared inches from his cheek and the soldier's foot pressed into the back of his neck. He gently laid his head back down on the tiles, knowing that the documents were lost and he would face a court martial and firing squad if and when he was repatriated to Germany. Hoenmanns intervened to calm the situation as he feared Rodrique was about to shoot the prostrate Reinberger; explaining that he only wanted to kill himself and not to harm his captors.

Two hours later, the detainees and the remains of the documents were in the hands of the Belgian Security Services; the documents being translated and the information they contained communicated to Allied Headquarters. An order for general mobilisation quickly followed.

Thursday 11 January 1940 –
Lille, Northern France.

A few minutes past midnight, the lights in the barrack rooms were switched on. Officers and non-commissioned officers yelled for the soldiers to get up, get their equipment on and get outside. Bedframes were kicked to encourage those who did not react immediately. On the parade square the platoons formed in section ranks. It was pitch dark and the men stood in pouring rain. Vehicles of all types were started up and parked in lines behind the parading troops, their lights illuminating the scene. Shouted commands were drowned out by the sound of the engines.

Company Sergeant Major McCann walked calmly between the ranks, telling the men to get their rain capes on while the Platoon Sergeants called the roll to ensure everyone was present. McCann found a soldier struggling with his cape, obviously woken from a drunken sleep. He grabbed him by each side of his head and shook him violently, causing him to immediately vomit. Those on either side were splashed, and stepped aside as the soldier vomited three times in all. When he stopped, they reformed the ranks, only for him to vomit again.

"Feeling better now, son?" McCann asked.

"Yes, Sir. Sorry, Sir." came the weak reply, as the soldier wiped vomit from his chin and spat out the remains in his mouth.

"Never worry yourself, son." said McCann reassuringly. "You haven't done anything wrong."

Officers gathered around vehicle bonnets on which maps were spread, trying to illuminate them with torches. The order to load the trucks was given and the men climbed aboard. Boxes of ammunition were hurriedly thrown inside and the tailgates slammed closed. With the revving of engines and clouds of exhaust fumes, the vehicles left barracks in a long line. The single line of vehicles moved east through the dark, rain soaked and deserted streets of Lille, the continuous sound of the engines of passing vehicles and crunching of gears causing dogs to bark and bedroom curtains to twitch. The vehicles moved out of the city into the countryside, switching to side lights only as per standing orders when travelling in the dark, and at a planned point split into individual company packets; company officers now responsible for the routes taken.

The experienced soldiers in the back of the trucks tried to sleep, knowing that the chance of rest when they arrived at their destination would be unlikely. Filled with a mixture of trepidation and anxiety, the younger men could not take advantage of the opportunity. The D Company convoy left the road and travelled about a quarter of a mile along a narrow country lane with deep drainage ditches on each side. The vehicles stopped and cab doors slammed as the officers dismounted and ran forward to gather around the Company Commander's vehicle. Torches flicked back and forward in the darkness as they studied a folded-out map. After a few minutes' deliberation, Lieutenant Chadwick appeared at the door of Sergeants Preston's vehicle, gesturing for him to open the window.

"We've taken a wrong turn." he began, the rain running from the rim of his helmet onto his shoulders. "We need to go back, but the road is too narrow to turn. You'll have to reverse." Preston nodded his understanding as did the driver who had leaned across the cab to listen to the conversation. Gears crunched as the vehicles were put in reverse, the last vehicle in the convoy having to move first to create space for the others to follow. As some of the trucks were civilian vehicles taken from trade due to the shortage of transport, they were not four-wheel drive, as the purpose-built military vehicles were. The heavy rain had turned the track into a muddy slime, and the civilian vehicles could not get satisfactory traction on the slippery surface. The sleeping soldiers were ordered out to reduce the weight and told to push. They struggled to see in the dark, slipping and falling in the mud which was getting worse by the minute as the rain was now falling heavier than before.

Captain Roberts was getting frustrated and angry at the situation. He approached the Company Commander discreetly. "Sir, order the vehicles to turn their lights on so we can get this mess sorted out." he suggested.

"What about the threat of aerial attack?" Major Crawley replied sarcastically.

"There are no planes flying in this weather." Roberts responded, holding his arms out to emphasise the falling rain. "No one can see a bloody thing and we'll be stuck here all night." Crawley nodded unwillingly and Roberts ran down the line of trucks ordering the lights to be switched on and mustering the men required to get the struggling vehicles moving again. One by one the vehicles reversed back down the lane in turn until they reached the road, the now soaking wet and mud-covered soldiers climbing back in. Roberts gathered the Platoon Commanders together and using his own map, briefed them on the route to take in case they became separated. He then replaced Major Crawley in the cab of the front vehicle to lead the convoy.

The convoy slowed and flicked back to side lights only as it neared its planned rendezvous. A torch flashed in the road in front, and Captain Roberts ordered his vehicle to stop, dismounting and going forward on foot. A few minutes later he returned, directing the vehicles into a small wood at the side of the road. He ordered foliage to be cut and placed over the windows before daylight, to prevent reflection from the glass indicating their position to enemy reconnaissance flights. The men were told to remain in the vehicles while the officers went forward to meet the liaison officer and be led onto their proposed positions. Major Crawley reasserted his authority, now that the vehicle move was complete.

The liaison officer was from a reconnaissance unit that had been sent ahead to guide the arriving infantry into position. He took the officers to pre-prepared defensive positions, dug by other units of the British Expeditionary Force, as the West Staffords had done elsewhere along the line. D Company were to be the reserve company, situated behind the other three companies in the battalion who occupied the front line. Once the platoons had been assigned their specific positions, the men were called forward from the wood to occupy the trenches.

As dawn broke, the company area became visible. They were in a well-prepared defensive position, complete with underground shelters and wire obstacles in front. A fit for purpose latrine had been constructed to the rear. Major Crawley and Company Sergeant Major McCann visited each platoon, ensuring rosters were created so the men could eat, rest and get dried out after the night move. When the rain stopped, the temperature began to drop and it became bitterly cold.

The Commanding Officer and the Adjutant arrived as the last stop of a routine visit to all companies. Major Crawley showed the Commanding Officer around the position and then into the command bunker where warm tea was offered. Colonel Chambers seemed happy with the situation and Major Crawley's briefing, relaxing somewhat as they chatted over the very welcome hot drink. McCann listened as the Commanding Officer outlined the situation around the sudden deployment to the Belgian border, based on captured enemy documents which suggested an imminent German offensive.

McCann suddenly became conscious of Major Crawley sniffing loudly; his attention drawn to two streams of fluid forming below his nostrils. As Colonel Chambers continued speaking, McCann noticed Crawley's tongue running along his upper lip. Sensing that Crawley was about to lick the forming fluid streams, he tried to attract his attention by staring at him and shaking his head to dissuade the intended action. Colonel Chambers suddenly stopped speaking mid-sentence, and McCann knew what had just happened. He set his tea down and abruptly told his Adjutant it was time to be getting back to his headquarters.

Friday 12 January 1940 –
France / Belgium Border.

The temperature had dropped below freezing overnight, the men waking the next morning to find their damp webbing equipment had frozen solid while they slept or stood guard during the night. The sky was clear and air sentries were assigned to watch for any approaching aircraft. Soldiers were ordered to carry their personal equipment for any movement around the position, including visits to the latrines. As the sun came up, tea was brewed, the hot metal mugs being appreciated as much for warming cold hands as for the liquid they held. Sergeant Major McCann made his way around the platoons to check on the men. He made a point of sitting with Kyle and sharing a mug of tea. McCann produced some chocolate from his equipment and the two chatted together for a while as they shared the snack.

"Any news from your mother, son?" McCann asked.

"Yes, Sir. She writes to me every week." replied Kyle. "She's well, but understandably worried about me."

"And I trust you write back every week to reassure her?" McCann replied with a grin, knowing that was probably not the case.

"Maybe not every week, but I write when I can." answered Kyle honestly.

"Good lad." replied McCann with a nod of his head. He moved closer and lowered his voice so no one else would hear. "If you need anything, you come to me. Alright?"

"Yes, Sir. Thank you, Sir." answered Kyle appreciatively. McCann patted him on the shoulder as he got up to leave.

* * *

Major Crawley had done his rounds of the position and had spoken with all three of his Platoon Commanders to appraise them of the latest situation. He felt the need to visit the latrine, and in compliance with his own orders, put on his equipment before making his way to the rear. The latrine had been situated on the edge of the wood where the vehicles had been parked, a hessian screen erected around a deep water filled pit with a six-foot-long wooden plank suspended across the hole. Newspaper had been cut into squares and hung from a wire hook at the entrance. Crawley pulled two pieces off as he passed.

Corporal Thomas and McCafferty were there already, their equipment and weapons stacked neatly in front of them. They sat at opposite ends of the plank, leaving Crawley with the only available option to sit between them. No one spoke, and tried to avoid eye contact with each other. Major Crawley unbuckled his equipment and set it on the ground in front of him, undoing his battledress blouse and dropping his trousers before positioning himself on the plank. He looked between his legs as his excrement landed on the frozen surface of the water, lying there for a few seconds before melting through the ice and disappearing.

A voice beside him said "W...wiping n...now." and he instinctively looked round at the sound, straight into the ginger haired buttocks of McCafferty, being wiped with a piece of newspaper only inches from his face. He reclined at the sight, uttering an exclamation of revulsion. McCafferty dropped the soiled paper into the pit, pulled up his trousers, picked up his equipment and left. Seeing Crawley's shock at what had just happened, Corporal Thomas explained the shared plank protocol, in that a declaration of imminent wiping allowed anyone else present to look the other way.

"Let's try again, Sir." said Thomas. "Wiping now." As he stood up, Crawley had learnt his lesson and turned his head away.

* * *

At mid-afternoon, orders were received that the prospect of a German offensive had receded, the deployment was over, and all troops were to return to barracks. All along the French / Belgian border, deployed units packed up and mounted their vehicles for the journey back. Company Sergeant Major McCann had the Platoon Sergeants confirm that all D Company personnel were present before any vehicles moved. In the back of the trucks, the damp, cold and exhausted troops were soon asleep.

Wednesday 7 February 1940 –
North Atlantic Ocean.

Captain Heinrich Pau of the Altmark had noted the phases of the moon rising and setting every day for a month, and then related these to the speed of his ship. If he was to make it back to Germany, what he regarded as dangerous areas close to submarine and air patrol lanes, allied island bases and convoy routes, would have to be passed during the early February new moon period. He travelled at twelve knots during daylight hours, allowing his lookouts to scan the horizon and giving him time to react to anything he felt was suspicious, increasing to twenty-three knots at night under the cover of darkness. His radio operators listened on a continuous watch, clearly picking up Morse signals from ships in the vicinity. Although they did not understand the content of the signals, the Altmark's officers were able to calculate the position of the ships from these transmissions, and set a zig-zag course between them.

On entering what he knew were the Atlantic shipping lanes, and after a sleepless night prowling the bridge, Captain Dau was preparing for a nap on the couch in his cabin when the sudden buzz of the telephone made him jump. In less than a minute he was on the bridge, the lookout having reported a sighting. Dau squinted through his binoculars, observing a ship with two masts, a funnel, and an imposing superstructure. He immediately ordered the Altmark into a stern-to-stern position, in effect hiding her silhouette from the unknown vessel should she be observed, and thus reducing the chance of a positive identification. The radio operators held their breath and clasped their hands over their headphones, pressing them tightly against their ears. They strained their senses against the vibrating hum of the ship's engines to hear any messages that the unidentified vessel might send, possibly indicating that they had been sighted. They heard nothing, and once out of sight of the unidentified ship, the Altmark returned to her course heading, North-North-West. Before the day had passed, they would have sighted six ships, and repeated the stern-to-stern procedure six times.

Sunday 11 February 1940 – Summa, Mannerheim Line, Finland.

The platoon defences at the Muolaa Church, were the furthest forward Finnish positions on the Summa sector of the Mannerheim Line. The command bunker had been established near the protective stone walls of the church cemetery, the unfortunate drawback of such a location being that an exposed coffin offered an obstacle that had to be crawled over to enter the dugout. Prior to an assault, Russian Engineers had rigged chain link charges along the belt of anti-tank rocks that the Finns had dug in prior to the invasion, the detonation of which would create gaps for the armour. Immediately after the explosion, a four-hour bombardment reduced the churchyard to a smouldering ruin, scattering disturbed bones and partly decomposed remains across the pitted and blackened surface. As the concussion caused by the exploding shells began to subside, the unmistakeable sound of grinding tank tracks took its place. Platoon Commander Kuusala moved among the dugouts to reassure his men. He had always found the sound of tanks more frightening than the sight of tanks, as the sound gave no indication of number or direction of attack. When the tanks appeared, at least the threat was tangible. He knew the men would feel the same as he did, and calculated that his physical presence among them at this specific time would have a reassuring effect.

For two months now the Russian tactics had been the same. The tanks would advance with impunity, knowing that Finnish anti-tank weapons were restricted to satchel charges, grenade clusters or Molotov Cocktails. They would stay a safe distance back, suppressing the defenders with machine gun fire and flame throwers, whilst their own infantry pushed forward to drive the defenders out. And for two months now, the liaison between Russian armour and infantry had not been good enough for the tactics to work. As long as the Finnish defenders held their nerve, they were able to keep the Russian infantry separated from their armour, and thus deal with the different threats independently. Kuusala had briefed his men carefully, detailing off those individuals who would attack the tanks after his machine gunners had driven off the Russian infantry.

The tanks came on as usual, without interference from the defenders, stopping thirty yards away from the churchyard wall. Here, they sprayed the dugouts with their machine guns and flame throwers to cover their advancing infantry who were following three hundred yards behind. The suppression of the defensive positions was ineffectual, the area behind the tanks being swept by Finnish machine guns, which the Russian infantry could not cross. They took cover, and the attack stalled; like all previous attacks. When dusk fell, the infantry withdrew, leaving dozens of bodies lying in the snow. The Russian armour formed a protective circle for the night with their lights switched on to illuminate any potential attackers, their on-board machine guns covering interlocking arcs.

Kuusala gestured to his assault teams to move forward and leapt from his trench, disappearing into the gathering darkness. Snipers shot out the tank lights, and with their intimate knowledge of the ground in front of their own positions, the Finns crept forward slowly and silently. Flashes of light from distant artillery created fleeting illusions of movement on the pitted snowscape. Bursts of machine gun fire came from the tanks as nervous crews fired at the shadows in their bid to keep the Finns at bay. Between the bursts, the tank crews fell silent to listen for the tell-tale noises of unseen assault teams climbing on their hulls to attach grenades or satchel charges, or burying mines below their tracks. The tank commanders see-sawed their machines a few yards forwards and backwards if they suspected an attacker was near the tracks, to crush them or disturb their work. Even expertly placed, the weapons available to the Finns were unlikely to destroy a tank; but would easily disable it or set it on fire, causing it to be abandoned.

The black outlines of the tanks were clearly visible against the white backdrop of snow as Kuusala crawled closer. His breath condensed in the night air and the undisturbed snow squeaked gently in protest beneath the weight of his forearms as he pulled himself forward through it. Lying perfectly still as the artillery flashes or flares lit the landscape, he took the chance to move rapidly when darkness returned, while any observers' eyes readjusted to the dark. He had left his rifle behind in the dugout to enable him to move more freely, carrying only a pistol on his belt for close combat. Slung across his shoulders were two satchel charges, each weighing thirty pounds, enough explosive to blow the track off a tank and damage the drive sprockets. Some of his men had simply strung grenades together which performed the same job. Others who had no access to explosives, carried only crowbars, which they used to break the track pins and cause the track to be thrown off the sprocket when the tank moved. This latter method was particularly risky due to the metallic noise it created when being performed, and the necessity to stand up in order to generate the required force to break the pins.

Kuusala approached his chosen vehicle from the side, sliding a charge off his shoulder and crouching upright with his back against the road wheels. Although not the safest direction to approach from a point of visibility, it was certainly safer if the tank commander got nervous and suddenly moved the machine backwards or forwards to crush any potential attacker. He waited for the flares to die before setting the fuse, quickly jamming the satchel charge between the road wheels and the track and sprinting to the nearest shell crater before the charge detonated. Pressing himself low into the disturbed earth and holding his hands over his ears, he braced for the explosion. It came without the ferocity he was expecting, and he untensed, only to be struck by a second explosion seconds later which violently shook his unprepared body. Lumps of ice and rock landed around him and he shielded his head with his arms to protect himself from the falling debris. The first explosion was the result of an almost simultaneous successful attack on a nearby tank by one of his platoon members. The second explosion was from his own charge.

The night was now consumed by violence as the alerted tank machine gunners shot wildly in every direction, tracer bullets bouncing from the frozen ground and arcing into the blackness of the sky before burning out. The machines lurched into life, shuffling backwards and forwards and spinning on their tracks as they tried to keep the Finnish assault groups away. In the midst of the noise, distinctive pistol shots were heard, indicating the death of a crew trying to escape from their burning machine, joyfully dispatched by their waiting attackers.

The Russian artillery now added their weight to the scene. Illumination shells descended slowly on parachutes, hoping to expose the attackers to the tank machine gunners. Ghostly shadows caused by the flickering of the falling flares danced across the snow-covered, shell pocked earth. More and more illumination shells began to fall, turning the night almost into day. The tank that Kuusala had attacked attempted to move forward, running off the broken track and imbedding the road wheels into the earth. The track on the undamaged side spun helplessly, churning up the frozen soil as it struggled for traction but without success. The turret moved in his direction, its machine gun firing wildly but blindly. He knew he was close enough to be in the safe space under the maximum depression of the weapon, and crawling back close to the hull of the tank before he got to his feet, he surveyed the scene in an attempt to plan his escape.

Running between shell holes, he used the temporary cover they provided to work out his next move. He jumped into an abandoned Finnish trench position and knew he was now close to his own lines. But as he raised his head to determine his next move, the ground around him began to shudder with the vibration of an oncoming tank. It was moving directly towards him at speed, obviously having seen him go to ground, and was coming with the intent of collapsing the trench around him. Machine gun bullets splashed all around the lip of the trench as the gunner attempted to keep him pinned down. The squeaking of the tracks grew louder and more threatening by the second as the machine raced towards him at top speed, when suddenly the light from the illumination flares disappeared, cut out by the hull of the tank as it stopped over the trench.

The engine revved noisily as the driver began to pivot the machine over the trench, collapsing the sides and showering Kuusala with earth and rocks. He began to furiously dig through the loose soil as it fell on him, shoving it below his body in an almost swimming-like motion to prevent himself from being buried. Involuntary yelps of terror and desperation came from his lips with each breath as he struggled to keep himself from being overwhelmed by the cascading soil. The noise of the tank engine faded as the debris covered his head; the last thing he remembered was trying to create an airspace with his arms in front of his face, and an enormous pressure on his back.

His men had watched horrified and helpless from thirty yards away, spraying the hull of the tank with small arms fire in pure desperation and pointless defiance. As the machine turned away and moved off, believing its job done, the watching soldiers scrambled forward to where Kuusala had been buried, tearing at the ground with their bare hands to free him. The hood of his snow smock appeared through the soil and he was jerked to the surface by his rescuers pulling on the fabric. The tank had broken off the attack too early to complete the job, and although disorientated and in a state of shock, Kuusala was able to assist in his own extraction from the collapsed trench. He was helped back to his own bunker where his smock was removed, and the contents of a water bottle poured over his face to wash the dirt from his eyes, nose, and mouth. Captured Russian vodka was liberally administered to settle his nerves and his gasping breaths slowly returned to a normal rhythm as the shock and fear subsided. There was no outwardly visible sign of injury as he responded positively to requests to move his arms and legs, until his shirt was removed so he could wash himself down. His back displayed a series of purple welts which matched the track pattern of a Russian T28 tank.

By midnight, the ever-present prospect of a decisive Russian breakthrough on the Mannerheim Line had materialised. Not in the expected hammer blow, but through a salient among scores of other reported salients that the counterattacking Finns simply did not have the resources to close off. It came at an elbow bend in the Mannerheim Line, north of Summa; a potential weak point that had concerned the Finnish High Command since before the invasion. The Russians had spotted this too, and having rehearsed the planned assault to improve joint infantry and armour tactics, they accepted the infantry casualties that would be necessary to create the breakthrough. The Russian tanks drove right up to the Finnish bunkers and parked across the firing ports, rendering the machine guns inside useless. Individual Russians wriggled through the firing ports of the bunkers and hand to hand combat raged inside.

The Finns were forced to abandon the bunkers to fight in the open and had simply been overrun. Finnish reserves earmarked for counterattack were sucked into hotspots as the Russians deliberately continued to attack along the whole front to create these exact circumstances. A counterattack to close the salient could not be mounted until Tuesday 13 February; but lacked the manpower to be effective. The Russians had broken the Mannerheim Line.

Sunday 11 February 1940 –
Lille, Northern France.

The shouts to get out of bed from non-commissioned officers in the early hours of the morning were met with an understandable verbal response from the soldiers. As they formed into platoon groups on the parade square their mood was no better, but their level of preparedness was increasing each time the exercise was conducted. They loaded their equipment and extra ammunition into the trucks quickly and efficiently, the vehicles getting underway as soon as a route to their designated rendezvous had been agreed. Once the required distance had been driven and the convoys had proven they could stay together, they were allowed to return to barracks, where the equipment was unloaded again.

In response to the apparent difficulties of the deployment over 10 / 11 January, General Montgomery had ordered that frequent exercises were to be conducted at different times of the day and night. These exercises specifically practiced rapid deployments and vehicle convoy drills over similar driving distances that could be expected to be covered if and when a genuine deployment was required. To ease the difficulty of travelling in convoy at night, Montgomery had ordered illumination aids to be fitted on the vehicles, so tactical movement could be conducted efficiently in darkness. The rear axles of the trucks had been painted white, and were lit by lamps positioned under the body of the vehicles, meaning they could be seen in the dark; but only from directly behind.

Tuesday 13 February 1940 –
North Sea.

It was 5 a.m. and Captain Dau was hunched over his charts with a protractor in his hand, a feint map light being the sole illumination on the otherwise pitch-black bridge. Smoke rose from a smouldering cigarette lying in an ash tray and spiralled through the beam of light before disappearing into the darkness. He called to his first officer, Leutnant Paulsen.

"We are entering Norwegian territorial waters." he declared. The two officers looked at each other. No words were necessary; their beaming smiles conveying what verbal communication could not adequately express. Dau looked eastwards, and as the sun gently rose, the outline of the Norwegian coast was unmistakable. He had steered his vessel between Iceland and the Faroe Islands and then across the North Sea, remaining undetected by the Royal Navy. But he knew there was not the slightest chance the Altmark would escape detection as she hugged the Norwegian coastline on the last leg of the journey home. "We are now protected by Norwegian neutrality." he murmured, as if to reassure himself.

Wednesday 14 February 1940 –
Norwegian Territorial Waters.

As the Norwegian torpedo boat moved alongside, Captain Dau could clearly see the name "Trygg" on the hull. He had once again been woken from an exhausted sleep and was in no mood to be civil to the unwelcome visitors. Trygg hoisted a flag ordering the Altmark to stop, at the same time sounding the letter "K" on her siren, the internationally recognised audible signal with the same meaning. As the Altmark slowed, a Norwegian officer was already in the Trygg's launch on his way to board her.

He was greeted by Dau on the bridge, the German forcing himself into pleasantries as he complied with the Norwegian's request to inspect his ship. Dau quickly insisted that the Altmark was an unarmed tanker, and after a cursory look around the navigation cabin, the Norwegian made an entry in the Altmark's log to the effect that the ship had been searched. The Norwegian saluted as he departed the Altmark, Dau returning his compliment with a forced smile. Hardly had the Norwegian stepped off the ladder, when the Altmark was moving again, heading towards Alesund where Dau had arranged to pick up pilots to assist in coastal navigation. The Trygg followed in her wake, much to the annoyance of Dau.

Thursday 15 February 1940 – Norwegian Territorial Waters.

As Altmark approached Alesund, Dau ordered the vessel to slow as a rowing boat drew alongside. His mood suddenly darkened as it became clear the expected coastal pilots were accompanied by a Norwegian Naval Officer. Immediately he set foot on the deck, and without exchange of even forced pleasantries, the Norwegian officer demanded information on the Altmark's proposed course, cargo, and any weaponry on board. Despite Dau's repeated protests that the ship had already been visited and details given, the Norwegian continued to question him as he was shown around the deck, bridge, and the captain's cabin. Leaving the Norwegian in his cabin momentarily, Dau quickly ordered that all the ship's cargo winches be started immediately. He had heard distinct rumblings from below decks, and assuming the British prisoners were trying to attract attention, had ordered the starting of the winches to drown out the noise.

Below decks, chaos was being created, as believing neutral vessels were nearby, the prisoners were hammering anything metal with their hands and feet, beating lavatory drums with sticks, rattling mess tins and mugs and shouting as loud as their weakened physical condition would allow. With every cargo winch turning, Dau returned to his Norwegian guest who was by now visibly impatient to leave. Murmuring his apologies at the delay, Dau escorted the Norwegian officer to his waiting boat, remaining long enough to see him pull away back towards the Trygg.

"Put the hoses on them. Turn out the lights down there." shouted Dau as soon as he was content that the inspectors were out of earshot. Hoses were immediately inserted into the hatches, and in the darkness, water gushed into the prisoners' quarters. The men were drenched, and the lavatory drums flooded over, human waste washing across the surface of the decks. It was 6 p.m. before the Altmark was underway again with the prisoners subdued and in misery. The hatch was pulled back and a notice, signed by Captain Dau, was handed down by the German guards. It stated that due to the behaviour exhibited during the day, normal meals would be withheld tomorrow, being replaced by bread and water only.

As the prisoners huddled together to keep warm in soaked clothing amid the stench of the overflowing lavatory drums, they felt they had been forgotten. But, unknown to them, having been spotted and positively identified as the Altmark by an observer in the approaches to Bergen, the information was in the British Embassy in Oslo within thirty minutes. A coded signal flashed between the Naval Attaché and the Admiralty, *"Altmark steaming two miles off Norwegian coast north of Bergen."*

Far from forgotten, the prisoners in the Altmark were very much in the thoughts of Captain Philip Vain on-board the destroyer HMS Cossack as his vessel made top speed towards the Altmark's estimated position; his orders to find her, board her and liberate the prisoners.

Thursday 15 February 1940 –
Karelian Isthmus, Finland.

At 4 p.m. Mannerheim ordered the abandonment of the front-line defences and a general retirement to the Intermediate Line; in itself a difficult decision to take, but utterly transformational to diplomatic efforts which had crystallised that very same day. Embarrassed by their inactivity around the German invasion of Poland, both Britain and France had been working on a plan to assist Finland. The proposed physical aid to Finland was in fact a secondary aim, the primary aim being the positioning of Allied troops in strategic ports and key locations in Norway and Sweden to disrupt the supply of iron ore to Germany.

Through his own diplomatic sources, Stalin was aware of the Allied plan, yet he was in no rush to conclude a compromise. His initial demands for the ceding of Finnish territory would have to be met, with added interest for his troubles; and he needed a military victory, either in reality or impression, to maintain the credibility of his armed forces.

The Finns themselves had not remained inactive diplomatically, with discussions having been underway since 10 January. Also aware of the Allied plan, the Finns had finally agreed among themselves to offer a swathe of the Karelian Isthmus, albeit a sparsely inhabited semi-wilderness, and the island of Jussaro, in return for financial compensation from Russia and an end to the conflict. The Finns were in effect buying time for political machinations as they withdrew to the Intermediate Line. With sparse concrete bunkers joined with scratched out trenches and barbed wire entanglements, the position was by no means as impressive as the First Line had been. Access to road junctions heading west were still relatively open, around which the Finns sited their remaining guns.

On the afternoon of 18 February, Russian armour reached the Intermediate Line and immediately launched massive attacks. In their desire to maintain the momentum of the last few days, they reverted to the tactics used in December; the tanks rushing ahead of their infantry, and suffering the same extreme casualties they had endured before.

Friday 16 February 1940 –
North Riding of Yorkshire, England.

At 7:30 a.m. the crews of "K" King and "F" Freddy, two Hudson coastal reconnaissance aircraft, took their seats in the front row of the briefing room at RAF Thornaby. The wall behind the stage where the Intelligence Officer stood held a map of most of Northern Europe, which had been marked out with red tape to show flight paths and boxed off areas of interest between Denmark and Norway. As the crews listened intently, the Intelligence Officer informed them they would be joining the search for the Altmark. A buzz of chatter briefly passed between the crews before their attention returned to the stage. The Intelligence Officer continued with the briefing. Their mission was to locate the tanker and record her position, direction, and speed.

"The ship must on no account be attacked." the briefing officer was at pains to make clear. The puzzled look on the aircraft crews' faces led him to elaborate. "We believe she is carrying hundreds of British seamen prisoners." he explained. "Note her exact position and report in." He held up a photograph of a hand drawn sketch of the vessel, clearly capturing her bold and distinctive outline, giving one to each crew to take away.

The weather was bright but cold, a perfect day for the type of mission they had been assigned. Pilot Officer McNeill in "K" King pushed the throttles forward and the aircraft jerked as he released the brakes. As the machine accelerated, the rhythmic noise of the tyres on the joints in the runway blended into a constant vibration through the airframe, instantly disappearing as McNeill pulled back on the column and the wheels left the surface of the concrete. At 8:25 a.m. they crossed the English coastline, and over a stunningly blue sea, set a course for Denmark.

Friday 16 February 1940 –
Norwegian Territorial Waters.

By 8 a.m. Altmark had covered a distance of one hundred miles during an uneventful night. As Captain Dau returned to the bridge after a few hours' sleep, the Norwegian pilots were changing over. Leutnant Paulsen formally reported the ship's position to the oncoming captain as just north of Stavanger. In another hundred miles, with the treacherous shallows and hidden rocks of the Norwegian coastal waters behind him, he could dispense with the need for pilots and their accompanying Norwegian Navy vessel, and make a dash for home across the deep waters of the Skagerrak.

The Danish coast was dotted with vessels which the Hudson reconnaissance aircraft dived low to inspect, before separating to cover a larger area as they expanded their search out to sea. At 12.55 pm, Pilot Officer McNeill saw a dark shape about fifteen miles north of his course. Easing the aircraft onto the new bearing, the dark shape formed into that of a ship as he got closer. She was heading south, steaming at a speed of about eight knots, evidently a large tanker. McNeill alerted "F" Freddy and his own crew as he descended to get a better look. He swept low in a wide arc to get a broadside view and let his co-pilot compare the ship's profile against the photograph provided by the Intelligence Officer at Thornaby. He flew just above the waves at deck level, and dipping under the bow saw the name clearly displayed on the hull – Altmark. The positive identification, position and heading were transmitted as McNeill turned for home.

The message was received on-board HMS Cossack, Captain Vain reacting instantly to direct the ships in his flotilla to the target. Destroyers Intrepid and Ivanhoe were nearest, and ordered to intercept at once. The cruiser Arethusa and Cossack herself made best speed towards the reported position. On Altmark, Captain Dau had watched the aircraft swoop around him with increasing agitation and powerless frustration, trying to keep it in his binoculars as it dived and turned away. He watched until it was out of sight, then switched his attention to the western horizon, where he knew the next threat would come from. An hour later at 2:45 p.m. simultaneous shouts from both Dau and the lookout alerted the waiting officers to the silhouettes of three vessels approaching from the southwest.

"English Warships." Dau hissed through his teeth without taking the binoculars from his eyes; his experience telling him one was a cruiser. Arethusa assumed a parallel course with Altmark, overtly threatening in the sheer majesty of her sleek lines and shallow bow despite a camouflage pattern designed to disrupt her outline. She flashed a repeated signal to "Steer West." Dau did not react. He paused for a few seconds before giving the order to continue on the same course at half speed.

"They will not dare touch us in neutral waters." retorted Dau, as if to convince himself, as much as the officers crowded around him. The standoff continued for a further thirty minutes, Dau mesmerised by the movements of the British ships as Intrepid and Ivanhoe moved closer and closer. On board HMS Intrepid, Commander Gordon had a thirty strong boarding party standing by on the deck, having raised signal flags ordering the Altmark to "Heave to." Dau again ignored the signals and continued on his course until a flash from Intrepid's four-inch gun preceded the whistle from a warning shot as it flashed past the Altmark, impacting on the Norwegian shoreline. The sound echoed off the mountains and returned to be heard several times until the energy dissipated. It was quickly followed by another shell, which this time impacted in the sea on Dau's intended course heading. It was Gordon's intent to place Intrepid between Altmark and the coast, in a position where she could force Altmark out to sea and into international waters.

His actions by firing within Norwegian territorial waters had violated Norwegian neutrality, and the Norwegian gunboat Skarv who had been shadowing the Altmark approached the British vessel, her captain shouting his protests through a megaphone. Gordon ignored the Norwegian's protests, continuing on his course to get between Altmark and the coast. The captain of the Skarv resolutely held his ground between the antagonists, only a few metres now separating all three vessels. In a mix of despair and fear for the safety of his ship, Dau turned to port, making for the entrance to Jossing

Fjord, ordering full speed from the powerful engines to maintain his momentum as the vessel entered the frozen waters of the inlet. The ice cracked and splintered as the Altmark's bow cut through, causing a juddering vibration along the full length of the vessel, unbalancing the sailors on deck and throwing the prisoners below into heaps of struggling limbs. Dau cursed the Royal Navy for attacking him in neutral waters, and then cursed himself for believing they would not. He was now trapped; the towering mountains on each side of the fjord seeming to lean in towards him, increasing his feelings of incarceration. Following behind, he saw the Skarv tracking his course through the broken ice, the surface of the dark green water filled with floating, glistening chippings. Shortly, the Skarv was joined by another Norwegian vessel, the Kjell; both boats subsequently lying side by side in silent protection.

Through the narrow neck of the fjord, Dau could see the two British destroyers that had tried to intercept him, but he was not aware that Cossack had now joined the force. Using the delay created by the protective stance of the Norwegian vessels, Dau signalled the German Legation in Oslo, giving an outline of the situation and requesting instructions. Almost simultaneously, Captain Vain was signalling the Admiralty outlining his position and requesting the same; the message reaching Churchill in his role as First Lord. This was more than a purely naval matter, and not wanting to risk a diplomatic incident, Churchill immediately telephoned Lord Halifax, the Foreign Secretary, to seek his advice. Despite the risk of antagonising the Norwegians or worse still, an armed encounter with the Norwegian vessels in Jossing Fjord, the order was given for Vain to board the Altmark and liberate the prisoners, only firing on the Norwegians in response to being fired upon first.

At 10 p.m. Cossack entered Jossing Fjord. To the men of the boarding party lined on the deck, the full moon revealed a fairy-tale landscape. The windows of the isolated houses around the fjord were lit up with a warm orange glow, contrasting against the glistening snowfield. Fir trees sparkled with ice crystals. The shrill voice of the lookout warning of pack ice to starboard brought them back to reality as the ice crunched against the hull. Cossack's searchlight probed ahead, like a long finger feeling its way through the inlet. Lying still, Altmark was a black silhouette against a white mountain backdrop and a leaden grey sky; almost sinister in its silence.

It was just past 11 o'clock when Captain Dau gave the order to start engines. The entire crew of the Altmark had been "stood to" when Cossack's searchlight had drawn attention to her presence. The ice which held her gently that afternoon had thickened in the cold of the evening, a distinct crack signalling that she had pulled clear from its grip. Dau took his ship further into the fjord, positioning her so that he could get a better view of the opening to the sea. He directed his own searchlight onto the advancing Cossack, lighting up her bows as she cut through the water towards the Altmark, before switching to the bridge in an attempt to blind the officers directing the action. Realising what was happening, the boarding party, whose vision was unimpaired, shouted situational updates from the deck. Despite the ship's crew being already stood to, the Altmark's siren sounded an alarm. Dau waited until he felt the Cossack was committed to her course before ordering full speed astern to ram the approaching destroyer. Using the shouted updates from the deck, Vain changed course at the last second, deflecting the intended blow from the Altmark; the two vessels glancing off each other with a screech and groan of protesting steel before separating again.

The boarding party, who had removed the deck rails on the starboard side to facilitate their planned action, rushed to the port side where the Altmark now lay four feet away. Lieutenant Commander Bradwell Turner leapt outwards and upwards, grasping the Altmark's rail, steadying himself as he drew his revolver from its webbing holster. He looked back, encouraging his men to follow and in an instant, Lieutenant CM Parker was beside him. Tossed rifles began landing on the Altmark's deck as the ratings threw their weapons across before jumping the slowly increasing gap. As the vessels began to drift apart, Petty Officer Atkins' leap was not high enough to reach the top rail, leaving him dangling helpless from the bottom rail. Looking down at the dark green foaming water below, he let out a terrified yell, his feet thrashing thin air as he struggled to find a foothold on the Altmark's hull. His cries alerted Lieutenant Commander Turner who grabbed him by the collar, heaving him upwards to land in a crumpled heap on the deck. The ships had now moved too far apart for any other boarders to make the leap, the handful who had already boarded temporarily left isolated. Captain Vain expertly manoeuvred Cossack to bring her alongside again, the vessels crunching together for a second time. Boarding Party reinforcements poured across the gap as the ships engaged in an awkward embrace.

From the Altmark's bridge, Captain Dau could hear shouts in both German and English, quickly followed by the sight of three men in British steel helmets and carrying rifles running across the catwalks on the stern deck. As Cossack came alongside again, he saw more men jump from the destroyer and fix bayonets once safely on the Altmark's deck. Shots rang out from two German sailors carrying rifles, only to be answered by a hail of bullets from the boarders. The echoes returned from the surrounding mountains, to find the wounded Germans sprawled on the deck. Cossack's searchlight whipped back and forth across the Altmark's deck, illuminating groups of men engaged in hand-to-hand scuffles, and then plunging them into darkness again as it swept away.

Able Seaman James Harper, an electrician on Cossack, had jumped with the second boarding party. His specific task, allocated by Turner, was to find the main power switch and prevent the crew of Altmark plunging the ship into darkness. As he pushed his way along the port catwalk, striking out in the darkness at indistinguishable friend and foe alike to clear his path, shots cracked past him through the air. He returned fire with his revolver in the direction of the incoming rounds. Locating a hatch, he descended the ladder, only to find himself in the steering compartment and forced to retrace his steps. A German rushed him as he re-emerged, Harper calmly levelling his revolver at the oncoming enemy. A sickening click told him the chamber was empty, but in a single movement he flicked the weapon over, grabbed the barrel and struck the German across the head with the butt just as their bodies met. Both men fell to the deck as the weight of the lunging German landed on Harper. They lay entwined and motionless for a few seconds before Harper gathered his wits, pushing the now unconscious German away to allow himself to stand up. The wooden grips from his revolver lay in pieces beside him, smashed by the intensity of the blow on the German's skull. Slightly stunned from his physical encounter, Harper shook his head to refocus. The sounds of the battle still raged around him, three of his fellow sailors both taking and returning fire crouched behind the steel superstructure close by. Paying no attention to the bullets splintering the deck around his feet, he set off again to find the main power switch.

Bradwell Turner had kept the most important task for himself; to reach and capture the Altmark's bridge; detailing off a small party to accompany him under the command of Petty Officer Barnes. After hauling Atkins on deck, he realised that he could not wait for further reinforcements and would have to move with the men he had, running along the catwalk towards the superstructure with Barnes and his party close behind. They reached a steel door fastened with eight metal clips, Turner and Barnes releasing them with the butts of their weapons. As the door swung open, Barnes noticed a German taking aim at them, leaning over the rail from the wing of the bridge above. Thrusting his bayonet with all his might through the walkway grill towards the enemy sailor, he heard a scream of pain and the German disappeared. Turner was already through the door and running down an internal accommodation corridor towards a ladder he hoped would take him to the bridge. As Barnes followed, the door closed behind him, and the commotion outside generated by the arrival of the second wave of boarders was replaced by the low vibrating hum of the Altmark's engines.

The corridor had a low ceiling and was lit by dim bulkhead lights. As Barnes raced after Turner, a German sailor stepped from a cabin door with a pistol in his hand, the men almost bumping into each other in mutual surprise. Barnes reacted first, pushing his bayonet against the German's throat, causing him to drop his pistol which clattered to the floor. Gesturing with his bayonet, and determined to keep his prisoner in shock, Barnes shouted at the top of his voice for the German to move down the corridor and stand in the corner. Doors opened all along the corridor to investigate the shouting, and as German faces appeared, Barnes shouted for them to come out with their hands up, herding them along until twelve prisoners now stood together.

As Turner started to climb the steel ladder to the bridge, he was caught in two minds, whether to approach quietly and possibly take those on the bridge by surprise, or to burst in, giving them little time to react. His first steps on the ladder negated any choice, the scraping of his boots on the rungs removing the chance of a stealthy approach. He climbed as quickly as his legs would allow. Six men stared at him as he burst onto the bridge, a mixture of shock and fear displayed on their open-mouthed faces. A very brief period of uneasy silence followed, broken when Turner ordered them to raise their hands, backing up the verbal command with a gesture of his revolver. He heard steps on the ladder, the appearance of Sub-Lieutenant Craven and a Naval Rating easing his sudden nervousness. Craven was a Naval Volunteer Reserve Officer who was Paymaster on Cossack. He spoke several Scandinavian languages and had been ordered to take part in the boarding operation by Captain Vain for this very reason. He had come aboard as part of the second wave, jumping onto Altmark's deck from a torpedo davit moments before it was crushed as the vessels collided the second time. Knowing that Norwegian pilots could be aboard, Craven asked any Norwegian officers to step aside. No one moved.

Content now that he would not cause a diplomatic incident, Turner roughly pushed the prisoners aside to access the telegraph, moving the pointer to stop. Taking stock of the captured officers, Turner was drawn to the eldest, trying to look dignified and thrusting out his chin. On questioning by Craven, Dau revealed himself as the captain, and complained it was an outrage that a ship's captain was required to keep his hands up. Craven let him rest his hands on his head as a concession to his age and position. A sudden bump caused all those standing on the bridge to stagger before regaining their balance. The lights flickered then returned to continuous illumination. Two further less violent bumps quickly followed. Altmark had run aground and settled on the rocks at the edge of the fjord.

The sound of Altmark grounding was much louder and infinitely more worrying to the prisoners in the holds. The men crowded around the ladders leading to the hatch, positioning themselves for the best chance of escape should their worst nightmare be realised, and the hull be breached. They could hear muffled voices from the deck, but the sound was confused and chaotic. Silence fell as they heard the distinctive sound of the hatch being opened, the rush of cold fresh air carrying the sound of shouting and the crack of gunfire into their confines. It was too dark to make out the faces that peered over the rim of the hatch, but the clear strong voice of Warrant Officer John Smith caused uproar amongst the prisoners.

"Any Englishmen down there?" A chorus of three hundred voices answered in unison with yells and cheers. "Come up then. The Navy's here." The words were repeated over and over between themselves as the prisoners hugged each other in an outpouring of relief and emotion. Ascending the ladder in a hurried but orderly fashion, they were helped through the hatch onto the deck and directed to a gangplank that had been established between Cossack and Altmark. To the ratings who helped the men out and hurried them along, the stream of prisoners seemed never-ending.

Petty Officer Barnes was still preoccupied with his prisoners when he became aware of someone standing in the doorway struggling for breath. Warrant Officer Smith was being held upright by a rating, clearly in a weakened state.

"I'm afraid I've been hit, Barnes." Smith's words were barely audible. Quickly ordering the rating to watch the prisoners, Barnes replaced him as the support for Smith who was by this time almost a dead weight. Opening his duffle coat, Barnes saw Smith's woollen jersey stained red under his right arm. Smith slumped against the bulkhead and slid down to a seated position, pulling Barnes off balance as he tried to break his fall. Stepping forward, one of the German prisoners gently pushed the rating's bayonet aside, declaring himself to be the ship's doctor and willing to help. Between them, Barnes and Doctor Tyrolt manhandled the now unconscious Smith into the doctor's cabin, laying him on the bed. Tyrolt exposed the wound, quickly identifying a severed artery. He opened his medical bag that had been in his cabin, applied a tourniquet and was bandaging the wound when the rating left on guard stuck his head round the door.

"Hurry up. We've got to get out." he yelled. Barnes shouted after him to get a stretcher, which quickly arrived complete with bearers. Ignoring Tyrolt's advice not to move him, Barnes helped load Smith on the stretcher and sent the bearers on their way back to Cossack. Returning to the prisoners, Barnes and the rating began moving them out through the door on to the deck.

On Cossack's bridge, Captain Vain watched as the released merchantmen filed across the gangplank; urging his officers to hurry them along. A loud hailer message telling the boarding party to re-join Cossack at once resounded in the stillness of the cold night air. On Altmark's bridge, Craven and his accompanying rating still kept guard over the captured officers. Although the message did not mention what to do with any prisoners, Craven shepherded the Germans down the ladder on to the deck, then marched them in single file to the fo'csle where all the Germans had been gathered. He then joined the dwindling queue at the gangplank as the last of the boarding party and merchantmen stragglers were checked on board the Cossack. The Germans looked bewildered as they did not know if they were to be taken off Altmark into captivity or left behind on their own ship.

As the searchlight swept the length of Altmark for the last time, the signal that all merchantmen and boarding party had been accounted for was shouted to Captain Vain on the bridge. On his command, the gangplank was pulled back on board and with a barely audible revving of the engines, Cossack gently moved away from Altmark, manoeuvring towards the open sea and England. It was five minutes to midnight.

They left behind seven German dead, killed in the fighting with the boarding party, drowned or shot as they tried to escape across the ice towards land, and eleven wounded, six of them seriously. The only British casualty was Warrant Officer Smith.

Tuesday 20 February 1940 –
Berlin, Germany.

When the customer bell rang on the door of the book and stationery shop, the owner looked up from his counter where he was cataloguing new publications. It was not unusual to see uniformed soldiers on the streets of Berlin at this time, but the red facings on his greatcoat lapels depicting the rank of a General Officer made the owner pay particular attention to this customer. He nodded as the officer went past, but obviously being deep in thought, the gesture was not seen and remained unacknowledged. The shop owner continued to observe the officer indirectly from his counter as the General browsed the Baedeker tourist guidebooks, and he continued watching while placing the newly catalogued books on the shelves. The General eventually returned to the counter with three guide books, purchasing them all.

Since the Altmark affair, Hitler doubted the determination of Norway to remain neutral. Britain had ignored Norway's status, and in his opinion, Norway had not responded appropriately. This had convinced him that in order to maintain the supply of Swedish iron ore through Norway, so critical to the German war effort, that an invasion of Norway was now necessary. General der Infanterie, Paul Nikolaus von Falkenhorst, had that morning been asked by Hitler to command the forces for such an invasion and to present his initial plan later that day. Von Falkenhorst knew very little about the country and not having the time under Hitler's imposed deadline to obtain military maps, had bought a Baedeker guide to assist his planning process; disguising his intentions with the purchase of several other tourist guides at the same time.

He worked in his hotel room that afternoon, and as instructed, presented his plan directly to Hitler at 5 p.m. His concept was to mount simultaneous attacks against the cities of Tromso, Narvik, Trondheim, Bergen, Stavanger, Kristiansand and Oslo; in a tri-service campaign to include the Navy, Luftwaffe and Army. Von Falkenhorst included measures to take control of key telephone and radio communication centres, and to take charge of civil administration in Oslo in order to keep the country subdued. Capturing the port of Narvik intact was also critical to the operation, as this was the facility through which the vast majority of high-grade Swedish iron ore was transported to Germany. The necessity of using airborne troops, combined with the flying distances involved, would require the use of Danish Airfields; in effect, demanding the invasion of Denmark as a precursor to the invasion of Norway. Hitler was delighted, and accepted the plan immediately. Von Falkenhorst's appointment to the role was formally announced the following day.

Wednesday 28 February 1940 –
Karelian Isthmus, Finland.

The Russians had planned an all-out offensive across the whole of the Intermediate Line, preceded as had become routine, with a massive artillery bombardment. They were not aware that their shells were falling on mostly empty trenches, Mannerheim having given orders the previous night for the withdrawal to the Third Line. Only specially selected delaying positions remained manned by the Finns, mostly on road junctions and likely tank access routes. At one such position, the defenders waited for the armour and infantry advance after the bombardment lifted, but nothing came.

A patrol was dispatched to confirm the reason for the delayed assault, subsequently finding hundreds of dead Russians in a two-acre concentration area, killed by their own bombardment which had fallen short. Recovered documents showed they had just arrived from Leningrad; all were clean shaven and wearing brand new uniforms. The Forward Artillery Observer, whose job it was to direct the bombardment, was found dead in a sitting position, clutching his map and a telephone receiver, killed as he was trying to redirect the fire.

Thursday 29 February 1940 –
Helsinki, Finland.

On 25 February new Russian demands had been delivered, which included the cession of all the Karelian Isthmus, the cession of the Hanko peninsula as a Russian base for thirty years, and the signing of a mutual assistance pact between Finland and Russia; clearly designed to put a land buffer between Russia and Germany in the event of future hostilities. A response deadline of 1 March was imposed. In light of the military situation and the inability of the western powers to agree and present a viable assistance plan, the Finns had no option if they wished to continue as an independent state. They would accept the terms in principle and were willing to enter immediate peace negotiations. When word of the accepted terms reached Paris, French Prime Minister Daladier immediately promised 50,000 French troops and an air fleet of one hundred bombers, being dependent of course on continued Finnish resistance.

Having been taken unawares by the French proposal, the British promised to activate their plans for an amphibious expedition to assist the Finns through neutral Norway and Sweden, for which the Norwegians and

Swedes had not given consent. The peace process was frozen as the Finns sought clarification from the western powers, only to be disillusioned when the true extent of military support that would actually reach Finland became obvious. Their only solace was the thought that the prospect of Allied intervention in the conflict would moderate the Russian negotiating position; but it had the opposite effect when negotiations began on 7 March. From a position of steadily increasing military advantage with a total of thirty divisions, 1,200 armoured vehicles and 2,000 aircraft pitted against the Third Line, the Russians increased their demands to include cession of the Rybachi Peninsula in the north of the country and a further area in the Salla district.

Wednesday 13 March 1940 –
Helsinki, Finland.

The Finnish Government met on 12 March to reach a final decision and agree the document that would give the peace delegation currently in Moscow the authority to conclude the hostilities on Russian terms. As President Kallio signed the document, he was heard to utter *"May the hand wither that is forced to sign such a document as this."* A few months later he suffered a stroke that paralyzed his right arm.

With permission given to the Finnish delegation, the treaty was concluded in the early hours of 13 March; the ceasefire to take effect at 11 a.m. Fifteen minutes before the agreed ceasefire time, the Russians opened a furious bombardment onto the defensive positions on the Third Line. Without any military necessity or reason, hundreds of Finns were killed in what was nothing more than a gesture of Stalin's vindictive rage.

Thursday 4 April 1940 –
Copenhagen, Denmark.

Using a civilian Lufthansa flight, the German Battalion Commander tasked with the impending capture of Copenhagen had flown there under the guise of a civil servant. He was able to examine the proposed landing quay in the heart of Copenhagen where his troops would be put ashore, and the defensive citadel in the north of the city that would be his objective. He was shown around the citadel by a Danish Sergeant on a tour which included the garrison quarters, the communications centre, the watch towers and the entrance gates. After sharing a beer with the Sergeant, he flew home to plan his attack.

Saturday 6 April 1940 –
Scapa Flow, Orkney Islands, Scotland.

To disrupt the supply of iron ore from Sweden to Germany through the Norwegian port of Narvik, the Allied War Cabinet directed a mine laying operation in the sea passages between Norway and Germany. The crew on one of the boom defence vessels protecting Scapa Flow, watched the departure of the battlecruiser HMS Renown, minelayer Teviot Bank and sixteen escort destroyers to conduct the operation. From the bridge of the destroyer HMS Hardy, Captain Bernard Warburton-Lee was sighted vigorously waving his cap to the crew of the boom ship. A gramophone record was being played over the ship's hailer at full volume. The sound of *"A-hunting we will go."* reached the spectators on the boom ship as they returned Warburton-Lee's wave.

Sunday 7 April 1940 –
Baltic Coast, Germany.

On 5 April the first of twenty-six merchant ships set sail from Stettin, packed with troops, horses, equipment and combat supplies. For reasons of secrecy and security, the boarding had been done at night, and the troops ordered to remain below decks. Those vessels with less far to travel set sail the following day, so that all would arrive simultaneously at their target ports, which by their planned arrival time, would already have been captured and secured by designated warship groups. Over 7 and 8 April, eleven warship groups set sail for Denmark and Norway, their strength directly related to the importance of their specific task. Sixteen vessels including three warships sailed for Oslo. Ten destroyers sailed for Narvik. By the night of 8 April, German warships sat poised all along the Norwegian coast to simultaneously attack Tromso, Narvik, Trondheim, Bergen, Stavanger, Kristiansand and Oslo, just as von Falkenhorst had planned.

PART 3
THE STRIKE NORTH

Tuesday 9 April 1940 –
Germany / Denmark Border.

On 8 April, Danish truck drivers delivering fish to Hamburg had warned of a thirty-mile-long column of German vehicles containing troops and equipment, approaching the Danish border. The reports were discounted by the Danish Government. Sightings of nearly one hundred German Navy vessels and merchant ships sailing north from German ports were also disregarded. Thus, when German forces crossed the Danish border at 4:15 a.m. on 9 April, the country was ill-prepared. Motorcycle troops led the assault, followed by armoured cars, light tanks and truck mounted infantry. Marching infantry units with horse drawn artillery followed some distance behind.

Danish troops felled trees to create roadblocks and engaged the fast-moving German columns with anti-tank weapons, however, the Danish guns were of insufficient calibre to penetrate the armour of the German Mark II Panzers, but did destroy some more lightly armoured Mark I Panzers and armoured cars. Any resistance was quickly swamped by sheer weight of numbers as the German columns raced north. Simultaneously, German warships, minesweepers and trawlers landed infantry at key port facilities all across the country. The first combat use of paratroopers took place at 7 a.m. when they successfully seized the airfields at Alborg, and connecting bridges between the main Danish islands. Later that day, a battalion of infantry was airlanded at Alborg airfield, which when secured, was subsequently used by aircraft flying on to Oslo.

Tuesday 9 April 1940 –
Copenhagen, Denmark.

At Copenhagen, the mine layer Hansestadt Danzig, a converted passenger ship, and the icebreaker Stettin entered the harbour with infantry on board. The Danish commander of the fort protecting the harbour ordered a warning shot to be fired, but excess grease in the gun breech prevented loading of the shell and the vessels sailed past unhindered. On docking, Hansestadt Danzig disembarked the infantry who ran to the Citadel and blew open the gates with hand grenades. They entered and captured the facility, setting up radio equipment they had brought with them in the Hansestadt Danzig.

Close by, the Royal Palace and Parliament were surrounded, with the Danish Cabinet inside; conferring while a gun battle between the Germans and the King's Personal Guard raged outside. As daylight broke over Copenhagen, twenty-eight Heinkel bombers dropped leaflets calling on the Danes to offer no resistance; such a show of arial superiority clearly implying the threat of bombing as an alternative. On realising the hopeless odds, orders were issued by the Cabinet at 6:35 a.m. to end any resistance. This order was broadcast to the nation when the national radio station came on air at 7 a.m. and the surrender was in effect by 7:20 a.m. By this time, the German columns had advanced twenty-five miles from the border.

That afternoon, the elderly King Christian took his customary horse ride through Copenhagen, where German officers saluted him as he rode past. The King did not return the compliment. Pre-prepared regulations for food rationing and control of radio and newspapers were immediately put in place, enforced by Danish Police Officers who had been allowed to retain their firearms.

Tuesday 9 April 1940 –
Oslofjord, Southern Norway.

On the afternoon of 8 April, the Norwegian Navy had been contacted by the Danish Navy, reporting German warships and merchant vessels crammed with troops steaming north. Despite this, Norwegian defensive preparations were confused and uncoordinated. The lengthy Oslofjord was not undefended, with a series of forts, naval gun batteries and torpedo pens; but which to a great extent were to remain undermanned despite the Danish warnings. Late on 8 April, Warship Group 5, under command of Konteradmiral Kummetz in his flagship Blucher, approached the entrance to Oslofjord, followed by the pocket battleship Lutzow and the light cruiser Emden. The Blucher was carrying an extra thirty-one tons of ammunition for the Army, above its own capacity, meaning by necessity that it had been stored above the armoured deck. As the warships passed the outer forts in a thick fog, they were engaged by the gun positions and illuminated by searchlights. The Germans blinded the fort's observers with their own searchlights before disappearing into the fog. Just before midnight, the German squadron stopped to offload infantry landing parties into the accompanying minesweepers, dispatching them to attack the forts in the outer approaches of Oslofjord that had engaged the vessels, and the Norwegian Naval base at Horton.

Moving at reduced speed, the squadron entered the inner fjord at 3:38 a.m. to be illuminated again by a searchlight from the shore, sweeping the entire length of the Blucher as it approached the gun battery at Oscarsborg

Island fortress. At 4:21 a.m. the Oscarsborg battery fired two 475lb high explosive shells, both striking the Blucher on the superstructure and starting fires. Blucher immediately returned fire which silenced the battery, but having witnessed the attack, the smaller battery forts engaged the Blucher with multiple rounds of smaller calibre shells, which although not penetrating the armoured deck, increased the number and intensity of the fires in the superstructure. Increasing speed and steering away, the Blucher was then attacked by the hidden torpedo pens, being struck twice, midship and stern. With the engine room flooding, the Blucher dropped anchor to prevent drifting on to the shore as the crew fought the fires. The deck stored ammunition and a freshening wind fed the flames, exploding the ship's gun magazines. At 6 a.m. the order to abandon ship was given, and the Blucher sank at 6:22. From the crew, nine hundred and twenty survivors reached the shore and were taken into military custody, only to be released later that day.

Landing parties were set ashore to attack the Norwegian batteries and torpedo pens that had engaged the Blucher, the surviving warships bombarding Oscarsborg with the assistance of Heinkel 111 bombers. The individual forts resisted until their ammunition ran out, not surrendering until that night; but it was clear the strategic capture of Oslo would not be achieved by the German Navy, whose ships did not enter Oslo until 10:45 a.m. on 10 April.

Tuesday 9 April 1940 –
Fornebu Airfield, near Oslo, Southern Norway.

To supplement the naval assault, two companies of paratroopers were scheduled to drop on Fornebu airfield near Oslo at 8 a.m. under cover provided by Messerschmitt 110 fighters. The fighters, being well beyond their fuel return range, would subsequently be forced to land at the captured airfield or be crashed and lost. Once in German hands, the airfield would then act as an airbridge to land two infantry battalions in transport aircraft following twenty minutes behind. Another two infantry battalions with the heavy equipment for all four, would be delivered to Oslo port by the approaching German merchant ships.

With the noise of the battle at Oscarsborg audible at Fornebu, the Norwegian defenders were put on alert. The fog that had influenced the naval operation now influenced the airborne operation, with the transport planes carrying the paratroopers unable to locate the airfield and returning to Denmark. The transports carrying the air landing infantry arrived over the unsecured airfield twenty minutes later, just as the fog cleared. The supporting Messerschmitt fighters had strafed the field and were circling waiting to land, desperately short of fuel.

As the parachute drop had not taken place, the Junkers transports carrying the infantry tried to land on the unsecured airfield, but being greeted by machine gun fire from the Norwegian defenders, aborted the landing attempts in most cases. In desperation, the out of fuel fighters landed, their crews dismounting their machine guns from the aircraft and engaging the defenders from the ground. The fighting continued until 10 a.m. when the defenders began to run out of ammunition, their resistance faltering, and allowing more German infantry to land. Once in control of the airfield, the Messerschmitt fighters were refueled for further operations and the paratroopers that had diverted earlier due to the fog were flown back. By midday, six infantry companies had been landed and set out for Oslo on foot. The first Germans to arrive appeared in the city at 2:30 p.m. and by the end of the day, reinforcements from subsequent landings had raised the total to 2,000. Curious Norwegian civilians crammed the streets to watch the Germans marching in, with a Norwegian Police guard at the head of the parade.

Having survived the sinking of his flagship, Konteradmiral Kummetz took a bus into Oslo that evening, as it was now under German control. Von Falkenhorst arrived in Oslo by air the next day, and established his headquarters at the Royal Norwegian Automobile Club.

Tuesday 9 April 1940 –
Olotfjord, Narvik, Northern Norway.

The weather could not have been worse on the journey north for Warship Group 1, assigned to capture Narvik. Sailors and deck stored equipment had been washed overboard in the storms and the soldiers locked below decks suffered from terrible seasickness. The Warship Group arrived off Olotfjord at 11 p.m. on 8 April and by midnight, much to the relief of the seasick troops, was in the much calmer waters of the fjord that led to Narvik. On board the ships were 2,000 specialist mountain troops, Luftwaffe anti-aircraft troops and guns, and specialist radio operators with their equipment. Their plan was to land and capture the coastal batteries, the Norwegian armoury at Elvegardsmoen and the port facilities at Narvik; establishing a perimeter that included the small airfield at Bardufoss and the railway line to Sweden along which the iron ore was transported. They carried with them leaflets for distribution to the locals explaining why they were there.

Having received reports of German ships in Danish waters, Norwegian patrol vessels had been positioned at the mouth of the fjord. At 3:20 a.m. patrol vessel Kelt reported to Norwegian Naval and Army Headquarters that nine German destroyers had entered the fjord at high speed. The tenth destroyer in the flotilla had become separated due to technical difficulties and arrived unseen some hours behind. The troops that were set ashore to silence the coastal batteries found them empty of both enemy and guns, quickly returning to the ships.

At 4:15 a.m. the lead destroyer Wilhelm Heidkamp approached the harbour at Narvik, when a warning shot was fired by the Norwegian coastal defence vessel, Eidsvold. The Germans sent across a small boarding party inviting the Norwegians to surrender, which was refused, and both sides braced for what would undoubtedly be a very uneven fight. The Eidsvold moved towards the Wilhelm Heidkamp at full speed, intending to ram her, but was struck by three torpedoes and sank almost immediately. Three destroyers were dispatched to capture the armoury at Elvegardsmoen while the remainder closed in to the harbour, where they were engaged by the deck guns of a second coastal defence vessel, Norge. Torpedoes from the German destroyer Arnim struck home and the Norge capsized. By 5 a.m. six hundred German soldiers had been safely landed at Narvik, where, under the threat of the German naval guns, and in consideration of the town being packed with civilians, the Norwegian garrison surrendered.

* * *

At 4 p.m. Captain Warburton-Lee stopped at the pilot station at the mouth of Olotfjord, where, in a mixture of German and English he tried to establish precise information on the German activity around Narvik. He held what could only loosely be described as a discussion with the Norwegian pilots stationed there, and a small boy, who due to the language barrier used a combination of gestures and diagrams drawn in the snow to describe what he had seen. The boy claimed to have seen at least six destroyers and a U-Boat passing up the fjord towards Narvik; yet confusion reigned due to the poor visibility, with scepticism around the credibility of the boy's statement. In frustration, the small boy's parting remark was that they would need twice as many ships than they currently had.

Warburton-Lee signalled the Admiralty with his intention to attack at dawn next day, still unaware that ten German destroyers had entered the fjord. His plan was to use destroyers Hardy, Hunter and Havoc to attack whatever ships they found in the harbour, with Hotspur and Hostile remaining outside to engage shore batteries; also keeping watch for German reinforcements and covering the withdrawal of the attacking ships by smoke and fire if necessary.

Tuesday 9 April 1940 –
Oslo, Southern Norway.

Shortly after midnight, triggered by the fighting in Oslofjord, the air raid sirens sounded in Oslo. A meeting of the Norwegian Cabinet was called for

1:30 a.m. in the Foreign Office building. Situation reports relating to German activity were being received from all along the Norwegian coast, and the Government issued an order to Naval Command at 4:20 a.m. to fire on German warships. At 4:30 a.m. German ceasefire demands were presented through the Foreign Office but were quickly rejected; the Norwegian response being to announce mobilisation on national radio at 7 a.m.

At the same time, the King and Government departed Oslo by train for Hamar, eighty miles inland and nearer to the Swedish border, where they arrived at 11 a.m. The Government reconvened at 12:30 p.m. for an updated military situation briefing which reported that most major ports and cities were in German hands, and that Denmark had agreed to German demands. The meeting was adjourned until 6 p.m. to allow generation of, and discussion around, a viable course of action.

The location of the Government was announced on the radio, which meant a large number of civil servants and diplomats began to arrive, but also that a German column was closing in with the aim of capturing the King and the Government. At 6:30 p.m. the terms of another German ultimatum were read, and the military situation was updated. With the German column getting closer, the Government moved again, this time to Elverum, where it met in a school gymnasium. They had decided not to negotiate with the invaders but to fight, and at 10:25 p.m. the meeting ended with tears and the singing of the national anthem. It would not convene a full sitting again until 1945.

Wednesday 10 April 1940 –
Narvik, Northern Norway.

The British ships entered Olotfjord at midnight on 9 April under a blanket of snow which reduced visibility to four hundred yards. Stern lights had to be kept on to maintain formation despite the possibility of detection by a German U-Boat screen suspected of being deployed in the area. The German destroyers had by this time disembarked their troops and were lying in and around Narvik harbour and its adjoining fjords as they waited their turn to refuel from the oiler Jan Wellem. As the U-Boat screen had not seen the British ships pass in the snow storm, the Germans in Narvik were taken completely by surprise.

At 4:30 a.m. HMS Hardy entered the harbour, closely followed by Hunter and Havoc, making a circuit, firing torpedoes and engaging the German vessels with their main armament of 4.7-inch guns. From almost point-blank range, a torpedo from Hardy struck the German destroyer Heidkamp, blowing off the stern and killing the enemy force commander, Commodore Bonte, in his bed. The Anton Schmitt was struck by two torpedoes, broke in half and sank immediately. Roeder was set ablaze by shell fire rendering the vessel unseaworthy, with the Ludemann and the Kunne also set on fire. Hotspur was called forward to fire her torpedoes, and sank two merchant ships. The Germans now replied with shells of all calibres, including shore batteries and small arms fire from the infantry units that had disembarked. Through the smoke from the burning German ships, tracer rounds streaked across the harbour towards the British destroyers.

Due to the British ships remaining largely undamaged, Warburton-Lee decided on another attack. This time the destroyers remained outside the harbour, their 4.7-inch guns firing almost blindly into the smoke from the burning German ships, and duelling with the shore batteries. HMS Hostile was the exception, firing her torpedoes from the harbour entrance. At close to 6 a.m. and with all their torpedoes gone, the British prepared to withdraw, just as three German destroyers, the Zenker, Giese and Koeller arrived from Elvegardsmoen to join the fight. They had been anchored northwest of Narvik in the Herjangsfjord, and only alerted to the battle in the harbour at 5:15 a.m. Shells from their bigger guns rained down on the withdrawing British destroyers who made smoke and zigzagged as they tried to escape westward down the narrow fjord towards the open sea, the three German destroyers in pursuit.

Two more German destroyers, the Theile and von Arnim, which had been anchored in Ballangenfjord, and bypassed unseen that morning in the foul weather, appeared across the British destroyers' line of withdrawal. They concentrated their fire on the leading vessel, HMS Hardy, which was moving ahead of the smoke screen cover. As shells smashed into his ship, Warburton-Lee signalled the flotilla to *"Continue to engage the enemy."* It was his last command, as a shell burst on the bridge, killing or wounding all those present. On fire and out of control, the ship veered at high speed towards the shore of the fjord where it grounded on rocks three hundred yards from land. HMS Hardy was last seen on fire, but with a gun still firing to keep the enemy at bay while the crew scrambled over the side into the freezing water and tried to make for the shore.

With Hardy gone, Theile and von Arnim switched their fire onto HMS Hunter. Ablaze and badly damaged, Hunter lost power causing a collision with HMS Hotspur which was running close behind at full speed. The two ships locked together, creating an inviting target for enemy fire. Hotspur managed to extricate herself, but the combined effect of the ramming and enemy fire caused Hunter to sink in the middle of the fjord. Havoc and Hostile rallied around the damaged Hotspur, engaging the Thiele and von Arnim at point blank range, and forcing them to retire damaged. At 6:30 a.m. with their path now clear, the three remaining British destroyers retired towards the open sea.

Saturday 13 April 1940 –
Narvik, Northern Norway.

With only three destroyers left undamaged after the Warburton-Lee raid, and half of their ammunition stocks used, the Germans worked feverishly to make their ships seaworthy for an attempted breakout and return to Germany. The Royal Navy had other intentions, and blockaded Olotfjord while another raiding party was assembled. On 13 April, nine destroyers led by the battleship Warspite, with its armament of eight 15-inch and twelve 6-inch guns, entered Olotfjord at 11 a.m. Sighted at noon by the German destroyer Koellner, the already badly damaged vessel hid on the southern side of the fjord with the intention of launching torpedoes at the British ships as they passed, before what would be her inevitable destruction. With Koellner being spotted by Warspite's Swordfish biplane, the British were prepared for the attack and the opponents fired almost simultaneously as they saw each other. The crew of the Koellner managed to fire only a single salvo from her torpedo tubes and guns before the combined gun and torpedo attack from two British destroyers struck home. Warspite followed up with her 15-inch shells, firing at almost point-blank range, blowing the Koellner apart.

The Swordfish that had spotted the Koellner flew ahead towards Narvik and caught sight of U-64 on the surface. Whilst in the dive to drop its bombs, the crew of U-64 engaged the Swordfish with their deck gun, but to no avail. Two bombs struck the conning tower, and by the time the aircraft banked around again, the submarine was already sinking. The crew on deck of U-64 remained at their posts, still firing at the Swordfish with the deck gun as the boat sank.

Having been warned of the approaching British ships, the remaining seaworthy German destroyers exited Narvik harbour just before 1 p.m. Leaving the immobilised Roeder behind, they initially engaged the approaching British vessels with their remaining torpedoes, and subsequently their deck guns. The Erich Giese was set on fire at the harbour entrance and abandoned, the remaining German destroyers retiring past the harbour entrance and further up the fjord. Stuck in the harbour, the Roeder engaged and damaged HMS Cossack with the last of her ammunition before the bigger guns of Warspite silenced the German vessel. The surviving crew abandoned the Roeder after setting depth charges which blew the ship apart.

Chasing the fleeing Germans, HMS Eskimo engaged the stranded Georg Thiele which had been deliberately run aground by her captain so his crew could escape. The last torpedo fired by the Georg Thiele struck Eskimo in the bows, causing massive damage. Despite this, Eskimo did not sink, but the ship was so badly twisted that some of the dead could only be recovered after making port at Barrow-in-Furness on 5 June.

The aircraft from Warspite now reported the three remaining German destroyers round the next bend in the shoreline. As the British approached it was obvious that the German ships, out of ammunition, had been deliberately run aground. The crews had abandoned the vessels and were climbing the sides of the fjord, making their way inland. Two of the destroyers were visibly sinking while the third was ablaze. The Germans had lost a total of ten destroyers at Narvik, while the British lost two. The commander of the flotilla, Admiral Whitworth, acutely aware of the remaining U-Boat threat or an aerial attack in the confines of the fjord, pulled his ships back towards the sea. He signalled to Admiralty that an immediate land assault would have the best chance of success while the enemy, now without Naval assets, were still reeling from his actions that day.

Sunday 14 April 1940 –
Harstad, Northern Norway.

The force to retake Narvik departed from Scottish ports on 12 April, but as the ships approached Olotfjord in the early morning of 14 April, orders were received to split the convoy in half. In the two days it took for the crossing, the strategic priorities had been reassessed. The signal from Admiral Whitworth on 13 April, citing the destruction of all enemy naval assets at Narvik, had created further options for the force currently sailing for Northern Norway. While the attack on Narvik was to go ahead as initially planned, the rear half of the convoy was diverted to conduct a simultaneous attack on Trondheim, some four hundred miles to the south.

Trondheim was the ancient capital of Norway, but now occupied the hub of the two main routes from Oslo, the main route east from Norway into Sweden and the only road and rail link north to Narvik that could be used for relief or resupply. It had a functional port and a nearby airfield, essential requirements if a military force was to be established there. With Norwegian political pressure also in the mix, it was believed that the recapture of Trondheim in central Norway would provide a much greater military and political impact than the capture of Narvik in the far north. Prior to a direct attack on Trondheim, British forces from the diverted convoy were to be established north of the town at Namsos, also south of the town at Andalsnes.

The undiverted half of the convoy continued on its planned route, and being unable to immediately launch an attack on Narvik due to equipment and loading issues in Scotland, was instead directed to the small port of Harstad, some seventy-five miles from Narvik by sea; the only town in the area that could support a landing force.

Wednesday 17 April 1940 –
Namsos, Central Norway.

Namsos was a small port situated directly on the western coast, and selected as the base for the northern pincer attack towards Trondheim, which lay eighty miles to the south. Lacking information on the strength of any German presence there, a Royal Marines detachment had been put ashore. They reported that Namsos was clear of Germans but would be unsuitable for troop transport ships, having only single concrete and wooden piers. The troops were subsequently cross-loaded from the transport ships onto five destroyers which arrived in Namsos on 16 April, landing a total of 1,000 men by daybreak on 17 April. That night, more troops and stores were landed including three battalions of French mountain warfare specialists, the Chasseurs-Alpins.

The splitting of the convoy on the route to Narvik, which had made a mockery of the ships' loading plans, resulted in both the British and French at Namsos being ashore with no artillery and almost no transport. The French had arrived with skis, but lacked the straps to attach them to their boots. The Germans quickly became aware of the landing and bombed Namsos, reducing the mostly wooden town to ashes, including any military stores that had already been landed.

146 Brigade, commanded by Brigadier Phillips, immediately deployed eighty miles south through deep snow to support Norwegian troops holding a strategic bridge at Verdal, over which passed the road and rail link between Trondheim and Narvik. Positioned here, as the northern pincer, they could block any relief for Narvik and influence the proposed attack on Trondheim by drawing off German strength. The Norwegians they encountered holding the bridge were in a desperate state, with only a single day's supply of ammunition left. The relieving British were unable to redistribute their ammunition due to the Norwegian weapons using a different calibre of round.

Wednesday 17 April 1940 –
Harstad, Northern Norway.

On making shore at Harstad, General Mackesy, the Army Commander of the Narvik operation, met with the Norwegian forces operating in the area and was briefed on the German strengths and dispositions. It was estimated the Germans had a force of 4,600 men, of which 2,600 were naval personnel from the lost destroyers, positioned to defend Narvik town and the railway along which the ore supplies came from Sweden. Once disembarked, the infantry was positioned to implement General Mackesy's plan for a two-pronged attack to capture Narvik, the priority being to cut the railway, while the Royal Navy blockaded the port.

The tactical loading of vessels is meant to ensure that essential equipment needed first is loaded last, so as to be immediately available on docking. The loading of the vessels for this operation had been conducted to save space rather than prepare for operations and would result in significant delays to Mackesy's deployment, as all the equipment had to be unloaded and laid out on the dock before being sorted into requirement priority. The operational readiness of the force at Harstad was further reduced due to the convoy having been split without prior warning; critical equipment required for the Narvik operation being diverted south to Namsos or Andalsnes.

Thursday 18 April 1940 –
Andalsnes, Central Norway.

One hundred and fifty miles south of Trondheim, Andalsnes had a good harbour and a nearby airfield, making it suitable as a base from which to launch the southern arm of the Trondheim pincer. After their voyage south, 148 Brigade, commanded by Brigadier Morgan, arrived there on the evening of 18 April. His primary aim was to join up with Norwegian forces in the area to secure the communications hub at Dombass, fifty-five miles south of Andalsnes, thereby cutting the road and rail links to Trondheim for the German forces advancing from Oslo. His secondary aim was to threaten Trondheim from the south as part of the proposed pincer operation, drawing away German forces from the town prior to the main attack. Again, because the loading plans were upset by the convoy split, the Brigade was put ashore in deep snow with no armour, no artillery or mortar ammunition, no maps, no transport, and crucially, ineffective communications with the northern pincer formation at Namsos.

Suitable vehicles were requisitioned locally, which was still woefully inadequate; the remaining infantry being restricted to movement on the roads only due to the unavailability of snow shoes. A battalion was immediately sent south to Dombass, with the remainder of the Brigade preparing to move north to threaten Trondheim. On finding the Norwegian troops around Dombass completely exhausted, and the Germans advancing north from Oslo with armour and artillery supported by aircraft, the situation demanded a change of plan; the entire Brigade being redirected to Dombass on 20 April.

Sunday 21 April 1940 –
Trondheim, Central Norway.

Due to the presence of the naval blockade, the Germans realised that Narvik could only be resupplied by air, for which the retention of Trondheim as a staging post was critical. The garrison there was reinforced by air-lifted troops and stood at around 3,000 men. In response to 146 Brigade's movement south from Namsos, the Germans advanced north from Trondheim to meet them and regain control of the vital bridge at Verdal.

146 Brigade were strung out over a frontage of some fifteen miles, anchored on the bridge with their western flank on the shore of the Beitstad

fjord. At 4 a.m. on 21 April, two hundred Germans were landed on the fjord shore by a destroyer from Trondheim and moved towards the Verdal bridge. The German column moving north from Trondheim, supported by air and naval guns from the destroyer in the fjord, simultaneously attacked and outflanked the over-extended British, threatening to cut them off. The British attempted an orderly withdrawal during the night of 21 / 22 April to a new defensive line, but at 8 a.m. on 22 April, German planes marked their new positions with flares, initiating a mortar and machinegun attack that forced a further withdrawal.

From mid-morning onwards, German bombers attacked behind the front lines to disrupt communications and resupply as the British withdrew through very deep snow. With the main road north falling to the Germans just before nightfall, the withdrawing British were forced off the road and dug themselves in along the forest edge. They managed to hold this position until 3 p.m. the following day until ordered to retire. They now faced a withdrawal of some eighty miles back to where they had started at Namsos, where the scattered 146 Brigade would attempt to reform.

Sunday 21 April 1940 –
Dombass, South of Andalsnes, Central Norway.

Having moved south from Andalsnes and established a defensive line to the south of Dombass, the battle-weary Norwegians were able to withdraw north through 148 Brigade positions on 21 April. As the German armour continued to advance north from Oslo, spotter aircraft located and reported the British deployment. German ski troops who could operate in the deep snow, easily outflanked the British who were confined to operating on the roads and tracks only, forcing them to withdraw back north.

An orderly British withdrawal was impossible in the unforgiving terrain without transport, and as the Germans simply bypassed any resistance, the Brigade cohesion fragmented very quickly. Outflanked British units scattered into the hills and forests without appropriate clothing or supplies, to try and make their way back through the deep snow into Dombass where they could reform and make a stand. Those that could not move quickly enough were rounded up over the next few days and became prisoners of war.

Wednesday 24 April 1940 –
Narvik, Northern Norway.

While not understanding the considerable equipment issues under which the force was operating, such as having no machine guns or mortar ammunition, London was pressing for quick action against Narvik; in the form of a frontal assault by infantry under cover of a naval bombardment. The Irish

Guards were selected for the attack, but having only a single landing craft available meant that just one platoon of infantry could be put ashore at a time; with a thirty-minute shuttle time delay before another platoon could be landed. It would take up to five hours to put the Battalion ashore, if nothing went wrong.

As the town was blanketed under deep snow right down to the waterline, this first platoon to land would be exposed and unable to manoeuvre while under German fire until reinforcements arrived. With this consideration brought to light, the plan was adjusted, the Irish Guards only to be put ashore if the Germans evacuated the town or offered surrender. It was hoped the naval bombardment on its own would be enough to achieve this, and thus render unnecessary what was certain to be a very risky infantry landing. On the morning of 24 April, the navy pounded assumed German positions in Narvik for three hours, but failed to dislodge the enemy. With no hope of a successful infantry assault, the Irish Guards were disembarked and returned to Harstad.

Wednesday 24 April 1940 –
Lake Lesjaskog, Central Norway.

With German bombing attacks during daylight hours against deployed British troops operating in the Namsos, Dombass and Andalsnes area being almost relentless, urgent action was required against the air superiority of the Luftwaffe over the whole Trondheim region. The response was an operation to position a squadron of Gladiator fighters in a makeshift airbase on the frozen Lake Lesjaskog, midway between Dombass and Andalsnes. Eighteen aircraft were taken across the North Sea on aircraft carriers to within one hundred and fifty miles of the Norwegian coast, ready to be flown into the airbase once it had been prepared. RAF ground staff arrived at Lake Lesjaskog over 23 / 24 April to make the site operational, with the aircraft scheduled to arrive on the second day.

Having landed safely, the pilots found that fuel was only available in four-gallon cans, milk jugs having to be borrowed from a nearby farmhouse to transfer the fuel from the cans to the aircraft a few pints at a time. On opening the cans, the fuel was found to be the wrong octane for the Gladiators, which although usable, caused the engines to overheat. The lubricating oil was also too thin, causing it to freeze during the night, and meaning the engines had to be started by hand cranking on the morning of 25 April; a process that took two hours.

German spotter planes had noticed the creation of the airfield and it was continuously attacked by bombers the day after the arrival of the Gladiators, destroying five aircraft on the ground. Those fighters that managed to take off, were able to engage with the waves of bombers attacking the airfield, and also support the infantry fighting both north and south of Trondheim with some success. Continuous German attacks caused the ice on the lake to break up thus rendering the makeshift runway almost unusable, and with only four serviceable aircraft and no ammunition remaining, the airfield was abandoned on 27 April. The remaining aircraft were deliberately destroyed to prevent their use by the enemy.

Thursday 25 April 1940 –
Dombass, South of Andalsnes, Central Norway.

The critical situation developing in central Norway required reinforcement to prevent the Germans moving any further north towards Trondheim. 15 Brigade, consisting of 2,700 men under Brigadier H.E.F Smyth, was rapidly withdrawn from France, back across the English Channel and up to Scotland for passage to Norway. Smyth's mission was to prevent further northerly advance of the Germans coming north from Oslo, but also to protect Andalsnes from attack by the Germans coming south from Trondheim, who had been substantially reinforced by air. Arriving with anti-tank and anti-aircraft weapons, 15 Brigade were much better equipped to meet the German threat than 148 Brigade had been.

At 7 a.m. on 25 April, 15 Brigade arrived in Dombass, moving south through the town; and were in action against the enemy by 11 a.m. The Germans continued with the tactics that had been successful against 148 Brigade; armour advancing along the roads supported by accurate artillery, and infantry moving around the flanks in the higher ground. Having held out all day, the Kings Own Yorkshire Light Infantry withdrew that night to avoid being cut off by the flanking Germans. The German attacks began again at 5:30 a.m. the next morning, but the armoured advance was stopped by the newly arrived anti-tank guns, forcing the Germans off the roads. They moved through the hills and forests where they gradually infiltrated the British positions during the course of the day and into the hours of darkness, resulting in a further withdrawal that night.

With the prospect of a German breakthrough against the crumbling Norwegian forces fighting to the east and south from Trondheim, 15 Brigade and the remains of 148 Brigade were ordered back to the crucial transport hub at Dombass. On 27 April, they dug in along a defensive line five miles south of Dombass to delay the Germans long enough for the Norwegians to withdraw behind them.

Sunday 28 April 1940 –
Dombass, South of Andalsnes, Central Norway.

The Luftwaffe saw the tide of battle turning and began to bomb any structure that could offer comfort or cover against the elements to the withdrawing British. During the day, there were small but vicious engagements as the British repelled the German attacks from their prepared defensive positions. Evacuation orders were received that same day, and the British were faced with having to break away from an aggressive and more mobile enemy to withdraw one hundred miles back to Andalsnes along a single road and rail track. The Norwegians took this development very badly, feeling the British were abandoning them, but promised their assistance as required. While a rearguard waited for the Germans, the bulk of the remaining forces withdrew towards Andalsnes by train from Dombass station. At 1:30 p.m. on 30 April, the rearguard withdrew in trucks that had been pre-positioned for them, destroying road and railway bridges as they passed over, to delay the German pursuit.

Monday 29 April 1940 –
Molde, Western Central Norway.

Having been told by the Swedish authorities that if King Haakon sought refuge in that country he would be detained and incarcerated, the Royal Party and Government officials moved north through the snow-covered forests and mountains to Molde on the west coast of Norway, thirty-seven miles from Andalsnes. Late in the evening of 29 April, the cruiser HMS Glasgow, escorted by two destroyers, took on board the King, Crown Prince Olav, Norwegian Government Ministers loyal to the Allied cause and remaining members of Allied political delegations. A total of two hundred and eighty persons, along with twenty-three tons of Norway's gold reserves were taken six hundred and twenty miles north to Tromso, where a provisional capital was established.

Tuesday 30 April 1940 –
Andalsnes, Central Norway.

With the Germans now sure that the British were attempting to evacuate their forces from Andalsnes, bombing raids were conducted around the clock, aimed at both the docks and the vessels in the port. As the infantry began to concentrate in the town, evacuations had been arranged over the nights of 30 Apr – 1 May, and 1 – 2 May, for what was estimated to be 5,500 men. A total of four cruisers, six destroyers and a troop transporter took part in the operation, the anti-aircraft cruiser HMS Calcutta attempting to keep the Luftwaffe at bay while the evacuation took place. Ignoring the danger of aerial attack, two of the cruisers berthed in port to load troops directly, a third being loaded outside the port by destroyers acting as ferries. Illuminated by the burning town, a total of 1,800 exhausted men were rescued that first night, most without any weapons or equipment.

The following night, two cruisers and five destroyers stood by for evacuation. The destroyers moved back and forth as ferries to lift the troops from the quay out to the waiting cruisers Birmingham and Manchester, which were too large to berth in port. In the space of an hour, 1,300 men were transferred and the ships sailed for home, leaving Calcutta to lift the rearguard when it arrived. Expecting to rescue only two hundred and forty men, Calcutta took on board a total of seven hundred in only fifteen minutes. Over 1,400 men from 148 and 15 Brigades were left behind; either killed, wounded or prisoners of war.

Tuesday 30 April 1940 –
Clacton-on-Sea, Essex, South East England.

Late in the night of 30 April, a German Heinkel 111 twin-engine bomber, piloted by 25-year-old Oberleutnant Hermann Peter Vagts, was on a mine laying mission off the coast of Essex when it was struck by anti-aircraft fire from the Thames estuary. With one engine destroyed, Vagts circled low over the town of Clacton-on-Sea fighting to keep the aircraft airborne while searching for a suitable area to attempt an emergency landing. He knew this would be a difficult and dangerous manoeuvre as two undeployed mines were still on board. As the noise of the crippled aircraft continued for thirty-five minutes, some town locals came out of their homes to see, until the second engine caught fire and the bomber lost height rapidly. Out of control, it came down in Clacton High Street, striking a chimney stack and a tree before skidding along the road and crashing into two houses, completely demolishing them.

The damaged aircraft was ablaze as residents rushed out onto the street. The fire prevented anyone from getting close enough to attempt a rescue of the residents from the ruined houses or the aircraft crew from the burning machine. A few minutes after the crash, a huge explosion caused severe damage to the area as a mine that was still on board detonated. One hundred and fifty-six residents were injured in the explosion, thirty-four of them seriously, as windows were blown in and ceilings collapsed under the force of the blast. Windows were smashed in houses two miles away such was the ferocity of the explosion.

Soldiers, Air Raid Wardens, and Police threw a cordon round the area and kept people back. For some hours there were distressing scenes as relief workers searched amid the debris and in damaged houses for the injured whose cries they could hear. The rescue work went on all night, the efforts illuminated by the burning aeroplane. In one of the demolished houses, husband and wife Frederick and Dorothy Gill were killed; becoming the first civilian casualties of the war in mainland Britain.

Thursday 2 May 1940 –
Namsos, Central Norway.

As at Andalsnes, the Germans threw everything at Namsos when it became clear a withdrawal was taking place. One French and two British cruisers, one French and four British destroyers and three French troop ships were gathered for the operation, prepared to evacuate an estimated 5,400 troops.

The plan was to lift half the force using the troop ships on the night of 1 – 2 May, and the remainder using the destroyers and cruisers on the night of 2 – 3 May. As the ships entered the Namsos fjord on the night of 1 May, they were enveloped in dense fog which reduced visibility to zero and prevented entry to the port. It was not until 5 a.m. the next morning that, using their sonar to define the topography, the destroyers reached Namsos. They found the port clear of fog, but also clear of any soldiers, who had waited for evacuation on the quay all night before being dispersed with the coming of daylight.

Due to the worsening military situation, it was decided to compress the timescale for the operation and attempt to lift the entire force over the night of 2 – 3 May. In the fading light, the French transport ships were led in to dock by the destroyers, and tied up at the concrete pier to load troops directly on board. The destroyers then ferried troops out to the other ships waiting in the fjord from the alternative wooden pier. The transport ships were dispatched as soon as they were loaded, each accompanied by a destroyer for protection on the route home, the last ship clearing the pier at 2:30 a.m. on 3 May. The destroyer HMS Alfridi stayed behind to embark the rearguard, using its guns to destroy the abandoned lorries that had delivered them, now neatly parked in straight lines on the pier. With a short delay due to a friendly competition between the rearguard to see who could be the last man to withdraw, Alfridi was able to get away just as it was becoming light.

With the convoy stretched out across the North Sea, German air attacks began at 8:45 a.m. The French destroyer Bison was hit almost immediately, and the Royal Navy destroyer HMS Grenade moved rapidly to assist. Having departed last, the Alfridi had caught up with the rest of the convoy by this time, and also drew alongside the listing Bison to take off survivors. With three static targets attracting further attacks, the spilled oil from the damaged Bison was soon set ablaze, making recovery of survivors even more hazardous. Sixty-nine men were transferred across or pulled aboard the Alfridi from the sea before the Bison sank at 2 p.m.

Now separated from the protection of the convoy again due to the rescue of survivors, and racing to catch up, Alfridi was a prime target for further Stuka attacks. Just as she rejoined the convoy, Stukas attacked simultaneously from different approaches to mitigate the ship's evasive action; striking the Alfridi twice and setting her ablaze. Many men were trapped by the fire in the forward mess decks and screamed through opened port holes for help. HMS Griffin pulled alongside to cross load survivors, the rescuers being able to touch the extended hands of the trapped men; but the portholes being too small for them to escape through. At 2:45 p.m. the Alfridi sank taking the trapped men with her. Thirty of the sixty-nine rescued earlier from Bison were lost.

The Luftwaffe attacks continued for seven hours until the convoy moved out of the range of the aircraft, a distance of some two hundred miles from the Norwegian coast; not arriving back at Scapa Flow until 5 May. All Norwegian troops south of Trondheim, who had held back the Germans to allow the British to get away, surrendered at 5 a.m. on 3 May.

Tuesday 7 May 1940 –
House of Commons, London, England.

Following the military reverses in Norway, combined with the prospect of a German offensive in Northern Europe, public criticism on the handling of the war was increasing. On Sunday 28 April, newspapers accused ministers of complacency in decision making and questioned the competency of the Cabinet. The Labour Opposition called for a debate on the war situation in the House of Commons on 7 May, which ran until 9 May, during which time Prime Minister Chamberlain and his Cabinet Ministers were bitterly attacked from all sides of the House, including Chamberlain's own backbenchers. The most notable personal attack on the Prime Minister came from his fellow Birmingham MP, Leo Amery. Against a background of uproar, Amery quoted Oliver Cromwell's demand to Parliament made in 1653, when he thought it no longer fit to conduct the affairs of the nation.

"You have sat too long here for any good you have been doing. Depart I say, and let us have done with you. In the name of God, go."

The Opposition called for a vote of no confidence. Forty-one MPs who normally supported the Government voted with the Opposition, while an estimated sixty other Conservatives deliberately abstained, although the government still won the vote by 281 to 200. With his credibility mortally wounded, and unwell from bowel cancer that he had concealed from his colleagues, Chamberlain left the chamber pale and grim. Over 9 and 10 May, Chamberlain attempted to form a coalition government with the Labour Party and the Liberals, but they refused to serve under him; although they made it clear they were willing to accept another Conservative as Prime Minister.

Thursday 9 May 1940 –
Berlin, Germany.

Just before noon, Hitler was briefed on the weather forecast for the next day, which was set fair, and to remain fair for as far ahead as could be accurately predicted. On Hitler's direction, General Wilhelm Keitel, Supreme Commander of the German Armed Forces, signed the order for Fall Gelb (Plan Yellow) bringing the military to readiness, and initiating preliminary moves to designated start lines for the offensive in the west. Hitler boarded his armoured train, initially heading north, having briefed his press officer he was going to visit shipyards in Hamburg. Just after 9 p.m. the codeword "Danzig" was transmitted, confirming the attack would begin at 3:45 a.m. the following day.

The plan had been revised many times, not least since the loss of the original in January; but now three German Army Groups were poised to strike. Army Group B in the north would move into the Netherlands, drawing the Allied Armies forward from their prepared positions into Belgium; Army Group C in the south would fix French forces opposite the Maginot Line. This left Army Group A as the main effort on a surprise strike through the Ardennes, to cross the major obstacle of the river Meuse and race to the channel coast, cutting off and trapping the Allied Armies in the north.

Shortly after midnight, the armoured train changed lines and turned south west, arriving at the station of Eifel near Euskirchen shortly before dawn. The journey to the new purpose-built Fuhrer Headquarters at Munstereifel, codenamed Felsennest (Rock Eyrie), was completed by car. As the party dismounted the vehicles and gathered near the entrance to the bunker, the horizon was lit up by the flashes of heavy artillery, followed by a distant rumbling. The offensive in the west had begun.

A special message from Hitler had been read to all personnel about to engage in operations on the Western Front.

"The battle which begins today will decide the fate of the German nation for the next thousand years. Now do your duty. The German people give you their blessing."

PART 4

THE STRIKE WEST

Friday 10 May 1940 –
Hennweiler Airfield, Western Germany.

The airfield at Hennweiler, like countless others in western Germany, came to
life at 4 a.m. on the morning of 10 May. Still in semi-darkness, the aircrew did
their final checks on their airframes and instruments, while the torches of the
armourers flicked back and forward under the aircraft as they attached bombs
to the fuselage. With the pilots strapped into their Stukas, the mechanics
brought the engines to life with starter handles. The sound of the spluttering
engines cut through the silence of the early morning as the pilots revved, and
the aircraft gently rolled forward to prepare for take-off. One by one they
disappeared into the slowly lightening sky.

Their part in the overall plan was critical. To attack enemy airfields and
destroy as many aircraft on the ground as possible before they had the
chance to join the battle; securing the skies for the insertion of the airborne
forces.

Friday 10 May 1940 –
Ostheim Airfield near Cologne, Western Germany.

Oberfeldwebel Helmut Wenzel had been awake for twenty-two hours. He
lay on his bed trying to sleep but could not stop his mind from running
through the plan again and again. The final briefings had finished well before
midnight and all personal and mission equipment had been checked, allowing
the opportunity for four hours rest before the operation was to begin. He
was not the only one that sleep eluded. Men sat smoking and talking quietly
so as not to wake anyone who was lucky enough or exhausted enough to
sleep. Preparations for this operation, originally planned for mid-January,
had been continuous since November the previous year, but repeatedly
delayed by bad weather and strategic changes. After many false starts, it was
on at last. The order had arrived early on 9 May to concentrate at Ostheim
and Butzweilerhof airfields near Cologne. The paratroopers had travelled by
train to Cologne where they boarded busses to Ostheim airfield. As they
stepped from their transport, they saw lines of waiting Junkers 52 transports
and the now very familiar DFS 230 gliders.

Wenzel lay with his hands behind his head and his eyes closed. It felt as if his whole life had been building to this moment; and he hoped he would pass the test he knew was coming. Preparations had started in Czechoslovakia the previous winter, living in isolation in the Altvater area. They had been practicing attacks against captured Czech border fortifications that had been remodelled to resemble their planned objective; which he now knew to be the Belgian fortress at Eben Emael. Three miles north of Maastricht, the fortress dominated three bridges over the Albert Canal, the Veldwezelt, Vroenhoeven and Canne. The plan called for the bridges to be captured intact by other airborne groups, and held until the armoured columns of the advancing ground forces arrived. If their attack on the fortress failed, its heavy guns would destroy the bridges, regardless of the success or failure of the other groups.

Their training had been conducted under the upmost secrecy. They had existed in isolation for six months, with no member of the group allowed home or to even leave the camp. Their equipment had been delivered disguised in furniture vans to avoid raising suspicion, and all identifying insignia had been removed from their uniforms. They had studied reconnaissance photographs taken by high flying Dornier aircraft with super lens cameras. Exacting models had been constructed which everyone had been forced to commit to memory. Oberleutnant Witzig, the officer in command of "Granite Section" as their group was codenamed, had ensured that everyone knew the role of every other member. If someone was killed or injured, there was always another trained to take his place and do his job. They had all been instructed on and practised in the use of newly designed "shaped" explosive charges that were to be used to destroy the rotating steel gun cupolas, also flame throwers to neutralise defensive machine gun emplacements. It appeared to Wenzel that nothing had been left to chance.

Even as Wenzel closed his eyes, he could see the models and photographs that were imprinted in his brain. The fort was seven hundred yards east to west and eight hundred yards north to south, surrounded by a twenty feet deep ditch. Machine gun posts with interlocking arcs of fire covered both the ditch and the flat, grassed upper surface of the fort. The gun emplacements and observation posts were constructed of steel and reinforced concrete, housing 2.5, 3 and 4.5-inch guns which dominated the surrounding approaches and the canal bridges. Ammunition magazines and accommodation galleries were buried deep inside the structure, connected by three miles of tunnels for ease of movement of men and ammunition. The ventilation ports were sited on the one hundred and sixty-feet sheer face above the canal to reduce the chance of gas attacks. It had been estimated up to one thousand troops could be inside at any one time. A glider assault was the only way to ensure the concentration of the required force in a small area; an effect a parachute drop could not guarantee. Granite Section had a strength of only eighty-five paratroopers, to be landed in ten gliders.

Wenzel must have dozed off, as a hand shaking his shoulder caused him to sit up with alarm. Oberleutnant Witzig told him to waken the men for breakfast and get them ready to move.

* * *

Although they had trained using the gliders, it was only now that they were finally to face the enemy, that Wenzel realised just how flimsy they were; tubular steel frames covered with stretched canvas, offering absolutely no protection from incoming fire or a hard landing. Eight paratroopers were squeezed together inside, four down each side with their equipment stowed on the floor between them and their personal weapons between their knees. He struggled to free him arms from the crush to pull up his sleeve and check his watch. It was 4:30 a.m. The engines of the Junkers 52 tug aircraft were revving, and he felt the glider lurch gently forward as the tow rope tightened and the Junkers tug began to taxi for take-off.

As he looked around him in the semi-darkness, he felt a sense of confidence in the men he had trained with for so long and so hard. He knew the equipment and the weapons they carried were the best available, but the immediate future was out of his control. The tug and glider pilots now had the job of delivering the paratroopers to the target; to land them safely, and in a condition to fight. His mind turned to Oberleutnant Witzig who was being transported in a separate glider; a deliberate tactic to give the best chance of one of them getting to the target safely should enemy interference or pure bad luck play a part. He turned his head and glanced into the cockpit. The pilot was busy with the controls as the glider picked up speed and the wheels bumped over the grass runway. The pilots had also undergone intense training in Altvater, honing their skills to place their machines within sixty feet of a designated spot. Barbed wire had been wrapped around the front skid of the gliders, designed to dig in on the grassed surface of the fort on landing and reduce the stopping distance of the machine. The pilots had been trained to fight alongside the paratroopers once they had delivered their deadly cargo. There was no space on the operation for passengers.

A total of forty-two Junkers tug aircraft, each towing a glider, left the fields of Ostheim and Butzweilerhof airfields at thirty second intervals and soared into the air; before joining up into their separate assault groups and turning south towards their specific targets. As the tugs joined their formations, the last pilot in Granite Group was forced to dive sharply to avoid a collision, causing the rope connection with his glider to snap. The powerless machine lost height rapidly as the pilot banked harshly in an attempt to return to the airfield, however, having insufficient height to complete the desired manoeuvre, he was forced to land short in a field near Cologne. As the glider came to a halt, an enraged Oberleutnant Witzig emerged through the door to hear the drone of the aerial armada fade into the distance. He could not use his radio to tell of his plight as the operation was to be conducted in radio silence. With his officer left behind, Oberfeldwebel Wenzel was now in command of Granite Group, but was as yet unaware of his new responsibility.

* * *

Due to this imposed radio silence, the pilots were forced to follow a string of beacons used as direction finders to guide them west towards the Dutch / Belgian border. The last beacon and the signal to release the gliders was a searchlight pointing directly upwards, at which point the tugs were to be at 8,500 feet; calculated as the height required on release to allow the gliders to cover the remaining twenty-two miles to their targets. This was also deemed far enough away that Belgian and Dutch sound location early warning systems would not detect the tug planes, allowing the gliders to approach with the element of surprise on their side.

A following wind meant that the tugs arrived at the release point earlier than expected and not at the required height for successful glider release. Having to delay the release of the gliders until the correct height could be reached, the tugs entered Dutch airspace, inadvertently alerting the early warning systems and attracting anti-aircraft fire. Defensive fire streamed up from the ground as Dutch anti-aircraft gunners engaged the tugs and gliders. Leaning forward to look through the cockpit window, Wenzel could see red tracer rounds streaking past in front of his glider in the slowly lightening sky, then felt a jolt as the tug rope was released. The tug pulled away to the right and the glider banked gently to the left, dropping quickly to pick up speed. They were on their own now, and totally dependent on the skill of the pilot to get them to the target and set them down in one piece.

* * *

Oberleutnant Witzig climbed the fence around the field and stood in the road to try and orientate himself. He had set his men the task of clearing a makeshift runway and they were busily pulling out fence posts and cross beams to create the required space. As car lights appeared, Witzig frantically waved his arms to get the driver to stop and was soon on his way to the nearest military establishment, from where the commander rushed him back to the airfield to organise a replacement tug aircraft.

**Friday 10 May 1940 –
Fort Eben Emael, Belgium / Netherlands Border.**

Major Jean Jottrand, the commander of Eben Emael, was woken by an orderly with reports from the units on the Albert Canal bridges that an aerial formation was heading their way; but in his semi-conscious state could not comprehend the information that the aircraft seemed to hang in the sky without any engine noise. He ordered his men to their battle positions when the sound of gunfire from the canal reached them; the defenders on the bridges engaging the silent, dark shapes that swooped down on them. Jottrand rushed to the surface of the fort and together with his men watched mesmerised as the noiseless machines got closer and closer; their weapons remaining silent, unsure if they should fire or not.

"Are they Belgian?" screamed Jottrand at his gunnery officer who replied that he was sure they were not. "Then shoot for God's sake." Jottrand yelled.

Wenzel ordered his men to brace for landing and they linked arms and raised their feet; and although told not to stiffen their bodies they found it hard to resist the overwhelming urge to do so. The glider jolted violently as it struck the grassy surface and the men inside were concertinaed towards the front of the aircraft. The barbed wire wrapped around the landing skid and the effect of an arrester parachute deployed by the pilot on the descent brought the glider to a stop within the sixty feet parameter, and before any enemy fire had been received.

All across the surface of the fort, the pilots had identified their specific targets and put their machines down as close as possible. Although potential enemy approaches from the ground had been strewn with wire obstacles, the top surface of the fort had been left clear so it could be used for football matches amongst the garrison. The paratroopers spilled out of the gliders on to the surface of the fort and immediately sprayed any defensive machine gun positions and viewing ports with small arms fire. Wenzel identified his team's specific target and dispatched the engineers to destroy it. The new shaped charges came in two 40lb packs, one carried in each hand by the assault engineers, which were then joined together and placed on the target. As the assault engineers raced towards the gun turrets, the defensive positions were engaged by the remaining paratroopers with grenades and flame throwers.

The resulting explosions caused devastation, blowing holes directly through the concrete, shredding the bodies of the crews inside and wrecking the guns. The engineers immediately reached through the breaches, firing at anything that showed signs of life and dropping grenades down the steps of the access shafts. The steel doors leading to the gun access shafts were slammed shut by the defenders, keeping them safe inside the fort for the moment, but out of the fight.

His specific aim achieved; Wenzel looked around at similar scenes being repeated all across the surface of the fort. Turret after turret was being collapsed, and the guns inside put out of action. The noise was tremendous and the devastation caused by the new charges was shocking; almost unbelievable. The months of training had paid off, his teams reacting instinctively without commands being given. Wenzel's thoughts now turned to the defence of the foothold from counterattack; a task that would require appreciation of the situation by the commander, and subsequent orders.

Wenzel looked to where Oberleutnant Witzig's glider should have been. It was not there, and Witzig's specific target, the casemate holding the 4.5-inch guns covering the bridges was still intact, although silent. As Wenzel began to re-organise the paratroopers into defensive positions, it became clear that two gliders were missing, two paratroopers had been killed and eight wounded. This left him only sixty-two men to contain the garrison and repel any attempted counterattack from the Belgians. Wenzel set up machine guns to cover the approaches of Belgian infantry from the west and tried as best he could with the remaining paratroopers to cover any doors that would allow the defenders who had been driven underground to gain access back to the surface.

Machine gun fire was still coming from a damaged building at the northern end of the fort, with a killing area in front too deep for the Germans to cross. Some fire onto the bridges was also coming from a retractable 3-inch gun cupola in a casemate that was damaged but not silenced; a second assault being rendered impossible because of the covering machine gun position to the north. Belgian artillery now began to land on the surface of the fort, pinning down the Germans in whatever makeshift cover they could find. Somewhere in the devastation, a Belgian Artillery Observer was still operating effectively, directing the incoming fire onto the German positions.

Wenzel needed to silence the gun still firing on the bridges and searched for Leutnant Delica, Granite Group's Luftwaffe Liaison Officer, to get him to call in air support. Delica was trapped in a pocket of isolated paratroopers on the southern end of the fort surface; the ground in between him and Wenzel being swept by Belgian machine gun fire. Wenzel carefully wrote out his air support request in his notebook and tore out the page. Forcing it into the pocket of the closest paratrooper, he sent his selected messenger through the machine gun fire in the direction of Leutnant Delica. Wenzel pulled his men back away from the casemate that was the air support target and rolled onto his side, turning his attention to the sky.

Under his breath, he was urging Delica to hurry up as two black shapes circled above, gradually getting larger. He heard the distant wail of the siren get louder and louder as the first Stuka dived towards its target, unable to break his gaze as the aircraft fell vertically from the sky. As he saw the bomb released, he rolled onto his front, burying his face in the grass of the fort surface. The impact felt as if a giant foot had stamped on the ground as the shock wave travelled through his body from the earth. He instinctively gripped the grass in a futile gesture, as he imagined he would be thrown into the air. Lumps of soil and smashed concrete landed around the paratroopers closest to the casemate. Having no time to gather his senses, another wailing Stuka forced his face back into the soil and he braced himself for another strike. The giant stamped his foot again, and Wenzel thanked God he was not on the receiving end of Leutnant Delica's devastating work. When the smoke cleared, it was obvious that the casemate had not received a direct hit, but the cupola was retracted and played no further part in the battle for the bridges.

Wenzel was about to turn his attention to the Belgian artillery that was still falling around them, and the machine guns that were still restricting the movement of the paratroopers, when a rapidly moving shadow streaked across the ground in front of his position. It was the sound of glider skids on the fort's grassed surface rather than a visual confirmation which told him that another machine had just landed. Oberleutnant Witzig was first to emerge, darting for cover through the machine gun fire and exploding shell splinters; the rest of the glider passengers close on his heels. He had managed to secure a replacement tug aircraft and had taken off from the rapidly cleared strip his men had prepared in the field where the glider had landed. Three hours after the rest of his group had attacked the fort, he was able to join the battle.

Having sprinted to join him, Wenzel slumped down beside Witzig to be greeted with a broad smile and a handshake. He pulled a printed plan of the fort from the front of his smock and briefed the officer on the current state of the battle, using a plucked blade of grass to point out specific casemates and enemy gun positions on the paper as he orientated it to the structures on the fort. The casemate assigned to Witzig's glider had not yet been attacked. It contained heavy 4.5-inch guns which could easily reach the bridges, and although up to this point had remained silent, the threat still existed that Belgian shells would destroy the structures before the approaching German armoured columns could get across the river. Witzig assembled the engineers from his own glider and sent them to attack the cupola, ordering every other paratrooper not in the assault team to suppress the machine gun covering the approach to the structure. The charges were placed and detonated successfully, lumps of concrete being scattered in all directions, but not collapsing the casemate itself. There still being no response from the guns, Witzig assumed they had been put out of action by the blast.

Witzig now turned his attention to the defence of the position against counterattack from Belgian forces stationed to the west of the fort, and from those defenders forced to take refuge inside. Believing all the guns were now disabled, Witzig positioned his paratroopers to cover the approaches from the west; the most likely area from which a counterattack could be expected.

Using conventional demolition charges, the engineers sequentially set about breaching the access doors from the fort's passages onto the surface. Further charges were dropped down the access stairwells once entry had been gained; muffled blasts, shouts and screams being heard from inside, before falling silent.

* * *

Major Jottrand was experiencing decision paralysis. Standing in his operations room, he was receiving frantic reports from the casemates as the guns were being knocked out by devastating explosions. Terribly wounded men were lying in the passageways as medical orderlies tried to stem their bleeding and prepare them for carriage to the fort's hospital by stretcher bearers. Reports of poison gas caused panic among the inexperienced conscript artillerists, and made command and control even more difficult as gas masks were donned for protection. No poison gas was used, the fumes from broken bottles of cleaning fluid being mistaken for chlorine. Smaller explosions indicated the Germans were now breaking down the access doors to the surface and would soon be inside the fort. Jottrand overcame his thought paralysis and gave orders for sandbag barricades to be built across the access doors. If he could contain the Germans on the surface, he believed there might still be a chance that he could organise a counterattack and drive them off. His telephone operator began passing the messages to the casemate control rooms and the defenders hurriedly set about their tasks.

The external telephone to headquarters in Liege suddenly rang. The line had been dead since the attack began, and both Jottrand and his telephone operator stared at the device in shock and surprise. Jottrand snatched the handset from the cradle and held it to his right ear, putting his left hand over his left ear to deaden the noise of running feet and wounded men from the passageway outside. The telephone operator only caught snatches of heated conversation between Jottrand and headquarters as he continued to pass the access blocking orders to the casemates. Jottrand slammed down the handset.

"Connect me to the commander of Cupola 120 immediately." he demanded. Cupola 120 housed two 4.5-inch guns, carefully pre-plotted on Vroenhoeven Bridge, one of the three bridges over the Albert Canal. The gunnery officer in command had received no orders to open fire and as such had taken no part in the battle up to this point. His cupola had been attacked, but the charge had not penetrated the armour. Jottrand quickly checked with him that the cupola was operational before giving the order to open fire. With ammunition already loaded in the guns, almost immediately, two shells left the cupola in the direction of Vroenhoeven Bridge. "Now get me every available officer here as fast as possible." Jottrand told the telephone operator.

* * *

On the surface, Witzig still believed all the guns had been silenced, and was positioning his men to deal with expected counter attacks from both inside the fort, and from a relieving force stationed at Wonck, three miles away. There was an estimated strength of around five hundred men in Wonck, who manned the fort on rotation for a week at a time. They knew the approaches to the complex, and most importantly, they knew their way around the inside of the fort. Witzig was determined they must not be allowed to join the battle.

The sudden and unexpected action of Cupola 120 stopped Witzig in his tracks. These large calibre guns were the most dangerous in the fort as they could easily destroy the canal bridges, rendering his men's exploits to date useless; and ultimately result in the failure of his part in the operation. An engineer explosive team did not wait for orders, and were already making their way back through the harassing machine gun fire to attach another shaped charge to the cupola. As they stood up to assemble the device, a burst of fire swept across them, putting the complete team out of action. Oberfeldwebel Wenzel was on his feet in an instant. He knew as Witzig did that their mission was on the point of failure. As bullets ripped up the grass around him, he made a crouched dash straight for the gun barrels which only protruded about two feet from the cupola, the vast majority of their length being inside the protective dome. Exposing his head and shoulders only, he fused and dropped a small charge directly down one of the gun barrels before throwing himself flat on the ground. The fuse burned as the device slid down the barrel, detonating the charge in the open breech of the gun as a second shell was being loaded by the crew. The blast sent a huge pressure wave around the inside of the cupola, disabling the crew and filling the turret with choking, toxic fumes. Cupola 120 was out of action; this time permanently.

Wenzel's action was not without personal cost. Blood was pouring down his face from a head wound, which both at the time of injury and on realisation of wounding, he had felt no pain. He pulled his field dressing from the pocket inside his smock, and finding the wound with his fingers, pressed the pad against the torn flesh.

* * *

Major Jottrand could sense the reticence from his officers as he gave orders for a counterattack against the Germans on the surface of the fort. They were conscript artillerists, called up after the invasion of Poland in September 1939, and here he was, asking them to engage in combat with highly trained enemy parachutists. He had requested a bombardment on the surface of the fort just prior to the planned counterattack, which would also be supported by an advance from the relief garrison in Wonck. He dismissed his officers to organise their men, with instructions to assemble in the access shafts as the bombardment fell on the surface. At the cessation of the shelling, they were to burst out and engage any Germans they found, driving them off the fort.

He glanced at his watch and felt his stomach knot with nerves. The relief garrison would already be forming on the approaches to the fort. He could do no more now; just hope. Stepping outside the operations room, out of sight of the telephone operator, he vomited in the corridor.

* * *

Witzig's paratroopers took cover as best they could in craters and folds in the ground as Belgian artillery from the neighbouring forts of Pontisse and Barchon began to fall among them. Any warning whistle from approaching shells was drowned out by the explosions of the continuous and accurate fire. Witzig knew this was the prelude to a counterattack, but there was nothing he could do except wait it out. He tried to force himself deeper into the ground with each explosion, feeling helpless and useless as the shells seemed to suck the ability for logical thought out of him. He was not in control of the situation and was in no position to regain it while the shells were landing. It was not a feeling he was accustomed to, and he didn't like it. He forced himself to think by gauging the rate and pattern of the explosions. If the rate or impact pattern changed, then the chances were that the bombardment would be ending, and the counterattack would follow immediately or very soon afterwards. His speed of reaction on cessation of the bombardment would be crucial, and he was determined to give his men the best possible chance against the impending attack.

This was it. The frequency of falling shells was decreasing rapidly; a few smaller shells landing seconds after the violence of the bombardment had declined. Witzig yelled for his men to prepare themselves to fight again, his voice sounding muffled to them through the whistling in their ears caused by the noise from the exploding shells. They retrieved their weapons from under their bodies where they had placed them to protect the working parts from falling dirt and debris. They crawled to the edges of their craters, set up their machine guns and prepared for combat.

The distinctive clang of metal bolts being slid open gave notice to the Germans that the defenders were about to emerge from the fort onto the surface. The sounds also indicated what access doors were to be used, the defenders not having thought to unlock the doors during the bombardment to disguise the sound of the sliding bars. The Belgians only possessed bolt action rifles, no automatic weapons and very few grenades. As their officers emerged through the doors into the sunlight, German machine guns ripped their bodies to pieces. Non-commissioned officers pushed men through the exits out onto the surface and into the maelstrom. Not being combat trained, practically no fire was returned from the Belgians. The result was slaughter. As German bullets came in through the open doors and ricocheted round the walls, those who had not yet been pushed out onto the fort surface slammed the doors closed and bolted them shut; leaving those already outside to their fate.

The paratroopers covering the approaches from Wonck saw around two hundred men moving steadily towards them across the fields. Witzig watched them through his binoculars and rightly assumed they were the relief garrison. He had already ordered Leutnant Delica to prepare an air support request for such an eventuality, and now called for its implementation. Once more the wail of Stuka sirens could be heard, this time six machines falling upon the approaching Belgians caught in open ground. As Witzig watched, the Belgians scattered in all directions for cover at the sound of the approaching aircraft. He saw the first bombs detonate, hurling debris and bodies into the air before the sound of the explosions reached him. One after the other the Stukas dropped their deadly loads, taking it in turn to dive almost vertically before pulling up at the last second and releasing their bombs.

As the last aircraft disappeared into the distance and the smoke from the explosions cleared in the breeze, Witzig could see black scars on the landscape where the bombs had impacted. Men were moving quickly between the prone figures of injured or dead comrades, all being conducted in a macabre silence after the violence that had just been visited upon them. He was glad he was not close enough to hear their agonised cries for help. As he continued to watch, some order was restored and a unified direction of movement of the Belgians became obvious again. Groups of uninjured men were running towards the fort, with slower moving individuals following or being helped along behind them. This was not an assault; they were seeking refuge inside the complex.

* * *

A Captain reported to Jottrand in the operations room. His face was covered in dirt, clean streaks showing where sweat was running from beneath his steel helmet. Jottrand listened almost expressionless as, between gasps for air, the account of the Stuka attack was related by the officer. One hundred men had been added to the garrison strength, and another forty to the hospital register. Sixty men lay dead on the approaches to the fort. Jottrand thanked the captain for his report and assigned the extra men to the construction of the internal barriers. He then lifted the handset on the external line to Liege to update headquarters.

As darkness fell, dull sounds of activity from inside the fort could be heard on the surface as the garrison worked on their barriers. The paratroopers lay exhausted and parched in their shell holes as harassing fire continued from Belgian artillery somewhere in the distance. The paratroopers had twinned together, allowing some to try and sleep while others remained alert. Witzig was woken by Wenzel with a beaming smile. Beside him stood an Army engineer whose men had crossed the Albert Canal in assault boats as a prelude to the advancing tanks and infantry. His offer of assistance was as welcome as the drink from his water bottle.

Friday 10 May 1940 –
Moerdijk Bridges, Western Netherlands.

The German strategy to capture bridges of critical importance by airborne assault was attempted simultaneously in the Netherlands. In anticipation, structures considered as vital infrastructure had been prepared for demolition by the Dutch military in case of German invasion. The Moerdijk road and rail bridges over the Hollands Diep, sixteen miles south of Rotterdam, and with a span of over half a mile, was known by the Germans to have been prepared as such. The 2nd Battalion of the 1st Fallschirmjager Regiment was assigned the task of capturing these bridges intact, and holding them open until the tanks of the 9th Panzer Division could race forward and relieve them. Due to the long bridge span, the German plan was to attack both ends simultaneously. The commander of the 2nd Battalion, Hauptmann Fritz Prager, was in hospital leading up to the events, having been diagnosed with terminal cancer. On hearing of the attack plans, and determined to lead the men he had trained so thoroughly for combat, he signed himself out of hospital and resumed his command position.

The Dutch plan was to demolish the bridge when it became threatened by the Germans approaching from the south, and explosives had been placed for this purpose. This decision resulted in sparse defences on the southern side, which would be abandoned prior to demolition; with reliance on a substantial mutually supporting concrete bunker complex on the northern side to prevent enemy encroachment to the north bank. The firing ports and loopholes in the blockhouses on the north bank all faced south, towards the perceived enemy approaches. No loopholes faced sideways or to the rear.

At dawn, German bombers and fighters attacked the Dutch positions around the bridge, and as the sound of aircraft engines faded, the Dutch watched in horror as dozens of white parachutes opened in the brightening sky, over both the south bank and behind the defenders on the northern bank. The German paratroopers jumped at an altitude of three hundred feet, unusually low, but necessary to avoid their forces being too widely dispersed. They flung themselves at the defenders in a race against time to prevent detonation of the demolition charges, only to discover on seizing both ends of the bridge, that the detonation wires had not been installed, as no demolition authority order had been received by the defenders. Capture of this bridge effectively isolated the centre of Holland from relief by any Allied forces attempting to come to the aid of the Dutch from the west.

Within the first hour of action, Oberleutnant Alfred Schwartzmann, who had won three gold medals for Germany at the 1936 Berlin Olympics, was shot through the lung and taken prisoner by the Dutch. Not expected to survive his wound, scarce resources were not allocated to evacuate him for medical treatment. Siem Heiden, a Dutch soldier and former Olympic speed skater and world record holder, recognised the critically injured Schwartzmann and personally arranged his evacuation to a Dutch medical facility.

Friday 10 May 1940 –
Willemsbrug Bridge, Rotterdam, Northern Netherlands.

At 5 a.m. twelve Heinkel He 59 seaplanes swept in low over the centre of Rotterdam just as dawn was breaking. They approached along the length of the Niew Mass river, their engines slowing as they hit the water, then revving again as they taxied to the river banks. One hundred and fifty German soldiers from the 16th Infantry Regiment in the airlanding role, clambered into inflatable boats and frantically paddled towards the embankments at both ends of the bridge. Dutch civilians on their way to work watched the spectacle in amazement. Some thought they were Allied troops and helped them up the steep sides of the embankment.

Initial Dutch military reaction was practically non-existent, allowing the Germans to quickly establish themselves at each end of the bridge; any available Dutch troops having been deployed in defensive positions protecting The Hague. Once confirmed as secure, reinforcements parachuted into the football stadium south of the river and commandeered passing trams to get themselves to the bridge. The commandeered trams were then used to block the northern approaches to the bridge against possible Dutch counterattack. The Dutch command system recovered from the shock of the assaults and reacted by sending the destroyer Van Galen up the river to engage the Germans on the bridge and in their landing zones. The approaching ship was attacked by the Luftwaffe, damaged, and ran aground before it could influence the battle.

There was no mass exodus of refugees as the Germans arrived; the invaders behaving courteously towards the civilian population who they came into contact with. German soldiers queued alongside bemused Dutch civilians in shops to buy chocolate; a product that had been rationed in Germany.

Friday 10 May 1940 –
Sauer River, Central Luxembourg.

The leading elements of German Army Group A crossed the border into Luxembourg at 5:35 a.m. where a squad of infantry rushed across the bridge over the Sauer, disarming the Luxembourg Border Police guard. Combat engineers destroyed the concrete block obstacles on the existing bridge and began to construct three additional bridges to cope with the expected volume of traffic, taking only forty minutes to complete their task.

Motorcycle troops, armoured reconnaissance vehicles and combat engineers led the way for the infantry and artillery to begin their advance. In three hours, they had moved thirty miles through Luxembourg to reach the Belgian border, meeting no opposition.

Friday 10 May 1940 –
Ardennes Forest, Germany / Belgium Border.

At first light, three hundred Luftwaffe bombers had attacked twenty-two airfields and rail hubs in Holland, Belgium and Luxembourg which had immediately alerted those countries to impending military action. As a result, in the Ardennes sector, the Belgian defenders had hurriedly destroyed bridges and mined the narrow curving roads, making them impassable to vehicles. These obstacles were then covered by machine gun positions in overlooking buildings or from higher ground. The German motorcycle troops, racing ahead of the advancing armoured columns, were the first to encounter these obstacles, coming under fire from the defenders. The Germans were under orders to maintain momentum at all costs, and the motorcycle troops fought as dismounted infantry to quickly suppress the enemy while the supporting engineers cleared the roads and repaired or replaced damaged or destroyed bridges.

As the German armour was still many miles behind, struggling over complicated routes entirely unsuitable for heavy vehicles, no tanks had as yet been involved in the engagements. Combat reports from defenders to their headquarters therefore did not mention the presence of tanks and raised no suspicion that this assault could be the German main effort. The Luftwaffe kept Allied aerial reconnaissance planes away, again preventing reports of mobile German armoured columns from reaching Allied headquarters. These combat reports encouraged the Allies to move their forces forward into Belgium where they believed the enemy main effort to be; and straight into the German trap.

Friday 10 May 1940 –
Lille, Northern France.

At 2:30 p.m.10 Platoon was in a PT lesson when the sight of officers and non-commissioned officers running between the accommodation blocks suggested that something out of the ordinary was happening. Orders were shouted to the instructor to curtail his lesson and get everyone into the cookhouse. Against a backdrop of the sound of vehicles moving and shouted orders from outside, the Commanding Officer briefed a stunned and silent gathering that the expected German offensive had begun that morning; with enemy columns advancing into Belgium and the Netherlands.

"We will not be manning the positions that we previously prepared, but have been ordered into Belgium and will take up positions on the river Dyle, east of Brussels." the Commanding Officer confirmed. Officers looked at each other in disbelief, as this was a huge variation on the deployment for which they had been practicing. "Reconnaissance elements are already on their way to secure the position and will meet us there on arrival." he continued. "All company officers are to stay behind after this briefing to be assigned routes and timings. Your officers will be able to answer any questions you may have later."

At this, the soldiers were dismissed and a flurry of activity began, packing personal equipment, loading food, fuel cans and defence stores onto the lorries and filling ammunition belts for the machine guns; all conducted to the accompaniment of shouted commands, vehicle doors slamming and the sound of nailed boots running. It was late afternoon by the time everything was packed and ready to deploy; the men sitting in the loaded vehicles waiting for their officers, who arrived with maps tucked under their arms and gave the orders to move. Two hours later, the convoy passed over the French border and into Belgium, leaving behind the prepared positions the men had worked on for months.

The reconnaissance elements of the Expeditionary Force reached the river Dyle that night to secure the allotted positions for the following infantry. A trickle of refugees was already crossing the river, passing through the reconnaissance screen, moving west.

Friday 10 May 1940 – Mo, Northern Norway.

With the withdrawal of British forces from around Trondheim, the road to Narvik now lay open for the Germans, who continued to advance as fast as the terrain would allow. Two hundred and fifty miles south of Narvik, was the narrowest part of Norway, being only seventeen miles from the tip of the Saltdalsfjord to the Swedish border. At the mouth of the fjord was the port of Bodo. As a last-ditch attempt to stop the German push north at this natural bottleneck, British forces had been set ashore at Bodo, which could be easily supplied by sea from Harstad. A smaller force landed one hundred and thirty miles further south at Mo, to deny this potential advance route north to the Germans, and prevent paratrooper or naval capture of the port as a potential resupply hub.

From Mo, a reconnaissance screen pushed out a further forty miles south to Mosjoen to destroy any still usable bridges, and block the road north. Between 7 – 9 May, German pressure against the reconnaissance screen increased, forcing the British back into Mosjoen. In a bold outflanking operation on 10 May, three hundred Germans were landed by destroyer at

Hemnesberget, fifteen miles west of Mo, with heavy equipment supplied in two Dornier seaplanes. This landing effectively cut off any potential withdrawal route for the British back towards Mo, forcing an evacuation of the reconnaissance screen by sea from the harbour at Mosjoen. With Mo now directly under threat, the port was reinforced on 12 May by three companies of Scots Guards. Brigadier Colin Gubbins was ordered from Harstad to Bodo with 24 (Guards) Brigade, consisting of practically all the remaining British forces in northern Norway, with orders to hold Bodo indefinitely, and Mo as long as possible.

Friday 10 May 1940 –
10 Downing Street, London, England.

Triggered by the news of the German attacks into Belgium and the Netherlands on the morning of 10 May, Chamberlain decided to stand down as Prime Minister; and advised the King to send for Churchill as his successor. As the news of the German attack spread, all across the nation, families at home and workers in their workplaces huddled around crackling radio sets, hungry for news. That evening, Neville Chamberlain addressed a stunned nation from the Cabinet Office at Downing Street.

> *"I sought an audience with the King this evening and tendered to him my resignation, which His Majesty has been pleased to accept. His Majesty has now entrusted to my friend and colleague, Mr Winston Churchill, the task of forming a new administration on a National Basis. And in this task, I have no doubt he will be successful. For the hour has come when we are to be put to the test, as the innocent people of Holland, Belgium, and France are being tested already. And you and I must rally behind our new leader, and with our united strength, and with unshakable courage, fight and work until this wild beast, which has sprung out of his lair upon us, has been finally disarmed and overthrown."*

Having gained the support of both Labour and the Liberals, Churchill formed a Coalition Government. Chamberlain remained Conservative Party leader and was given a position in the War Cabinet by Churchill. He resigned from this position on 22 September due to ill health and succumbed to cancer only a few months later on 9 November.

Saturday 11 May 1940 –
Fort Eben Emael, Belgium / Netherlands Border.

Reinforced with both men and equipment, the paratroopers and engineers began at dawn to drop demolition charges down the casemate entrances into the stairwells and to blow open the bolted access doors to the surface. Witzig sent men inside the fortress to dismantle the barricades hurriedly thrown up by the garrison, and to begin clearing out the defenders. Battles raged in the connecting corridors as the Germans fought their way in, their automatic weapons and grenades spraying the walls inside with bullets and fragments; a weight of firepower that the defenders could neither match nor resist. German tanks were now across the canal and pushing forward around the fortress; their supporting infantry joining Witzig's paratroopers on the surface, and being immediately fed into the battle raging inside the fortress.

With the sounds of combat clearly audible in the background, Jottrand made it clear to headquarters in Liege that unless a counterattack was mounted immediately, the fortress would be lost. He listened intently to the reply, then without affirmation, he reached out to replace the handset in the cradle. His hand was visibly shaking, so much so that the handset did not seat properly, falling off and left swinging on the cable. Jottrand didn't notice. He slumped into the wooden chair beside the telephone operator who expected orders; but received nothing.

When he had gathered his thoughts, Jottrand convened a meeting with his surviving officers and non-commissioned officers in the briefing room beside the operations room. He was not giving orders but taking council, and the calmness of his voice disguised the torment he was feeling inside.

"There will be no relieving force." he explained to his ashen faced subordinates. "The decision whether to surrender or withdraw has been left to me." No one else spoke; not even a murmur came from his audience. The lights flickered as an explosion sent dust falling from the ceiling; as if deliberately planned to add more drama to the situation. "The fort is lost; without question." he continued. "We can either try to fight our way out or surrender to the Germans." Having witnessed the consequences of German occupation as a young man during the Great War, Jottrand had already made up his mind on his favoured course; but was not prepared to send more men to their death in a potentially fruitless attempt at withdrawal if their heart was not in the fight. "I want your views." he said.

Having formally offered the choice, the shackles of military etiquette were off, and the room erupted in clamouring voices as everyone tried to make their opinion heard. The telephone operator from the operations room handed Jottrand a message he had hurriedly scribbled down. It read, *"Main entrance under attack from enemy armour and infantry."* Jottrand's question to his officers had become nugatory. The option to break out had been removed and Jottrand knew at that point his war was over. He glanced at his watch. It was 10 a.m. But there was one final gesture to make before he became a prisoner of war.

* * *

Oberleutnant Witzig heard his name being called. His presence was required inside the fortress. He was met by one of his junior non-commissioned officers at the top of a spiral metal walkway leading into the complex, and was requested to follow the young paratrooper. The sound of their boots on the metal steps echoed around the confined stairwell. He was amazed the electric lighting was still operating. Had he been defending the fort, he thought, it would have been turned off long ago to make a disorientated enemy fight in the dark. At the bottom of the steps, corridors opened out in all directions. Empty bullet cases littered the ground as Witzig was led past sandbag obstacles and metal bedframes that had been used by the defenders in a futile attempt to block the way. There was a strong smell of propellent and explosive in the air from the fighting. On a wooden bench sat a Belgian officer who sprang to attention as Witzig approached. He saluted and Witzig returned the compliment. The Belgian explained that he had been sent by the Fortress Commander, Major Jottrand, to discuss surrender terms with the Officer Commanding the German forces.

* * *

At fifteen minutes past noon, a bugle was heard from inside the fort; the call being repeated several times. The doors to the main entrance were opened and the garrison began to file out, blinking in the bright sunlight, their hands raised above their heads. The Germans hurriedly began to process their prisoners, removing and searching their equipment and personal belongings. Steel helmets and gas masks were returned to their owners in line with the Geneva Convention, and the prisoners were moved away. Major Jottrand approached the commander of the engineer battalion, introduced himself, opened his holster and handed across his pistol. The engineer Hauptman asked for assurance that no delayed action charges had been left in the fort. When Jottrand gave his word, his pistol was returned and he was directed away to join his men. The German engineers found the Belgian medical staff still attending to their wounded in the fort's hospital, but every other item of stores and equipment had been destroyed before the garrison had departed; Jottrand's last order being to deny anything of use to the enemy.

* * *

Witzig and his paratroopers stood in the village of Eben Emael and watched as columns of tanks and supply vehicles streamed past them, sending a choking dust cloud into the air, and mixing with the engine exhaust fumes. The village was deserted; abandoned by the inhabitants when the fighting had started. The cafe door they tried was not even locked, and the paratroopers, their job done, helped themselves to the fruits of victory from behind the bar.

Saturday 11 May 1940 –
Moerdijk Bridges, Western Netherlands.

In the area around the bridge, an almost continuous bombardment by Dutch artillery failed to dislodge the German defenders. The sky was full of German planes whose dive bombing not only harried the Dutch artillery, but cleared the path for the 9th Panzer Division column racing to relieve the bridge from the south. In the afternoon, a French reconnaissance unit, the 5e Groupe de Reconnaissance de Division d'Infanterie, with the assistance of a Dutch border battalion, attempted an attack on the southern bridgehead; but their armoured cars were heavily bombed by Stukas and forced to retreat.

Saturday 11 May 1940 –
Willemsbrug Bridge, Rotterdam, Northern Netherlands.

As the Dutch military command structure reacted to the numerous German incursions and parachute drops across the country, the Rotterdam garrison was reinforced by an infantry regiment, which immediately flung themselves against the German bridgehead on the northern bank of the Maas. Despite being vastly outnumbered, the German defenders continued to resist from what was by now a single occupied office building, protected by a canal to their front and supported by machinegun fire from the southern bank. Aware of the perilous position, permission had been granted for a withdrawal, an option the defenders were loathed to accept despite there being no possibility of immediate relief or resupply. The only two remaining operational Dutch bombers mounted an attack, but failed to destroy the bridge.

Saturday 11 May 1940 –
Neufchateau, River Semois, Southern Belgium.

There was little sleep for the soldiers in Army Group A over the night of 10 / 11 May. After resupply of ammunition and fuel, and weapon and vehicle maintenance; soldiers slept where they lay down, using their packs as pillows. Officers wrote combat reports and received and issued orders for the next day. The objective for 11 May was the Semois river, being the last natural obstacle before the Meuse. By dawn, German reconnaissance vehicles were already in contact with a French forward screen, which conducted a fighting withdrawal to a defensive line between the towns of Librament and Neufchateau. Although most German armour was confined to the rear by a combination of deliberate deception and unfavourable terrain, some tanks were used to exploit a gap around the town of Neufchateau, penetrating deep into the defensive positions and causing confusion in the French rear.

The panzers arrived at the Semois river before dark, and attempted a crossing over two bridges that were destroyed just in time by the French defenders. With the tanks' advance now frustrated at the destruction of the bridges, the accompanying infantry crossed the river using a ford, and with the support of Stuka attacks, established a bridgehead on the western bank. Further success was achieved to the south when a motorcycle unit seized an intact bridge at Mouzaive, the Germans crossing just after midnight. By the end of the day, Army Group A had achieved its objective; it was across the Semois.

Although reports of German armour at Neufchateau got back to headquarters, they were still not taken as significant by the French, who continued to push forces into northern Belgium where panzer columns were at the forefront of the action; and where they still believed the main German thrust was developing.

Saturday 11 May 1940 –
River Dyle, Central Belgium.

The British vehicles had driven all night, cab passengers deliberately talking continuously to the drivers to keep them awake, while those in the back tried to sleep as best they could. At dawn, the drivers were changed and the passengers were allowed out to stretch their legs and relieve themselves. They emerged from the canvas covered vehicles, blinking in the light, to see a lush green landscape; far removed from the grey and smoke-stained industrial area of France they had become accustomed to over the last months. Officers gathered and confirmed their location and route that would take them through Brussels, indicating that it would be close to dark before they arrived at the river Dyle. The order to get back into the vehicles was softened somewhat by the promise of another halt in a few hours, with time then to be allowed for the preparation of a hot meal.

* * *

It was late evening before the convoy reached Brussels. The British were met with cheering crowds, the noise from which drowned out the sound of their engines and vehicle tracks on the cobbled streets. Women ran beside the vehicles, throwing flowers, fruit and sweets to the passing troops who had rolled up the canvas sides of the trucks to reach out, shake hands and accept the gifts. With crowds of civilians jamming the streets, the progress of the convoy was slowed, not covering the further sixteen miles to the river Dyle before it was dark.

As the infantry dismounted from their vehicles, they saw the roads were full of refugees, some in horse drawn carts and a few cars with their possessions loaded on the roof; but with the vast majority on foot, pulling hand carts or pushing wheelbarrows. The refugees made no sound, only the grinding of the cart wheels on the roads breaking the eerie silence. The reconnaissance force that had secured the position agreed to let the newly arrived soldiers sleep after their journey, and maintained watch during the night.

Sunday 12 May 1940 –
Moerdijk Bridges, Western Netherlands.

Shortly after noon, German armoured cars from the 9th Panzer Division made contact with the southern perimeter of the Moerdijk bridgehead; met by cheering paratroopers who emerged from their defensive positions to greet their relief column. This in effect ended any prospect of assistance to the Dutch from Allied forces. By 4:45 p.m. tanks had reached the bridges themselves.

A final artillery barrage was ordered by the Dutch Commander, General Winkelman, in a last-ditch attempt to destroy the bridges before the Germans could cross, but to no avail; causing only slight damage to the huge structure. Being pessimistic about the general situation at this point, Winkelman also ordered the strategic oil reserves of Royal Dutch Shell to be set on fire, denying their use to the enemy.

Sunday 12 May 1940 –
Willemsbrug Bridge, Rotterdam, Northern Netherlands.

In Rotterdam and around The Hague, again little was done against the paratroopers ensconced on the bridge. Most Dutch commanders, still afraid of a presumed Fifth Column operation by collaborators or German agents dressed in civilian clothes, limited themselves to security measures for the protection of the Government sector.

Sunday 12 May 1940 –
Veldwezelt Bridge, Belgium / Netherlands Border.

Early on the morning of 12 May, the aircrews of 12 Squadron, Royal Air Force were called to an emergency briefing at their base in Amifontaine, near Rheims, where they learned that the Germans had seized intact several bridges over the Albert Canal; across which vital war material and fighting units were flowing into Belgium. Several previous attempts by the RAF to destroy the bridges had been unsuccessful due to enemy fighter cover and anti-aircraft guns; orders now being received that the bridges had to be destroyed at all costs. The emergency briefing was to inform 12 Squadron that they had been selected to mount the next attack against the bridges, but that due to the high attrition rate of previous attacks, this mission was for volunteers only. Every member of aircrew volunteered, more than enough to man the five available Fairey Battle light bombers. Invariably, lots were drawn to select the crews.

21-year-old Flying Officer Donald Garland was chosen to lead his section of three aircraft against the Veldwezelt Bridge. After a low-level flight under the 1,000 feet cloud base, Garland's section approached the bridge as the escorting Hurricane fighters struggled to keep enemy aircraft away and give the dive bombers a clear run. Garland led his section in a shallow dive from 1,000 feet through a storm of German anti-aircraft fire to release his bombs over the bridge, but was struck multiple times and crashed into the ground. The second Battle to attack was in flames even before it began its run in and was forced to land nearby. The third aircraft was blown apart in flight. The Hurricane pilots in combat above the target reported that the bridge was obscured by the bombs bursting on it and near it. As the smoke from the attack cleared, the western end of the Veldwezelt Bridge was seen to be badly damaged.

Sunday 12 May 1940 –
River Semois, Southern Belgium.

The attacking front of Army Group A expanded as it broke free of the logistical and terrain constraints imposed by their assigned route of advance. Reconnaissance units now raced towards the Meuse from both north and south of the Semois bridgeheads, sweeping aside the Belgian and French defenders. In the afternoon of 12 May, aerial reconnaissance identified an intact bridge being used by refugees over the Meuse at Yvoir; but it was demolished by its French defenders just as the leading elements of General Rommel's 7th Panzer Division reached it.

As the Germans pushed along the east bank of the Meuse in search of an alternative crossing, a motorcycle patrol found an undefended weir a few miles to the south, which connected the mid-river island of Houx to both banks. It was the exact spot where the Germans had crossed the Meuse in the 1914 invasion. The French realised the danger and pushed reinforcements into the area. When darkness fell, German infantry managed to ford the river but were held in a tiny bridgehead on the west bank by the French reinforcements.

Sunday 12 May 1940 –
Sedan, River Meuse, France / Belgium Border.

The 1st Panzer Division, fighting forty miles further south, had spent a number of hours overcoming ferocious French opposition before the town of Sedan, but as the division finally fought their way into the town that evening they heard loud explosions, indicating that the final bridges over the Meuse, that had been held open for the French to withdraw, had now been destroyed. With just a pinprick of a bridgehead on the west bank of the Meuse at Houx, and most of the Army Group's tanks still miles behind the leading elements, it would take many hours before the Germans would have the strength to attempt a crossing in force. The French were planning on it taking many days.

Sunday 12 May 1940 –
River Dyle, Central Belgium.

Dawn broke to reveal the position on the river Dyle; at a point where the river was narrow with wooded areas on each bank. With the reconnaissance unit happy that D Company were in position, they moved east across the river to form a defensive screen to frustrate any German reconnaissance efforts, and give advance notice of the approaching enemy. To provide immediate protection, two-man holes were dug in which the soldiers could take cover from enemy air or artillery attack while the company officers prepared a defensive plan for the assigned sector.

Captain Roberts assessed likely enemy approach routes and river crossing points, and the defensive plan was then built around these considerations. Some isolated farm buildings were dotted around the area and these were used to disguise the larger anti-tank weapons, sited to cover likely enemy armour approaches. Smaller machine guns were disguised in chicken sheds and outhouses, carefully selected to dominate areas of open ground. Once these major weapons were established, considerable efforts were made to disguise their presence within the fabric of the buildings by positioning them back from windows. To widen and improve arcs of fire, bricks were removed to allow traverse barrel movement for the machine guns. Over the next few days, the gun crews would remove any small trees and shrubs that might obstruct their view of the created "killings areas," in which it was planned to inflict maximum casualties on an attacking enemy.

With the priority work completed, the company was at least in a position from which it could fight if required. The remaining time before the expected German assault would be spent enhancing the individual platoon positions, but that night the men climbed down into their holes and collapsed into an exhausted sleep, still wearing their equipment and cradling their rifles.

Monday 13 May 1940 –
Moerdijk Bridges, Western Netherlands.

Having relieved the German defenders in the southern bridgehead the evening before, the tanks of the 9th Panzer Division were resupplied and split; some to pursue the French reconnaissance force that had attacked the southern bridgehead two days earlier, and the rest to push north towards Rotterdam. This second group began to cross the bridge at 5:20 a.m. In response, at 6 a.m. the last operational Dutch medium bomber, a Fokker T.V. dropped two bombs on the bridge. One hit a bridge pillar but failed to explode, with the aircraft subsequently being shot down. Dutch artillery batteries tried to prevent the crossing by shell fire, causing slight damage to the bridge, but were hindered in their efforts by German dive bomber attacks. A last-ditch attempt was made to restrict the German armour by the opening of canal sluice gates, hoping to flood the area. The gates failed to open and the strategy was unsuccessful; the panzer spearhead pushing relentlessly forward on the road to Rotterdam.

Monday 13 May 1940 –
Willemsbrug Bridge, Rotterdam, Northern Netherlands.

In Rotterdam a last attempt was made by two Dutch Marine Companies to blow up the Willemsbrug Bridge. They stormed the bridgehead and after a period of two-hours fighting, reached the bridge itself. With only fifty defenders remaining in the final occupied building, and down to their last magazines of ammunition, the Germans were on the point of surrender. They had unsheathed their fighting knives for a last stand when the tanks of 9th Panzer Division appeared on the southern end of the bridge. The Dutch Marines were driven off by heavy fire from across the river.

Monday 13 May 1940 –
Sedan, River Meuse, France / Belgium Border.

Having continued to move all through the night, the Units of the 1st Panzer Division were still arriving in the assembly areas around Sedan as dawn broke. French aerial reconnaissance had by now clearly identified armoured columns with bridging equipment moving west, and the process of moving reserves towards the area had begun. The west bank of the Meuse was part of the newly extended Maginot Line, having concrete bunkers, mines and wire obstacles as part of an interlocking defensive system. The worsening situation in central Belgium and the Netherlands continued to occupy the minds of French commanders, but they felt the defences on the Meuse were strong enough to hold any German attempt to cross the river, and thus paid little attention to developments in that area.

Beginning at noon, the Luftwaffe mounted continuous raids on the French defensive positions. The Germans on the east bank watched transfixed as the west bank of the Meuse was continually bombed by Stukas and strafed by fighters for four hours. At the designated assault time of 4 p.m. the aerial attacks were transferred against French artillery positions in the rear in order to prevent interference with the crossing; and from 5.30 p.m. until dusk, the Stukas switched again to interdiction of French reserves moving towards the area.

As the rubber boats carrying the first wave of Germans entered the water, they immediately came under fire from French defenders who had survived, and recovered from the Luftwaffe bombing. Machine gun rounds kicked up the water all around the vulnerable boats, many striking home to sink the loaded craft and cause casualties. With the crossing point specifically chosen for the short distance between banks, the Germans were soon across, and began to systematically silence the French guns. Using grenades and flamethrowers, the attackers blew the doors off the defenders' bunkers, before setting the occupants on fire. The bridgehead was secured by 5 p.m. and allowed the Corps Commander, General Guderian, to cross to the west bank in the second wave; where he directed the development of the battle from the front line.

As dusk fell at 9 p.m. and exhaustion began to impact the attackers, Guderian pushed them on relentlessly, determined to create the right conditions not only to facilitate the bridge building operations that would have to be performed that night, but to allow space on the west bank for the tanks and armoured vehicles that would subsequently stream across. After eight hours fighting, a penetration of five miles into the French defensive positions had been achieved.

While the fighting raged in the bridgehead on the western bank, eight miles away to the north east, the panzers waited in a forested assembly area. Crews rested as the mechanics carried out essential running repairs and the vehicles were rearmed and refuelled ready for their part in the battle. Anti-aircraft artillery was hurriedly concentrated around the bridge construction sites, in preparation for Allied air attacks that were sure to be launched the next day.

Monday 13 May 1940 –
Houx, River Meuse, Southern Belgium.

Sixty miles further north, the Germans had managed to maintain the bridgehead at Houx overnight; so that by 5:30 a.m. three infantry battalions began to cross the weir in single file. Clearly exposed, they took heavy casualties from French machine guns, their commanders forcing them on past the dead bodies of their comrades floating in the water, until they got across in sufficient strength to subdue the resistance. By the end of the day, they had managed to advance the bridgehead more than two miles.

South of Houx, at a point dominated by rocky outcrops on the west bank, two battalions attempted a crossing in rubber boats under cover of a morning mist. General Erwin Rommel paced the bank nervously as the crossing began, encouraging his men until he was content that a foothold had been gained. He then moved just over two miles north to Leffe, where he found another attempted boat crossing in serious difficulty as reinforcements to the tenuous bridgehead faltered under heavy fire. He screamed orders in an attempt to motivate the reinforcement effort, even crossing the river in a rubber boat himself to direct the establishment of the bridgehead on the western bank. He returned to the east bank when he was content everything was in order, moving south again to the crossing below Houx. Here, he was seen up to his waist in the river assisting the engineers to construct the bridge that would support his armour; over which he would be one of the first to cross in his command vehicle. By evening, all three of the 7th Panzer Division's bridgeheads had been linked.

Monday 13 May 1940 –
River Dyle, Central Belgium.

Captain Roberts spent the morning visiting the flanking companies; and in liaison with their officers, formally agreed the overlap of arcs of fire to close any gaps in the defensive line. Likely approaches for enemy armour were mined, as were any likely river crossing points and areas of dead ground that could not be covered by the machine guns or anti-tank support weapons. There were a few scattered concrete pillboxes of Great War vintage which provided cover for the infantry, but most of their work that day was in the enhancement of the small holes they had already dug. Time was spent making them deeper and wider to allow ease of movement and provide better cover from enemy artillery. Barbed wire obstacles were created on the approaches to the trenches to slow any enemy advance, and detain them for longer in the created killing areas. The signallers from Company Headquarters laid telephone cable to the three platoon positions, which the infantry soldiers helped to bury in order to provide some degree of resilience to the communication system.

Sergeant Major McCann moved around the trenches continually, making the soldiers camouflage their positions with branches cut from the woods to the rear in order to thwart enemy aerial reconnaissance efforts. He warned against the temptation to look up or shoot at aircraft flying overhead, as the contrast of a face against the landscape or smoke from a fired weapon invariably attracted the attention of the aircraft crew. He spent time with Captain Roberts and an Artillery Liaison Officer in the wooded areas on the river bank. These were the places that would offer the best cover for an assaulting force, and would demand specific plans for defence or indeed counterattack should the enemy gain a foothold. The Artillery Liaison Officer was plotting and code numbering targets on maps for fire support on both the east and west banks of the river; which could then be bombarded quickly in an emergency by using the appropriate code number. He left copies of the marked maps for Roberts to distribute to each platoon commander.

"Tell me this." asked the artillery officer as they assessed the requirements and worked out a plan between them. "Why did we leave prepared positions in France to come here and have to prepare all over again?"

"Damned if I know, Sir." McCann replied. "Maybe the Belgians thought they could remain neutral as they did in the last war." he suggested.

"It would appear the Germans have now taken away that choice." Roberts added. The stream of refugees that had been steady through the previous day now became a flood, indicating to the soldiers dug in and waiting, that the enemy was getting closer.

Monday 13 May 1940 –
Bjerkvik, Northern Norway.

Due to the unfavourable topographical considerations at Narvik, proven by the failed frontal assault attempt on 24 April, a revised plan to capture the town by an overland assault had been devised. Lieutenant General Claude Auchinleck had replaced General Mackesy on 11 May with the twin aims of capturing Narvik and slowing the German advance north from Trondheim.

The operation to slow the German advance would be an all-British affair, while the renewed attack on Narvik would be conducted by elements of the French Foreign Legion via a beach assault at Bjerkvik, ten miles north of Narvik. The ground around Bjerkvik would enable a sizeable force to get ashore quickly, which could then move the short distance to Narvik. Norwegian and Polish units would be used in support of the French attack, moving overland to capture strategic positions on the higher ground overlooking the town.

At midnight on 12 / 13 May, although still in daylight due to being so far north, a naval bombardment fell on Bjerkvik as landing craft loaded with French Foreign Legionnaires and five Hotchkiss tanks moved towards the beach. Simultaneously, Norwegian troops were engaging Germans on the dominating high ground overlooking Narvik, forcing them back into the town. Sporadic resistance was soon overcome by the French tanks, and the German garrison at Bjerkvik withdrew south east towards Narvik.

Monday 13 May 1940 –
House of Commons, London, England.

An emergency sitting of the House had been called to announce the formation of a War Cabinet, and to take a vote of confidence in the new Government. The now Prime Minister, Winston Churchill, rose to his feet and approached the dispatch box. The House fell silent.

"It must be remembered that we are in the preliminary stage of one of the greatest battles in history. That we are in action at many points in Norway and in Holland. That we have to be prepared in the Mediterranean. That the air battle is continuous, and that many preparations have to be made here at home. I would say to those in the House, as I have said to those that have joined the Government, I have nothing to offer but blood, toil, tears and sweat. We have before us an ordeal of the most grievous kind. We have before us many, many months of struggle and of suffering. You ask what is our policy? I would say it is to wage war by sea, and in the air with all our might and with all the strength that God can give us. You ask what is our aim? I can answer in one word. Victory!"

Tuesday 14 May 1940 –
Willemsbrug Bridge, Rotterdam, Northern Netherlands.

As German tanks prepared to cross the bridge into central Rotterdam, Dutch defences began to concentrate on the northern bank. German Luftwaffe General Kurt Student requested a limited air attack to disrupt these defences, and allow German tanks to break out of the bridgehead. Student stipulated that severe urban destruction must be avoided, as it would only hamper the tanks trying to advance through rubble strewn streets, most certainly containing civilian corpses; against an enemy now motivated by rage and revenge at the destruction. Embracing the concept, the head of the Luftwaffe, Reichsmarshall Herman Goering, agreed to such a raid, but against the advice of Student, planned to go further. He was becoming increasingly frustrated with the Dutch defence and was concerned about the continued attrition of his prized airborne troops fighting in the streets of Rotterdam. Unbeknown to Student, Goering was determined to force an immediate Dutch national capitulation by demonstrating German airpower through a much more extensive bombing raid.

At 9 a.m. a German messenger crossed the Willemsbrug Bridge to bring an ultimatum to Colonel Pieter Scharroo, the Dutch Military Commander of Rotterdam. The ultimatum demanded the capitulation of the city; under threat of destruction by the Luftwaffe. Colonel Scharroo did not receive the message until 10:30, with a reply deadline of two hours. Not empowered to make this decision without referral to higher authority, Scharroo asked Dutch Supreme Commander, General Winkelman, for orders. In the knowledge of the fate of Warsaw, he warned that if a positive answer had not been received within two hours the "severest means of annihilation" would be unleashed against them. Despite misgivings by Goring's subordinates, at 11:45, ninety Heinkel He 111 bombers took off from Delmenhorst, Munster and Quackenbruck; destination Rotterdam.

The German messenger returned at noon and confirmed delivery of the ultimatum, followed fifteen minutes later by a Dutch envoy seeking clarification on the demands, and requesting an extension of the deadline to allow internal discussions to take place. Instructions to postpone the bombing raid were immediately sent by radio, citing that negotiations were still underway. Recall signals were transmitted to the bombers, but their trailing aerials had by this time been pulled in, and they continued on their mission unaware of the change in orders. It was reported back that the aircraft were underway and radio communication was no longer possible; adding that the bombers could now only be stopped by using the emergency protocol of firing red flares above the target.

An hour later at 1:20 p.m. the Dutch envoy had just received the requested clarification, and an extended deadline until 4:20 p.m. when two formations of Heinkels appeared in the sky over Rotterdam, one approaching from the east and one from the south west. Red flares were fired as ordered to signal the aircraft to break off the raid, but due to fires from burning buildings and Dutch anti-aircraft fire, only the formation making its approach from the south west saw the flares, abandoning its attack after the first three planes had dropped their bombs.

The other formation approaching from the east saw nothing, all of the aircraft releasing their bombs. The high explosives destroyed the inner city, killing 814 civilians, but also hit a margarine warehouse, starting a major blaze. The watermains had been broken in the attack and the city's fire brigade could not contain the blaze with wheeled hand pumps. At 3 p.m. Colonel Scharroo ordered the garrison in Rotterdam to cease fire, and at 3:50, with the approval of General Winkelman, he offered the surrender of the city.

Winkelman was horrified at the reports of the destruction in Rotterdam, and under German threats of the bombing of Amsterdam and Utrecht, that evening gave orders for a national capitulation. The Dutch would surrender the following day with their army virtually intact. The ensuing fires in Rotterdam destroyed close to 24,000 houses, making almost 80,000 inhabitants homeless. German fire engines were dispatched from as far away as the Ruhr to assist the Dutch, and try to save what was left of Rotterdam.

Tuesday 14 May 1940 –
Sedan, River Meuse, France / Belgium Border.

German assault engineers worked through the night at Sedan to construct bridges over the Meuse that could support the weight of their tanks. Having been awake for over twenty-four hours, and exhausted by their efforts right through the night, they still managed to cheer and wave as the tanks rolled across their bridges at 7:20 a.m. the next morning. The tank crews waved back, acknowledging the engineers' efforts. As the first tanks arrived on the west bank, Guderian directed them to a ridge to meet a French counter attack that had just been launched. They were engaged by French armour as they approached the ridge, being severely mauled, but holding the feature until more tanks arrived to solidify the position. The French counterattack was further disrupted by Stuka attacks and anti-tank guns that had been brought across the river during the night and expertly placed to cover major road junctions.

With the bridgehead now secured from ground attack, it began to fill with armour and support vehicles coming across the bridges; creating a priority target for Allied air attacks. These began at 5:30 a.m. and would last until midnight. With a combined total of one hundred and fifty-two Allied bombers available for operations, coordination problems between the RAF and the French resulted in twenty-seven separate piecemeal attacks, whereas fewer combined massed attacks, with their weight of numbers, would potentially have had a greater chance of success.

The German anti-aircraft assets placed around the bridges for exactly this scenario, took a heavy toll on the Allied machines. The largest raid by seventy-three RAF bombers in the late afternoon saw forty aircraft shot down. Despite the obvious danger, Guderian stood in the centre of one of the bridges during an attack to ensure the passage of vehicles continued through the raid. Six hundred tanks and 60,000 men were moved into the Sedan bridgehead during 14 May; which by nightfall had expanded to twelve miles wide and nine miles deep.

Tuesday 14 May 1940 – Leffe Bridgehead, River Meuse, Southern Belgium.

Further north at Leffe, the 7th Division probed forward at first light. As Rommel followed the armoured spearhead in his command vehicle, he came under fire from a French anti-tank gun. Hit several times, his driver took evasive action resulting in the vehicle sliding down an embankment and the main armament becoming wedged in the ground. The vehicle had to be abandoned, Rommel emerging through the turret with a nasty facial wound. As in the Sedan sector, the French tried to mount a counterattack, but bad coordination and roads clogged with refugees and withdrawing French troops meant it did not materialise that day; being postponed until the morning of 15 May. By nightfall, the Leffe Bridgehead had expanded eight miles west of the Meuse, reaching the town of Flavion.

Tuesday 14 May 1940 – River Dyle, Central Belgium.

To those unfamiliar with the sound of approaching tanks, the high-pitched squeal from the tracks of metal rubbing on metal made them inquisitive. To those familiar, it caused delight, as it signalled that armour support was arriving. Matilda tanks could be seen moving along the roads to the rear of the position, struggling to make progress against the stream of refugees moving in the opposite direction. A troop of three tanks had been assigned to the battalion and could be used by the Commanding Officer to plug any gaps created in the line or to lead counterattacks against enemy river crossings. The tanks carried a 2-pounder gun and a machine gun which used the standard .303-inch small arms round.

"Thank God for that." McCann said as the sound of the tanks were heard at Company Headquarters. Captain Roberts looked visibly relieved as he knew he could use their extra firepower should his counterattack plans have to be activated; now being able to call on both artillery and armour support. His relief was short lived as the drone of numerous aircraft engines sounded from the east. Shouts to take cover spread rapidly around the position, the men running and diving into their trenches. As they lay and waited, the drone got louder, almost rhythmically rising and falling in intensity. Kyle and Farthing were together in the bottom of their trench, seated and curled up, squeezed against the bare soil sides, the rims of their helmets digging into the exposed earth as they tried to make themselves as small as possible.

The first explosions came as bombs landed on the east bank, moving closer, landing in the river and then on the west bank. The two soldiers closed their eyes and flinched involuntarily as the ground shook around them, the noise nothing like they had heard before; more violent than they could ever have imagined. Within seconds the attack had passed over. The silence was eerie. No one wanted to move in case another bomb landed. Then voices began to call out, asking if anyone had been wounded. Kyle stood up to see Corporal Hutchinson moving between the trenches to check on his section.

"Everyone alright in here?" he asked Kyle as he passed.

"Yes, Corporal." Kyle answered as Hutchinson moved to the next trench. Farthing emerged and the two soldiers looked around. They could see a bomb crater on the far bank of the river, like a brown wound torn in the green grass, but could see no strikes around their own position. They grinned at each other, feeling euphoric that they had survived an attack by the enemy. The feeling did not dissipate as the day wore on, the two soldiers still grinning as they ate lunch consisting of cold bully beef from a tin at the bottom of their trench. Corporal Hutchinson returned after lunch and jumped down beside them in the trench.

"You will hear some explosions soon." he began. "Our forward reconnaissance has identified the German advance and will soon be withdrawing back across the river. The bridges will then be destroyed." The men nodded their understanding. "Any movement on the far bank after these explosions will be the enemy." They nodded again. Hutchinson gently slapped each one on the helmet in turn and climbed out of the trench. As warned, explosions followed, the sound of debris falling into the river clearly audible after the blast.

At mid-afternoon, the feint sound of a motorcycle engine was heard from the east bank. It revved and slowed as it picked its way through the wooded area, eventually a cycle and sidecar combination emerging from the cover of the wood and stopping in the open on the sloping river bank. An officer stepped from the sidecar and spread a map over the frame of the machine. Another motorcycle and sidecar combination appeared, which again stopped on the bank in full view; the officer being joined by the passenger from the second sidecar. They made no attempt to conceal themselves, even talking loudly enough for those watching from the west bank to hear. They remained in full view for a few minutes, the rider of the second cycle feeling secure enough to dismount his machine and urinate in the open.

Three, almost simultaneous, bangs wrecked the silence as mortar shells fell around the Germans, throwing them to the ground. Bullets ripped up the grass between them as a machine gun joined the engagement. One man lay motionless and the other three ran towards the woods they had emerged from, one obviously wounded and staggering, before falling over and lying still. The other two Germans made it into the cover of the trees. The two machines lay wrecked and burning on the grass.

Those soldiers in the trenches simply watched in silence, mesmerised by the burning machines and the bodies of the two dead Germans. Not knowing what further enemy forces were present on the opposite bank, no one left their trenches, raising their heads just far enough above the lip of their trenches to see. Thirty minutes after the engagement with the Germans, half a second of a whistling noise was all the warning that the dug in soldiers got before artillery shells fell on the west bank. Unlike the earlier bombing attack, the artillery bombardment was almost continuous; shells falling on the trees, the obvious concrete pillboxes and the scattered farm buildings. Splintered branches landed on the trenches, along with stones and earth from nearby ground impacts. Men huddled together in their trenches, gripped with fear as the ground shook around them; causing panic and claustrophobia as the sides of their trenches started to crumble around them under the weight of the explosions, the soil falling on their helmets and shoulders.

Kyle and Farthing held their hands over their ears in what was a vain attempt to stop the concussion from the explosions, their bodies jumping with shock each time a shell landed nearby. Then there was silence. Kyle was afraid to open his eyes as he felt strangely protected by his self-induced darkness. Slowly squinting through the settling dust, he saw Farthing still curled up in the corner of the trench. He shouted to confirm that Farthing was unhurt, but his own voice sounded muffled and distorted by the whistling in his ears and the sound of his own heart racing. He shook his head to try and clear his senses but to no avail. He began to untangle his body from the curled-up ball he had created, and tried to stand up. He shook Farthing but found him stiff with fright although apparently uninjured.

Looking over the lip of the trench he saw some figures running and then felt a hand on his shoulder. Startled, he looked round to see Corporal Hutchinson, his mouth moving but with no words coming out. Kyle pointed to his ears, signalling to Hutchinson that he could not hear. Hutchinson jumped down into the trench and tried to pull Farthing away from the wall. After some resistance, his body moved and he also began to unwind himself from the knot of limbs he had created. Hutchinson took Farthing's water bottle from his equipment, pulling out the cork and forcing him to take a drink. Kyle took a drink from his own bottle.

Having confirmed both soldiers were uninjured, Corporal Hutchinson climbed out and moved away to the next trench. The two soldiers embraced each other for comfort, sitting back down in the trench and drinking more water.

"I think I've shit myself." said Farthing meekly, as he unbuckled his equipment and undid his battledress blouse. Sliding his braces off his shoulders, he dropped his trousers and underwear. "Shit confirmed." he said as they both giggled at his predicament. He tipped the deposit out onto the floor of the trench and got dressed again, before taking his entrenching tool from his webbing, lifting the shit on the blade of the shovel and throwing it out of the trench onto the surface.

A single shot rang out followed by a yell. Slowly raising his head above the lip of the trench, Kyle saw an unidentified khaki clad figure on the ground, obviously injured and dragging himself towards the nearest cover.

The call of "Sniper" was shouted from trench to trench, Kyle turning his head towards the next trench and repeating the message. Further shots rang out as the men raised their heads from their trenches and positioned their weapons to fire. German snipers had moved into the wooded areas on the east bank during the artillery barrage and were intent on keeping the defenders occupied until their advancing columns could arrive and attempt a crossing.

"Watch for movement in the trees." came the next call; as some rounds were fired into likely enemy positions on the far bank. When someone thought they had seen a sniper, they concentrated the fire of their section in the same place. Leaves and small branches flew as the defenders' fire smashed into the suspected sniper position, the soldiers relishing the chance to strike back at the enemy after enduring the bombing and artillery bombardment. The sniper duel continued until late evening, but just as the sun was setting the body of an enemy soldier fell from the trees, hanging suspended on the rope he had used to tie himself in position. A cheer went up from the defenders, acclaiming their first personal victory against the enemy.

Tuesday 14 May 1940 –
Harstad, Northern Norway.

At 6 p.m. the Polish liner Chobry left Harstad bound for Mo, containing the Irish Guards, Brigade Headquarters staff, and a troop of three tanks from the

3rd Hussars. The Commanding Officer of the Irish Guards, Lieutenant Colonel Faulkner, gathered his officers for a briefing on the conduct of what could potentially be an opposed landing at Mo, hammering home the continuing German aerial threat. At midnight, as the soldiers slept, the Chobry was attacked by three Heinkel bombers while still thirty miles from its destination. A bomb detonated midships where all the senior officers were accommodated, killing Faulkner, his Second in Command, Adjutant and four Company Commanders. The resultant fire separated the non-commissioned ranks, housed forward, from all the other officers housed in the stern.

With the vessel ablaze and the battalion's stored ammunition exploding in the heat, Regimental Sergeant Major Stack assembled the Guardsmen on the foredeck, lining them up as if on parade. With enemy planes still overhead, the accompanying destroyer HMS Wolverine came alongside and secured a gangplank between the vessels. Despite an imminent threat of Chobry exploding, the Guards filed across the gangplank in perfect order, a total of six hundred and ninety-four men being evacuated in sixteen minutes. It took seven hours for the return journey to Harsted, being bombed continually by the Luftwaffe all the way.

Wednesday 15 May 1940 –
Sedan, River Meuse, France / Belgium Border.

The high ground at Mont Dieu, which overlooked the bridgehead at Sedan, was recognised as crucial by both sides. For the Germans, it would secure the southern flank of the bridgehead. For the French, its possession would ensure freedom of movement to launch a counterattack into the German flank. In the centre of the area was the village of Stonne, made up of a small collection of farm buildings. The Germans attacked at first light with a mixed force of infantry, tanks, anti-tank guns and assault engineers, capturing the village after vicious hand to hand combat. A French counterattack retook the village, only to be driven out again when the Germans regrouped. The village was to change hands seventeen times over the coming days, neither side able to hold their gains.

Unwilling to wait for a conclusive result on his left flank at Mont Dieu, and accepting the risk this carried, Guderian pushed his forces west out of the bridgehead. The terrain was close, with the French defence based on a series of fortified towns and thus not suited to the advantages that fast-moving German armour could offer. The German infantry battalions were at the end of their strength as night began to fall, and it was only exceptional leadership by their officers that enabled the last village to be taken, opening up more favourable terrain for the tanks. On the northern edge of the bridgehead, four hours of similar close combat had taken place before a breach was made in the French defence. The tanks streamed through the gap, advancing thirty-five miles by the end of the day, reaching the town of Montcornet.

Wednesday 15 May 1940 –
Leffe Bridgehead, River Meuse, Southern Belgium.

At 10 a.m. the 25th Panzer Regiment spearhead from Rommel's 7th Division fell upon the French in their assembly area near Flavion, where they were preparing their delayed counterattack against the Leffe bridgehead. When German reinforcements arrived an hour later at 11 a.m. Rommel withdrew his spearhead tanks and pushed them west into much more favourable tank country as Guderian had done at Sedan; leaving the reinforcements to continue the battle with the French counterattack forces. Stuka attacks prevented more French tanks from joining, and also those trying to leave to refuel, enabling the outnumbered Germans to prevail against the odds. Rommel's tanks reached speeds of up to 40 mph on the westward thrust, and by the end of the day had reached Froid-Chapelle, a further advance of twenty miles.

Wednesday 15 May 1940 –
French Army Headquarters, Chateau de Vincennes, Paris.

The success of Army Group B in Belgium and the Netherlands had pushed the French back to the river Dyle, against which the Germans were now pressing. The positioning of German Army Group C continued to pin thirty-eight French Divisions on the Maginot Line to the south. Reports of panzer columns from Army Group A speeding west from the Meuse bridgeheads made the French Commander in Chief, Maurice Gamelin, realise that he had fallen into the German trap. From his headquarters at Chateau de Vincennes, he issued orders to fall back from the river Dyle and form a defensive line to protect Paris from Guderian's panzers in Army Group A. He had not even considered the possibility of Guderian striking for the coast rather than the capital.

That night, Gamelin telephoned the Defence Minister, Edouard Daladier, to appraise him of the situation. Daladier was stupefied and demanded an immediate counterattack.

"With what? I don't have the reserves." Gamelin replied.

"Then the French Army is finished?" asked Daladier after a pause.

"It's finished." replied Gamelin.

Wednesday 15 May 1940 –
Louvain, River Dyle, Central Belgium.

As dawn broke, the body of the German sniper that had been hanging from the tree was gone, removed during the night by his comrades. There seemed to be no other enemy activity on the east bank opposite 10 Platoon positions.

After the first light stand to was rescinded, they took the opportunity to clean their weapons and make a hot meal, one man in each trench cooking and cleaning in rotation while the other remained alert. Lance Corporal Tetlow went around each trench replacing ammunition that had been used in the duel with the snipers the previous day, and resupplying tinned rations.

At mid-morning, word was passed that the Germans had crossed the river Dyle at Louvain, less than a mile north of the West Stafford's positions. Although the bridge had been deliberately destroyed by demolition charges, the Germans had managed to cross the damaged structure by wedging planks between the girders. Reinforcements were being taken from unthreatened positions on the British line and rushed to the area of Louvain to bolster the defence. 10 Platoon were ordered to prepare to move, the men making their way back to the wood behind their position where they gathered to await further orders. Lieutenant Chadwick, Sergeant Preston and the three Section Commanders knelt in a huddle, Captain Roberts briefing them over a map that had been spread out on the ground.

"The Germans have pushed infantry across the bridge at Louvain, and it appears they are moving to capture the railway station." he began. "Loss of the station will seriously disrupt our ability to move both men and supplies into the Dyle area." He looked directly at Lieutenant Chadwick before speaking again. "Take your platoon as far as you can towards Louvain in the trucks, then the rest of the way on foot." He paused to let the situation sink in before continuing. "Go directly to the railway station as marked on the map, and find the senior British officer in command there." Chadwick nodded his understanding. "You're moving on the road in daylight so watch out for enemy fighters. Leave the vehicles at the slightest sign of aircraft and continue on foot."

The men removed the canvas canopies from the back of two trucks to allow them to watch the sky as they drove, and climbed on board, Chadwick in one and Preston in the other. They arrived at the outskirts of Louvain without incident and disembarked; taking cover against the walls of houses and in the neatly kept gardens. Chadwick confirmed his position on the map and signalled for the men to follow him as he set off towards the station, their weapons held ready for immediate action if required. The streets were deserted, and the sound of fighting could be clearly heard coming from the direction of the river. Chadwick found a Major in a hurriedly created command post inside the station, and was quickly directed to reinforce a defensive perimeter just inside the structure. 10 Platoon ran across deserted platforms, past abandoned bread and tobacco stalls and took up positions with other infantry units facing the direction of the river. They smashed the windows in the shops to create fields of fire covering the approaches to the station. The building had a glass roof, suspended high above the platforms, giving the impression of the station being outdoors. Birds fluttered around the inside of the roof; their normally quiet roosts disturbed by the noise of the fighting.

Grey / green uniformed figures suddenly appeared moving quickly from door to door along the approach roads to the station, remaining still for a few seconds before moving again.

"Here they come." shouted Chadwick. "Prepare to fire on command." he ordered. The men cocked their weapons, ready to fire. There was an open square in front of the station that offered no cover, Chadwick waiting until the Germans emerged from the cover of the side streets. There was a sudden rush as the Germans tried to cross the square, Chadwick's order to open fire cutting them down as if a giant hand had swiped them aside. The British fire then switched to those who had remained in the cover of the side streets, forcing them to back away. The birds inside the station took to flight, squawking in fright at the sudden noise of the rifle fire. As their squawking subsided, a stillness fell on the scene; the defenders reloading their rifles as a dozen motionless bodies lay on the cobbled square.

The silence only lasted as long as it took a German officer to request mortar fire against the station; the glass roof shattering with the explosions and showering the men below in deadly shards. They huddled against the walls as the glass landed around them, bouncing off their helmets and shoulders. German machine gun bullets struck the outside walls around the windows, fragments of stone and brick shooting in all directions. With no glass left in the roof to impede their trajectory, the mortar bombs began to land and explode inside the station, razor sharp slivers of red-hot metal adding to the chaos. The defenders remained hunched against the walls, helpless to respond to the violence going on around them.

Chadwick knew the enemy fire would slacken or stop before another infantry assault could be mounted, and waited for the coming lull in the firing. The Major commanding the defence of the station appeared beside him.

"Bring two sections of your men and follow me." he yelled above the noise of the incoming mortars and bullets. "Leave a section here to hold this position." Chadwick shouted to attract his Corporals' attention, and as they looked, he tapped his own helmet to signal for their sections to gather on him. Running hunched double, they followed the Major in single file around the internal wall of the station, the broken glass from the roof crunching under their feet. He led them to a platform terminal, the tracks stretching away to the outside, blue sky and the roofs of buildings visible in the distance. "The Germans are trying to get in by coming down the tracks." he told Chadwick. "Position your men here to hold them back." Chadwick nodded his understanding. "You've got to hold them here." the Major repeated, the sincerity in his voice reinforcing the importance of the task. He patted Chadwick on the shoulder and moved off the way he had come.

Chadwick positioned his Bren guns together in a group, pointing straight down the tracks where their field of fire was greatest. The riflemen took up positions in the arched brickwork along the sides of the platform;

and although this restricted their view outwards on their own side, they had clear views of the approaches across the other side of the track onto which they could offer covering fire. Their colleagues positioned on the other side of the railway line offered reciprocal cross track covering fire. Chadwick returned to the Bren gunners, kneeling between them as they lay prone on the platform floor, and had been in position only a matter of seconds when figures became visible from the open track end, silhouetted against the sunlight.

"Wait." he said to his gunners, holding his hands above their shoulders. "Wait." he repeated as the figures moved closer, getting bolder and venturing down the middle of the tracks. Chadwick waited until the Germans saw him and raised their weapons before dropping his hands onto the gunners' shoulders and ordering them to open fire. The wooden sleepers splintered and bedding stones jumped as the bullets tore into them, the Germans stranded in the tracks spinning and yelling as they were struck. Those Germans following behind ran towards the cover of the brick arches on either side of the platform, where the waiting riflemen cut them down before they reached the perceived safety. Chadwick called a stop to the slaughter when nothing moved, the echo of gunfire from the arches dying shortly afterwards.

"Reload." shouted Chadwick to his gunners, expecting another assault. They unclipped the magazines from the top of their weapons and fitted fresh ones, whisps of smoke from the hot barrels and open breeches spiralling upwards. With dry mouths and racing hearts they waited for signs of another assault, but none came. They could hear the sounds of combat from the centre of the station behind them, but it was the sound of British Bren guns firing, and Chadwick was content the resistance still held firm. When the noise of combat had completely stopped, the Major reappeared and recalled Chadwick and his men back into the station. Further British reinforcements had arrived and Chadwick watched as soldiers ran in all directions.

"You did well today, Lieutenant." the Major remarked. "Get your men some food and a hot drink before going back to your unit." 10 Platoon found a quiet area among the battle damage and away from the running troops, sitting together in silence while they brewed tea and ate some tinned food. Sergeant Preston handed Chadwick a mug of hot tea and a lit cigarette.

"I don't smoke." Chadwick said as Preston held the cigarette in front of him.

"I know, Sir" Preston replied, "But you'll feel better after." He offered the cigarette again and Chadwick took it gingerly and placed it between his lips, puffing gently.

"You did a good job today, Sir." said Preston as Chadwick screwed up his face at the taste of the tobacco. Chadwick nodded his acknowledgement then felt his head go light as the nicotine entered his bloodstream. He coughed, shook his head and handed the cigarette back to Preston. The chatter between the platoon started as the hot tea and their own cigarettes began to take effect. They were soon recounting their experiences to their colleagues, embellishing how crucial their individual efforts had been in holding off the German assaults.

Preston had chatted to some of the reinforcements that had arrived in the station and reported back to the Platoon Commander.

"It appears the Dutch have surrendered." he whispered, not wanting the men to hear. "I expect things will get a bit hotter for us now."

"Get the men gathered, Sergeant." Chadwick said, getting to his feet. "Let's get back to the battalion."

* * *

Immediately on arriving back at the company location, Chadwick was called to receive orders from Major Crawley, held in an abandoned farm building that had been taken over as the Company Headquarters. The Company Second in Command, Company Sergeant Major and the three Platoon Commanders were all confirmed present before Major Crawley began to speak. He confirmed that the Dutch had surrendered that morning and the Germans had broken through the French positions on their right, who were now streaming back towards Paris.

"This leaves us no option other than to withdraw, otherwise we will be cut off." continued Crawley. "We will be forming a new defensive line here, on the river Lasne, three miles to the rear." As he spoke, he pointed to his opened map case which he had spread on the floor, on which the new positions had been marked in wax pencil. "Reconnaissance parties have already gone to mark out the new position and will meet us there when we arrive."

Major Crawley described how the battalion would withdraw during the night under cover of an artillery bombardment. The companies had been given specific withdrawal times and routes, which Crawley then allocated to the three platoons. 10 Platoon would not withdraw until 1 a.m. the next morning. When the orders were finished, Chadwick returned to his platoon location and briefed his Section Commanders. He told them to ensure everything was packed immediately in case their withdrawal slot was altered at short notice, then to eat and sleep in rotation.

Chadwick tried to sleep, but thoughts of his first combat action that morning kept him awake. When darkness fell, he walked around the platoon position, visiting the individual section trenches to ensure everything was packed up and the sentries were awake and alert. Just before midnight, the sky to the west lit up with artillery muzzle flashes, the sound of the guns arriving some seconds later. The covering barrage under which they would withdraw was timed to last for two hours; firing off the ammunition that had been transported forward, and which the pressures of time and logistics meant could not be moved back.

Thursday 16 May 1940 –
Montcornet, Eastern France.

Armed with the knowledge provided from his reconnaissance units, Corp Commander General Guderian met with his Divisional Commanders at Montcornet on the morning of 16 May to direct the continued advance. He had been assured the route to the next major obstacle of the river Oise lay open, and was determined to exploit the opportunity. Travelling with the 1st Panzer Division, Guderian reached the river that night and seized the Ribemont bridge, some ninety miles beyond the Meuse Bridgehead.

However, the unprecedented speed of the panzer advance and the lengthening lines of communication were causing some concern at Army Headquarters in Berlin, with Hitler himself becoming very nervous about the possibility of a French counterattack into the left flank of the panzer spearhead. Claiming poor communications, Guderian had blatantly ignored radio orders not to move beyond Montcornet until infantry could be brought up for flank protection; but he could not ignore a written order to the same effect pushed into his hand by a staff officer at 1 a.m. on 17 May. He returned to Montcornet, leaving his panzers to develop the bridgehead over the Oise at Ribemont.

Thursday 16 May 1940 –
Froid-Chapelle, Southern Belgium.

After essential maintenance and refuelling, leaving very little time for rest, Rommel's tanks covered the ten miles west from Froid-Chapelle and crossed the French border at 6 p.m. The border was defended by the extension to the fortifications of the Maginot Line which Rommel then attacked in the direction of Avesnes. Just as Guderian had done when he encountered the Maginot extension after crossing the Meuse into France at Sedan, Rommel pushed his assault engineers forward to neutralise the concrete bunkers with grenades and flamethrowers. They were supported by direct fire against the bunkers from the tanks, and indirect fire from his artillery engaging French positions in depth.

The attack began at 6:30 p.m. and as dusk fell, the full combat weight of the division was brought to bear on the defences in an attempt to unblock the roads heading west. As the tanks opened the roads, motorcycle infantry and reconnaissance vehicles raced through the gap, overrunning the French artillery line and reaching five miles into France at Solre-le-Chateau by 11 p.m. Without stopping, the spearhead pushed on a further six miles, encountering and crushing unsuspecting French motorised units, and reaching Avesnes by midnight.

PART 5

THE WITHDRAWAL

Thursday 16 May 1940 –
River Lasne, Central Belgium.

10 Platoon stood in silence in the wooded area behind their location, the soldiers in full marching order, their loaded packs cutting into their shoulders and making them lean forward to reduce the strain on their backs. The Section Commanders had reported to Sergeant Preston that everyone was present and Lieutenant Chadwick was waiting on the order to move. With only three miles distance to the next defensive position, the battalion was to move on foot; all available truck space loaded with the equipment that had been brought forward and was now being taken back. The sky was still being lit by the flashes of the guns; so continuous that it appeared dawn was breaking in the west and not the east.

When given the order to move, 10 Platoon led the way for D Company, firstly passing through the battalion checkpoint where the Regimental Sergeant Major confirmed their withdrawal, and then back along the road they had used to advance only a few days before. They moved in single file on each side of the road, intermittent convoys of vehicles passing them in the same direction. The muzzle flashes of the supporting artillery stopped at 2 a.m. just as the battalion arrived at the river Lasne. Captain Roberts had been part of the reconnaissance party, and met Chadwick as the lead element of D Company as he crossed a footbridge onto the west bank of the river. Major Crawley moved to the front of the line and spoke with Roberts for a few seconds before leading the company into their designated positions.

Having been given their place in the new defensive line, the Platoon Commanders placed their sections in temporary positions until dawn, pending a realignment in daylight. Major Crawley and Sergeant Major McCann moved around the platoons at first light, making minor positional adjustment before giving the order to dig in. The soldiers immediately began to dig fox holes to provide them with cover in case of air or artillery attack. The fox holes were subsequently joined and widened to accommodate two men, then camouflaged using any available foliage before the men were allowed to sleep or eat. The day passed without incident, solitary enemy reconnaissance planes flying high over the positions.

The Platoon Commanders were called to receive orders that afternoon. It transpired the battalion would be moving again that night, back a further seventeen miles to the river Senne which flowed through Brussels. The withdrawal would begin at 10 p.m. under the cover of darkness; initially on foot but with the prospect of vehicle transport being made available further along the withdrawal route. Chadwick returned to the platoon and passed the orders to the Section Commanders. Again, he ordered the men to eat and sleep as circumstances allowed before the withdrawal began.

Thursday 16 May 1940 –
French Foreign Ministry, Paris, France.

Churchill had landed in a sun-drenched Paris accompanied by General Sir John Dill, vice-chief of the Imperial General Staff, and his deputy Hastings Ismay, along with Air Marshal Joubert de la Ferté, deputy chief of the Air Staff. As their car swept through the entrance to the Foreign Ministry that afternoon, they saw French soldiers throwing bundles of files onto fires that had been lit on the lawns. The sense of panic in the air was palpable. On meeting their counterparts, the British delegation found the French General Staff verging on paralysis, their faces expressing complete dejection.

General Gamelin briefed the latest reports on the military situation from a map two yards square, balanced on an artist's easel. Black lines marked the German positions in the Netherlands, Belgium and around the area of the River Meuse. He specifically concentrated on the bulge in the marked line around Sedan, striking the map with a pointer as he spoke. He explained that the Germans had torn open a forty-mile-wide hole in the French defences and from the latest reports had already advanced forty-five miles past Sedan. He admitted that he did not yet know whether their objective was Paris or the coast. When Churchill asked about the strategic reserve, Gamelin replied that there was none. Churchill looked at Daladier in silent disbelief, and it was clear the news was not a surprise to the French Defence Minister.

On the flight home, Churchill began discussions with his advisors around continued support for the French, in relation to sending more troops and aircraft across the channel. In his mind was the primary pillar of British Defence Policy, the protection of the nation and its people. Should France fall, he had to maintain the means to defend the British Isles.

Friday 17 May 1940 –
Montcornet, North Eastern France.

At 7 a.m. Panzer Group Commander Ewald von Kleist's plane landed at Montcornet airfield. Guderian was waiting to meet his superior officer, in the knowledge he would have to explain his actions from the previous day. Without returning his salute, von Kleist immediately began to berate his Corp Commander for what he deemed to be disobedience to the Fuhrer's direct orders, and demanded he stop his panzers immediately. When Guderian realised that his tactical assessment would not even be considered by his superior, who he believed was intellectually inferior, he offered his resignation. In his rage, von Kleist immediately accepted, appointing General Veiel, his senior Divisional Commander, in Guderian's place. Guderian immediately ordered all his units to stop where they were, and handed command over to General Veiel.

In an act of total disrespect for the chain of command, Guderian then went over von Kleist's head and gave a full account of the situation by wireless to the Commander of Army Group A, General Gerd von Rundstedt. Later that afternoon, and in the knowledge that the channel coast and not Paris was now the target of the panzer thrust, von Rundstedt overruled von Kleist and reinstated Guderian. He soothed both egos by limiting Guderian to "fighting reconnaissance patrols" and thus was seen to restore von Kleist's authority. These patrols were to be instigated the following day, as the enforced operational pause had allowed the infantry to catch up, and provide the required flank protection that had been so concerning to Army Headquarters and Hitler.

As if to justify Hitler's fears, French Colonel Charles de Gaulle, recently given command of the 4th Reserve Armoured Division comprising 5,000 men and eighty-five tanks, advanced towards Montcornet just as the German Generals were fighting amongst themselves. The French struck from the south west, and after gaining some initial success with the destruction of a convoy of German supply trucks, it looked as if de Gaulle's forces would significantly disrupt the lines of communication of 1st Panzer Division. The prompt action of German logistics officers in redirecting anti-tank and anti-aircraft guns that were moving through the area, and bringing into action some tanks in a repair workshop, subsequently blunted the French assault. The attack was finally repulsed when Stuka support was hastily arranged.

Friday 17 May 1940 –
Avesnes, North Eastern France.

As with Guderian, Rommel blamed bad communications for his non-compliance with Hitler's order to halt the drive west; continuing to push forward from Avesnes through the hours of darkness on the night of 16 / 17 May. While leaving some of his tanks to engage the remnants of shattered French armoured units, Rommel pushed on to take the bridge over the Sambre river at Landrecies, a further eleven miles west. Again, leaving some of his tanks to protect the captured crossing, he only stopped the advance at 6:30 a.m. on 17 May at Le Cateau, to allow rest and resupply of his exhausted force.

His actions caused a dilemma with his superiors. He had potentially disobeyed orders, but had travelled a distance of forty-five miles in 24 hours. In stark contrast to the treatment of Guderian, Rommel received the Knights Cross for his significant contribution to the operation, rather than being disciplined.

Friday 17 May 1940 –
Brussels, Belgium.

Having left the area of the river Lasne at 10 p.m. the previous night, and walked for almost three hours, D Company eventually met with their promised transport; Bedford trucks driven by Royal Army Service Corps drivers. The men tried to board the trucks only to find them crammed with stores, leaving no room to accommodate passengers. Orders were quickly given to prioritise the movement of men, and the stores were unceremoniously unloaded to make room before the convoy moved off towards Brussels. The vehicles passed through a defensive screen of armoured cars and tanks on the outskirts of Brussels, only to become stuck in the mass of refugees fleeing along the main roads into the city. The sullen refugees looked accusingly at the soldiers, as if blaming them for their plight. Shouts of derision had replaced the euphoric welcome received from the same population only six days prior.

Just as it was getting light, the convoy was stopped at a Royal Military Police checkpoint, the Sergeant in command advising the Company Commander to separate his vehicles into smaller packets, and to use the side streets which were relatively free of refugees. The company split up, and Chadwick directed his two platoon vehicles off the main road. Turning into a side street, he noticed Belgian troops without weapons, wandering in disarray and breaking into shops and houses, scavenging for food. Still being early morning, the vehicles made better progress along deserted narrow streets, past terraced houses with small tidily kept gardens at the front. Chadwick followed the route closely on his map, giving instructions to the driver as they approached junctions.

The vehicle suddenly screeched to a halt, Chadwick looking up from his map, startled.

"What's the problem?" he asked.

"I think I just hit an animal, Sir." came the reply as the driver opened his door and jumped out of the cab before Chadwick could stop him. The driver waved down the following vehicle, signalling for it to pull in behind, then he walked back along the road. Only a few yards away, a cat lay on the pavement at the gate to a house, raising its head to look at him as he got close. He returned to the cab where a now frustrated Chadwick told him to get going again.

"I just need to put a cat out of its misery, Sir." the driver pleaded. "I won't be a second." He retrieved a shovel from the space between the cab and the load compartment of the truck, returning to where the cat lay. Raising the shovel above his head and arching his back to increase the force, the driver brought the shovel down with all his strength on the cat's head, a loud clanging noise accompanying the action.

The upstairs curtain of the house was pulled aside, as the owner, having been woken by the sound of the truck engines, slamming vehicle doors, and the sound of the shovel on the pavement, looked out to see what was happening. His mission of mercy complete, the driver returned the shovel to its bindings behind the fuel tank, but as he opened the cab door to get back in, he froze. Squashed on the front wheel was the body of a cat that he had not seen when he got out. Realising that he had just killed an uninjured resting animal, probably belonging to the resident that was now looking out of the window, he quickly jumped back into the cab and started the engine.

"In one hundred yards, take the left junction." said Chadwick, unaware of the driver's predicament; and with a crunching of gears the vehicle quickly moved off. Flashing lights from the vehicle behind caused the driver to stop again.

"The second truck wants us to stop, Sir." said the driver nervously as he applied the brakes. Having run forward from the second vehicle, Sergeant Preston appeared at Chadwick's door, tapping at the window,

"Hold on, Sir." he said, breathless after his sprint forward. "Hamill's not back yet."

"Where the hell is he?" questioned Chadwick in frustration.

"He needed a shit, and took the opportunity to get out when we stopped." Preston explained.

"For God's sake! He's got ten seconds or we're leaving him." Chadwick snapped; getting angry at the continuous delays.

"Hamill, move yourself!" Preston shouted as he ran back towards his own vehicle. Hamill emerged from the same garden gate at which the cat had been killed, stepping over the dead animal and buttoning his trousers as he was pulled over the vehicle tailgate by Private Bell, who had been watching from the open canvas cover. His exit from the garden was followed by the shouts of the houseowner, who had opened the window and released a tirade of verbal abuse, accompanied by vigorous arm waving. Preston told his driver to flash the lights as a signal to move off, and the two vehicles departed in a haze of fumes.

"Well, we've done our bit for Anglo-Belgian relations." remarked Bell, as Hamill squeezed in beside him. "I can see the headlines now." he said, holding his hands apart and moving his head from side to side as if reading a newspaper. "Who are these British monsters who kill Belgian pet cats?"

"The same British monsters that leave a yard of shit in their front gardens." Hamill added with a giggle. "God help any German that has to take cover behind that garden wall."

* * *

Chadwick's directions brought the two vehicles closer to the river, and taking what he calculated would be the last turn, was relieved when he saw the bridge in front of him. Armoured vehicles were positioned on the east side, their weapons pointing in the direction of enemy approach. The vehicles were again stopped by Military Police, and after a cursory check were allowed to proceed over the bridge where Royal Engineers were busily preparing the structure for demolition. Once across, they were reunited with the other vehicles from D Company.

Captain Roberts led the platoons to their allocated positions and defences were prepared in what was the new setting of an urban environment. Buildings that dominated main approaches or crossroads were occupied and fortified as best as possible, with furniture being repositioned inside to provide greater protection for the defenders. Staircases were blocked to restrict the movement of an attacking force should they enter the house, and holes were created in the attics between the houses to allow covered movement for escape routes or counterattacks. The armoured vehicles that had been guarding the bridges withdrew when all the expected British units were across; moving directly west through the new defensive positions.

"That will be them off to secure the next defensive line." McCann said to Chadwick as they toured the section positions together.

"You think we'll be moving again soon, Sergeant Major?" Chadwick inquired.

"Guaranteed, Sir." McCann answered confidently. "This is an organised withdrawal as we're a step ahead of the Germans. It could all turn to shit very quickly if they catch us up." He paused for thought. "Allow me to offer some advice, Sir." he continued. Chadwick nodded expectantly. "Expect chaos, accept it as unavoidable, and get used to operating in it."

Before Chadwick could answer, an explosion made them look around. The bridge they had crossed earlier had been demolished; pieces of masonry, steel and wood flying into the air before landing in the river and on the banks. Chadwick pulled out his binoculars, twisting the focus wheel to get the best view. To his surprise he saw motorcycles moving along the streets on the far bank. The Germans had caught them up already.

Friday 17 May 1940 –
Harstad, Northern Norway.

The South Wales Borderers departed Harstad in the cruiser HMS Effingham with a destroyer and anti-aircraft escort, bound for Bodo. At 8 p.m. that evening in perfect sea and weather conditions, the force entered the Saltdalsfjord to dock at Bodo when Effingham shuddered to an abrupt halt and keeled to one side before righting again. Fearing a torpedo attack, passengers and crew rushed on deck where it became obvious that the ship had run aground, tearing a hole the length of her hull. The engine room soon flooded and the ship lost all power.

As Effingham began to sink, the escort vessel HMS Echo, came alongside and towed the ship to shallow water where she settled on the bottom. Realising there was now no immediate danger of sinking, the crew took the opportunity to gather their personal possessions. They emptied the canteens and bars, handing out food, alcohol and chocolate to the soldiers patiently waiting on the deck for rescue. Echo transferred 1,400 crew and passengers to the anti-aircraft support vessels and returned to Effingham for the remaining two hundred crew who were preparing for the ship to be abandoned. Once the remaining crew had been evacuated, Echo then destroyed the Effingham with two torpedoes. All the survivors were returned to Harstad.

Friday 17 May 1940 –
Mo, Northern Norway.

On 17 May, the Germans attempted to outflank the Scots Guards in their positions around Mo. Reinforced by the landing of one hundred and fifty paratroopers, the German attack began at 9:30 p.m. resulting in a withdrawal order the next day. The Scots Guards withdrew through Mo at 2 p.m. on 18 May, destroying bridges and burning stores of petrol and ammunition that had been deposited in the town and could no longer be used.

Dismayed at reports of the sudden withdrawal, Brigadier Gubbins left Bodo at 8:30 p.m. to drive one hundred and thirty miles south to Mo and see what was going on for himself. His journey by car along the only route available for either reinforcement or withdrawal took seven hours; which included crossing a twenty-mile-wide snow belt along a single track, bordered on each side by twenty feet deep snow drifts. Gubbins identified this as an obvious tactical weak point, as any movement along this track in daylight would be extremely vulnerable to attack by German aircraft.

Gubbins arrived at the Scots Guards' positions early on 19 May, openly displeased that the town had been lost; but on seeing the seriousness of the situation for himself, agreed to a further withdrawal north the next day. Left with only the food and ammunition that the men could carry on their person, Gubbins arranged for extra stores to be pre-positioned at selected points along the planned withdrawal route.

Bunny hopping back through their own company positions, the Scots Guards had formed a defensive line along the southern edge of the snow belt by midnight on 20 May. The Germans attacked the position the next evening, and fearing being caught exposed in daylight on the snow belt during any further withdrawal, the Scots Guards withdrew during the night of 22 / 23 May. Using locally sourced buses driven by Norwegian troops, they crossed the snow belt and were established in defensive positions at Viskiskoia on the northern side by the early hours of 23 May.

Saturday 18 May 1940 –
River Oise, Eastern France.

Being careful to be seen to be in compliance with von Kleist's orders, Guderian used the enforced pause to create better conditions for the continued advance when his constraints would be lifted. He expanded the bridgehead over the Oise, moving the tanks of the 1st Panzer Division over the river to the western bank, positioning and resupplying them for a renewed advance on the approaches to Peronne, across the old Somme battlefields of the last war.

Saturday 18 May 1940 –
Landrecies, Eastern France.

Illustrating limited and grudging compliance to the constraint of only permitting fighting reconnaissance patrols, Rommel pushed his tanks forward from Landrecies to capture Cambrai, taking the total distance of his advance to one hundred and seventy miles. This reflected Guderian's similar plan, using the halt order to create a springboard for further offensive operations when von Kleist's constraints were eventually removed. Here at Cambrai, Rommel waited in frustration for his supporting infantry and technical troops to catch up.

Saturday 18 May 1940 –
River Senne, Brussels, Belgium.

Having spent a reasonably comfortable day with the chance to sleep in the beds and armchairs in the abandoned houses, and prepare a hot meal in their kitchens; first light brought another withdrawal. The men stood ready as dawn broke, feeling a bit more rested and their packs full of food that had been left behind when the Belgians evacuated their houses. The next defensive position was to be established on the river Dendre; a twelve-mile march in daylight with no transport available. An artillery barrage began as the British left their positions; an attempt to keep the Germans on the east bank of the Senne under cover and prevent an immediate river crossing attempt. It would be only a matter of time however, before the barrage stopped and the Germans would resume the chase.

The battalion was spaced out along the road as they left the urban surroundings of Brussels and entered the countryside. Cobbled streets gave way to rough limestone tracks with drainage ditches on each side. Scattered farmhouses rested on the higher ground, surrounded by fields of crops and abandoned animals. A file of soldiers marched on each side of the road with Belgian refugees in their carts or on foot slowly trudging down the middle. A huge dust cloud was being created by the combination of military boots, the occasional military truck and the wheels of the refugees' carts.

"What a target for German aircraft." said Sergeant Preston to Chadwick as he looked upwards into a cloudless blue sky.

"At least we can jump into the ditches for cover." Chadwick replied. "It's the refugees that will take the worst of any attack."

A rest halt was called and the men slumped down into the cover offered by the drainage ditches, taking their helmets off, unhooking their equipment and retrieving their water bottles. Some cows in the adjoining field came close to the wire fence that bordered the ditch.

"Hear that noise?" said Bell, remarking on the bellowing of the cows. "That's the sound a cow makes when it needs milking." He pulled himself to his feet to get a closer look. "The farmers have just left them." he added. He climbed out of the ditch and approached the cows that were gathered by the fence. Being accustomed to human contact, they did not pull away as he reached over the wire and scratched the head of the nearest one. "Right, who wants some milk?" he declared, satisfied the cows would not shy away. "La La, fetch your mess tin and get up here."

McCafferty unpacked his mess tin and climbed up beside Bell. They pulled the wire strands of the fence apart and stepped through. Bell kneeled down beside his selected animal, McCafferty holding the mess tin at arm's length underneath the udder. After a few seconds, milk was gathering in the tin as McCafferty watched fascinated.

"W...where d...did you learn that?" he asked.

"I was raised on a farm you fool." replied Bell abruptly. "Now get me another mess tin quickly." McCafferty shouted into the ditch and empty mess tins were passed up, as the full one was passed down and shared among those waiting. Bell had managed to fill three tins before the call came to get moving again. As they climbed back through the fence, Bell noticed two young children staring at him from the road. He waved at them to come closer and each got a drink from his mess tin, the awkwardly shaped vessel causing dribbles to run down their chins onto their dusty clothes. He was startled by a shout as their mother pulled them away roughly, Bell's feelings left hurt that his gesture had been misinterpreted so badly.

Close to noon, the marching troops moved through a screen of armoured vehicles parked on the east bank of the river Dendre, guarding a bridge. The crews were in their vehicles and looked tired, their faces covered in dirt except where their dust goggles had been, now pushed up on top of their heads while the vehicles were stationary. No words passed between the troopers and the infantry as they passed, the vehicle crews' gaze fixed on the sky and the roads leading east, as if expecting attack at any time. Once across the bridge, the platoons were directed to defensive positions on the west bank, where they began to dig fox holes for cover as before. Chadwick was called to receive orders almost immediately; Company Headquarters having been set up in a tent.

"Tell the men not to get too comfortable." Major Crawley began. "We'll be staying the night and moving again tomorrow, probably around noon." He pointed out the next defensive line on the map, along the river Escaut, a distance of twenty-eight miles further west. As he continued to speak, Chadwick noticed how tired Major Crawley looked. There were dark rings around his eyes and he looked as if he could fall asleep at any second. He was not filled with confidence at the Company Commander's appearance. He began to think how he looked to his own soldiers, and was determined not to show any signs of the tiredness that he knew was building within himself. "Brussels and Antwerp have fallen to the Germans." Crawley concluded. "They will be snapping at our heels, so make sure the men stay alert and ready for action at a moment's notice."

Captain Roberts stopped the three Platoon Commanders as they left the tent. "Site your support weapons to cover the river." he began. "Remember to tie in with the neighbouring platoon and cover each other's blind spots if necessary. I'll come round later to make sure everyone is happy." He left them to return to their men and went back inside the tent. Chadwick began the process of siting the trenches and support weapons immediately on return to the platoon position, and as the men worked, he brought the Section Commanders together for briefing; covering the expected move the following day, and reinforcing that they could expect enemy action at any time.

As arranged, Captain Roberts visited the platoon locations that afternoon. He adjusted the arcs of the machine guns to fire into the flanks of any attempted river crossing, making them more effective, and just as importantly, making identification of their position more difficult. Once the weapons were sited, the positions were camouflaged with cut branches and at last the soldiers were allowed to clean their weapons, eat and sleep.

At 8 p.m. the sound of tracked vehicles could be heard as the reconnaissance screen withdrew over the bridge, meaning it had been prepared for demolition. As night fell, small fires became visible on the east bank of the river Dendre as the arriving German troops settled down for the night and prepared themselves for an attempted river crossing the next morning.

Sunday 19 May 1940 –
Peronne / Cambrai, Eastern France.

Direction was received from Berlin that the advance was to resume the following morning. The stream of reinforcing infantry and technical troops continued all day; who then worked against the clock to maintain and repair the tanks that would break loose again the next morning. Rested and resupplied, six German armoured divisions now lay along a line from Peronne to Cambrai, poised for the next move.

Sunday 19 May 1940 –
River Dendre, Central Belgium.

The sounds of enemy activity continued all through the night; the occasional artillery flare causing them to dive for cover in case they were engaged by the watching British. Dawn revealed a partially constructed pontoon bridge, made of rubber boats with planking across the top. Expecting to be attacked at first light, there were no Germans to be seen; the pioneers only reappearing to continue the construction of the bridge at the observed absence of enemy activity. The West Staffords were under orders to remain hidden until the bridge was finished, planning to subsequently engage the much more inviting target of combat troops trying to cross. The men remained absolutely still in their foxholes, neither talking, eating or smoking as they watched the German bridge get closer to the west bank.

Kyle felt beads of sweat running down his chest. His shaking hands gripped his cocked rifle, his finger on the trigger ready to fire. This was a different feeling than returning fire when being attacked. He was now going to initiate violence against the Germans he could clearly see working on the bridge. He thought about his mother, then thought about their mothers. His stomach was knotted with nerves, which he tried to justify to himself as hunger, but knew were in reality the product of fear. He slowly let his head fall forward until the rim of his helmet rested on his rifle, took some deep breaths to compose himself and then returned to the alert position. He glanced across at Bell standing beside him in the trench. He noted how calm he looked, the concentration on his face, and what he thought was the absence of fear. Bell felt he was being stared at and gently turned his head towards Kyle, smiled and winked and resumed his alert position. As the sun got stronger, the air noticeably warmed very quickly. The smell from the cut greenery they had used for camouflage increased, and flies began to buzz around the men waiting in the trenches, attracted to their dirty and sweaty uniforms; the temptation to swat them away denied by the risk of disclosing their positions with any sudden movement.

There was a flurry of activity on the eastern bank of the river, shouted orders initiating the starting of motorcycle engines as the machines and accompanying infantry were ordered across the newly constructed bridge. Kyle's nerves increased as he readied himself to open fire, waiting for the signal from the machine guns. The Germans were nearly across when fire from machine guns on both flanks tore into men and motorcycles alike. Kyle pulled his trigger at the signal, cocking and firing his rifle as fast as he could. The motorcycles slewed off the bridge into the water, the infantry falling down as if swept aside by an invisible scythe. Those Germans who had just started to cross tried to withdraw, but were cut down as they became entangled with those on the east bank waiting to use the bridge. The machine guns then switched fire against the rubber boats supporting the bridge surface, tearing them to shreds and collapsing the wooden roadway into the water. As firing ceased, moans of wounded enemy soldiers could be heard; their cries fading as they slid off the collapsing remains of the bridge and sank in the river.

Kyle unclipped his now empty magazine, and replaced it with a full one from his ammunition pouch. The knots in his stomach were gone. He had managed his fear, followed his training and done his job.

* * *

With confirmation received that the battalion would withdraw again at noon, the experienced soldiers immediately prepared food, primarily to give them energy for the move, but also because they could not be sure when the next opportunity for the luxury of a hot meal would present itself. Weapons were cleaned in relay to maintain a defensive capability, although it seemed the Germans had abandoned the plan to cross at this point of the river. If the chance to sleep presented itself, even for a few minutes, it was taken.

As 10 Platoon left their trenches and moved to the rear, the sound of transport vehicles manoeuvring was a welcome relief; indicating that the men would not have to march, for what would have taken a full day, to reach their next location. Captain Roberts was waiting at the concentration area and took Chadwick aside. Spreading out a map, Roberts pointed out the main features, areas of population and the route to be taken.

"These maps are in short supply, so it's only one per platoon. You'll have to keep your vehicles in convoy but under no circumstances let them bunch up, otherwise you're sure to be attacked by enemy fighters." Chadwick nodded his understanding and called his Section Commanders to him for briefing as the men climbed on board the trucks. As he described how he wanted vehicle spacing maintained on the withdrawal under the threat of air attack, his orders were interrupted by a loud explosion; the bridge they had crossed the previous night being deliberately destroyed by the Royal Engineers before the withdrawal.

* * *

The roads were slightly raised above the surrounding fields, with drainage ditches on each side. There were uninterrupted views over the surrounding farmland with absolutely no cover; Chadwick posting air sentries in each vehicle who continually scanned the skies in all directions. Scores of Luftwaffe bombers in formation flew high overhead, their intended target somewhere further to the west.

"Someone's in for a pasting!" remarked Bell to no one in particular from his position as air sentry. "At least it's not us this time." he added. Progress reduced to a crawl as the roads became jammed with refugees, their possessions loaded onto hand or horse drawn carts. Exhausted children slept on top of the bundles. Some pushed bicycles with loaded baskets on the front, their progress too slow to enable them to be ridden. Military vehicles of all types were mixed in with the refugees, the sounding of their horns in an attempt to clear a path being totally ineffective in the melee.

"Aircraft south!" came the warning from the air sentry. All eyes turned south towards three small black dots in the sky just above the horizon, which then disappeared from view.

"Keep your eyes peeled everyone!" yelled Sergeant Preston; those who had fallen asleep in the heat in the back of the vehicles now very much awake. The movement on the road had now almost stopped. A huge pall of smoke rising into the sky in the distance. Lieutenant Chadwick took a bearing on his compass and confirmed the city of Tournai was ablaze. The German bomber formations that had been seen earlier had attacked the city, cutting the main access across the river Escaut, and effectively stopping all movement on the approach roads. The convoy crawled forward for a few more minutes before the alert was raised again.

"Aircraft south!" No sooner had the call gone out when three Messerschmitt fighters in line abreast approached from the south at almost ground level, the characteristic zipping noise from their engines causing everyone to crouch as they streaked overhead at right angles to the road. They arched gracefully into the sky to the north, the sun glinting off their canopies, before dropping down and disappearing from sight.

Without any alarm or warning, bullets tore into the road a split second before a single Messerschmitt fighter approached from the east. Screams from the refugees could be heard above the sound of the engine and the aircraft's guns as they scattered in all directions. Soldiers jumped from vehicles and dived into the ditches on each side of the road, mixing with the refugees that sought shelter. An elderly man remained standing in the road, trying to control his terrified horse, the contents of the cart it was pulling spilling out. Two more fighters attacked from the same direction, one on each side of the road, firing into the drainage ditches now filled with civilians and soldiers alike. The old man still struggled with his horse as the bullets smashed into the road around him, the animal eventually pulling the elderly man off his feet and breaking away across the fields.

Soldiers fired their weapons at the fighters as they disappeared towards the west, more in an act of defiance rather than offering any meaningful threat to the aircraft. Farthing lay back down in the ditch to reload his weapon, having fired a full magazine at the aircraft. He found himself beside a civilian in a business suit. The man patted his trousers to remove the dust from the ditch, straightened his tie, and lifting his briefcase, climbed back up onto the road. As the soldiers emerged from cover, they saw Sergeant Preston examining the trucks. The rear vehicle had punctured tyres, steam was coming from the radiator and water was running onto the road.

"The truck's had it." he said as they approached. "Get your kit out of the back." As the soldiers climbed in to retrieve their equipment, they were shocked by the bullet splintered wooden seats where they had been resting only minutes before.

"Bloody Hell." said Bell as he passed equipment out to those waiting. "Just as well we weren't in here." As he jumped down from the now empty truck, the scene was strangely quiet after the violence of the attack. The screaming had stopped, and those trying to recover their scattered possessions spoke in hushed voices. Two young boys stood beside their mother's body. She lay face down in the road with no obvious sign of wounds. The elder of the boys, who Bell estimated to be about six, was gently pushing her as if trying to waken her on an early Sunday morning, repeatedly calling "Mama." The younger boy just stood watching in silence. An old man wearing a horizon blue steel helmet from the previous war stood defiantly, shouting and shaking his fists at the sky. His family seemed embarrassed as they tried to quieten his obscenities. Bell saw Farthing staring at the boys trying to rouse their dead mother. He gently tried to move him away, but met resistance from Farthing's stiffened body. Being more robust, he gripped Farthing by his shoulders and turned him around.

"There's nothing you can do here, Penny." he said, looking into a face that showed both anger and despair in equal measure. "Gather up your kit and let's get moving." Without saying a word, Farthing bent down and lifted his equipment, slung it over his shoulders and moved away. Sergeant Preston reallocated some of the platoon to the undamaged vehicle, the remainder that would not fit in having to walk. The speed of the vehicle on the crammed and wreckage strewn road was such that those walking behind had to reduce their pace to a shuffle. Lieutenant Chadwick leaned out of the window of his vehicle and called Sergeant Preston forward. From the height of the cab, he had noticed three British vehicles together in a farmyard set back from the road; ordering Preston to take some men and investigate.

As Preston approached, it became obvious the vehicles had been destroyed in what had probably been an air attack. The canvas canopies had been shredded and whisps of smoke still swirled from the burnt cabs. As the patrol moved closer, khaki clothed bodies could be seen hanging from the vehicles and lying scattered on the ground. Preston hurried the men forward to check for any survivors. All those who had been present at the scene were dead, their clothing dishevelled; either by their owners looking for family photographs for comfort before they died, or by looters looking for money or food. Preston ordered the patrol to collect any remaining identity tags and paybooks and bring them to him, before hurrying back to the road.

"All dead, Sir." he told Chadwick as he handed across the recovered tags and paybooks. "Looks like they ignored the order not to bunch up. Made a perfect target for a fighter all parked together like that." He shook his head gently. "Got hit while still in the vehicles." Chadwick took the recovered items and secured them inside his tunic.

As they trudged along, Farthing was becoming irate. He noticed both French and Belgian soldiers, mostly without weapons, apparently uncaring about the plight of the refugees.

"Look at these soldiers, Tom." he said to McEnearney in despair as he walked along beside him. "These are their people, and they're doing nothing to help."

"There's not a lot they can do, Penny." McEnearney replied.

"They can try to help!" replied Farthing, getting so exasperated that he approached a young woman of his own age in a brightly coloured summer dress, struggling to carry her possessions over her shoulder in a knotted sheet. Gesturing that he would carry her burden, she unleashed a tirade in French, waving her free arm as she passed a shocked and chastised Farthing, turning around and walking backwards as she continued her abuse. She turned back to face her direction of travel, still muttering to herself.

"What was all that about?" Farthing asked McEnearney, clearly hurt that his gesture had been rebuffed.

"Apparently she blames you personally for her situation; and doubted your parentage for good measure." McEnearney summarised in translation. He laughed at Farthing's hurt innocence as he slapped him on the shoulder. "Come on, forget about it. Maybe you're just not her type."

The truck in front had stopped, and Sergeant Preston was ordering those who had been travelling inside to get out, replacing them with the members of the platoon that had been walking.

"Get inside, eat something and sleep if you can." he suggested as the walkers happily climbed on board. They unbuckled their equipment and slumped down on the benches, glad to be out of the heat and dust.

"Aircraft east!" came the warning shout, only a split second before a single Messerschmitt fighter passed only feet above the heads of the refugees along the axis of the road, its machine guns blazing. It pulled up in a graceful arc, dropping away to the west as the refugees and soldiers on the road dived for cover in the ditches; those of 10 Platoon who has just alighted the vehicle jumping out again and taking cover. Returning to ground level, the fighter attacked again, this time from the opposite direction.

Every available Bren gun and rifle the length of the aircraft run opened fire as it came at them head on. The engine spluttered and the pilot tried to climb away, a trail of leaking fuel being left in the sky. The machine stalled in the climb as the engine began to fail, hanging almost motionless in the air before slowly dipping back towards the ground and gaining speed. Those watching stood mesmerised by the fate of the aircraft as it looked like it would crash, before pulling up at the last moment and flying level as the engine spluttered and died. It glided silently parallel to the road for a few seconds before belly-flopping in a cloud of soil and dust, spinning around and coming to rest facing the opposite direction to its approach. Stopping only a hundred yards from the road, the soldiers dashed across the field towards the downed machine, reaching it just as the leaking fuel sprayed onto the hot engine and burst into flames. The first arrivals climbed onto the wing and smashed the canopy with their rifle butts, pulling the pilot from his cockpit as the fire gained hold.

Carrying the rescued pilot away from the burning aircraft, the soldiers laid him gently on the ground to assess his injuries. There was a bullet hole in his throat, which not being immediately fatal, had allowed him to manoeuvre his machine to crash land before he died. As there was nothing they could do, they stood in silence looking at the dead pilot, the first enemy they had seen face to face. The silence was broken by loud shouts, as enraged refugees that had run to the crash site began beating the dead German with their fists and feet and stones they lifted from the ground. The watching soldiers initially tried to prevent the mutilation of the pilot's body, but became the target of the violence themselves and were ordered back to the road.

The remaining vehicle had been damaged in the attack, its windscreen shattered; but it was still serviceable and able to resume the withdrawal. Wounded refugees lay moaning in the road, their families offering what assistance they could. As the soldiers climbed into the vehicle, Farthing saw a lifeless body in a brightly coloured dress lying at the side of the road. It was the girl who had refused his assistance. She was lying face down with her head to one side, blood running from her mouth; her eyes wide open. The back of her dress was covered in blood and she still clutched the knotted sheet bundle which now lay beside her. Farthing slumped to the ground beside her body, reaching out to touch her hair, but pulling back before his hand made contact.

"Up you get, Penny." said Corporal Hutchinson, putting his hands under Farthing's armpits and pulling him to his feet. "In the vehicle as quick as you can." Farthing climbed into the vehicle and sat down on the bench with his head in his hands. McEnearney offered him a drink from his water bottle. He just shook his head, said nothing and continued to stare at the floor of the truck.

Surrounded by refugees and withdrawing Allied soldiers, 10 Platoon crossed the designated bridge over the Escaut at 9:30 p.m. just as darkness was falling. On identification of their unit, the Military Police at the checkpoint directed them to their battalion area, where they were met by the Regimental Sergeant Major. He took a record of any wounded or missing, and Lieutenant Chadwick passed across the documentation and tags that had been recovered from the destroyed vehicles on the road. They were directed to their company location, where the platoons were gathering under the supervision of the Company Sergeant Major. Chadwick reported 10 Platoon all present, and was told by McCann to let the men sleep; however, he was to report to Major Crawley immediately to receive orders.

Sunday 19 May 1940 –
French Army Headquarters, Chateau de Vincennes, Paris.

General Gamelin had been visiting his subordinate commanders, delivering orders for a counterattack against the German incursion. On returning to his headquarters at Chateau de Vincennes, he found general Maxime Weygand with official notification of his replacement. Weygand had a glittering military career. He was part of the negotiations team at the signing of the armistice in Compiegne in 1918 to end the Great War, and held the office of Chief of Staff of the French Army and Vice President of the Supreme War Council; retiring in 1935, before being recalled to service on the outbreak of war. Gamelin cleared his desk and offered Weygand a situational brief before handing over command. Weygand refused the offer, and subsequently cancelled the orders for the counterattack that Gamelin had given that afternoon.

Monday 20 May 1940 –
Peronne, Northern France.

When the advance was renewed at 7 a.m. Guderian set his sights on reaching the coast that day. On his southern flank, the 1st Panzer Division raced thirty-five miles to Amiens and seized a bridgehead over the river Somme. Here, Guderian met some resistance from scattered units of the British Expeditionary Force for the first time. Further north, the 2nd Panzer Division thrust fifty-five miles across the old Somme battlefields of the previous war, and meeting no resistance, reached the mouth of the river at Abbeville at 8.30 p.m. Without stopping, they continued the advance west, reaching the Channel coast at Noyelles the next morning at 2 a.m.

The possibility of an Allied withdrawal south over the river Somme was now gone; the trap had closed, and Hitler's plan had worked. Forty-five British, French and Belgian divisions were now sealed in a pocket one hundred and twenty miles long and eighty-five miles deep.

Monday 20 May 1940 –
Cambrai, Northern France.

When given the order to advance, Rommel began his push from Cambrai towards Arras. His reading of the situation prompted him to expect stiff resistance, as Arras was the vital pin in the British Expeditionary Force's southern flank. He tempered his previous cavalier attitude however, ensuring that any enemy interference against his lines of communication were completely controlled before he pushed on. As he approached Arras and skirted around the city, he was engaged for the first time by the British troops defending it, inflicting significant casualties on Rommel's force, and making progress difficult.

Monday 20 May 1940 –
River Escaut, Western Belgium.

As dawn broke, Sergeant Preston woke the men.

"Did anyone else hear Dinger snoring last night?" Orpin asked no one in particular as the men packed away their blankets and groundsheets.

"C...could h...have given us away to the G...Germans!" McCafferty interjected.

"I think the Germans know we're here already, La La." Orpin replied. "He probably kept them awake as well." Lieutenant Chadwick gathered the platoon together for briefing.

"Situation reports tell us that the Germans have broken through between us and the French to the south. It would appear they are heading for the Channel rather than Paris."

"What does that mean for us, Sir?" questioned Corporal Hutchinson.

"Continued defensive actions for now I would assume." Chadwick replied. "Until a defensive front can be stabilised. After that I can't be sure; maybe a counterattack of some kind. We'll just have to sit tight and await further orders." The men looked at each other nervously.

"So more of the same until told differently?" Hutchinson confirmed.

"That about sums it up, Corporal." Chadwick replied. "You will see that we still hold the bridges over the river, but it is shallow enough in places to wade across." he continued. "We will be covering one of these potential crossing points when the Company Commander assigns our place this morning." He paused for any questions. There were none. "Get some food inside you and be ready to move in thirty minutes." As soon as the Platoon Commander had finished speaking, the Section Commanders triggered a flurry of activity, dividing work between food preparation and weapon cleaning.

* * *

Major Crawley placed 10 Platoon on a bend in the river where the action of the flowing water had eroded the bank on the west side, creating a beach like shelf at water height and a cutting behind about twice the height of a man. Scrub, shrubs and wooded patches dotted the bank and scattered isolated buildings were set back from the river. The men began to dig in, Captain Roberts carefully siting their trenches in mutually supporting positions to make the most of the attached machine guns and anti-tank weapons. As before, an Artillery Liaison Officer visited the positions, assessed likely enemy concentration areas, assigned them a code number and marked them on his map. Bren gun carriers ferried backwards and forwards, bringing ammunition for the heavy weapons, rations and water. Any sick or injured from the withdrawal the previous day were taken to the rear for medical treatment.

The positions had been dug and camouflaged by mid-afternoon when the sound of artillery landing further north on the defensive line was heard. The men dived into their trenches, but gingerly emerged again when it was clear they were not the target of the bombardment. But as the sound of shell impacts came closer, they instinctively took cover again. Then the bombardment fell around them. Half-second duration whistles from the falling shells were the prelude to fountains of earth being thrown into the sky. It felt as if the ground moved beneath them as soil fell from the exposed earth sides of their trenches. Shells impacting on the trees sent huge wood splinters into the trenches that had been sited below, the steel helmets of those crouched inside deflecting the deadly shards. Screams of terrified men could be heard between the explosions as they fought with the knowledge that only luck would save them from terrible injuries or death. The attack stopped just as quickly as it had begun. Sergeant Preston was first out of his trench.

"Anyone injured?" he yelled; but his ears were ringing so badly he could barely hear his own voice let alone any replies. He tried to run between the platoon trenches, stumbling and disorientated from the effect of the explosions, unable to see because of the smoke and dust.

"Over here, Sergeant." came a muffled reply.

"Keep shouting." Preston yelled back.

"Over here." came the reply again. "Over here." Preston got a fix on the voice, getting closer as he stumbled through the slowly clearing smoke. Then he was on top of the trench. Kyle was standing up, his head and shoulders protruding over the lip.

"It's Moore, Sergeant." he shouted, the panic evident in his voice. "He's been hit in the shoulder." Moore was curled up in the bottom of the trench, his ashen face stark against the brown of his uniform and the earth walls of the hole.

"Can you stand up, Moore?" asked Preston. With no response from Moore, Kyle helped him to his feet and he began to moan in pain. Preston could see splinters from the smashed trees imbedded in his left shoulder.

"Let's get him out." continued Preston. "You lift and I'll pull." Grabbing his right arm and the equipment strap on his right shoulder, Preston pulled Moore upwards. Kyle put his arms round his hips and lifted up, setting Moore in a seated position on the edge of the trench. "Alright, lad." said Preston reassuringly as Moore sat propped up on the edge of the trench. "You can lie down now if you want." Moore reluctantly leaned back with a wince, but visibly relaxed once he was flat on the grass. "Do you think you can walk?" Preston asked.

"I'll have a go, Sergeant." Moore replied in a voice distorted with pain. Lance Corporal Tetlow had arrived, and between him and Sergeant Preston got Moore on his feet.

"I'll get him to the Aid Post." offered Tetlow, supporting him under his uninjured shoulder and slowly moving to the rear.

"Are you injured?" Preston asked Kyle as Tetlow and Moore walked away.

"I'm alright, Sergeant." replied Kyle, although his disposition said the opposite. He looked confused and unsteady, turning very pale very quickly. Preston jumped down into the trench, realising quickly that Kyle was having an adverse reaction to seeing his friend wounded.

"Stay in here and get your brew kit out." began Preston. "Get some hot tea inside you with plenty of sugar in it." He pulled out his cigarettes and offered one to Kyle, who shook his head to decline. Preston returned his cigarettes to his pocket without taking one himself. Kyle slumped down in the bottom of the trench and unpacked his brew kit as advised, Preston ensuring he was capable of the task before climbing out of the trench and moving off to check on the rest of the platoon.

* * *

Kyle felt the calming effects of the tea as he sat in the bottom of the trench with his back against the wall, his eyes closed and both hands cupped around the metal mug. He could hear voices and activity going on above him when Sergeant Major McCann's face appeared, peering over the edge of the parapet.

"Mind if I join you?" he asked, jumping in without waiting for an answer and sitting down beside Kyle. "Moore will be alright." he began. "I just saw him at the Aid Post, and he said he was in the same trench as you." Now happy that Kyle was uninjured, McCann changed the subject completely. "Have you been writing to your mother?" he asked. Kyle was a bit flustered at the question, but holding his mug of tea in one hand, he reached into his tunic, pulling out an envelope.

"I had this ready to go just before we got deployed." he said, holding up a letter addressed to his mother. "Just haven't had the chance to get it posted." He chuckled at the understatement of his excuse.

"I'll take it." said McCann, tucking the envelope inside his tunic. "It will go into the company dispatches and be sure to get away." There followed an uneasy silence, as if McCann was building up for something.

"Your dad saved my life in the last week of the war, you know?" He paused. "November 1918." He paused again, as if recalling a painful memory. "We were attacking Valenciennes and the Germans were in headlong retreat. I remember the rain was torrential. Everyone knew the war was nearly over, and all they had to do was stay out of trouble and they'd get through it." He took a deep breath. "But still, we were thrown into the attack and that's when it happened. A German barrage landed right among us, and I got hit." He touched the scar on the back of his head. "Your dad risked his life to come and get me and carry me back. He was awarded the Military Medal for his actions that day."

McCann unbuttoned his tunic pocket and took out a battered photograph, holding it out for Kyle to see. "That's your dad and me the day he was awarded his medal." Kyle had not looked up from his tea until this point. He met McCann's gaze and could see tears in his eyes. He took the photograph, seeing two smiling soldiers with their arms around each other's shoulders. As he handed it back, McCann continued with the story.

"He left the Army and I stayed in. I couldn't go home to Ireland due to the civil war, and the fact I had fought for the British. We were sent to India shortly after and I only saw him once again; when I was Best Man at your parents' wedding." There was a long silence as McCann seemed to be carefully considering his next sentence. "He gave your mother a terrible time with his temper and his nightmares; and he knew it because he told me. Couldn't hold down a job and provide for the family. The Police report said he fell off the station platform and was hit by a train." McCann gathered himself before continuing. "I didn't find out for weeks by the time your mother's letter reached me, but I visited when next back from India. You probably don't remember as you were so small, but I have tried to keep in touch ever since."

"I don't remember much about that." said Kyle. "Dad was there, then he wasn't. I remember that mum cried a lot when I was growing up." Both men sat quietly for what seemed an age; one unburdened and one enlightened.

"What will happen now, Sir? I mean, if the Germans reach the Channel." asked Kyle, hoping McCann would maybe have more information than had been disseminated earlier.

"Just you let the officers worry about that, son." said McCann, gripping Kyle's knee. "Write home as much as you want, and give me the letters. Alright?"

"Alright, Sir. Thank you." Kyle replied.

"I'll get someone else to share your trench." said McCann as he climbed out.

Monday 20 May 1940 –
Dover Castle, Channel Coast, England.

As the War Office started contingency planning with the Admiralty for the evacuation of the British Expeditionary Force from the continent, an order from Churchill was received in the operations room in the tunnels carved into the white cliffs below Dover Castle. They were to begin assembling small civilian and trade craft as a precautionary measure.

The planning of the operation fell to fifty-seven-year-old Vice Admiral Bertram Ramsay, lured out of retirement by Churchill and given command of the Dover area of operations. As Ramsay and his staff began to make arrangements to gather the vessels, the codename "Dynamo" was assigned to the rapidly developing plan to lift the Army from the beaches and ports of the French and Belgian coast, which at that time included Boulogne, Calais, Dunkirk and Ostend. Churchill personally visited Ramsay in the operations room at Dover the next day to discuss the plans, and Dynamo was formally initiated.

Tuesday 21 May 1940 –
Arras, Northern France.

As Guderian consolidated his Somme bridgehead at Amiens and secured his stretched lines of communication and resupply to Abbeville and Noyelles, Rommel completed his advance around the south and west of Arras. His aim was to isolate the British in the city, then to sweep north to the Channel ports, cutting off the possibility of resupply or evacuation of the Allies by sea. By 3 p.m. the German spearhead, with Rommel leading, had moved to the west of the city when a hastily arranged and badly coordinated Franco-British counterattack struck the German right flank two miles south of Arras.

Eighty-eight British and sixty French tanks were massed for the attack, with infantry in close support. But lacking any maps and with insufficient time to fully establish the communications net, the British armour quickly became separated from their infantry. Due to poor coordination, they were initially fired on by the French, before being reunited with their infantry at Wailly, just as they attacked a German motorised infantry column. Without their own tank support, the Germans suffered considerable losses of equipment and many casualties; burning vehicles blocking the streets of Wailly, and creating panic which delayed the formation of a defensive line.

On receiving reports of the incident, Rommel rushed back to the scene with his Aide de Camp, Leutnant Most; where he personally coordinated the German response. Siting artillery and anti-aircraft weapons, Rommel and Most ran between the guns, identifying targets and controlling the fire, as bullets and shrapnel hissed around them. Just as the tide of the battle turned, Leutnant Most fell at Rommel's feet, blood gushing from his mouth. He died almost immediately. As darkness fell, the British and French were withdrawing, hastened on their way by Stuka dive bombing attacks. By midnight, the engagement was over.

Tuesday 21 May 1940 –
River Escaut, Western Belgium.

Reunited with Bell in the same trench, Kyle had shared sleep and sentry duties with his friend during the night. There had been continuous noise for most of the night from the east bank, and it was obvious the Germans were preparing an attempt to cross the river. Just before dawn, Kyle woke Bell on the call of "Stand To" and both strained their eyes and ears for a sign of the inevitable attack. All was now silent on the far bank and a thick mist hung over the river, which would conceal any enemy movement as long as they remained quiet. Kyle gripped his rifle tightly, happier on this occasion that his hands were not shaking.

Streams of green tracer bullets suddenly appeared from the east bank, followed a split second later by the characteristic sound of MG 34 machine guns with their tremendously high rate of fire. Kyle thought it sounded like material being ripped as he quickly ducked down into the trench.

"Bloody Hell. Here we go." yelled Bell as he joined Kyle below the lip of the trench. The tracer seemed to be passing just over their heads, but was impossible to judge accurately in the semi light. Both men thought it was more prudent to keep below ground level anyway. The similarly characteristic sound of Bren guns was now heard in response, their red tracer streaking in the opposite direction and disappearing into the mist. Orders were shouted between the trenches to watch out for boats crossing the river.

"We better have a look then." said Bell, slowly lifting his head above the trench lip and peering out over the water. Through gaps in the mist, he saw rubber boats full of German assault troops, hunched over for protection and paddling furiously to reach the west bank. The German machine gunners now raised their fire further up the west bank to avoid hitting their own men, and suppress the British trenches in depth positions. "Boats in the water." shouted Bell as loud as he could, then raised his rifle to his shoulder and began to fire. "Boats in the water." he shouted again as Kyle stood up beside him and began to fire at the fleeting glimpses of the enemy through the mist.

The Bren guns had channelled the Germans into the cover of the cutting on the west bank, where they were concentrating in a bridgehead. The growl of engines from behind indicated that tracked vehicles were approaching, the Bren gun carriers moving forward to get better fields of fire onto the river, passing between the front-line trenches and down towards the water. The carriers were attempting to position themselves where they could shoot directly into the currently hidden bridgehead, and moved onto the river bank to give themselves a direct line of sight. As they did this, they were exposed to the German machine guns, their bullets ripping through the side plates of the lightly armoured carriers at such close range, and killing the crews before they had a chance to engage the Germans who had landed. The German guns now sprayed the west bank on each side of the bridgehead with fire to keep any defenders suppressed as more boats began to cross.

Shouts of "Where's Bell?" could be heard above the sound of the German guns. It was Sergeant Preston.

"Over here, Sergeant!" yelled Bell. Preston was crawling along the ground towards the trench, pulling two wooden boxes behind him. He stopped about twenty yards away.

"Remember you beat me at throwing grenades?" Preston yelled over the noise. "Well, I need you to do it again."

"Will you make me crawl through nettles after?" answered Bell sarcastically.

"Just get your arse over here now, Dinger." replied an increasingly frustrated Preston. Bell jumped out of the trench and crawled towards Sergeant Preston. They took a box each and crawled further back into the trees before standing up and disappearing in a crouched run. They approached the German bridgehead in the cutting from the higher ground above, but due to the covering fire from the machine guns could not get far enough forward to drop grenades over the lip onto the Germans below. Staying as far back as they estimated Bell's arm could throw, Preston primed one of the grenades they had carried; Bell getting up onto his knees and throwing as hard as he could. It landed just short of the lip, detonating on the surface of the high ground.

"Another few yards, Dinger." Preston encouraged. Bell rotated him arm in an exaggerated way to loosen the muscle and let out an almighty grunt as he threw the next grenade, which cleared the lip and fell into the cutting below. The two men heard screams as the grenade exploded, the Germans now trapped on the bank with nowhere to go. "Same again." said Preston as he handed Bell another grenade. Screams continued as the following grenades exploded; eventually only the sounds of the detonations reaching the throwers. With the boxes empty, the two men lay back on the grass to recover from their exertions. Preston then tapped Bell on the leg to signal it was time to go. They crawled back the way they had come until it was safe to stand up and run to cover.

Bell returned from his exploits with a beaming smile, relating the story to Kyle in infinite detail, and again on repeated occasions throughout the afternoon. With the attempt to create a bridgehead having failed, the German machine guns only conducted sporadic harassing fire onto the positions on the west bank, but enough to prevent unhindered movement between the trenches, or work to strengthen the defences.

* * *

Distant black dots appeared in the sky to the east, slowly getting bigger.

"They don't look like fighters." remarked Bell as he squinted through the brightness of the sun. "Wrong shape and moving too slowly." Six aircraft could be counted as the distance decreased, the now clearly visible gull wing profile and high canopy of Stuka bombers aiding their identification. They began to circle above, confirming identification of their target, before an individual aircraft pulled away and began to descend, followed by another, then another.

Shouts of "Take cover!" spread across the position as the first Stuka came closer, its siren now wailing to increase the psychological impact of the impending attack. The men huddled in their trenches, eyes closed and shaking with fear as the sound of the siren got louder. Kyle felt completely helpless, fighting to control his emotions as he braced himself for the impact that was about to come. He heard himself whimper as the bomb struck and he felt as if the ground was trying to spit him out of the trench. He heard lumps of earth that had been flung into the sky falling back down, and strangely, the sound gave him comfort that he had survived. The emotions returned as he heard the wail of the next aircraft on its dive. His fingers dug into the earth wall of the trench as the ground shook with the second bomb. The third bomb fell among the trees, severed branches falling around the trench. He had seen six planes, and tried to convince himself that if each was to drop one bomb, then he was half way through the attack and his chances of survival had just doubled. The next three bombs fell further away, as the buildings to the rear housing the support weapons were attacked. Then silence. There were no screams of injured men, no machine guns firing. Kyle slowly raised his head above the trench lip. There was a huge hole in the ground one hundred yards in front, the brown soil like a scar in the green grass. Lumps of soil and boulders had been scattered everywhere.

"Are you alright, mate?" asked Bell from the bottom of the trench.

"I think so, Dinger." Kyle replied, wiping dirt from his eyes and spitting out dust that had got into his mouth. "That one was close." he continued, pointing to the crater in front. Bell stood up to look.

"Shit!" he shouted. "That's a 2 Section trench." Bell was on the surface and sprinting towards the crater before Kyle realised what was happening. The trench had been covered by the soil thrown into the air with the force of the nearby bomb blast and Bell began to dig with his bare hands. "Help here!" he yelled; other members of the platoon reacting and running to assist. Some arrivals quickly assembled their entrenching tools from their webbing and dug in panic and desperation at the loose soil covering the trench. The German machine gunners on the east bank noticed the activity and began to fire into the area; the rescuers now forced to dig lying down as a battle between the respective machine gunners was waged around them.

As the soil was removed, helmets and khaki uniforms began to appear, Bell jumping into the hole and pulling the buried men free. They were lifted to the surface, helmets removed and laid out flat; water from the rescuers' bottles being poured over their faces to remove the dirt and identify them. Two Medical Corps non-commissioned officers arrived, their visible white armbands causing the Germans to cease firing. Corporal McIlwaine came running and identified the men as Watts and Warren. Taking a water bottle, the Medical Corporal cleaned the dirt from their mouths and noses as the concerned soldiers looked on. There was blood coming from their noses and ears which the medic washed away. He pulled open their eyelids. What should have been the whites of their eyes were completely red.

"There's nothing we can do." he said. "They have been killed by the blast." Corporal McIlwaine grabbed Watts by the tunic and began to shake him, as if to waken him up. The medic grabbed his arm to stop him. "They have been turned to jelly inside, mate." he said firmly but calmly. "They wouldn't even have known what hit them. Cover them with their groundsheets until we can get them collected." The medics left; those remaining on the scene sitting silently looking at their dead comrades. It was Corporal McIlwaine who broke the silence.

"Take out their groundsheets and wrap them up." he said. Bell returned to his trench, leaving the members of 2 Section to deal with their dead. He jumped in beside Kyle.

"Watts and Warren are dead." he blurted out. Kyle immediately tried to climb out of the trench. Bell pulled him back.

"Don't go over there, mate." he pleaded. "Let their section mates deal with them." Kyle kicked and punched the walls of the trench in anger and frustration, the soil becoming dislodged and falling onto his boots. After a few moments he appeared to control himself and assumed his alert position. He stifled any sounds of his emotions as his body gently rocked backwards and forwards, but tears ran down his cheeks and dripped onto the sights of his rifle.

* * *

Corporal McIlwaine returned with Company Sergeant Major McCann and Corporal Hutchinson, carrying two stretchers. The two Corporals unfolded the stretchers and laid one beside each body. Hutchinson took the head and McIlwaine the feet and lifted each body in turn onto the stretchers. As Watts was being lifted, the groundsheet slipped off. Looking down at his now ashen face, Hutchinson remembered the promise he had made to Watts' mother at the station in Lichfield; a promise he had failed to keep. He leaned down and straightened Watts' unruly tuft of hair, just as she had done when she said goodbye to her boy, then covered him again with the groundsheet. They carried the bodies to the Regimental Aid Post where their details were recorded and the bodies prepared for burial in temporary graves.

***

At orders that evening, Major Crawley began by mentioning that two soldiers in 10 Platoon had been killed that day, and three soldiers in 11 Platoon had been severely wounded when the farmhouse they were occupying was bombed. The usual situational update confirmed that the Germans had reached the Channel coast at Noyelles, but that a counterattack had been launched at Arras, and early reports were encouraging.

Orders were then given for the battalion to withdraw the next day, back to the original defensive line they had helped prepare the previous year on the French / Belgian border. 10 Platoon would remain behind to guard the bridge over the Escaut, that they had crossed two days prior, and still being held open for the evacuation of refugees and rearguard Allied units. They were to follow on when the bridge demolition was completed. To finish, Major Crawley mentioned the threat of "Fifth Columnists" that were believed to be hiding among the refugees, whether they were German sympathisers, communists or indeed German soldiers in civilian dress; being intent on slowing the Allied withdrawal by whatever means they could. Reports had been received of deliberate disruption of communications, planned demolitions and destruction of stores. Crawley reinforced to Chadwick the need to remain vigilant against this potential threat.

Tuesday 21 May 1940 –
Esquelmes, River Escaut, Western Belgium.

The Germans had crossed the river Escaut in inflatable boats near the village of Esquelmes, and were holding a fragile bridgehead as they waited for reinforcements to cross. At 11:30 a.m. a company of Grenadier Guards counterattacked under the command of Lieutenant Reynell-Pack, supported by three Bren gun carriers and the battalion mortars. The tracked vehicles charged at top speed and got to within fifty yards of the Germans before being stopped by machine gun fire at close range, with all vehicle occupants killed. The dismounted infantry was then pinned down by three enemy machine gun positions and taking heavy casualties. Despite being wounded in the arm by shrapnel, Corporal Nicholls dashed forward with a Bren gun, and firing from the hip on the move, put an enemy machine gun out of action. Carrying extra magazines for the Bren gun, Guardsman Nash followed Nicholls as they dashed forward in short rushes, reloading the weapon each time they stopped. Wounded again, Nicholls continued his assault and put the two remaining enemy guns out of action.

Moving to a ridge overlooking the river, he then engaged the German infantry who had already crossed, and sank two boats carrying reinforcements. With enemy incoming fire striking the ground around him, and being wounded

271

twice more, Nicholls continued to engage the enemy, forcing them to withdraw back across the river. Corporal Nicholls had been grievously wounded in the action and fell unconscious. With incoming fire still landing around them, Guardsman Nash withdrew, leaving Nicholls where he lay, believing his comrade to be dead.

Tuesday 21 May 1940 – Bardufoss, Northern Norway.

With the loss of the temporary airstrip at Lake Lesjaskog, and the capture of an increasing number of airfields as the Germans advanced north into central Norway, the Luftwaffe was now mounting continuous attacks against Allied shipping and the bases established around Narvik. With the operational constraints upon using Fleet Air Arm aircraft operating from the carriers sitting offshore, another solution to the maintenance of air cover was required.

An existing Norwegian Military airfield at Bardufoss, sixty miles north of Narvik, was identified as a potential solution. With the removal of nearly 1.5 million cubic feet of lying snow by Norwegian soldiers and civilians working in ten-hour shifts, an eight-hundred-yard runway was created, which received its first Gladiator fighters on the morning of 21 May. The next day, sixteen Gladiator aircraft conducted over fifty operational sorties.

Tuesday 21 May 1940 – Bodo, Northern Norway.

With Auchinleck desperate to hold back the German advance from the south in order to allow sufficient time for completion of operations around Narvik; he dispatched the partially equipped Irish Guards who had survived the sinking of Chobry. They arrived in Bodo on the evening of 21 May; the continued occupation of the town viewed by Auchinleck as the last chance to prevent the German relief of Narvik from the south. Secondly, the loss of Bodo would reduce to one the usable ports in Northern Norway for resupply from Britain, or in a worst-case scenario, evacuation.

24 Brigade Headquarters staff and half of the South Wales Borderers had arrived the previous day and were already deployed. After a twenty-one-hour journey from Harstad, the Irish Guards slept that night among the miscellaneous stores lying on the dock at Bodo that had been recovered from the stricken Effingham; the Guards using the opportunity to supplement their equipment holdings where possible. On the morning of 22 May, they left Bodo and moved south a distance of sixty miles to meet the advancing Germans at the town of Pothus.

Wednesday 22 May 1940 –
Boulogne, Channel Coast, Northern France.

The attack on Rommel's extended column south of Arras on 21 May caused another failure of nerves in Berlin; with a further twenty-four-hour curtailment of offensive operations imposed. With 1ˢᵗ Panzer Division preparing to move on Calais, and 2ⁿᵈ Panzer Division poised to attack north from Noyelles towards Boulogne, this new delay caused massive frustration for Guderian who could see the importance of the Channel ports to the Allies, for either resupply or potential evacuation. Like Guderian, General Gort also saw the importance of the Channel ports and sent a brigade of infantry for their defence; with orders to hold the towns at all costs.

As the Allied perimeter shrank under increasing German pressure, the reduction in frontage to be defended released assets to start forming a new defensive line along the Aa canal, a mere ten miles from Dunkirk. A determined defence of the Channel ports would delay the German advance and buy valuable time for this defensive line to be properly prepared. Almost 2,000 men of the Irish and Welsh Guards arrived in Boulogne that morning, along with 1,500 men of the Auxiliary Military Pioneer Corps, sent for evacuation. The Pioneers were mostly construction workers and not front-line combat troops; but were soon assigned a combat role regardless.

With the imposed delay period expired, the 2ⁿᵈ Panzer Division attacked Boulogne in the early evening, striking the Irish Guards in the southwest of the town just as they were preparing their defensive positions. The battle raged into the night. The 10ᵗʰ Panzer Division replaced the 1ˢᵗ Panzer Division in the drive for Calais, allowing the latter to be redirected towards Dunkirk, the only other port with the facilities to mount a large-scale evacuation.

Wednesday 22 May 1940 –
Arras, Northern France.

Rommel remained in the area of Arras throughout the period of the offensive restriction order. He used this time to reorganise the forces that had been attacked the previous day, while also receiving reinforcements. He positioned these reinforcements with the aim of widening his armoured corridor. This reduced the likelihood of another counterattack breaking through and being able to link the allies on either side of the corridor. Meanwhile, his reorganised forces prepared for an assault on the city of Arras itself.

Wednesday 22 May 1940 –
River Escaut, Western Belgium.

Since the attacks the previous day, the dead had been buried and any wounded personnel evacuated by the now empty Bren carriers which had brought up ammunition, food and water during the night. At first light, the Germans tried to cross the river from where the woods ran down to the bank, giving them a covered approach; and at points where the depth of the water permitted an attempt to wade or drive across. At some of these shallow points, German reconnaissance vehicles had managed to reach the west bank, desperately firing into likely defensive positions as they emerged from the water. As a counter, the British had placed their machine guns and anti-tank guns in flanking positions to give better fields of fire, breaking the momentum of the infantry and destroying the German vehicles.

There had been no further attempted crossings in the West Stafford's area, and when the designated time came, they left their trenches and made their way west; apart from 10 Platoon who moved north to their bridge security task. A medic had been attached from the Regimental Aid Post to supply medical assistance if required. Refugees were still streaming across the river and 10 Platoon simply moved in the opposite direction to the flow, which led them to the bridge. When they arrived, Chadwick approached a Royal Engineer Warrant Officer and identified himself as the designated security detail. With a look of obvious relief on the face of the Warrant Officer, he was directed to Captain Riley, the officer in charge of the demolition. Captain Riley, who introduced himself as "Wiley" due to a speech impediment, was also delighted to see them. His men had been held back by refugee marshalling demands instead of demolition preparation, and he could now get them back working on what they had come to do.

He explained to Chadwick that the greatest risk was premature destruction of the bridge by the enemy or Fifth Columnists while Allied units were still on the far bank. His orders were to hold it open as long as possible, only destroying it when the enemy were about to cross. He had placed two lines of minefield marking tape which restricted refugee access to a central path across the bridge, keeping them away from the wiring and explosives on the sides. He requested a Bren gunner be placed to cover this "sanitised space" between the refugee corridor and the bridge sides, with authority to shoot anyone who strayed outside the marked path. The river was narrow at the bridge site, but much deeper and fast flowing, so Riley had also strung ropes across the water to prevent the enemy using the fast flow to float a raft containing explosives downstream and detonating it under the bridge.

Chadwick queried why the Germans wanted to destroy the bridge when they could use it for themselves. Riley explained that preventing the evacuation of British forces still on the east bank was their priority, and if required, they would build a new bridge within a matter of hours to continue their assault. Chadwick's suggestion was to take two of his sections to the east bank to control refugee access, and leave a section with Riley on the west bank to provide physical protection for the bridge. Riley agreed. Chadwick called Corporal Thomas and told him to select six good men with two Bren guns for bridge security duties. The remainder, Chadwick took across the bridge to the east bank.

* * *

The refugee situation on the east bank was chaotic. The few engineers that were there had almost lost control completely. They were standing behind some access control obstacles, constructed of a thick wooden pole with an "X" shaped stand on each end; the whole device wrapped in a coil of barbed wire. They had fixed bayonets and had adopted a confrontational stance. The refugees were fighting with each other to get through the small gap in the obstacle, at which no security checks were being made. Chadwick sent the engineers back across the bridge and took control of the gap in the obstacles. Anyone of fighting age or who raised suspicion due to their demeanour was taken aside and searched before being allowed to proceed. McEnearney repeatedly announced in French to those passing through the gap to stay between the white lines when crossing the bridge. A withdrawing Belgian soldier was pressed into service in return for food and cigarettes to make the same announcement in Flemish for those who did not speak French. The remainder deployed further forward, ushering the refugees into a semblance of a queue and prioritising any withdrawing Allied troops to the front.

Corporal Thomas had positioned Lance Corporals Tetlow and White on either side of the bridge, their Bren guns trained down the space between the designated refugee path and the bridge sides. He stayed close to Captain Riley so that any change in circumstances could be passed quickly. Riley had established his command post close to the exit from the bridge, having dug down a few feet and used the removed soil to build up the sides with filled sandbags. His detonation device was in the base of the position, wires running out to the explosive charges that the engineers were attaching to the bridge supports. He had communications to his headquarters through a radio set which sat beside the detonation device in the bottom of the position.

Corporal Thomas listened to Riley as he updated his headquarters on the radio. He reported the bridge was ready for demolition, pronouncing it as "bwidge" due to his speech impediment. Corporal Thomas looked around his men, then deliberately selected McCafferty, calling him over. "Run forward to Lieutenant Chadwick and report the bwidge is now prepared for demolition." he ordered, within clear earshot of Captain Riley.

"Y...yes, C...Corporal." answered McCafferty, setting off towards the east bank to deliver the message. Riley stared at them hard, not quite sure if Thomas and McCafferty were mocking him or not. Thomas then addressed the two Bren gunners and the rest of his section.

"Be aware the bwidge is prepared for demolition." he announced loudly, again drawing a stare from Riley, who was now completely sure of his motives. Lance Corporal White gestured him across.

275

"What is it, Chalky?" Thomas asked.

"That engineer officer is giving you dagger looks, mate." he whispered.

"I'm just having a bit of fun." Thomas replied. "What's he going to do anyway?" he questioned. "Send me to the front?"

"Keep Wobbly Gob away from him or he'll think you're really having a go." White suggested, and both men giggled at the thought. Thomas' attention was drawn when he heard Captain Riley calling him. He made his way quickly to the command post.

"Cowpwal, help me test this ciwcuit." said Riley. He told Thomas to place his fingers across the electrical posts on the plunger device. "You should feel a slight tingle if the ciwcuit is complete." Riley warned, then without further delay pushed the plunger down hard. A massive shock went up Thomas' arm, and he sucked air in between his teeth; but he fought the instinctive reaction to pull away.

"That seems to be wowking. I hope it wasn't too uncomfowtable." Riley asked him grinning, knowing exactly how nasty a shock Thomas would have received.

"Not at all." Thomas replied, when all he wanted to do was shake his arm. "It was weally quite enjoyable." he added, remembering to keep up the pretence of his own speech impediment despite the level of discomfort he was experiencing.

Shots suddenly rang out from Lance Corporal Tetlow's Bren gun, everyone's attention drawn to the sound. Out of Tetlow's line of sight, an elderly male refugee had tripped on the bridge planking, stumbling over the line and steadying himself on the side of the bridge, causing Tetlow to open fire as ordered. There were screams from the refugees as bullets splintered the wooden bridge decking, the old man twisting in agony before falling to the ground without uttering a sound. A middle-aged woman shouted "Papa", but was held back by those around her as she struggled to reach the stricken man.

"Stop firing!" shouted Corporal Thomas as he realised what had just happened; the woman now struggling free and throwing herself on top of the old man. Lieutenant Chadwick had run towards the sound of the firing and was met by Corporal Thomas who explained the event.

"Get the medic and McEnearney here." ordered Chadwick, Corporal Thomas running towards the east bank shouting for the two individuals. The medic had heard the shooting and was already on his way when intercepted by Corporal Thomas and directed towards the casualty. He bent down beside the old man, gently pulling his distraught daughter away from the body so he could assess the man's condition. He had been struck multiple times in the upper legs and body; his vital organs smashed by the bullets. The medic looked up at Chadwick and shook his head. His daughter was now standing, pulling at her own hair, howling in grief and distress. Chadwick felt helpless and touched the woman's shoulder in an act of sympathy. She pushed his arm away and stared straight into his eyes. Without breaking her gaze, Chadwick told the recently arrived McEnearney to say the shooting had been a mistake and express how sorry he was. As McEnearney translated, the woman spat in Chadwick's face and hissed a reply through streaming tears and clenched teeth.

"She said you are doing the Germans' work for them, Sir." translated McEnearney. They both watched silently as she turned away and male refugees lifted the dead man off the bridge. Chadwick's embarrassment had not subsided when the sound of aircraft made everyone look up. Machines were circling above like a swarm of insects, which from experience of the last air raid suggested they were preparing to attack. A single aircraft peeled off, then another, diving vertically towards the bridge. The soldiers took cover as the refugees trapped in the queue on the bridge screamed and abandoned their possessions as they tried to run forwards or backwards to escape. The Stukas' siren began to wail, adding to the panic. They watched mesmerised and helpless as the bomb was released, appearing to fall almost in slow motion as it wobbled slightly on its path downwards. Exploding in the river, the bomb sent a spout of water into the air, soaking those still trapped on the bridge and knocking them off their feet.

The soldiers and Bren gunners on either bank shot at the planes as they came in, adding to the noise and fear of those civilians close by. The second Stuka dropped its bomb, again seeming to hang in the air, before it landed in the queue of refugees that had been waiting to cross the bridge. Bodies and body parts were flung into the air as it detonated on the road. Only two planes had attacked from those circling above; Riley drawing a tactical conclusion.

"They appeaw be saving the bwidge for theiw tanks, meaning they awe close." he declared. His assumption was reinforced when the sound of the departing aircraft was replaced by the feint but characteristic metallic squeal of armoured vehicle tracks. A cloud of dust was visible on the eastern horizon. "Get youw men back acwoss, Chadwick." he yelled. "I'm going to blow the bwidge."

Chadwick ran to the east bank to gather the men. He found them mixed with the dead and injured refugees, escorting any survivors and lightly wounded away from the scene. The medic was trying to do an impossible job, treating terrible wounds with the limited supplies he had, and directing those refugees and stray Allied soldiers that had come forward to assist him.

"Get back over the bridge." Chadwick yelled, pushing his men in the direction of the bridge as they passed. He stopped Bell as he was passing. "Get down to the bank and cut those ropes." he ordered. "We don't want to give the Germans any help to cross." Bell slid down the steep bank and cut the ropes designed to stop a raft attack, he then scrambled back up and ran across the bridge. The current quickly swept the ropes away from the bank. Being reluctant to leave casualties untreated, the medic was the last one to cross the bridge, and Chadwick signalled to Riley that all his men were over.

"Move away from the bwidge and take covew." Riley yelled, the platoon finding suitable folds in the ground and disappearing from sight.

The resultant explosion was less than Chadwick had expected, the supporting legs collapsing from the carefully placed charges and the superstructure of the bridge falling into the river. When the dust had settled, Chadwick joined Riley and his Warrant Officer on the bank to inspect their handiwork.

"I was expecting a bigger explosion." remarked Chadwick as the two officers surveyed the remains of the structure.

"Not necessawy." replied Riley. "Just enough to knock the legs away and let gwavity do the west." Chadwick took out his binoculars and focused on the developing dust cloud on the eastern horizon.

"I think I can see vehicles." he remarked, handing the binoculars to Riley. There was no reply for what seemed an age as Riley stared hard through the lenses.

"I think they awe Bwitish vehicles." came the reply eventually, as he lowered the binoculars, rubbed his eyes and raised the lenses again. "Yes, definitely Bwitish." he confirmed, handing the glasses back to Chadwick. He ran back to his command post and Chadwick could see him operating the radio. The Royal Engineers Warrant Officer took the binoculars and studied the horizon himself, handed them back to Chadwick and joined his officer at the command post. Chadwick kept watch on the approaching vehicles, being rejoined by Riley.

"No one seems to be awawe of any Bwitish units on the east side of the wiver." he commented, as the vehicles continued to get closer. "Better tell your men to assume firing positions just in case." Chadwick shouted for his Section Commanders and briefed them to get the men organised, keeping Sergeant Preston with him at the now destroyed bridge and handing him the binoculars. Preston surveyed the approaching vehicles.

"There's no tactical formation." Preston concluded. "Looks to me like they're running away from something." Those watching from the west bank took cover as the first vehicles approached and halted on the east bank. Soldiers wearing British uniforms jumped from four wheeled Morris reconnaissance vehicles and Bren carriers, gathering at the destroyed bridge. On hearing their accents, Riley stood up and identified himself. The new arrivals shouted back, a Sergeant identifying his troop as Royal Lancers, and explaining they had been told this was the last bridge still standing.

"You're ten minutes too late." replied the Royal Engineers Warrant Officer. "We thought you were Germans." he added.

"There's a German armoured column less than thirty minutes behind us." came the reply. "Can you rig something to get the men across?"

"If you can throw a rope, then we'll attach it here." replied the Warrant Officer. "The men can swim across holding on to it." The Lancers ran back to see what they could find as more vehicles from their formation arrived.

"We'll have to leave you to it, Chadwick." said Riley. "More jobs to do fuwther back." He wished Chadwick the best of luck and they shook hands before Riley departed. In a few minutes the Lancers had returned.

"We've no rope, but have joined rifle slings together." their officer began. "I don't think it will reach your side, but have you someone who can catch it in the water?"

"Who's the best swimmer in the platoon, Sergeant?" Chadwick asked Preston.

"Orpin I would say, Sir." Preston answered immediately.

"Get him up here now and get all the rifle slings off the men." ordered Chadwick. Preston hurried off, shouting for Orpin. The Royal Lancers began to manoeuvre their vehicles into a semi-circle so that their weapons pointed in the direction of the pursuing enemy. Keeping the weapons manned, the other vehicle crew members began to gather on the east bank. Chadwick shouted instructions across to the Lancers.

"Go upstream and throw your line when our man is in the water. The current will bring the line to him." Orpin appeared with Sergeant Preston, rifle slings already attached together. "Tie the slings around your waist, Orpin." began Chadwick. "Wade out as far as you can then swim as far as the line will allow. We'll hold the other end so you don't get swept away by the current." Orpin nodded his understanding as he began to get undressed. "Catch the line thrown from the other side and attach them together, then use the line to make your way back." Orpin nodded again and began to tie the sling line around his waist.

Sergeant Preston gathered half a dozen men to hold the line as Orpin waded into the river. He managed to hold his own until out of his depth, when the current took him, those holding the line stopping him from being washed downstream. Preston fed out more line as Orpin struggled towards the centre of the river, the slings now stretched straight with the force of the water on Orpin's body. He kept disappearing under the surface, only to appear again a few seconds later, coughing and spluttering.

"Throw the line." Chadwick shouted to the Lancers who had moved further upstream. The slings splashed into the river half way across and began to float downstream. Orpin was swimming furiously to maintain his position when the end of the Lancer's line floated past, two yards away from his outstretched arm.

"Wade out as far as you can and try again." shouted Chadwick. The Lancers waved their acknowledgement, winding the line back in and wading into the river. The second attempt seemed to land further out, and began to move with the current, the Lancers wading downstream with it. "Come on Orpin." Chadwick whispered under his breath. As the end floated close, Orpin reached out again, disappearing underwater. He had not surfaced after ten seconds and it seemed as if all those watching were holding their breath for him. Orpin's head reappeared and he gave a thumbs up.

"Both sides pull apart." Chadwick yelled. A huge cheer went up from both sides of the river as the tension was applied and a complete line appeared above the surface of the water. Orpin ducked under and reappeared on the upstream side, using his hands to move along the line towards the west bank. "Right, get your men across." shouted Chadwick to the Lancers. Dumping their equipment and battledress blouses, the Lancers waded out one by one, holding the line for stability, swimming and using their hands to slide along when out of their depth. They were helped out by Preston and his men when they reached the west bank.

With their escape route now secured, the lancers set fire to their vehicles as they abandoned them, ammunition exploding in sparks among the thick black smoke of the burning oil and fuel. The Lancers Sergeant was the second last to cross, a burly Corporal taking the strain on the line alone. When his Sergeant was safely over, the Corporal tied the line around his waist and waded into the water, being lifted by the current and swept towards the bridge, relying on Sergeant Preston's team to pull him the rest of the way across.

With everyone secure on the west bank, Chadwick quickly ordered the group to get ready to move. The men fell in on the road and began to walk west, with a distance of eight miles to march to the next position. As the Lancers looked back, their vehicles were well ablaze, ammunition still exploding and a pall of smoke now hanging in the air.

Thursday 23 May 1940 –
Boulogne, Channel Coast, Northern France.

The 2nd Panzer Division's assault on Boulogne on the morning of 23 May concentrated along the coast from the south and also from the east. As with the previous evening, the Irish Guards took the weight of the attack from the south, a single company suffering ninety-eight casualties out of a strength of one hundred and seven men; but the line held. The attack from the east was more successful, resulting in a perimeter reduction and hand to hand fighting in the built-up area around the port. The destroyer HMS Vimy arrived to evacuate wounded and sent ashore a naval demolition team to destroy the port facilities, denying their subsequent use by the Germans. HMS Vimy also delivered Naval Gunfire Support, disrupting German logistics by landing large calibre shells among the supply chain moving men and materials towards the battle.

The Germans disengaged that evening and withdrew to allow a Luftwaffe strike on the town. As the bombs fell around them, the destroyers HMS Vimy and HMS Keith lifted nearly 4,500 men off the docks; the captains of both vessels being killed in the action. Four hundred men, mostly Welsh Guards, who had been on the wrong side of the last bridges as they were destroyed, were left behind. They only managed to get through to the port after the last ships had departed; and subsequently became prisoners of war.

Thursday 23 May 1940 –
Arras, Northern France.

The arrival of more panzers and motorised infantry enabled Rommel to push north through Arras. The British offered stern resistance, knowing that every hour they held the Germans would allow more time for their French and British counterparts to escape north. They were eventually forced to withdraw from what was rapidly becoming an exposed salient, back over the river Scarpe, where the French had prepared and now held a defensive line. The British Divisions withdrawing from Arras were hurriedly moved northeast to reinforce the Belgians who were coming under extreme pressure from German Army Group B.

Thursday 23 May 1940 –
Gort Line, Near Lille, Northern France.

Having crossed over the border into France and reached the designated concentration point in the late evening of the previous day, 10 Platoon were shown to their new positions by the Company Second in Command just as it was getting dark. This was the prepared defensive position, known as the Gort Line, that they had worked on through the previous autumn and winter; then bypassed as they moved forward into Belgium. As dawn broke, they found themselves in properly prepared defensive positions for the first time since being deployed on 10 May, although having been neglected since construction some months ago, minor repair work was required. The men cleaned their weapons in rotation and then had a hot meal before being set to work repairing the position.

"This is more like it." said Bell as he filled new sandbags to replace ones that had split from exposure to the elements. "Somewhere we can properly fight from."

"Whoever prepared this area did a good job." Smith added as he held open new bags for Bell to fill.

"I wonder who's in the bit that we dug?" Bell asked, knowing he could not possibly receive a meaningful answer.

"I hope they appreciate the work we did, whoever they are." Smith replied.

"As soon as we're finished here, I'm going to find a stream and have a wash." continued Bell. "I feel like my clothes could stand up on their own."

"I gave up caring about a week ago. Don't think I can get any dirtier." added Smith.

"Here comes the lucky bugger now." said Bell as they were joined by Orpin, who looked at him puzzled by the remark. "Got a nice swim and a wash in the river yesterday."

"I don't want to be doing that again." replied Orpin. "Swallowed about half the river Escaut I did. Probably lowered the level downstream."

"Allowed the Germans to just walk across further down you did." Bell teased.

"Well, they'll have a harder job getting past us here." said Smith as he lifted a filled sandbag up onto the trench parapet, beating it into place with the handle of his entrenching tool.

"That's if they let us fight." replied Bell. "I'm bloody tired retreating."

"You heard what the Platoon Commander said." continued Orpin. "The Germans have reached the Channel. There'll be nowhere to retreat to! We have to stand and fight now."

"The top brass will come up with something. We're not paid enough to worry about things like that." Smith concluded. "Right, Dinger. Don't stop working. Next sandbag please." said Smith as he held open a new sandbag for filling.

* * *

With the defensive line enhanced, the men were allowed to rest and had been fed. With no enemy action that day, morale had risen considerably and they now felt secure in a strong defensive position. As night fell, the sentry roster was implemented, some men sleeping while others stood ready. Bell and Farthing stood side by side on the firing step of the trench.

"I wonder if the brothel we visited is still open." queried Bell.

"Don't suppose there would be much demand at the minute with everything that's going on." answered Farthing.

"What was the name of that girl you were with?" asked Bell. "The well fed one." he added.

"Arlette." Farthing replied. "The beautiful Arlette." he sighed, recalling the memories of that night.

"I wonder if she's brushing up on her German. Just in case." Bell proposed.

"You're talking about the woman I love." protested Farthing, both men bursting out laughing.

Corporal Tetlow approached angrily. "What's all the bloody noise?" he hissed.

"Sorry, Corporal." Bell replied quickly. "We were just remembering the night in the brothel in Lille."

"Do your bloody remembering later." Tetlow snapped back. "Use your ears at night when you can't use your eyes." he reminded them. "You can't do that when you're bloody talking and laughing." He continued down the length of the trench, patting Farthing on the shoulder as he passed.

"What the hell has got into him?" Farthing whispered. "I was expecting a cuff around the ear there."

"Maybe he's remembering the visit to the brothel himself." replied Bell in hushed tones. "Just take it and be thankful."

Friday 24 May 1940 –
Aa Canal, Western Perimeter, Allied Defensive Pocket, Northern France.

With Boulogne surrounded and panzers now closing in on Calais, Guderian was able to turn his forces east, away from the channel ports, into the western side of the Allied pocket. He seized crossings over the Aa canal, putting the 1st Panzer Division only ten miles to the southwest of Dunkirk. Rommel continued the push up from the south and Army Group B advanced west from Belgium. The defensive pocket was being squeezed from all sides, when another halt order was received. Guderian's tanks were to stop on the Aa Canal, with Rommel's drive north from Arras also halted. Only the advance of Army Group B westwards towards Lille was allowed to continue, but using infantry only.

With his armoured formations now badly depleted after two weeks of continuous fighting, Hitler was convinced they needed rest and refitting before turning south for the impending push on Paris. He felt that the terrain and water obstacles around the Allied pocket would further degrade his tanks, and conditions were now best suited to an infantry battle. Herman Goring, head of the German Airforce, also convinced Hitler that his Luftwaffe could reduce the defensive pocket where the terrain was unsuitable for armour, especially around the ports. Hitler saw this as the ideal solution, where he could continue the pressure against the pocket, but also preserve the armoured force for the next phase of the battle.

Friday 24 May 1940 –
Gort Line, Eastern Perimeter, Allied Defensive Pocket, Northern France.

Just after first light, German recce vehicles approached the defensive line, the defenders taking up their positions in the trenches. With their weapons firing into what they believed were likely enemy positions, the German vehicles raced forward towards the British line, hoping to find a weak spot and break through. The Bren carriers that were being held just behind the front line for such an event, were now deployed to the areas the Germans were attacking. As before, the British machine guns and anti-tank weapons had been placed to fire along the defensive line, striking the German vehicles in their thinly armoured flanks as they came forward. When the crews jumped from their disabled vehicles, the defenders in the trenches engaged them with rifle fire, mercilessly cutting them down as they tried to run to the rear.

In thirty minutes, the attack was over. The vehicle hulks burned furiously, muffled explosions coming from inside as stored ammunition was detonated by the heat. German dead lay scattered on the ground or hung from the vehicles in grotesque shapes. The defenders watched, somehow mesmerised, as their dead bodies were slowly consumed by the flames, the smell of their burning flesh mixing with the acrid fumes of scorched metal. Major Crawley visited the position after the failed attack, accompanied by Lieutenant Chadwick.

"The heavy armour will be a number of hours behind." Crawley said as he walked down the line chatting with Chadwick. "But their reconnaissance will have reported our positions and we can expect a more concerted attack later when they bring up the artillery." he continued. "In the meantime, the Company has been given a time slot at the Mobile Bath Unit and the Company Sergeant Major will let you know when it's 10 Platoon's turn." A cheer erupted from those within earshot, the prospect of a wash and change of clothes too good not to be celebrated.

* * *

Having been relieved by a platoon from the reserve company, Chadwick gathered his men at the rear of the position and marched them to the location of the Royal Army Ordnance Corps Bath Unit. It was a tented location centred on a large water boiler from which pipes ran out in every direction. The men were handed a towel and a bar of soap and then stood in the queues that had formed at the multitude of smaller tents that contained the baths. After their bath, the men returned the towel and were issued clean underwear before getting dressed again. The Section Commanders accounted for their men as they waited for the platoon to reform.

"I will never take feeling clean for granted ever again." Kyle said to Farthing as they waited for the others to finish. Both stood with their eyes closed as if in ecstasy.

"I'm now scared to get dirty again." Farthing replied. "I washed my socks in the bath water and I'll hang them up to dry when we get back."

"I don't think anything we are asked to do tonight will ruin this feeling." Kyle continued. "A good dinner, and I'll be the happiest man in France." he muttered through a permanent smile.

The platoon was marched back and resumed their place in the line, morale immeasurably improved after their bathing experience; only to be told on arrival that the entire British Expeditionary Force had been put on half rations. The elation of being clean was soon forgotten when dinner was distributed. As he ate his meagre portion of meat and vegetables from the mess tin he had balanced on the trench lip, Kyle looked at the German vehicles that had long since burned themselves out. Enemy dead still littered the ground and he found himself thinking about Watts. He remembered the time they had spent together at Depot and his mother sharing their table at lunch. He wondered if she knew yet that her son was dead, how the news had been passed and the impact this would have had on her; and on consideration, he found his perspective on the issue of half rations had changed.

Friday 24 May 1940 –
Viskiskoia, Northern Norway.

The Scots Guards had only one day to establish positions in Viskiskoia before the Germans crossed the snow belt and attacked during the early afternoon of 24 May. Under pressure from a flanking operation with aircraft, mortars and machine guns, another withdrawal was ordered; which began at 4 p.m. By the early hours of 25 May, the Scots Guards had withdrawn fourteen miles to Pothus, where the Irish Guards had been placed in a defensive line only a few hours prior.

The Irish Guards watched in silence as the Scots Guards moved through their positions, shocked by their physical appearance. There were none of the usual exchanges of friendly rivalry when Guards Battalions met, the toll of having withdrawn one hundred miles in a week, through appalling weather and under constant aerial attack, clearly visible on the retiring troops as they trudged back towards Bodo.

Friday 24 May 1940 –
10 Downing Street, London, England.

Facing a military disaster in France and the potential German invasion of Britain, Norway had become a side show; but one that was absorbing much needed ships, equipment and soldiers desperately required for home defence. To this end, the War Cabinet ordered the complete evacuation of Allied forces from Norway, but only to be enacted after the capture of Narvik and the destruction of the iron ore handling facilities there. The retention of Bodo had suddenly become critical to an orderly and controlled evacuation from Norway.

Saturday 25 May 1940 –
Calais, Channel Coast, Northern France.

Trapped in the burnt-out railway station in Boulogne, under fire from German artillery and mortars, and running out of ammunition, the remaining defenders surrendered in the early afternoon of 25 May. Calais still held out, and had been reinforced with troops on 22 May, that due to the haste of their deployment from England were unfortunately not ready for battle. The tanks had been delivered straight from the factory having been prepared for a sea deployment, their guns uncalibrated and still covered in protective mineral jelly. The soldiers had been put ashore during a bombing raid a few days prior, with no maps and untested radios, with orders to simply hold the town. After forward reconnaissance had confirmed the coming onslaught, they had purposely established themselves in the centre of the town where the advantages of the battle-hardened German armour would be reduced by the closeness of the environment.

An order to prepare for evacuation on 25 May had triggered the destruction of supplies and equipment that could not be taken back, some tanks being set on fire to deny their use to the enemy; before the order was later rescinded. The British now dug themselves in behind the seventeenth century walls, designed for siege defence, but which now, three hundred years later, held firm against a twentieth century bombardment. The shelling stopped at 8 a.m. and the defenders emerged to fend off German infantry assaults. As the Royal Air Force strove to keep the Luftwaffe bombers away, two Royal Navy Destroyers assisted with Naval Gunfire Support against the German encirclement, resulting in a duel between the ships and German tanks which returned fire.

**Saturday 25 May 1940 –
Arras, Southern Perimeter, Allied Defensive Pocket,
Northern France.**

As Rommel prepared to resume his push north, the French defenders on the Scarpe river who had held their positions to allow the British to withdraw from Arras were now able to withdraw themselves from what was becoming a dangerously exposed salient. They moved north towards Lille, where the emphasis now fell on the British defending the eastern perimeter to hold the line long enough for the French to pass through and establish themselves in defensive positions in the town.

**Saturday 25 May 1940 –
Gort Line, Eastern Perimeter, Allied Defensive Pocket,
Northern France.**

The night had passed without incident and after the dawn stand to, the routine of weapon cleaning and eating was followed as normal. Expectations of a German attack that day were high after the engagement with the enemy reconnaissance force the day before. The sky was clear and the sun beat down on the men as they waited in the trenches, the heat stirring flies and other insects into activity, much to the increasing annoyance of those whose exposed hands, faces and necks they chose to alight on. Formations of enemy bombers could be seen at high altitude heading west, the rhythmic drone of their engines fading as they left the range of vision. A single enemy reconnaissance plane attracted sporadic small arms fire as it buzzed backwards and forwards from the eastern horizon.

"That's an artillery spotter plane." remarked Sergeant Preston. "We can expect some activity soon." he predicted. Not long after, dust clouds appeared on the horizon; the use of binoculars revealing infantry dismounting from their transport. Kyle felt his stomach tighten with nerves as the word was passed to prepare for action. The split-second warning whistle of incoming artillery sent the men diving into their underground shelters, where they sat huddled together as the shells exploded on the surface above them. The ground shook and soil fell from the roof of the shelter onto their helmets as the German artillery swept across the defensive position. The sheltering men began to cough as they breathed the dust filled air. The ferocity of the explosions began to decrease as the larger shells were replaced by those of a smaller calibre; an artillery tactic which allowed the attacking infantry to move closer without taking casualties, yet still keeping the defenders under cover. Sporadic shells were still falling when the shouts of the non-commissioned officers told the men to get outside.

Kyle took up a crouched position on the fire step of the trench and blew hard on his rifle to remove any dirt from the working parts. He checked his sights and made sure the magazine was tightly fitted, then lifted his head above the lip of the trench. Shells were still bursting among the barbed wire obstacles as the German artillery tried to clear a path for their infantry. Through the dust and flying clumps of earth Kyle saw grey / green uniforms darting furiously between shell holes as they tried to weave their way through the wire. Muzzle flashes exposed the enemy positions as the Germans fired from their cover. The guttural shouts of their officers and non-commissioned officers could clearly be heard as they encouraged their men to move forward.

Kyle cocked his rifle and flicked off the safety catch. The nerves in his stomach had disappeared as he took aim and fired on the advancing enemy. He had emptied a magazine without realising, dropping down into the trench and undoing the catch on his ammunition pouch to get a replacement. As he fitted the new magazine, he looked up to see Bell standing beside him, slowly and meticulously firing.

"I can't seem to hit anything." Kyle shouted above the noise of the firing.

"Watch for them taking cover." Bell yelled back. "Then shoot as they get back up."

Kyle stood up, and as instructed watched as a German soldier jumped into a shell hole. Keeping aim on where he disappeared, Kyle fired as he saw his head emerge; the man slumping backwards as Kyle's bullet struck home. He whooped in delight at his success, but his celebrations were cut short as soil was kicked up beside his head, small stones cutting into the skin on his cheek. He immediately ducked down below the lip of the trench. Bell ducked down beside him.

"You have to change your position every few shots." Bell shouted above the noise of the firing. "Otherwise, they will get a bead on you. It works both ways." Kyle nodded his understanding and rubbed has face where the stones had hit. He looked at his hand and saw a smear of blood. Taking a deep breath, he stood up again to continue the battle.

The individual crack of rifle bullets was suddenly replaced with the chattering sound of machine gun fire. The support weapons had been traversed to fire across the front of 10 Platoon, the surface of the ground seeming to spit soil as the rounds landed among the attacking Germans. With men spinning and falling as they were hit; the momentum of the attack was broken. As the Germans disengaged and fell back, shells began to impact on the defensive positions again, the enemy artillery attempting to cover the infantry withdrawal. Kyle crouched down as the artillery began to fall, his back against the front edge of the trench, his legs pulled in tight to his body. In a few minutes it was over. Dust and the smell of cordite hung together in the air. There was absolute silence as no one moved or shouted orders. Kyle felt a wave of relief wash over him. He had survived another engagement, helped by some soldiering skills; but mostly by a huge degree of pure luck.

As the defenders began to emerge after the last bombardment, shouts for assistance and medical attention broke the silence. Bell told him to stay put and remain alert, as he left to answer the calls for help; and as Kyle looked out over the ground in front of his trench, he saw more bodies had been added to the scene. Some hung on the barbed wire, entangled uniforms suspending their lifeless forms, like puppets being held on strings. Muffled moans from the direction of the enemy reached his ears; wounded men who could not suppress their agony. He could see feint signs of movement, as those that could still move their limbs attempted to crawl back towards their own lines. Some lightly wounded struggled to assist their comrades, their movement drawing unwanted attention to themselves.

Individual shots rang out, quickly followed by shouted orders not to fire at the wounded unless fired upon first. Kyle watched mesmerised and yet horrified at the same time; realising that he may well be partly responsible for the plight of the wounded. He had felt no compassion as he fought, but as he surveyed the aftermath, he now felt guilty for the part he had played in the action and the suffering he may have caused. He thought about his mother and how she would react if someone had to tell her he was dead. He thought about the mothers and wives of the dead Germans he saw lying in front of his position. Who would tell them? How would they tell their children their father wouldn't be coming home?

German medics, who had come forward with the assault, began to move between the wounded. They wore combat uniforms and equipment, but were unarmed. They had red crosses painted on their helmets, wore white bibs with a large red cross in the middle of their chest and carried medical backpacks with the red cross symbol displayed on the closing flap. A German ambulance came slowly forward, red cross symbols clearly displayed on the side of the vehicle. Medical personnel jumped out carrying stretchers and under the direction of the medics already present, carried selected individuals back to the vehicle.

Lieutenant Chadwick appeared in the trenches, ordering that trench walls and shelter roofs that had been damaged by the German bombardment be quickly repaired. The platoon placed sentries to give warning of any further potential attack as they dug out collapsed shelters and replaced damaged sandbags in the trench walls. As soon as they were finished, weapons were cleaned in rotation and any food that was found in personal packs was shared out. When the work was finished, those not on sentry duty were allowed to sleep. Bell made himself comfortable in the nearest shelter, using his personal equipment as a pillow, and within seconds was asleep. Kyle closed his eyes and tried to sleep, but his mind was racing after the events of the day and he lay awake listening to Bell gently snoring. Corporal Hutchinson came past to check on the section position and looked into the shelter, shaking his head at how Bell could sleep so soundly.

"How the hell does he manage that?" he asked Kyle.

"No idea, Corporal." replied Kyle. "I wish I could."

"I wish I could as well." added Hutchinson.

* * *

"We are in a pocket being attacked on three sides." Major Crawley explained as he began his orders session that evening, pointing at the map on the wall of his command shelter as he spoke. "We are currently fighting to retain Calais and a defensive line has been created along the Aa canal in the west." He traced the Aa canal line with his pointer. "The French have withdrawn from Arras and will be dropping back to Lille to form a defensive position there. We will provide protection for them to move behind us, and then they will hold the line while we move north to Messines." He pointed at Messines on the map, and the route to be taken through Armentieres, moving his pointer north as he continued. "The Belgian sector to our north east is collapsing but is being reinforced by our forces who withdrew from Arras two days ago. At Messines, we will form part of a new defensive line being created around Ypres."

With the situational outline completed, he sat down to go through the finer points of the orders, referring to his notes that he took at the Commanding Officer's orders session earlier.

"The French will be in Lille tonight and we will withdraw as soon as it gets dark. Runners will be sent to call the platoons back. There is no transport available, so everything that cannot be carried is to be rendered useless." He stopped to let his statement sink in. "There will be no move before twenty-two-hundred hours, so get the men fed, packed up and prepared by then." As the session finished, the Platoon Commanders marked their own maps from the master copy on the wall and left to brief their men.

* * *

10 Platoon ate in silence after the briefing by Lieutenant Chadwick. Everything had been packed and anything of value that could not be carried had been destroyed. The platoon had gathered together to eat, waiting for the order to move. There was a sense of despair in the atmosphere as cigarettes were passed around after the meal, and Chadwick could feel it. Corporal Hutchinson articulated what the men were thinking.

"Were we not doing alright, Sir?" he asked. "Holding the Germans back like we did."

"We were doing fine, Corporal." Chadwick answered, knowing what was coming next.

"So why are we pulling back again, Sir?" came the expected question.

"It's not us, Corporal." said Chadwick slightly frustrated. "As I said in the brief, the Belgians have collapsed and if we don't move to support them, then the Germans will capture the coast and we'll be cut off."

"So that tells me there's a plan to lift us from the coast." Hutchinson came back quickly.

"Either that, or a plan to reinforce us through the Channel ports." Chadwick replied, unable to answer the question directly.

"Evacuation would be my bet." Corporal Thomas added, to a murmur of agreement from the gathered men.

"10 Platoon?" came a questioning voice from the dark. It was Private Cockcroft, sent as the runner from Company Headquarters.

"Over here." Sergeant Preston replied.

"Follow me." said Cockcroft.

Saturday 25 May 1940 –
Pothus, Northern Norway.

The Irish Guards took up positions astride a one-hundred-yard-wide river, protecting a steel constructed road bridge that was prepared for demolition. Forests covered the hills that swept down to the river on each side, providing cover for both the defenders and a screened approach for the German attackers. Brigadier Gubbins' aim was for the defences to hold until the evening of 26 May to let the Scots Guards and South Wales Borderers prepare the next defensive position on the approaches to Bodo. The Norwegian Army supplemented the defence at Pothus with mortars and machine guns, which were immediately in action with the first German attack being only two hours after the Scots Guards had passed through on their withdrawal north. Mortar and machine gun fire were exchanged from the early hours on 25 May, the Luftwaffe joining the battle with the strafing of the Allied positions from the air.

Late in the morning of 26 May, Brigadier Gubbins came forward from his headquarters to see for himself what was happening. On assessing the situation, he subsequently gave the order for withdrawal. The bridge was demolished and the Irish Guards broke away that evening under cover of a detachment of RAF Gloster Gladiators that had been sent south from Bardufoss to a temporary airstrip at Bodo. Evacuation had been arranged through the small port of Rognan, ten miles from Pothus, using locally provided boats for the fifty-mile journey back to Bodo. It was now obvious to the Germans that a withdrawal was taking place from Bodo, prompting a heavy bombing raid by the Luftwaffe against the town on the evening of 27 May, striking the jetty and the makeshift airfield from which the Gladiators had been operating.

Sunday 26 May 1940 –
Calais, Channel Coast, Northern France.

After the lull in night operations, a tactic favoured by the Germans to allow resupply and receipt of new orders; the assault on the town resumed at 7 a.m. A Stuka raid at 9:30 a.m. forced a reduction in the defensive perimeter and the Germans infiltrated the port. In the late afternoon, having run out of ammunition, the defenders either surrendered or attempted to evade capture by moving in small packets through the German lines back towards Dunkirk.

The British knew they could not hold a continuous defensive line on the Aa Canal once the German attacks against the Dunkirk pocket resumed; and using the respite from the enforced halt in the German offensive, had established mutually supporting strongpoints centred on the scattering of small towns behind the canal line. The plan was to delay the Germans for as long as possible, buying more time for the developing evacuation effort. The flames and smoke from Calais could clearly be seen from this new defensive line, and it was no surprise when news came through that the town had fallen to the Germans.

In the chaos of conflicting information and communication, the RAF dropped supplies into Calais the next morning, meant for the defenders, but gratefully received by the German occupiers. With Calais secured, the German artillery was moved forward to within range of Dunkirk, also bringing the most direct shipping route from Dover under fire. This necessitated the use of a safer alternative route, in effect doubling the length of the sea passage between England and France.

Sunday 26 May 1940 –
10 Downing Street, London, England.

That morning, Anthony Eden, Secretary of State for War, sent a message to Gort's temporary headquarters at Houtkerque in Northern France, ordering a withdrawal to the coast for embarkation. Just before 7 p.m. Churchill authorised Operation Dynamo to begin, and less than two hours later, the first vessel was dispatched to Dunkirk; which was by this time the only port suitable for large scale evacuation remaining in Allied hands.

The steam turbine passenger ship, Mona's Isle, arrived in Dunkirk at midnight and during an air raid; but managed to embark nearly 1,500 troops, departing again at dawn. On the return route, the vessel came under fire from German shore batteries, being struck but with the shells failing to explode. A near miss smashed her rudder, but differential use of the port and starboard engines meant she could still be steered. A Messerschmitt fighter attacked the defenceless vessel in daylight, killing twenty-three and wounding sixty. Mona's Isle arrived back in Dover just before noon on 27 May.

Sunday 26 May 1940 –
Temporary German Airfield, near Calais.

The shadows from the slowly turning Messerschmitt BF109 propellor flicked across the canopy before coming to rest as the engine stopped. Squadron Leader Wilhelm Balthasar leaned back against the seat, pulled his leather flying helmet down over his face and silently thanked God that he had landed safely. Balthasar had come up against RAF Spitfires for the first time while operating over Calais, had seriously underestimated them, and was realising that he was lucky to have escaped unscathed. He pushed the release lever on the canopy and flipped it open. It clunked back against the hinge and a rush of fresh air entered the cockpit, laced with a hint of burning oil from his overheated engine. Remaining still in his seat emotionally drained, he didn't know whether he was relieved or elated.

Fearing the worst, the ground crew raced across the grass and climbed onto his wings as their Squadron Leader had not emerged from the cockpit. Shocked back to reality as his crew and squadron pilots appeared beside him, he released his harness, remembering to cover his Spanish Cross medal with his hand as it always caught on the harness when released. His crew pulled the harness clear, allowing him to lever himself out of the seat. He stepped out onto the wing, then jumped to the ground. Having landed their own aircraft nearby slightly before him, his junior officers began to gather excitedly around him.

"How many, Herr Hauptman?" they quizzed. He couldn't answer immediately from sheer emotional exhaustion, simply raising two fingers of his gloved hand.

"Spitfires, Herr Hauptman?" came the supplementary question; to which he nodded gently. His response was met with wild celebrations from those around him.

Sunday 26 May 1940 –
Lille / Armentieres Road, Northern France.

The platoon had been walking for two hours, and had reached the outskirts of Lille when a rest halt was called. Leading D Company, 10 Platoon had been following 9 Platoon from C Company; the night sky being clear and visibility good. As the men sat down at the side of the road to rest and drink from their water bottles, the drone of enemy bombers at high altitude moving west reached their ears; even more ominous than usual in the darkness. Lille appeared deserted, no lights in any of the houses and not even a dog barking.

"Where is everyone?" asked Orpin as he slumped down beside Kyle at the side of the road. "The place is deserted."

"Either left or locked in their cellars I suppose." replied Kyle with a tilt of his head. "I think I brought too much in this pack." he added, slipping it off his shoulders to give himself a break from the weight.

"Let me have a look." said Orpin, unbuckling the straps on the pack. He pulled out the contents as Kyle looked on, setting the items out on the grass. "Keep the greatcoat and rain cape." he suggested. "I don't think you'll be needing your PT kit, this spare shirt, gloves and spare underclothes." he said giggling. "Right, try that now." he added, helping Kyle sling the pack back on.

"Feels better thanks." Kyle said relieved, just as the order was given to stand up and prepare to march. "Do we not need to destroy that kit, rather than just leave it lying there?" he quizzed, looking at his discarded clothing.

"If some poor German feels the need to put on your sweaty PT kit or underwear, then I think he deserves to have it mate." replied Orpin.

* * *

They had another break two hours later and then walked for a further two hours before arriving in Armentieres, just as it was beginning to get light. Like Lille, the town was deserted, although had been badly damaged by German bombers. The houses had lost their windows and roof tiles lay in piles on the road, the remaining wooden joists pointed and stark against the lightening sky. The order came to rest and take cover in the ruined houses. Grunts of relief could be heard as the men left the road and took off their packs, settling themselves among the remains of the houses where some furniture was still intact. Tea was quickly brewed and the opportunity to eat and have a hot drink was gratefully accepted. Those that could, lay on the dust covered beds that remained in the ruined houses, even the few minutes sleep that they managed being better than nothing.

The bombing that had destroyed the town had also damaged the nearby lunatic asylum. As the column left Armentieres, the now unconfined asylum residents lined the road to stare at the passing British troops. Two elderly female residents, cackling with laughter like pantomime witches, lifted their nightgowns and exposed themselves as the soldiers marched by.

"Dear God boys, look at that!" said Bell as he passed the two women only feet away. "Somebody keep Lance Corporal Tetlow under control." Those within earshot laughed loudly, adding another layer of absurdity to the scene.

* * *

After a further two hours marching, the column came close to Messines. The soldiers fell silent as they passed the memorials and cemeteries from the battles fought there during the last war. The order came to rest and the men moved off the road, finding cover in the dilapidated Great War trenches that still survived. Having marched all night, the men were grey with fatigue and covered in dust. Most were quickly asleep and they were allowed to rest until it was just getting dark. From Messines they continued north towards Wytschaete, passing artillery batteries in the fields to the left of the road that were firing over their heads. A battle was raging in the east to keep the withdrawal corridor open; the night sky filled with flares. The white gravestones in the military cemeteries around Wytschaete glowed in the muzzle flashes of the guns and flickering light from the flares.

It took just under two hours to reach Ypres and their designated defensive position, centred on the Ypres Canal as the most formidable natural obstacle in the area. D Company was placed on ground that was dotted with orchards, hedges and small clusters of houses and farms, the officers doing their best in the dark to form a continuous defensive line with the other companies in the battalion.

Monday 27 May 1940 –
Aa Canal, Western Perimeter, Allied Defensive Pocket, Northern France.

As it became clear to Hitler that the Luftwaffe on its own would not destroy the Allied pocket around Dunkirk, despite Goring's personal promise, the halt order was rescinded on 26 May, under the proviso that the artillery was to be moved within range of Dunkirk as a priority. Freedom of action was returned to the panzer commanders at 8 a.m. on 27 May, and as instructed, the artillery of 1st Panzer Division was moved within range of Dunkirk to hinder reinforcement or evacuation.

As expected, the terrain was quickly found to be unsuitable for heavy armour, and the attacks against the British defensive line along the Aa Canal were resumed using infantry and lightly armoured vehicles only. The line was breached with little difficulty, but the interlocking strongpoints centred on the towns behind the Aa held firm into the night of 27 / 28 May, allowing British units withdrawing from the south to move behind the line and into Dunkirk.

Monday 27 May 1940 –
Dunkirk Port, Channel Coast, North East France.

At 6 a.m. the Royal Navy Destroyer HMS Wolfhound arrived in Dunkirk in the middle of a German air raid. On board was Captain WG Tennant RN, who was to be Admiral Ramsey's representative; with the hastily agreed title of Senior Naval Officer Ashore at Dunkirk. He had been sent by Ramsay, not so much to assess the options for evacuation, as Dunkirk was by this time the only option remaining, but to decide what could potentially be achieved and allocate resources to best effect. He brought with him a party of twelve officers and one hundred and fifty ratings who set to work immediately.

The docks were surrounded by old fortifications and a formidable bastion in which the French had established the headquarters for the coastline sector. The harbour was protected by two moles, long wooden structures that jutted out into the water from the coast, designed as breakwaters and not for the docking of ships. The furthest west mole was joined to the oil refinery, which had been set ablaze by German bombing, rendering the structure useless. The east mole was five feet wide and just short of a mile long. Further east beyond Dunkirk, sixteen miles of coastline stretched into Belgium with very gently sloping beaches; so shallow that even small craft could not get closer to the beach than one hundred yards without grounding. The beaches were backed by undulating dunes which Tennant envisaged could be used for troop assembly areas. Within two hours of arrival, Tennant sent a signal to Ramsay:

"Please send every available craft to the beaches east of Dunkirk immediately."

Tennant went to the bastion where he met with the French Commander Falgade, and British General Adam, who had been assigned to organise the evacuation. They had already agreed that the perimeter defence would be manned by the French in the west and the British in the east, forming an inner pocket thirty miles long and seven miles deep at its widest point. When established, the perimeter would run along existing canals and waterways, connecting the towns of Gravelines, Bergues, Furnes and Nieuport; now designated as "fortress" towns and defended accordingly. The ground behind was to be deliberately flooded by the opening of the sea dykes, to impede both vehicle and infantry movement.

Monday 27 May 1940 –
Messines, Eastern Perimeter, Allied Defensive Pocket,
Western Belgium.

At first light, work began on strengthening the defensive line. Adjustments were made to ensure interlocking arcs of fire for the machine guns and anti-tank gun positions that had been hurriedly established the previous night. Bushes and shrubs were cut down to improve visibility over potential enemy approaches. Firing ports were created in the walls of the buildings and reinforced with sandbags, and external doors blocked by repositioning of furniture. Internal doors were removed and holes dug in the internal walls to ease movement around the inside. Once the work had been completed, weapons were cleaned and ammunition unpacked and distributed; before the men were allowed to eat whatever they had carried, or could find in the abandoned houses.

With restrictions on offensive operations having been removed, the full weight of the German assault fell on the defensive positions. At 8 a.m. German artillery heralded the attack, falling all along the line, closely followed by reconnaissance vehicles searching for weak points they could exploit. Although dry, the canal cutting prevented any further advance by enemy vehicles, the British anti-tank weapons taking a heavy toll as the reconnaissance vehicles were forced to stop. The obstacle did not hinder the German infantry however, who climbed or jumped down into the dry canal. Defensive artillery fire fell among them as they negotiated the canal bed, but once across, the scattered woodland and houses on the far bank provided ideal terrain for infiltration between the British units.

As 10 Platoon waited, Chadwick heard the battle moving closer. The sound of British Bren guns to their front being sequentially replaced by the sound of German MG34 machine guns as the British positions fell to the Germans. He had positioned 1 Section in a line of forward foxholes, overlooked by 2 Section in a line of buildings one hundred yards further back. 3 Section were in the same line of buildings, but to the right of 2 Section. Chadwick knew the platoon was about to meet the enemy at close quarters and that if his positions fell, the integrity of the company line would be broken. He had placed Sergeant Preston in command of 3 Section, and designated this as his reserve section; knowing that with minimal direction, he could trust his most experienced soldier with the role of plugging any gaps that formed in the platoon position.

Some running soldiers appeared in front of 1 Section's position, but were instantly identified as British from their khaki uniforms and the outline of their helmets. They were waved across by the incumbents and jumped into the foxholes. As Chadwick watched, a scuffle broke out in one of the forward trenches, a recent arrival trying to climb out of the hole to continue his withdrawal, while its occupant tried to hold him back. The man broke away and continued to run until a stream of enemy tracer bullets followed him across the ground. His back arched and he took a few more faltering steps before falling face down, remaining motionless. A whisp of smoke rose from the wounds in his back as the heat from the tracer rounds burnt his clothing. Further streams of tracer now concentrated on the 1 Section positions, throwing lumps of earth into the air as the bullets struck around the edges of the foxholes, the occasional tracer round ricocheting off hard ground and shooting upwards into the air, before disappearing as the tracer burnt out.

Grey / green clad figures began to appear, the outline of their coal scuttle helmets clearly visible, crouching low as they ran towards where the machine gun rounds were impacting around the foxholes. The sections in the houses reacted immediately to the sight of the enemy, engaging the advancing infantry with well-aimed rifle fire; some Germans falling as the rounds hit home. The enemy machine guns then switched their attention onto the houses to suppress the return fire, isolating the 1 Section positions and providing cover for their leading infantry to assault the forward trenches.

Chadwick dropped below the window in the house he had chosen as his command post as brickwork flew in all directions with the impact of the machine gun bullets around the window frame. From the relative safety of his sandbag reinforced wall, he heard the explosion of hand grenades as the battle continued for possession of the forward trenches. The impact of the bullets around his window stopped as the German guns switched targets to another window, and Chadwick quickly raised his rifle and resumed firing in support of the forward trenches. He could see the men from the other houses rejoining the battle as the German fire moved away. Their supporting fire caused the German infantry to withdraw, but the action had highlighted the exposed position of 1 Section's forward trenches; and feeling they may not withstand another assault, Chadwick decided to move them back. He signalled with his arm for them to withdraw, Corporal Hutchinson acknowledging his instruction. 1 Section quickly jumped out of their foxholes and sprinted back towards the houses occupied by 2 and 3 Sections. They spread themselves among the line of buildings that overlooked the now vacant trenches, taking up firing positions in preparation for the next attack.

The Germans also appreciated the vulnerability of their failed frontal assault over exposed ground, being unable to suppress the depth positions sufficiently for their infantry to capture the forward British trenches. Instead, they began to infiltrate through a wooded area on the left side of the platoon positions and attacked the first house in the row; the arcs of supporting fire from the other houses being limited to the tiny gable wall windows of the adjoining house. The German machine guns concentrated their fire on the next house in the row as their infantry advanced from house to house. The sound of grenades exploding inside the buildings told Chadwick the Germans were working their way through the position from left to right, taking the buildings in sequence. He ran upstairs and looked through the gable window to see his men jumping out of the windows of neighbouring houses as grenades exploded inside, then running back to the next building in the row. He called Sergeant Preston to him.

"They're working their way through the woods to the left and taking us in the flank." he began. "Take 3 Section and recover the lost buildings on the left. I'll take the rest of the platoon and try to stop their reinforcements coming through the woods." Preston nodded. "Wait until you hear us fire before you begin your assault, otherwise you'll be on your own." confirmed Chadwick.

Sergeant Preston gathered the reserve section around him and told them to get as many grenades as they could carry. Chadwick took the rest of the platoon out the back of the houses, sprinting into some dead ground one hundred yards away, before moving to the right towards the wooded area. As he got closer, he could see Germans slowly moving between the trees in single file towards the buildings he had just vacated. Chadwick placed the men in a firing line facing into the wood, and gave the order to open fire. Having been taken completely by surprise, the Germans stopped and took cover behind the trees before the weight of fire forced them back the way they had come, leaving their dead and wounded behind.

Above the noise of the firing, Chadwick heard the shouts of 3 Section as they began their assault on the occupied buildings; before their voices were lost in the almost continuous sound of exploding grenades. He shouted to the firing line to watch out, and within a few minutes Germans started to appear between the trees from their right, withdrawing from 3 Section's counter attack. They were stopping momentarily and turning to return fire as they withdrew. Chadwick waited until their numbers filled the frontage of his line and again gave the order to open fire.

The volley slammed into the withdrawing Germans; those not being killed instantly trying to take cover behind the trees. Soil and wood splinters from the trees flew in all directions as Chadwick's firing line pinned the withdrawing Germans in place. Carefully watching for the arrival of 3 Section from the right flank, Chadwick yelled "Switch fire left." as the outline of British Brodie helmets appeared. The men in the firing line realigned their weapons to their left to avoid hitting the advancing 3 Section, yet still keeping the German withdrawal or reinforcement route covered by fire.

Faced with the onrushing 3 Section, the Germans broke cover and made a dash for safety; Chadwick's firing line cutting them down as they ran between the cover of the trees. Sergeant Preston came running through the woods at the head of 3 Section, bayonets attached, weaving between the trees. Chadwick called "Cease Fire!" as 3 Section ran across the front of his firing line, still chasing the retreating enemy. Chadwick rolled onto his back and breathed heavily for a few seconds, pleased that his plan had worked; the men in the firing line beginning muted celebrations at their successful engagement.

"Quickly, back to the houses." Chadwick shouted, the men reacting instantly and running after him. The violence of 3 Section's assault was evident as they reoccupied the recovered buildings. Blast marks of grenades were visible in every room, empty bullet cases littered the ground and dead Germans hung from windows, killed as they were trying to escape the assault. Private Henry from 3 Section lay wounded, propped against a wall in the first house Chadwick re-entered, his field dressing self-applied to his leg. He raised his rifle to fire as Chadwick appeared, letting out a sigh of relief and lowering his weapon when he recognised the Platoon Commander.

"Where's the rest of the section, Sir?" he asked.

"I think they'll be nearing Berlin by now!" Chadwick replied jokingly.

"Did we do alright, Sir?" asked Henry.

"You were bloody marvellous." replied Chadwick with a broad grin, patting him on the shoulder. Chadwick ordered the men to assume their former firing positions and reload their magazines in preparation for another possible German attack. He then moved between the houses, checking the men were prepared for further action, ordering the removal of the dead Germans and ensuring no one was concealing a wound or injury. Sergeant Preston re-appeared with 3 Section in tow. He was beaming from ear to ear, adrenaline still pumping through his veins after combat.

"Brilliant work, Sir!" he exclaimed, holding out his hand to Chadwick. "You've changed my opinion on officers." he continued. Chadwick tentatively shook his hand, unaware if Preston was being serious or not. Preston took out two cigarettes and lit them both at the same time; taking one from his lips and passing it to the Platoon Commander.

"I don't smoke, thanks." Chadwick reminded him.

"I know." replied Preston, offering the cigarette again. "You deserve it and you need it." he continued. Chadwick gingerly accepted the cigarette and took a puff. His head began to swim as the nicotine entered his bloodstream, but a sense of calm flowed through his body. Preston sat down on the floor and Chadwick joined him, feeling unsteady as the nicotine continued to do its work.

"That was some assault." Chadwick began. "I thought we might never see you again."

"Just like fighting in Glasgow on a Saturday night." Preston replied. "Once the red mist comes down, it's hard to stop." The two men laughed out loud. Chadwick leaned his back against the wall, now enjoying the calming effect the cigarette was having.

"I need to get myself some of these." said Chadwick, taking the cigarette from between his lips and looking at it as the smoke spiralled into the air. Preston undid the top pocket on his battledress blouse and took out his packet of cigarettes, dropping them in Chadwick's lap.

"Take these in the meantime." he said standing up, throwing down his cigarette butt and rubbing it out with his boot. "I need to get any wounded moved back and an ammunition resupply sorted."

* * *

Kyle and Bell were taking turns to keep watch while the other had some food and cleaned their weapon. Kyle stood in cover to the side of a now empty window frame, scanning the area to his front.

"What are you thinking?" he asked Bell without averting his gaze from the area in front.

"I'm thinking I could do with a proper dinner." Bell replied, kicking out at an empty tin of meat and vegetables on the floor, that he had just eaten cold. He licked his spoon and wiped it clean on the leg of his trousers before putting it away in his haversack. "Right, your turn." he said to Kyle as he got to his feet and took over the sentry position. "Do your rifle first, then get a bite to eat."

"What are you thinking?" repeated Kyle as he sat down, not getting the answer he had been hoping for earlier. "I mean, how do you feel?" he clarified.

"About what?" Bell asked.

"About the fighting today?" replied Kyle.

"I don't feel anything." answered Bell, bemused by the line of questioning.

"That's what I'm on about." Kyle blurted out in frustration. "Should you not feel something?" He paused. "After all, we could have easily been killed today."

"At least our skills can help us in a fire fight like today." Bell replied. "A shell could land on us when we're sleeping and there's nothing we can do about it." He continued when Kyle did not reply. "Look mate, if your number's up, then your number's up! Just like Watts. Had he been the best soldier in the world there was nothing he could have done; nothing anyone could have done." Sensing his friend's unease, he sat down on the floor beside him. "You just do your best when you can. Like you did today." he began. "The rest is pure luck and no amount of worrying can change that." Kyle remained silent, staring at the floor between his legs. "Now, put this out of your head and get some food inside you." Bell stood up again and resumed his watch. As he scanned the ground in front, he became concerned that Kyle was overthinking things. "You'll be no good to me if you're worrying instead of fighting." he concluded.

***

The Company Commander and Company Sergeant Major visited each platoon location that afternoon. Lieutenant Chadwick showed them around the 10 Platoon positions, Major Crawley concentrating on the layout of the defence, Sergeant Major McCann taking the opportunity to chat with the soldiers. It was clear from the conversations that all the platoons had seen action during the day, some sustaining greater casualties than the single 10 Platoon wounding. Chadwick got the impression that Major Crawley was exhausted; just going through the motions. He asked the expected tactical questions on interlocking fields of fire and counterattack plans, but did not seem to be listening to the replies. McCann took the time to properly engage with the men, relating his last known update on the strategic position and offering his opinion on what would happen next. Using this interaction, he gauged the attitude and morale of the men from their physical appearance and content of their conversation. He deliberately sought out Kyle, checking on both his mental and physical state; and surreptitiously taking a letter to his mother for inclusion in the company dispatches.

***

Major Crawley had called the officers together for an orders session in the occupied house being used as Company Headquarters. He had just returned from battalion orders with the Commanding Officer, and had an important update to pass on.

"The British Expeditionary Force is to be withdrawn from Dunkirk." There was a stunned silence from those attending. "With the fall of Calais, Dunkirk is the only port left in Allied hands large enough for such an operation; from where we will be lifted by the Royal Navy and returned to England." He waited for the information to sink in before continuing. "The Belgians are on their last legs, which could mean the collapse of our north east flank. If the Germans get between us and the coast then the game's up. Reinforcements are being rushed there as we speak to strengthen the line, but there is no guarantee they will arrive in time. So, we will withdraw north, leapfrogging through these defensive lines from Ypres to Dunkirk as marked." A 1:250,000 map hung on the wall, showing the perimeter of the Allied pocket, and marked with a series of lines running east to west between their current location and the port. Crawley identified the lines on the map with his pointer as he spoke. The shocked silence continued as Crawley went through the detailed arrangements for the withdrawal. With his mind numbed by the developments, Chadwick wrote down everything that was said, hoping that he could make sense of it later when his head cleared.

* * *

10 Platoon had been assigned two Bedford trucks for their transport, the men splitting themselves equally between the vehicles; Chadwick in the cab of the front vehicle with a Royal Army Service Corps driver, and Sergeant Preston in the cab of the second vehicle with another driver. It was already dark when the transport moved off, no lights being allowed for reasons of security. A long line of trucks carrying the whole battalion in convoy moved steadily north, driving nose to tail. Chadwick's driver was not in the mood for conversation, intently staring at the illuminated axle of the vehicle in front.

Chadwick drifted in and out of sleep, his mind free of the responsibility of map-reading for the convoy. Muzzle flashes from British artillery lit up the sky to the west, the convoy moving in a corridor below the outbound shells. In the distance to the east, the flashes of German artillery could just be seen, locked in a deadly duel between the opposing guns. Chadwick lit a cigarette, before offering one to the driver who took it and put it behind his ear for later. When he opened the cab window to let out the smoke, the noise of the guns supplemented the light display.

"Was it our fault, Corporal?" Orpin asked Corporal Hutchinson, squeezed together in the back of the lorry. "Having to withdraw, I mean."

"You heard the Platoon Commander as well as I did, Orpin." Hutchinson replied. "The Belgians are collapsing, and if we stayed, we'd have been cut off."

"So, we're not to blame then." Orpin replied, relieved that his professional pride was maintained.

"No, we're not to blame." Hutchinson reassured him. "And if I was you, I'd try and get some sleep while you can. God knows what we'll have to face tomorrow."

Monday 27 May 1940 –
Le Paradis, Pas-de-Calais, Northern France.

The unmistakeable sound of a BMW motorcycle engine could be heard approaching at some speed along the Rue de Paradis, when two rifle shots rang out in unison from a small farmhouse on the southern side of the road. The motorcycle and sidecar combination swerved viciously, the tyres squealing, and came to rest in the hedge surrounding the house. Standartenfuhrer Hans Friedemann, commander of Totenkopf Infantry Regiment 3, and son of German Field Marshal Götze, along with his Aide-de-Camp, Haupsturmfuhrer Sparmann, lay dead in the road. Oblivious to the identity of their enemy but knowing that they had now revealed their position; the British soldiers responsible ran from the house and crossed the road into Druries Farm, the current headquarters of the 2nd Battalion, The Royal Norfolk Regiment. News of the death of their commander soon spread among the soldiers of Totenkopf Infantry Regiment 3, who now approached Druries Farm driven by revenge.

The Norfolks had been spread out along the north bank of La Bassee Canal but were driven back as the Germans crossed, first in rubber boats, then bringing armoured vehicles across using sunken barges. They had subsequently centralised their defence around Druries Farm. The farm construction was typical of the area, with a three-storey farmhouse to the south, a central courtyard with a cowshed and barn to the north and west, and a brick wall with a gate to the east. There was a small pond in the centre of the courtyard. At 11 a.m. that morning, their Brigade Commander, Brigadier Warren, had given the Norfolks orders to fight to the last man and the last bullet. The men had subsequently prepared the buildings for defence by knocking out bricks in the farmhouse and the east wall to form loopholes, and splitting the metal sheets in the corrugated iron barn to create firing positions. They had stacked bales of straw around the firing positions to give them some protection from artillery and mortar splinters. An observation post had been established at the small window on the top storey of the farmhouse, giving a commanding view of the surrounding countryside.

For added protection, the Battalion Headquarters and the wounded were co-located in the cellar, where the medics did what they could to ease the suffering; while the signallers struggled to maintain communications with Brigade Headquarters and the other companies. As they watched and listened, the noise of battle from the village of Le Paradis reduced, as elements of the Norfolks who had taken up position in the village church were gradually overcome. As the heat of the day grew intense, mortars began to rain down on the farm. There was no warning noise as the mortars fell silently from the sky, imbedding razor-sharp splinters of red-hot metal into bricks, wood, straw and bodies alike. Fire began to take hold of the buildings, prompting the movement of the wounded from the cellar to the cowshed at the rear of the courtyard. Company Sergeant Major Whitlam moved among the wounded with a jar of issue rum, giving each man a large swig in turn. As a trained radio operator, Private Bill O'Callaghan remained in the cellar of the burning building, manning the radio. He watched the Commanding Officer, Major Lisle Ryder, move around the positions inside the farm complex encouraging the men in their defence. The men were very fond of Major Ryder, a calm and considerate officer, and brother of Victoria Cross winner Robert Edward Ryder.

Splinters of glass and plaster suddenly flew through the cellar as two large explosions above rocked the building, filling the air with dust.

O'Callaghan was thrown to the floor along with the seven other men in the room. He raised his head to see them covered in dust and rubble, the dust appearing darkened where it soaked up blood from their injuries. O'Callaghan's head whistled from the noise of the explosions, and looking around the room, dust clad figures were rising as if in slow motion from the rubble strewn floor. He became aware of Major Ryder shouting at him, but although he could see his lips move, no sound could penetrate the ringing in his ears. He deciphered the words "Are you OK?" being formed by the officer's mouth, and nodded his head in acknowledgement.

Contact with the other companies had now been lost, and Major Ryder scribbled out a note summarising the situation, passing it to O'Callaghan, who tapped it out on the Morse key to Brigade Headquarters. The reply brought no solace; ordering continued resistance until darkness fell; after which a fighting withdrawal could be attempted. Major Ryder read the reply and left the cellar, moving to the cowshed where he spoke with the wounded and those men already inside. On his return he ordered the radio equipment destroyed and all documentation and maps burned.

"When done, make your way one at a time to the cowshed." he said. O'Callaghan and those left in the cellar busily began to smash up their equipment. A fire was started in the middle of the floor, in which all the papers, log books and maps were burned. One at a time the men moved up the cellar stairs to the courtyard and dashed the twenty yards to the cowshed. As O'Callaghan took his turn to cross, he noticed broken rifles in the courtyard pond. Their previous owners were either dead or wounded beyond the capacity to fight; their weapons being smashed and then discarded to deny their subsequent use by the enemy. As O'Callaghan approached the cowshed, the door was opened from the inside and he flung himself through the gap. The building was constructed of red brick, about ten yards long and seven yards wide, divided into straw covered cement floor mangers, separated by brick partition walls. The heat and sweet smell of the straw struck him instantly, in contrast to the stale and dusty atmosphere of the cellar. He remembered that their packs had been centralised there on arrival, and quickly searched out his own. It contained two hundred cigarettes that had been taken from an abandoned NAAFI, which he now unpacked and distributed among the pockets in his battledress blouse.

Major Ryder was moving among his men, checking enemy movements through the windows and talking to the wounded who were laid out in neat lines being treated by the medics. He got the Company Sergeant Major to establish silence before he addressed those present. With a shaking voice he offered them a stark choice of fighting on or surrender, reiterating carefully that they had done more than their duty had asked, and that no shame would be attached to anyone who chose the latter path. He wanted them to talk among themselves and be ready to answer in a few minutes.

In a state of shock, the soldiers gathered in groups, seeking the wisdom of the older and more experienced among them. They talked in hushed voices, and although a majority decision was reached, it was by no means unanimous. Knowing they were to be outvoted, Privates Brown, Hagen and Leven said farewell to their comrades and ran back across the courtyard, through the burning farmhouse and out a side door into a ditch. It was a decision that was to save their lives.

Major Ryder took the presence of those that remained to be their answer to the question. He ordered Company Sergeant Major Whitlam to find a towel and tie it to a rifle. A desperate rummage found a soiled towel which Sergeant Curson attached to the barrel of his rifle. The back door of the cowshed opened onto a meadow about one hundred and fifty yards wide, from which the Germans were firing at the building. Sergeant Curson opened the top half of the split door and waved the towel until the firing stopped. He opened the bottom half of the door and gestured for the men to follow. Six men in total had passed through into the meadow when a German machine gun resumed firing, cutting down the Sergeant and three of the men who had managed to get outside. The remaining two tried desperately to return to the cowshed but the crush of those trying to leave prevented them from gaining immediate entry. Someone yelled to fall back, and a gap was created to allow the terrified men back inside. The firing stopped immediately they re-entered the building. As the two survivors lay shocked and breathless on the floor, the rest of the men looked at each other in fear, and at their officers for direction. Major Ryder tried to bring some calm to the scene.

"We'll wait a few minutes and try again." he said reassuringly.

After five minutes, Major Ryder signalled to try again. Removing the towel from the rifle, a junior officer shouted that they were coming out, and boldly stepped through the door furiously waving the towel. When he was met by silence rather than gunfire, the others began to file out behind him. Looking around the meadow there seemed to be Germans everywhere, now standing up waving and celebrating. Individual Germans approached, keeping their weapons pointed at the surrendering men and indicating for them to raise their arms. Those wounded and holding their comrades for support stopped, raised both arms to show they had no weapons, before regaining their support and limping forward again. They were formed up on the road and shepherded into an adjoining meadow where they were halted.

A German officer addressed them in good English, getting them to kneel down and put their hands on their head; which he then demonstrated as if he had not spoken to them in their native tongue. While kneeling, Bill O'Callaghan very slowly moved his head to look around and get his bearings, trying not to draw attention to himself with the movement. The men had been gathered beside a corn field, the yellow crop swaying gently in the warm breeze. Insects buzzed around, drawn to the sweat on the men's clothes and to the blood-stained dressings on the wounded. He noticed a few artillerymen who were not part of their own unit, and even a prisoner in French uniform. With the heat of the sun on his back, he suddenly felt tired to the point of nausea. Almost falling asleep, his head jerked forward which brought him back to reality. Gentle moans could be heard from the wounded. German voices were talking excitedly, the movement of their men around the field signalled by the rattle of their metal equipment clinking together as they set up a prisoner processing area.

The German officer addressed them again. They were to move forward five men at a time to the trestle tables that had been placed at the side of the field. Behind each table sat a clerk who was there to process each man through the recording of prisoners' procedure. As each man approached his respective table, their webbing equipment and gas mask were removed. They were then physically searched and their personal items placed on the table in front of the clerk. Pay books, photographs and even their cigarettes were returned after details had been recorded by the clerks. Once processed, the prisoners were taken to the area where they had entered the meadow, and sat back down with their hands on their heads to await the rest of their party.

Bill O'Callaghan approached the table when it was his turn and placed his personal effects in front of the clerk. The English-speaking officer who had been moving between the tables stopped beside him.

"You have a knife?" the officer asked.

"No." replied O'Callaghan, not remembering he had a utility knife attached to his belt. The officer stepped behind him and removed the knife, setting it on the table. A German soldier who was waiting beside the next five prisoners in line stepped forward and struck O'Callaghan viciously in the lower back with the butt of his rifle. Pain and shock hit him simultaneously and his knees buckled, but he refused to fall and forced himself upright again. The processing by the clerk continued as if nothing had happened. While waiting his turn, Private Albert Pooley noticed that the wounded had been allowed to sit down, and as he was bleeding from a few minor wounds, he took it upon himself to join them. No sooner had he began to feel the comfort of sitting, than a German hurriedly approached and kicked him in the back and legs, gesturing him to stand up. Pooley quickly got to his feet and showed the German his wounds. He received another kick for his trouble and replaced his hands behind his head as before.

Just as all the prisoners completed the registration process and were reconstituted as a single group at the entrance to the meadow, another German officer approached with eight men in tow. He moved amongst the prisoners, regarding them with disgust. Pooley was drawn to his sharp, angular features; his face reddened by anger. He was wearing a spotted, loose fitting camouflaged smock with ties at the neck which hung loose, allowing the smock to gape. Underneath, Pooley could see a field grey tunic with a dark green collar bearing a Deaths Head Skull, embroidered in silver thread on a black rectangle. The rest of the section wore similar insignia on their tunic collars, but woven in white cotton. The newly arrived officer became involved in a heated conversation with the English-speaking officer who had been overseeing the prisoner registration procedure to this point.

The squad that had arrived with the angry officer got the prisoners to stand, and forming them into three ranks, marched them back onto the road where they were searched again. This time, personal items such as wallets, watches and rings were removed. Bert Pooley struggled to hide his feelings of contempt for his new captors, an attitude that did not escape the SS trooper who was searching him. The silent confrontation came to a head when Pooley had his cigarettes removed, and his face displayed his inner feelings. His searcher took a step back, giving him room to take a swing, and Pooley received a rifle butt to the face, catching him just under the nose. Staggering backwards through the ranks, his comrades prevented his fall. His head was spinning; his ears were ringing, and his mouth filled with blood. Pushing his tongue forward he felt the jagged edges of his broken teeth. The inside of his upper lip was split wide open. Finding his balance again, he returned to his position in the ranks; ignoring the unspoken body language invitation of his assailant to react and receive another blow. Pooley simply tilted his head forward and spat out the blood and tooth fragments that were still in his mouth.

The prisoners were held for several minutes where they stood, witnessing the clearly heated conversation between the German officers; the angry officer who had intervened being the most vocal. On his orders, the column was marched two hundred yards down the dusty road to a crossroads junction with the Rue De Paradis, where they were again halted. As they stood there, columns of German trucks carrying men, stores and ammunition passed along the Rue De Paradis, creating clouds of dust and choking engine exhaust fumes. The prisoners attracted inquisitive glances from the vehicle passengers and drivers as they sped past. A body of marching German infantry slowed to look; some of the soldiers breaking ranks to demean the prisoners and assault them with rifle butts and kicks.

A sharp German voice shouted "Come!" and the column of prisoners moved forward, turning immediately right at the junction. About twenty yards on the left was a red brick building, clearly visible over its surrounding hedge. The column passed the building and were directed left through a small gate into the meadow directly behind it. Bill O'Callaghan noticed the angry officer standing just inside the meadow, with his arms folded, watching the prisoners as they passed through the gate. The building was about forty-five feet long with a door in the middle and windows on either side. There was another door on the second story, giving access for loading hay or grain bags in the upper rooms. Some of the tiles were missing from the roof, but commensurate with the rest of the building, seemed to be from neglect rather than battle damage.

There was a shallow pit about one third of the way along the front of the building; the prisoners stepping in and out again as they moved towards the far end of the structure. As the rear of the column reached the building wall a command was given in German to fire. Two machine guns that had been concealed in the hedge immediately opened fire, starting at opposite ends of the column and moving towards the centre. Shouting and screaming began as the guns cut down the men like a scythe cuts corn. Bill O'Callaghan was in the centre of the column and had the split-second thinking time offered by his position to dive behind the falling men in front of him. He landed at full stretch and felt a searing pain in his arm; knowing immediately he had been shot. Gripping the earth, he felt men fall on top of him as death cries left their throats. His face was in a patch of thistles but he dared not move. The firing abruptly stopped, and the moans of the wounded became audible.

At the same instant, Bert Pooley lay a few yards away. He too was injured, being hit twice in the legs. Above the cries of the wounded, he heard a command in German, and the unmistakable sound of bayonets being unsheathed and attached. The sound of more screams and pistol shots came closer, and he braced himself for a bullet or even worse, the thrust of a bayonet. A man below him shifted as the Germans approached, inviting two shots from a pistol. Both bullets hit and lodged in Bert Pooley's legs, but with amazing willpower he neither moved or made a sound. He now had four wounds. Through squinted eyes he saw Major Ryder sitting propped up against the brick wall of the building, obviously still alive, and following the approaching Germans with his eyes. Ryder stared in defiance at his murderer who walked briskly towards him and finished him with a single shot.

Bill O'Callaghan felt a sense of peace flood through him. He thought of his family as he prepared for death. He could feel a wounded man on top of him move as the Germans approached. The SS man stood on O'Callaghan's back as he pulled the wounded soldier from between his legs and shot him; despite his pleas for mercy. He felt the lifeless body fall back on top of him and the German stepped away.

A shrill whistle blast signalled the end of the killing, and the Germans left the scene. O'Callaghan squinted along the length of his outstretched arms and saw a tangle of motionless bodies, now silent, their mouths and eyes frozen open in horror. His mind shut down with a combination of exhaustion and trauma, and he fell into a semi-conscious sleep.

* * *

Bert Pooley lay motionless, not daring to move. He had heard nothing that sounded like enemy troop movements for what felt like hours, although even the silence seemed to menace him now. The pain of stiffening muscles throughout his entire body added to the agony from his wounded legs. Very slowly he began to move his head; his thought process being that unless someone was deliberately watching him, the movement would not be discernible. He watched flies settling on the exposed brains of a dead soldier inches from his face. He recognised the features of Alf Spinks despite the protruding tongue and glassy eyes, but it was the deathly pallor of his skin that disturbed him most. Pooley averted his gaze and decided to wait for darkness before making any further movements.

* * *

As darkness fell it began to rain. The moon shone between the rainclouds, casting moving shadows and adding an extra eeriness to the scene of death. Pooley felt the silence almost crushing him, when he heard the sound of someone snoring. Bill O'Callaghan had been asleep for some hours when he became aware of increased pain in his wounded arm. Someone was tugging at the material of his battledress sleeve.

"Who's that?" he whispered.

"It's me!" a whispered voice answered.

"Who the hell is me?" O'Callaghan questioned back.

"Pooley." came the reply. "You've got to help me before Jerry gets back."

"I'm O'Callaghan. Are you badly hurt?"

"My legs are smashed up pretty badly. You've got to help me out of this." O'Callaghan began to push the dead bodies of his comrades away to give himself room to move. He manoeuvred his arm under Pooley who yelped in pain as his position changed.

"Keep your voice down." O'Callaghan hissed as he eased Pooley from the tangle of dead; and both men lay side by side on the grass to catch their breath and ease the pain of their wounds. The now heavy rain was a welcome relief on their parched lips, but soaked their uniforms through to their skin. As their eyes became accustomed to the dark, they saw some outbuildings nearby. O'Callaghan struggled to his feet and silently made off to check them out, leaving Pooley alone on the grass. He returned a few minutes later with a discernible sense of urgency.

"We've got to get away from here, Bert. That barn is full of Germans. I was lucky they didn't hear me." he whispered.

"Where shall we go?" asked an increasingly nervous and excited Pooley.

"I don't know, but we'll keep away from the main road. There will still be lots of Jerries there." O'Callaghan whispered back.

Bert Pooley was over six feet tall, and Bill O'Callaghan struggled to get him lifted up and onto his shoulders. Moving away from the barn and the road, O'Callaghan managed to carry his groaning comrade for two hundred yards, skirting around a burning outhouse, before his legs gave out and both men tumbled to the ground with a dull thud. Lying exhausted and panting, Pooley begged O'Callaghan for some water. Directed to his pocket, Bill O'Callaghan took a cigarette tin from Bert Pooley's battledress, emptied the contents into his hand and returned the cigarettes to Pooley's pocket, before making off with the tin to find water. The heavy rain had gathered in a track rut and O'Callaghan skimmed the surface to collect as much clean water as he could in the tin. Pooley drank eagerly and asked for more; O'Callaghan having to make three more trips to the puddle before Pooley was satisfied. Both men crawled a few more yards to the scant shelter of a young fruit tree, where shock and loss of blood began to impact their bodies. They sat upright with their backs against the tree and began to shiver almost uncontrollably.

Pooley had spotted two civilian corpses covered in blankets near the German occupied barn, and pleaded with O'Callaghan to go back and get them. As he made off in a crouching run back towards the barn, Pooley could see him silhouetted against the burning outhouse and realised the risk he had asked him to take. As O'Callaghan got close to the dead civilians, the roof of the burning outhouse creaked and collapsed inwards, sending sparks and flames shooting into the sky. Night turned to day, and O'Callaghan instinctively threw himself flat on the grass. Despite his actions he was clearly visible as the flames danced, casting a long, flickering shadow of his prostrate body across the meadow. He lay perfectly still, braced for the enemy reaction, assuming he would be seen at any second. But no reaction came, and he crawled the whole way back to the tree.

As the flames began to die and there was no sign of the enemy leaving the comfort of the barn, O'Callaghan decided to have another go at retrieving a blanket. He retraced his route from the previous attempt, his steps getting shorter and the noise of the Germans talking and laughing getting louder as he approached the barn. From ten yards away he made a dash, grabbed a blanket and sprinted back to Pooley. The two men placed the wet blanket over their heads and bodies, their hands shaking as they lit a cigarette under the cover of the wet wool. O'Callaghan took a long drag and handed the cigarette to Pooley. As the nicotine took effect it seemed to soothe their minds of the horrors they had endured. Their world became almost silent, apart from the rain falling on the leaves above their heads and on the sodden blanket stretched over their bodies. They began to process what had happened to them.

"I can't believe what they did to us. Why did they do that to our lads?" O'Callaghan asked as if wanting to hear it was all a dream or that he had not seen what he thought.

"It was that fucking officer." hissed Pooley. "I shan't forget his face. Ever."

"We have to get out of here before it gets light." whispered O'Callaghan. "I'll have a look around and try to find the best way out." At that, he lifted the blanket off his head and tucked it in around Pooley; before making off into the dark and the rain. He moved in the opposite direction to the burning barn, remaining in cover as best he could by using the dead ground that the slope of the meadow provided. He came to the boundary of the meadow, a ditch six feet wide, lined with reeds and filled with water due to the rain. O'Callaghan stepped into the water to test the depth. It came up to his thighs. The obstacle this would present to the almost immobile Pooley was obvious, but the only other alternative was discovery and execution.

O'Callaghan returned to Pooley and explained the situation, who agreed it was the only option. Manhandling his wounded comrade onto his shoulders once again, O'Callaghan headed back towards the ditch; sitting on the bank momentarily to rest before sliding down into the water. Pooley moaned as the water reached the wounds on his legs and O'Callaghan felt the grip around his neck tighten as Pooley's body reacted to the pain. In a few steps he was across the ditch, and he turned his back to gently unload Pooley on to the far bank. Scrambling through the reeds and up the bank, he pulled Pooley clear of the water. Both men lay flat on the grass breathing heavily; one in exhaustion, one in agony, the rain still falling heavily on their saturated uniforms.

"We're on the edge of a cornfield, Bert. Do you think you can crawl through it for a bit?" inquired O'Callaghan.

"I'll give it a go, Bill." replied Pooley, fully appreciating the effort his friend was making, when it would be so much easier for him to go on alone. O'Callaghan led the way, crawling and carrying the precious blanket, with Pooley pulling himself along backwards in a seated position behind him. The corn was only shin height so provided little cover from view, the men lying down frequently to hide, snatch a rest, and listen for enemy activity. The only sound was artillery fire in the distance.

The men had lost all track of time and distance covered when they arrived at a barbed wire fence bordering the field; from where the dark outline of another farm complex was just visible. As they edged along the fence towards the complex they came to a gap in the wire, and using the last of his strength, O'Callaghan lifted Pooley onto his shoulders again and carried him towards the buildings. As they got closer, the complex outline separated into that of a farmhouse and a detached open-sided Dutch barn. Thinking the barn was the safer choice, O'Callaghan headed for that, finding piles of clean straw inside onto which the men collapsed. Stripping him out of his wet uniform, O'Callaghan covered Pooley in some sacking, before removing his own uniform, wrapping himself in more sacking and falling into an exhausted sleep.

Tuesday 28 May 1940 – Lommel, near Lille, Northern France.

To impress the importance of applying continuous pressure against the withdrawing French, and to stop them concentrating their forces against him, Rommel had moved forward to visit his Reconnaissance Battalion in the village of Lommel, just west of Lille. He was in discussion with the Battalion Commander, Major Erdmann, who had removed his leather gloves for the purpose of pointing out the position of the enemy forces to Rommel on his map. Reacting to the split-second warning whistle of an incoming artillery strike, both men had begun to move before the first shell landed. From the direction and the size of the impact it was obvious these were German 155mm shells, mistakenly firing on their own troops.

Erdmann and Rommel ran towards the signals vehicle to order the lifting of the bombardment, with Erdmann just a few yards in front, when a shell struck the house outside which the vehicle was parked. When the debris settled and the smoke cleared, Erdmann was lying face down, dead; his head shattered and a gaping wound in his back. His leather gloves were still clutched in his hand. Although other officers and men were also injured in the same blast; Rommel was shaken but unharmed. However, having narrowly escaped injury or death yet again, he ensured the subsequent orders were issued to contain the French breakout.

Tuesday 28 May 1940 –
Dunkirk Beach, North East France / North West Belgium.

As he watched the evacuation efforts, Tennant realised that the operation from the beaches was too slow, and decided to call forward ships directly to the east mole. That morning, six destroyers came alongside under RAF fighter protection. The soldiers waiting on the mole quickly filed onto the ships but remained on the decks, being reluctant to go below in case of sinking. The crammed decks not only prohibited full use of the ships' guns, but rendered the vessels top heavy and harder to steer as they zigzagged away to avoid the German dive bombers. Witnessing how efficient this process could be when properly controlled, Tennant decided this would be the principal method of evacuation. Later that afternoon, in response to Tennent's request the previous day, the first little ships appeared on the horizon opposite the evacuation beaches.

Inside the perimeter, General Gort set up his headquarters in what was formerly King Albert of Belgium's holiday villa in La Panne. The villa had a direct phone line to England that King Albert had installed to keep track on his investments on the London Stock Market while on holiday, and thus provided a perfect location for Gort.

Tuesday 28 May 1940 –
Ypres / Poperinghe Road, Western Belgium.

The West Stafford's convoy moved slowly right through the night, dawn revealing carefully positioned roadside route markers and Royal Military Police traffic controllers. The signs indicated the road to Poperinghe, which Chadwick quickly located on his map.

"This is going to get messy." he said to the driver. "The roads to Poperinghe all merge further ahead." As predicted, movement soon became difficult, the vehicles moving forward ten yards then being forced to wait, then moving again a few minutes later. The driver, who had been awake all night, fell asleep each time the vehicle stopped, Chadwick having to continually waken him to move the truck forward.

Such a slow-moving convoy made a perfect target for the Luftwaffe, Messerschmitt fighters crisscrossing the blocked road at tree top height, picking out individual vehicles to attack. Trucks exploded in huge fire balls, causing further delay until the wreckage could be cleared from the road. A towed Bofors Gun fired at the attacking aircraft while on the move, by pure luck hitting a fighter and knocking off part of a wing; the aircraft flipping over and spiralling out of control before smashing into the ground. A huge cheer erupted from those in the trucks who witnessed the event.

The road move soon ground to a halt completely, and with a timetable to meet in the leapfrog defence line plan, D Company were ordered to leave their vehicles and proceed on foot. Just as they emerged from the trucks it began to rain. Seeing the men alight, a Military Police Sergeant spoke to Major Crawley, advising him to avoid areas where the Germans had reportedly broken through the eastern defensive line. Crawley pulled the three Platoon Commanders together and highlighted the route they would take along minor roads. He set them off in platoon sized groups, 10 Platoon to bring up the rear. In worsening weather, the men pulled out their rain capes and put them on before they set off.

"At least the rain will keep the Luftwaffe grounded." remarked the Military Police Sergeant as he stood beside Chadwick, watching the other platoons walk away. "Best of luck, Sir." he added, before moving off down the line of stationary vehicles.

The ground turned into slippery mud almost instantly as the heavy rain came down too quickly to be absorbed by the parched soil. The men's rain capes were soon breached by the weather, water running in around the neck closure and the run off soaking their trousers.

"I b…bloody h…hate the rain." complained McCafferty as he trudged along.

"Would you rather be sitting in a lorry waiting for a German fighter?" Orpin asked him.

"I c…could be killed any m…minute now!" McCafferty replied. "A…at l…least I would die d…dry in a l…lorry." Orpin just shook his head in disbelief.

***

Chadwick saw the leading platoons stopped beside a parked lorry ahead. As 10 Platoon got closer, they could clearly see men in the back handing out boxes to those soldiers gathered round, who then moved off.

"You're just in time, boys." said a Service Corps Corporal, standing in the back of the packed lorry as the platoon approached. "Take anything you want."

"What's the deal?" asked Sergeant Preston.

"The lorry's broken, Sarge." said the Corporal. "Our officer has buggered off and I'm not leaving this for the Germans." continued the Corporal, pointing over his shoulder with his thumb at the stacked boxes. "What you don't carry away right now is getting burned."

He had unpacked cigarettes and food to give to the other platoons, and held out tins of beef stew and cartons of cigarettes, offering them to the quickly gathering 10 Platoon soldiers. Unable to resist the temptation, the men filled any empty space in their packs, some stuffing cartons of cigarettes down the front of their battledress blouses. Chadwick took some tins of stew and a carton of cigarettes. "This new habit was working out well." he thought to himself. He had yet to pay for any cigarettes.

"Don't go near the main roads." Chadwick told the Service Corps Corporal, as the platoon prepared to depart. "Walk north on the minor roads or across the fields." As the platoon moved off, the Corporal was throwing petrol from a can over the remaining boxes, preparing to set his vehicle on fire.

Less than a mile further on, the platoon came across a military staff car that had apparently skidded off the mud-covered road and was stuck in the ditch. A Major stood beside it looking bemused, and on seeing Chadwick's officer rank, called him over. The Major was considerably overweight, rolls of fat hanging over his shirt collar and the buttons on his tunic straining against the stretched material.

"Get your men to push my car out, Lieutenant." demanded the Major. Chadwick quickly gathered some men together to comply, Private Hamill jumping into the ditch to assess the task. He called Chadwick across.

"Sir, the axle's broken. This car isn't going anywhere." Hamill told him. When Chadwick passed on the assessment, the Major exploded in a fit of rage, accusing the men of being idle and demanding the car be pushed back onto the road. Sergeant Preston witnessed the exchange between the officers and stepped in, ordering the men to push the car back onto the road. As many men as could fit around the vehicle climbed into the ditch or pulled from the road. Lifting and pulling together, the car slid back onto the road, coming to rest with its chassis on the road surface and the rear wheels sitting at an angle.

"There you go, Sir." said Preston sarcastically to the Major as the men climbed out of the ditch. "She's all yours." Chadwick saluted the Major politely and ordered the men to move off. As Preston passed Chadwick he leaned towards him. "That's why I hate most officers." he whispered. As they passed the stranded officer, Farthing noticed the RASC shoulder titles on his uniform.

"What does RASC stand for?" he asked Hamill.

"Usually, it means Royal Army Service Corps, Penny." replied Hamill loudly enough for the Major to hear. "But in his case, it means Run Away Someone's Coming." A ripple of laughter passed along the line of men as the joke was repeated.

"I want that man on a charge for insubordination." shouted the Major as the platoon moved off. "Did you hear me?" he yelled as he was left standing alone beside his disabled car in the pouring rain.

* * *

Major Crawley called a halt to the withdrawal in mid-afternoon, establishing his headquarters in a farm complex consisting of a small house, a yard and a barn. The three platoons created a defensive ring in the fields surrounding the buildings where they waited for further orders, rigging shelters with their rain capes to get some respite from the weather. The heavy rain had exposed the potatoes that were growing in the fields and the men pulled them up and cooked them to supplement the meat they had received from the broken supply truck earlier that day. Inside the farmhouse, Sergeant Major McCann had managed to get the stove going and hot tea was being brewed.

A motorcycle messenger came into the yard, sent from Battalion Headquarters and carrying a sealed envelope of orders for the Company Commander. It was the Battalion Intelligence Officer, Captain Heath. Major Crawley asked McCann to give the soaking wet officer some hot tea; McCann seating him in front of the stove, handing him a metal mug and a blanket from the farmhouse to dry himself off while Crawley opened the sealed orders.

"What's happening, Sir?" McCann asked the officer quietly, who he knew from the position he held at Battalion Headquarters would be aware of the strategic situation.

"The Belgians have surrendered and the north east Belgian Sector is under severe pressure, but holding." began Heath. "We are being squeezed into a pocket around the port of Dunkirk with the Germans trying to move east along the coast from Calais, and west along the coast from Belgium to cut us off. The Luftwaffe are dropping these." He produced a leaflet from inside his tunic, showing a rudimentary map of the situation, and calling on the British forces to surrender. "There have been reports of the shooting of prisoners, but nothing has been confirmed." Heath continued. McCann took the leaflet and tucked it into his pocket. "It looks like an evacuation is being planned from the beaches east of Dunkirk."

"They want to lift a quarter of a million men off the beaches?" McCann asked in disbelief.

"That appears to be the intent." Heath replied.

"Jesus Bloody Christ." McCann whispered.

Major Crawley had cleared a space on the dining table in the middle of the farmhouse main room and sat with his maps and orders book spread out.

He had opened the sealed orders and was reading through. He suddenly appeared beside Captain Heath, slapping the mug from his hand and sending it clattering across the stone floor, its contents leaving a steaming trail of spilled tea. He pulled the blanket off Heath's shoulders and threw it to the floor, lifting the officer out of his seat by his equipment straps and pushing him towards the door. McCann stood up, stunned by the actions of his Company Commander, but Captain Heath had already been ejected from the house before McCann could intervene.

"Sir, what the hell is going on?" McCann asked, stunned by Crawley's actions.

Crawley said nothing and sat back down at the table. McCann asked again and was handed the written orders that the messenger had delivered.

"We're to be the bloody rearguard on a defensive line." Crawley blurted out. "The last ones to leave."

* * *

The orders session had been arranged in the barn for 9 p.m. Paraffin lamps hissed and the rain made a continuous noise on the corrugated tin roof. The smell of wet wool uniforms mixed with the sweet odour of stored hay. A map had been attached to an upright stall beam, with hay bales arranged in a semi-circle for seating. All officers and non-commissioned officers had been summoned to attend; an unusual occurrence.

Major Crawley began by explaining the current strategic situation, pointing out the perimeter edges of the Allied defensive pocket on the map. He then described the withdrawal plan to Dunkirk, with the aim of lifting the Expeditionary Force from the beaches. A withdrawal corridor was being held open at Ypres, down which the battalion would move that night, to take up defensive positions on the Yser canal, north of Poperinghe. He pointed out the canal on the map.

"We will then hold this position as the designated rearguard until the troops holding open the corridor at Ypres can withdraw back across the canal." Those who had sufficient service, knew the implications of the phrase "designated rearguard". A murmur went up across the gathering as this was announced. "We will remain in these positions until ordered to withdraw." continued Crawley, reinforcing the importance of the task. He then addressed the unusual attendance of all the non-commissioned officers at the orders session.

"I have asked you all to attend for a very good reason. You are getting these orders directly from me." He paused to draw attention to the importance of the next statement. "There is a distinct possibility that we will have to withdraw from the Yser Canal while still engaged with the enemy. Should you become separated during this process, you are to make your own way to a rally point here, at Furnes." He tapped the map with his pointer to highlight the location of the town. "We must be beyond Poperinghe by first light tomorrow to reach our objective of the Yser canal in time. We move in one hour."

Tuesday 28 May 1940 –
Narvik, Northern Norway.

After the landings of the French at Bjerkvik, and operations by the Poles and Norwegians on the high ground overlooking Narvik on 13 May, German General Dietl was effectively left with only a single course of action. His forces were not in a condition to fight their way south and attempt a link up with the German column advancing north from Trondheim; a withdrawal along the line of the ore railway towards Sweden being his only viable option. If Narvik was attacked, his plan was to hold open this withdrawal route to Sweden as long as he could, giving his forces in Narvik both the time and the corridor to escape. He had positioned his forces to this end.

With a direct attack on Narvik beach having already been found unfeasible, the Allied forces were to be put ashore at Orneset, two miles north east of Narvik town. The naval bombardment started at 11:40 p.m. on 27 May, with men from the French Foreign Legion going ashore at midnight. The naval guns specifically targeted known enemy positions to neutralise the defenders, also bombarding railway stations and tunnels to hinder any planned German withdrawal. By 3:30 a.m. on 28 May, a battalion each from the French Foreign Legion and the Norwegian Army had been landed. Two tanks were put ashore to assist the assault, but both got stuck in the soft ground on the beach. While the German infantry fought hard to keep the Allies away from the railway and their only means of escape, the Luftwaffe attacked the ships providing the naval gun support and machine gunned the infantry fighting to establish the beach bridgehead. The attackers were successfully held off until midday, by which time most of the Narvik garrison had managed to escape. As the German rearguard withdrew down the railway, they blew up the tunnels as they passed through, in order to delay any potential Allied pursuit. Narvik was at last in Allied hands. After the withdrawal, the Germans re-established themselves in the mountains between Narvik and the Swedish border; and prepared for a defensive battle that did not come.

Once secured, the Allies found the ore handing facilities and the electricity supply to Narvik had been completely destroyed during the bombing and naval bombardments; and twenty sunken vessels blocking the harbour. Continued Luftwaffe bombing added still further to the destruction of the town. On 4 June, the troops at Narvik destroyed the remaining tunnels and the railway tracks to the docks, finally being lifted from the jetty and returned to Harstad. The aim of temporarily rendering Narvik useless for the transport of iron ore to Germany had been achieved, and attention could now be focussed on the complete evacuation of Allied forces from Norway.

Tuesday 28 May 1940 –
Creton Farm, Le Paradis, Northern France.

O'Callaghan woke with a shock that made him sit bolt upright, his mind's anticipation of danger renewed once total exhaustion had been dispelled by some sleep. It was daylight and birds were singing outside. He let out a sigh of relief that he was not in imminent danger and lay back down on the straw as his shock subsided. The thought entered his head that the events of yesterday might be a dream, until he turned and saw the injured Pooley still asleep beside him.

His shirt and underwear had dried on his body as he slept, but he realised he was stiff and sore all over as he reached to recover his battledress that lay on the straw beside him. The material was still wet, and on inspection he found four holes in the sleeve. He rolled up the corresponding shirt sleeve to see a superficial wound and a long track where one of the German bullets had cut a groove the whole length of his lower arm between his elbow and wrist. Slipping on his battledress blouse and trousers, he gently moved away from Pooley to let him sleep and cautiously peeped out of the barn side opening. It had stopped raining, with only wisps of cloud in the sky. Looking across the cornfield they had crawled through last night, he could see the farm complex where the massacre had taken place, about five hundred yards away. Smoke was still rising from the burning barn.

In the corner of the farm yard, he saw a clump of spindly trees and a large woodpile. The farmhouse and the outbuildings formed a square, with a brick cowshed and another brick barn making up the other sides. The brick barn was damaged and showed signs of a fire. O'Callaghan assumed there had been fighting at this complex also, and that the farmhouse would subsequently be deserted. He could see a few chickens pecking at the ground and heard the sound of a pig grunting, but could not identify its whereabouts.

Daylight revealed that the open-sided barn he had chosen for cover in darkness was very exposed, and not a good place to hide. He stood quietly for a few moments, listening for other noises that would indicate an enemy presence, before cautiously moving out from the barn to find a better location. He checked the woodpile which was protected by a hedge at the back and offered a small open space with the entrance concealed by a large shrub. Squeezing past the shrub he surveyed the space. It would offer little protection from the elements but was concealed from all sides and was much less obvious than the barn. He returned to the sleeping Pooley and gently woke him to prevent initiating a shock response. Pooley was badly disorientated initially, but soon gained his senses.

"We need to move to a better place, Bert." whispered O'Callaghan. "There's a good place behind the woodpile in the yard. Let's get you dressed." Before getting Pooley dressed, O'Callaghan decided to have a proper look at his wounds. Pooley winced as O'Callaghan straightened out his leg. He had been hit four times, and with only two exit wounds visible, at least two of the bullets still remained in his flesh. The machine gun wounds were big enough to put his fist in, covered in congealed blood and dirt from the ditch and cornfield.

After dressing him, O'Callaghan assisted Pooley to his feet and supported him as he hobbled across the yard to the woodpile. Pushing him past the shrub and into the space, O'Callaghan headed back to the barn for the blanket, sacks, and Pooley's blouse that had been hung up to dry. On the way back he heard vehicles moving on the road at the front of the farmhouse but knew he could not be seen from that direction. He stuffed some straw into the sacks to create makeshift bedding, lifted those in his left hand, threw the blanket over his shoulder and retrieved Pooley's jacket in his right hand. As he turned to leave the barn, he heard a cough and froze with fear. He looked up slowly and saw a German soldier standing at the door of the damaged brick barn, appearing to look directly at him. The disappointment was overwhelming after all the effort they had put in to escape and stay hidden.

He raised his arms in surrender but the German did nothing. "Surely he must see me!" O'Callaghan thought, but then realised he was being screened by the support girders of the barn. The German walked into the yard, and O'Callaghan moved to the side, keeping the girder between himself and the enemy; before the German turned around and entered the farmhouse. O'Callaghan took his chance and sprinted to the woodpile while the German was in the house, slipping past the shrub and into the hideout.

"I saw a Kraut in the yard!" blurted Pooley as O'Callaghan dropped down beside him.

"Best not talk." whispered O'Callaghan, pushing Pooley back down from his seated position. The two men lay perfectly still, with the blanket draped over them. Their hideout was good at concealing them, but also limited their vision outwards, with only the yard and a section of the road outside the farm visible past the shrub. They had no idea if the German was still there or not. They lay quietly for what seemed like hours, not daring to make a sound; their hearing the only sense they could use to assess the danger of their situation. A light breeze blew, which occasionally brought the sound of artillery fire, and rustled the hedges and shrubs around them. After what they agreed was a safe duration without further indication of an enemy presence, they decided to risk a cigarette. The nicotine calmed them, but shifted their minds to other things.

"Can we get a drink anywhere, Bill?" pleaded Pooley. O'Callaghan had noticed a hand pump in the yard and was on his way past the shrub, when he first heard a vehicle engine, and then glimpsed a German lorry that appeared to be slowing as it passed through his sight picture of the road. The noise of the engine got louder and the lorry emerged into the yard, coming to a halt at the gate leading into the cornfield about ten feet from where they were hiding. The engine remained running. The two men pushed as far back into their hideout as they could, hardly daring to breathe. The tailgate was dropped, making a metallic thump, and at least two sets of boots landed on the cobbled yard surface.

The Germans were talking easily amongst themselves, with no indication of any danger or imminent action. A scraping noise was heard and the lorry moved off into the field, the voices growing weaker as the soldiers who had alighted followed the vehicle on foot. O'Callaghan inched forward on his front and poked his head around the shrub to see what was going on. The gate to the cornfield was open, which explained the scraping noise, and the vehicle had moved one hundred yards further into the field. The two soldiers who had jumped from the back were lifting bodies of dead Germans and loading them into the lorry. O'Callaghan could see more dark shapes lying scattered around the field, testimony to the fighting that had taken place around the farm.

"They're picking up their dead." O'Callaghan whispered to Pooley, who had remained at the back of the hideout. Confident that they were not the purpose of the enemy visit, the two men lay back down and remained silent until the Germans had completed their task and drove away.

After another period of waiting and listening to confirm the enemy had left, O'Callaghan returned to his task of finding water. Pushing past the shrub, he made directly for the hand pump only to find it was not working. He heard the pig grunting again and traced the noise to the damaged brick barn. Entering through the wooden door which was already ajar, he found himself in a passageway, half blocked by some farm equipment. He pushed the equipment aside and squeezed through the gap he had created. The noise of the equipment being moved stimulated more grunting and he followed the sound down a side opening. There, he saw two pigs, their skin marked by the smoke and fire which had previously damaged the building. Their stye was about ten feet square with a semi-circular opening at the far end for light and a similar opening at the near end separating it from a small store area. In the store he found a sack of potatoes, some knives and some metal dishes.

Picking up a dish he scouted the rest of the barn, and finding nothing more of use moved back to the yard. He stopped at a puddle and using the dish, scooped some water from the surface, before re-joining Pooley behind the woodpile. As Pooley gulped the water, O'Callaghan explained that he had found a better hiding place. The fact that it was a pigsty brought a sarcastic look to Pooley's face, of which O'Callaghan was unsure had been caused by the pigsty comment or by the taste of the water.

In preparation for occupancy, O'Callaghan released the pigs and scraped the floor with a wooden board to remove as much dirty straw and pig faeces as he could. He then fetched a bale of fresh straw from the Dutch barn and spread it on the floor. Still wary of being discovered, he retrieved the sacks and blanket from the woodpile hideout before carrying Pooley across the yard to their new home. As soon as they were settled, O'Callaghan retrieved some of the potatoes from the sack that he had found in the store; peeled them with one of the knives, and the men ate them raw.

Now they were reasonably safe, O'Callaghan conducted a proper assessment on Pooley's leg. He sterilised the knife with a match, and after splitting the trouser seam, scraped away the dirt and congealed blood from the wounds. During the procedure, Pooley bit on the sleeve of his battledress blouse to prevent crying out. All O'Callaghan could do was bathe the wounds in the water from the puddle before applying the field dressing that he had in his battledress pocket. As darkness fell, O'Callaghan tried to fetch more water, but the puddle had drained away. During the night, Pooley suffered terrible stomach cramps and diarrhoea.

Wednesday 29 May 1940 –
Dunkirk Beach, North East France / North West Belgium.

The small boats, manned by civilian crews, approached the beach at dawn and took on board as many men as their vessels could safely carry; returning them directly to England. Queues of soldiers stood in line on the sand and waded into the water as the boats approached. The boarding process became panicked as the boat captains struggled to keep within the safe limits of what their vessels could carry; order being restored by officers firing warning shots with their issue revolvers. Use of the individual boats was then lost for the length of time taken on the return journey to England and back to France.

Wednesday 29 May 1940 –
Yser Canal, Western Belgium.

D Company had marched all night. The men were exhausted, almost asleep as they trudged through the rain; concentrating on the man in front, being just a feint outline in the gloom. The area around Poperinghe was lit with flares as the Germans continued to attack all through the night; but by first light as planned, D Company had bypassed the town. As they looked back, the weather had cleared and formations of Luftwaffe bombers were dropping their ordnance on the town.

By 8 a.m. they had reached the Yser Canal, crossing to the northern bank over rickety wooden foot bridges. British reconnaissance vehicles held the road bridges open, having repulsed sporadic attempts by German reconnaissance troops to cross the obstacle; those same crossing points now prepared for demolition. The men were grey with fatigue as they slumped down in the buildings that lined the canal bank. 10 Platoon were placed furthest east, at the end of the battalion line. Some machine guns, and Bren carriers were already in position, having been carefully placed to provide interlocking arcs of fire. Their crews were delighted to receive infantry support, knowing they would cover the areas of dead ground between the heavier weapons. Rifles were cleaned after the night march in the rain before anyone was allowed to sleep; and then in shifts for only an hour at a time to ensure everyone had at least some rest. Without defence stores such as sandbags and barbed wire, very little could be done to enhance their positions among the buildings on the northern bank of the canal. Furniture and mattresses were piled against the windows to provide a degree of protection from artillery and small arms fire.

The sound of loud explosions further to the west indicated that the last safe moment for demolition of the bridges had come, and heralded an imminent attack. Some British transport vehicles that could not reach the bridges before they were destroyed appeared on the south bank, their passengers running across the remaining foot bridges after rendering their vehicles unusable by pushing them into the canal. At 3 p.m. artillery began to fall around the defensive positions on the north bank, to cover attempted crossings by German infantry in rubber boats. The machine gunners let them get half way across before cutting the boats and their crews to pieces. 10 Platoon had little to do other than shoot at individuals floundering as they tried to reach the south bank after their boats had been sunk. The cries of the wounded and those being pulled underwater by the weight of their equipment soon faded, leaving only the sound of a continuing battle further west along the canal; where the Germans had constructed a pontoon bridge and established a foothold on the north bank. Reinforcements were now streaming across the pontoon, developing the bridgehead by working along the banks and pushing the British away from the canal.

"That battle's getting closer, Sir." Sergeant Preston remarked to Chadwick. "It sounds like it's also moving north now, away from the canal."

"I agree." confirmed Chadwick, a worried look on his face. "I hope somebody knows what's happening. I would hate to get cut off here."

"Shall I send a runner to 11 Platoon to check if they've heard anything?" asked Preston.

"Good idea." Chadwick replied. "Pick a good Corporal to go and see." Preston hurried off to find Corporal Hutchinson. Twenty minutes later, Hutchinson returned and reported to Chadwick.

"I spoke with Lieutenant Coburn, Sir." began Hutchinson, a little out of breath from running between the positions. "He went to Company Headquarters himself, and was told to stand his ground until ordered to withdraw."

"Thank you, Corporal." said Chadwick. "Go back to your section." Chadwick waited until Hutchinson was out of earshot before he spoke again with Sergeant Preston. "I want to be ready to move the second any order comes." he said to the Platoon Sergeant. "Get around the sections and make sure everything is packed up and ready to move at a moment's notice. I'll stay with 3 Section on the right, so any runner bringing orders from Company Headquarters can find me easily."

"Right, Sir." replied Preston, moving off quickly to visit the section positions.

* * *

It was starting to get dark as Chadwick sat in the furthest west house occupied by 10 Platoon. Corporal Thomas, the Section Commander of 3 Section sat beside him. They both agreed the sound of German machine guns was getting closer, replacing the sound of the British Bren guns as the defensive positions to their right were progressively being overrun.

"I'm going to have a look myself." Chadwick said to Thomas as the concern became too much to bear. "Come with me in case I run into trouble." Thomas called Lance Corporal White across and told him they were leaving the position.

"We're going out that way, Chalky." he said, pointing out some dead ground behind the house. "And we'll come back in the same way. So don't go shooting us in the dark." Lance Corporal White nodded his understanding and the two men left quickly. They ran crouched through the dead ground behind their position towards 11 Platoon, stopping as they approached where the other platoon should be. There was no sign of movement and no sentry challenged them.

"Where the hell are they?" Thomas whispered.

"This is the left edge of their position, so they should be here." Chadwick whispered back. "Let's go a bit further." The two men crawled on their elbows further into the 11 Platoon position, seeing no sign of anyone.

"They've gone!" Thomas exclaimed.

"Shit, shit, shit!" cursed Chadwick, hitting the ground with his fist.

"What now, Sir?" whispered Thomas.

"I need to confirm the company has withdrawn." added Chadwick, rising back to his feet. "I'm going on." Thomas said nothing, dutifully following his Platoon Commander as he adopted a crouched run. They turned north behind 11 Platoon's position to where Company Headquarters should have been, expecting a challenge from a sentry, but again finding no one.

"They've gone without us." he confided to Thomas.

"How the hell did that happen?" Thomas replied, stunned and confused.

"How it happened doesn't matter now." Chadwick said. "What we do next is what matters. Let's get back to the platoon." The two men moved as fast as they could, while trying to maintain a low silhouette, slowing to a walking pace as they approached 10 Platoon positions. They returned through the agreed point, where Lance Corporal White was waiting.

"Come ahead, Sir." he whispered as he recognised the two figures in the dark. Sergeant Preston was waiting for Chadwick.

"The company has withdrawn without us." Chadwick told him.

"What the hell happened?" Preston asked.

"The runner carrying the orders could have got lost or killed; God knows." Chadwick replied impatiently, "But it's happened, and we have to deal with it." He gathered his thoughts before continuing. "We will have to make our own way back to the rally point at Furnes." He pulled his map from its case and spread it on the ground. "Pass the word and get everyone back here as quickly as possible. I'll work out the route." Preston ran off to gather the platoon, leaving Chadwick on his own. As he got out his torch and compass, his Sandhurst doubts around his suitability for command suddenly returned. There was no direction or support from Company Headquarters, and Chadwick felt totally alone. A huge weight of responsibility descended upon him, and he felt too exhausted to care anymore. For an instant, he contemplated disappearing into the darkness, and would have given anything for someone else to take command at that point, when he heard some of the men talking together as they began to gather.

"You mean the others have left us here?" questioned an unidentified voice in the dark, having just been told of the situation.

"Don't worry." replied another voice. "Mister Chadwick will get us out. He's got us this far, hasn't he?" The words hurt him and reinvigorated him at the same time. He felt ashamed that he had contemplated leaving the platoon to its fate, his thoughts returning to the map spread out on the grass, and the requirement to calculate a route to Furnes.

* * *

Chadwick had set a bearing directly north towards Furnes, hoping to outrun the German advance by moving through the night; when from experience he knew the Germans were usually inactive. He ordered single file formation with himself in the lead and Sergeant Preston as the last man; moving as quickly and yet as silently as possible using the darkness to avoid detection by any German patrols. The men were told to stay close enough to maintain visual contact with the man in front to avoid separation in the darkness. Staying off the roads, they skirted around buildings and wooded areas where the enemy may have taken cover for the night.

Chadwick suddenly stopped and signalled everyone to take cover. He could see small fires to both left and right of his chosen route between sparse trees and shrubs. Leaving the platoon lying in cover, he took Corporal Hutchinson, the second man in the line, to investigate. As they approached, they heard German voices, talking loudly and laughing as they sat around their cooking fires; obviously feeling confident enough in their tactical position to pay little or no attention to security.

The clinking of mess tins against a metal gas mask container alerted them to the presence of a German sentry. Both men froze, hardly daring to breathe as the sentry came closer; trusting the darkness to hide their presence. They heard the sound of splashing on vegetation and a moan of relief as the German relieved himself, only feet away from where they lay. Refastening his clothing, the clinking of his equipment faded as he made his way back towards the group gathered around the fire.

"I think he splashed me there." whispered Hutchinson, rubbing his battledress blouse. Despite the seriousness of the situation, both men suppressed the urge to laugh.

"Go back and lead the men through here." Chadwick whispered. "Total silence to be observed." As Hutchinson made his way back to collect the rest of the platoon, Chadwick trained his rifle on the Germans, hoping the visual attraction of their flickering fires would keep them looking inwards. Corporal Hutchinson quickly reappeared at the head of the platoon, Chadwick signalling for the line to move past him. He winced at the light crunch of the men's feet on the fallen twigs and leaves as they passed, and subconsciously urged them to hurry up. After what seemed like an age, Sergeant Preston tapped him on the shoulder to signal that he was the last man; Chadwick standing up and following after the line.

Thursday 30 May 1940 –
Dunkirk Beach, North East France / North West Belgium.

To bring some order to the use of the growing number of small boats, Rear Admiral Frederic Wake-Walker was dispatched to Dunkirk, tasked with the coordination between these vessels, and the larger Royal Navy vessels that could not get close to the shore. Through the morning mist he witnessed lines of soldiers wading into the sea up to their necks and masses gathered in the dunes behind the beaches.

Wake-Walker established a system using the small boats to lift soldiers from the beach and bring them to the large Navy ships stationed offshore, returning immediately to the beaches in a ferry system rather than heading straight back to England with their load. Royal Engineers constructed piers using vehicles driven into the sea and decked with planks, allowing the men to board the small vessels without wading into the water. Wake-Walker established wireless communication with Tennant in Dunkirk port, subsequently dispatching the larger ships directly into the harbour for loading at the mole when requested.

Thursday 30 May 1940 –
Southern Perimeter, Allied Defensive Pocket,
North East France.

An unusual battlefield situation had developed along the southern perimeter defensive line due to the terrain. Both defenders and attackers were confined to fortified houses and outbuildings because of the flooded ground. With the absence of armoured vehicles and no ground cover due to the lying water, any troop movements were easily identified and broken up by machine guns established in the buildings. The Germans reverted to shelling and mortaring the defensive positions, but this had only a limited effect, and the line held firm. Stuka attacks which may have made a greater impact, were restricted due to low cloud.

Thursday 30 May 1940 –
Eastern Perimeter, Allied Defensive Pocket,
Western Belgium.

There was a concerted German effort to attack into the east flank at Nieuport and roll up the defences along the Belgian beaches towards Dunkirk. This was frustrated by the British "Last Stand" mentality that had developed when the Dunkirk perimeter formed, and also the problems of transport congestion for the German resupply vehicles due to the number of refugees on the roads.

Thursday 30 May 1940 –
Yser Canal / Furnes Road, Northern Belgium.

Just before dawn, Chadwick ordered a halt, positioning the men out of sight in roadside ditches as they waited for the sun to come up. Some fell asleep instantly while others took the opportunity to eat whatever rations they still had. Using the welcome daylight, Chadwick scanned the area through his binoculars. There was no sign of Allied or German troops; Chadwick deeming it safe to continue. Sergeant Preston went down the line, getting the soldiers to their feet, some now so exhausted they seemed drunk.

With the coming of daylight, Chadwick separated the platoon back into mutually supporting section formations, two abreast and one behind; and staying off the roads, continued to move north across the fields. He knew that a water resupply would soon become urgent, and headed towards what looked like a small farm complex he had identified from the map. As they got close, Chadwick stopped and surveyed the complex through his binoculars, acutely aware that the needs of enemy soldiers were the same as his own. Through the lenses he saw what looked like British military vehicles in the yard, but decided to get closer for confirmation. Moving the platoon closer to the complex behind the cover of some sparse trees, he could now see two ambulances and a Bedford truck; but with no sign of any crews or movement of any kind. Chadwick positioned his Bren gunners to provide covering fire if required as the platoon moved stealthily towards the farm; then rushed into the yard with their weapons at their shoulders ready to fire.

A few chickens that were scratching around the yard took fright, shedding some feathers as they squawked and rushed towards the safety of the barn. Chadwick signalled for the following sections to check the barn and the farmhouse, and maintaining their alert posture they disappeared inside. Chadwick approached the nearest ambulance and pulled up the handle on the back door. A medic who was kneeling over a wounded man on a stretcher inside jumped with shock and squinted as the light streamed in. He relaxed and stood up when he identified the British uniforms.

"Thank God. I thought for a second you were Germans!" he blurted out when realisation hit.

"They won't be far behind." replied Chadwick. "What happened here?"

"We're a Regimental Aid Post." the medic continued. "We had been told to set up here, but were attacked by a swarm of German fighters." He paused as he gathered himself prior to continuing. "Everyone was hit except me. There are three injured in here and I've put the dead in the other ambulance." His voice then tailed off. "Captain Kenny, the Medical Officer is in the other vehicle."

"You stay where you are." Chadwick ordered the medic. "I'll see if there is anything we can do." He closed the ambulance door and shouted for Sergeant Preston; reciting the medic's story when he arrived. "I'd like to get the wounded back to Furnes if we can." Chadwick said quietly to Preston.

"If we can get the ambulance and the truck working, then we can all make a dash for it together." Preston suggested.

"Right. Get some men to check out the vehicles and I'll talk to the medic to see if the wounded can be moved." he replied.

The medic confirmed he was content to move the wounded as long as he travelled in the ambulance with them, meaning platoon members would have to drive both the truck and the ambulance. Although superficially damaged, both vehicles were found to be serviceable; tents, stretchers, blankets and various medical supplies having to be unloaded from the Bedford before the men could get in. While the vehicle was being unloaded, all the water bottles were filled from the hand pump in the centre of the yard. Chadwick opened the door of the second ambulance to retrieve the identity discs of the dead. He was met with the sound of buzzing flies that had already begun to crawl over the corpses in the heat, making his recovery of the discs and paybooks particularly unpleasant.

Lance Corporal Tetlow and Private Hamill sat in the front of the ambulance, with Sergeant Preston and Chadwick in the front of the Bedford.

All others were crammed into the back of the Bedford; having to stand to ensure everyone got on board. The two vehicles pulled out of the farm complex and took the road to Furnes, the ambulance leading; and with consideration for the comfort of the wounded, driving only as fast as the medic in the back of the ambulance would allow.

Chadwick was conscious that as they were now on a deserted road in broad daylight, they were inviting an attack from the air, or risked being identified by enemy artillery spotters. He ordered Sergeant Preston to keep a safe distance behind the ambulance to give a better chance of survival in case either vehicle was attacked. Some military stragglers began to appear on the road, moving in the direction of Furnes, and attempting to wave down the Bedford; becoming animated and abusive when the vehicles did not stop. Their abusive gestures were returned by those riding in the back of the Bedford, much to the amusement of their fellow passengers, but only adding to the anger and frustration of those still walking.

As the ambulance approached a crossroads, there was a flash of light followed by a loud explosion, the rear of the vehicle lifting into the air and crashing back onto the road, rolling forward slowly before coming to a halt. Sergeant Preston stiffened his arms against the steering wheel of the Bedford and pressed the brake pedal as hard as he could, guiding the skidding truck to a halt.

"Get us off the road." yelled Chadwick, realising that enemy artillery was targeting the crossroads. Preston steered the vehicle into the adjoining field, stopping a hundred yards away from the junction.

"Everyone out. Get out." screamed Chadwick as he opened his door and jumped down onto the grass. The men were falling out of the back of the truck in their hurry to get clear, running for cover in any depression in the ground they could identify. Disregarding his own urge for self-preservation, Chadwick ran to the damaged ambulance. The back doors had been torn off by the force of the blast, the vehicle body looking like a roughly opened food can. The bodies of all those inside had been torn apart by the blast, and were now unidentifiable as individuals from the severed limbs and entrails that remained. Chadwick felt his stomach heave as the smell of blood, disrupted bowels and burnt flesh hit his nostrils, turning his head away from the sight. He was aware of a uniformed figure running past him towards the front of the vehicle; platoon members ignoring the risk of further shelling in an attempt to rescue their comrades.

The cab of the ambulance had been squashed from the back as the shell exploded, but remained intact. Both Hamill and Tetlow were conscious but confused and disorientated. Hamill tried to open his door, but the panel was bent and jammed closed. He kicked it open and fell onto the road as he tried to step out. Tetlow was sat back in the driver's seat as if sleeping, but moaning gently; his arms motionless by his sides. His door was also jammed closed and he was unable to move to attempt to release it. Failing to open the driver's door from the outside, Private Bell climbed into the cab through the now open passenger's door.

"Are you injured, Corporal?" he asked nervously.

"I can't move my arms, Dinger." Tetlow replied without opening his eyes, but lucid enough to realise who was speaking to him. Bell positioned himself to get a kick at Tetlow's door, and after a few blows, it swung open.

"Go easy!" Bell called to the men who had gathered around the cab as they began to pull Corporal Tetlow from his seat. Tetlow moaned again as willing hands pulled at his legs and supported his body as he was lowered to the ground. Chadwick waved the Bedford forward onto the road, and the two injured men were lifted into the back and laid flat on the floor.

"Everyone inside quickly." he ordered, pushing the men towards the vehicle, conscious that the crossroads was an obvious artillery target. Farthing was standing silently, mesmerised by the scene in the back of the ambulance.

"Get in the truck, Farthing." Chadwick shouted, pulling him away from the back of the ambulance. With men now standing on the dropped tailgate and holding on to the canvas canopy, Chadwick climbed into the cab and the vehicle moved away, leaving the wrecked ambulance and its grisly contents behind.

* * *

The road to Furnes got steadily busier with both military vehicles and refugees the closer they got to the town, eventually slowing to a crawl in nose to tail traffic. About a mile out from the town, the truck reached the front of the queue at a Royal Military Police checkpoint. Chadwick wound down the window and was asked for his identification by a Warrant Officer.

"You are about a mile away from the perimeter defences, Sir." explained the Warrant Officer. "You won't be able to take the vehicle across the canal, so I suggest you abandon it as close as you can get. Pick a good approach road to block and destroy it there. Stops the Germans using it later you see." Chadwick explained there were wounded on board and was told there was an Aid Post directly on the other side of the canal bridge.

The surrounding fields were waterlogged due to deliberate flooding, denying freedom of movement for both enemy tanks and infantry. The only remaining raised road to Furness was lined with abandoned vehicles and equipment, and soldiers walking north towards the perimeter, some with their tunics open and equipment unbuckled, carrying their weapons across their shoulders with their arms resting on them.

"Look at the state of them!" remarked Sergeant Preston as the truck went past, his head swivelling around to stare at them out of the side window of the cab. "They're a bloody disgrace to whatever regiment they are." He wound down the window in a fit of temper. "Sort your bloody selves out."

he shouted. "At least try and look like soldiers." His comments were greeted with shouts of derision and abusive gestures. He wound up the window, his face red with anger.

"I think this is as far as we'll get." said Chadwick changing the subject quickly. "There's a raised road on the left, turn in there. We can block that." Preston pulled the vehicle onto the raised road and stopped. "I'll get the men out while you disable the truck here." Chadwick instructed as he jumped down from the cab. Moving to the back of the truck he ordered the men to jump out.

Corporal Hutchinson was first out. "I think Corporal Tetlow's arms are broken." he told Chadwick. "Probably smashed them on the steering wheel when the vehicle was hit. But he can still walk." Both wounded men were helped down from the truck, and although still shaken up, both confirmed they were in a condition to walk without assistance. Corporal Tetlow had been bandaged to support his arms; two shell dressings having been applied to make rudimentary slings. Hamill looked pale and unsteady but otherwise uninjured, and was adamant he could continue on foot. Chadwick heard the truck engine revving as Sergeant Preston jammed the accelerator down. He then took out his entrenching tool and punctured the radiator.

"She'll overheat and the engine will seize." he confirmed to Chadwick. He tapped the bonnet affectionately as he passed, as if saying goodbye to a friend, and joined the rest of the platoon walking north.

* * *

Mixed with what seemed like thousands of withdrawing soldiers, 10 Platoon passed through a defensive screen of reconnaissance vehicles and then over the bridge at Furnes. Royal Engineers scurried around with boxes of explosives and spools of wire as they prepared the structure for demolition. The bridge was being secured by a battalion of Guards, their uniforms and demeanour immaculate in comparison to the bedraggled men crossing over. A Guards Officer directed Chadwick to the town of La Panne where he said an orderly evacuation was being arranged via separate Corps embarkation points; but recommended staying off the roads which were under continuous attack by the Luftwaffe. Corporal Tetlow and Hamill were taken to the medical facility beside the bridge as identified by the Military Police Warrant Officer, a temporary tented structure, marked with red cross flags draped over the tents and stretched out on the ground to deter aerial attack.

Deciding a short rest was required before continuing, Chadwick followed a tourist sign to a café, finding the tables and chairs undisturbed inside. The men eagerly removed their equipment and slumped into the chairs, although a cursory check quickly proved nothing of any use remained in the building. On the way to the café, a sign on the NAAFI requested that anyone could "Help Yourself", although most seemed too tired or disinterested to accept the offer.

Private Bell could not resist and returned with a bulging large pack, throwing a carton of cigarettes and a bar of chocolate onto each table in the café.

"How long are we staying, Sir?" Farthing asked. Chadwick looked at his watch.

"We'll rest for another hour before heading for La Panne." he replied.

"I would like to check on Lance Corporal Tetlow at the dressing station with your permission, Sir." requested Farthing.

"By all means, if they'll let you in." replied Chadwick. "But be back within the hour." he warned.

* * *

Farthing quickly covered the short distance back to the dressing station, entering the reception area. Wounded were being brought through, some walking and some on stretchers, the medical staff directing the new arrivals to the appropriate area. Despite the many raised voices requesting assistance and giving directions, there was a feeling of control and calm. Farthing stopped a medic who was rushing past and was directed to a Medical Corps Sergeant entering figures onto a gridded blackboard.

"Excuse me, Sergeant." he began meekly. "I'm looking for a Lance Corporal Tetlow who was brought in earlier with arm injuries."

"I can't help you, mate." said the Sergeant, not even looking round from his board. "He might still be in the triage area if he wasn't badly hurt. Outside and turn right."

Farthing didn't reply, but turned around and left the tent, turning right. There were rows of men, some lying on the ground, some on stretchers, each with a paper tag attached to their uniform with string. Farthing walked between the rows of men, none seeming particularly badly hurt, patiently waiting their turn for treatment. A medic was moving around the men doing continuous assessments, checking dressings and offering water where appropriate. Farthing spotted Tetlow lying on the ground in one of the rows.

"Alright, Corporal?" he said as he approached, Tetlow opening his eyes on recognising the voice.

"I'm alright thanks, Penny." he replied quietly. "They've given me some morphine for the pain. Smashed both my arms." He tried to raise his bandaged arms in demonstration of his injuries, but yelped in pain and rested them back across his chest. Farthing examined the paper tag attached to Tetlow's tunic, but could make no sense of the information it contained.

"We're moving off towards the beaches soon," Farthing began, "and I came to check on you before we go."

"That's kind, thanks Penny." he said. "Hopefully they can get the injured away too," Tetlow continued, "otherwise, I'll be spending some time in a German Prison Camp." He tried to laugh to make light of the situation, but the attempt died in his throat.

"I've got something here in my battledress for you." said Farthing confidently. Tetlow went quiet, remembering what he had done to Farthing in the toilets in Aldershot. He closed his eyes, expecting the worst as he was now helpless because of his injuries. He felt a finger touch his upper lip, and screwed up his face in anticipation; then felt Farthing trying to push something into his mouth, when the smell of chocolate reached his nostrils. He relaxed, opened his lips and a piece of chocolate fell into his mouth. "I just wanted to make sure you would be alright." said Farthing. "I'll see you back in England, Corporal." He tucked the remainder of the chocolate bar under Tetlow's bandaged arms, and before Tetlow could reply, Farthing was gone.

* * *

The smell of the sea told the men they were getting close to the beaches at La Panne, and as they crested the dunes, they saw the horizon dotted with large naval vessels. A column of smoke from burning fuel stores was rising into the air fifteen miles away at Dunkirk, flattening as it hit high clouds, then spreading out like a blanket which hung over the port. Little ships were running ferry operations between the beach and the bigger naval vessels sitting offshore.

"Keep the men here." Chadwick told Sergeant Preston. "I'll try to find out where the embarkation point is." Preston pulled a red handkerchief from his pocket and tied it around the sling swivel on the butt of his rifle. Then, attaching the bayonet, turned the weapon upside down and stuck it into the sand.

"There's a marker to help you find your way back, Sir." he told Chadwick, getting the men to sit down together in a group in the dunes. Once seated, he surveyed a scene of chaos, like something from a nightmare. The troops waiting in the dunes had dug holes in the softer sand for protection. Stukas swarmed overhead like wasps, apparently unimpeded, with no discernible beach defence. Some individuals fired their rifles at the diving aircraft from sheer frustration, and with little chance of success, but probably felt that at least they were resisting. The falling bombs imbedded in the soft sand before exploding, the detonation throwing shrapnel mostly straight up in the air.

Lines of men waited on the shore, wading out into deeper water as the little ships came in. Messerschmitt fighters flew low over the lines of men, their machine guns blazing. Some Stukas attacked the larger ships, the guns on the waiting destroyers constantly in action, while the little ships zigzagged as their only means of defence. Designated beach parties marshalled the small boats, calling them in, ensuring they were not overloaded, and dispatching them out to the destroyers. Revolver shots could be heard as the officers struggled to prevent the boats being overloaded by men desperate to get away. The waiting soldiers watched as the little ships were bombed as they ferried between the destroyers and the shore, but stood patiently for their turn to run the gauntlet of the Stukas. Capsized ships were pulled back to the beach and refloated for another attempt. Having reached the destroyers waiting offshore, the little ships pulled alongside. Scramble nets had been hung from the rails, and the exhausted men struggled to climb up, crew members helping them over the rails onto the deck.

* * *

About an hour later, Chadwick reappeared with half a dozen men in tow. He explained to Sergeant Preston that men separated from their parent units were being assigned to platoon sized formations with an officer in command. Preston called Corporal Hutchinson to look after them, and make sure they had food and water. Chadwick took Preston out of earshot of the men.

"I've just been told that we will join the end of the queue for evacuation here or we can move to Dunkirk where the destroyers are lifting hundreds of men at a time directly from the port." He paused before continuing. "It's a fifteen-mile march to Dunkirk along the beach, but the chances of evacuation seem better. Do we stay or go?" Preston remained quiet while he weighed up the option in his head.

"The men are still in a good state, Sir." he began. "It can't be any worse than here. I think we should go for Dunkirk."

"Agreed." said Chadwick. "Get them to eat and prepare for the move." he ordered. "We'll leave when it starts to get dark."

* * *

With the plan briefed, and time to be filled before departure, food was shared out. The men took their boots off for the first time in days to get some air around their feet; preparing for what they hoped would be the last leg of their march. In the gathering gloom, Chadwick led the men down to the water's edge where the sand was firmer and easier to walk on. The beach was a jumble of abandoned rifles, clothing and equipment. Bodies were being washed ashore, and now that the air attacks had stopped for the night, work parties had been organised to gather and lay them in rows to aid identification. Identity discs were being collected and records made of the deceased.

In the distance, flames illuminated the smoke that was rising from the ruins of Dunkirk. As 10 Platoon trudged through the sand, it pulled on their already exhausted limbs. To the weary men, their destination seemed to get no closer as the hours passed.

Thursday 30 May 1940 –
Bodo, Northern Norway.

The Scots Guards and South Wales Borderers had formed a defensive line across the road to Bodo, south of Lake Soloi, five miles from the town. It was now the turn of the Irish Guards to pass through the Scots Guards as they made their way directly to Bodo, where everyone, less those on the defensive line, had concentrated in preparation to depart. Entering the town, they saw all the wooden buildings had been damaged or destroyed in the fires caused by the German bombing, only the brick chimneys of the houses remaining upright. Finding some element of cover amongst abandoned buildings still standing, they took the opportunity to wash and prepare a hot meal, some exchanging their torn underwear with clothes they found in the abandoned houses. Word was passed to move at midnight, and the Irish Guards filed to the docks where destroyers were waiting. As they reached the top of the gangplanks, sailors forcibly removed from them any equipment they deemed unnecessary and threw it overboard. The destroyers then sailed for Harstad.

The Scots Guards began their withdrawal at 7:15 p.m. on 31 May, a company at a time, an hour apart; the battalion being completely clear by midnight. Contrary to the routine of the previous night, the Scots Guards brought on board a considerable amount of ammunition and stores, even having time to drain the petrol from local garages to prevent its use by the Germans. As the Scots Guards boarded the ships, those soldiers from the South Wales Borderers providing the rearguard were told to dump all their equipment apart from their rifles, and run the last five miles along the road to Bodo. After a five-minute wait on the jetty, a destroyer came alongside and with the use of ten gangplanks, the complete battalion was embarked in only four minutes. The destroyer zigzagged away from the jetty as Stuka bombers attacked from a night sky, still lit by a sun that at this time of year, this far north, didn't set.

Thursday 30 May 1940 –
Creton Farm, Le Paradis, Northern France.

After two days surviving on raw potatoes and rain water, both men were incredibly weak. They had become used to hearing the natural noises of the farm and the countryside; when in stark contrast, O'Callaghan thought he heard a woman's voice and the chatter of a child. He peeped out to see a woman and young boy approaching the yard from the road. The woman was in her mid to late thirties, with fair hair and the ruddy complexion of a farm worker. As she viewed the wreckage of the farmhouse, she became distressed; the child clinging to her dress in alarm at his mother's sobs. Both men lay back down on the straw, unsure how to deal with the probability that they would soon be discovered.

The pigs that O'Callaghan had released when he took over their stye were running noisily around the yard, expecting to be fed now that their owner had returned. She herded them towards the brick barn, calling for her son to help move the farm equipment that was blocking the passageway. As she bent down to move the machinery, she saw a uniformed leg stretched out in the stye. Her terrified scream shocked O'Callaghan into action. He jumped the stye wall, wriggled past the machinery, and chased after the woman, calling out to her in English. As he came out of the barn, he could see her leaving the yard in the direction of the village, her child following behind as fast as he could. O'Callaghan ran out onto the road, still calling after the woman, before realising he was completely exposed in the open and turned to make his way back to the yard.

The realisation that the soldier had been wearing a khaki-coloured uniform and had shouted after her in English suddenly dawned on the woman. As she stopped and turned, she saw O'Callaghan disappearing back into the yard. Gathering her son who had just caught up with her as she turned, she hurried back towards the departing soldier. O'Callaghan heard her footsteps as she returned, and he waited just outside the entrance to the barn, stepping out into the yard as she got close. She continued to approach but visibly slowed the closer she got, holding her sons head into her chest as if trying to stop him looking. O'Callaghan noticed the fear in her eyes as if she might turn and run again at any moment, and beckoned to her reassuringly.

"Soldat Anglais." he stuttered as he pointed to the insignia on his uniform. Receiving a flicker of recognition, he thought he would try his luck. "Monche." he said more convincingly, pointing to his open mouth.

"Je comprends." replied the woman with a gentle smile. She released her son from her grip, and taking his hand turned to walk back towards the village. The boy kept turning to stare back at O'Callaghan as his mother tugged at his hand to hurry him along.

The two men waited, not knowing if she was going for food as indicated, or going for the Germans. Thirty minutes had passed when they heard footsteps again, and peeping out, O'Callaghan saw the woman accompanied by a tall, strongly built man. She was carrying a basket. Pooley and O'Callaghan were almost tearful with a mixture of relief and excitement when the basket contained bread, milk and eggs. The woman brought some water from the wrecked farmhouse, and introductions were made as a fire was lit and the eggs were boiled.

Madame Pauline Duquenne-Creton owned the farm along with her husband, who was at that time a prisoner of war. Her son was called Victor. He was twelve years old. The man with her was Eugene Francis Joseph Le Comte, a road builder from Le Paradis. He had been burying British soldiers left lying in the fields when he had met Madame Creton. After boiling some more water, Madame Creton cleaned Pooley's leg before she and Eugene left for Le Paradis; with a promise to return the next day. As they lay on the straw that night, Pooley and O'Callaghan felt their luck had turned. Since their ordeal had begun, they talked for the first time about their families, feeling confident now that they would see them again.

Friday 31 May 1940 –
Dunkirk Beach, North East France / North West Belgium.

Royal Engineers had installed telephone cables between Tennent's Beach Party Commanders and the Corps assembly areas in the dunes behind the beaches. This reduced the time that soldiers had to stand exposed to German fighter attacks in queues on the beach waiting for small ships, as they could now be called forward from the relative cover of the dunes when vessels were in place to pick them up. As dawn broke, the small boats could be seen on the horizon preparing to come in.

When Tennant called the destroyers in to the mole, they approached with their guns pointing skywards, firing at the German bombers circling overhead. They continued to fire for the duration when berthed during the embarkation process, and as they zigzagged away from the mole once loaded. The Stukas still attacked despite the defensive fire, bombs landing all around the destroyers and transport ships, the columns of water from the explosions soaking the defenceless men crammed on the decks and on the mole. A paddle steamer loaded with three hundred soldiers was hit and burst into flames. Hearing the screams of the men trapped inside the burning vessel, the captain was attempting to beach the slowly sinking steamer to allow the men to escape, when a second hit sank her almost instantaneously, drowning everyone; and undoubtedly saving some from a slower death by burning.

Despite his protestations, Lord Gort was ordered back to England by Churchill on the night of 31 May, when the strength of the British Expeditionary Force was reduced to Corps level by the developing evacuation. Appropriate to his rank and seniority, General Harold Alexander was appointed Senior British Officer in France.

Friday 31 May 1940 –
Eastern Perimeter, Allied Defensive Pocket,
North West Belgium.

After four days of desperate defence, the French that had been holding Lille were forced to surrender. Now that the Lille salient had been reduced, and with consideration of the coming offensive push south of the river Somme towards Paris, German Army Group A was withdrawn from the perimeter battle. The reduction of the Dunkirk pocket thus became the sole responsibility of Army Group B, with its commander, Field Marshal Fedor von Bock, being put under increasing pressure from Berlin to end the embarkation operation.

The Germans probed all along the perimeter attempting to find a weak spot, increasingly shelling road junctions that the Allies were using to move troops inside the pocket for counterattack against perimeter breakthroughs, or towards the evacuation points on the beach and the mole. Once again, the Germans attempted to cross the Furnes canal, and once again they were frustrated by strong counterattacks. Under cover of a smoke screen, the attack from the east towards Nieuport was renewed, but a change in the wind direction dispersed the smoke screen and the now exposed German infantry were beaten back by machine gun fire.

The evacuation of the Belgian sector began that night at 9 p.m. with a new perimeter being established on the French border. Aided by the German dislike of fighting at night, British and Belgian forces had completely disengaged by 2 a.m. the next morning. Prior to the withdrawal, all remaining artillery ammunition was fired off and the guns abandoned, but not before being disabled by removing the optics and breech blocks. Those forces withdrawing were not involved in the creation of the new perimeter and moved directly to the beaches for evacuation. With an exceptional level of planning, reception areas had been established in the dunes behind the beaches where the withdrawing units were reformed and could eat and rest prior to their evacuation.

Friday 31 May 1940 –
Dunkirk Port, Channel Coast, North East France.

It was daylight before 10 Platoon reached Dunkirk port. A blanket of smoke hung over the port and funnels of sunken ships protruded from the water. The wreck of a destroyer sat beside the mole, having been blown in half by German bombs. A clearly marked hospital ship was trying to dock; Stukas pouncing on it as it pulled alongside the mole. The impact of the bombs almost lifted the ship out of the water, and knowing it was doomed, its captain steered it away from the mole before it sank.

Chadwick was stopped by a Beach Party Commander and handed a ticket with a number on it. He was briefed that a stacking system was in operation, and his group would be called forward when a vessel was available for them. They were directed to Malo-les-Bains, a suburb of Dunkirk which overlooked the port.

"You'll probably get away tonight," confirmed the officer, "so keep your men together and report to the mole when your number is called. Strip out your packs and dump anything that is not absolutely essential."

Chadwick led the men away from the port into Malo-les-Bains, which due to the ongoing battle had been reduced to burnt-out buildings; the streets blocked by wrecked vehicles. The sections occupied three adjoining houses, destroyed above ground level by enemy shelling, but with cellars still intact. They collapsed exhausted, using their equipment as makeshift pillows, sleeping soundly for four hours.

* * *

Corporal Hutchinson came looking for Chadwick.

"Sir, would you like to help us empty our packs of non-essential items?" Still not fully awake, Chadwick both looked and felt confused.

"I'm not sure what you mean, Corporal." he answered quizzingly.

"We have some pack issues that require your personal attention, Sir." Hutchinson continued. "Will you come this way?" Chadwick struggled to his feet and followed Hutchinson into his section cellar. Laid out on a groundsheet were three bottles of port, a block of cheese and a box of cigars.

"Where did all this come from?" asked Chadwick.

"I liberated it from the NAAFI in Furnes, Sir." Bell replied smugly. "We have to destroy everything of use to the Germans, so let's destroy this lot." Chadwick shook his head in disbelief and sat cross-legged in the ring that 1 Section had created around the items. The port was uncorked and poured into waiting mess tins. Kyle watched as Bell cut the cheese into slices with his penknife and then declined the offer of a piece. He smiled knowingly to himself as everyone else accepted.

The chat grew raucous as the port took effect on exhausted bodies and minds, the cumulative stress of the last three weeks at last finding a release valve. With three empty port bottles lying in the middle of the groundsheet, it was time for a cigar. The men had made seated support out of their equipment and packs, leaning back like gentlemen in a members' club and blowing the cigar smoke up towards the ceiling of the cellar.

"Why have you not got four names then, Sir?" asked Bell randomly, his reticence to speak openly in front of an officer reduced by the consumed port.

"I don't know what you mean." replied Chadwick, bemused and slightly drunk.

"I thought all officers had to have four names." Bell clarified.

"Well, I have three." replied Chadwick. "William Dudley Chadwick." he said smugly. "William after my grandfather, and Dudley after the place I was conceived."

"Dudley near Wolverhampton?" asked Bell incredulously.

"The very place." replied Chadwick, blowing cigar smoke at the ceiling. "My parents honeymooned there just before the end of the last war."

"Bloody Hell, Sir. Who said romance was dead?" blurted out Corporal Hutchinson; the entire cellar descending into laughter.

"If I was called after where I was conceived, my middle name would be haystack." added Bell, triggering another outburst of laughter.

"I...I'd be L...Lawrence L...Lime Street S...Station McCafferty." said La La. The whole cellar was now in convulsions of laughter, as each individual tried to outdo the last with even more outrageous made-up names. As he looked around the men who had just come through so much, Chadwick wondered what anyone hearing the commotion would think, surrounded by death and destruction, and soldiers still managing to find humour despite their circumstances.

* * *

Messengers from the mole moved among the British positions in Malo-les-Bains at dusk, calling out the numbers of the formations to be evacuated. When their number was called, Chadwick gathered the platoon together and moved back down towards the port. The men coughed and spluttered as the sea air cleared the cellar dust from their lungs. On reaching the beach, their number was checked and they were shepherded into a long queue, the lines of men lit up from the fires still raging in the town. They slowly shuffled forward as those at the front were moved onto the mole; the sound of the battle on the perimeter line clear in the night air. Chadwick hoped the covering of thick low cloud and the onset of darkness would provide some protection from the Luftwaffe, but was to be disappointed.

Some of those waiting in the line dug depressions in the sand to protect themselves from aerial attack; and as the queue moved forward, fortunate individuals were able to occupy a depression dug by someone else. Having spotted such a depression being vacated, McCafferty pushed Orpin aside and jumped into a pre-dug hole as the queue moved.

"Y...you d...dirty bastard!" he yelled as he landed in fresh excrement, left by the previous occupant.

"Serves you right, La La. That should have been me covered in shit right now." giggled Orpin, as his friend tried to scrape the excrement from his clothes with his bayonet.

As 10 Platoon got close to the mole, a fighter came in low below the clouds and machine gunned the waiting queue. Hundreds of men lay down in unison, the sporadic crack of rifle fire following the aircraft as it arched upwards and disappeared again into the clouds. From the beach the men could see the destroyers departing the mole as soon as they were loaded, and another arriving having been called forward. In the gathering gloom, Stukas launched their final attacks of the day, screaming down towards the packed destroyers, their pilots defying the constant stream of fire coming up from the deck guns. With nowhere to take cover, the men packed on the decks stood completely helpless as the bombs fell, getting soaked from the columns of water as bombs narrowly missed their target.

As they approached the mole, the soldiers were marshalled into a queue twenty men wide, and packed onto the structure. French soldiers were being evacuated from the same mole, the British forming their queue on the right side and the French on the left side.

"Look at these buggers!" remarked Corporal Thomas as he stood beside the French troops. They had no weapons, but many of them carried suitcases. "Must think they're going on their bloody holidays." Many of them understood enough English to stare back angrily.

German artillery now replaced the Stukas as the last light disappeared. Gaps being created in the queue as men were simply swept away by the shells landing on the mole. Any dead were just pushed into the water and planks placed over the gaps in the decking created by the explosions. Men gingerly walked across the narrow planks, with only the stanchions of the mole and the long drop to the sea below them. The soldier in front of Farthing lost his footing crossing a plank and disappeared into the darkness below, his cries stopping with a dull thud as his body hit the stanchions and then splashed into the water. On seeing the man fall to his death, Farthing froze; shouts of impatience quickly coming from those in the queue behind him, who then tried to push sideways to where other crossings points were still operating normally. A Naval Petty Officer appeared on the far side of the gap, come to investigate the hold up and the commotion.

"Move yourself, soldier." he yelled, his offensive approach making Farthing even more reticent.

"Give me your rifle, Penny." said Kyle who was standing directly behind him, pulling the weapon from his grasp. "Now hold your arms out to balance yourself as you go across." Farthing began to slowly shuffle out onto the plank, his arms outstretched, the shouts of impatience from behind getting louder. He was half way across when a shell landed in the water close by, the spray soaking everyone in the area of the breach. Farthing wobbled as the weight of the water hit him, lifting one foot off the plank as he tried to rebalance himself.

"Make a dash for it, Penny." screamed Kyle as Farthing took some faltering steps and looked certain to lose his balance. The Petty Officer on the far side took two steps out onto the plank and grabbed Farthing by the arm, pulling him across; both falling in a tangle of limbs on the far side.

"Right, next man." yelled the Petty Officer, struggling to his feet. Kyle stepped confidently out onto the plank, a rifle in each hand, and was across in seconds. "Next man." yelled the Petty officer again, determined to keep the queue moving. Farthing was still sprawled on the decking when Kyle got across. Helping him up, Kyle handed him back his rifle and pushed him forward towards the waiting destroyer.

A Royal Marine stood beside a huge cooking pot, offering stew to those who still had a suitable receptacle. Kyle quickly got out his mess tin and the Marine almost filled it with one serving from a huge ladle. Sharing a spoon, Kyle and Farthing devoured the stew while shuffling along as the queue continued to move forward.

Ladders had been placed from the edge of the mole onto the deck of the destroyer, lines of men being able to board simultaneously. Kyle went first with Farthing holding on to his equipment belt behind, carefully looking at his feet as he placed them on the rungs. Just as Farthing stepped onto the ladder, a shell clipped the edge of the mole near the destroyer. A bite shaped hole appeared in the structure, collapsing some of the ladder bridges and throwing the men on them into the water between the ship and the mole. Fighting against their fear, Kyle and Farthing stood up and continued across their ladder, the slight incline downwards towards the ship's deck helping their forward momentum. As they stepped off the ladder, a Naval Rating took their rifles, placing them in a neat pile, and telling them to move to the far side of the deck to allow others to board. Kyle looked around for other platoon members and heard Sergeant Preston and the other non-commissioned officers shouting for 10 Platoon to gather. He pulled Farthing towards the shouts through the rapidly growing crowd. The Section Commanders counted their men and reported to Sergeant Preston when they were all present.

"That's 10 Platoon all present, apart from Private Smith, Sir." Preston told Chadwick. "It appears he might have been hit in the last artillery strike."

"Keep everyone together here." Chadwick told Preston. "I'll try and find Smith." He stood up on the rail to try and see, but the deck was just a mass of khaki uniforms. Pushing against the flow on the increasingly crowded deck, he made his way to where the wounded had been laid out on stretchers. Army and Navy Medics moved between the rows doing what they could with the medical supplies available. Checking the ashen faces, Chadwick had walked past Smith before he recognised him without his glasses. He knelt down beside him.

"Can you hear me, Smith?" he asked gently. Smith opened his eyes and smiled.

"Don't worry, Sir." he whispered. "I'll be fine. It's just a bit of shrapnel in my side." His demeanour then changed. "I'm really thirsty. Can you get me some water?"

"I'll ask the medic if you're allowed water." said Chadwick, getting to his feet and looking around for a medic. In a minute he was back. "Small sips only. Where's your equipment?"

"At my feet, under the blanket." he replied. As Chadwick lifted the blanket, he noticed the stretcher fabric was covered in blood. Not allowing himself to show any reaction, he located the equipment and took out Smith's water bottle. He pulled out the cork and held the bottle to Smith's lips, letting some water dribble into his mouth. Smith lifted his head slightly to accept the drink, then swallowed weakly and lay back down.

"I've lost my glasses and can't see a thing without them." he continued. "There's a spare pair in my haversack." Chadwick went back to Smith's equipment, found the case and took out the glasses. Opening the legs, he put them on Smith's face.

"Thank you, Sir." he whispered. "That's much better." Chadwick, dribbled some more water into his mouth.

The casualty beside Smith, who had been silent up to this point, suddenly regained consciousness, lifting his blanket and looking underneath. Then, throwing the blanket to the side, rolled off the stretcher onto the deck. Chadwick saw that both his legs were missing from the pelvis, only tattered flesh remaining where his genitals had been. Using his forearms, he dragged himself across the deck to the rail, and disappeared overboard. Chadwick remained frozen at what he had just seen, losing his perspective on time; only brought back to reality by the voice of a medic doing his rounds of the wounded.

"You can leave him now, Sir. He's gone." Chadwick stared at the medic, not having registered what he said. The look of confusion on his face prompting the medic to repeat himself. "This man's dead, Sir. There's nothing more you can do here." Chadwick slowly stood up, mental and physical exhaustion removing his ability for rational thought. He found that he was still holding Smith's glasses case and his water bottle, handing them to the medic in a pointless gesture.

"Why don't you go to the Wardroom and get a drink, Sir?" suggested the medic. Chadwick just nodded and turned away without answering. He felt as if his mind was outside his body, somehow being able to watch himself slowly walking across the packed deck, pushing his way through the jostling soldiers. The ship shuddered as it pulled away from the mole, and a cheer went up from those on deck. The vessel quickly gained speed as it zigzagged out to sea.

Chadwick felt the heat as he stepped inside from the chill of the night air; the noise from outside almost disappearing as the door swung closed behind him. A Naval non-commissioned officer welcomed him and handed him a glass from a silver tray he was holding. There was a buzz of conversation in the Wardroom from a mixture of Navy and Army Officers, but no one paid him any heed as he found a seat at a round topped table. He looked at the glass he had been given, and could smell Gin. He drank the contents without stopping and laid his head across his forearms on the table.

Friday 31 May 1940 –
Creton Farm, Le Paradis, Northern France.

True to her word, Madame Creton came back, alone this time, but with more food and hot coffee. The two men held the hot liquid, smelling it, reluctant to drink it and deprive themselves of the sensation. She had brought hydrogen peroxide and bandages for Pooley's wounds. O'Callaghan held his leg steady as she poured the liquid into the bullet holes. The fluid foamed, pulling the dirt and pus to the surface where she wiped it away. Pooley stiffened, but self-pride would not let him cry out in front of a woman he barely knew. She left O'Callaghan with instructions to repeat the process in twelve hours.

Saturday 1 June 1940 –
Southern Perimeter, Allied Defensive Pocket,
North East France.

In an act of desperation to disrupt the evacuation, the Germans swam the canals to get a foothold on the opposite bank. Last ditch counterattacks through knee deep water by the remaining defenders failed to drive them back but did prevent further incursion into the pocket. The Allied plan was for the British to withdraw from their positions that night, to be replaced by French troops; and similar British counterattacks happened all along the perimeter throughout the day to maintain the line that was to be handed over to the French.

As darkness fell the British withdrew and the French replaced them, the medical orderlies and the walking wounded being among the last to get away. Those who were too injured to move, but could still operate a weapon, had their casualty tags removed so they could fight under the protection of the Geneva Convention, which forbad the carriage of arms by personnel designated as under medical care. The French began to replace the British defenders on the perimeter at 8 p.m. and throughout the course of the night, all perimeter defensive responsibilities were assumed by the French. Once relieved, the British made their way to the beaches and the mole for evacuation.

Saturday 1 June 1940 –
Dunkirk Beach, Channel Coast, North East France.

General Montgomery remained on the beach until 3:30 a.m. on 1 June to ensure his men who had just withdrawn from the Belgian sector of the perimeter all got away safely, and were settled into the reception areas he had ordered be created. As he stood beside Montgomery, his Aide de Camp, Charles Sweeney of The Royal Ulster Rifles, was wounded in the head by an exploding shell. Montgomery immediately berated Sweeney for not wearing his steel helmet, until it was pointed out by the wounded Sweeney that Montgomery was not wearing his either.

Those soldiers withdrawing from the Belgian sector found the tide out when they arrived on the beach, and the lorry piers which had made the beach embarkations so much more efficient, were rendered temporarily useless. Rather than have them wait, Montgomery directed them along the beach towards the harbour at Dunkirk, being warned to stay off the roads which the Germans were shelling.

In Dunkirk harbour, Tennant was calling forward destroyers and transport ships for the men queued up on the mole. Once loaded, the ships then zigzagged as they pulled away to upset the targeting of the dive bombers and the German artillery which was now in range. With the numbers of German aircraft exceeding those seen on previous days, both the ships at the mole and those waiting out to sea came under relentless aerial attack throughout the hours of daylight; a total of thirty-one vessels being sunk, including HMS Keith with Rear Admiral Wake-Walker on board.

Taken off in a launch to Dunkirk, Wake-Walker was able to continue his work from the town. At 6 p.m. Captain Tennant suspended any further daylight embarkations due to heavy shipping losses from enemy aircraft. The evacuation began again when it got dark, beginning to take away those who had withdrawn from the Belgian sector the previous night and were now arriving at the mole; soon to be joined by those who had just handed their sections of the perimeter over to the French.

Saturday 1 June 1940 –
Canal de Bergues, Southern Perimeter,
Allied Defensive Pocket, North East France.

During the night of 31 May / 1 June, B Company of the 1st Battalion, East Lancashire Regiment, commanded by Captain Harold Ervine-Andrews, had been ordered to hold a line of 1,000 yards along the Canal de Bergues, about three quarters of a mile south of Dunkirk town and five miles from the beach. Ervine-Andrews was a professional soldier who had served in India prior to the war, on the North West Frontier, where he had been Mentioned in Dispatches for bravery. After intense artillery, mortar and machine gun fire, the Germans attacked at dawn and crossed the Canal de Bergues on both flanks of B Company. By this time, the company had been reduced to forty men and had centralised in a barn which held a dominating position overlooking the canal.

Climbing onto the thatched roof, Ervine-Andrews killed seventeen Germans with rifle fire. He then disrupted the attack by sweeping the ground with a Bren gun, forcing the Germans to take cover in the flooded fields. Throughout the action, mortar bombs were bursting on the thatched roof, setting it ablaze, but Ervine-Andrews had gained time for the wounded to be evacuated in the only remaining Bren gun carrier. Only eight unwounded men remained fighting from the barn, and as their ammunition ran out, the Germans regained forward momentum. With the barn almost surrounded, Ervine-Andrews led the remaining men back through the flooded landscape, wading in water up to their necks for over a mile. On reaching the safety of their battalion position, B Company resumed defensive duties.

Saturday 1 June 1940 –
Folkstone Docks, Southern England.

Chadwick woke with a start when the Naval non-commissioned officer shook his shoulder. He was still holding the empty glass, which the steward gently took from his hand.

"We're in England, Sir." he said quietly.

Still in a state of high alert, Chadwick jumped to his feet, disorientated as to where he was and what was happening. He looked around the room and saw officers in various states of consciousness, some awake and some still in exhausted sleep. Suddenly realising where he was, he rushed out without speaking, leaving a bemused steward holding his empty glass.

It was dawn, and the white cliffs of southern England reflected the rising sun, making them shine. Chadwick moved as quickly as possible to where the platoon had been, stepping between sleeping soldiers that completely filled the deck. Sergeant Preston was awake, leaning on the rail looking at the coast. The rest of the platoon lay huddled together on the deck around him. Preston broke into a beaming smile as Chadwick approached.

"You did it, Sir." he began, slightly emotional. "You got us home safely." Chadwick's response was cut short by the sound of the ship's klaxon, announcing their arrival in England. The deck seemed to come to life, sleeping forms suddenly stirring and moving at the sudden blast. The klaxon sounded again, as if to call the men to their feet. Naval ratings scurried around the decks as the ship prepared to dock, the engine revving as the vessel manoeuvred against the wharf.

"Keep everyone together as we disembark." Chadwick told Preston. "Don't let them wander off until we find out what is happening." Preston kicked the feet of those still sleeping to waken them, getting them upright and ready to move. Gangplanks were slid into place and the deck slowly began to clear as the men descended onto the wharf. As Chadwick led the platoon towards the gangplank, he spoke to a Naval Rating supervising the disembarkation.

"Where are we?" he asked.

"You're in Folkstone, Sir." came the cheerful reply. Treading carefully on the sloping gangplank, Chadwick led 10 Platoon off the destroyer, a sense of utter relief washing over him as his boots touched English soil.

Ladies from the Women's Voluntary Service had set up tables on the docks, trays of buns and lines of tea filled enamel mugs arranged for collection as the men filtered past. There were many shouts of "Well done." from the ladies as the men helped themselves to the food. As the disembarked men stood waiting for direction, the wounded were carried off the destroyer. The blankets covering their wounded bodies were carefully folded, exposing their pale, pain wracked faces; in stark contrast to the sunburnt faces of the survivors who stood watching. Then stretchers with the dead came last, the bodies completely covered by blankets. Chadwick watched as the dead were taken past, knowing one of them was Private Smith.

All officers were called together for briefing. They were told that returning troops were to be temporarily housed in Training Depots across the country, until units could be identified and reassembled. Chadwick noted that the West Staffords, among other units, were to be taken to Wheaton Cavalry Barracks, between Stoke and Birmingham, the journey expected to take around eight hours by train.

* * *

Sergeant Preston confirmed that all were on board, then settled down beside Chadwick in the carriage. As the train moved off, Chadwick was already asleep, his head slumped awkwardly to the side, the weight of responsibility finally lifted. Preston stood up and putting his hands under Chadwick's armpits, adjusted his position to straighten his neck, before resuming his seat and falling asleep himself.

* * *

Sergeant Preston was woken by someone hammering on the carriage window. The train had stopped at a station and a civilian was tapping the window with beer bottles. Preston stood up and opened the window flap at the top, the civilian reaching the beer through the gap.

"Thank you. Well done, lads." the man shouted as Preston took the bottles from him. Corporal Hutchinson woke up at the noise.

"Well done lads?" he repeated the statement as a question. "I thought we got beat."

"Maybe he knows something we don't." replied Preston. "Maybe they got the Army out."

"Well in that case, we deserve a drink." said Hutchinson, holding out his hand for a bottle. "Shall we waken Lieutenant Chadwick and offer him some?"

"Let him sleep." replied Preston. "He needs it. And anyway, there's only two bottles."

* * *

Having been collected at the railway station by Bedford trucks, all the units sent to Wheaton were assembled in the gymnasium. The Camp Commandant addressed the gathering, thanking them for their efforts and telling them that each and every one was a hero. Like most of the others there, this reception was hugely unexpected by the survivors of 10 Platoon, who believed they would be ridiculed for the performance of the Expeditionary Force as a whole. They were served, for most anyway, their first proper meal in three weeks, issued razors, soap and towels, fresh socks and underwear; finally, being allowed to sleep on camp beds arranged on the gymnasium floor.

Saturday 1 June 1940 –
Creton Farm, Le Paradis, France.

Madame Creton seemed more agitated than normal that day when she arrived with the usual bag of food. As the men ate, she tried to convey through a mixture of gestures and broken English that some villagers suspected there were soldiers hiding at the farm, and feared German reprisals. Receiving no recognition of understanding from the men, she ended the visit distinctly frustrated, speaking her native language in a tone that suggested to Pooley and O'Callaghan she was chastising herself for her failure to communicate. When she left, the two men discussed their impression of what she was trying to tell them. They agreed that whatever she had been saying involved the Germans, and the result would not be good.

Two hours later she reappeared with a well-dressed male. As they entered the building, Madame Creton was speaking so quickly that neither Pooley nor O'Callaghan caught a single word of what she was saying. She gesticulated at the two men with both her arms and then symbolically stood back, as if offering her acquaintance the stage on which to play his part. His English was excellent and he confirmed what the men had suspected. The villagers feared German reprisals should they be found to be helping British soldiers, and he gently advised them to hand themselves in. He confirmed that the German soldiers now occupying the village were Regular Infantry and not SS. Having paused for a few seconds, and received no immediate response, he tried another angle; stressing the need for Pooley's wounds to receive proper medical attention, something that could not be provided by the villagers.

O'Callaghan looked at Pooley, who gave him a slight nod, before giving their permission for their new host to report their presence to the Germans. The man partly turned his head to the left and gave a single, slow nod. He then relayed their decision to Madame Creton, who immediately launched into another tirade in her native tongue. She broke off from her conversation just long enough to acknowledge Pooley and O'Callaghan with a nod and a wave, before following the interpreter out of the building, still talking.

Sunday 2 June 1940 –
Dunkirk Pocket Perimeter, North East France.

Having withdrawn from their positions the previous night and handed responsibility for the defence of the perimeter over to the French, no British troops were in direct action against German land assaults that day. The Germans had crossed the canal barrier at 11 p.m. the previous night, and the French were fighting heroically to limit their encroachment into the perimeter to allow the British to get away.

Sunday 2 June 1940 –
Dunkirk Beach, Channel Coast, North East France.

All evacuations stopped again at 3 a.m. as the sky began to lighten; the mole still packed with troops who hadn't managed to get to the front of the queue and board a vessel. They were all sent back into Malo-les-Bains to wait until darkness returned that night. As the sound of battle was getting closer, those remaining British and Belgians in the town formed a defensive position in the remaining buildings in case the Germans broke through. With all remaining British and Belgian troops now concentrated in Malo-les-Bains, General Alexander moved among them, calming them and raising their morale by his professional behaviour and sheer presence. Fortunately, the defensive position was not to be tested, as the French still fighting on the perimeter held firm. With naval vessels banned from the mole during the day, a hospital ship tried to enter Dunkirk harbour, expecting the appropriate internationally accepted markings as to its purpose to be respected by the Germans. It was bombed and sank.

The queues for embarkation were formed again as soon as darkness fell, and despite the soldiers being illuminated by the flames from burning buildings in the port, there was no interference from the enemy. Just before midnight, the channel ferry Saint Helier took the last members of the British Expeditionary Force on board. Tennant and Alexander moved up and down the beach in Tennant's launch, calling through a megaphone to anyone who possibly remained. Receiving no response from the now deserted beaches, they headed out to sea and boarded a destroyer. Tennant signalled Dover Command.

"BEF evacuated."

Sunday 2 June 1940 –
Wheaton Cavalry Barracks, Stoke, England.

Although a late breakfast had been arranged, most of the men were already awake hours before. The gymnasium was alive with chatter between both individuals and different units about where they had been and what they had endured; eager for news on what was happening in France. After breakfast, every individual was given a blank Field Card to fill in as a way of letting their next of kin know they were safe and well. As information from returning units was collated, each man was interviewed by non-commissioned officers of the Royal Military Police in relation to their knowledge of missing colleagues, whether they were assumed killed, injured or a prisoner of war.

The men were very much left to their own devices until they were transferred to alternative locations, where their units were being reassembled. The non-commissioned officers and other ranks remained in the gymnasium; the officers being offered accommodation in the houses of Depot Staff Officers who lived on site.

Sunday 2 June 1940 –
Creton Farm, Le Paradis, Northern France.

Bill O'Callaghan had taken the opportunity offered by a bright sunny morning to leave the barn, and was sitting behind the woodpile enjoying the feeling of the sun on his face and the warmth on his stiff and aching limbs. As the sound of sporadic vehicle movement on the road at the front of the complex was normal, and he had taken care to conceal himself from view, he felt safe and relaxed, stretching out full length on the grass with his hands behind his head. He had unbuttoned his battledress blouse and the first few buttons of his shirt. As he moved, wafts of his body odour reached his nostrils, and he realised how filthy he had become. He wondered how bad he smelled to other people.

Insects buzzed through the air, and some small birds swooped in and out among the swarms of creatures to feed. He began to feel himself doze off in the heat, until the sound of a motorcycle engine slowing down made him sit up. He scrambled to his feet and peeped from behind the woodpile to see a German motorcycle with a single rider precede an army staff car into the yard. In the car sat a German officer and another man in a civilian suit. The car stopped behind the motorcycle and the driver quickly dismounted, opening the car door for the occupants to step out.

The man in civilian clothes led the way straight to the barn where Pooley was in the pigsty. The German officer and driver followed, the motorcyclist remaining seated on his machine. O'Callaghan cursed himself that he had let his alertness slip and been unable to warn Pooley. He turned his head away, and closing his eyes slid down the woodpile into a sitting position. Both he and Pooley were separated and helpless. He fully expected to hear pistol shots, but no sound came. His excitement growing again, O'Callaghan resumed his watching position. The three men left the barn and resumed their seats in the staff car. The motorcycle engine roared back to life and the visitors left the yard.

O'Callaghan sprinted across the cobbles and into the barn, not knowing what he would find. Pooley was seated in his usual position, a packet of German cigarettes on the straw beside him, with one already between his lips. O'Callaghan began to ask questions but changed his mind after starting each one; his eventual outburst making no sense at all. Understanding O'Callaghan's impatience, Pooley explained that the Germans were a Medical Officer and his orderly; the civilian was the Mayor of Le Paradis. In good English, the Medical Officer had explained that he knew there were two British soldiers here that required medical attention, and requested the whereabouts of the other.

"I told them you were out looking for food. I thought it best not to let them think the locals had been feeding us." explained Pooley.

"Just right." replied O'Callaghan. "We don't want to land them in it."

"I'm glad you think so, Bill, because the orderly gave me some sausage and bread from his food bag. I had to wolf it down to make them think I was starving, but I did manage to save you a bit." Pooley handed over a piece of sausage and some crusty bread. As O'Callaghan ate the remains of the sausage, Pooley recited that the Medical Officer had examined his wounds and suggested hospital treatment.

"They're going to come and collect us in a few days, Bill. The military hospital is currently full and they need to clear some space first. In the meantime, they have made the mayor responsible for our custody and the locals can openly care for us without fear of reprisals. Good news, eh?" questioned a very upbeat Pooley.

* * *

As night fell, the two men had a serious discussion. Since they knew they would soon be prisoners of war, they agreed never to mention the massacre until they were released from German custody and back home. They could not be sure of the reaction they would get being possibly the only witnesses to a mass murder by German soldiers, and vowed to remain silent no matter how long it took. Pooley took a turn for the worse during the night, his leg becoming discoloured, and emitting a foul smell. Any movement caused him agony, and he became delirious. The pair spent a fitful night, hoping the Germans would return for them soon.

Monday 3 June 1940 –
Dunkirk Port, Channel Coast, North East France.

By late afternoon, the Germans had reached the outskirts of Dunkirk, and fierce street fighting was taking place in the ruined buildings about two miles from the mole. The French commander in Dunkirk judged they could not hold another day and planned for hostilities to end sometime that night. He established an inner rearguard around the port, requesting they hold until 2 a.m. on 4 June in order to mount a final evacuation operation.

In a last effort with exhausted crews, which included the French Navy, Ramsay gathered a total of sixty-three vessels, coordinated by Commander HR Troup. The usual reduction in the intensity of night operations by the Germans facilitated the withdrawal of the French defenders through their inner rearguard and onto the mole. Queues of men waited to the sound of sporadic machine gun fire as the rearguard held. The last ship to leave was the destroyer HMS Shikari as dawn broke at 3:40 a.m. on 4 June, carrying three hundred and eighty-three passengers. As the Shikari pulled away, the mole was still packed with French soldiers who, along with the British medical personnel who had stayed behind to tend the casualties, would soon become prisoners of war.

Monday 3 June 1940 – Paris, France.

Having moved their armoured assets away from Dunkirk and prepositioned them for an attack across the Somme River into central France, the German High Command turned its attention to Paris. An air raid was mounted against selected targets of direct military value such as airfields, bridges and railways, and also factories and warehouses. At this stage in the conflict, the Luftwaffe bombers who took part in the raid lacked the sighting technology for precision attacks; the damage that resulted from the high-level attacks being mostly random, insignificant to the war effort and quickly repaired. However, in terms of civilian morale, the effect of Paris being bombed was enormous.

Monday 3 June 1940 – Creton Farm, Le Paradis, Northern France.

In the morning, Madame Creton arrived with some food. As usual, she dressed Pooley's wound while the men ate, but the look on her face when she saw the worsening state of the injury betrayed her concern. She tried to conceal her anguish by being upbeat and cheerful, but the false exaggeration of her mood told the men all they needed to know. When she had recovered her now empty bag and other possessions, she hurried from the barn towards the village.

That afternoon, a man and his two daughters arrived in the yard. The man simply stood there doing nothing, as if waiting for something to happen, while his daughters chased each other around the yard laughing. Their childish sing song voices brought an as yet unheard language to the ears of the soldiers. O'Callaghan sensed the awkwardness of the scene and left the cover of the barn to speak to him. He turned out to be a Polish refugee, but little further sense could be made of his attempts at conversation. He gathered his daughters and left the yard, heading in the opposite direction from the village, towards the city of Bethune. The girls skipped after him, still laughing and chattering in their unusual language.

Late that afternoon, both men were in the barn. Pooley was in a restless sleep and O'Callaghan was still trying to make sense of the strange circumstances of the visit earlier that day. The sound of a vehicle engine brought O'Callaghan quickly back to reality, and to his feet at the same moment. Looking out onto the yard he saw a clearly marked cream coloured civilian ambulance drive towards the woodpile and then reverse back towards the entrance to the barn. Two uniformed men got out, and while one opened the rear doors of the ambulance, the other made his way to the barn. O'Callaghan met him as he entered. He wore a military style black tunic over a shirt and tie, but most noticeably to O'Callaghan, had red cross insignia on his sleeve. The man greeted him warmly in French, then English, saying they were here for the wounded soldiers. O'Callaghan led him to where Pooley was lying in the pigsty and the second ambulance passenger joined them, carrying a wood and canvas stretcher. Setting the stretcher down beside Pooley, the two men gently lifted him onto the stretched canvas, stood up, and carried him out of the barn, placing him onto a metal frame in the back of the vehicle before sliding the stretcher smoothly inside. They then removed another stretcher from the back of the vehicle and set it on the cobbles beside O'Callaghan.

"For you, Monsieur." said the medic who had spoken to O'Callaghan before. O'Callaghan explained that he was not seriously wounded and could easily walk. "We were told two English. We must take two English." The medic became quite irate, but then clarified his actions. "If you walk the Germans will not allow you in hospital." O'Callaghan nodded his understanding and lay down on the stretcher; being lifted and placed in the vehicle beside Pooley. The inside of the ambulance smelled like a wet tent; the canvas stretchers having been washed but not yet fully dried. Pooley turned his head and looked at O'Callaghan. Now being too weak to speak, he just smiled. His face was ashen, and O'Callaghan suddenly realised what a poor state he was in.

The back doors slammed and the interior of the ambulance went almost dark. There was a small round window at face height in the side panel of the vehicle. Looking through, O'Callaghan caught a glimpse of the damaged farmhouse and the barn as the vehicle manoeuvred before leaving the yard. He then saw Madame Creton standing at the side of the road waving as the ambulance turned towards Bethune and the events of the last few hours made sense. She had realised that Pooley was in serious trouble, but had arranged a non-local to raise the alarm, still not wishing to invite German reprisals on the village.

Pooley winced and moaned as the ambulance bumped over the road, uneven and damaged by the passage of heavy military vehicles. Through the small window O'Callaghan could see a war-scarred landscape of shattered buildings and burnt-out vehicles. The ambulance passed over a temporary bridge on the Aire Canal, still under construction by German Military Engineers who clung to the girders as they made the structure secure; and into the city of Bethune. On arrival, the men were separated; Pooley taken almost immediately into surgery, and O'Callaghan to a post-surgical ward, where he had the opportunity to wash and clean himself up. He was looking forward to a restful sleep in a fresh bed when a German orderly arrived. Without nicety or conversation, the German copied the details from O'Callaghan's identity discs and recorded his civilian address in England. He was officially in German military custody.

Tuesday 4 June 1940 –
Dunkirk Beach, Channel Coast, North East France.

At 9:40 a.m. the German infantry arrived on Dunkirk beach. The mole was still packed with French soldiers who had not managed to embark, and they were searched before being marched away into captivity, many to remain prisoners of war until 1945. As the Germans wandered in curiosity along the beach, they found it littered with abandoned weapons and personal equipment. Half buried steel helmets protruded from the sand, gleefully collected by the Germans as souvenirs and tried on for size, to the laughter of their comrades. Piles of boots and clothing still lay where their owners had undressed before attempting to swim out to the boats. Small arms of all descriptions lay abandoned, mixed with heavier weapons that had been disabled to deny their use to the enemy.

The sound of the sea had replaced the sound of battle, bodies of the dead on the shoreline being gently lifted and set down as the waves broke on the sand. A pall of smoke still hung in the air from the burning oil storage wells in Dunkirk, intermittently broken by sunbeams that caught the masts and rails of sunken vessels that protruded above the waves. The breeze broke up the foam carpet that had formed where the waves finished, pieces rolling across the sand, until coming to rest against dead bodies and the debris of a defeated army. A total of 40,000 Allied troops, mostly French, went into captivity; and a delighted Hitler ordered bells to be rung throughout Germany for three days.

Tuesday 4 June 1940 –
Dover Castle, Channel Coast, England.

Admiral Ramsay stood on the balcony at the entrance to his headquarters under Dover Castle. Across the channel he could see the pall of smoke that hung over Dunkirk. Shortly after 2 p.m. he called the Prime Minister and gave him the latest available figures from the evacuation. Having initially believed that 45,000 men could be evacuated, a total of just over 338,000 had been lifted from the mole and the beaches at Dunkirk. Of the thirty-eight destroyers that had been involved, six had been sunk and fourteen damaged. Of the forty-six transport vessels of the Merchant Navy and ferries taken from trade, nine had been sunk. At 2:23 p.m. Ramsay officially called an end to Operation Dynamo.

Tuesday 4 June 1940 –
House of Commons, London, England.

With civilian morale destroyed after the defeat and withdrawal of the Expeditionary Force from France, and only half the population of Britain expecting the Government to fight on, Prime Minister Churchill rose to his feet in the House of Commons to give what he did not yet know would probably be the most important speech of his life. No contemporaneous recording was made; however, a transcript was read out by newsreaders on radio broadcasts across the country that night.

"I have, myself, full confidence that if all do their duty, if nothing is neglected, and if the best arrangements are made, as they are being made, we shall prove ourselves once more able to defend our island home, to ride out the storm of war, and to outlive the menace of tyranny, if necessary for years, if necessary, alone. At any rate, that is what we are going to try to do. That is the resolve of His Majesty's Government – every man of them. That is the will of Parliament and the nation. The British Empire and the French Republic, linked together in their cause and in their need, will defend to the death their native soil, aiding each other like good comrades to the utmost of their strength.

Even though large tracts of Europe and many old and famous States have fallen or may fall into the grip of the Gestapo and all the odious apparatus of Nazi rule, we shall not flag or fail. We shall go on to the end. We shall fight in France, we shall fight on the seas and oceans, we shall fight with growing confidence and growing strength in the air, we shall defend our island, whatever the cost may be. We shall fight on the beaches, we shall fight on the landing grounds, we shall fight in the fields and in the streets, we shall fight in the hills; we shall never surrender. And even if, which I do not for a moment believe, this island or a large part of it were subjugated and starving, then our Empire beyond the seas, armed and guarded by the British Fleet, would carry on the struggle, until, in God's good time, the New World, with all its power and might, steps forth to the rescue and the liberation of the Old."

PART 6

COLLAPSE AND ARMISTICE

Wednesday 5 June 1940 –
River Somme, Northern France.

While the Germans had been fighting to destroy the Allied forces around Dunkirk, the French had turned their attention to preventing the Germans from advancing south, and the protection of Paris. They had begun and were still consolidating what was to become known as the "Weygand Line", a defensive barrier running for a total of two hundred and twenty-five miles from the mouth of the Somme on the Channel coast to the still intact Maginot Line on the German border. During the race to the coast two weeks earlier, the Germans had seized crossing points on the river Somme, and now planned to use these as the means to quickly shatter the Weygand Line and subsequently break out into central France.

The French aim was to engage the Germans in a protracted defensive battle of attrition, a type of conflict that they had equipped and trained for, and were better suited doctrinally to conduct than the Germans. The defenders planned to counter the German momentum, that had been so destructive in the campaign to date, by creating a deep band of strongpoints offering mutual fire support; and all available manpower had been employed on this task in a race against time before the Germans attacked. The length of front to be covered precluded a continuous defensive line, so instead, fortified "hedgehogs" in a checkerboard pattern were constructed to delay the attackers, along with the creation of an armoured mobile reserve capable of being called forward to stem and force back any breakthrough.

Prior to their attack, the Germans had built up a detailed picture of French positions from reconnaissance flights, while their air superiority denied the French any similar source of information. At first light on 5 June, the German attack began with a massive air and artillery bombardment; quickly followed by the infantry and engineers to clear a path for the panzers. As far as possible, the tanks would then deliberately avoid the hedgehogs identified by aerial reconnaissance, choosing instead to strike deep into the French positions to identify weak points. Using this method, Rommel's 7th Panzer Division had advanced eight miles in the direction of the river Seine by the end of the first day.

At 4 a.m. the British 51st Division, which had been separated from the rest of the Expeditionary Force when the Germans reached the coast on

20 May, came under direct attack to the south of Abbeville. The length of front they had been expected to hold was too wide for their resources, and they were quickly forced to withdraw south west, towards the mouth of the Seine at Le Havre.

Thursday 6 June 1940 –
River Somme, Northern France.

The Germans attacked at what they believed to be weak points all along the length of the defensive line, but did not have it all their own way; the French putting up notable resistance. Their assaults bounced off and manoeuvred around the defensive hedgehogs; but as the armour pushed ahead, the assaulting infantry were subsequently caught up in the defensive checkerboard web; the defenders continuing to fight even when bypassed. Rommel's tanks advanced a further thirteen miles the second day, as French counterattacks were restricted to the hours of darkness by the continuous daytime presence of Stuka bombers, which attacked any columns of vehicles or troops that presented themselves.

The direct pressure on the 51st Division had slackened, but only because the German armour was advancing inland. A map appreciation of the German advance highlighted a danger of the division being cut off in the Havre peninsula. The Divisional Commander, Major General Victor Fortune, reported his assessment, requesting permission to withdraw. His request was denied; being ordered to hold the position at all costs.

Friday 7 June 1940 –
River Somme, Northern France.

While the German infantry continued to struggle against the French infantry in their defensive hedgehogs on the Weygand Line, the situation around the 51st Division was deteriorating badly as they were forced south towards Le Havre, with Rommel's panzers advancing a further sixteen miles that day. The Weygand Line would hold its cohesion for a further three days before the continuous German pressure resulted in a fighting withdrawal all along the front. This withdrawal was conducted in such a way that the German pursuit was delayed long enough for the French to establish a new defensive position along the rivers Loire and Rhone, running from the Atlantic coast to the Swiss border.

At the highest political level, the Allied Supreme War Council had been discussing the concept of a Brittany Redoubt. By forming this redoubt between the mouth of the Loire and the coast at Saint-Malo, the French could fight on, reinforced by the British and resupplied across the English

Channel. To fulfil their part of the plan, the British 52nd Division was ordered to Southampton for transportation to France.

Friday 7 June 1940 –
Tromso, Northern Norway.

With the imminent withdrawal of all Allied troops from Norway, to be followed by the cessation of Norwegian armed resistance; the continued presence of the Government and Royal Family on Norwegian soil lost its rationale. Under the strictest security measures which included radio silence, HMS Devonshire lifted four hundred and sixty-one members of the Norwegian Royal Family and Government from Tromso on 7 June, bound for England. Once safely delivered to London, King Haakon and his Cabinet set up a Norwegian Government in exile which operated from the British capital until the end of the war.

Saturday 8 June 1940 –
Rouen, River Seine, Northern France.

To protect the approaches to the ports in the Havre peninsula that would be necessary for the reinforcement or withdrawal of the division, the British established roadblocks on the roads from Rouen, the direction from which it was identified that the panzers were advancing. French refugees moving ahead of the panzers swamped the British positions, a column of French tanks moving with the refugees being waved through the roadblocks. The tanks had been captured and were being operated by German crews, who once through the roadblocks, turned and attacked the British positions from the rear, allowing the main panzer force to continue their advance unhindered. That night, General Fortune received permission to withdraw; but the order arrived too late, as the 51st Division had already been cut off as he had predicted. The Germans entered Rouen on the morning of 9 June, and that night began to move towards the coast.

Saturday 8 June 1940 –
Harstad, Northern Norway.

The aircraft carriers Ark Royal and Glorious arrived off the coast of Norway on 2 June, their on-board fighters specifically tasked to provide cover for the planned evacuation from Harstad. In a secondary role, Glorious would be used as a platform to recover the fighters still operating from the airfield at Bardufoss. The evacuation plans envisaged units being allocated to specific ships at specific times from specific boarding points, all running against a carefully worked out timetable. Six pre-war luxury liners waited one hundred and eighty miles off the coast, being called in closer two at a time, to where destroyers ferried out soldiers that had been lifted from the shore. The destroyers worked non-stop to the timetable, embarking 15,000 soldiers onto the liners. Low cloud for an extended time during the evacuation, combined with the presence of the carrier-based fighters, resulted in very little Luftwaffe activity over this critical period. On 5 June, the Irish Guards and the Scots Guards were lifted from the shore. The same day, the French Foreign Legion were taken off, sailing straight to join the battle for France; where they arrived home just in time to hear that Paris had been occupied.

To cover the evacuation, the two squadrons of Gladiators and Hurricanes at Bardufoss were kept operational until the last moment. At 11:45 p.m. on 7 June, ten Gladiators left the runway at Bardufoss for the last time, heading for Glorious; the Hurricanes leaving shortly afterwards to ensure the Gladiators landed first. As soon as the aircraft had departed Bardufoss, the airstrip was deliberately dug up to prevent its use by the enemy. In the early hours of 8 June, Hurricane fighters successfully landed on the deck of Glorious, the first time this type of aircraft had been landed on the deck of a carrier.

As the destroyers were now required to protect the loaded troop ships off the coast, three smaller Irish Sea Ferries docked at Harstad to lift the South Wales Borderers and the rearguard of Engineers and Military Police who had been managing the evacuation process. The Ulster Monarch was the last vessel to depart, joining the waiting convoy which sailed for Britain on 8 June. The remaining Norwegian units, still fighting to cover the Allied withdrawal, were ordered to disengage in the early hours of 8 June, to coincide with the completion of the evacuation. All fighting ceased at midnight on 9 June, with the formal surrender of all remaining Norwegian forces being signed at the Britannia Hotel in Trondheim at 5 p.m. on 10 June.

Saturday 8 June 1940 – Norwegian Sea.

After the indifferent performance of the German Navy in the battle for Norway to date, Admiral Raeder was determined to return the Kriegsmarine to the struggle and save some face with Hitler initially, but also with the Army and Luftwaffe who had both performed extremely well. Capital ships that had been damaged earlier in the campaign had been repaired and were now ready for sea again. His proposal was a sortie into the Norwegian Sea to disrupt supplies of men and equipment from Britain to Northern Norway, potentially attacking the base at Harstad or relieving the German garrison at Narvik. Scharnhorst, Admiral Hipper and Gneisenau left Keil at 7 a.m. on

4 June with such an operation in mind; but as it became obvious the Allies were withdrawing, the focus of the German force changed to an attack on the westward bound convoys. Scharnhorst and Gneisenau altered course to intercept the convoys, allowing the Admiral Hipper to continue to Trondheim.

At 2:53 a.m. on 8 June, the aircraft carrier HMS Glorious detached from the convoy, and along with two destroyer escorts, Acasta and Ardent, were soon a few hours sailing time ahead of the main force. At 3:45 p.m. in perfect conditions, the lookout on Scharnhorst spotted smoke, and the two German battlecruisers closed at top speed to investigate. Twenty minutes later, the Germans were spotted by the destroyer escort who immediately generated a smoke screen as Glorious turned away. At 4:32 p.m. the 11-inch guns of the German ships engaged Glorious at a distance of fourteen miles, well beyond the range of any of the British guns. Glorious immediately sent a radio distress signal which was picked up by HMS Devonshire only one hundred miles away, but under the imposed radio silence due to her Royal passengers, could not be re-transmitted so as to keep her location secret.

To protect the carrier, the two destroyers placed themselves between Glorious and the German ships, initially to draw off their guns, but also to get close enough to launch their torpedoes. The Germans engaged the destroyers with their smaller secondary armament, 4.7-inch shells smashing into both, while maintaining the bombardment on Glorious with their larger main armament. At 5:25 p.m. HMS Ardent capsized while still firing, sinking at 5:28 p.m. with her last torpedo passing only a matter of feet from Scharnhorst.

With Glorious now on fire and listing, the order to abandon ship was passed at 5:40 p.m. with nine hundred men entering the sea; of which only forty-eight would survive. Glorious sank thirty minutes later at 6:10 p.m. Now alone, HMS Acasta continued the fight through a torrent of shells, moving close enough to the enemy ships to engage them with torpedoes and her deck guns. Acasta struck Scharnhorst with both a torpedo and shells from her guns, causing considerable damage before she succumbed. Acasta sank at 6:12 p.m. with Leading Seaman Nick Carter the only survivor, being rescued from the sea by a Norwegian trawler three days later. Able Seaman Roger Hooke was the sole survivor from the Ardent crew, picked up five days later from his life raft by a German seaplane which spotted him in the sea and landed beside him. A total of 1,519 British officers and men from the three warships were lost.

The damage caused to Scharnhorst by Acosta, required an immediate passage to Trondheim for repairs, subsequently preventing the German vessels from locating and engaging the larger convoy of British troop ships returning to Britain.

Sunday 9 June 1940 –
Paris, France.

The French Government had never planned to defend Paris in its streets and squares, having convinced itself, and the population, they could sit securely behind the Maginot Line. The raid by the Luftwaffe on 3 June, news of the defeat at Dunkirk, and the sight of retreating troops moving through the city being enough to trigger a mass civilian exodus. Railway stations became overwhelmed, with people crowded outside as the platforms were soon full. Those who chose to leave by road became locked into slow moving columns of overloaded cars, carts and any other wheeled transport that could be pressed into service.

After the destruction of non-essential papers, the critical instruments of the decision-making apparatus of Government were moved to makeshift locations at Tours on the Loire, with Governmental Departments spread across the town in different buildings; more often than not without adequate communications. On the same day, Weygand moved his Headquarters from the Chateau de Vincennes to the Chateau de Muguet on the Loire. Here, he had access to a single telephone, which could not be used over the period when the operator was at lunch.

Monday 10 June 1940 –
Saint-Valery-en-Caux, Channel Coast, Northern France.

With the Germans closing in all around, Rommel's panzers reached the coast at Veulettes, blocking the route south to La Havre and by doing so immediately reducing the evacuation options of the 51st Division to either Saint-Valery-en-Caux or Dieppe. With the news that Dieppe was about to fall into enemy hands, General Fortune began to make arrangements for an evacuation from Saint-Valery, where he was told that ships would be waiting. Over the night of 10 / 11 June, the 51st Division concentrated at St-Valery-en-Caux, along with the remnants of French units in the area.

Monday 10 June 1940 –
Rome, Italy.

At 6:00 p.m. Benito Mussolini emerged onto his balcony overlooking the Palazzo Venezia. In the shadow of a huge Italian flag, with his uniform bedecked in medals and his thumbs tucked into his belt, he addressed a crowd of 60,000 jubilant Italians. Urging them to *"Rush to arms and show your tenacity. Your courage. Your Valour."* he declared war on

France and Britain, to take effect just after midnight. Fifty-five Italian Savoia-Marchetti SM.79 Sparviero bombers from Sicily struck Malta the next morning, beginning the siege of the island that was to last until November 1942.

In response to the declaration of war, French engineers destroyed the transportation and communication links across the border with Italy, but there was little ground activity other than exchanges of fire between forts on either side of the line. Both adversaries had long-standing defensive strategies in the border area, but due to the difficult terrain, which restricted offensive operations, the French took no further action in this area for the remainder of the war. Italian air operations continued in the Mediterranean on 12 June, when SM.79 bombers from Sardinia attacked French targets in Northern Tunisia.

Tuesday 11 June 1940 −
Saint-Valery-en-Caux, Channel Coast, Northern France.

With the coming of daylight, Fortune had most of his division in defensive positions occupying a wide perimeter around the town; while the still withdrawing rearguard units struggled through disorganised and aimless French troops that were clogging the roads. The Germans attacked at 2 p.m. and as the infantry battled in the suburbs, Rommel's panzers broke though and seized the cliffs that overlooked the town from the west. From his headquarters in the centre of the town, Fortune arranged ships for an evacuation attempt that night.

As darkness fell, the men formed queues at the port in the pouring rain, silhouetted against the burning town. Fog began to roll in from the sea, and being deemed too thick, the ships did not come. Some ships made it to the small fishing port of Veules-les-Roses, still within the defensive perimeter and fog free, taking off more than 2,000 British and French troops while holding the Germans back with their deck guns. At 3 a.m. Fortune ordered the men to resume their perimeter positions, hoping for another rescue attempt that night; and for a change in the weather.

Tuesday 11 June 1940 −
Libya / Egypt Border, North Africa.

The border between Italian controlled Libya and Egypt consisted of metal posts with four single strands of wire supporting barbed wire coils, overlooked by several small stone-built forts from which Italian forces monitored and patrolled the border area. During the night of 11 / 12 June, Morris armoured cars of the 11ᵗʰ Hussars penetrated the border on a reconnaissance mission to establish the Italian strength and deployments, capturing seventy surprised Italian prisoners. Two days later on 14 June, they were reinforced by elements of the 7ᵗʰ Hussars, and felt strong enough to attack the major Italian base in the area at Fort Capuzzo. Just before the ground assault, the fort was attacked by RAF Blenheim bombers, and after a token resistance, the entire garrison of two hundred and twenty-six Italians surrendered.

Wednesday 12 June 1940 –
Saint-Valery-en-Caux, Channel Coast, Northern France.

White flags appeared all through the town at 8.15 a.m. as the French began to act on an order from their own Command Headquarters to stop fighting. Although theoretically under the same French command structure, Fortune did not comply and continued to resist. But as any further French resistance melted away, Fortune realised he could not hold out until dark in the hope of a renewed evacuation attempt, and at 10.30 a.m. gave the order for his division to stop fighting. The order was disseminated by Major Thomas Rennie, serving on Fortune's staff. Thirty minutes after ordering the ceasefire, Fortune received a signal from Commander-in-Chief Portsmouth, confirming the request for the planned evacuation that night.

A total of 46,000 Allied troops were captured at Saint-Valery-en-Caux, of which 8,000 were from the 51ˢᵗ Division.

Thursday 13 June 1940 –
Cherbourg, Atlantic Coast, Northwest France.

Having been promoted to Lieutenant General, Sir Alan Brooke had been put ashore at Cherbourg early that morning to take command of a second British Expeditionary Force, bringing with him the 52ⁿᵈ and Canadian 1ˢᵗ Divisions. They were to be joined by those forces recently lifted from Le Havre and the already in theatre 51ˢᵗ Division.

Brooke's orders were to take command of all the British forces in France and join with the promised French forces to create the Brittany Redoubt. All non-essential support troops still in France were to be evacuated. On arrival, he learned that the 51ˢᵗ Division had surrendered the previous day, and after subsequent discussions with British Liaison Officers at Weygand's Headquarters, he was convinced the French Army could not continue to fight for more than a few days longer. He made arrangements to meet Weygand personally the next day to confirm his assessment.

Thursday 13 June 1940 –
Paris, France.

During the night, Government notification posters appeared on the walls of public buildings in Paris.

"Paris having been declared an open city, the military government asks the population to abstain from all hostile acts, and hopes that the people will remain calm and dignified in a manner which appears appropriate in the circumstance."

As they crowded around the posters, jostling for a place to read the information, relief was the prominent emotion of those civilians that remained in the city, now knowing they would not become another Warsaw or Rotterdam. To the sound of distant artillery fire, the last military transport vehicles left the city that afternoon. As the famous landmarks of Paris passed from view, those soldiers aboard who watched in silence through dusty windows or canvas truck canopies felt a mixture of anger and shame. With all shops, offices and factories shut, and unsettled by the sound of approaching gunfire, the remaining civilians went home. Having been taught since their first years at school not to trust the Germans, they were afraid and worried the hated enemy may not honour the declaration.

Thursday 13 June 1940 –
Tours, River Loire, Western France.

Churchill left Hendon Airfield in bright sunshine, but landed at Tours in a thunderstorm, where the French Government had established itself since moving from Paris on 9 June. He had travelled by air at some personal risk of being attacked by German fighters to attend another Supreme War Council with French Government and Military representatives. At the meeting, Churchill was told by Prime Minister Reynaud that he believed it was too late for the Brittany Redoubt plan to be effective. Despite this declaration, Churchill was still convinced the French would continue to fight until all political and military options were exhausted, and before leaving the meeting, committed to do all he could to assist.

The political options included an approach to the United States of America to enter the war on the side of the Allies, and a proposal by the now General Charles de Gaulle, for the British and French nations to combine into a single nation. These options were discussed during a French Cabinet meeting after the War Council meeting; a formal appeal to Washington being made that day, while the single nation proposal was to be further discussed at the next meeting. After the Cabinet meeting, the Government vacated

Tours and moved further away from the advancing Germans to Bordeaux on the Atlantic coast, from where they awaited the response from American President Roosevelt.

Friday 14 June 1940 –
Paris, France.

Paris was practically deserted. Only the bakeries were open for the usual early morning purchases from the now sparse populace. In the face of no resistance, the German 87th Division entered the city from the northwest. A ceremony was conducted by German officers at the tomb of the unknown soldier below the Arc de Triomphe, watched by a crowd of Parisiens who had gathered out of morbid curiosity. Then a swastika flag was unfurled on the monument and columns of soldiers marched through, led by a military band.

The soldiers were not dressed for a ceremonial parade, with scuffed helmets, dusty boots and grubby uniforms; carrying machine guns and combat equipment. Metal gas mask containers clinked against their canteens and mess tins as they marched, their nailed boots crunching on the cobbled streets. General von Bock stood on the pavement of the Champs Elysees with his entourage, smiling and saluting the troops as they marched past. Infantry, cavalry, horse drawn artillery and armoured vehicles all passed with their officers saluting the General from horseback or from their vehicle seats. When the parade was over, the swastika flag was removed from the Arc de Triomphe.

That afternoon, a German military car with a loudspeaker attached drove slowly through the streets, a German accented voice speaking French, and advising of an 8 p.m. curfew. While the German infantry was parading through Paris, their panzers had in the meantime crossed the Seine, driving south.

Friday 14 June 1940 –
Maginot Line, Eastern France.

With the German thrust into central France leaving those troops manning the Maginot Line isolated, they were ordered to withdraw in stages, the first tranche being taken out over the night of 13 / 14 June. A German advance against the forts on 14 June was repulsed, but reducing manpower due to the ongoing French troop withdrawals allowed the Germans to penetrate between the forts the next day. Despite being surrounded, almost continually bombed by Stukas and heavily shelled by German artillery, the now isolated strongpoints continued to hold out.

Friday 14 June 1940 –
Orleans, Northern France.

Lieutenant General Brook was driven one hundred and seventy miles from Le Mans to Weygand's Headquarters at Orleans, where he received a map briefing on the military situation. During the meeting, Weygand admitted the French Army could undertake no further meaningful resistance and the Brittany Redoubt plan would not work from the French perspective, as he could not provide the promised military support. But he insisted that the British continue with the plan as it was an order from the Supreme War Council meeting held the previous day. Weygand made no mention of the fact that he had already asked the Germans for an armistice.

On leaving the meeting, Brooke sent a telegram to General Dill, Chief of the Imperial General Staff, saying that in his opinion the Brittany Redoubt plan should be reconsidered. After the one-hundred-and-seventy-mile drive back to his headquarters, Brooke telephoned Dill requesting that all further movement of troops to France be stopped and arrangements be made for the evacuation of those already in place. Brooke's request met political resistance and it was only after a thirty-minute telephone call with Churchill that evening that authority was given for the evacuation to begin the next day. The codename "Aerial" was assigned to this new evacuation effort.

Saturday 15 June 1940 –
Bordeaux, French Atlantic Coast.

As Bordeaux was overflowing with refugees, the French Cabinet meeting was held in the best available place, a rearranged school classroom. There was heated discussion and rejection of a proposal to move the Government to North Africa and continue resistance from there. De Gaulle's proposal on French and British unification, it was argued, would mean joint financial and economic policies, joint defence and foreign policies, and joint citizenship of both countries. The Cabinet rejected this as they believed the French would lose their colonies and be reduced to dominion status under the British. Now, the only remaining hope of salvation was if America entered the war.

Saturday 15 June 1940 –
Atlantic Ports, Brittany, Northwest France.

Evacuation of the 52nd Division from Cherbourg began almost immediately with both trade and Royal Navy ships lifting soldiers from ports all along the

Brittany coast. The Royal Air Force sent squadrons based in England to support those still based in France, fighting to keep the Luftwaffe away from the gathering ships. False rumours spread of the imminent arrival of German forces, resulting in the deliberate destruction of vast quantities of equipment stored on the docks. As the evacuations continued practically unhindered for the next two days, the destroyed equipment could mostly have been recovered, given the resultant time that was actually available.

Sunday 16 June 1940 –
Bordeaux, French Atlantic Coast.

Official notification was received by the French Cabinet that the United States had refused to join the war. With Reynaud's last hope of being able to continue the fight now gone, he resigned as Prime Minister, recommending that Petain be appointed in his place. Petain immediately approached the Spanish Government as an intermediary to offer the Germans a cessation of hostilities. The British forces still fighting in Brittany were not informed of the French intentions.

Sunday 16 June 1940 –
Libya / Egypt Border, North Africa.

Incensed at the British incursions across the border four days prior, an Italian battlegroup was dispatched to the area south of Fort Capuzzo. This column was spotted on the border at Ghirba and attacked by armoured cars of the 11th Hussars. With their firepower limited to their vehicle mounted Vickers machine guns, they called forward Cruiser tanks of the 7th Hussars, which encircled the column, adding their cannon fire to the battle. In what became a one-sided engagement, the Italians lost sixteen tankettes, four field guns and thirteen trucks. Over fifty Italians were killed, over one hundred captured, and all without a single British casualty.

Sunday 16 June 1940 –
Bruly-de-Pesche, Southern Belgium.

At his temporary Fuhrer Headquarters in Bruly-de-Pesche, Hitler received the French offer for cessation of hostilities with laughter. Unused to seeing any displays of emotion from the Fuhrer, his staff officers watched in amazement as he stamped his feet and waved his arms in celebration.

368

Monday 17 June 1940 –
Saint-Nazaire, Loire River, French Atlantic Coast.

Ferries from the Dover / Calais route made up part of the waiting vessels off the coast at Saint Nazaire, including the Cunard Cruise Liner Lancastria. The service personnel embarking were mostly support troops, including engineers, labourers, tradesmen and mechanics of the Royal Army Service Corps and Royal Air Force who had been stationed at Nantes aerodrome; along with British Embassy staff including their wives and children. With a normal passenger manifest of around 1,700, the severity of the situation resulted in an estimated 6,700 being taken on board the Lancastria. The crew and passengers could see vapour trails as fighters and bombers fought over the Loire estuary, and watched nervously as other vessels close by were attacked. At 3.45 p.m. German bombers penetrated the fighter cover and struck the Lancastria.

The ship immediately keeled to starboard, then righted itself and keeled to port. The command was given to clear away the lifeboats, and those that were undamaged quickly became swamped from the disproportionate passenger numbers being carried. Men walked down the exposed hull and stepped out into the water. Others wearing life jackets jumped from the high decks only to be severely injured as they hit the water; the impact on the jackets jerking their heads back. Above the sounds of the panic of escape, the yells of men trapped inside could be heard as the ship began to settle in the water.

The German bombers returned, dropping flares into the leaking fuel oil and setting it alight; burning alive those that had already escaped into the water. Rather than jump into the burning sea, men clung to the hull as the ship sank, choosing a death by drowning rather than burning as the Lancastria disappeared. The smaller vessels in the area managed to rescue almost 2,500 people, but around 4,000 perished.

Monday 17 June 1940 –
Bordeaux, French Atlantic Coast.

Without waiting for a response from the Germans regarding the offer of peace, Marshall Petain, as the new Prime Minister, broadcast to the French nation. Citizens gathered around radio sets in total silence wherever they could find them, whether this was the privacy of their own homes, cafes or in village squares.

"*Frenchmen,*

At this grave hour in the life of our country, I am addressing you tonight to tell you that the armistice was signed today at 6 o'clock. This act will

369

become effective tomorrow at 0.35. Hostilities will cease on all fronts at that time.

The duration of the armistice has been fixed at thirty-six days. During this time, negotiations will be undertaken with a view to concluding a definitive peace.

The French Army has laid down its arms. I ask all Frenchmen who may find themselves in contact with the enemy to observe strictly the rules of discipline and good conduct.

Long live France!"

The speech was greeted with a mixture of shock for some and joy for others. Refugees saw it as an end to their misery and immediately turned for home; although the fighting continued, and those using the roads were still attacked by the Luftwaffe. The French military were relieved that an armistice was being sought but resistance to the invaders continued with varying degrees of commitment, as officers rallied their men to fight on. Elsewhere, huge numbers took the opportunity to surrender rather than risk their life further for France when they saw the war was finished.

No effort was made to inform the British, Brooke becoming aware when he heard the speech on the radio.

Tuesday 18 June 1940 –
Atlantic Ports, Brittany, Northwest France.

Evacuations from Cherbourg finished on the afternoon of 18 June, just as Rommel's tanks arrived at the outskirts of the city. The 1st Canadian Division evacuating from Saint-Malo; Brooke departing along with the rearguard units from Saint-Nazaire. Almost 192,000 fighting men were evacuated including British, Canadians, French, Polish, Czechs and Belgians.

Tuesday 18 June 1940 –
House of Commons, London, England.

To report the successful evacuation of the vast majority of British and Commonwealth soldiers from France, Churchill rose to his feet at 3:49 p.m. and weaponised the English language.

"However matters may go in France or with the French Government, or other French Governments, we in this Island and in the British Empire will never lose our sense of comradeship with the French people. If we are now called upon to endure what they have been suffering, we shall

*emulate their courage, and if final victory rewards our toils, they shall
share the gains, aye, and freedom shall be restored to all. We abate
nothing of our just demands; not one jot or tittle do we recede. Czechs,
Poles, Norwegians, Dutch, Belgians have joined their causes to our own.
All these shall be restored.*

*What General Weygand has called the Battle of France is over. I
expect the Battle of Britain is about to begin. Upon this battle depends
the survival of Christian civilisation. Upon it depends our own British
life, and the long continuity of our institutions and our Empire. The
whole fury and might of the enemy must very soon be turned on us.
Hitler knows that he will have to break us in this island or lose the war. If
we can stand up to him, all Europe may be freed and the life of the world
may move forward into broad, sunlit uplands. But if we fail, then the
whole world, including the United States, including all that we have
known and cared for, will sink into the abyss of a new Dark Age made
more sinister, and perhaps more protracted, by the lights of perverted
science. Let us therefore brace ourselves to our duties, and so bear
ourselves that, if the British Empire and its Commonwealth last for a
thousand years, men will still say, this was their finest hour."*

Wednesday 19 June 1940 –
Rivers Loire and Rhone, Southern France.

Having penetrated the Weygand Line, Guderian's panzers flooded south on
12 June, leaving their infantry to deal with the bypassed strong points. As the
tanks pushed ahead, the French conducted a fighting withdrawal from the
Weygand Line against the pursuing German infantry as they moved towards
the next natural obstacle, the river Loire. In the race to the Loire, the German
plan was for encirclement of the remaining French forces, rather than a
battle of destruction they felt would be a struggle to conduct. This was due
to the increasing concern about the cumulative effect of battle on the fighting
power of their weary troops and worn-out vehicles.

Bypassing any resistance, they nursed their vehicles south, advancing
sixty miles a day, sometimes faster than information on their position could
be received and processed by their commanders. The tanks now displayed
swastika flags on their decks to signify their origin to roving Stuka pilots
who had been given free rein to attack anything that moved. After the radio
broadcast from Petain on 17 June, they were pushed even harder to capture
more ground and add strength to the coming armistice negotiations. On
19 June, Guderian's panzers stopped west of the Loire at Vichy, and on the
river Rhone at Lyon. The escape route of those French troops withdrawing
from the Weygand Line had been cut, and the battle of encirclement was
complete.

Friday 21 June 1940 –
France / Italy Border.

In the knowledge that Franco-German armistice discussions were about to begin, and with Mussolini determined to be regarded as a significant player on the European stage; the Italians launched a ground offensive through the Alps. At 3 a.m. Italian troops crossed the French border at points all along the Alpine Front, the main attacks coming in the northern sector and along the coast. Against weakened French defensive lines, stripped of soldiers to fight the Germans in the north, the offensive enjoyed some initial success, advancing about five miles before becoming bogged down due to topography and badly planned logistics. The Italians suffered 3,000 casualties of which over 2,000 were from frostbite, with a further six hundred missing and 1,100 taken prisoner.

Friday 21 June 1940 –
Compiegne, Northern France.

It was 3 p.m. on a bright sunny afternoon in a clearing in the forest of Compiegne, forty miles north of Paris. The German Army and Luftwaffe honour guard presented arms, the military band struck up, and his personal standard was raised as Hitler and his entourage walked past. Hitler returned the gesture with his characteristic straight arm salute. The site, personally chosen by Hitler, was the scene of the signing of the Armistice that had ended the Great War in November 1918. It had been turned into a place of commemoration for the French public to visit and celebrate, and a site of continued humiliation for the German Army and the German nation. A Nazi Battle Flag was symbolically unfurled to cover the Alsace-Lorraine statue, depicting a German Eagle impaled on a sword, a symbol of the defeat of Germany in the 1914 – 1918 conflict.

Prior to entering the converted railway dining carriage, Hitler paused to look at the statue of General Ferdinand Foch who presided over the Armistice negotiations and had become a French national hero. The carriage was part of Foch's personal train, finished in polished wood and studded leather chairs, and had been kept on site in a purpose-built museum to commemorate the event. Hitler had ordered it removed from the museum and placed in the exact spot where it stood in November 1918.

The German delegation sat cramped around the same table placed in the middle of the carriage, with cardboard name tents showing where the delegates were to sit. Hitler occupied the same seat used by Foch twenty-two years earlier. The Germans all stood as the French delegation arrived, returning the salutes of the French officers as they entered the carriage and took their seats. Hitler sat in silence as General Keitel stood and read aloud the terms of the armistice; his face unable to hide the distain and ultimate revenge he now felt for the way Germany had been humiliated in the 1918 Armistice proceedings. When Keitel finished reading, Hitler stood up and left, again without saying a word, just as General Foch had done in 1918, in a symbolic gesture that there was no negotiation to be done, and French agreement was a matter of course. At the bottom of the steps leading from the carriage, Hitler paused and replaced his uniform gloves that he had removed for the indoors meeting. Twenty-two years of hurt had been healed.

The head of the French delegation was General Charles Huntziger, who after being handed the terms by Keitel, reported by telephone back to the French Government in Bordeaux. There was no discussion to be had, as Hitler had intimated by his actions. The proposed armistice established a German occupation zone in Northern and Western France, including all English Channel and Atlantic Ocean ports. The remaining rump of the country was to be unoccupied and under French administration from the resort town of Vichy, where a Government of Collaboration was to be established. The French were permitted to retain control of their overseas territories and colonies, and the French Navy was to be left intact for this purpose, although disarmed. The French Government tried to soften the terms but to no avail, and the following day, Huntziger was given authority to sign the document, which he did at 6:50 p.m. on 22 June. At 7:06 p.m. Keitel messaged Hitler to confirm that the armistice had been signed and the war with France was over. It would come into effect on 25 June at 1:35 a.m. Keitel then sent a message to the German Armed Forces.

"The young German Army has passed it severest test before the whole world, before history and before itself. The distress and disgrace that descended over our people after the World War has been blotted out by your loyalty and bravery.

Long Live the Fuhrer."

Sunday 23 June 1940 – Paris, France.

Fresh from his personal triumph at Compiegne, Hitler arrived in Paris in a convoy of black Mercedes cars. It was 5:30 a.m. and the sky was just beginning to lighten with the impending dawn. In deserted streets, Police Officers awkwardly saluted their new overseer as the cars swept past.

A rigidly orchestrated programme began at the one place above all that Hitler wanted to visit, L'Opera at Palace Garnier. An elderly attendant patiently showed the visitors around the building, answering questions on the architecture and recent renovations, but curtailing his deference at the end of the tour by refusing a 50-mark tip. The convoy stopped for a propaganda photograph of the "Fuhrer at the Eiffel Tower", before a brief visit to the tomb of the unknown soldier at the Arc de Triomphe. Longer reverence was shown at the tomb of Napoleon in Les Invalides, an experience that Hitler labelled as *"the greatest and finest moment of my life."* He was subsequently motivated to demand the remains of Napoleon's son be returned from Vienna, where he had died of tuberculosis at the age of twenty-one, in order to lie beside his father. The last stop was at the highest point in Paris, the Sacre Coeur Church on Montmartre. The church had been constructed as a reminder of the moral decline of the French people, said to have been responsible for defeat in the Franco / Prussian War of 1871. Hitler took a moment to admire Paris from this viewpoint, while newspaper sellers and churchgoers ignored him as they filed past on their way to morning mass. He left for Le Bourget airport before 9 a.m. having spent only three hours in Paris.

That evening, Hitler summoned his architect, Albert Speer. He confided in Speer that Paris was beautiful, demanding that Berlin was to be made "Far more beautiful." He then ordered the destruction of two Great War memorials in Paris, one to General Charles Mangin, the leader of France's colonial troops which showed the representation of four black soldiers; and the monument to British nurse Edith Cavell, a Matron in a nurse training college in Brussels, executed by the Germans in 1915 for helping allied prisoners of war escape.

Sunday 23 June 1940 –
Rome, Italy.

At 3 p.m. three German aircraft landed in Rome, carrying the same French delegation, led by General Huntziger, that had just completed the armistice negotiations at Compiegne. The first meeting took place at 7:30 p.m. in the Villa Incisa on the Via Cassia, lasting just twenty-five minutes. On receiving Italy's terms, Huntziger immediately requested a recess so he could confer with the French Government. Mussolini had determined to eliminate the Anglo-French domination of the Mediterranean, and worded the armistice to allow occupation of the French territory his forces had captured in the offensive of 21 June; also granting concessions relating to the demilitarisation and Italian use of French colonies in the Mediterranean.

At 7:15 p.m. the next evening, having received his government's authority, General Huntziger signed the armistice on behalf of the French, with Marshal Badoglio signing for the Italians. It would come into effect on 25 June, at a time to coincide exactly with the Franco-German Armistice.

Tuesday 25 June 1940 –
Maginot Line, Eastern France.

Of the fifty-eight fortresses in the Maginot Line, only ten had fallen to the Germans by the effective date of the Armistice. Several of the forts continued fighting for a further week, displaying the same courage and tenacity their countrymen had shown in the Dunkirk perimeter and on the Weygand Line; but which had been sadly missing from the earlier battles of the German invasion.

Sunday 30 June 1940 –
Whittington Barracks, Staffordshire, England.

The West Staffords had been reconstituted at their Regimental Depot, Whittington Barracks in Staffordshire. The Commanding Officer had been evaluating the performance of his Headquarters Staff and the Rifle Companies over both the deployment to, and evacuation from France. He was determined to implement some changes of personnel over the coming months, and also asked the Battalion Second in Command to design a training programme to address the weaknesses he had identified. The implementation of this programme kept the unit very busy during the week, but gave them a well-deserved break at weekends.

Private Hamill had concocted a plan to supplement the bland rations that were the daily fare in barracks. He had found a crutch in an unused locker and decided to put it to good use. Himself, Orpin and McCafferty attended church meetings around the area on Sunday evenings, to elicit sympathy from the mostly elderly Christian women who frequented such gatherings. Orpin hobbled with the aid of the crutch, claiming injury at Dunkirk, and happy to tell an invented account of his own bravery under fire to anyone who would listen. Hamill related the tragic circumstances of Private McCafferty to the elderly ladies; who had been so badly affected by the fighting, that he had developed a speech impediment as a result. Hamill explained that both his friends were very self-conscious of their injuries and afflictions, but that all were eternally thankful to God that they had been delivered home alive from the horrors of war. As a result of their fictitious religious beliefs and battle experiences, all three were showered with tea and sandwiches at every meeting they attended; supplemented with buns and cake in brightly coloured tins to take back to the barracks.

Wednesday 3 July 1940 –
Mers-el-Kébir, Mediterranean Coast, French Algeria.

After the Armistice with Germany and Italy, Admiral François Darlan, commander of the French Navy, assured the British that the surviving French ships that had sailed to North Africa would not fall into Axis hands. However, Darlan repeatedly refused British requests to move his ships to the French West Indies, out of Axis reach, or place the vessels in British custody. With negotiations at a standstill, and the threat of seizure of the ships by Italian troops in Libya looming, the British War Cabinet assessed the risk as too great.

On the morning of 3 July, a British Fleet appeared off the naval base of Mers-el-Kébir in French Algeria, and demanded the surrender of the French vessels. French Admiral Marcel-Bruno Gensoul, who commanded the ships in Mers-el-Kébir, was affronted that the surrender terms were offered by a less-senior officer than himself and refused to negotiate directly, using a Lieutenant Dufay as a go between. This led to delay and confusion, and it became clear that an agreement was unlikely. When the French began to prepare their aircraft for action and dispatched four submarines to take post off the port, Churchill ordered the British ships to open fire at 5:57 p.m.

The joint air and sea attack by the Royal Navy resulted in the sinking of a French battleship, and damage to five other vessels. A total of 1,297 French servicemen lost their lives. The French retaliated for the Mers-el-Kébir attack by bombing Gibraltar on 18 July.

Wednesday 10 July 1940 –
Whittington Barracks, Staffordshire, England.

The battalion had been assembled in the cinema for an announcement, and rumours abounded on what they were about to be told.

"Look, I'm telling you, straight from the horse's mouth." Orpin began. "We're going back to France. My mate who was in Battalion Headquarters heard the Commanding Officer talking about it." he continued; full of confidence in his information source.

"With what equipment?" asked Hamill "We've no tanks, no guns and no vehicles. We left them all on the beaches at Dunkirk."

"I reckon we're off to the south coast to face the German invasion when it comes." chipped in Farthing, unusually, offering an opinion on anything. The Regimental Sergeant Major brought the room to attention as the Commanding Officer entered and stepped up onto the stage. There was no lectern or map displayed.

"Gentlemen." he began. "British forces have been engaged with Italian troops on the Libyan border with Egypt since 11 June. The Italians have now been heavily reinforced with 225,000 men." The audience remained completely silent as he paused for effect. "Italian forces invaded Sudan on 4 July, and in conjunction with insurgent activity in Cairo, these combined forces now pose a significant threat to the Suez Canal."

"Where the hell is the Suez Canal?" asked Orpin quietly as the Commanding Officer paused again.

"British forces currently in Palestine are being transferred to Cairo as we speak, and we will be joining them." A loud murmur broke out across the audience. The Commanding Officer held out his hands and quiet was restored. "Gentlemen, while those left in Britain will face a possible German invasion, we are off to Egypt."

EPILOGUE

A total of 338,226 men were lifted from the beaches and the mole at Dunkirk during Operation Dynamo. A further 191,870 were lifted from the French Atlantic ports during Operation Aerial. These included soldiers from Britain, France, Belgium, Poland and Czechoslovakia. The British Army lost 68,111 men killed in action, wounded, missing or prisoners of war. Equipment lost included 2,472 guns, 84,427 vehicles (including tanks and motorcycles) and 492,637 tons of ammunition and supplies. In the battles on the continent, the Royal Air Force lost 931 aircraft, either failed to return, destroyed on the ground or damaged beyond repair; with the loss of 1,526 personnel killed in action, died of wounds, lost at sea or taken prisoner. 272 vessels of all descriptions were lost, including 6 destroyers sunk and 19 damaged.

With the fall of France, newly acquired airfields enabled Luftwaffe attacks on the United Kingdom and coastal shipping in the Channel and the North Sea. Long range Focke-Wulf Condor bombers could now directly attack Allied shipping far out into the Atlantic, and direct U-boat packs to the convoys. Using the ports on the Biscay coast, U-boats had direct access to shipping lanes in the North and South Atlantic. With the loss of the French Navy, the Italian battlefleet and Air Force posed a major threat to shipping transiting the Mediterranean, immediately lengthening the route to Egypt from 3,000 to 13,000 miles round the Cape of Good Hope, and the route to Bombay from 6,000 to 11,000 miles.

Foreign Minister Joachim von Ribbentrop.

In early September 1940, Ribbentrop initiated negotiations with the Japanese Foreign Minister with a view to an anti-American alliance; the result being the signing of a Tripartide Pact by Ribbentrop, Italian Foreign Minister Count Ciano, and Japanese Ambassador Saburō Kurusu in Berlin on 27 September. Later that year, Ribbentrop made a sustained but ultimately unsuccessful effort to have Spain enter the war on the Axis side.

In December 1942, Ribbentrop met French Chief of the Government, Pierre Laval, in East Prussia, where he quickly agreed to Hitler's and Ribbentrop's demands to increase French Police antisemitic activity and transport hundreds of thousands of French workers to labour camps in Germany to support the country's war industry. Between 1943 and 1945, he had the task of trying to keep Germany's allies from leaving her side as the war turned against them, but his power and influence diminished as the value of diplomacy decreased. When Germany surrendered, he went into hiding in Hamburg under an assumed name of Herr Reiser, but was arrested on 14 June.

Ribbentrop was a defendant at the Nuremberg trials, where he was convicted on four counts: crimes against peace, deliberately planning a war of aggression, committing war crimes, and crimes against humanity. He was executed on 16 October 1946, his hangman using a short rope, rather than a long rope which breaks the condemned man's neck; the result being that Ribbentrop was in agony before he died, being slowly strangled for fourteen minutes. His body was cremated at the Ostfriedhof Cemetery in Munich, and his ashes scattered in the river Isar.

Sturmbannfuhrer (Major) Alfred Naujocks.

Soon after the Gleiwitz incident, all the other operatives involved in the raid bar Naujocks, met untimely deaths at the hands of the SS. In early 1940, Naujocks was put in command of the counterfeiting unit of the Sicherheitsdeinst (known as the SD), charged with Operation Andreas; the forging of millions of pounds in Sterling bank notes in an attempt to undermine the value of the UK currency. By late 1940 Naujocks had been removed from this position after falling out of favour with his superiors.

In 1941, he was dismissed from the SD after disputing one of Reinhard Heydrich's orders; was demoted, and sent to the Eastern Front, where he served with the 1st SS Panzer Division (Leibstandarte Adolf Hitler). Wounded in action, he returned to Germany in 1943, and while still in recuperation he was sent to Belgium the following year where he served as an economic administrator for the German occupation forces.

In November 1944, Naujocks defected under an assumed name and turned himself over to American forces, but when his true identity was disclosed, he was handed over to the British for interrogation. When all useful intelligence had been gleaned, he was returned to the American Zone in Germany, four months after the end of the war. Although he was not prosecuted at the Nuremburg Trials, his witness statements were used as evidence in the proceedings. On request, he was extradited to Denmark for war crimes trials on charges of murdering Danish resistance fighters, subsequently found guilty, and sentenced to fifteen years imprisonment in 1949. In 1950 his sentence was reduced to four years, which meant with time already served in custody, he was deported back to Germany having served barely a year in a Danish jail.

Following his release, he lived in obscurity in Hamburg under a false name. He worked as a businessman and was allegedly involved in the handling of contracts with the Spanish Government to supply passports and arrange funding for alleged former Nazi war criminals escaping to

South America. He eventually sold his story in the form of a book entitled *"The Man who Started the War"* in which he denied shooting Honiok. He died of a heart attack in Hamburg on 4 April 1966, aged 54.

Captain Gustav Kleikamp.

After the Danzig operation, Kleikamp commanded the Schleswig-Holstein during the invasion of Denmark and Norway in the role as the flagship of the warship group which occupied the Danish ports in the early morning of 9 April 1940. After the fall of France, Kleikamp was appointed Head of Calais Command, specifically commanding the transport fleet for Operation Sealion, the codename for the planned invasion of Great Britian. With the postponement of Sealion, Kleikamp was appointed head of the military office responsible for warship construction in December 1940, where he gained promotion to Rear Admiral in 1942. In 1943 he became Commanding Admiral in the Netherlands and was promoted again to Vice Admiral.

With the loss of the Netherlands to the Allies, he became responsible for the defence of the German North Sea coast until the end of the war. He was captured by the British at the cessation of hostilities, being released in April 1947 due to ill health, and remained unemployed until spring of 1952. After a short period of work as a commercial clerk in the export department of Hugo Stinnes in Mülheim, he died on September 13, 1952.

Danzig Post Office Aftermath.

Upon surrender, sixteen wounded prisoners were sent to the Gestapo controlled hospital, where six subsequently died, including 10-year-old Erwina, who succumbed several weeks later from her burns. The surviving prisoners were put on trial and all were sentenced to death as illegal combatants under the German Special Military Penal Law of 1938. The prisoners were executed by firing squad led by SS Sturmbannfuher (Major) Max Pauly on 5 October, and buried in a mass grave near Danzig Airport. Pauly later became Commandant of the Neuengamme Concentration Camp.

In Poland, the episode has become one of the better-known episodes of the Polish September Campaign and is portrayed as the heroic story of David and Goliath; being a group of postmen who held out against German SS troops for almost an entire day. In 1979, the "Defenders of the Polish Post Office" monument was unveiled on the site of the Post Office in the renamed Polish city of Gdansk. In 1991, during construction work at the airport, the mass grave was found in which the executed postmen were buried. The defenders were then officially re-buried in 1992 at the "Cemetery of Victims of Nazi Germany" in Zaspa.

Tadeusz Jasiński.

Communist administration of Poland ended in 1989 with the Polish Republic being restored in 1990. Under the restored regime, on 14 September 2009, Tadeusz Jasiński was awarded the Commander's Cross of the Order of Polonia Restituta by decree of the President of Poland for heroism shown during the defence of Grodno.

Captain Otto Schuhart.

For his actions on sinking HMS Courageous on 17 September 1939, Schuhart was awarded the Iron Cross First Class and the entire crew of U-29 the Iron Cross Second Class. After a further six war patrols, Schuhart was withdrawn from operational duties and became Commander of the 1st U-boat Training Division and later, the 21st U-boat Flotilla. In total, Schuhart claimed thirteen vessels sunk, totalling 67,277 tons of Allied merchant shipping and one warship of 22,500 tons. He was awarded the Knights Cross of the Iron Cross on 16 May 1940.

He spent the last months of the war at the Naval Academy at Murwik, and worked in various civil jobs after the war, before rejoining military service with the Bundesmarine of the Federal Republic of Germany in 1955. He retired in 1967 and died on 10 March 1990 in Stuttgart.

HMS Courageous Sinking Aftermath.

The sinking of HMS Courageous was the first U-boat success against the Royal Navy, but more importantly, Schuhart's victory prompted the Admiralty to withdraw all three remaining Royal Navy carriers from the Western Approaches, not to return to those waters for another four years. This was precisely what Admiral Donitz had wanted, as the reduction in anti-submarine assets allowed his U-boats to continue with their attacks unabated. Hitler was not so enthusiastic however, as he was at this stage in the war still hopeful of a diplomatic solution, and did not want to antagonise Great Britain further.

At the beginning of 1941, U-29 was removed from front line duty and reassigned as a training vessel, remaining in this role until 17 April 1944 when she was decommissioned and used for instruction. The vessel was scuttled in Kupfermuhlen Bay on 5 May 1945 to avoid falling into Allied hands.

Captain Gunter Prien.

Unknown to Prien at the time, and the reason behind Scapa Flow being almost deserted, was that a sortie into the North Sea by the Kriegsmarine's new battle cruiser Gneisenau, had emptied Scapa flow of major capital ships as they sailed out to intercept. Only the ageing Royal Oak remained as she was too slow to keep up with the modern fleet.

The few days taken for the return journey after the attack were spent running on the surface at night and stationary on the sea bed during the day. The crew listened eagerly to news broadcasts from Grossdeutsche Rundfunk, confirming that Royal Oak had been sunk by suspected enemy U-boat action. The reports of Prien's exploits sent Germany into a frenzy even before the vessel was back. U-47 was met by two destroyers and escorted into Wilhelmshaven to be welcomed by cheering crowds lining the docks. The vessel was met by two beaming admirals, Donitz and Raeder, who decorated Prien with the Iron Cross First Class and all other crew members with the Iron Cross Second Class.

Hitler was ecstatic and anxious to meet the Reich's new hero. That afternoon, the entire crew of U-47 was flown to Berlin in Hitler's personal plane; where they were paraded in a motorcade through the city. Thousands turned out, cheering and lining the streets, throwing flowers and gifts into the open topped cars of the motorcade. At the Reich Chancellery, with the sound of the crowd outside still audible, Prien was further decorated with the coveted Knights Cross of the Iron Cross, bestowed personally by Hitler, and the first U-boat commander to receive the award. The Fuhrer then walked along the line of crew men, thanking each one personally, and individually shaking their hands. Everyone then sat down to lunch together. That evening, Prien gave a press conference and a speech at the Wintergarten Theatre.

Under Prien's command, submarine U-47 was credited with sinking thirty-one Allied ships, totalling about 200,000 tons. While at sea on 21 October 1940, Prien received a message that he had been awarded the Oak Leaves to his Knights Cross the day before. He was the fifth member of the Armed Forces and the first Naval Officer to be so honoured.

U-47 went missing on 8 March 1941 after intercepting Convoy OB 293 west of Iceland. Prien was caught in a rapid depth charge attack from the escorts and is believed to have been sunk during an action by the corvettes Camellia and Arbutus, and the destroyer Wolverine. The ships took turns covering each other's ASDIC blind spots and dropping patterns of depth charges until U-47 rose close to the surface before exploding with an orange flash; clearly visible to the British crews. The news of the loss of U-47 was kept from the German public, only being released through a radio announcement on 23 May, saying that Prien and his crew were missing.

HMS Royal Oak Sinking Aftermath.

Ken Conway, Alf Fordham and Norman Thackery were picked up by rescue boats and ferried to HMS Pegasus. They were stripped and washed in paraffin to remove the oil from their skin and hair, dressed in coveralls and allowed to sleep. News of the fate of Royal Oak was released to the British public the next day. On 17 October, the First Lord of the Admiralty, Winston Churchill, spoke of the tragedy in the House of Commons. He paid tribute to the feat of arms whereby a submarine had managed to penetrate the defences, launch an attack and escape without detection. The sinking of Royal Oak cost 833 lives from a crew of 1,219. Of the 163 Boy Sailors on board, 126 were lost. From the 37 Boy Sailors who survived, only 18 saw the war through.

A Board of Inquiry was convened which found the state of Scapa Flow's defences clearly inadequate, laying the blame firmly at the door of the Admiralty. Admiral Sir Wilfred French, the senior Naval Officer Commanding Orkneys and Shetlands, was deemed responsible and forced to retire from active service. He was posted to Washington in an administrative role.

Bandmaster (Royal Marines) Arthur James Golding died when Royal Oak sank. His remains were never found. His widow, Dorothy Golding was reunited with her husband in death on 14 October 2000, when her cremated remains were taken by divers and placed in the body of the wreck, exactly sixty-one years to the day after the attack in which Arthur was killed.

General Carl Gustaf Emil Mannerheim.

At the conclusion of the Winter War, Mannerheim remained Commander-in-Chief of the Finnish Armed Forces for the next five years. He led the Finnish Defence Forces in the subsequent invasion of Russia alongside Germany in 1941, cooperating with the Germans for reasons of national security from the Russian threat, rather than through ideology. In July 1941 the Finnish Army retook the territories annexed by the Soviet Union after the Winter War and took part in the 872-day siege of Leningrad.

With the prospect of German defeat, the Finnish Parliament appointed Mannerheim as President of Finland in 1944, and although in declining health, he oversaw peace negotiations with the Soviet Union. He resigned the presidency in March 1946 and spent much of his remaining life in Switzerland, where he wrote his memoirs, dying from a bowel obstruction on 27 January 1951. He was buried with full military honours on 4 February 1951 in the Hietaniemi Cemetery in Helsinki.

Colonel Paavo Juho Talvela.

With the German invasion of the Soviet Union in 1941, Talvela, by this time a Major General, commanded an Army Corps which recovered the ground ceded to Russia in settlement of the Winter War. He was promoted to

Lieutenant General in 1942 and transferred to Germany as the Finnish representative in the German High Command. He was recalled to Finland in February 1944 as the Russians once again threatened the Finnish border, returning to Germany in July, where he remained until the breaking of the cooperation agreement between Finland and Germany.

Talvela left the Army in September 1944, relocating to Rio de Janeiro until 1949. On returning to Finland, he served as a member of Helsinki City Council between 1954 – 1960. He died on 30 September 1973 and was buried in Kulosaari Cemetery in Helsinki.

Captain Hans Wilhelm Langsdorff.

After the scuttling of the Spee, Captain Langsdorff and his crew arrived in Buenos Aires on the morning of 19 December to be interned in the Marine Arsenal there. The Argentine Government were sympathetic to the Nazi cause, and although theoretically in detention, Langsdorff was allowed to host a dinner that night for the German Ambassador, some members of his staff, and the officers of the Spee. Langsdorff was in high spirits and behaved as the perfect host, engaging with all his guests in animated conversation. The next morning, he was found dead in his room, having shot himself in the head. On his desk lay a letter to the German Ambassador, whose contents explained the tactical rationale behind the destruction of the Spee and his acceptance of full responsibility for this. It made clear that he feared his actions would be misinterpreted by those who would choose to do so, and hoped his death would remove any dishonour apportioned to him.

Commodore Henry Harwood.

For his actions in the crippling and eventual destruction of the Spee, Harwood was promoted to Rear Admiral and Knighted. From December 1940 – April 1942 he was Lord Commissioner of the Admiralty and Assistant Chief of Naval Staff. Promoted to Vice Admiral in April 1942, he took the role of Commander-in-Chief Mediterranean Fleet. In April 1944 he became Admiral Commanding Orkneys and Shetlands, retiring in August 1945 through ill health. He died in Goring-on-Thames in 1950.

Major Erich Hoenmanns.

The lost documents of Plan Yellow contained the orders for the German land grab operation in Belgium, Holland and Northern France, specifically designed to facilitate air operations against England. The operation was due to begin on

17 January 1940 and, contrary to popular belief, was not cancelled due to the loss of the plan, but due to bad weather. It was only after Field Marshall Erich von Manstein discussed with Hitler over dinner the concept of a "sickle cut" through the Ardennes to trap the Allied forces moving into Belgium, that Plan Yellow was adjusted; the weight of armour being subsequently transferred to Gerd von Rundstedt's Army Group A in the south.

Erich Hoenmanns was tried in absentia for the crime of transporting secret documents by plane without authorisation. It was a capital offence, and he was condemned to death, although the verdict would never be implemented. After a spell in a Belgian internment camp in Huy, he was evacuated during the German Blitzkrieg in 1940, firstly to Britain and then to Canada. Hoenmanns' wife Annie was interrogated by the Gestapo, suspecting her husband to be a traitor. She denied this, but subsequently died as a consequence of the severity of the interrogation. Hoenmanns' two sons were permitted to serve in the army and were killed in action during the war. Hoenmanns was released in 1943 as part of a prisoner of war exchange programme due to deteriorating health, being put on trial on his return to Germany, but subsequently pardoned.

Major Helmut Reinberger.

Reinberger was also tried in absentia, and likewise condemned to death. He was moved to Britain, then Canada, returning to Germany on the prisoner of war exchange programme in 1944. At his subsequent trial he was not held accountable for the consequences of Hoenmanns' transgressions and was acquitted.

Captain Philip Louis Vain.

Vain was awarded the Distinguished Service Order for his actions in rescuing the merchantmen from Altmark. He would receive a bar to his award for his part in the evacuation of Namsos during the Norwegian campaign, and a second bar for actions during the hunt for the Bismark. In July 1941, Vain was promoted to Rear Admiral, shortly afterwards taking command of a taskforce of cruisers and destroyers as part of the Mediterranean Fleet, escorting convoys to Malta. He commanded naval forces during the invasion of Sicily and mainland Italy in 1943; experience gained during these operations setting him up for a pivotal role during the invasion of France in 1944. During Operation Neptune, the naval contribution to Operation Overlord, Vain commanded the Eastern Task Force, responsible for landing the British 2nd Army on D-Day and subsequently guarding the eastern flank of the invasion fleet against German counterattack.

With the naval war against Germany nearly over, he was sent to command the carrier force of the Eastern Fleet at Trincomalee, Ceylon, in November 1944. His carrier force took part in the battle for Okinawa, all four of the British carriers being hit by kamikaze planes. Vain remained in the Far East after the war, returning to Britain in 1948 to serve as Fifth Sea Lord, in command of naval aviation. Between 1950 − 1952 he commanded the Home Fleet, being promoted to Admiral of the Fleet on retirement. He died at his home in Berkshire on 27 May 1968.

Lieutenant Commander Bradwell Turner.

Bradwell Turner was awarded the Distinguished Service Order for his actions during the boarding of Altmark. Despite being responsible for the violation of Norwegian neutrality, he became British Naval Attaché in Oslo after the war.

Warrant Officer John Smith.

Smith survived his wound from the Altmark boarding, having been treated by the Altmark's surgeon, and was awarded the Distinguished Service Cross for his actions that night. He remained in the Royal Navy until the mid-1950s, dying in 1973. He never told his family about the part he played in the Altmark incident, only hearing the story of his actions from his former colleagues at a memorial service after his death.

Captain Heinrich Dau.

Dau supervised the repairs to the Altmark, which was re-floated, returning to Keil on 28 March. He did not receive a warm welcome, being relieved of his command and forcibly retired. He committed suicide on the day of Germany's surrender in May 1945. The Altmark was renamed "Uckermark" and returned to service, when on 30 November 1942 in Yokohama Harbour, Japan, a suspected gas explosion wrecked the ship, killing fifty-three of the crew, most of whom had stayed in service from the Altmark days.

General der Infanterie Paul Nikolaus von Falkenhorst.

For his role in the planning and conduct of the invasion of Denmark and Norway, von Falkenhorst was promoted to Generaloberst (Colonel General), awarded the Knights Cross on 30 April 1940, and appointed commander of all German forces in Norway. Von Falkenhorst was known as a ruthless commander. He implemented the infamous "Commando Order" which required captured British Commandos to be handed over to the Gestapo for execution.

After the war, von Falkenhorst was tried by a joint British-Norwegian military tribunal for violating the rules of war. His defence council argued that von Falkenhorst was acting under superior orders, but he was convicted and sentenced to death in 1946. This sentence was later commuted to twenty years imprisonment, although he was released from Werl Prison in July 1953, on grounds of ill health. Following a heart attack, Nikolaus von Falkenhorst died in Holzminden, Germany, on 18 June 1968 at the age of 83. He was buried in the Holzminden Cemetery.

Captain Bernard Warburton-Lee.

A wounded Captain Warburton-Lee was taken off Hardy and brought ashore on a stretcher strapped to a float, but was found to be dead on reaching land. He was posthumously awarded the Victoria Cross for his gallantry and leadership during the engagement at Narvik, and lies alongside eleven other officers and men from Hardy and Hunter in Ballangen New Cemetery, Norway.

Clacton-on-Sea Aftermath.

The bodies of the four German crew were later recovered from the wreckage of their aircraft and buried by the Royal Air Force with full military honours, including swastika flags on the coffins and a volley of shots over the graves. Oberleutnant Herman Vagts now rests with his crew in Cannock Chase German Military Cemetery. Vagts had three brothers, all of whom lost their lives in the war.

An unexploded parachute mine was discovered in the wreckage of the Heinkel, having originally been confused with what was thought to be a water cylinder from a wrecked house. Surprisingly it had not detonated when the other mine had exploded or indeed been set off in the fire that consumed the wreckage. It was defused by a Bomb Disposal team.

In a bizarre twist to the tale, the graves of Frederick and Dorothy Gill are unmarked.

Oberleutnant Rudolf Witzig.

Witzig was awarded the Knights Cross of the Iron Cross for his actions at Eben Emael, being decorated by Hitler on 16 May on his return to Germany, and given early promotion to Hauptmann. All the officers who had taken part in the assault were likewise decorated and all soldiers awarded the Iron Cross and promoted one rank; apart from one individual who was found to have filled his canteen with rum instead of water prior to the assault.

Rudolf Witzig led the 9th Company of the Parachute Assault Regiment during Operation Mercury, the airborne invasion of Crete, being wounded in the battle for Maleme Airfield. On 10 May 1942, he was given command of the Corps Parachute Pioneer Battalion and was promoted to Major on 24 August 1942. From November 1942, he and his battalion served in Tunisia, escaping to Sicily in a small motor boat before the Germans were pushed out of Africa in May 1943.

Witzig served as the Commanding Officer of the 21st Parachute Pioneer Regiment from 15 June 1944, winning the Oakleaves to his Knights Cross in Russia in November 1944. He then commanded the 18th Parachute Regiment from 16 December 1944 until the end of the war, seeing action in Holland and the Rhineland before going into captivity with his regiment on 8 May 1945.

Rudolf Witzig re-joined military service in the newly created Bundeswehr of the Federal Republic of Germany on 16 January 1956. He retired on 30 September 1974 holding the rank of Oberst, having given 28 years of service to his country. He died on 3 October 2001 in Oberschleissheim.

Oberfeldwebel Helmut Wenzel.

Wenzel was awarded the Iron Cross First and Second Class for his actions at Eben Emael, and the German Cross in Gold in 1943. He was taken prisoner by the British on 8 March 1943 in Sedjenane, Tunisia, and spent until 1947 in a prison camp in Canada. On returning to Germany after the war, he worked as a forester in Celle, dying there on 24 January 2003.

Hauptmann Fritz Prager.

Despite having an operation the previous month, Prager led his men in an assault on an enemy bunker at Moerdijk Bridge and was severely wounded. He received the Iron Cross First Class that day. He was decorated with the Knights Cross of the Iron Cross by Herman Goering, the Head of the Luftwaffe, on 24 May.

Prager was promoted to Major on 19 June 1940 and on 1 July took command of the 3rd Parachute Regiment's Second Battalion. His illness caught up with him and he died of cancer on 3 December 1940 in Braunschweig, being buried at Taucherfriedhof in Bautzen.

Oberleutnant Alfred Schwarzmann.

Schwarzmann rose to fame at the 1936 Olympics in Berlin, winning six medals, three of them gold; becoming the icon of Aryan athletics. On joining the armed forces as a Paratrooper, he took part in the German invasion of Poland in 1939 and then the Netherlands in 1940, where he was severely wounded assaulting the Moerdijk Bridges. His life was saved by a fellow Olympian, speed skater Siem Heiden, now a Dutch soldier, who recognised him and took him to a Dutch hospital facility. Schwarzmann was returned to German medical care after the Dutch capitulation, subsequently receiving the Iron Cross First and Second Class on 25 May for his part in the assault; and the Knights Cross of the Iron Cross on 29 May.

This did not sit easily with his paratrooper comrades who believed the medals were awarded for propaganda purposes rather than personal courage. He continued in service until becoming a prisoner of war in Italy in 1945. Returning to his athletics career after the war, he once again graced the Olympic stage at the age of forty, representing West Germany in 1952 and upgrading the bronze medal he won for the horizontal bar in 1936 to a silver medal. He continued his service to gymnastics by becoming the German national gymnastics coach. Schwarzmann died in Goslar on 11 March 2000, aged 87.

Flying Officer Donald Garland.

Flying Officer Donald Garland and his navigator Sergeant Thomas Gray were both posthumously awarded the Victoria Cross. A year later, Donald Garland's mother attended the investiture at Buckingham Palace to receive her son's award. The citation read:

> *"Much of the success of this vital operation must be attributed to the formation leader, Flying Officer Garland, and to the coolness and resource of Sergeant Gray, who in most difficult conditions navigated Flying Officer Garland's aircraft in such a manner that the whole formation was able successfully to attack the target in spite of subsequent heavy losses."*

Donald Garland was the first Royal Air Force Victoria Cross winner of the war. His mother was to lose three more sons in the course of the war, all serving with the Royal Air Force:

- Pilot Officer Desmond William Garland – killed in action in Belgium on 5 June 1942, aged 27.
- Flight Lieutenant John Cuthbert Garland – died on 28 February 1943 of pulmonary tuberculosis, aged 32.

- Flight Lieutenant Patrick James Garland – killed in action in Holland on 1 January 1945, aged 36.

Vice Admiral Bertram Ramsay.

For his role in Operation Dynamo, Ramsay was made Knight Commander of the Order of the Bath. He was then given responsibility for defending the Channel from the expected German invasion, a role he kept for two years before being transferred to become Deputy Naval Commander for the Allied invasion of North Africa.

When the Axis powers were ejected from Africa, he was made Naval Commanding Officer, Eastern Task Force, responsible for the preparation of the amphibious landings on Sicily. After promotion to Admiral on 27 April 1944, Ramsay was appointed Naval Commander-in-Chief of the Allied Naval Expeditionary Force for the invasion of Normandy, coordinating an invasion fleet of almost 7,000 vessels delivering over 160,000 men onto the beaches on D-Day.

He was killed in a plane crash on 2 January 1945 at Toussus-le-Noble Airport, southwest of Paris, while en route to a conference in Brussels with Field Marshall Montgomery, being subsequently buried in Saint-Germain-en-Laye New Communal Cemetery. A statue of Ramsay was erected in November 2000 at Dover Castle, close to where he had planned the Dunkirk evacuation.

Squadron Leader Wilhelm Balthasar.

On Sunday 26 May, the last day of the siege of Calais, six Spitfires had been lost of which two were accredited to Balthasar. He emerged from the Battle of France as Germany's leading fighter ace with twenty-three aerial victories, nine in a single day on 6 June, and was awarded the Knights Cross of the Iron Cross on 14 June 1940.

On 16 February 1941, Balthasar was appointed Wing Commander of Jagdgeschwader 2 "Richthofen" named after the World War One fighter ace Manfred von Richthofen (The Red Baron). During the Battle of Britain his total reached forty victories, and to mark the milestone he was awarded the Oakleaves to his Knights Cross on 2 July 1941. The next day he was killed in action near Saint-Omer, when his wing collapsed, being overstressed in a turn whilst engaged with Spitfires.

Wilhelm Balthasar was posthumously promoted to the rank of Major and buried at the World War One German Cemetery at Illies, France, in the same grave as Hauptman August Balthasar, who had been killed in action in the opening months of the conflict, on 25 October 1914. He was the only

World War Two casualty to be buried here, as was his wish that if killed in combat, to share a common grave with the father he never knew, who died when his son was just nine months old.

Corporal Harry Nicholls.

After the bitter engagement at the village of Esquelmes on 21 May, both sides sent out reconnaissance patrols that night. A German patrol found Nicholls still alive, took him into custody, from where he was subsequently admitted to a German Field Hospital. Missing presumed killed on the evidence of Guardsman Nash, Harry Nicholls was posthumously awarded the Victoria Cross for his act of valour. His citation was published in the London Gazette on 31 July, which read:

> *"He was wounded at least four times in all, but absolutely refused to give in. There is no doubt that his gallant action was instrumental in enabling his company to reach its objective, and in causing the enemy to fall back across the river Scheldt."*

With no news to the contrary, Harry's wife Connie attended an investiture at Buckingham Palace on 6 August 1940, receiving Harry's medal from King George VI on his behalf. In September 1940, Connie Nicholls was contacted by the Red Cross, notifying her that her husband was alive and held as a prisoner of war. Overjoyed, Connie returned the medal to the Army for safe-keeping. While held as a prisoner in Poland, Harry Nicholls was presented with his VC ribbon by the German Camp Commandant and allowed to wear it on his battledress tunic.

On repatriation at the end of the war, Corporal Harry Nicholls attended an investiture at Buckingham Palace on 22 June 1945 to receive his medal in person; marking the only occasion in the history of the Victoria Cross that the medal has been presented twice. Having continually suffered from lingering health problems because of his wartime wounds, he died on 11 September 1975 in Leeds.

Captain (RN) William George Tennant.

For his contribution to the evacuation from Dunkirk, Tennant was appointed Companion of the Order of the Bath on 7 June 1940. On 28 June he was appointed Captain of the battlecruiser HMS Repulse, which subsequently saw action against the German battleships Scharnhorst, Gneisenau and Bismark. In December 1941, Tennant and Repulse were sent to Singapore to counter the Japanese threat in the Pacific. Repulse sailed for Malaya when the Japanese landed, being attacked on 10 December by torpedo bombers. Despite avoiding nineteen torpedoes dropped by Japanese aircraft, Repulse was hit five times, sinking within twenty minutes with the loss of twenty-seven officers and four hundred and eighty-six men. HMS Prince of Wales was sunk in the same engagement.

Tennant survived the sinking, and on 6 February 1942 was promoted to Rear Admiral. In June 1944, he was responsible for the transport and construction of the Mulberry Harbours that provided the necessary port facilities for the invasion of Normandy. He was appointed Commander of the Order of the British Empire for his part in this operation. Tennant was promoted to Vice-Admiral on 27 July 1945 and his Order of the Bath was upgraded to Knight Commander in recognition of his war service. He was promoted to Admiral on 22 October 1948 while in the post of Commander of America and West Indies Station; a position he held between 1946 and his retirement in 1949. He was subsequently named Lord Lieutenant of Worcestershire, serving in this capacity until his death in the Worcester Infirmary in 1963.

Rear Admiral Frederic Wake-Walker.

For his contribution to the evacuation from Dunkirk, Wake-Walker was appointed Companion of the Order of the Bath. As Rear Admiral commanding the 1st Cruiser Squadron, over the period 23 − 27 May 1941, from his flagship HMS Norfolk, Wake-Walker played a role in the detection, tracking and eventual destruction of the German Battleship Bismark. For his part in this engagement, he was appointed Commander of the Order of the British Empire.

On 6 April 1942, Wake-Walker was promoted to Vice-Admiral and took up the appointment of Third Sea Lord and Controller of the Navy, with the specific task of creating a fleet of landing craft in preparation for the invasion of North Africa, and subsequently, Sicily and Normandy. In 1943 he was appointed a Knight Commander of the Order of the Bath, and promoted to Admiral on 8 May 1945. He assumed the role of Commander-in-Chief in the Mediterranean in September that year, but died unexpectedly at home in London on 24 September 1945, aged 57. He was buried in East Bergholt Cemetery, Colchester.

Major Charles Raymond Patrick Sweeney.

Being an Ulsterman, General Montgomery had selected Charles Sweeney as his Aide de Camp from the Royal Ulster Rifles, who were part of the division that he led to France with the British Expeditionary Force. He had

393

known Sweeney from service in Palestine before the outbreak of war in Europe, taking him onto his staff in early 1940. Sweeney was an orphan, and their relationship became so close that Montgomery became his surrogate father.

After Dunkirk, Sweeney returned to his parent battalion, but joined Montgomery's staff again as a Liaison Officer in January 1945. He was killed in a road traffic accident on 9 May 1945, a few days after the end of the war, when his car left the road and crashed into a tree. He was buried at Becklingen War Cemetery near Soltau on 13 May; the by then Field Marshall Montgomery, attending his funeral.

Captain Harold Marcus Ervine-Andrews.

Captain Ervine-Andrews was lifted from Dunkirk on 2 June aboard Royal Navy Destroyer HMS Shikari, arriving in Dover on 3 June with the remainder of his battalion. He learned that he had been awarded the Victoria Cross on 30 July at a restaurant in the west end of London when the radio was switched on for the 9 o'clock news and he heard the announcement. He received the award from King George at Buckingham Palace on 6 August. The citation read:

> *"For most conspicuous gallantry on active service on the night of 31st May / 1st June 1940. Throughout this action, Captain Ervine-Andrews displayed courage, tenacity, and devotion to duty, worthy of the highest traditions of the British Army, and his magnificent example imbued his own troops with the dauntless fighting spirit which he himself displayed."*

He survived the war and returned home to live in County Cavan in his native Ireland, but was pushed out by the local IRA. He lived out the rest of his life in Cornwall, where he died on 30 March 1995, aged 83. He was cremated at Glyn Valley Crematorium in Bodmin, and his ashes scattered at his home, Trevor Cottage, Gorran, Cornwall.

Le Paradis Aftermath.

A total of ninety-seven British prisoners were killed at Le Paradis, the Germans forcing French civilians to bury the bodies in a shallow mass grave the next day. The bodies of those killed in the massacre were exhumed in 1942 by the French, but only about fifty of the ninety-seven were successfully identified. The bodies were then reburied in Le Paradis churchyard, which now forms part of the Le Paradis War Cemetery. A memorial plaque was placed on the barn wall where the massacre took place, and a large memorial was subsequently erected beside the church.

The British received no information about the massacre until the summer of 1943, when Bert Pooley, who had spent the last three years in a German hospital due to his injuries, was declared medically unfit and repatriated. British authorities did not believe Pooley's story, as it was thought that the German army were incapable of such atrocities. It was not until Bill O'Callaghan returned to the United Kingdom in 1945, upon his liberation from a prison camp, that Pooley's story was confirmed and an official investigation begun.

The massacre was investigated by the War Crimes Investigation Unit and Knöchlein's company was identified. He was tracked down and arrested in 1947, being arraigned on charges of war crimes in August 1948; to which he pleaded not guilty. He was tried before a war crimes court in Hamburg, being found guilty after a two-week hearing, and sentenced to death. No other German soldiers or officers were prosecuted for their roles in the massacre.

Private Albert Pooley.

Bert Pooley spent almost four years in hospital in France at Bethune as a prisoner-of-war and was eventually repatriated to Britain in 1943 by the Red Cross. Despite his story being doubted, Pooley refused to give O'Callaghan's name as corroboration while he was still being held prisoner in Germany. After the war, Bert worked in the Post Office, in charge of the "telegram boys".

Bert's legs, which had been shattered by German bullets, never fully healed and both were eventually amputated. Bert's last wish was to have his ashes buried along with the bodies of those he referred to as "my boys" in the cemetery at Le Paradis, a request the Pooley family were able to honour. Bert's ashes were interred at the foot of the Cross of Sacrifice within the cemetry.

Private William O'Callaghan.

Bill O'Callaghan recovered from his wounds and spent the rest of the war in prisoner of war camps in Poland and Bavaria. Throughout his time as a prisoner, he never mentioned the massacre for fear of German retribution, and it was not until he arrived back in Britain that he could corroborate Bert Pooley's story. He was discharged from the Army on 18th January 1946, and returned to Norfolk where he gained employment as a metal polisher and welder. He was diagnosed with a terminal illness in May 1975, and made two trips to Le Paradis before his death on 26 November the same year, at the age of 61.

Following his death, Bill had a sheltered housing scheme in Becclesgate, Dereham, named after him. William O'Callaghan Place, is a reminder of his bravery.

Hauptsturmfuhrer (Captain) Fritz Knöchlein.

Rumours of a massacre spread through the neighbouring German Divisions, but subsequent investigations were deliberately frustrated. After the French campaign, Knöchlein was appointed Company Commander of an anti-aircraft artillery battery in the Totenkopf Division and he served in this capacity on the Russian Front until summer 1942. He was then appointed Sturmbannfuhrer (Major) in command of the 3rd Regiment, Totenkopf Division, being awarded the German Cross in Gold on 15 November the same year. In October 1943, he became Commander of No 36 Regiment, of the newly formed 16th SS Panzer Grenadier Division (Reichsfuhrer–SS), was promoted to Obersturmbannfuhrer (Lieutenant Colonel), and appointed commander of a Norwegian SS volunteer unit from March 1944 to January 1945. He was awarded the Knights Cross of the Iron Cross on 16 November 1944.

At the end of the war, Knöchlein was captured by the Americans and sent for internment in their camp in Yorkshire. After his identification, the subsequent investigation and guilty ruling, Knöchlein was hanged on 28 January 1949 in Hamelin, aged 37. The hangman at Knöchlein's execution was Englishman Ted Roper, a colossus of a man weighing over twenty stone and standing well over six feet tall. He had the following to say about Knöchlein:

> *"He was very pompous and unrepentant to the end, and when asked his religion, snarled 'atheist'. Accordingly, he was not given the usual attendance of a minister. As I led him to the scaffold after securing his arms, he stared hard at me and made a noise in his throat as if to spit. I was too quick however and bundled him unceremoniously onto the trap door. He disappeared shouting "Gott Strafe" but was too late to get out the last word which was presumably 'England'."*

"Gott Strafe England" was a slogan initially used by the German Army during the First World War and literally means "May God punish England."

Major Thomas Rennie.

Having been captured at Saint-Valery-en-Caux, Major Rennie subsequently escaped nine days later and returned to England. He was made Commanding

Officer of the 5th Battalion, The Black Watch in 1942, leading them in action at the Second Battle of El Alamein in October of that year. On promotion to Brigadier and being appointed Commander of the 154th Infantry Brigade, he led that formation during the invasion of Sicily in July 1943.

On 12 December 1943, Rennie was promoted to the rank of Major General and assumed command of the 3rd Infantry Division, which had been training in a combined operations role in Scotland. In April 1944 the division was moved to southern England to prepare for, and take part in the invasion of Normandy. As the Normandy bridgehead expanded, the 3rd Division arrived at Saint-Valery-en-Caux on 1 September, the 5th Seaforth and 5th Camerons meeting in the town square. Major General Rennie put his headquarters in the Chateau at Cailleville, which had been the location used by General Fortune in 1940, and from where as a staff officer, Rennie had passed the order to surrender.

Rennie was killed in action leading the 51st Highland Division in the Rhine crossing operation in March 1945. He was buried in Reichswald Forest War Cemetery.

Compiegne Aftermath.

Three days after the armistice was signed, Hitler ordered the site to be destroyed. The museum which had housed the carriage was blown up and the Alsace-Lorraine monument smashed. The site was dug over and re-grassed, apart from the statue of Foch, which Hitler ordered to be left intact, and thus honour only an empty field. The railway carriage was taken to Berlin and displayed to the public at the Brandenburg Gate. It was burned by the SS in the final months of the war and the remains buried to prevent it returning to Allied possession; and perhaps being used for another German surrender ceremony. After the war, the site at Compiegne was restored using German prisoners of war, and an identical carriage from the original train is now on display.

General John Standish Surtees Prendergast Vereker (6th Viscount Gort).

Gort was criticised and credited by historians in equal measure for his actions as Commander in Chief in France in 1940, but Churchill was convinced that what he considered to be the rout of the British Expeditionary Force made Gort an unsuitable field commander. He was subsequently given the post of Inspector of Training and the Home Guard. Gort became Governor of Gibraltar from 1941 – 1942, and Governor of Malta from 1942 – 1944.

He was promoted to Field Marshall on 20 June 1943, and witnessed the signing of the surrender of Italy in Valetta harbour on 20 September 1943.

When the war ended, he was made High Commissioner for Palestine where he strove to build good relations with both Arabs and Jews; being greatly admired by both communities. He stepped down from this post on 5 November 1945 due to ill health and returned to England, being admitted to Guy's Hospital where inoperable liver cancer was diagnosed. He died in Guy's Hospital on 31 March 1946, aged 59. His body was entombed in the family vault at St. John the Baptist Church, Penshurst, Kent.

Major General Bernard Law Montgomery.

On his return to Britain, Montgomery was made a Companion of the Order of the Bath for his part in the Dunkirk evacuation. In July 1940, Montgomery was appointed acting Lieutenant General and was placed in command of the 5th Corps, responsible for the defence of Hampshire and Dorset. In April 1941, he became commander of the 12th Corps, responsible for the defence of Kent, Sussex and Surrey; the most likely area for a German invasion. During this period, he initiated a rigorous training regime for both officers and other ranks, ruthlessly sacking those who he felt unsuitable for combat command positions. He was to continue this ethos right through the remainder of his service.

On 13 August 1942, Montgomery replaced William Gott as Commander 8th Army in North Africa; his appointment transforming the fighting spirit of the force. He co-located his headquarters with the Royal Air Force to better coordinate joint operations for his planned offensive, which he unleashed on 23 October at El Alamein. He pursued the Axis forces relentlessly across the whole of North Africa, driving them from the continent in early May 1943. Montgomery then led the 8th Army in the invasion of Sicily in July 1943 and the subsequent invasion of Italy in September. Dissatisfied with the conduct of the campaign, he was delighted to be recalled to England in January 1944, to take command of 21st Army Group preparing for the invasion of France.

Disagreements with Supreme Allied Commander General Eisenhower and his American peers dogged the landings in Normandy, the breakout battles, and the Allied advance east through France, Belgium and the Netherlands, culminating in the failure of Montgomery's Market Garden plan to capture the bridge over the Rhine at Arnhem. He was promoted to Field Marshal on 1 September 1944. Relations soured even further during the German Battle of the Bulge offensive in December 1944, and the crossing of the Rhine in March 1945. Montgomery accepted the surrender of German forces in North West Germany, Denmark and the Netherlands at Lüneburg Heath on 4 May 1945.

After the war, Montgomery became the Commander-in-Chief of the British Army of the Rhine (BAOR), the name given to the British Occupation Forces in Germany. To recognise his contribution to the Allied victory in Europe, Montgomery was made a Knight of the Garter and 1st Viscount of Alamein in 1946. He succeeded his mentor Alan Brooke, as Chief of the Imperial General Staff from 1946 – 1948, and became Eisenhower's Deputy at Supreme Headquarters Allied Powers Europe on the creation of NATO. On the death of his mother in 1949; Montgomery claimed he was too busy to attend the funeral. He served in this post under Eisenhower's successors until his retirement in 1958 at the age of 71, when he wrote his memoirs.

He died on 24 March 1976 at his home in Isington, Hampshire, aged 88. After a funeral ceremony at St George's Chapel, Windsor Castle, he was buried in Holy Cross Churchyard, Binsted, Hampshire.

Lieutenant General Alan Francis Brooke.

Brooke was created Commander of The Most Honourable Order of the Bath on 10 June 1940 for his role in the withdrawal from France. Having been evacuated from France twice, he was appointed Commander United Kingdom Home Forces in July 1940, responsible for preparing to receive a German amphibious invasion. He believed this could be best achieved by a thin defensive line on the coast supported by a fast-moving mobile reserve.

In December 1941 he was appointed Chief of the Imperial General Staff (CIGS), the top job in the British Army, and in March 1942 became Chairman of the Chiefs of Staff Committee, the top job in the UK military and foremost military advisor to the British Prime Minister. His responsibilities included the appointment and evaluation of senior commanders, and allocation of manpower and equipment to theatres of operations. He would retain this role for the duration of the war.

Initially his focus was on the Mediterranean theatre, to drive the Axis from North Africa and knock Italy out of the war, thus securing safe passage through the Mediterranean and weakening Germany before considering a cross-Channel invasion of Western Europe. This approach led to heated arguments with his American peers who wanted an earlier attack into occupied France. He was promoted to Field Marshal on 1 January 1944.

During his time as CIGS, Brooke had a mixed relationship with Churchill, although both men deeply respected each other; borne out by the fact that Churchill kept Brooke in post despite their many disagreements and arguments. In a diary entry on 10 September 1944 Brooke wrote of Churchill:

"Never have I admired and despised a man simultaneously to the same extent."

At the end of the war, Brooke was created Baron Alanbrooke of Brookborough in the County of Fermanagh in his native Ulster. He was made Viscount of Brookborough in 1946 and appointed Order of the Garter. Very much turning his back on military life, although he held the honorary position of Colonel Commandant of the Honourable Artillery Company from 1946 – 1954, he served on the boards of both industry and banking firms while working on his memoirs. He served as Chancellor of The Queen's University in Belfast from 1948 until his death. Having been educated in France, he spoke the language fluently, also being fluent in German, Urdu and Persian.

For the Coronation of Queen Elizabeth II, he commanded all military forces taking part in his appointed role as Lord High Constable of England. On 17 June 1963, Lord Alanbrooke suffered a heart attack and died quietly in his sleep at home in Hampshire, aged 79. He was given a funeral in Windsor Castle and buried in St Mary's Old Churchyard, Hartley Wintney.

Major General Harold Alexander.

On returning to England after the Dunkirk evacuation, Alexander remained in command of the 1ˢᵗ Corps, with a role of guarding the Yorkshire and Lincolnshire coast. He was promoted Lieutenant General in July 1940, and in December of that year took over Southern Command, responsible for the defence of South West England. He was appointed Knight Commander of the Order of the Bath on 1 January 1942 and sent to India as Commander British Forces in Burma on promotion to General. He oversaw the fighting withdrawal into India before being recalled to Britain and given the role of Commander in Chief Middle East, responsible for the conduct of the campaign in North Africa. For his success in removing the Axis powers from Africa, Alexander was elevated to Knight Grand Cross of the Order of the Bath.

As Commander of 15ᵗʰ Army Group, Alexander conducted the Allied campaign in Sicily and invasion of Italy. In a slow and costly advance up the length of Italy, Alexander's forces captured Rome in June 1944. He was promoted to Field Marshal in December 1944 and appointed Supreme Commander of Allied forces in the Mediterranean, taking the German surrender in Italy on 29 April 1945. As a reward for his efforts in the Mediterranean theatre, he was created Viscount Alexander of Tunis, and of Errigal in County Donegal, to reflect his Irish heritage. At the end of the war, he chose to retire from the Army and became Governor General of Canada.

In 1952, Alexander was asked by Churchill to return to London and take the position of Defence Minister in the British Government, where he served until 1954, when he retired from politics. He died on 16 June 1969 of a perforated aorta; his funeral being conducted at St. George's Chapel, in Windsor Castle. He was buried in the churchyard of Ridge in Hertfordshire.

Charles de Gaulle.

Refusing to accept his government's armistice with Germany, De Gaulle fled to England and exhorted the French to continue the fight in radio broadcasts from London; inviting all French colonies still supporting Vichy to join him and the Free French forces in the fight against Germany. The Vichy regime subsequently sentenced de Gaulle to four years' imprisonment and held a court martial in his absence, which sentenced him to death. He reached an agreement with Churchill that Britain would fund the Free French military effort with the bill to be repaid after the war.

He became head of the Provisional Government of the French Republic when the Allies invaded in June 1944, and arranged for French troops to liberate Paris; the German garrison surrendering on 25 August. De Gaulle subsequently refused any British representation at the victory parade. He resigned from his post in 1946, but was recalled as President in 1958 during the political instability caused by France's war in Algeria. He pursued a policy of national independence, resulting in France becoming a nuclear power in 1960.

De Gaulle was re-elected President in 1965, resigning in 1969. He died suddenly from an aneurism on 9 November 1970, aged 79, at his country estate in Colombey-les-Deux-Églises, 120 miles southeast of Paris. The funeral on 12 November 1970 was the biggest such event in French history. His grave is in Colombey-les-Deux-Églises.

General Heinz Wilhelm Guderian.

After the defeat of France, Guderian led the 2nd Panzer Army during Operation Barbarossa, the invasion of the Soviet Union, in 1941. With the failure to capture Moscow leading to the prospect of a protracted campaign, Guderian was dismissed from command and appointed to the role of Inspector General of Armoured Troops, with a responsibility to rebuild and train new panzer forces.

As a committed Nazi, he was appointed Chief of the General Staff of the Army High Command following the 20 July 1944 plot to assassinate Hitler, taking on responsibility for the discharge and trial of Army personnel implicated in the assassination attempt. Guderian surrendered to the Americans on 10 May 1945 and was interned until 1948. During this period of captivity, he informed on his ex-colleagues and co-operated with the Allies, claiming he was not a Nazi; and for which in return he evaded prosecution for war crimes.

Guderian was released from internment in 1948, many of his peers receiving long prison terms. He retired to Schwangau in Southern Bavaria, and began a successful career as a writer, recording his wartime experiences. Guderian retained an affinity with Hitler and National Socialism, remaining an ardent German Nationalist for the remainder of his life. He died on 14 May 1954, aged 65 and was buried at the Friedhof Hildesheimer Strasse in Goslar.

Major General Johannes Erwin Eugen Rommel.

After the surrender of France, Rommel's 7th Panzer Division was sent to Bordeaux to prepare for the invasion of Britain. When this operation was cancelled, Rommel was appointed Commander of the newly created Afrika Korps on 6 February 1941, promoted to Lieutenant General, and arrived in Tripoli on 12 February. On 21 June 1942 he was promoted to Field Marshall, but by this stage in the war North Africa had become a costly side show compared to the campaign in Russia. Rommel was withdrawn from Africa on 9 March 1943 and returned to Germany.

He was posted to Italy as commander of the newly formed Army Group B in August 1943, with his headquarters at Lake Garda. On 21 November, Hitler gave Kesselring overall command of the Italian theatre, moving Rommel and Army Group B to Normandy, with the role of defending the French coast against the much-anticipated Allied invasion.

On 17 July 1944, his staff car was attacked by Allied fighters, causing the vehicle to leave the road and crash into trees. Rommel was thrown from the car and fractured his skull in three places. While recuperating, he was implicated in the 20 July 1944 plot to assassinate Hitler. Due to his status as a national hero, he was spared the ignominy of a public trial, disgrace and execution, being offered suicide in return for his continued reputation and the guarantee his family would not be persecuted. It was announced that Rommel had died from his wounds and he was given a state funeral. He was buried in Herrlingen, west of Ulm.